ON THE EDGE

F. PARKER HUDSON

ON THE EDGE

A JAN DENNIS BOOK

THOMAS NELSON PUBLISHERS
Nashville

Copyright © 1994
F. Parker Hudson
On the Edge
by F. Parker Hudson
A Jan Dennis Book
Thomas Nelson Publishers
Nashville

Published in Nashville, Tennessee, by Jan Dennis Books, an imprint of Thomas Nelson, Inc., Publishers, and distributed in Canada by Word Communications, Ltd., Richmond, British Columbia.

Scripture quotations are from the NEW KING JAMES VERSION of the Bible, Copyright © 1979, 1980, 1982, Thomas Nelson Inc., Publishers.

Library of Congress Cataloging-in-Publication Data

On the Edge: A Novel / F. Parker Hudson
    p. cm.
  ISBN 0-7852-8294-7 (pbk.)
  1. Family—United States—Fiction   I. Title
PS3558.U289705 1993   93-27310
813'.54—dc20   CIP

2 3 4 5 6 7 8 9 — 99 98 97 96 95 94

For My Wife

Alida

Whose voice of encouragement over many years
is the reason for this book

JANUARY

S	M	T	W	T	F	S
1	2	3	4	5	6	7
8	9	10	11	12	13	14
15	16	17	18	19	20	21
22	23	24	25	26	27	28
29	30	31				

FEBRUARY

S	M	T	W	T	F	S
			1	2	3	4
5	6	7	8	9	10	11
12	13	14	15	16	17	18
19	20	21	22	23	24	25
26	27	28				

MARCH

S	M	T	W	T	F	S
			1	2	3	4
5	6	7	8	9	10	11
12	13	14	15	16	17	18
19	20	21	22	23	24	25
26	27	28	29	30	31	

APRIL

S	M	T	W	T	F	S
						1
2	3	4	5	6	7	8
9	10	11	12	13	14	15
16	17	18	19	20	21	22
23	24	25	26	27	28	29
30						

MAY

S	M	T	W	T	F	S
	1	2	3	4	5	6
7	8	9	10	11	12	13
14	15	16	17	18	19	20
21	22	23	24	25	26	27
28	29	30	31			

JUNE

S	M	T	W	T	F	S
				1	2	3
4	5	6	7	8	9	10
11	12	13	14	15	16	17
18	19	20	21	22	23	24
25	26	27	28	29	30	

JULY

S	M	T	W	T	F	S
						1
2	3	4	5	6	7	8
9	10	11	12	13	14	15
16	17	18	19	20	21	22
23	24	25	26	27	28	29
30	31					

AUGUST

S	M	T	W	T	F	S
	1	2	3	4	5	
6	7	8	9	10	11	12
13	14	15	16	17	18	19
20	21	22	23	24	25	26
27	28	29	30	31		

SEPTEMBER

S	M	T	W	T	F	S
					1	2
3	4	5	6	7	8	9
10	11	12	13	14	15	16
17	18	19	20	21	22	23
24	25	26	27	28	29	30

OCTOBER

S	M	T	W	T	F	S
1	2	3	4	5	6	7
8	9	10	11	12	13	14
15	16	17	18	19	20	21
22	23	24	25	26	27	28
29	30	31				

NOVEMBER

S	M	T	W	T	F	S
			1	2	3	4
5	6	7	8	9	10	11
12	13	14	15	16	17	18
19	20	21	22	23	24	25
26	27	28	29	30		

DECEMBER

S	M	T	W	T	F	S
					1	2
3	4	5	6	7	8	9
10	11	12	13	14	15	16
17	18	19	20	21	22	23
24	25	26	27	28	29	30
31						

FOREWORD

What follows is a fictional account of a family in America today, including their friends and business associates. I hope to show what happens when these thoroughly modern individuals rely on their own strengths and resources to solve the problems that naturally occur in their lives. I also hope to communicate the different results when their lives are submitted to the Lord and the Holy Spirit is set free to act as our God has promised He will.

These words are by no means my own. As may be obvious from the first, I am neither a theologian nor a pastor; I am a businessman. Much of what is written here has been inspired by listening to other godly men and women, who have had the patience and the gift to teach, to preach, and to minister the Word to me and to many others. And while I don't want to appear presumptuous, the words are not mine because they seemed to flow, as I wrote, from a higher source.

I have tried to describe the spiritual warfare that is raging today, at this hour, for the hearts and souls of our family members, neighbors, business associates, government leaders, media executives, and others. In describing this warfare, I have used some visual images which may not be traceable to particular verses in the Bible, but I hope will nevertheless communicate the battles, which I know are going on even as you read these words.

I must warn you that there are a few events and descriptions in this book which are not particularly pleasant or Godlike. I take no joy in including these. I have tried to choose words that are as inoffensive as possible to describe these situations. I have included them because my heart breaks at what we are doing to ourselves, as individuals and as a nation, and it is my conviction that we must understand exactly what is happening to have any chance of being set free from it. If these events offend you, I cannot change them, because they are all too real. If my choice of words offends you, then I sincerely apologize.

Let me also be quick to say that before Christ came into my life and made a new person of me, I had experienced many of the situations described herein. I am, in that sense, the chief of sinners in this book. But I have also experienced firsthand the infinite power of His Holy Spirit to change lives, instantly and permanently. I give Him all the glory and all the praise for what He has done in my life, and in the lives of my wife and children. The power *is* there if we just ask for it.

Besides our Lord, I also want to thank the following people, who have helped me over many years of teaching and/or have delivered particular messages that have stuck with me through the years. They are Michael Youssef, Roy Ludwig, Joe Spence, Adolph Coors, IV, John Guest, Archie Parrish, Ed Silvosa, and Mark Rutland. Some of the images and statements in this book began with ideas I heard first from these men.

I also want to thank a wonderful group of people who made specific suggestions and gave encouragement on early versions of this book. They are Gil and Bonnie Meredith, John and Laura Wise, Caroline Kerr and her daughters Caroline and Helen, Margie Wynne, Bob Morgan, Bo and Paula Smith, Carrie Guest, Bradley Fulkerson, Betty Lee Hudson, Sue Cortese, Dot Vick, and Bob Hupka, Gene Hall, Byron and Florence Attridge, and Tony and Rae McLellan.

To them and to the Lord belong the thanks for any words you find helpful as you consider what is happening today. If any words are not helpful, then let that responsibility be mine alone.

May God bless you and your family as you read these words and consider His promises to each one of us.

Book One

1

TUESDAY, APRIL 18 ■ It was only midafternoon, but already it was gloriously dark to Balzor. One of Satan's most experienced demons, Balzor was not visible to human eyes. But he was no less real. And just like a devastating, invisible wind, he was no less deadly. From his vantage point high above the northwest section of the city—his personal responsibility for forty years now—the sun's position was really irrelevant. His whole area had grown progressively darker during his years there, and he was immensely proud of his accomplishments. As he shifted his dark form and exhaled a breath of broiling sulfur, he watched his minions going about their tasks below, content that the long war was now almost won.

Richard Sullivan had a problem. The contract documents for the McKinney and Smith corporate expansion had to be reviewed with Bruce McKinney in the morning, but he had not even looked at the file their investor's attorney had delivered to his office before lunch.

Kristen. Kristen Holloway. They had spent all of lunch—and two hours more—tossing and turning in her penthouse apartment bedroom. For almost three months now they had been meeting there "for lunch" a couple of times every week. A small voice seemed to tell him at times that it was wrong, but it only took one look at her long reddish-brown hair, her young face, and her nearly perfect body to drown out any voice of reason. He had tried to stop, but he was lost in her. Consumed by the passion which swelled in them both—a passion he and his wife of eighteen years had once shared, but which she could no longer understand, he was convinced. And now he had to call her and make excuses for why he had to work late.

The receptionist at the television station recognized his voice on the telephone and put him straight through to the programming director.

"Janet Sullivan," said the voice in the receiver—a voice which twenty years ago in college, he momentarily reflected, could by itself make his heart leap. But not now; not for years. *Why?* he started to think, but then stopped himself.

"Hi, uh, honey, it's me. I've had a terrible day and I'm way behind on reviewing this important contract for Bruce and David. It's the capital expansion for their company they've worked on for months. I've just got to get it finished tonight, to review it with them first thing in the morning."

"But Richard, tonight is Tommy's first game, and he thinks the coach may give him a chance to play in the infield. You told him you'd be there. Even Susan is cutting tennis practice to come. Can't you work on the contract in the morning?"

"I wish I could, but it's too important to chance it. There will be lots of other games, and maybe I can sneak in late if I get through in time. It's at Riverside isn't it?" he added, sounding hopeful, but realizing as he spoke that a late appearance never really happened. "Anyway," he said, trying to end the discussion quickly before it became another argument, "don't bother to fix me anything for dinner. I'll grab something on the way."

"Oh, all right," Janet acquiesced, "but, Richard, you've really got to spend more time with the kids. They're teenagers now, and they need you."

He could feel the hurt and the pain in her voice, but before he could respond with something that met her feeling, a voice welled up inside him and reminded him that all she did was nag. He knew the kids were important, but what about his work? How was he supposed to pay for all the things his family needed and wanted? Not on Janet's salary! And Kristen never nagged like this. Why couldn't Janet understand him and his needs like Kristen did? Janet was always too busy being an "executive"!

Barely holding back his anger, which erupted almost instantly when Janet's words hit his own suppressed guilt, he lashed out at her, lying as sternly as possible: "Look, I've had a very busy day—I've worked very hard—I'm doing the best I can—I'll be there as soon as I finish this contract. OK?" Hearing his own voice speak the words, he convinced himself that it was in fact his work, and not his affair with Kristen, that was keeping him from his family. That felt much better.

After Janet's quick but unhappy goodbye, he replaced the receiver and took out a handkerchief to wipe his suddenly sweaty hands before he picked up the contract file. Kristen. He smelled her perfume—he had used the same handkerchief only two hours before to wipe the sweat of their passion from her forehead. As he put the handkerchief back in his pocket, he was already visualizing Thursday's luncheon appointment.

He could hardly wait.

Tommy ran up the aisle of the school bus, chasing his baseball cap as it sailed from teammate to teammate. His was the latest cap to suffer this fate on the way to Riverside High, and upon successfully retrieving it, he stuffed it into his back pocket. As he retreated down the aisle, he defended his cap against several spirited grabs and did a fake slide into his seat next to Brent Holcombe, who had already removed his own cap in self-defense.

Tommy was a ninth grader on the fence. Like many fourteen-year-old boys, caught awkwardly in between, he didn't know whether he was a child or a man. A few of his childhood friends seemed very mature now and acted almost as if they knew something he didn't. And maybe they did. He was not very sure of himself. Some of the guys were dating regularly now and talked obtusely about their latest conquests. He doubted that much of their talk was true, but he really didn't know. How could he? A little skinny, with a shallow chest which had apparently not read the health texts about filling out, he sometimes wondered if the girls in his grade would ever even know he existed.

Brent Holcombe shared his uncertainty and his doubts. They had become good friends ever since Brent transferred to Northpark last year. They were similar, almost like soulmates. They were neither popular nor unpopular. They were neither superior athletes nor bookworms. They were squarely in the great middle, by almost any "standard," and in a large class it was easy for them to be lost in the crowd. So he and Brent stuck together, a two-boy support team, defending themselves as best they could from those who were bigger, smarter, faster, better looking. And sharing almost everything together, including the outfield on their baseball team

Having a popular big sister at the same high school didn't help matters. Tommy was always Susan's little brother. Not that Susan was the most popular or most beautiful girl in the junior class—she wasn't. But she was pretty enough and good at most things. People, both boys and girls, just seemed to like her and enjoyed being with her.

And she was generally OK to him. Oh, they had experienced a few knock-down fights several years ago. But as their outside interests grew, an undeclared truce settled on their relationship. Tommy would have to admit, if anyone ever pushed him, that their truce was also a reaction to the escalating war between his parents, which neither he nor Susan understood or talked about much. But on those occasions when the strange mixture of anger and ice that was now their parents' relationship invaded their own world, he and Susan sometimes exchanged glances, trying to reassure one another.

Without being able to explain it, he felt sorry for his mother. Dad seemed to have no time for any of them, and Tommy could almost see his mother slowly wilting before their eyes. Lost sometimes, she just seemed like she didn't know what to say or to do. And he couldn't help her. He was confused and inexperienced and wanted someone to explain life and women and relationships to him. How could he help his mother? Why didn't his father make her happy? They had almost everything they could ever want. Wasn't that important? What was going on? Were anyone's parents happy? Had he done something? Was it his fault? He didn't know how or why, but he clearly knew that his parents were unhappy, and that added sadness, anger, guilt, and fear to the naturally volatile feelings that swirled around inside him every day.

"Awesome," said Brent, holding open for Tommy the *Petgirl* magazine he had smuggled on the bus in his team bag.

"Look at that," he whispered to Tommy. The boy's reaction was immediate and predictable; the pictures depicted beautiful women in poses he could not have imagined with a fourteen-year-old mind unless they were captured for him. He wanted to see more, but the bus was nearing the ballpark, and Brent buried the magazine in his bag. Tommy was left with an empty feeling, as if some of the wind had been knocked out of him. A voice seemed to tell him that he needed to see more, but for now he had to think about baseball.

Maybe tonight something good would happen. His ninth-grade team had their first spring game. His dad had said he would be there. Mom and Susan too. His coach had hinted that maybe he would play in the infield. It had happened almost by chance. Everybody knew that only the best players played in the infield, and Tommy had been tagged as an outfielder since Little League. For years he had tried not to let it bother him. He never had the confidence to upset a practice by pushing a coach to give him a chance in the infield.

But deep inside he wanted to play shortstop or second base. To be noticed. Perhaps by Becky Thornton, his pretty classmate whose twin brother, Patrick, was on his team. To make a great play. To make his mom and dad proud. To see them smile together again, like they used to, because of him.

And then yesterday, after he had charged and fielded a grounder cleanly in center field, coach told him he was playing well and that perhaps he would get a chance in the infield! Maybe tonight would be a good time for the whole family. If Tommy had known how to pray, that would certainly have been his prayer.

The ever-growing darkness was gratifying to Balzor, but he knew its cause was the even more wonderful noise. If a human could have perched above the city at his height, taking in everything from the river on the west to the university on the east, he would have heard nothing. But to the black, horrendous Balzor there was the cacophonous din of thousands and thousands of voices—some whispering, some shouting—all lying! The combined noise was a terrible, frightening mixture of roars and screams, slowly rising to new peaks as yet more voices were added. To Balzor it was eternal music, and he planned that it would grow even louder, day by day. And as the noise grew louder, his sector of the city would grow darker still.

Down below, just above the trees, the well manicured lawns, and the expensive houses along Devon Drive, the voices did not combine to a single roar for Streetleader Nepravel. At his level, he could make out distinct sentences now and then, as he went about his appointed tasks, his dark shape moving from house to house. From centuries of habit, his blood-red eyes darted constantly for the occasional angel who might still be around, despite the lack of prayer, as he sowed lies and discord with impunity. The spiritual lights were now almost out on his street, and as a part of the darkness, he could move almost anywhere, unchecked.

Tonight he was bringing the demon Envy into the McKinneys' house at the north end of Devon Drive, to recharge the voice of Bruce McKinney's envy for his neighbor's new second home. As Bruce sat down in his armchair before dinner with a new European car catalog, Nepravel nudged Envy right up behind him; and Envy began speaking words into Bruce's ear, which Bruce heard in his own voice.

"That Tom Bryant is one lucky guy. Where does he get the money to buy a new mountain house in this economy? Isn't he in real estate development? And last weekend when we were up there together with them, Diane commented that the furnishings alone must have cost a fortune. She's already implied we're some sort of failures because we drive a perfectly good four-year-old domestic car. And the kids always want something new. Tom and Nancy only have Amy; we've got four little ones to raise. Is it my fault our new business has taken all of my money, and everything else costs so much?"

Once Envy had started it, Nepravel knew that Bruce McKinney's own internal voice of envy, without anything to stop it, would take over, repeat it, build on it, improve it, and continue the cycle until Bruce had to act. Humans were so predictable. A single session with lies from a demon could start a voice replaying which could last for months, even years!

So long as nothing interfered.

Nepravel pulled Envy back and smiled grotesquely at him, smoke and sulfur escaping from his hideously smoldering mouth. He wished for a moment that Bruce could see them and smell the putrid stench that flowed from them like sewage. But Nepravel knew that there would be plenty of time for that; it didn't look like anything was going to sidetrack Bruce McKinney's rendezvous with him and the other demons when he passed. Oh, how he looked forward to the look in these stupid humans' eyes when they finally came face to face with him, with Balzor, and with the others! Hopefully some would pass tonight in their sector. He never tired of watching that first realization of where they were going and how they had been deceived. That was what he had lived all these millennia for!

As Nepravel and Envy floated up through the rafters and out of the McKinneys' house, they shared together a final hideous laugh of hatred for Bruce, and for the whole human race, as they heard him say to himself, with his own internal voice: "Tom Bryant has been looking for a way to one up me ever since Diane and I bought that boat which Nancy likes so much. He may be our friend and neighbor, but he can't stand having to go out on our boat all the time. Now I'll bet he'll want to go to their mountain house instead. Well, we can't quite afford a second home right now, but when this capital infusion comes through for the company, we'll at least buy—or maybe lease—a new car to make Diane feel better. And then maybe next year a new home even nicer than Tom's—maybe at the beach." Bruce heard just one of the tens of thousands of deceiving voices working in the northwest section of the city that night, virtually drowning out the few isolated voices that were speaking and praying the Truth.

Nepravel nodded to Envy in mutual satisfaction as Envy headed off for another appointment to the south. Sometimes Nepravel lapsed and felt that creating envy over something like a new home was not really very important. But then he remembered that it was a higher power than he who made these assignments. And he had to admit that his meeting with Guilt, which he was now hurrying to make, was to solidify the uncrossable gulf between a mother and her daughter, which started after an explosive argument over just the same sort of small thing. Others like Sectorchief Balzor obviously had the assignments worked out, and Nepravel could certainly see with his own beady eyes that the process was working well.

Still later that evening he had to rendezvous with a demon so powerful and so vile that he almost single-handedly sucked light into himself: Pride. On one of his regular rounds of the street, Nepravel had overheard Mark Davidson, who lived in the middle of the block, near the city park, listening to a tape which a Christian friend had given him on salvation, and Nepravel was petrified to hear almost nothing coming from Mark's internal voice of pride. Someone must have been praying for Mark or talking to him about that accursed Jesus, and Nepravel had missed it! He would have to watch Mark closely for a while, but for tonight he would personally insure that pride was turned up again within Mark. With pride playing loudly again in his head, Mark would never admit that he needed help or imagine to get down on his knees and submit to the Lord.

Nepravel knew he had dodged a close one there. Balzor's wrath flared mercilessly on those rare occasions when someone in their sector was saved from hell by that unmentionable blood of the Lamb. Thankfully, as the voices grew louder year after year, and the city grew darker, fewer and fewer were saved. And he was particularly proud that Devon Drive was almost completely dark now. That one old couple, the Halls, across the street from the Sullivans, had the accursed Light burning in them, and they prayed together every day. But they were almost finished—good riddance—and no one listened to them anyway.

And there was that teenager out in the suburbs, Bobbie Meredith. Every night Nepravel had to watch the answers to her prayers, incoming from heaven, for the Sullivan and Bryant families, like clockwork. Streaks of bright light in an otherwise gloriously dark sky. But by themselves these few answered prayers had little effect on the voices. It wasn't like the old days, when people really prayed, lighting up the whole city, causing Balzor's horde real problems. What could these few prayers do to silence so many wonderful, harmonious, lying voices on his street?

Susan Sullivan lay back on the only part of her bed not covered with the books and papers from her homework, talking on the phone to Amy Bryant, who lived next door to her. "Did you see that ridiculous sweater Mr. Demetry was wearing today? Didn't he look dorky? Do you think he's trying to win the Worst Dressed Faculty Award in the yearbook?"

Amy laughed. "Maybe he's trying to impress Mr. Peters. Petey wears stuff like that, and maybe Mr. Demetry wants to be a principal too, someday. Wouldn't he be just perfect!"

The thought of young Mr. Demetry as a principal made Susan laugh along with Amy—it seemed so absurd. The girls had finished their homework and were comparing notes on the day, before supper.

"Was that Drew walking with Sally after gym class?" Amy asked.

"Yes, but she said they were just talking about the school newspaper; he didn't ask her out or anything."

"Susan, dinner's ready," her mother called upstairs. "We've got to hurry to make it over to Tommy's game."

"Hey, I gotta go. No, not tennis. I told Tommy I'd go to his first game, and now it's turned into a family thing. You know."

"OK, Mom!" she yelled towards the hall.

She told Amy goodbye, slid off the bed, and carefully arranged all of her books for school in the morning. Susan looked around her room: from the top of her desk to the row of stuffed animals collected since she was a little girl, everything was in order. She stopped in front of the mirror over her bureau to check her hair and makeup, and then she bounced down the stairs to the kitchen with a spring in her step.

The world was reasonably OK to Susan Sullivan. Except for her parents' relationship, which seemed to worsen every month, everything else was, like her room, in the neat order that most firstborns seem to appreciate. She was a consistent B+ to A- student, a member of student council, one of the junior members of the varsity cheerleading team, and a strong tennis and basketball player in her own right. As importantly, Susan just seemed to exude confidence and quiet strength. She was popular, but she was good-natured and genuinely concerned about others, particularly her friends, of whom there were many. But Amy and Bobbie were her best friends.

Occasionally Susan was struck by how different they all were, yet she truly loved them both. The three of them had been together since sixth grade. Amy Bryant was good looking and very popular with the senior boys; she had even dated one or two college freshmen when her parents were out of town. Amy hinted once or twice to Susan that she was quite knowledgeable about boys and had even come close to "doing it" with a college date. That was all so incredible to Susan that she simply dismissed it as Amy's occasional bragging.

An average student, Amy tended to view her world through how others viewed her. Sometimes the resulting anxiety would make Susan laugh, and she would tease Amy for being so uptight about her appearance. But acceptance and approval meant a lot to Amy, and she sought it through friends, boys, and athletics.

Amy laughed a lot and kidded almost everyone, but she used Susan as her rudder to push her back on course when she became too distracted by contradictory opinions about anything—from the color of her skirt to where they should think about going to college. She even once told Susan that it was as if there were a lot of different voices in her head, and she could only really trust Susan's.

Bobbie Meredith was just the opposite in many ways. Not nearly as striking as Amy, Bobbie was nevertheless quite popular with most of the girls and with many of the boys. While Amy bounced from boyfriend to boyfriend, Bobbie quietly dated two of the brighter boys in their class and one senior. Like Susan, she tended to stay in one "serious" relationship for quite a while. Unlike Susan or Amy, she was not at all athletic, but she made the best grades of the three. She did not live on Devon Drive with

Susan and Amy; her family had a slightly smaller home on the northern edge of their school district.

The main thing about Bobbie was her faith. One day, when she was fourteen, she told Susan and Amy that with her father the previous evening she had prayed to have Jesus come into her life. Although she did not parade her faith, she did tell her friends on a couple of occasions in the intervening two years that events or testimonies at her Spirit-filled church had really moved her and that she felt like a different person because she knew that Jesus lived inside her. It had once struck Amy that Susan was quietly strong and confident because she was born that way. Bobbie, on the other hand, was just as strong and just as confident, but it was as if those qualities had been added later to Bobbie. And Bobbie herself occasionally almost marveled that these qualities had been given to her as gifts.

Susan—and Amy and the other kids in their class—knew of Bobbie's faith, and most respected her for it. Only a few kidded her now and then; one or two actively ridiculed her. She was pretty good-natured about it, never seeming to get angry. But Susan, like the others, did not really understand it. On the few occasions when Susan had spent the night at Bobbie's home and gone to church with her parents and two brothers, she had definitely felt something different, particularly from the youth minister, Glenn Jamison. He just seemed to understand teenagers. But Susan's own family didn't go to church, and Richard Sullivan thought that organized religion was unnecessary to a caring, moral person. His voice Susan heard every day, not just on an occasional Sunday. So whatever it was that Bobbie had was definitely noticed by her friends; but it went no further.

Susan, Amy, and Bobbie were best friends, unconsciously respecting their differences and enjoying each other's company. They shared everything with each other. They kidded each other. They supported each other. They imagined that they would always be together. And as their junior year was drawing to a close and they were preparing to look at colleges in earnest, they sensed that a special year was beginning for them, culminating in graduation in just over twelve months. They were looking forward to being seniors.

That thought put the bounce in Susan's step as she walked into their kitchen early that spring evening to find her mother finishing a large salad for their supper. "Where are Dad and Tommy?" she asked.

"Your father is working late," Janet said, a little too icily, concentrating on the salad bowl, "and Tommy took the team bus over to Riverside. The game starts at 7:30, so we've got to eat and get going to be there on time."

"Isn't Dad going to make it? I heard him tell Tommy at breakfast that he'd be there."

"I know, dear. He called and said he has to work late, but he'll try to come directly to the game." Janet said it as positively as she could, but it was part of an earlier battle for her—a battle she had lost. And she didn't have the energy to recall it again with Susan. She hoped Susan would not press her with it, as she herself had pressed earlier with Richard.

Susan sensed the weariness under her mother's voice, despite the otherwise normal tone, and decided not to push further into the uncharted water of her parents' relationship right then. So she played the game with her mom, gave a reassuring smile, and said, "I hope so too."

While Bruce McKinney was listening to the voice of Envy, Richard Sullivan, his neighbor and attorney for almost ten years, sat behind his desk downtown and reviewed the contract for the capital investment which Bruce's company needed to survive.

If the other attorney did a good job, maybe this will be simple and I really can make Tommy's game. God knows I'd rather be there than here, he thought, as he glanced out the window at the long shadows being cast by the tall buildings in the sunset. It was quiet in their space—only one other attorney was working late. For a moment he allowed himself to picture Tommy, Susan, and Janet. *How did life get so complicated? Were other families on the same treadmills? When did it start? How would it stop? When could he spend more time with his children?*

But then, before those thoughts could build, another voice came up, blocking them out. *What else can I possibly do? The mortgage on the house and the overhead at the firm have to be paid every month. Janet stopped trying to understand me years ago; she's so caught up in that idiot TV station that she's forgotten how to be a wife. Susan and Tommy do need me, and I'll try to spend more time with them; but even more they need a roof over their heads. And besides, Bruce is counting on me to represent him in this deal. I've just got to review this contract now.*

He turned off that one sided debate and waded back into the contract, still hoping to finish in time for the game. Forty-five minutes later, he knew it would be impossible. He exhaled a long sigh and cursed the other attorney. *He's got these conditions for closing all wrong, at least as Bruce explained them to me. I'll have to redraft this whole section.* Reaching for his dictating machine, he blotted out a momentary thought of Tommy. *I'll make it up to you, son.* Then he began dictating.

As so often happens, the baseball game itself was an anticlimax. The important events were those that did not happen, because they had the most lasting effects.

In the bottom of the first inning, standing in center field, Tommy could pick out his mother and sister in the visitors' stands; but he could not see his father. He imagined that his dad would arrive late, directly from work.

Tommy spent the first four innings in his usual places, center field and on the bench, alternating with Brent. He realized in the top of the fifth inning that he might have made a mistake by mentioning the infield to his mother. While his team batted with a two-run lead and he and Brent sat together, watching, their coach walked in front of them, studying his lineup card. Tommy summoned the courage which had built during the whole day and asked, a note of hope in his voice, "Hey, coach, you remember about me maybe playing in the infield?"

"What? . . . Oh . . . Oh yeah. Sure. I meant in practice, to see how you do. Someday. This is a close game, Tommy. We couldn't put you in now." And he said it just loud enough for four or five of the starters sitting nearby to hear, besides Brent. The other boys turned for a minute to look at him, or rather to look through him, as if he were not there. Several smiled. In an instant he knew the coach was right, that he had been stupid, and that he should never have brought it up. How many more kids in his class would hear this story by lunch tomorrow? What a fool. Now he just turned red in the dark of the dugout and wished he could hide, but there was no place to run.

"No sweat," Brent whispered to him under his breath, as if to say he understood Tommy's agony. At least Tommy had one good friend.

In the sixth inning Tommy made a spectacular catch over his shoulder; the runner on first was as surprised as Tommy was to see the ball caught cleanly in his glove. The runner had to turn around and race back toward first. Tommy saw a chance for a double play—something he had never done before—and heaved the ball toward his teammate on first, who was waiting with outstretched glove.

Unfortunately, Tommy was off with his throw; the ball sailed up and to the right of the first baseman. By the time the catcher ran after the ball, the base runner had tagged and was standing on second. Tommy cursed. A voice told him it was always like this. Even when he lucked out and did something right, he messed up the next thing. Infielders don't make bad throws like that, he reminded himself.

After the game, which Northpark won by a run, the players, families, and friends all milled around together between the dugout and the concession stand. Janet found Tommy and said, "Good game; you made a great catch. Your father had to work late, Tommy. He called this afternoon and said he'd try to make it, but he was working on a contract for Mr. McKinney, and I guess it just took too long."

Tommy had a long face. Inside he was stumbling through the complex emotions of what to tell his mom and sister about not playing in the infield, and of whether to be upset or glad that his father had not been there to see it. Before he could say anything, Brent, who had been standing next to him, said, "Mrs. Sullivan, can Tommy come with me and my parents to get some ice cream?"

Janet sensed the general disappointment in her son. She wanted to reach out and hug him to her. Just a few years ago she would have done exactly that; but now he was fourteen, and she felt she couldn't. "I guess so. Sure, Brent, if your parents say it's okay." The boys turned together and ran off, leaving Janet with a smile, intended for Tommy, frozen on her face and unseen by him.

Just then Susan walked up with one of the boys from her class. "Mom, this is Drew Davidson. He was here watching his brother in Tommy's class. We want to go get a Coke, and then I'll be home in a little while."

The daughter and mother exchanged looks, unseen by Drew, which communicated: "I really want to go with him—he's neat—pleeease." . . . "Can he be trusted? I don't know him. Is he a good driver? Will you be home on time?" . . . "Yes, yes, yes, yes."

Then Janet spoke, "Well . . . all right. Sure. Hi, Drew. I'm Janet Sullivan. Have a nice time, but please have Susan home by 10:30. OK?"

"Yes, ma'am. We won't be late. Thank you. Nice to meet you."

And as quickly as that, Janet Sullivan was all alone.

As Janet drove home by herself, her mind bounced back and forth between her marriage, her children, and her job. Only her daughter Susan provided a bright spot; her strength and normally positive outlook sustained Janet in what was otherwise a troubling night.

Raised as a Catholic in a parochial school, Janet's primary association with religion was overreaching guilt. As a girl she had been made to feel guilty about almost every indiscretion, no matter how slight. Consumed by guilt, she had finally rebelled completely in college and never looked back. She had decided in those heady days that people—either individually or as the government—could solve their own problems, without any help from God, were He even really around.

As an adult, she knew she could not sit through a Catholic mass, yet she felt out of place in the few Protestant services she had attended over the years. Richard had been raised as a Presbyterian; and after their marriage, the easiest way to solve their religious difference—it was really religious indifference—was simply not to attend church at all.

When the children came along, they had half-heartedly tried some different churches in their neighborhood. Usually one of them dropped the kids off at a Sunday school, then came back an hour later. When they did attend, it seemed that half of the sermons were about raising more money. Finally, when the children were older and complained about having to go to Sunday school, they gave up entirely.

They even had a discussion about it a few years ago, convincing themselves that if they taught their kids the right, moral ways to behave and set good examples themselves, then that was what really mattered. What more could God actually want in these complicated days, anyway, if there really was a God? And that conclusion had the happy result of freeing up their Sundays for other things.

But when Janet reflected on the past several years as she drove home alone on that dark spring evening, genuine guilt started to speak to her. For an instant it occurred to her that even if their theory was right, were they now very good parental examples? And when was the last time they had done something together that was fun on a Sunday—or on any other day? And what about Richard, and their marriage?

As her mind wandered to her husband, the potentially positive voice of convicting guilt, which could have led to real change, was overtaken by the louder voice, planted in her long ago, of personal, unworthy guilt.

"What have I done to our marriage? Is it my job at the station? Should I have stayed home these last five years, like Richard wanted? Was I too selfish in wanting to continue my career after the children were older? Have I valued myself over them? What have I done to drive Richard away? When was the last time we were intimate—not sex—just lying quietly together on the big sofa, or holding hands? Is it all my fault? What can I do? Is he going to leave us?" That thought hit her like a shot, and she almost steered off the road.

A jerk of the wheel snapped her attention back to driving. Her mind rested for a minute, without resolution. Almost in defense, she started thinking about her work, where she generally found satisfaction as the director of programming, responsible, as many told her, for the real operation of the station. She knew that such accolades were flagrant exaggerations, but she didn't mind the compliments, which otherwise were few and far between in her life.

She had taken the job at TV5 four and a half years ago, hoping to put her college training to work. She started as the promotion assistant, under Tom Spence. But she was a quick study, and soon her talents for organization and communication had been noticed by management. Two years later, when the position unexpectedly opened, she was asked to be the programming director, a fantastic opportunity for her. Now she balanced, like so many other women, the dual responsibilities of home and office, some days wishing she could stay at home again, other days filled with exuberance by what her team at work was accomplishing.

But even at work there seemed to be a problem brewing. The network was promoting a new show for the fall lineup to be called "911 Live." For years several syndicated shows which reenacted ambulance, police, and fire department emergencies had won very high ratings. True to life, these shows were immensely popular. Because they were reenactments, they were edited and generally wound up with happy endings.

But "911 Live" planned to take this concept one step further. The producers intended to put tiny cameras and dish transmitters on two hundred ambulances, police cars, and fire trucks in ten of the nation's largest cities. Then when the show came on the air every week, the directors would monitor the activities at these two hundred potentially live sites from a central control room and cut to the city where the "action" at that moment was the "best." Anything could be happening. Anyone could be involved. Fires, accidents, murders, rapes, drug busts—anything that the cameras could catch. Real. Live. No script. Anything could happen. A helicopter would be on standby in each city in case something really big started, so that a live reporter could cover it.

The problem was that a couple of the old timers at the station had already told her boss, Bill Shaw, that they thought the show was unsuitable, particularly for the early evening time slot for which it was planned. The scuttlebutt from network was that the producers hoped to capture the first live killing on TV since Lee Harvey Oswald. Or at least a burn victim jumping from a tall building.

These employees, whom Janet labeled as "Christian fundamentalists," asked Bill in a meeting she had attended not to air the program in their city. They said it just went too far in its potential for death and violence. Real death and real violence. And during the family hour. They even suggested that the wrong people in those ten cities, of which theirs was one, might start planning their violence for the specific day and hour of "911 Live," hoping to achieve some perverted recognition on national television.

Bill Shaw had listened quietly and promised to take their views under consideration before making a final decision. But after they had left, he confided to Janet that he thought they were squeamish God-squaders, trying to censor America's right to see and to experience whatever technology made possible. The problem for Janet was that she found herself agreeing with these Christians; she simply thought about her own children and what they might see and hear on this show. But the experience of agreeing with them was so unusual, and the issue was so difficult, that at this point she didn't know what, if anything, she should do.

With all that on her mind as she neared their home, hoping to find Richard's car already in the garage, she hardly had time to reflect on Tommy. She felt his confusion and his sadness. It pierced her. But she had been unable to talk to him tonight, not even one word. She had a sickening feeling that they were losing him. She did not know to where. She did not know exactly when it had started or when it would finally happen. But he was withdrawing, from them and from others, slipping through their fingers as they watched. Richard was too busy, and she didn't know how to begin. She wanted to stop and run the tape back, like at the station—about five years—and then start it again. But she couldn't. She had no one to turn to. She would have to force Richard to listen. He had to do something. Tommy was their precious son, and they were losing him.

Even before she clicked up the garage door from the driveway, she knew that Richard was still not home. The lights in the house were on exactly as she had left them.

Thirty minutes later Tommy came through the front door. She called from the kitchen, where she was cleaning up the few dishes from supper. Tommy moved quickly through the breakfast room, opened the refrigerator for an apple, and headed upstairs, mumbling as he went that he had to take a shower and finish his homework.

Susan came home right on time. *Thank God for Susan,* Janet thought. Susan said she and Drew had shared Cokes and frozen yogurt at the shopping center near the mall. Drew was new for Susan; he had transferred to their school last year, and he was only now being "noticed" by the girls in the tenth and eleventh grades. Susan offered few details and Janet didn't mind—it was just nice that someone in their family was happy.

After Susan went upstairs, Janet's sadness and distress settled in again, like a dull weight on her chest. She didn't know what to do or where to turn. She could have gone to see her sister, but Caroline lived hours away and had much younger children. Janet doubted that she would understand. And Janet suspected that Caroline was still tied to religion—she would probably tell her to pray! A lot of good that would do.

Following a bath and a glance at the news, hoping that Richard would come home so that she could at least tell him about Tommy, about the game, and about the TV station, she finally went to bed, alone. As she lay her head on the pillow, a small voice said "There has to be a better way" . . . but a louder voice despaired, "How will any of this ever change?" Despair coursed through her that night; dull, aching despair. What scared her most was the realization that she was used to it, that it was almost "normal." A tear wetted her pillow as she finally drifted off to a fitful sleep, alone, in the darkness of her bedroom.

As midnight drew near, Streetleader Nepravel broke off from Devon Drive and headed up for the nightly rendezvous with Sectorchief Balzor and the other fallen angels who now virtually controlled this part of the city. They gathered above the city in an invisible demonic swarm, like black vipers writhing in a nest, bent on human destruction by any means possible.

Although they did not "talk" in a human sense, they communicated well enough with one another. Balzor was very much in charge, meting out praise when it was due; and disciplining with demonic brutality whenever one of his soldiers fell prey to a plot by members of God's diminishing army on earth.

All of the streetleaders reported the important events in their areas, emphasizing their successes, because they knew that Balzor then had to report to the lord of the city, Alhandra, and he had been known to blast even a sectorchief back to hell for too many failures. Each demon in the city lived in fear of Alhandra, whose bitter hatred for God, angels, and humans was well known and well documented. It was rumored that Alhandra had once been a member of Satan's own ruling council and that he wanted to be there again, no matter what it took to make this city a showplace for demonic power over human lives.

So Nepravel reported his close brush with Mark Davidson and the Christian tape in a way which emphasized his own alertness and his own brilliance, particularly the way he brought Pride in quickly to counter the tape with a strong, clear voice. Balzor congratulated him but also warned him to watch Davidson and his friends closely for the next several months.

As their cabal broke up and Balzor headed off for Alhandra's palace, Nepravel flew back to his neighborhood next to Zloy, a streetleader with a station just to the north of his own.

"Can't you do anything about that Meredith girl?" whined Nepravel. "Every night her prayers for the Bryants and Sullivans spoil our otherwise quiet street. Each answered prayer hits and diminishes one of our voices just enough to make a lot of extra work for me. Can't you quiet her down?"

"That little twit," Zloy snarled, "and her whole family. They all pray! Constantly. It's terrible. You're not the only one I hear from. I get complaints and groans from as far away as England, where they have friends. They pray for lost souls everywhere, by name, so they make the prayers stick. I hate them. Ever since the Light came into that family, I haven't had a moment's rest. Can you believe that they have a neighborhood Bible study going on our street? So I not only have to fight them with the voices, to try to throw them off track personally, I also have to run around the whole neighborhood, countering the Word wherever I can, turning up the volumes, hoping that no one else will learn the truth. It's awful! If they don't stop, someone else will repent soon and surrender his life, and I'll get blamed, and I'll have two families at it. Have you got any ideas?"

Nepravel started to boast about how he had dimmed the Light in an entire village, back when the Word was really spoken and most families actually tried to follow God, and about how this particular village had stopped praying altogether, rendering them no threat to anyone else. But just as he was warming to his own key role in this success, he whirled, sensing a passing on his street. "Oh—got to go—a death on my street to handle!" he blurted behind himself to Zloy, as he darted for the fruit of his long labors, leaving a trail of dark smoke in the night.

"Who could it be? One of the Halls, finally?" he hoped. As he neared Devon Drive he saw the soul rising from a house near the Davidsons. It was Hugh McEver! Only thirty-eight years old—Nepravel knew instantly that he was dead in the shower from a massive stroke while he was talking through the door to his wife, Betty. Left three children, all under twelve. Fantastic!

Hovering near to McEver's spirit, which had virtually the same appearance as his earthly body, only translucent, Nepravel waited for the only moment he hated during this otherwise enjoyable task: dealing with one of God's holy angels. The light was already coming; soon he knew it would almost blind him. Fearsome creatures—he was glad that his master, Satan, had dominion over the earth and that prayer was now rare, so demons like him only had to deal with angels on special occasions like this one.

On the angel came, flying down from heaven. The light became brighter still. Six massive wings! Two heads like eagles! Eyes covering his body! Two legs ending in sharp, taloned feet! Nepravel knew firsthand that many real angels were nothing like the wispy characters in human books and films. This creature was simply awesome in his power and his might. On several occasions in years past he had seen lesser demons such as himself crushed and exploded back to hell in those powerful talons. But tonight there would be the usual truce. There was no need in fighting now for

McEver; the battle for his soul was obviously over. Nevertheless, Nepravel could hardly imagine that he and some of his fellow God-haters had long ago looked like this, before their rebellion against God, which Satan had led, and their expulsion from heaven.

The light temporarily blinded McEver's soul as well. Although by ancient tradition an angel and a demon accompanied each soul to the judgment seat, the angel often arrived at the scene of the death first. Balzor had laughed at a recent midnight rendezvous and told them that it was because angels didn't have too much else to do on Earth these days! At any rate, the light was very bright; on those few occasions when a soul had left someone's body prematurely and then returned, the subsequent report almost always emphasized the light.

But as the angel, unspeaking, took his station on the right side of McEver's soul, Nepravel slid silently up on the left. Nepravel loved this moment. Because of the blinding light, it was usually the smell which the eternal soul first noticed about him. Now it was a real smell, no longer separated by the slight gulf between the physical and the spiritual. The stench of putrid death was overwhelming, and McEver's spirit, like countless before him, involuntarily turned to discover its source. There! This was the one moment when Nepravel was glad for the bright light. He knew that it must have made his hideous, smoldering form all the more grotesque to the just-released soul, which had until recently lived in McEver's mortal body. Nepravel smiled his practiced smile, revealing the fire in his face, as if to say, "You're mine now." McEver recoiled in revulsion and in terror.

Only a few seconds before had McEver actually realized that his body was dead, but that his spirit was still living. And somehow he also knew, with his body gone, that he would now live forever. Forever. The light had been so bright and powerfully peaceful. But now this, this evil blob of dark, as powerfully dark as the other was light. Instantly a freezing fear surged through his soul: if this thing was part of his future, he wanted no part of it. Surely there had to be a mistake. Whom could he tell?

He turned back toward the light from the angel, to try to ask why this evil monster was with them. After all, he had been as good as anyone else. He hadn't murdered anyone; everyone said he was a good guy. But before he could point these things out to the light, they were already moving, the three of them, away from his home of ten years, away from his wife, away from his children, from his new car, from his business deals, and from everything else he had known. They were headed together to the judgment seat, where the holy Lord of Lords waited to review McEver's entire life, his every act, and all of his thoughts. He was naked. What would he say to God Almighty? Would "as good as everyone else" be good enough? He had believed the voices that had said so. But what would God Himself expect? Somehow McEver knew their destination and that his place in eternity was about to be proclaimed. His soul suddenly began to weep and to wail. But Nepravel continued to smile.

■   ■   ■

The contract rewrite had taken much longer than Richard had imagined possible, but finally he had finished and was pulling into their driveway. He hoped the one light on in the living room meant that Janet was already asleep. What a day!

Just as he turned in, he noticed the red flashing lights of the ambulance stopped several houses away, near the McEvers'. He made a mental note to check in the morning; he hoped that everything was OK with Hugh and his family.

Richard put on his pajamas in the bathroom, hoping not to wake Janet. As he came out and the light from above the sink fell across her sleeping face, his stomach turned with an involuntary reaction to what he was doing to her and to his family. A small voice pleaded with him to stop his affair with Kristen, to talk to Janet, to love her, to spend real time with Susan and Tommy. For just that one moment, he froze with the enormity of his betrayals. He opened his mouth, as if he might speak out loud, his mind confused.

But then the other voices kicked in. "You're tired—you've had a very difficult day. It will be all right tomorrow. You haven't done anything that everybody else isn't doing. And look at the house, the car, and the education you're providing. Take it easy on yourself. You deserve a little on the side. It's not really hurting anyone. Janet seems the same. You'll spend more time with the kids, but this weekend you've got to make that meeting in Atlanta. Next weekend will be better."

And with those half truths and outright lies, the voices inside Richard Sullivan once again overcame the one honest whisper from the real truth. The real truth could not grow in Richard, because the other voices were not checked or silenced, and like weeds, they choked out the Word.

As Richard slipped silently into their bed, careful not to touch Janet, his mind was almost back at peace, completely fooled by the lies which he constantly and unconsciously told himself. Even before he turned out the last light in their home that night, it was already almost completely dark there, as seen by the red eyes of those who hovered and smiled.

2

WEDNESDAY, APRIL 19 ■ With the morning came the familiar routine that smoothed the peaks and valleys of the emotions from the evening before. It also brought the possibility of a new beginning, combined with the necessity to get ready for school and for work. Like families everywhere, the Sullivans began this day with an unspoken willingness to look to the future and to temporarily, at least, forget the unpleasant past.

As Janet returned to their bedroom with two cups of coffee, Richard sat up in bed. "I'm really sorry I was so late and missed the game. Bruce's contract had to be completely rewritten. How did Tommy do?"

"OK. He made a great catch, but then threw the ball away. He never did play in the infield." If Richard had been home the previous evening, she would have said much more; but now they were all in their usual morning rush, and Janet just wasn't up to a battle. It occurred to her that they had many other issues to discuss, but later. Then the telephone rang.

"Oh, my heavens," she exhaled. Covering the mouthpiece, she said to Richard, "It's Nancy Bryant. She just got a call that Hugh McEver died last night of a stroke!"

Richard was shocked and told Janet about the ambulance. He thought for a moment about Hugh, who was a friendly competitor with another law firm. What a shame.

"He was four years younger than you," Janet said, hanging up the phone. "I think Betty has some family here in town. Nancy is going to call me later at work to let me know what we can do for them. Those three sweet young children!"

The death of their neighbor filled what passed for discussion at family "breakfast." More correctly it was a loose twenty minutes when the four Sullivans passed each other in the kitchen and breakfast room, each fixing and eating some sort of prepackaged morning food. Richard did ask Tommy about the game and told him that he hoped they could hit some balls together next weekend following his business trip. Tommy said something in reply that only another teenager could perhaps have understood. Richard surmised that it was a short sentence, but it sounded like a grunt.

He was about to ask for a repeat when Susan walked in with her books and told him she had enjoyed a short date with Drew Davidson after the game. As the two of them began talking together, Tommy withdrew to get his school work.

"Isn't it awful about Hugh?" Bruce McKinney asked, as he and his partner, David Smith, entered Richard's conference room that morning.

"He and I talked together on Saturday afternoon. He was out working in their yard, and I had just finished jogging. I guess you never know."

Each man gave a respectful shrug or glance at the floor. Death was just not something anyone lingered on. Better to avoid the thought and get on with business—something each one could understand.

"Parts of this contract look like they were written for another deal," Richard began after they were seated. "I had to rewrite several sections to match what you've told me. Are you sure you and Patrick Tomlinson had a meeting of the minds on his investment in your company?"

"Of course," Bruce replied. "I bet it's all just his lawyer, Marty Tsongas, trying to earn his keep. Give us some examples."

"Well, the closing can't take place until his father's estate is settled. Frankly, that could still take months. His father was very wealthy and has a complicated estate, as you know from your work with him. And then it's further contingent on the price of Fairchild Textile stock being at twenty or better for the week before the closing. Did you agree to that? And they want your personal guarantees on the accounts payable disclosure schedule."

David and Bruce looked at each other. David spoke. "Those are specific points we had not discussed in detail, but Tomlinson did mention in general that the money had to come from his father's estate. I guess that's just his attorney's way of protecting him."

"I wish we could close much sooner, like tomorrow," Bruce added. "We really need his capital, Richard, and Patrick Tomlinson is the only investor we've found who will put up all the money we need for expansion and still let David and me continue to run the company as we think best. It's a deal made in heaven for us. I guess we'll just have to work with the conditions. Fairchild Textile is at thirty-six now, and hasn't been below twenty in years, so I'm not worried there. And David and I will just have to guarantee whatever he wants. But can't you push them on the closing date? We really need his money."

"I'll try, but if the money is coming from the estate, and he won't borrow it, then I'm afraid we're all at the mercy of the estate process."

After another twenty minutes of discussing the details, Richard promised that he would call Tomlinson's attorney and do the best he could to win some concessions, without killing the deal.

As they rose to leave, Bruce asked, "Have you and Janet been up to Tom and Nancy Bryant's new mountain house yet?"

Richard had heard that their mutual neighbor's new home was well done, but they had been busy the month before when Tom had invited them up. "No, not yet. How is it?"

"Spectacular. Really nice. I don't know how Tom does it with real estate development the way it is today. Those of us in securities are just scraping by. But if we can close this deal, Richard, maybe David and I can also do something big for our families. Maybe Diane and I can get a beach house for the whole neighborhood to enjoy!"

"I hope so," said Richard. Incredibly, as he smiled to himself, what popped into his mind was a vision of Kristen, sprawled seductively on the deck of Bruce's new imaginary beach home. "I sure hope so," he repeated with a visible grin.

"Please, Susan," Amy Bryant asked, as they walked to their lockers between classes, "Billy asked me to go out Saturday night, to a party at his fraternity house. He has a friend who he says is a cute guy for you to go with. My parents want to spend the weekend at our new mountain house, but I'd rather stay here and go out with Billy. They'll let me stay with you, if you invite me, and we can meet Billy and his friend at the restaurant. We'll be home on time. You'll love the party. No one will ever have to know."

"Well, my folks don't want me dating college boys yet, and I've never really lied to them before on something like this."

"You don't have to lie. We'll just tell them we're going out for dinner. We don't have to tell them that there will be a little detour from the parking lot!" Amy smiled. "And besides, we're almost seniors now. We drive ourselves. What right do our parents have to tell us we can't date college guys? They're just guys. Believe me, you'll really have a great time."

Susan thought for a minute about her parents and their icy relationship, which seemed to be falling apart. "What do they really know about dating and kids these days?" a voice asked her, echoing Amy's logic. "Why should you suffer because they can't agree on anything?" the voice added in righteous indignation.

"OK," Susan agreed, to Amy's delight. "But let's keep it under control and be in on time. I don't want a hassle. Tonight I'll ask my mom if you can spend the weekend with us. And let's not tell Bobbie. She won't understand."

"I know you probably think I'm crazy," Tom said, after he and Janet had ordered sandwiches at the cafe around the corner from the television station. "But I've been at this for more than twenty years. A lot has changed. It's not the way it used to be, I know. But this '911 Live' is just too much. Have you seen the promos? Do you know they're already outfitting several ambulances and police cars here in our city for a test run this spring, before the show starts in the fall? Can you imagine what might wind up in people's living rooms at 7:30?"

Janet had known Tom Spence for almost five years; she respected his professionalism as the head of their promotion department. His job was to promote the station, to increase their ratings, and thereby to increase their advertising income. She had begun her career at the station as his assistant. He had been her early mentor, but now the student had equalled the teacher. The fact that he was opposed to this new show was particularly troubling to Janet because she knew in fact that he was not crazy. His opposition virtually demanded her attention.

"Tom, I don't know as much about it as you do, but I must say that what I've seen so far does trouble me. Are they not going to have any controls at all on what is televised?"

"Not according to Network, and I've called the people who should know. They're just going to let it all happen, in the name of realism and 'true life in the city'."

"What about the FCC? Aren't there some standards?"

Tom laughed, as the waitress brought their iced teas. "Are you kidding? There used to be. This show would have been impossible just a few years ago. But the American Civil Freedoms League brought all those lawsuits, and the networks and cable stations have been competing with each other to push beyond the old standards. The result is that there aren't any standards at all any more. If you'll excuse a quote from the Bible, Janet, it says at the end of Judges, 'In those days there was no king in Israel; everyone did what was right in his own eyes.' That seems to be about where we are today."

The quotation reminded Janet of the other thing about Tom: she knew that he was a Christian. Despite herself, a voice warned her that she should watch out; he probably had some hidden religious agenda.

"It does seem like Network may be going too far with this one. I certainly would not want my kids, much less younger children, seeing firsthand, live and in color, the worst scenes of what happens in our city. Without any editing or masking or explanation. But what do you expect to do about it?" They paused while their sandwiches arrived.

"I asked you to lunch because you obviously have Bill Shaw's ear and his confidence. A group of us feel so strongly that, if something doesn't change, we may threaten to quit if our station carries this show. It would be better if it could be stopped at Network, by opposition from enough local stations. But if that's not possible, at least we can stand up here for what's right. We would like you to join us—or at least be helpful and run interference for us with Bill."

"Good grief, Tom. You're willing to lose your job over this one show, in a sea of other shows which are almost as bad? What about Sandy and your two girls? You know jobs are not easy to come by now."

"I know. It's tough. A group of us are praying." Janet raised her eyebrows. "Sandy is praying too. She feels just as strongly as we do. I don't know what will happen. But I do know that this show is not right, and someone has to try to stop it. I guess we feel that if it is not us at this station, then who will it be?"

"Well, I doubt I'll be praying," Janet smiled, and a voice laughed quietly within her at her little put-down. "But I do agree that this show, if it's as you say, seems to be going too far. I tell you what I'll do: you get me the details that you have from Network on the format. I'll read it over and discuss it again with you. If I still agree that the show is lousy, then I'll set up a meeting for your group with Bill, and I'll attend and add my voice. But I don't plan to risk my job over this show or over any other show."

"Fair enough," said Tom. "We appreciate whatever help you can give us. I'll make you a copy of the information right after we get back."

"Can you come over and spend the night on Saturday?" Brent asked Tommy as school was letting out. "You can come home with us after the game. We'll probably all go to the pizza place. My brother is having a friend over too. Maybe we'll get to see some of those movies!" With that he rolled his eyes and grinned.

"Sounds good to me. I'll check with Mom when I get home and call you. I think my dad is going somewhere this weekend, so she probably won't mind."

"Mr. Sullivan, it's a gentleman named Robert Meredith on line three," Mary, his secretary, announced on the intercom.

The name was familiar, but he could not place it. "OK," he said, "I'll take it."

"Richard, this is Robert Meredith, Bobbie's dad. How are you today?"

"Fine," Richard replied, but a voice was already screaming inside to watch out; he vaguely remembered something unpleasant.

"Remember a while back when we were at that parents' meeting at school, and I mentioned that this spring we were going to have a men's prayer breakfast with Benjamin Fuller as the speaker? Well, it's coming up in two weeks. You said you'd like to hear Fuller, and I'd like to invite you as my guest. It's two weeks from Thursday at 7:30 at the Palace Hotel. Can you make it?"

Oh great, Richard thought, *a prayer breakfast. Just what I need at 7:30 in the morning!* A voice was telling him to make an excuse, but for some reason it had a little less volume than usual. Perhaps it was Hugh McEver's death last night; maybe that made him pause. But he was still about to say no, when he thought again about Benjamin Fuller. Richard had practiced corporate law for years, and Ben Fuller had been one of the premier merger and acquisition lawyers in the nation for two decades. Richard had always wanted to hear him. He finally decided that he could sit through whatever else happened at a prayer breakfast in order to see and hear Ben Fuller firsthand.

"Oh, sure, Robert. I remember. I guess I've never been to a prayer breakfast before, but I'd like to hear Benjamin Fuller. So count me in."

"Great, Richard. I know you'll enjoy it. It will be in the Grand Ballroom at the Palace. I'll have them send you an invitation. See you there." And they said goodbye.

Richard couldn't even remember what Robert Meredith did for a living. He would have to ask Susan, so he could carry on a civil conversation at that early hour. He wrote the meeting in his appointment book, wondering as he did what sort of businessman had enough spare time to invite other men to prayer breakfasts!

■ ■ ■

As Janet worked in the kitchen that evening preparing their supper, she shook her head and smiled to herself, thinking back on her short conversation with Richard that Wednesday afternoon. They usually checked with each other to find out what, if anything, had come up to modify the family's routine for that particular evening. She smiled because for the first time in weeks, they were all four actually going to be home, and they might really sit down to a meal together. No baseball practice, no cheerleading assignment, no late taping session at the station, no crisis in the law practice.

With a hint of sadness, Janet reflected through her smile that a supper together had become the exception. Whatever else had been wrong in her own home growing up, at least they had almost always dined together as a family. Oh, well; thank God for small blessings.

Susan and Tommy had been home from school for some time, doing their homework. Now Susan was on the phone, as usual, and Tommy was two blocks away at Brent's house. Janet was not only cooking supper, but also preparing a casserole to give to Nancy Bryant to deliver to Betty McEver tomorrow. She wanted to talk to Betty and ask about the children, but she decided that she should wait a day or two.

Tommy came home as it started to get dark, and Richard was virtually on time, right behind him. A few minutes later, Richard sat at the breakfast room table, looking at the paper with one eye and the evening news with the other. When Susan and Tommy came in, Richard asked them about their days at school and listened to brief reports. He then reminded Janet that he had to leave late the next day for the law conference in Atlanta, returning home Sunday afternoon.

Susan used that opening to ask if Amy could spend the weekend with them, since her neighbor didn't want to go to her family's new mountain house again. And Tommy asked if he could spend Saturday night at Brent's, after their baseball game. Janet agreed to both requests, and as she dished up supper, there followed a general discussion about their weekend schedules, all of which Richard would miss.

They ate dinner together, interrupted only once by the telephone. And during the rest of the evening, each Sullivan pursued his or her own activity, from homework to the newspaper to the television. Richard reviewed another draft of the McKinney contract and some other work he had brought home. Janet read through the material on "911 Live" which Tom Spence had given her. She was appalled by some parts of it, and she made some notes to discuss with Tom in the morning.

It was a thoroughly normal evening, partly because they were all a little exhausted from the hectic night before. Later, as they sat together in the den, watching a television show, Susan asked her father what would happen to the McEver children. He replied that it depended a lot on how much life insurance McEver had. Between programs, Tommy asked both parents whether they thought McEver's soul had gone to heaven. Richard and Janet looked at each other briefly. Richard responded that he believed everyone probably went to heaven: how could a just God do anything else? Tommy thought about it for a moment and then nodded.

Nepravel, who had been listening from the ceiling, smiled hideously and gave a thumbs up to Richard; he couldn't have said it any better himself! If only Richard could have seen McEver as *he* had last seen McEver! Sometimes this was almost too easy, with the fathers teaching the children the same lies it had taken the demons years and years to build up. Could Richard still repeat the lie which Confusion had fed him way back in college? "Yes," chortled Nepravel, as Richard looked right at Tommy and told him with the voice of parental authority that the Bible never really mentioned hell anyway, so he didn't have to worry about it. Fantastic! Confusion was passing from generation to generation, and all Nepravel had to do was watch. Weren't these voices just incredible, when nothing interfered with them?

Later that night, after the kids had gone to bed, Janet reflected in the bath on how wonderfully sane and normal their evening together had been. Not a single argument. They'd actually talked about issues of life and death. The dark note was that Richard was going away for the weekend, but even he had seemed a little sad about it, like he wanted to stay home. Why couldn't they have more times like this?

After her bath, she selected a particularly revealing nightgown, which she had not worn in a long time, and she put on Richard's favorite perfume. He was already in bed, reading. She turned off all but one light in their bathroom—she knew that he liked a little light—and sat down on the bed next to him.

When he looked up, she smiled and said, "I really enjoyed having you home with us tonight. It was great just talking together. I wish we had evenings like this more often."

Janet meant her words as a genuine compliment, trying to break the ice between them with words and with looks, reaching out to her husband as best she knew how. Trying desperately to use the good fortune of a pleasant evening together to bridge the widening gulf. But Richard saw her, and instead thought of Kristen, fifteen years and two children younger. He heard Janet's words, but a voice told him that it was an attempt to make him feel guilty for not being home more often. And the involuntary guilt over his affair with Kristen, whom he would see again in just twelve hours, touched off that volatile mixture. His words exploded out too quickly, almost as if they were spoken by someone else in advance: "Janet, you look so cheap in that get-up. I'm glad we were all home, too. But I'm tired tonight, and I have to travel tomorrow. Let's just go to bed. OK?"

His words stung her, and he knew it. He wanted to take them back, and he almost reached for her. But a voice told him that after years of ignoring his needs, trying to be a big executive, she had some nerve suddenly getting dolled up, rolling her eyes at him, and expecting him to respond like Pavlov's dog! Well, he wouldn't do it. He had pride too. What about all the times he had almost begged her, only to be told that she was too tired?

Let's see how she likes that line for once! So the emotion that began as remorse only a second before was whipped instead into a self-righteous put-down. Score one for him.

She recoiled, his reaction so contrary to her own feelings of the past hour that she was genuinely speechless. "But, Richard . . ." she finally started, not knowing how to finish. Uncertain of her feelings. Uncertain of his motives. Uncertain of her femininity. Not trusting her senses with him. Feeling terrible, as if the wind had been kicked out of her. For an instant she almost started crying; she almost reached for him. But the look in his eyes raised her own defenses. Pride started to take over. She would show him! But then she simply couldn't do it. It had all just been too much, all these many months. She caved in. She *did* start to cry. She *did* reach for him. She lay down on his shoulder and sobbed, saying nothing, not knowing what to say.

And, as he lay there, his book on the bed, Janet's tears wetting his shoulder, Richard's heart melted. A new image came to his mind, of Janet in their college days. Of their great times together, before law firms and television stations. Of Susan and Tommy being born. Of tricycles and swing sets. Of a simpler and happier life. His hand came up to stroke her head, and he whispered two very difficult words: "I'm sorry." And he meant it.

He turned her to him and cupped her face in his hands. "I'm sorry. We've both just been too busy for each other. I did have a great evening tonight with you." Smiling, he added, "And you don't look cheap . . . You look great."

Janet smiled, tears still all over her face. "I'm sorry, too. Let's try harder, both of us, to be together. OK?"

"Yes," he replied, feeling better than he had for months. "We will."

They went on to make love together that night, for the first time in a very long time. The release, particularly for Janet, was overwhelming. She cried and laughed and hugged him to her.

Once the lights were completely out and he lay with his arms around her, Richard wondered to himself what on earth he was going to do with Janet and Kristen.

At midnight's unholy meeting above the north side of the city, the news from eight different demons was about the upcoming prayer breakfast. Sectorchief Balzor fumed. "It's one thing when one or two of those pastors preach their cursed Word about Jesus in churches; we can contain that. But when they come outside where we're in control, it really makes me angry. Does any one of you know yet what they're really up to?"

"They've invited in Benjamin Fuller. He can be very dangerous," snarled Tymor, one of several menacing demons who everyone knew was vying for Balzor's position, should he ever make a slip. "In Pittsburgh last year a revival started in the financial sector and in two big downtown churches when he spoke. We're still having big problems up there. We even lost some of our strongest voices when several young ministers became Christians."

"That won't happen here!" railed Balzor. "What else?"

Abalat, another pretender to Balzor's power, said, "It's those three ministers—Stephen Edwards, Jim Burnett, and Michael Andrews—who are behind this. There hasn't been a move toward the businessmen in this city in years, and they're pushing it."

"But we've got them separated in different denominations! Two are white, and one is black. How did those three get together?" Balzor looked around accusingly, as his assembled cadre of people haters and family destroyers writhed in anticipated pain. But no one spoke. Any one of them would have sold his fellow demon back to hell to escape that fate himself, but no one answered.

After a long pause, Balzor continued, "This is potentially very dangerous. If business leaders find out the Truth and then repeat it, others will listen to them. And you all know what usually happens to families when the husband goes over. We almost always then lose the wife, the children, friends, and others. It's a mess! We've got to go to work to make this prayer breakfast ineffective. How are they preparing for it?"

"That," answered Tymor, rising to his full height in front of the ranks, "is the good news so far. This is their first stab at a prayer breakfast. They don't really know what they're doing. Thankfully there has been almost no prayer support, just a few general statements, but nothing by name. Their follow-up committee hasn't even met yet; I've kept the chairman out of town on business all week. I recommend that we get Discouragement and Fear in here immediately to work on the hosts. Then even if Fuller does come and speak well, we can contain their paltry results, and they'll never try another one." He ended his recommendation with a nod toward Balzor, who had been listening along with the others.

"Yes, yes, right away. Get them here tonight so we can plan," Balzor ordered Tymor, reclaiming his position of authority by turning the suggestion into a command. "And," he said, looking out at all of his demons, "put the usual measures into effect at once: illness, telephone confusion, concern about the costs, missed meetings, schedule conflicts. And, of course, the voices. You've got to redouble your attention and be sure that all the voices on your streets and in your businesses are operating at full volume. We don't know who might be invited to this thing, or when. We've got to be sure they don't go; but if they go, we've got to be sure they don't hear! We've perhaps grown a little too soft in the past few years with all the help from the media; but this is a real test, and I want every one of you on the alert. We will not lose souls that belong to us to an old attorney and three amateur preachers! I want a report from each one of you, every night, until this is over. Now go!"

Nepravel and Zloy again flew back to their neighborhoods. Tonight it was Nepravel's turn to worry. "Just as I was leaving Devon Drive a little while ago to come up to our meeting, I flew through the Sullivans' house for a final evening check. I couldn't believe it! I came in on the tail end of a reconciliation! They both told each other that they were sorry. They held each other. She cried. He felt bad about his affair with that real estate agent. It was sickening. Balzor has big things planned for them, and now this! I'm glad our exalted leader was so upset about the prayer breakfast that he didn't even ask for our usual reports. I've got to do something, and quickly."

"Hold on," breathed Zloy as they neared the familiar rooftops of the commercial district between their two neighborhoods. "Was He involved?"

"I don't think so, from what I could see in those few minutes. This wasn't about faith; they just looked at each other for the first time in many months and realized how, one inch at a time, they had moved miles apart. They longed to get back to where they were years ago, and they both said they would try. But neither of them talked about Him," Nepravel replied, with a derisive slight to the final word.

"Then don't worry. If they're trying to fight you themselves, relying on their own power and ability, you know they'll fail. How can they battle against the voices and the lies and the pride that you've sown in them over the years? They may reconcile for a while, but on their own they're too far gone to ever get back. You've done a good job—I've watched. If I can just confuse that Bobbie Meredith into stopping her prayers for that family, there will be no interference at all with your work."

Once Nepravel considered Zloy's words and agreed with them, he smiled again his malicious grin. "Thanks. I hope so. We've got a lot invested in them. He's well respected in the legal and business communities. When we bring him down, it will discourage hundreds of others. And speaking of sowing and reaping," Nepravel added, "would you like to hear about McEver last night? He was truly one of the most surprised I've ever seen! I think it must be this new generation. They really believe what we've been telling them, because they hear it all day, every day, from every imaginable source. Like Balzor was saying, maybe it *is* getting too easy for us, with the media and the movies and the records, but I sure do like it! And are they ever surprised when they find out that *all* of that has been lies!

"And then when He tells them from the judgment seat that the Bible really is Truth, and asks them why they haven't believed it, it's almost too funny to watch. They feel so betrayed. McEver pleaded for another chance in his next life! Can you believe that? More and more they tell Him that same New Age stuff we've been feeding them about reincarnation. Since I hate Him so much, after what He did to us, I do like to watch Him when they try that. I'm almost feeling sorry for Him; how must it feel to lose so many of your own creation? They're all so stupid! You're right, Zloy. Thanks. The Sullivans haven't got a chance on their own."

■   ■   ■

THURSDAY, APRIL 20 ■ The next morning Janet awakened with more energy
than she had felt in months. Before Richard awoke, as she packed his
necessities in a small suitcase for his trip to Atlanta, she was actually
excited about the challenges on her "do list" for the day, and she was
already thinking about Richard's return on Sunday. One new item for her
executive goal list was going to be "Spend more time with Richard." She
felt she had a small opening to save their marriage, and now she had to
make a conscious effort to work on it.

Richard also awoke that morning feeling better than he had in a long
time. He lay in bed and listened to Janet humming softly as she moved
around their room, back and forth to his suitcase, and he thought back
happily to how this habit had begun. When they had only been married
about a month, he was called to an interview with a big law firm, and he
had to be gone over the weekend. Janet, who had grown up with only one
sister and no brothers, was intrigued by all things male; and she had asked
him to show her exactly what he would take for his trip. So they had
packed his bag together, laughing as he pulled out and explained each
item. Unknown to Richard, she had slipped love notes into the folds of his
underwear and the pockets of his trousers; he found them during that
weekend, reminding him of her. There was even a photo of herself, which
he happened to pull out of his pocket in the middle of his interview. They
had laughed about that for months. The love notes had long since stopped,
but Janet still always packed his bag for him.

He rolled over and smiled. She pecked him on the cheek and smiled
back. "I bet you need some coffee, after I kept you up all night. How ya
feeling, 'boy attorney'?" It was a name she had not called him in years.

"Fine. Just fine. You need to take it easy on this old man, though," he
added.

"No way," she smiled over her shoulder as she headed to the kitchen
for two cups of coffee.

But Richard wasn't really fine, and he knew it. He lay quietly in bed,
thinking. What had happened last night? Was Janet a new woman; was
he a new man? Was she really going to work less, to spend more time with
him and the kids? Was he? Was last evening the dying gasp of an
impossibly wrecked marriage, or a new beginning? And, more to the
immediate point, what was he going to do about Kristen, whom he was
supposed to see in a few hours?

The next hour went according to the Sullivan household routine, and
soon they were all headed for their destinations. As he said goodbye,
suitcase in hand, Janet gave him a warm hug, looked up into his eyes, and
said, "I really do love you, Richard. Last night was wonderful. Come home
as early as you can, and let's do it again!" He smiled a genuine smile,
hugged her back, and promised that he would.

As he drove to work that morning, the competing voices in Richard's
mind threatened to cause him sensory overload—the debate was almost
audible. Should he stop seeing Kristen? Was Janet really going to be

different? Was *he* going to be different? Shouldn't he wait and see? Should he call Kristen and make an excuse for today? What if Janet found out about them? What if he lost *both* of them? What about the kids? Could he really try hard with Janet, while still seeing Kristen? Was that fair to Janet? If Janet hadn't really changed, what if he dumped Kristen too quickly? Then where would he be? The voices kept up at this pace all the way downtown, through the parking garage, and even into the elevator, as he rode up to the thirty-seventh floor.

But in the hundreds of questions he asked himself that morning, not once did he push past the most cursory thought about his own responsibilities. Richard had grown up in a generation quick to claim its rights, but slow to face its responsibilities. He was convinced that Janet didn't understand him or his "needs," that she had changed once she had gone back to work. Only the dimmest of voices got through, once or twice that whole morning, that perhaps he also had responsibility for their relationship over the past few years. But another voice always countered that it was primarily the wife's job in a marriage to work on keeping them happy. It was hard to imagine that he had to do anything or change anything about himself.

He felt badly about his betrayal of Janet; but, doggone it, she had asked for it, by ignoring him for what seemed like years, working so hard on her job at the station. But on the other hand, she *was* his wife, and they had shared so much together. This morning he found himself imagining for a moment that their marriage might just really work out. He would have to say something to Kristen, to put some distance between them. But now Kristen loved him, too, she said. And did he love her? He didn't really want to; he hadn't originally planned to; he simply didn't know.

In the end, the only decision he could make was to wait and see. He would try to back Kristen off a bit, if the opportunity presented itself, to buy some time with Janet. And that thought made him wish that the problem could just somehow go away. His life was getting very complicated, almost too complicated. He was debating with himself, and he could see both sides very clearly. How had he gotten into this mess?

"Tom, my problem is that I can see both sides of this issue very clearly," Janet frowned, as they talked in her office with the door closed. "Certainly there is the public's right to know, even if the communication of that knowledge is not particularly attractive."

He started to protest her choice of words, but she held up her hand. "But I also appreciate your concern about showing this program unedited to an audience which will almost certainly contain children. Especially when they're already exposed to enough violence on television and in real life."

"That's important, Janet," Tom finally replied, "but just as important is the precedent. I mean, look how far we've come from just a few years ago; and we've done it one small but significant step at a time. If I had told you when Susan was born that on television today we'd have male and female nudity, couples obviously having orgasms in bed, gays hugging and kissing, bloodbaths on every local news show, and almost every comedy hit dripping with sexual *double entendres*, would you have believed it?

"Of course not, but here we are. How did it happen? One show tries something as a daring 'experiment,' and the next season everyone is doing it. A year later it becomes the new norm.

"Now if this show gets on as another 'experiment,' where do we go next? Public executions? Broadcasts of graphic evidence during trials? Teenage suicides videotaped and shown on the six o'clock news? Satanic rites with animal sacrifices? Janet, we have to stop this somewhere. Draw the line and say, 'Not here, not on my watch. I won't be part of this.' If we don't, then in a few years there will be a 911 channel, broadcasting the worst moments and most devastating personal tragedies from across our nation—and from around the world—for all to see, twenty-four hours a day."

"OK. OK. I know how you feel, and as I said, I agree. It's probably too much. But I can also see the other side. The anti-censorship side. And I can understand how the show could boost our ratings. We have to think of that in this economy."

"Censorship? We're not talking about censorship. I almost wish we were, but the government weenied out on this one years ago. We're talking about our own network, or at least our own station, making the corporate decision that this show is not appropriate. And the ratings argument is all wet. If this goes on, then in six months the other networks will copy it, and we'll be right back where we were—except that we've torn away another brick in the foundation holding up our society."

"Now, Tom, don't get too philosophical on me."

"I happen to believe that very strongly. We in the media have been tearing away those bricks for the last twenty years, until there's almost no foundation left. And someday, just maybe someday, there might actually be a backlash, if people ever wake up and realize how far we've sunk, and why. Then what about the ratings? I hate to think."

"I'm not too worried about that; but, again, I do share your concern about this show. I'll set up a meeting with Bill for early next week. Besides the two of us, who else do you want to attend?"

Richard had devised a simple but virtually foolproof ruse to carve out his Tuesday and Thursday "lunches" with Kristen, thanks to technology. Janet had been bugging him about his waistline. So he joined the Downtown Health Club, conveniently located near Kristen's top-floor apartment at Park Place. He told Mary, his secretary, and Janet that he would probably be jogging or working out in the weight room, so he bought a telephone pager he could wear as he exercised. He told both of them not to bother to call the club if they needed him. It would be much quicker and simpler just to page him directly, and he would return the call.

In the almost three months that they had been meeting, he'd only been to the health club two times. He had returned several calls to his secretary, and one to Janet, from Kristen's bed. And he had smiled to himself, a month later, when he realized that by just eating some fruit on those two days and by "exercising" as they did, he had actually lost a few pounds! And the health club cover explained his shower in the middle of the day. On several occasions a voice had congratulated him for being so clever with these arrangements; they had certainly worked well so far.

But today he wasn't feeling very clever, as he walked toward Park Place a little before noon. The catharsis—a word he remembered from English lit in college—with Janet last night, and the debate in his head that morning, had drained his emotions. He even wondered if he could perform as expected. All morning he had been thinking of Janet, of how they had loved and laughed together for so many years. Of how beautiful she really was, even now; of how she had suffered the pain of childbirth twice for them; of their real joy until . . . *when? Several years ago. What had happened? Was it really just boredom? Was it her new job? Was it his job? With all their other responsibilities, had they both just forgotten to try? The little extra things they used to do for each other, the glue that said "I love you." When had they stopped doing them? Who had stopped first? Did that even really matter?*

And then he had met Kristen. He occasionally handled real estate closings, and Kristen had been the agent on a big home purchase for one of their firm's corporate CEO clients. Richard still remembered the electric effect she had on him when she first came to see him with some documents, the day before the closing. She had been dressed in a smart suit, all business in its cut, but all female in its shape. Her brown hair was piled behind her head; and her freckles added an incongruous impishness to an impression which was otherwise one of intelligence and vitality.

That day she had deferred to his legal authority and treated him with respect, asking him questions and seeming to be genuinely interested in his answers. It had been late in the afternoon, and Richard heard the voice of Lust, which Nepravel had been nurturing regularly, as his marriage with Janet began to unravel. "Why don't we adjourn to the pub across the street, and I'll finish the explanation?" he said suddenly, when that thought first entered his mind.

She agreed, and they sat and talked quietly for over an hour. The next afternoon was the real estate closing, and she asked him to lunch on the following day, as a professional gesture of thanks for help on her biggest sale so far. He gallantly accepted in front of the other participants at the conference table. That had been their one and only real lunch together. On their second "date," at a noisy bistro, they had not even read their menus when Kristen mentioned that her apartment was just around the corner and that it was much quieter there.

From that afternoon on, he had been lost in her. It had started as simple passion, ignited, he thought, by her attractiveness and by the inattention, he felt, of his "executive" wife. It never would have occurred to Richard to imagine where the voices that egged him on were coming from, or what was producing those powerful rationalizations whenever a more quiet voice tried to tell him that he was terribly wrong. And it certainly never occurred to him that someone was trying to help him destroy his life, his marriage, and his children. Whenever he was with her, it simply seemed "right."

This seed of passion, once planted and nurtured by their long afternoons together, soon grew into a real relationship. Richard quickly learned to respect Kristen's mind as well as her body. Not as old or as experienced as Richard (or Janet, for that matter), Kristen naturally deferred to him, which he loved, and which further fed his fast-ripening ego. But she had a quick intellect. What's more, they were interested in many of the same subjects, in real estate, law, and other areas. Here was a beautiful young woman, who told him that she liked him, talked intelligently with him, and shared many of the same interests. Soon Nepravel did not even have to maintain the voices at night; Richard was doing quite well with his own library of lies, all by himself. And there were no other voices in his recent past to diminish the volume of the lies he told himself. So he carried on, seeing her at least twice a week.

But today, for the first time, he had some slight doubts. Maybe there was a downside. Maybe he and Janet could and would get back together. How much better for the kids? What would Kristen do? Probably better for her, actually, because he never really intended to leave Janet or to marry her, anyway.

Those were his thoughts as he rode the elevator to the twelfth floor, knocked once, and let himself in with his key. She was barefoot, putting a fruit bowl on the table in the dining area, dressed in a tight khaki skirt and a crisp white blouse, unbuttoned half way down. She smiled when she saw him, and all the debates and all the arguments of the last three hours were instantly drowned out by the singular howl of his lust for her. He smiled back and shut the door.

Afterward, as they shared the same fruit bowl in bed, and the complexities of the last half of his day broke through his mind, he began to think of things he might say to slow down their relationship a bit. Not stop it, of course, but just apply some gentle brakes, in case he later had to force a full stop.

Before he could begin talking about all the work he had to do in the upcoming weeks, to hint that he might have to miss some of their lunches, Kristen turned to him, many more freckles now visible, and asked, "When are you going to tell Janet that you're leaving her?"

He gulped and drew back a bit. Sensing his reaction, she continued. "You told me a month ago you thought it was over between you two. You said it would be better for your kids if you stopped fighting at home with each other. And you've told me that you love me." Richard cringed inside—he had told her once or twice lately, in the middle of their passion, that he loved her. The words had just come from nowhere, but now they were being fed back to him by someone who remembered very well. "So when do I get you all to myself, every day, instead of just being an afternoon romp?" She leaned over on his shoulder and looked up at him with her bright brown eyes.

"I don't know, Kristen. That's a big step. I'm not so sure now about what it would do to the kids." Sensing an opening to turn the conversation more the way he had intended, he added, "I've really got to spend more time with them, especially Tommy. It's not their fault that Janet and I are so unhappy, and they shouldn't be punished for it."

"Well, when we're living together, you'll have plenty of time to be with them. Probably more time than now. I won't mind sharing you with your children. It's just Janet who bothers me."

This was the first time that either of them had mentioned living together. It occurred to him that two days before he probably would have been flattered and happy. But today it sent a cool chill down his back. Before he could respond, Kristen continued, "And I've figured out how to give you a first taste of what it will be like for us to live together all the time. I've got a surprise for you, Richard: I'm coming to Atlanta with you!"

His shock was apparent. She laughed. "I called your secretary, pretending to be a travel agent, to confirm your accommodations. Now we're booked on the same flights and in adjoining rooms at the same hotel. What do you think about that? We can do this again tonight! What will it be like for us to make love when it's dark outside?" she laughed again.

Knowing that he was licked, he caved in. Anyway, it was past time to get back to the office for a couple more hours of work before the flight. He had tried. He told himself that he really had tried. And he would try again, some other day. But now to the inner voice of Confusion there was added the mental picture of himself and Kristen alone for a weekend in a strange hotel. It was just too much. As Zloy had predicted, Richard was no match for the voices and his own visual images. He was trying to fight a forest fire with a bucket of water.

"And, oh, while I'm thinking about it," she said, reaching across him to take her purse from her night table, "I'd better leave this here." Lifting out a chrome Sig Sauer P-230 automatic pistol, she added, "It wouldn't do too well through airport security."

"Good gracious, Kristen. Why do you carry that?"

"Richard, I show houses at all hours of the day and night, and on the weekends, to I don't always know who. I just hope that this gun will give me a little edge if someone ever tries something. But I'll have you to protect me this weekend!" she said, as she leaned provocatively across him again to put the gun in her drawer, and then kissed him deeply.

Walking back to his office, Richard shook his head in disbelief. What do you do when two women love you? He conveniently skipped over the fact that one of the women he had only known for two hours at a time over just the past few months. The other he had solemnly promised before

God, eighteen years before, to love, to honor, and to cherish, in good times and in bad, in sickness and in health, forsaking all others, for the rest of his life. The lawyer in him might have asked to see that agreement in writing, if one still expected to enforce it today. He certainly no longer felt that particular promise to be binding or important. "After all, who else did?" he asked himself. And that particular voice sounded very reassuring. He began to look forward to their trip to Atlanta.

3

F RIDAY, APRIL 21 ■ Friday dawned cold and wet, and Janet thought for a second about the early spring front with its wind and rain, hoping that Richard's flight had been uneventful. She and the kids went through their normal morning routine, each glad that the work week was almost over.

"I hope this weather clears up for your game tomorrow," Janet mentioned to Tommy, as he gulped down a large bowl of cereal.

"Coach says it's supposed to," Tommy replied, not looking up.

"Amy is going home from school this afternoon and then bringing her stuff over," said Susan. "Her parents aren't leaving for the mountains until after five."

"That's fine. Just don't destroy the place until I get home from work," she said unnecessarily. "I don't know of any crises brewing, so I should be home on time. I may even try to sneak out a little early. Maybe we can all go out to dinner, since Dad's out of town," she smiled.

For the first time in over eighteen years of marriage, Richard awoke that morning next to a woman other than Janet. When he looked over at Kristen's sleeping form, a voice told him that he felt fifteen years younger. Nepravel had alerted his counterpart in Atlanta, and the demon was already on hand for this very important morning, playing the voices in Richard's head like a virtuoso. Not that they really needed much help, under the circumstances.

He and Kristen had arrived late, after a bumpy flight, just ahead of the front. But then they stayed up even later, playing like two teenagers let loose in the adult cookie jar. Kristen was determined to make the night memorable for Richard, and she succeeded.

Now he was late to the morning registration and first meeting. He slid out of bed to shower and to dress. A voice told him how great it was to feel so young and to be having such a great time! So easy and so much fun. Almost drowned out was the single pinprick which hit just once, telling him that this could not go on for long. He actually looked up from shaving when that thought hit him.

When he pulled a fresh pair of underwear out of the bureau drawer, a note fell on the floor. He reached and opened it. It was from Janet. "Last night was almost like old times. I love you and will try my best to make us a family again. Hurry home. Me." As he lowered the note, he saw Kristen's dozing body, and the freckles on her back. It occurred to him that his situation was simply bizarre. He was OK when each woman could be kept in her usual place. But when they both impacted his life at the same instant, it made his hands sweat. He had to keep the women separated to preserve his sanity. And the voices told him just to enjoy himself while he was away, and not to think about such things for now.

Richard slipped out of their room while Kristen was still sleeping. She had planned a day of shopping, since his meetings would continue until just before supper.

Later that morning, during a break, he phoned Mary at his office to check in. "Please call Bruce McKinney and tell him that Tomlinson's attorney and I have almost worked out all of the details. I should have a second draft of the contract for him to review early next week."

"How is the conference going?" Mary asked.

"It's very interesting, but of course being away from home is always tough," Richard replied.

Nepravel was making his usual early afternoon rounds, pleased to see that most of the televisions in the occupied homes were turned on, either to soap operas or to talk shows. He was pleased because that meant he had much less work to do, maintaining the voices, when humans watched these shows regularly. How could anyone know what "normal" was anymore? These shows regularly produced stories and situations which even he had not thought of in his best moments!

Oh, there it was again. He suddenly sensed another passing. Two in one week! Superb! But, on the other hand, one had to watch out. Too many deaths in a short time caused people to think. And that could become a problem.

But, at any rate, he saw as he rose above the rooftops, it was old Mrs. Hall. Her mortal body was dead at last! It was great to be finally rid of her: one less of the ever diminishing voices which prayed regularly. One less light in the ever spreading darkness.

But speaking of light, he could see that the blasted angel had already almost arrived. He must have been in the area. Why?

Mrs. Hall's spirit, like all of them, was momentarily confused by the transition out of her mortal body. In a matter of a few moments, her spirit had gone through the trauma of death and into the incredible confirmation of immortality, suddenly free of all the earthly aches and pains that had racked her body for so many years. It was a great deal, Nepravel knew, to experience in such a brief moment.

He took his position next to Jean Hall, just as he had done three days earlier with Hugh McEver. As with McEver—as with all of them really— there was again the involuntary turning to face him, as the closeness of his stench pierced through the dazzling effect of the angel's luminescence.

There was again the shock and the natural concern for her spirit, so close to so much evil and such obvious hate. But Nepravel could see in her eyes that there was not the fear. Blast! He sensed that it would go badly for them at the judgment seat. She was definitely questioning, looking back and forth between him and the angel. But—and he hated it—he could see her quiet confidence as well.

As the three of them flew off to their appointed rendezvous, Nepravel knew he would have to downplay this death at the midnight meeting. With the prayer breakfast already on Balzor's nerves, Nepravel would be afraid to linger too long on losing another soul, even if it was an old lady. Nothing stirred up the demons more than a soul being allowed to pass into heaven, being atoned for by the death of Jesus, because heaven was the one place to which they could never go again.

Down deep inside, what made the most fearsome demons hate even the most insignificant humans was jealousy. It was jealousy that fueled their bitter struggle and gave them the energy to work incessantly to utterly confuse humans about the Truth. They almost never talked about it, but what they hated more than anything else was the thought of any lowly human spirit going to where they once had been, but had lost forever. And only because they had wanted a share of the power. It was so unfair! Nepravel, like all the demons, was determined that no more human souls would slip through, inheriting what was rightly his! "Curse them all! And curse that Jesus who made it possible!" he seethed.

SATURDAY, APRIL 22 ■ Saturday brought broken clouds racing across the sky from northwest to southeast, signaling that the front had passed and that the sun would soon be allowed to do its warming work on the damp and cool ground below. Completely unknown to Janet, as she worked on their late breakfast, the events that would occur in their children's lives that day would change their family forever.

Tommy packed his overnight bag to take to their baseball game so that he could spend the night at Brent's home. Susan and Amy were seated at the breakfast room table, looking through the latest magazines and comparing notes on the latest spring fashions.

Tommy's game was to be late in the afternoon, so he and Brent spent the morning on their bikes, bouncing between their homes, the nearby commercial area, and the city park, located at the midpoint of Devon Drive. On one turn through the park later that morning, they ran into their classmates, the twins Patrick and Becky Thornton, watching and helping their younger brother, Jeff, who was trying to fly a kite. Becky's best friend, Anna, was also there, sitting on a park table with the Thorntons. All of them wore sweaters against the chilly wind.

As Tommy and Brent pedaled up the sidewalk toward them on their sleek racers, Becky waved. "You know Tommy is kind of cute," Becky said to Anna, before the boys were within hearing range. "It's too bad he's not a little older. I've always just thought of him as somebody who was 'there,' as Patrick's teammate. But in class lately he has really had some interesting things to say. He's not bad."

The boys stopped their bikes and everyone said hello. For a few minutes they helped Patrick teach his younger brother the finer subtleties of flying a kite. Then they walked back over to Becky and Anna. "Will you be at the game?" asked Tommy, smiling at Becky.

"I don't know. I'd like to, but the game is so late today. Ian is picking me up early and we're going to a movie, so I'll just have to see."

There it is, thought Tommy. *The wall.* Subtle but nevertheless very real. Becky's parents already let her date the older boys who could drive, and that was a gulf that he would not cross for eighteen more months. With that one statement she had reminded him that although they might be almost the same age, he was still relegated to childhood, while she was moving on.

"Oh, well. Yeah, I understand. But if you do decide to come, it ought to be a good game. Both of our teams are undefeated," added Tommy, trying to increase her interest.

The four of them talked for a while, soon joined by Patrick, once Jeff's kite was securely hovering in the blue, clearing sky. After a while Brent said, "Well, Tommy and I have to go buy some things at the store for my mom. We'll see you guys later. See you at the game, Patrick." And the two of them left, waving a thumbs up sign to the young pilot of the kite.

"You two sure are getting dressed up just go to out to dinner," quipped Janet, as Susan and Amy collected their coats and purses near the Sullivans' back door, leading out to their garage.

"Well, we may go to a movie afterward," smiled Amy, "and you never know who you're going to run into!"

Susan was glad that Amy had answered. She was not used to lying to her mother, and Amy clearly seemed better at it. So Susan just smiled in silence.

"I know, I know. I was young once, too, as hard as that is for you to believe," added Janet, putting her hands on both girls' shoulders. "Just have a good time, and don't do anything I wouldn't do."

Susan gulped. It suddenly occurred to her that her mother had seemed a little happier the last two days; but she could not figure out why. *Is it because Dad is gone?* she suddenly thought, with a sinking feeling. Well, now was not the time to think or to talk about her parents' relationship.

"I'll expect you home by 11:30, no matter what you do. And I would appreciate it if you'd call me from wherever you wind up, if you do go somewhere after dinner."

Both girls just smiled and gave Janet a wave as they went through the door. Richard had taken a taxi to the airport so that Susan could borrow his car when Amy spent the night. Susan drove them over to the parking lot in front of Austin's Restaurant.

Tommy's game started on time but went to extra innings before Northpark finally won on an inside-the-park home run down the first base line by their star shortstop. Janet had dropped Tommy off with his overnight bag. Holding down a full-time job herself meant that there was not much time for shopping or other household chores. So her Saturdays were always very full. But today she had also attended the funeral for Hugh

McEver, which had been packed with family, friends, and neighbors. The presence of the McEvers' children had upset her. "Why did this happen?" she had asked herself. And after the funeral, she had been so rushed that she had not been able to stay for even a few innings of Tommy's game.

After the game, Brent's parents drove them back to their home to clean up. Then they all went out for pizza. Actually there were six of them, because Brent's older brother, Zane, had a friend, Roger, from his eleventh-grade class, over to spend the night as well. And the great thing about Roger, as far as Tommy and Brent were concerned, was that his older brother attended the local university, and he had videos!

As a cover for their real intentions, the boys rented a mindless teenage comedy from the video store in the same shopping center with the pizza restaurant. They were careful to pick a title that would interest neither of Brent's parents. This was all new to Tommy, but he quickly got caught up in the shared secret, and in the camaraderie with the older boys.

Upon returning to Brent's home, the four teenage boys spent a few moments with Brent's parents in the den so as not to seem in too big a hurry. Finally, Zane suggested, "Let's go see that movie," and the four of them retired to the basement, where Brent's family had a television and a VCR.

Once downstairs, Zane took the one rented video out of its case and fast forwarded it for a few minutes, in case they had to insert it on short notice, should they be interrupted unexpectedly. He then took that video out of the VCR and pulled out the three videos he and Roger had stashed in the basement before supper, offering their explicit covers to the two younger boys, as if they were trophies. "Which one do you want to watch first?" asked Zane. "Since this is your first time, Tommy, you can pick."

Tommy was almost bursting with anticipation. He pointed to *Young Desires*. They moved the armchairs up close to the television. While Roger inserted the video and turned down the volume, Zane turned off the lights. Nepravel, who had arrived shortly after their return from the restaurant, sat invisibly on top of the TV and cheered them on. He knew that no voices would be needed here, with the visual images that were about to overwhelm them.

The rendezvous between Susan, Amy, Billy, and his college classmate, Jay Stembler, happened as Amy and Billy had planned. Billy gave Amy a knowing hug, which seemed more familiar to Susan than the casual relationship Amy had so far represented to her. Billy introduced Jay and then suggested that they all four go in his car, leaving Susan's father's car in the parking lot, since the fraternity party was just beginning over at the university.

Soon the four of them were driving off to the east, and the two boys offered Amy and Susan paper cups with ice, filled with an unknown liquid.

"We thought you two rising seniors would like a little grapefruit juice and vodka," smiled Billy, as he handed a cup to Amy. She took a quick gulp and then settled back in her seat, smiling, with a little toast in Billy's direction.

This was Susan's first experience with college boys on a date. She had decided earlier that day that she would follow Amy's lead. But as Jay handed her a cup as well, she became uncertain of herself. She quickly decided that it would be rude to refuse the offer, but she also decided that she would only take small sips. Whatever "fun" Amy had advertised as being in store for them this evening, she knew inside that getting drunk in the back of a car with a boy she did not know was simply not her definition of fun.

In the Holcombes' basement, the visual images had been going on for over an hour. For the first fifteen minutes, Tommy's eyes had almost popped out of his head. Then he settled back into his chair and watched with full attention while the video simply overwhelmed his senses, short circuiting his brain with pictures he could never have imagined only an hour before.

With the end of the first video, Brent chose *Slippery When Wet*, and they hardly missed a beat between the two. Pressure was building and building in Tommy. He felt like a teapot on high heat, about to boil over. Nepravel, who had left for a while to check on the rest of the neighborhood that Saturday evening, returned to the basement for the grand finale.

Billy's fraternity house, like the others on fraternity row that Saturday evening, was jammed with college students, letting loose after a demanding week of classes, swaying to the beat from the disc jockey's extensive library of new and old tunes. They found a spot to park not too far from the cul-de-sac. As they walked up the sidewalk, Amy managed to squeeze Susan's hand and whisper, "Let's have a great time tonight." Susan, who had never been to a fraternity party before, smiled and nodded her head.

The din would have been louder had it not been absorbed by all of the bodies. Billy motioned for Jay to turn to the right, into the living room and toward the bar. In a matter of moments Susan and Jay had lost Billy and Amy in the crowd.

Jay had grown up in Memphis, and he and Susan had talked in the back seat about his impressions of Susan's city, where he was finishing his first year as a freshman at the university. He was a nice enough boy, Susan thought. Too many college boys were so impressed with themselves. Jay seemed to be the exception. When she confessed to him that this was her first fraternity party, he seemed genuinely surprised and told her that he would do whatever she wanted to make their evening a success. Then he asked her what she wanted to drink.

"I think I'll just take a Coke, thanks," Susan answered.

"Aw, come on," he suggested. "How about some vodka and grapefruit juice?"

"No, thank you. Let me just edge into this a bit, OK? A Coke will be just fine," she found the strength to say.

"OK. That's fine with me. Whatever you want." And he seemed to mean it.

Drinks in hand, they pushed back towards the source of the music, and Jay introduced Susan to several of his classmates and fraternity brothers. Susan recognized a few girls from the senior class at her high school, and it suddenly struck her that Amy's plan for the evening had not allowed for the daughter of one of her mother's friends seeing them at this party. That thought threw her, and she began to worry. She would have to find Amy and ask her for an answer to that one.

Soon she and Jay were dancing, and the evening flew by. She enjoyed the party enormously. She and Jay took breaks to get away from the noise and to talk every now and then. She stuck to her nonalcoholic drinks, which Jay respected. Just to be friendly, she accepted a few sips from his vodka and tonic.

Before she realized it, she looked at her watch to discover that it was 11:00! She could not remember seeing Amy or Billy for what seemed like the whole evening. If she and Amy were going to be home by 11:30, they had to leave quickly to retrieve her father's car from the restaurant parking lot. She pointed out the time to Jay and yelled in his ear over the music that they had to find Amy and Billy, and then leave as quickly as possible. Jay nodded, and they started their search through the fraternity house.

Janet used the rare Saturday night alone at home to catch up on several small domestic projects and to bake another casserole for Betty McEver. Betty had so much family in town and so many new problems to work through that Janet and several of Betty's other friends were keeping her refrigerator well stocked.

After the girls had left that evening, the earlier feeling of being surrounded by unanswered questions returned to buffet Janet. She felt no better equipped to answer the questions which the death of their neighbor thrust upon her than did those three precious children, the backs of whose heads she had focused on during most of the funeral. As she prepared the ingredients for the casserole, unusual questions broke through in her mind, touched off by the funeral, and too strong to be suppressed by the routine voices of busyness that usually did so. Janet did not know the answers, and pride and busyness had always kept her from asking anyone else who might be able to help. But maybe, just maybe, the questions would linger long enough, like seeds in the earth, to be triggered into life and growth with the right stimuli and care.

Finally, later than she had originally hoped, Janet took a long bath and climbed into bed to read, waiting for the return of the girls. It was only then that it occurred to her with some surprise that Susan had never called all evening.

■　■　■

The visual images were searing Tommy's young mind. It was almost as if the screen of the television were aflame and he could feel the heat in his eyes. His mind had long since gone into overload. The pressure had built inside him to the point where he felt that he was going to jump out of his skin.

Something had to give. They either had to stop watching these videos, which *he* was not going to suggest, or . . .

It was then he realized that the quiet whistles, catcalls and guffaws of the past hour had now stopped in the dark basement. Only when he started to turn his head back to see Roger and Zane, sitting behind him, did he realize that the other boys in the room were already relieving themselves sexually.

"Go ahead," whispered Roger to him in a low, guttural voice. "It's the only way to fly."

Tommy thought about it, and for just a moment, he felt stupid. But the visual images and the pressure were just too great, and everybody was doing it. So he followed Roger's advice.

Susan and Jay had started at one end of the fraternity house and pushed their way through to the other, without seeing either Amy or Billy. It was only after Jay had returned from a fruitless search upstairs that Susan suggested they go find Billy's car. Jay told her that Billy would not leave without telling them, and so he was as surprised as Susan to find that Billy's car was, in fact, gone.

Susan's initial annoyance because of the late hour had already changed into mild apprehension, and now it was headed toward serious panic. Where could Amy be? How could she have left without telling Susan? Did she leave voluntarily? Was she all right? And what would Susan tell her mother?

It was fast approaching 11:30, and she had no idea what her mother would do if she were very late. It had never happened before, but she knew it would not be good. She sensed that whatever else happened, her best course of action was to go home. Even though her mother would be terribly upset and disappointed, she could then help Susan deal with what to do about finding Amy.

"Jay, I have just got to get home," said Susan, in a voice filled with anxiety. "Do you have a car? Can you get me back to my dad's car in the parking lot? If Amy comes back, can you call me and be sure she gets home safely?"

"Yes, of course," answered Jay. "I have a car here, and I'll do all of that."

As they drove in Jay's car to the restaurant parking lot, he tried to soothe Susan's raw nerves and imagination, assuring her that there must be some reasonable explanation and that Billy was really a good guy. Susan listened to him but did not hear—her mind was racing through the possibilities of what might have happened to her best friend.

Susan hoped that by some chance Billy and Amy would be waiting for them at her father's car, but it sat almost deserted in what had once been a full parking lot. Jay offered to follow Susan home, but she thanked him and declined. They exchanged phone numbers so that each could call the other with any news about Amy or Billy. Susan then thanked him for what had been, until forty-five minutes earlier, a great evening for her, opened the door to her father's car, and slid behind the wheel.

The familiar smell of her father's car suddenly hit her, perhaps because all of her senses were so much on edge, with all of the adrenaline pumping through her body. Her father. Where was he? What could he do to help her or Amy? What would he do when he found out how she had lied to her mother? Would she ever be able to go out again? And did she deserve ever to go out again, after what she had done?

Pulling out of the parking lot, tears filling her eyes, she almost did not straighten up in time, just missing a power pole. That snapped her attention back to the road, but she still had no idea of exactly what she would say to her mother. Under the circumstances, should she blame it all on Amy? Should she take the responsibility herself? Would her mother call the police? Would she call Amy's parents at their mountain home? What on earth had they done? How stupid could she have been, lying to her mother and going to a fraternity party with boys she did not really know? It suddenly occurred to her that she could just as easily be the one who was missing!

As she slowed and began to turn into her driveway, still not knowing what she would say to her mother, someone suddenly darted out from the bushes on her right and waved for her to stop. She stopped, leaned over, recognized the form, and flung open the passenger door. Amy jumped in, her clothes obviously in disarray, her cheeks stained from tears.

Susan's heart was pounding in her chest. "Where have you been? What are you doing here? Are you OK? My goodness, Amy, do you realize it's 11:30, and I've been looking for you all over, not knowing whether you were dead or alive? What happened?"

"Please, go on so we won't be any later," replied Amy, remaining in control of her emotions, for the moment, even though she was just as physically upset as Susan. Taking out a handkerchief and straightening herself as best she could, she wiped her face and said, "Let's just get past your mother for now, and then I'll tell you what happened. We were at my house, and it got so late that I knew you would be coming home. So I just waited outside in the bushes for you to get here."

Amy's partial explanation left Susan with her mouth open. The moment's circumstances were playing wildly on her emotions. In less than fifteen seconds she had gone from distress, to anger, to thankfulness that her friend was safe, to deep concern about what, if anything, to tell her mother if she questioned them. Would she lie? Could she? What if her mother already knew where they had been, somehow, from one of their mutual friends? Or what if she found out tomorrow? There was now no time to ask Amy or to prepare. They were home, the garage door was coming down, and they would have to go in. Susan, too, wiped her eyes and cheeks, then quickly put on a dab of make-up.

She opened the door from the garage to the breakfast room with her key, her heart in her throat. Mercifully, her mother was not sitting right there in the bright light. They closed and locked the door, then turned off the light, which left only the light from the stairway and the light coming down the hall from her parents' bedroom.

Amy started to go upstairs, but Susan grabbed her arm, and they walked down the hall in the direction of her mother's bedroom. "We're home," whispered Susan toward the light in the doorway.

To her dismay, her mother opened the door and walked down the hall toward them. But at least she did not turn on any more lights. "I'm glad to see you. What did you wind up doing? And, Susan, why didn't you call me?" asked her mother.

As Susan opened her mouth, still not knowing exactly what to say, Amy spoke up. "We went to a movie, Mrs. Sullivan. It was . . ."

It suddenly occurred to Susan that Amy must have prepared this explanation in advance, for it to be so quick and so positive. Amy must have done this before!

Before Amy could finish the sentence, Janet, who had been looking at their faces, interrupted. "Are you girls all right?"

"Oh, yes," said Amy. "We went to see *Wounded Soldier*, and it was very sad. I guess we both cried at the end," she smiled through her lie.

"And, Susan, why didn't you call?" repeated Janet.

"We were late finishing dinner," lied Susan. Once over that first lie, she warmed to the task. "We just made it to the theater on time, and there was a line, and I guess in the rush to get to our seats I just forgot. I'm sorry, Mom. I'll be more careful next time."

"All right. I'm just glad you're both home safely. Get a good night's sleep, and don't stay up too late talking." With a welcome home smile gracing her face, she gave Susan a quick kiss on the cheek and turned to go back to her own bed.

With the door to Susan's room safely closed behind them, the emotional roller coaster of the last hour suddenly took its toll on Susan. Her knees started to buckle. She grabbed Amy and pushed her so that they sat down on the bed together. "So what, in heaven's name, happened to you tonight? Why didn't you tell me where you were? Can you imagine how worried I was about you? And what about this movie? I've never seen *Wounded Soldier*! What if Mom asks me about it?" So many questions. So much had happened to these two junior girls in one simple evening, when they were supposed to be at a restaurant and a movie.

Amy, too, was obviously racked by emotion. She started to cry, gently. Susan could tell that Amy was not crying for effect. She was not like that, anyway. These were genuine tears and genuine emotions coursing through

Amy's body in front of Susan. In a moment the trickle of tears turned into quiet sobs. "Oh, Susan, it was awful."

Whatever her own emotions had been, Susan was now very concerned for one of her two best friends. She reached out for Amy and slid across the bed to her. Amy buried her face on Susan's shoulder and cried for a while, interrupting her tears with her explanation.

"Oh, Susan, I was such a fool . . . It seemed so sensible at the time, but now I know I'm an idiot . . . You see, Billy and I have had quite a few dates, and I really like him a lot. He's so sweet. And, you know, I drank two or three of those grapefruit and vodka drinks when we first got there . . . and I guess I just lost my head, or I don't know—Anyway . . ." She wiped her eyes with a new Kleenex Susan handed her, then took a deep breath and looked down at the floor, "anyway, Billy told me that we should go somewhere to be alone." Amy visibly exhaled. Susan's back straightened as she kept her hand on Amy's hand.

"From somewhere, I don't know why—I guess it was the drinks—I told him that my parents were away for the weekend and that no one was at our house."

"Oh, Amy." Now it was Susan's turn to inhale deeply.

"I know, I know," offered Amy, still looking at the floor. Susan took Amy's hand in hers. "We tried once to find you, but we must have missed you. He was so impatient. He said we'd be back before very long and that you wouldn't miss us. He fixed me another drink, and we left." Susan exhaled through her teeth, making a quiet sound.

"Anyway, he drove us to my home, and he turned off the headlights of his car when we came up the driveway so no one would see. I, uh, let us in, and, uh, we . . . went to my parent's bedroom and, uh, Susan . . . I guess I'm not a virgin anymore." She tried to smile as tears again rolled down her cheeks, and she held her abdomen with her free hand.

Susan was speechless, the visual image in her mind of Amy and Billy holding hands as they walked through Amy's darkened house, just next door, the same home which she had been in all those thousands of times herself. And then the familiar image of Amy's parents' bedroom. And Amy and Billy on the bed together. That's where the visual images stopped because Susan simply could not complete the picture.

"I, uh, we did it on my parents' bed." Amy now visibly hung her head, and the tears again turned to sobs. "I feel so stupid, and dirty. I guess I was drunk. I don't even remember what it felt like, except that it wasn't any fun. Now it hurts," she said, again holding her lower abdomen. "What a night. What a mess I've made of it all. It feels so bad. I'm so sorry." She paused, but Susan was still speechless.

"Like, again, I guess I was drunk. I guess I passed out. Anyway, the next time I remember anything it was after 11:00, and I knew you'd be looking for us, and I knew you'd be upset, and we rushed around and got dressed (for some reason, those particular words hit Susan very hard, as if her teenage friend with whom she had just the other day been playing dolls, was now talking like her own mother) . . . made up the bed, and by then it was so late that I figured you must already be on the way home . . . So I told Billy to head back to the parking lot in case you had not left yet, and I told him I would wait in the bushes, in case you were already on the way so we wouldn't miss each other."

Those words reminded Susan that she had Jay's telephone number and had promised to call him if she found Amy. Should she call now? Would Billy already have bragged about his conquest of Amy to Jay? That made her angry, and she was not sure she could have a civil conversation with him. While she thought about that one, Amy concluded, "So there I was, waiting in the bushes outside your home, and thank God you came along on time." And this time she smiled a genuine smile of friendship. "You always were dependable and punctual! So what do you think, I've pretty well trashed tonight? Lying to your mom. Making you lie to your mom. It's just been a great evening!"

"Oh, Amy," was all that Susan could say at first. Then, trying to make her friend feel better, and as a natural reaction to all of the immediate tension, she added, "What are we going to do tomorrow night?"

They both laughed a short, nervous laugh. Then Susan again reached for Amy, and hugged her close. "Well, I guess you've taken a pretty big step, in a way that doesn't sound like it was very much fun for you. I'm sorry it happened this way . . . and I'm very sorry we lied. But here we are. I guess we'll make it."

"One more thing," added Amy, as she pulled back a bit from Susan's embrace and again looked down at the floor, "thinking back on it, I don't remember . . . I don't think he used any protection."

"What?" asked Susan. "Amy, how could you both be so stupid?"

"I don't know. Like I said, I'd had too much to drink. He said he didn't have any and that anyway nobody ever got pregnant the first time. I don't know," and finally her eyes rose level to Susan's.

"Oh Amy, you know that's hogwash. Why have we had all those sex education classes in school?" Realizing that she was coming on pretty strong and that there was now nothing either of them could do about it, Susan backed off, smiled, and patted her on the shoulder. "You're a real dope, you know."

"Yeah, I know. I just hope it will be all right. On top of all this, I sure don't need to be pregnant." She smiled bravely. "Anyway, let's see . . . I need to tell you about *Wounded Soldier*. I saw it last week with Jessica. I'll tell you about the highlights, and you'll be able to cover for any of the questions anyone ever asks you about the movie. Then we'll just keep all this quiet. And, like you said earlier, let's don't tell Bobbie. She wouldn't have understood us going to the party, so I know she'll never understand what else happened!" Amy shook her head.

"OK . . . and I guess now that I've calmed down some, I ought to call Jay and let him know you're safe. Do you think Billy has found him?"

"Probably," said Amy, "but I guess you ought to call if you said you would. By the way, what sort of a date was he?"

Susan picked up her phone to make the call, and she and Amy drifted back to familiar ground, chatting about their dates, away from the difficult tightrope on which their emotions had been balancing for the past hour and a half. They both sensed that neither of their lives would ever be the same again, for many reasons, after the events of this evening. And their emotions now needed to fall back on older, more familiar ground, to reset the bond between them, which had been stretched further than ever before by what had just happened. Susan had disobeyed her parents' rules. Amy, at seventeen, was no longer a virgin and ran some risk of being pregnant. They had both lied to Susan's mother. But their friendship had survived and, if it were possible, had seemingly actually deepened.

While his children were enduring trials that would dramatically change their lives, Richard and Kristen decided to enjoy room service and each other that Saturday night. It is safe to say that neither Tommy nor Susan ever once crossed Richard's mind all night. While he was with Kristen, no voice told him that Tommy, in acting on his sexual fantasies, and Susan, in lying to Janet, were both growing up to be just like their father. The voices did not volunteer that kind of information, just the opposite. And, besides, Balzor and Nepravel were planning other ways for Richard to find out more about his offspring.

4

WEDNESDAY, MAY 3 ■ On returning from lunch that Wednesday afternoon, Richard picked up his telephone message slips and looked through them, walking down the hall to his office. One of the slips was from Robert Meredith, with a note written by the receptionist "Reminder: prayer breakfast in the morning at Palace Hotel at 7:30." Richard had already noted the event written in his appointment book, and he was looking forward to hearing Ben Fuller, even if it was at such an early hour.

Thirty minutes later Bruce McKinney and David Smith arrived, and Mary showed them into Richard's office.

"Did you see the For Sale sign in front of Hugh McEver's house on the way in this morning?" asked Richard after their initial greetings.

"Yes, I did," answered Bruce. "Do you have any idea what she's asking for the house?"

"No, I don't, but I'm going to ask a friend of mine in the real estate business. Janet told me the rumor is that Hugh didn't have as much insurance as he probably should have, and it's apparently going to be pretty tough on Betty and her kids. I just hope she doesn't dump the house and hurt the values of all our homes in the neighborhood!"

"I'll say," said Bruce. "So, what did you work out with Patrick Tomlinson's attorney? Are we ready to go?"

"Yes, I think so. Here is the final copy of the contract. Both of us have been through it twice, and Tomlinson has signed. I was able to clean up some of the legal wording in your favor, but the closing is still contingent on the settlement of his father's estate and also on the price of the Fairchild Textile stock. I did get them to agree that if we have not closed by September 30, then he will advance $100,000 to you as a working capital loan, until his equity actually comes in."

"September 30?" said David with real surprise. "Richard, we can't last until September 30 if this deal doesn't close earlier, or some other miracle doesn't happen. We have lots of other irons in the fire and transactions that should provide big commissions, but this is the closest thing to a real investment that we've got and we just can't wait that long."

"Well, I'm afraid that anything else is a true deal killer, my friend. He would not budge beyond the possibility of $100,000. But I suspect that if your funds get tight, you can take this contract to your bank and borrow at least some money on the strength of the contract," added Richard.

"Bruce, what do you think?" asked David, obviously disappointed.

"Well, it doesn't look like we have an alternative. I can't fault Richard. He did the best he could. Patrick's father must have taught him well because he apparently isn't going to budge on these two or three key issues." Turning to Richard, Bruce asked, "And does he still want our personal guarantees on all the representations and warranties?"

"Yes, he does, without limitation. He wants to hold your feet to the fire to be sure that the accounts receivable and payable, for example, are accurate as of the closing date."

"Well, David, I guess we'll just have to hope that the attorneys working on the old man's estate move along quickly. And if all else fails, like Richard has suggested, we'll try going to the bank with this contract to see if we can borrow against it. Thanks, Richard. We really appreciate your help. Here, David, let's start signing these contract copies so Richard can send them back to Tomlinson's attorney this afternoon."

After they left, Richard picked up his telephone and dialed a beeper number. A few minutes later his direct line rang. It was Kristen.

"Hey, how are you? . . . Listen, I really am sorry about yesterday, but that board luncheon rolls around every once and a while on a Tuesday. I hope we're still on for tomorrow," Richard said trying to put some extra enthusiasm in his voice. Smiling, he added, "And, listen. So that I can write off the cost of the food as a business luncheon, please check on the price of the McEvers' house down the street from us, and we'll discuss it over lunch!"

At baseball practice that afternoon, Tommy and Brent were lofting fly balls to each other in the outfield, waiting for the batting drills to begin. As Tommy threw the ball high into the brilliant blue afternoon sky, for some reason he thought of his father. All the past weekend he had waited for his father to say something about hitting a few balls with him, as he had promised before going to Atlanta, but he never did. The weather on Saturday had been a bit marginal, but by Sunday warm spring weather had settled in. His father had come and gone as usual that weekend, doing some work at the office for a few hours, paying bills at his desk in the den for a few hours, and even cleaning the leaves out of the gutters on his ladder on Sunday morning.

Tommy thought, as he ran a few steps to catch a throw from Brent, about how he had decided that Sunday morning—it was almost as if a voice told him—for once not to say anything to his father, but rather to test him to see whether he would remember on his own. Unfortunately, his father had failed miserably. And what had really made him mad was that Susan had asked him to play tennis on Sunday afternoon, and he had actually done it!

"I guess it hasn't changed since we were little," said a voice inside Tommy. "Dad just always has more time for Susan than he does for me." And he threw the ball back to Brent with an unusually high arc, from all of the frustrated energy released with that thought.

But at least, Tommy had to admit, his father had not yelled at his mother in the past ten days or so. There almost seemed to be some sort of truce or peace between them, for the moment. Nothing really specific had happened. It just seemed that his mother was happier and that his father did not yell as much. So maybe he should just be thankful for small blessings.

The coach blew the whistle and the two boys ran in together toward the group gathered around home plate. "Hey, Zane told me to tell you that Roger is coming over again to spend the night on Saturday night," Brent said to Tommy as they trotted in together. "He says he's got some new videos, and he wants to be sure you're invited. So, do you want to ask your folks if you can spend Saturday night with us?"

"Fantastic. Sure, I'll ask, and I think it'll probably be OK." Then Tommy joked, "But you know, after that sex education class we had yesterday, who needs those films?" And the boys laughed together as they took their places for batting practice.

At the television station, the meeting Janet had tried to set up the week before finally began that afternoon.

"Come in, come in." Bill Shaw motioned to the three of them. "Please have a seat there while I get my note pad," he said, motioning them toward the comfortable chairs around a small conference table on the side of his large office. "I'm sorry I couldn't meet last week, but as you know we had a Network Affiliates Conference in Phoenix. Anyway, I'm glad we can get together today."

Besides Janet and Tom Spence, the fourth person at their meeting was Connie Wright, one of the station's younger camerapersons. It was not usual for her to be at a meeting of management personnel, but Tom had requested her presence, presumably, Janet thought, because she shared both his fundamentalist Christian beliefs and his opposition to "911 Live."

"Now, Janet, you called this meeting," said Bill, who always seemed to be in a hurry and never suffered any time for small talk at station meetings. "I understand that this is about '911 Live,' but nothing else. What can I do for you?"

"Bill, Tom and I had lunch a couple of weeks ago, and he shared his concerns about this program with me. I must say that in the beginning I hadn't thought very much about it, but as I reviewed the information Tom shared with me after our lunch, I couldn't help but agree with him." Bill's eyebrows rose slightly to signal his surprise that Janet had joined forces with the folks who never tired of reminding everyone about how they were going to hell. So boring a thought! "At any rate, I thought we should revisit this one, and so I've asked Tom to review his concerns with you again, and he invited Connie to join us." Bill nodded in Connie's direction.

"OK, I'm all ears. Shoot," said Bill, leaning back in his chair and folding his arms across his chest.

Tom carefully built much the same case he had done with Janet at lunch two weeks before. Then Connie added that two years before she had lost her younger sister in a tragic apartment fire, and she would not have wanted that awful scene broadcast live and unedited into all of the homes in their city.

Tom concluded by saying, "We feel so strongly—and there are a few others besides Connie and me—that this show should not be broadcast that we will consider resigning from the station if we air it."

Bill, who had been sitting quietly in a frozen position during their presentation, suddenly rocked forward in his chair, put his hands on the table, and looked at Tom and Connie. "Are you crazy? You would resign over one show that might once or twice show something a little squeamish, when the airwaves are full of much worse already? . . . Janet," he said, turning to face her, "I hope you're not that crazy."

She looked down and shook her head in embarrassment, indicating that Tom and Connie were on their own with that notion.

Bill turned back to the other two and warmed to his subject. "This really is a bit too much. I do appreciate your sincerity, but you are way off base on this one. Why, '911 Live' was one of the two or three new fall shows everyone was talking about in Phoenix. It could singlehandedly recapture the Friday night ratings for us. And, remember, all we're showing is what is actually happening. It's not that we are making anything up. It's just live action. What's wrong with that? How can we be criticized for showing what is actually happening? Don't you think the people of this city, and everywhere else in America, have the right to know what is really going on?"

"Yes and no," answered Tom. "They do have the right to know, but we have the responsibility to present the information in a nonoffensive, nonhysterical, balanced way—particularly at an hour in the evening when a large part of the audience will be children. The fact that Connie's sister died in an apartment fire, for example, was of course in one sense news, and that particular fire was reported on our newscast. But here we are talking about families gathering around their televisions in the early evening for what we are portraying as entertainment, when it will actually be one personal tragedy after another, without having any way to know either about whom we are reporting or what the consequences might be. What if Connie had been sitting at her dinner table and first learned of her sister's death by seeing her body dragged out of the apartment?"

Connie squirmed in her seat and looked away. "I'm sorry, Connie," said Tom.

"No, that's all right. You had to say it. You're right."

Bill was not finished. "Responsibilities. Editing. That's all I ever hear about from people like you. If you ran the television industry, we'd still be in the Dark Ages. And, hey, you want to talk about responsibilities, let's don't stop with television. Have you been to the movies lately? Have you tried to listen to what teenage kids are listening to today on tapes and CDs? Hey, and while you're on your soapbox, let's go further. Every few months there seems to be a major exposé about how someone in our government has lied to us. And the church, which I presume you two support . . . last week one priest was arrested for child abuse, and another one made headlines when he figured out that over half of the verses in the Bible can't be right. And the schools. Have you seen what they're teaching in sexual education classes these days? In fact, go down after this meeting and look at the shots we're using tonight from the sex-ed classes in our own public schools. You probably won't believe them. But are you going to resign over that too? Come on. The whole world is different from the simple life you wish we still had. And, besides, the people of this city have a right to know and to see exactly what is going on. And '911 Live' will show it to them."

Caught off guard by the wide range of examples which Bill had used to defend "911 Live," Tom took a moment to reflect, while Connie looked at him, and Janet looked at the floor. "I know, Bill. You're right, the world *is* a more complex, and, in our opinion, a less inviting place than it was only a few years ago. And you're right about the examples you used. But I guess our point is that thirty years ago each of those examples would have been an isolated case. Today they all seem to be somehow connected together. And what is it that connects them in most cases? It is us, the media. We can make it all seem as bleak as you have painted it, and soon it all is, because everyone believes us and acts accordingly. We can create our own self-fulfilling prophecies, because we have the power to mold what people learn and what they think. Our point is that with that kind of power comes responsibility, whether you think so or not.

"Have you thought beyond this show?" Tom added. "The effect it will have on the situations which you have just described? Won't we be creating a stage at 7:30 on Friday nights for every hoodlum, arsonist, and gang in our city to parade their activities? Aren't we saying, in effect, 'Come on guys, give us some action!'? It seems to me that we in the media too often take the position of 'report first and think later.' There are simply bound to be disastrous effects from a show like this, both in individual lives and in our community, which we cannot begin to foresee today."

Bill started to speak, but Tom raised his hand. "One last thing. I appreciate that you think we're crazy. And you are probably right about the movies and the records, the government and the churches and the schools. But we don't work at those places. We work here. While we wish that those other things were not true, we can't do anything about them. Maybe if there were other people like us in those organizations, we wouldn't be where we are today. I just don't know, Bill. I don't want to make too big a thing out of our stand. But we are serious, and we again ask that you try to stop this show at the network . . . or at least preempt it here locally."

Bill thought for a moment before answering. "Look. I think you're spitting in the wind, if you'll pardon the expression. And I can't imagine bucking Network over this show, particularly when I think you're wrong. Frankly, the concept kind of excites me. But I tell you what I'll do. As I think you know, Network is going to run a test of the concept in a few weeks here in our city. The show will not actually be broadcast, but they will practice with the command and control links, the cameras, etcetera. I think I can arrange for the four of us to go along, either on the equipment itself or in a separate car. For your families' sakes and our station's sake, I hate to see any of you resign over something you haven't really seen firsthand. So I'm willing to keep an open mind, if you are. And we'll all agree to withhold a final judgment until we see how the test goes. Is that OK?"

Tom and Connie looked at each other and shrugged their shoulders. Connie nodded. "I guess so, Bill," Tom volunteered for both of them. "We doubt we'll change our minds, either. But I suppose we could be missing something. So I guess we'll go along. How about you, Janet?"

She smiled, trying to help defuse the tension in the room. "Sure, I'm game. I never told anybody, but as a little girl I always wanted to be a firefighter. And I guess now I will be." She had just finished speaking when she thought about Connie's sister and suddenly wished she had chosen a different example. She glanced quickly at Connie, who seemed not to mind and was returning her smile.

"OK, then. I'll set it up with Network and let you all know the details. I guess that's it," Bill said, standing up to signal that the meeting was over.

"So, the Bolsheviks really didn't overthrow the czar like they wanted everyone to believe," said Amy, sitting on one side of Susan's queen-sized bed, which Susan had "inherited" from her grandparents when they moved to a smaller home in the previous year.

"That's right," confirmed Bobbie, sitting in a chair, her feet propped up on the end of the bed. "The Bolsheviks actually overthrew Kerensky's government, which had been in power since that spring."

"Susan," her mother called up from downstairs, "supper will be ready in about twenty minutes. Do Amy and Bobbie want to stay?"

Susan, also sitting on the bed, turned to her friends. Amy closed her history book, "No, thanks. I've got to get home and hit this stuff one more time before our test tomorrow."

"Me, too," added Bobbie, putting her feet down and standing to get her book bag.

"Thanks, Mom," Susan raised her voice towards the open door of her bedroom. "They say they've got to get home. We'll all be down in a few minutes."

As Bobbie collected her things, Amy ran her finger along the pattern of Susan's bedspread. "Listen, guys," she said. "I don't exactly know how to say this, but I'm five days late, and I'm worried, and I don't know what to do. If I'm pregnant, I'm going to really need your help."

Susan, of course, knew what Amy was talking about, yet this news still sent a strong chill down her spine. But Bobbie, who knew nothing about their dates at the fraternity house, simply could not believe her ears. "What? ..."

"Listen, Bobbie, I've been meaning to tell you about this, but there really hasn't been quite the time or place until now." said Amy. And then she, with some help from Susan, gave Bobbie an edited version of what had happened ten days before, leaving out the details of their homecoming, but making it very clear that she was no longer a virgin.

Three waves hit Bobbie in immediate succession, each stronger than the other. First, there was simple shock that all of this had happened to her good friend. Then she felt extreme disappointment with Amy for choosing to take this step. Finally, she experienced an overpowering sympathy and concern for Amy, who, now that she noticed, really looked quite terrible. Although Bobbie had a strong faith, this was new ground for her. She instantly knew that it would do no good to dwell on what had already happened. Amy might really be pregnant, and she was obviously reaching out to her two best friends.

"It wasn't all that it's cracked up to be," said Amy, first looking at Bobbie and then lowering her eyes. "I guess I don't really remember a whole lot about it. But I did it. I wish I could take the days back and not do it, but I did. And now I'm really worried that I might be pregnant."

Susan shifted on the bed, drawing her knees up under her and putting her hand over Amy's. "Look, I know you're worried, but it has just been five days. That happens all the time. Let's give it a while longer before we really start worrying," Susan said, with as much optimism as she could muster.

"OK, I'll try. But if I *am* pregnant, I just know that I'm going to need you guys. I really don't want to have a baby. Can you imagine me as a mother? I think it would cut into my dating. What do you think?" Amy managed a small smile.

"Well, I've never had to deal with anything like this before," said Bobbie, moving around the bed next to Amy, "but I know that with my parents we pray about big things together, and I think this certainly fits that category. Would you two mind if we prayed together?"

Neither Amy nor Susan had ever prayed out loud before. But Amy was ready to try anything, and Susan wanted only the best for her friend, so she nodded as well.

"Then let's hold hands right here, and I'll pray." They stood together in the center of the bedroom. Bobbie bowed her head, holding her friends' hands, and the other two girls followed her lead.

"Dear heavenly Father, uh, we're praying today for our friend, Amy. There are . . . um . . . maybe some things which she will want to talk to You about herself later, but for now we, uh, are praying for Your perfect will in her life and that she will not be pregnant. We pray that each of us . . . um . . . will learn from this experience and will always try to seek You in all that we do. Please bless and protect Amy . . . Take away her worry and her doubt. Be with her and guard her and protect her, this night and always. Amen."

The girls raised their heads, and Bobbie and Susan both squeezed Amy's hands. "Thanks, Bobbie," Amy said. "I'm not sure exactly what good a prayer will do at this point, but I appreciate it, and I need all the help I can get."

"I'll add this particular prayer to my prayer list," said Bobbie, "and Susan and I will do everything we can to help you. But like Susan said, try not to worry too much right now."

The three girls collected their things and headed downstairs.

As they descended the staircase, Richard came in through the door from the garage with his briefcase, pecked Janet on the cheek as she stood over the stove, and smiled when he saw the "Three Musketeers" as he had called Susan and her friends for years now, coming through the breakfast room.

"Hi, ladies. How goes it?" he asked. They seemed a little subdued, which Richard assumed was from the studying they had been doing. But each greeted him with a smile.

"Fine, Dad," Susan spoke first. "But we've got a big history test tomorrow and all of the facts are spinning in our minds." Richard nodded back knowingly.

"My father told me that you're going with him to the prayer breakfast in the morning, Mr. Sullivan," Bobbie added to her usual greeting. Both Susan and Janet turned toward Richard, neither having heard this news before.

"Yes, well, I am . . . and I'm really looking forward to it, although I've never been to a prayer breakfast before. The speaker, Ben Fuller, is quite a well-known attorney, and I'm particularly looking forward to hearing him talk."

"Well, I know it's early tomorrow morning, but I hope you enjoy it," said Bobbie, as she took out the keys to her family's station wagon.

"See you tomorrow in school," Susan said to her friends as they went through the breakfast room door and out to the turnaround. "And be careful walking home, Amy," Susan said, realizing that she was already more worried about Amy than she had let on. The three friends waved, Bobbie got into the station wagon, and Susan closed the breakfast room door. Simultaneously, the front door opened and Tommy came in from baseball practice. "I'm starved," he called, as he vaulted up the stairs to clean up.

Their dinner that night fit the quiet pattern of the last two weeks. Both children had noticed a change, a slight improvement in their parents' relationship. Their father had not put their mother down during this period. Neither parent had yelled at the other. There was still some stiffness in their relationship—it wasn't warm and loving. But it was at least civil, and that was so rare that it was noticeable, and it was received happily by the two teenagers.

But Tommy had a hard time looking at his father. He just felt unconnected to him. He didn't think about it that much, but when he did, he could not remember the last time the two of them had ever done anything together. Pride's voice, just gaining a foothold in Tommy's fourteen-year-old mind, had convinced him that he should stop asking and suggesting. And though it hurt, with a pain in his throat when he thought about it, he was not going to push himself on his father. When the voice really got going, which it did more regularly, Tommy could convince himself that his father did not love him like his friends' fathers loved them. But the immediate result was that he simply had trouble looking at his father. And Richard sat only four feet away, at the head of the breakfast room table, thinking that Tommy was fine and not realizing any of the turmoil which was churning in his son. Or in his daughter, for that matter.

The four of them swapped information from their day, as families do around the dinner table. In answer to Janet's question, Richard explained in more detail about the prayer breakfast in the morning, as he understood it. Then he asked, "Susan, I'm embarrassed to admit it, but I'm not sure what Bobbie's father does for a living. Do you know?"

"Yes, I think he has a company that makes loans to people. I believe he's a mortgage banker, or mortgage broker, or something like that."

"OK, good. Thanks."

Tommy cleared the table, which was his chore for the week, and as Janet prepared some ice cream from the freezer, she asked, "Now I've got a question for the two of you kids. I know this is going to seem a little off the wall, but help me if you can. Late this afternoon at the station I saw a video about sex education in our schools. Frankly, I couldn't believe some of it. You may not have exactly the same program in your school, but Susan, in the eleventh grade have they had you actually putting condoms on bananas?"

Susan immediately turned crimson and averted her eyes. Her family had always been pretty open about any topic, including sex, which she appreciated. But as she and Tommy had grown older, she found that it became a little more difficult to talk about such things with her father and her brother around. Particularly since her brother was now leering from the kitchen sink. But what was really turning her crimson was remembering how embarrassed she had been a month ago in Mr. Burton's biology class, where the sex education section was taught, when she had, in fact, done as her mother described.

"Yes, ah, yes ... we did. We had to do it as part of the AIDS awareness section." Both her mother and father stopped to listen. "We teamed up in pairs...." Susan did not tell them that her partner had been Drew, which had completely mortified her. "And each of us had to open a condom and put it, or roll it, or whatever, onto a banana. I can't say that I particularly enjoyed it, but Mr. Burton said it was something we had to know how to do in order to protect ourselves someday."

"Richard," said Janet, "don't you think that's a bit much for the eleventh grade? Boys and girls putting condoms on bananas together?"

"Yes, well, it does seem a bit strange to me, dear," said Richard. "But this program is supposedly all researched and organized by the state board of education. It can't be too crazy, can it?"

"And what about in the ninth grade, Tommy," Janet asked. "What have they got you doing in sex education?" She paused as she placed the bowls of ice cream in front of her family, who were now all back at the breakfast room table.

"Well, I guess we haven't quite started on-the-job training, like they do in the eleventh grade," Tommy smiled at Susan and looked quickly to both ends of the table, where frowns greeted him. He tried to recover and said with more seriousness, "I don't know, we've just had drawings and charts. Only now we're into 'relationships.' Today we had a marriage counselor speak to us, and tomorrow we're having some people come in to talk about 'alternative lifestyles.'"

"What does that mean?" Richard raised his eyebrows.

"I'm not exactly sure. But Mrs. Duncan said we're going to have a lesbian businesswoman and a gay school teacher come and tell us about their lifestyles."

"You mean they're teaching you about homosexuality as part of your sex education class?" Richard asked, his voice rising in concern.

Sensing an opening to make his father squirm a bit, Tommy paused for a second and then answered "Well, I won't really know until tomorrow. But Mrs. Duncan said they're real nice people and we'll enjoy hearing what they have to say."

"You may be right, Janet. This does sound like it's a little bit too much. I wonder who actually put together this program? And I wonder why we haven't heard anything about it? How did you say you became aware of it?"

"One of our reporters is doing a story about it. Isn't it ironic," she said to all three of them, "that we find out about what's happening in our own children's schools by watching television!"

Maybe Bill Shaw is right, after all! she thought. *Maybe we do need television to tell it all, since it seems to be the only way we find out these days . . .*

The rendezvous over the city that night was a black, menacing storm. Demons were arriving late from their many assignments, as the city finally went to sleep. Balzor had asked for reinforcements from other sectors of the city, and even from other nearby cities, to help combat tomorrow morning's prayer breakfast. So far their strategies seemed to be working extremely well.

"Lieutenant Tymor," ordered Balzor, "give us a report on where we stand."

Tymor rose to address the unholy black hole of hatred. "Our early suspicions have been confirmed that this group is headed by Edwards, Burnett, and Andrews. Luckily they have not been well enough organized with their prayer support. Other than a few scattered individuals, they have only started praying in earnest tonight. We've been able to keep all of our voices speaking reliably in our own sector for the past ten days, without any interference from angels, because the prayers have been so few. In fact, the first angel has only just showed up outside the Palace Hotel." The demons could look down and see the powerful light darting back and forth around the hotel complex. "But certainly there are too many of us to be bothered by just one angel.

"The three ministers have delegated most of the work for inviting the businessmen and for following up after the breakfast to their lay leadership. In some cases, unfortunately, these men are quite good and quite dedicated. But Fear and Discouragement have been doing some particularly effective work on most of them, and I believe there will be many no shows in the morning, and only sporadic follow-up afterwards. If we can get through the first few days after the breakfast, we should never have to worry about one of these again."

"Good work, good work," added Balzor. "I think we have risen to the challenge magnificently, and some of them will actually be more confused than ever after this is over!" He cackled, and the others all followed him. "We'll dispense with the regular reports tonight. We still have a lot of work to do. All of you street leaders keep working tonight with Busyness and Discouragement, to have those voices playing as loudly as possible in the morning, when all these men wake up early. Maybe we can sidetrack a few more. And the rest of you, who have come here to help us, head down and flood the Palace Hotel with your wonderful stench! One lonely angel will be no match for all of you, and we should entrench ourselves completely in that building by the morning. We want all of the souls in that place, and particularly Ben Fuller's, to feel the power of our presence, despite the subject of their talk."

With that dismissal, all of the demons left to complete their appointed tasks. Nepravel descended through a wide arc back to his neighborhood, detouring over into the vicinity of the Palace Hotel. There he watched as the one mighty angel, irridescent but alone—there really had not been much prayer support for this breakfast. Nepravel could remember years ago when revivals would be protected by ten, perhaps even twenty, such angels—flew back and forth at the entrance, grasping futilely with his talons at the hundreds of demons who were entering the building from all sides and through the roof. Oops! One demon had strayed too close to the angel, on a dare from another demon, and paid the price. Well, Nepravel had learned to keep a safe distance, and he cruised back over to Devon Drive, where it was almost completely dark.

"What's that?" he snarled, as individual bolts of light appeared from the suburbs and landed at two of his houses. "Blast! What is that Meredith girl doing up at this time of night, praying for these two families? Now she's apparently added Amy Bryant to her prayer list. And tonight she's even praying for Richard Sullivan and the prayer breakfast! Her prayers have damaged our voices a bit. After the prayer breakfast, I'll have to build them up again. And Zloy has to do something about that girl, and her whole family. They're getting to be such a pain. I'm just glad there are not many like them."

5

THURSDAY, MAY 4 ■ Richard's alarm went off that morning a little before 6:00, and for an instant he could not remember why it was set so early. Then he remembered the prayer breakfast and lay there in bed thinking. Did he really have to go? Did he really want to go? It was so early. He had told Robert Meredith that he would be there, and wasn't his word important? People had probably spent money on his breakfast. What to do? The voices of Confusion and Defeat tried to dissuade Richard from going, but they were not as loud in his mind as they could have been, thanks to the prayers for Richard from both Robert Meredith and his daughter. So Richard finally slid out of bed and began to get dressed.

When Richard arrived at the Palace Hotel's main ballroom, he was surprised to see that several hundred men were already there. Many of them he knew well. He also noted that it was an interracial group, with whites, African-Americans, and Hispanics. Either Ben Fuller was quite a draw, or a lot more men attended prayer breakfasts than he had ever suspected.

A kindly lady at one of the tables in the atrium gave Richard a name tag and directed him inside to Table 15, where he found Robert Meredith and several other men already waiting. "Hi, Richard, Bob Meredith. I'm so glad you could make it this morning. Here, let me introduce you to the other guys."

After the introductions, Richard thanked Bob for inviting him. Then he asked about the sponsors for the breakfast, since the invitation had only said "Spring Prayer Breakfast," with a list of individual hosts.

"Oh, it's the pastors and laymen from several of the churches in our area. We decided to work together so that a larger audience could hear a national speaker like Ben Fuller."

As breakfast was served to the several hundred men and the conversation continued at their table, unseen to their eyes a spiritual battle of large proportions was being waged all around them.

There were now two angels, which were all that the late prayer cover could provide, and they were doing their best to grab and to destroy the demons who were still trying to get inside. But unfortunately, two angels were no match for the hundreds of demons who had already flooded the hall under Balzor's orders. Although individual demons were no match for one of God's angels, in large numbers the advantage was turned, and in tight quarters a swarm of demons could drive away an angel with thousands of sharp bites. So the two angels had to remain outside, and the grand ballroom where Fuller would soon speak was sadly almost as dark as midnight. Only the flames burning inside the many Christian men seated at the tables illuminated any of the eternal players in the ballroom.

Balzor himself, once he knew that the area was safe, had entered the hall surrounded by a horde of his lesser demons for protection. He had taken up his position directly across from the podium. The darkness, the terror, and the stench in that place would have completely overwhelmed any human spirit, should it have been unlucky enough to have passed during those ninety minutes!

Ben Fuller was seated at a table just below the podium with Stephen Edwards, James Burnett, Michael Andrews, and several of the prayer breakfast leaders. When he had arrived the previous evening and found that the leaders had only begun to pray sporadically for the prayer breakfast that night, Fuller had stayed in his room an hour before dinner, on his face before God, praying for all those who would attend the breakfast and for God's Word on his lips in the morning. It was as a result of his prayers, and those of the other leaders who began praying as well, that the second angel had been empowered to descend and to fight the demons.

The Reverend James Burnett gave the welcome and invocation, and Reverend Stephen Edwards introduced Benjamin Fuller.

As Fuller rose to speak, Balzor urged on his demons, like a coach on the sidelines of the Super Bowl. They had not seen a challenge like this, projecting the Truth into the business community, in many years. Balzor knew that his own future depended on his demons counteracting Fuller's words, and then destroying any follow-up which might try to save these men. Every streetleader, like Nepravel, had been called in from his sector. Each one knew where his men were sitting, and they darted from table to table, snarling and cursing, coaxing up the voices of hate and deception, which could be diminished by Fuller's words and by the few targeted prayers which were even now landing in the ballroom.

Benjamin Fuller, who had surrendered his life to God eighteen years before, began his Christian walk at that time. He knew the Truth which could free these men and their families from the lies and the pain which the world and Satan had laid on them. He personally knew the power which could overcome any problem, change any relationship, bring any result. But even as he began speaking, as he looked out at the hundreds of faces in front of him, his spirit was troubled. Perhaps he could sense the awful presence which had filled the room and which was battling against his single voice. But he nevertheless prayed a silent prayer, asked for God's help, and began.

Richard listened intently as Fuller recounted his more than thirty years as a Wall Street attorney. He mentioned several of his firm's merger and acquisition successes, stretching back several decades to a time before M&A work became the darling of the securities and legal industries. He then said an extraordinary thing, which certainly got the attention of Richard and most of the other businessmen in the room: Fuller claimed that he had turned away potential fees, amounting to millions of dollars, because he believed that some particular work his firm was asked to do, while certainly legal, was neither right nor moral. Richard simply could not believe these words coming from a hard-nosed New York M&A attorney. He started to become curious about this man, but then a voice inside him said that any attorney who would turn away that kind of business must not be "moral"—he must be crazy!

And so went the debate in Richard's mind throughout the rest of the prayer breakfast, as Fuller described his own submission to the will of God, and how it had changed his life and work forever. The demons, moving around with impunity, turned up the voices in each listener to discredit Fuller's testimony and Fuller himself.

A few words did manage to hit home with Richard. At one point Fuller implied that he had been doing something of which his wife would not have been proud. Although he did not come right out and say it directly, Richard imagined that Fuller must have had another woman at one point. When Fuller said that his actions were ruining his marriage and killing his wife, the words pierced Richard's heart. And especially since today, being Thursday, he was supposed to see Kristen in just a few hours.

But Nepravel and the other demons fought back. Several times during the talk, Richard actually daydreamed, or thought about problems and contracts at his office.

When Fuller said, "We borrow money we don't have, to buy things we don't need, to impress people we really don't like," Richard chuckled with the other businessmen, but as that thought started to sink in, a voice replied, "Sure, that's easy for him to say. He's already got it all, and doesn't have to impress anybody. But what about all the rest of us who haven't quite made it yet? Are we just supposed to chuck it all and move off to the top of a mountain? How would our families survive?"

As Fuller concluded, Richard found himself awakened from more thoughts about his office schedule that morning to hear Fuller saying, "It's this simple, men. You have to choose either to be on God's side, or on the other side. You cannot be on both. You will not get another chance after you die. And your soul *is* eternal. You don't have the choice of simply stopping at death and saying 'Thanks, that's enough for me.' Your soul *will* live in one of two places, forever. Forever. Think about that. And if you choose God's side, you can begin to walk with Him now and to build a relationship with Him like no other relationship you will ever know.

"As you walk with Him, His Holy Spirit will fill you each day, as I pray that He will do each day in my life, and you can begin to glimpse what eternity with Him will be like, right here on earth, right now. Starting today. I hope you will repent of all that you have done, choose God, and ask His Son, Jesus Christ, to come into your life this morning. To submit to Him and to ask Him to be the Lord of your life from this day forward. Let us pray."

Richard was astonished. Fuller must have said something important while Richard was daydreaming, he thought, because he could not imagine anyone making such a "hard sell" to this group of tough businessmen so early in the morning! Did he really expect men in thousand-dollar suits with Oxford button-down shirts to buy his story and make this choice after a forty-five-minute talk? As Fuller began to pray, encouraging the men in the audience to pray silently along with him, there was certainly no silence in Richard's mind. The voices were turned up to full volume, virtually laughing that Fuller would expect anyone here to change his life over a breakfast!

Fuller's prayer was basically an opportunity for each man in the audience to make the choice that morning and to submit himself to Jesus Christ at that time. In the prayer, he promised not immediate happiness, but immediate peace, which would grow if the men began seeking God's face in all that they did. Richard bowed politely, but Pride was running rampant inside him, and he wasn't about to submit to anyone or to anything, particularly in front of hundreds of men.

At the end of the prayer, Richard looked up and was astonished to see the face of the mechanical contractor to whom he had been introduced at the start of the breakfast. There were streaks of tears running down his cheeks! This big man, who must have weighed over 250 pounds, was crying like a baby, right across the table from him! And, as he looked around the room, there were other men wiping their eyes and several who still had their heads bowed in prayer. Richard was flabbergasted. These visual images affected him as much as, or more than, any of Fuller's words, and the volume of the deceptive voices was dimmed by what Richard suddenly realized had happened across the table from him. This man had apparently done as Fuller had suggested, and now he was crying and laughing at the same time, and holding onto Bob Meredith's shoulder, telling him that he felt freer than he had been in twenty years. Richard found himself staring, and wondering how this could possibly have happened. The man even looked different in his face. He really had changed!

Then Michael Andrews spoke from the podium, thanking all of them for attending and asking them to fill out one of the cards in front of them at their tables.

Richard looked down and saw that there were four lines on the card, below a space for his name. The lines read:

_____ I accepted Jesus as the Lord of my life for the first time this morning.
_____ I rededicated my life to Jesus this morning.
_____ Please let me know about future prayer breakfasts.
_____ Please keep me on the mailing list.

Richard almost did not fill out a card, but since all the other men were doing so, he elected to place a polite check on the last line and turned his card over.

Rising, Richard took Bob's hand and thanked him for inviting him to the prayer breakfast.

"We're going to have some follow-up sessions for a small group at my office, if you would like to attend, Richard," Robert Meredith said.

"Well, I'll think about it," said Richard. "Why don't you give me a call?" Bob nodded that he would. Then the mechanical contractor rose and shook Richard's hand, his own hand still moist from wiping away his tears. Richard suddenly felt vaguely uncomfortable around this man, as if he had taken a step which was denied to Richard. He just wanted to leave and get back to his office, where things were familiar. So he bade farewell to Robert and the men at his table and made his way towards the exit, shaking hands with several of the other men whom he knew.

Balzor was ecstatic. Yes, they had lost a few. In the darkness, he could see the spark of light begin to flicker in ten or twenty men, including the mechanical contractor sitting across from Richard. And he knew that seeds had been planted in many others which, if left unattended, might also grow and cause problems for them. But he had one of the best teams around, and he knew that they could choke off most such seeds before they did any real damage. Balzor felt great that they had lost only about twenty out of an audience of hundreds. At tonight's rendezvous he would have to be uncharacteristically strong in his praise for his demons. They had turned back the Light and had kept his sector intact. He waited for the "all clear" that the angels had departed, and then he and his people haters went back to their normal duties, glad that the prayer breakfast was over.

Nothing Richard heard that morning affected him enough to keep him from his luncheon with Kristen, particularly since they had missed their date on Tuesday. But as he walked toward her apartment, Ben Fuller's words about his own wife and marriage rang in Richard's ears.

Since their intense weekend in Atlanta almost two weeks before, he and Kristen had settled back into their previous routine of Tuesday and Thursday rendevous in her apartment. Richard knew, although he wasn't exactly sure how, that eventually his relationship with Kristen had to end. From the partial reconciliation with Janet two weeks ago, to their pleasant relationship during this same period, to Benjamin Fuller's words that morning, Richard knew that, ultimately and in the long run, he would have to figure out a way to make his life work with Janet. It now seemed to him that she wanted that, too, and was willing to try—though it was not clear how hard. Could they both give in some and make their marriage work? And what, more pressingly, to do about Kristen?

Those were his rational thoughts. But the tugs of his heart and the lust of his body were not quite ready for logic. Yes, he knew that ultimately he would have to make a break. But it was just so pleasant and convenient to spend each Tuesday and Thursday afternoon with this delightful, beautiful younger woman. If only Kristen would let it stay this way . . . and Janet never found out . . . and he could still be a good husband and father while having his affair . . . and he could keep these two situations in separate slots. How nice it would be . . .

Kristen greeted him at the door in only a teddy, which she had bought in Atlanta, and high heels. It seemed incongruous for meeting at noon, in broad daylight, but he definitely liked it. "I wore the teddy because we haven't seen each other for a whole week, dear, and I didn't want you to forget what I look like!"

"Well, I better have a look then," he said, as he reached for the top snap.

An hour later, lying in bed together, watching a soap opera which they had, for some reason, begun keeping up with in this way, Richard said to Kristen, "The most extraordinary thing happened this morning at the prayer breakfast I attended." And he went on to tell her about the mechanical contractor and his reaction to Benjamin Fuller's testimony.

"It was really strange. Here was this grown man, sitting across the table from me, having just heard the same thing I heard, crying like a baby. And he really, somehow, seemed to have changed. His facial expression was different from an hour before. Have you ever seen or heard of anything like that?"

"No, not for a long time. Back in Texas when I was a little girl, my parents sometimes took us to revivals, and people had all sorts of reactions. Some seemed real, some didn't. But I haven't seen anything like that since junior high school. Of course when I talk to my mother, she says that she prays for me every day, 'to get saved,'" Kristen smiled. She snuggled up and traced patterns through the hairs of his chest with one fingernail. "Now don't you go getting religious on me. It would probably be bad for our relationship!" And she pressed herself against him.

"Oh, I don't think you have to worry about that," Richard said, as he reached for her again. A voice added silently, "I think our relationship may be coming to an end, anyway." And then he kissed her.

FRIDAY, MAY 5 ■ That Friday night, much to Susan's delight, Drew invited her to the movies. It was their first real date, and, with Drew's permission, Susan arranged to meet Bobbie, Amy, and their two dates at the movie. Then all six planned to go together after the movie to a Chinese restaurant in their neighborhood.

Drew and Susan were in several classes together, besides biology. She enjoyed both his intelligence and his natural sense of humor. Among Susan's friends, Drew had developed a reputation as a "sweet" boy, good at tennis but always polite and pleasant. Amy and Bobbie shared Susan's joy that she had snagged Drew, at least for a first date.

Amy's situation was a little different. After some debate, Amy had finally convinced her mother that since she was almost a senior, it was OK to date a college freshman. The previous weekend, before she had begun to worry about her situation, she and Billy had gone to a professional baseball game. He had wanted to leave the game early, to spend more time with Amy, as they had done the Saturday night before.

Amy had resisted leaving the game early, and as they parked outside her house that same night, it was obvious to her that Billy now expected their relationship to include fairly regular sex, but she was not willing. The resulting tension strained their relationship, which became obvious when they talked on the phone during the week. This Friday night she was happy to go out with him, she said, and genuinely meant it. But she insisted that they join a group activity with her friends. Billy had reluctantly agreed, muttering that he was now in college and could not make a steady diet of high school-type events. But he went along.

The six young people arrived at the theater almost simultaneously. Bobbie was dating Thomas Briggs, who attended a different high school. She had met him through their church youth group. They had gone the previous summer on a mission trip to build a church in Mexico. The thirty kids on that trip had come to know each other quite well, and Bobbie very much enjoyed going out with Thomas. His one drawback was that Thomas loved to talk about airplanes, something Bobbie knew almost nothing about. He was working hard at school and hoped to apply to the Air Force Academy in the fall.

Since the three boys did not know each other, the girls had agreed that it would be OK to go to one of the "action" movies, which they figured the boys would like more. Susan had to close her eyes a couple of times as blood and brains ricocheted across the screen; and she was a little uneasy sitting next to Drew during the extremely graphic love scenes. *Why do the leading women always have to take off all their clothes in these movies?* Susan thought once to herself. But, at any rate, they survived the movie and went on to the Chinese restaurant in three separate cars.

As they ordered their dinners, Susan was sensitive to the tension between Billy and Amy, who had shared her concerns about him with her two best friends. The girls did their best to be pleasant and friendly. Susan was glad to see Thomas again. She knew that Bobbie really liked him. And she was surprised to learn that Drew had more than a passing knowledge of fighter aircraft. *Where do boys pick this stuff up, anyway?* she wondered. So Drew and Thomas were soon discussing the nuances of the combat differences between two naval and air force fighters.

There followed ninety minutes of pleasant conversation and a wonderful Chinese meal. At one point, watching her friends have fun, Susan thought how much saner this was than her earlier Saturday night at the fraternity house, and she was glad to be able to relax.

Billy kept a somewhat aloof attitude, being a "college man" among high school students. At one point Bobbie, looking at Billy and Amy together, wondered what his reaction would be if Amy were, God forbid, actually pregnant. Bobbie was opposed to abortion, but she had never had to confront the possibility so personally. She had been praying for two days that they would not have to discuss it further.

After dinner, the boys drove their dates home. Susan had plenty of time before she had to be in, and Drew seemed to be in no hurry, so they sat and talked in his car outside her home. She was delighted when, just before getting out, he leaned across and kissed her, smiled, and said "I've had a really wonderful evening. I hope we can do it again soon."

Just down the street, near the park, Billy had stopped a couple of blocks from Amy's home. He was obviously interested in more than just a goodnight kiss. And Amy had to tell him explicitly again that she was not.

"And what about two weeks ago?" asked Billy with an edge to his voice. "What about then?"

"I don't know, Billy. I had a lot to drink, and I guess it seemed right at the time. I don't know, maybe it will be again, but not now, not tonight. I'm just a little confused. I like you very much, but I don't want to do that now."

Billy acquiesced but was obviously distraught. The thought occurred to Amy that her mother had warned her. Oh, how many times had she lectured her that "once you give it away, that's all they will want, no matter what else they say." Could it be possible, it suddenly dawned on Amy, that her mother had been right?

Thomas chose this evening to kiss Bobbie for the first time, after their several dates, and they liked it so much that they kissed again. Bobbie realized that she might really like Thomas as they kissed for the third time and he hugged her tightly. She felt in her stomach the tension between human desire to do more than kiss, and her faith, which told her not to. She knew that Thomas shared her faith and that he was probably feeling exactly the same tension. After the third kiss, they looked into each other's eyes, and each could read the other's thoughts. They simultaneously broke into laughter, relieving the tension for the moment and making Bobbie like him even more.

"I'll see you Sunday at youth group," said Thomas. "And I hope we can go out again soon. Maybe next weekend." She nodded and smiled.

SATURDAY, MAY 6 ■ That Saturday was a normal weekend day for the Sullivans. Richard spent the morning at the office, catching up on his contract files. Janet had to do "big shopping," and she coerced Tommy into joining her for the trip to the grocery warehouse. Susan studied in the resulting quiet for a big math test. That evening Richard and Janet were scheduled to attend the last performance of the winter season at the local symphony. Tommy was to spend the night again at Brent's, and Amy had invited Susan to spend the night next door at her home. Janet, realizing that she and Richard would be home alone that night after the concert, hoped that their budding romance might continue.

That evening, Tommy and Brent drove with Zane, Brent's older brother, to pick up Roger and the videos and to have a quick dinner at the food court in the mall.

With Janet's approval, Brent's parents were going to a movie that night. Tom and Mary Holcombe regularly left the younger teenagers by themselves, so they thought nothing of leaving them in the "care" of the older boys.

As soon as the boys returned to the empty home after dinner, they headed straight for the basement and the VCR. Just then the doorbell rang, and Roger returned upstairs to welcome two more of his friends, whom he and Zane had invited to the showing. Tommy only vaguely knew these older boys, Derrick and Paul. He had always seen them together, kind of like himself and Brent. Derrick had two small earrings in one ear, and Paul wore clothes that looked like the hippie pictures from his father's college days. "I can't wait to see these flicks," announced Derrick, as they positioned themselves in front of the basement television.

After dinner at the Bryants', Amy told her parents that she and Susan were going to get some frozen yogurt. Once they were beyond Devon Drive, Amy turned in the opposite direction and headed east across town. "Hey, where are we going?" asked Susan.

"We'll get some yogurt in a little while," answered Amy. "But first I want to buy one of those pregnancy tests, and I don't want to go to a drugstore where we might be recognized. I thought it might be good to have you with me tomorrow morning, in case it turns out to be positive."

The girls drove on in silence for several minutes, each considering the gravity of Amy's possible situation.

As Richard and Janet took their usual seats at the symphony, he was surprised to see Kristen and another man moving across the rows of seats, two rows in front of them. Kristen had not noticed him yet, but he was appalled to see that she and her date were going to sit directly in front of them. As Kristen turned to take off her coat, she saw Richard, and she involuntarily smiled and waved. He nodded politely in her direction and raised his hand in acknowledgment, as the houselights went down and the conductor entered the hall.

"Who's that?" whispered Janet in his ear.

"She was the real estate agent on the Drucker home purchase several months ago. I think her name is Kristen something. I don't know who he is," Richard replied, as the symphony began.

The girls had no trouble finding the pregnancy tests in among the condoms and other personal hygiene items. Amy decided, after reading them all, to buy two different types of tests, just to be sure, since each one appeared to work differently.

They purchased the tests at the counter, and the cashier paid no more attention to the teenagers' purchase than if they had been buying candy bars.

■ ■ ■

Roger had come with new videos in his bag this time, and soon Tommy was once again virtually unable to contain himself because of what he saw on the screen. Given all of the hormones normally running around inside a fourteen-year-old boy, it was just too much for him to watch these graphic videos without short-circuiting inside. After viewing *Come Along with Me*, Roger reached again into the bag, and this time he triumphantly pulled out a sixpack of beer. "There's only one for each of us, so nurse 'em along," he said, as he handed out the tall cans. Tommy, who had never before had more than a sip or two of alcohol, popped the top on his beer and felt very grown up. And then Roger inserted *Four Play*. As this video began, Nepravel and two demons who had tagged along with Paul and Derrick arrived in the basement. Nepravel took up a position near Tommy, urging him to relax and to enjoy all of his feelings with his new friends.

Roger announced, "You guys are really going to like this one," and they settled back to watch the first segment, which featured four women together.

Even Richard knew that his emotions were bizarre. He and Kristen had never run into each other socially, and he realized that she had never mentioned dating any other men. On several occasions, in fact, she had told him that she had no time for "normal" dates, since she worked so often on the weekends. He knew that it was crazy, but now he actually felt somewhat jealous of the unknown man sitting next to her. *How ridiculous*, he thought, especially since he was thinking about ending their relationship. Nevertheless, there it was. *Is this guy going to go home with her, too?* Then, suddenly, he thought, *What about AIDS? Who exactly is this guy, and with whom has he been sleeping?* Even in the dark symphony hall, he turned pale. His mind started to race. *What if he himself now had AIDS and had given it to Janet? What have I been doing?* he thought.

Just then the first half of the performance ended, to loud applause. The Sullivans and the rest of the audience headed for the large theater hall, for champagne cocktails.

Given their previous greeting, Richard knew that he could not ignore Kristen. As he collected two drinks for Janet and himself, Kristen arrived with her date.

"Hello, Richard, I'm Kristen Holloway. Do you remember me from our real estate closing?"

"Yes, of course, Kristen. This is my wife, Janet." Janet extended her hand warmly, and Kristen shook it, smiling broadly.

"And I'd like you to meet an old friend of mine from San Francisco, Peter Dowling. He's a reporter out there, in town this weekend doing a story. We haven't seen each other in years, and we were able to get some last-minute tickets to the symphony," Kristen finished, looking directly at Richard and smiling.

Oh great, Richard thought. "San Francisco!" Richard said, "Nice to meet you, Peter," extending his hand. "What sort of story are you working on?"

Turning to Janet, Peter answered, "We think there may be a link back this way to a financial scandal that seems to be brewing, and I'm here checking with some local sources to see whether the pieces and the characters fit."

"I see," was all that Richard could add.

"Oh, Peter," Kristen said, "Richard is a lawyer who does a lot of financial work. Maybe he could help you," she smiled, appearing to Richard to be enjoying herself.

"Yes, maybe so," said Peter. "Would you mind if I called you? Does Kristen know how to reach you?"

"Sure, that would be fine," said Richard, thinking to himself that it wouldn't be.

"Tell me, Janet," said Kristen, changing the subject but still directing the conversation, "do you have any children?"

"Yes, two. A girl who will be seventeen next week, and a boy who is fourteen," Janet smiled.

"Well," Kristen smiled, speaking to Janet and then turning towards Richard, "you are certainly very lucky. I hope that one day I can get married and have nice children, too . . ."

Richard could feel the anger rising inside, that Kristen was playing *double entendre* with him in this way, and he hoped that he was not turning red enough for Janet to notice. He worked hard to keep his emotions in check.

Trying to end the conversation, Richard nodded to Peter and said, "Well, I wish you good luck with your investigation. Do call me if I can ever be of assistance to you," he lied. With a nod and a slight squinting smile toward Kristen, the Sullivans bade them farewell, and Richard maneuvered Janet by her elbow toward one of his partners, who was standing nearby with his wife.

After ninety minutes of almost uninterrupted hard-core sex coming through his eyes, and the urging of the voices turned to a fever pitch by Nepravel, Tommy was still physically in his chair, but his mind was no longer able to control his body. At this crucial juncture, the scene on the video changed, and it was four men together. At first Tommy was surprised and uncomfortable, "grossed out" might be a better phrase. But the other boys there in the basement seemed to be just as interested as they were in the previous videos, and Nepravel whispered in his ear to relax and to enjoy it. After all, he had just learned in school, this was a legitimate alternative lifestyle.

Ten minutes later, the pressure and the tension just became too much. One by one, the boys sought relief. At this point, as Tommy was most vulnerable, Roger got up, walked over to him, leaned down and whispered in his ear, "Can I help you?"

Tommy knew that he should say no. He tried to fall back on what he believed, but there was little there to help him, and other voices encouraged him to go ahead and to try anything once. It was all just too much. The boys on the screen certainly seemed to be enjoying themselves. Why shouldn't he? Unable to think or to control himself, he simply nodded.

6

SUNDAY, MAY 7 ■ The next morning, Sunday, the two girls awoke at Amy's house, and Amy pulled the pregnancy tests out of her drawer, while Susan remained in bed. "Well," Amy said, holding the tests up in front of her, "wish me luck." And she headed for the bathroom.

It occurred to Susan that she should try praying, and so she said quickly, "Dear God, please don't let Amy be pregnant."

But it was not to be. Within an hour, as the girls dressed, both tests confirmed that Amy was, in fact, pregnant.

When the first test turned positive, Amy sat on the bed, staring at it. Her first emotion was a genuine thrill, that a new life was actually growing inside *her*. How incredible! But then, like a pump evacuating water, the reality of her situation pushed the momentary joy right out of her and kept it out, almost completely. "I can't have a baby now," she heard a voice screaming inside her. Soon she began to cry. "Susan, what am I going to do? My parents will kill me if they find out. How could this happen to me? We only did it one time! I wonder what Billy will say!" she laughed derisively, sensing his answer. Turning to Susan, she said, "You can't tell anybody—and certainly not your parents—until I figure out what to do. Do you promise?"

"Yes, of course," Susan answered, sitting beside Amy and putting her arm around her shoulder. "You, Bobbie, and I will figure out what to do."

"Do you think we should tell Bobbie?" Amy asked Susan. "She will be so disappointed, and I know she'll want me to have the baby. And I just don't think I can do that."

"Yes, I know. But she already knows what you've done, so I don't think she can be any more disappointed. And we've been best friends for so many years. I think we should try to work this out together."

Amy nodded her acquiescence and wiped her tears with the tissue Susan offered. "Now we better go downstairs for breakfast," Susan concluded, smiling as best she could, "or your parents will think that something strange is going on."

When Tommy arrived home after lunch on Sunday, he seemed to be so withdrawn that even Richard noticed it. Smiling, Tommy offered a grunt of a hello to his parents and went immediately upstairs. Richard and Janet exchanged glances over the Sunday newspaper. Their relationship had healed a bit. Last night at home after the symphony had been particularly happy and enjoyable for Janet. It made Richard feel good too, but it also made him feel more like a heel, particularly remembering the way Kristen had behaved at the symphony. At any rate, he was able to accept Janet's next statement without any hostility.

"Richard, Tommy has gotten to be like someone in another family. You've really got to spend some time with him," she said quietly.

"You're right," Richard readily admitted, putting down the newspaper. "And I guess I'll start now." He rose and headed upstairs.

Richard knocked on Tommy's closed door and thought he heard a mumbled "come in" over the loud rock music, which had begun only seconds after Tommy had come home.

"Hi, son," Richard said upon opening the door. "How's it going?"

"Huh? Oh, fine, Dad. Just fine. But I've got to study for this English literature exam we have tomorrow."

"Well, would you like to take a break and go throw the baseball in the backyard? Or maybe we can get Brent and hit some down at the park."

"Well, Dad, I'd like to. Maybe later. But right now I've got to study for this test, since I haven't even read two of the stories yet," Tommy said, pleased to be able to disappoint his father for once, in the same way he had been disappointed so many times.

Dismayed that anyone would wait until the day before an exam to read the required stories, Richard felt his pulse quicken a bit, knowing as he spoke that it was a mistake, "OK, Tommy. But how can you possibly study for an exam with this loud music playing?"

Tommy just shrugged his shoulders. "I don't know, Dad, but somehow I get it done. Maybe my brain is just different from other people's." And he looked back into his book, signaling that he had to study.

Richard closed Tommy's door and retreated down the stairs to the den. "I blew it," he said to Janet. "I went upstairs trying to spend time with Tommy, and instead we managed to make each other mad. I guess I've lost my touch as a father."

"At least you tried, dear," said Janet, sympathetically. "I admit that I've lost touch with you. None of us can replace all of those lost hours in a twenty-minute baseball toss, or, in our case, one great night together. But the good news is, you tried. Maybe that will register with Tommy. You've got to keep trying. He's probably going to test you, to see if you really mean to spend more time with him, and in the beginning it will probably be rocky, just like us, perhaps. But please keep trying. And also don't forget Susan and me. We like having you around too." She smiled encouragingly.

Richard knew that Janet was right, and the positive events of the last two weeks combined to keep his possible anger in check. Instead, he accepted her criticism in the constructive way it was offered and resolved that he would try harder.

"You're right. I'll keep trying, and you keep reminding me," he smiled back. "I'll even give Tommy an hour and then ask him to play ball again."

Richard meant well, as did Janet. Unfortunately, Nepravel, who had been listening from the ceiling, had different plans for them and for their family.

■ ■ ■

Amy called Bobbie on Sunday afternoon and told her the news about her pregnancy. Bobbie was very concerned and told Amy that she would pray even more diligently for her. Amy smiled and suggested that she pray for a miscarriage. Then, more seriously, Amy asked Bobbie to meet her and Susan at lunch on Monday, which of course Bobbie agreed to do.

That night Amy had a hard time sleeping. She felt like such a fool. What had she been thinking? And why did this have to happen to her? And on her first time? It was so unfair . . . her father would be so disappointed in his only daughter, if he ever found out. Nepravel had the voices spinning loudly in her head. After crying quietly for more than an hour, she decided that crying was not going to solve her problem. She had some tough decisions to make, and it occurred to her that she needed some specific information. To get some peace, she finally got up and wrote down the steps she would take and the people with whom she wanted to talk. Putting those concrete thoughts in her notebook at least let her get a few hours of sleep.

MONDAY, MAY 8 ■ Richard had not been in his office very long the next morning when his private line rang. "I enjoyed meeting Janet," Kristen said into the receiver, the strained enthusiasm in her voice obvious. "And I hope you enjoyed meeting Peter."

"And just who is Peter?" Richard responded too quickly, realizing as he spoke that his voice sounded as jealous as he felt.

"Oh, I think we're a little jealous, Richard . . . Peter happens to be an old friend whom I dated years ago at the end of college. Is there anything wrong with that? After all, I've only got one man, unlike you, who shares his bed with two women."

"Have you . . . have you and Peter . . . been . . . ?"

"No, Richard, not for many years. He was a good boy Saturday night and went home to his hotel room. Why? Does that bother you?"

Richard knew he was trapped and that he sounded stupid. But the feelings were still there, and his male ego had been working in overdrive where Kristen was concerned since Saturday night. "No, well, I know you must have another life, but I guess I never really thought about it. And we've never talked about your past or present boyfriends," Richard added, fishing a bit.

"I'll be delighted to reveal my complete, sordid past to you, anytime you like," Kristen said, lightening her tone. "And . . ." Richard could feel her smile through the telephone. "I don't have any *real* boyfriends now except you, which is why I want you all to myself so much. What's going on with you and Janet? When are you going to leave her? She doesn't make you happy. We *are* getting together tomorrow, aren't we?"

Richard had firmly resolved the previous evening, after spending a wonderful weekend at home with Janet, to find some reason for canceling his luncheon appointment with Kristen on Tuesday. But now he had been trapped by his own conversation. "Of course, I'll be there, now that I know there won't be three of us," he returned her levity, and wondered for just a second how he was ever going to change having two women.

The three of them found a table in the corner of their large high school cafeteria and put down their trays. They were joined for lunch by Pitow, the demon in charge of their school, who had been alerted by Nepravel.

"Well," began Amy, "the main thing I've decided to do is not to panic. Not to make any decision for a few weeks. And to try to think through what my options are."

"How do you feel?" asked Bobbie. "Do you feel any different? Are you hungry all the time?"

"I have noticed a few differences. I get tired easily. My breasts are a little heavy, and my stomach feels fuller than normal. And, yes, I have a pretty good appetite. But that's about all, other than a little queasiness sometimes in the morning."

Susan had such mixed feelings. Obviously it was awful what Amy had been through and was about to go through. But she nevertheless could not help feeling a little bit jealous, in a strange way, of Amy's experiences. Amy was already living what she did not expect to experience—had not even imagined to experience—for several—no, many—years. Susan felt both intrigued and hopelessly inadequate that Amy was sharing her experience with them and looking to them for advice.

"And I'm definitely not going to tell my parents, at least not now. Not until I decide what to do. They would go crazy, especially my father." Pitow nodded his dark, smoking head in agreement.

"So far, I've thought of the following things . . ." and Amy ticked them off on her fingers. "I've obviously got to talk to Billy and find out what he thinks. Then I'm going to talk to the school nurse about what's involved with an abortion." She glanced at Bobbie, who looked back at her but did not otherwise change her expression, other than to make a slight frown. "And, Bobbie, I want to talk either to your priest or to your youth leader or whomever you think best, so long as they'll talk with me confidentially."

Susan was again struck with Amy's sudden maturity. A seventeen-year-old who only the day before had been weeping on her bed, now was explaining a reasonable plan of action for determining what to do about her own life, as well as the life of an unborn child. Susan marveled at the transformation.

"And, when I talk to Billy, I definitely want one or both of you to be there," said Amy, looking at each of them in turn. "I have no idea what his reaction will be, but I doubt it will be very positive."

"Of course," said Bobbie. "I certainly agree with what you're planning to do, but I think you should consider telling your parents now, instead of later. I'm sure they will be upset for a day or two, but eventually they will have to help you. They know so much more about these things than any of us does, and they will want to help."

"No way," replied Amy, tapping her finger on the cafeteria table. "And if you are even thinking about telling them, or your own parents, then please don't, and please just leave and forget about all of this. I mean it, Bobbie."

The emotional flare-up was short-lived, but it registered with Susan. Amy was going to have to be handled with kid gloves, she could tell.

"Oh, no," said Bobbie. "This is your call. I just thought I'd let you know what I feel. Please don't get mad when I do that. I love you and just really want to help you, but maybe there are others who can help you more."

"Yes, the school nurse and a priest," said Amy. "But not my parents. They will be so disappointed. I just cannot face them right now, OK?" The other girls nodded.

"Now I'm going to call Billy and tell him I want to meet him somewhere this week. Then I'll call you guys, and hopefully at least one of you can be there."

Susan and Bobbie looked at each other and again nodded. "You know that we'll do everything we can for you," Susan said, as they picked up their trays and headed for their afternoon classes. Pitow would report that night that the hellish plans were progressing as they had expected.

As he walked down the hall at the end of classes that day, Tommy was continuing the debate he had been having with himself since Sunday morning. His experience Saturday night had been so intense, so overwhelming. All of them had eventually participated together as a group, just like on the video. It had been wild, and he couldn't take his mind off of it.

He had liked it so much. Did that mean he was a homosexual, part of the alternative lifestyle that his sex education class had studied only last week? Or was this just an aberration, something that happened once, perhaps as with other boys his age, but then would never happen again? He actually smiled when he thought of what his dad would say if he knew. "Boy, that would get him." Hey, his dad had thrown the baseball with him, after asking twice, yesterday afternoon. Big deal! What about all the times he had stood him up? All of the unfulfilled promises, all of the games he had missed? The voices were winding up inside Tommy when Roger suddenly appeared next to him. "Hey, big guy. The same bunch is going to get together over at Derrick's house this Saturday night. Do you think you can figure out a way to make it?"

Tommy looked at Roger and a voice, planted by Nepravel and spun by Pitow, said "Why not? It's fun, it feels good, and it sure beats sitting at home and doing homework."

"Sure," Tommy said, smiling. "I'll talk to Brent, and we'll see if we can figure a way to get there. Thanks."

TUESDAY, MAY 9 ■ On Tuesday, shortly after Richard had his usual date with Kristen, his daughter Susan and her two friends waited for Billy at the same table in the park from which Jeff had flown his kite less than a month before. It was a beautiful afternoon, and Susan could not help watching the mothers with their young toddlers playing in the nearby sandbox and on the climbing toy, imagining that Amy could be one of those mothers while she was still a teenager.

Billy parked his car and walked up to join them a little after four, surprised to find Susan and Bobbie sitting with Amy.

"How ya doin'?" He waved to all three with a smile. Their set expressions and the lack of movement out of Susan and Bobbie told Billy that this was not going to be a happy occasion.

The three girls waved politely as he walked up. He awkwardly bent down and kissed Amy on the cheek, like a husband returning home from work. Susan felt that was strangely out of place in the park, but perhaps more appropriate than he imagined, she reflected.

"Hi, Billy," said Amy. "Glad to see you. Please sit down, so I can let you know something."

The girls had not really meant it, but Billy wound up sitting across the park table from the three of them, with Amy in the middle.

"Listen, it's best if I don't beat around the bush. I want you to know that I'm pregnant."

Susan had to admit that Billy didn't miss a beat. There was no change in his expression as he brought both of his hands up on the table in front of him.

"Oh, I see," he said, looking first at Amy, then at the other two. "Are you sure?"

"Yes, two tests have confirmed it, and now I can feel it myself."

"And I guess you've told Susan and Bobbie that I'm the father. Are you sure of that too?"

Susan was flabbergasted. Bobbie started to stand up, clenching her fists, but Amy put her hand on Bobbie's leg to stop her. "Yes, Billy," Amy said with some sting in her voice. "You are *definitely* the father. Either that, or, excuse me, Bobbie, we will shortly have the second virgin birth in just under two thousand years."

There was silence for a moment between them. Billy looked down at his hands as he alternately changed the position of his thumbs. "Well, OK," he finally said. "What do you want to do?"

"I guess that it's ultimately my decision," said Amy, again mustering the maturity that Susan had first felt the previous day. "But I would very much like to have your input. Can you imagine, for example, that we would get married and raise a child? Could either of our parents raise it? There are apparently a lot of people who want babies. Should I have it and put it up for adoption? Or should I just get rid of it and hope that I feel like it never happened?"

Again there was a long silence. Billy was obviously thinking. "Well, if I have a vote, I vote for an abortion. I'm finishing my freshman year in college, and as much as I like you, I can't imagine us getting married and raising a family. I don't think I'm ready for that yet."

Susan knew it was not all his fault, but she nevertheless thought to herself that he should have considered that particular point of view several weeks earlier.

"Well, if I do have an abortion and it costs something, will you help pay for it?"

"Sure, uh, sure. Of course," he added with more decisiveness. And with some relief, it seemed to Susan, since it appeared for the moment that abortion was to be the resolution of the problem.

Bobbie, who had not said anything yet, now spoke up. "I know that neither of you wants to hear this, but there is a baby living inside you now, Amy. He or she did not ask to be there, but it has happened. That baby is alive, just like the four of us. God has made him. Abortion may 'solve the problem' for you, but what about the baby? I hate to spoil it for you, but you will be killing that baby." Her voice rose slightly and she turned to Amy, her difficulty in speaking apparent to them all. "I hate this situation as much as you do. I wish it hadn't happened. I know having the baby would create all sorts of problems for you. But many, many other girls have gone through these problems, and a year later their lives are seemingly back in order. Some couple would love to adopt your baby, Amy. Please don't compound one terrible wrong by making an even greater mistake."

While Bobbie spoke, Billy blanched, then spoke. "You can't really be serious? Have the baby? How old are you anyway, Amy? Seventeen? That's absurd to imagine."

"It's obviously a lot simpler for you if Amy has an abortion," Bobbie said, her anger rising. "But maybe you should have thought about that earlier. Now there is a baby to think about, and you're just thinking about yourself."

"Now, Bobbie," said Amy, placing her hand over Bobbie's hand. "I told you we came here to find out what Billy wants to do, not to lecture him. If you're handing out lectures, then you better lecture me as well. Anyway, he's not going to make the final decision. I am. And I haven't decided yet, although I do think an abortion does make the most sense for us, in our situation. But," raising her hand to interrupt Bobbie's attempt to argue, "I told you that I also want to talk to your priest, or to someone. So please look into that. But please be discreet."

"Well, you know where to find me, Amy," said Billy. Sensing that he should be nice to her, since she was soon going to make a decision which could significantly affect his life, he added, "Would you like to go out one night this weekend?"

"I don't know," she said. "I guess I can't get any more pregnant, can I, Billy?" she said acidly, as a bit of the anxiety she had kept under check for the past few days finally came out.

Billy turned red and looked at the other two girls, who were smiling "at-a-girl" smiles at him. "No, Amy," he defended himself. "I like you, and under the circumstances, I thought you might want to go out and have dinner, that's all."

"Well, thank you, Billy. Let me think about it. I'm genuinely a little confused now." The control crept back into her voice. "That will probably be fine, but this hasn't been the easiest few days for me, and I need to think. I'll call you tomorrow, OK?"

"Sure, sure." And Billy rose to leave. He started to lean over toward Amy, then could not quite manage it and instead just held her hand for a moment, turned, and left.

"Well, we have now confirmed where he stands. I guess we should all go home and study. I'll try to set up an appointment with the school nurse during seventh period, which we all have free, in the next couple of days, if you'd like to come along."

Susan finally spoke, "Yes, Amy. We've gone this far together, we might as well see it all the way through. You know we want to help you."

Having literally considered matters of life and death at the playground that afternoon, the three teenage girls returned to their homes to study French verb forms and the underlying causes of World War II.

Upon returning from "lunch" at Kristen's, Richard found that Robert Meredith was one of those who had called him at midday. "Listen, Richard," Robert began, when Richard returned his call, "there's a small group getting together at my office on Wednesday mornings for three weeks, to talk about Ben Fuller's message. We'll have coffee and doughnuts and be finished by 8:45. Would you like to join us?"

Richard thought about it. He really thought about it. He was about to say maybe, when a voice inside him told him that even if he wanted to find out what that mechanical contractor had found, he certainly had no business talking about God when he had a mistress on the side, one whose perfume he could still smell from less than thirty minutes before. Men who seemingly talked to God wouldn't understand someone like him. The voice told him that if he ever wanted to have a relationship with God, he had first better take care of this mistress situation on his own. Then, maybe God might be interested in talking with him. But for now, there was no chance that God would have anything to do with someone like him.

"Listen, uh, Robert. I, uh, really appreciate your asking me. I certainly enjoyed Ben Fuller's talk, and it obviously had a tremendous effect on some of the men there. As I said on that card, please keep me on the mailing list. If you ever have another prayer breakfast, I'd like to try to come. But I just don't think I'm prepared to get involved in any kind of regular meetings or anything."

"Well, OK," said Robert, with obvious disappointment in his voice. "But if you'd ever like to have more information or ask any questions about what Fuller was talking about—I mean about letting God come into your life—please feel free to call me. Any time. I mean it."

"Yeah, thanks. I certainly will. Goodbye." Richard thought that Robert's voice sounded so certain, so in control of his life. Unlike Richard, who was trying to balance two women, a difficult law practice, a son who seemed to be withdrawing from him, and a daughter . . . a daughter who seemed OK. It suddenly occurred to him that maybe Bobbie Meredith, Robert's daughter, had something to do with his own daughter's apparent stability. *Maybe so,* he thought.

Yes, once he took care of the situation with Kristen, he might definitely give Robert a call and have breakfast with him. Try to find out what this stability, this peace really was. But God would definitely not want him as he was. So first he had to clean up his life, then find out about God.

As he put aside those thoughts and picked up another briefing file, Nepravel, who had floated in with Richard from Kristen's apartment, congratulated himself on this ruse, which he had used thousands of times in the past.

"If they start to look like they're leaning toward the truth," Balzor had reminded them on many occasions, "give them the Unworthy voice. It lets them think temporarily that they are on the right track, but it keeps them squarely under our control, without any help from Jesus or those cursed angels. And nine out of ten times they'll eventually forget about it and be right back where they were within a month." Yes, Nepravel thought. Unworthy was a great voice. And the great thing about it was, it was universally applicable to all of them!

FRIDAY, MAY 12 ■ That Friday afternoon at lunch in the high school cafeteria, Amy told Bobbie and Susan that their regular school nurse, Mrs. Simpson, had gone to a conference all week. Amy had not wanted to talk with the substitute.

"Mrs. Simpson will be back on Monday, and I'll try to set up an appointment for us early next week. I guess time is marching on," Amy said.

"And I'll talk to Glenn Jamison, our youth leader on Sunday morning," added Bobbie. "You'll really like him, Amy. He's young, has a wife and two children. He's a neat guy. Everyone in our high school group really likes him. I'll see if we can meet him one afternoon after school, maybe at the yogurt shop."

"Thanks, Bobbie. I think maybe the park, or even his office, would be better. I hate to talk about something like this in the yogurt shop, where some of our friends might come in," said Amy.

"Sure, OK. I'll talk to him and give you both a call on Sunday afternoon."

"Janet, it's all set up," said Bill Shaw, standing in the doorway to her office.

For a moment, she was uncertain what he was talking about. A questioning look confirmed it.

"You know, the '911 Live' test run. It's all set up to take place here in two weeks, and I've been able to wrangle the four of us permission to chase along with the equipment, sort of adding a local interest to the network production. I told them that we could use the footage to promote the show here in the city. It's scheduled for Friday next week. Are you still on?"

"Yes, of course," Janet replied. "I had just lost my train of thought for a moment. What time are we supposed to get together?"

"Probably about 5:30 in the afternoon. The network show in the fall is scheduled to run for ninety minutes, but it will have ten cities to pull input from. Since this test run will only take place here, they're going to give it four hours, from seven until eleven that evening. Will you tell the others?"

"Sure, Bill. And thanks for setting this up. I really appreciate your fair-handedness."

"Of course. It's the only way to manage a creative bunch like you. Fair-handedness . . ." He smiled as he left her doorway.

That weekend, Amy surprised her parents by accepting their invitation to spend a couple of days together at their mountain home. She had decided that whatever the next weeks would bring, this might be one of her last chances to be with her parents as she used to be, their innocent teenage daughter. She had called Billy and told him that she certainly wanted to see him again soon, but this weekend she needed to be away. He had understood and had immediately asked her out for the following Saturday.

Susan and Bobbie had individual dates with Drew and Thomas. Each of them needed a little familiar territory after the tension of dealing with Amy's adult problem.

SATURDAY, MAY 13 ■ Kristen had flown to Dallas. She had said on Thursday that it was to visit her family, but Richard couldn't help suspecting that perhaps she was going to visit Peter.

Richard and Janet went to Tommy's baseball game on Saturday afternoon. It was the first game Richard had attended that season. He was proud of the way Tommy handled a long fly ball in the third inning—his throw to the cut-off man was right on target, and that boy then threw out the runner at the plate.

"Maybe I ought to talk to the coach about Tommy playing in the infield," Richard said under his breath in the stands.

"No, I don't think you should," Janet patted his hand. "Let's just let Tommy handle that."

After the game, Richard and Janet congratulated Tommy and Brent on their win and on the fine plays they both had made.

"Would you boys like to go get a hamburger?" asked Richard.

"Thanks, Dad," Tommy replied, not wanting to annoy his father. "After we get cleaned up, we were planning to go to the mall with Brent's brother, to the food court and to the arcade," he lied. "Is that OK?"

"Sure, sure, Tommy. That'll be fine. You boys have a good time. Just don't stay out too late."

With both children gone, which seemed to happen regularly now, Richard and Janet decided to go to a movie themselves.

It was, all in all, a normal weekend, with one great exception. Tommy was being dragged further and further into a group of boys whose way of dealing with parental problems and adolescent rejection was to band together and to spend every Saturday night experiencing fantasies and each other—in a way which seemed right only because they imagined themselves to be rejected by those whom they loved, or by those whom they wanted to love.

What could have been an understandable one-time adolescent experience was instead becoming a way of life for them. When Tommy arrived home late that Saturday night, he felt even more cemented to this particular "alternative," because for the first time he had become an active, not just a passive, participant.

That evening, at their regular rendezvous over the city, the demons were a pretty contented and self-congratulatory group. Nepravel and several others reported major advances in the destruction of families along their streets.

"I think the prayer breakfast has almost blown over," reported Tymor. "As we all know, there were some immediate conversions ten days ago, which is highly regrettable, but understandable. Happily, due to the hard work of so many of us, no major revival was kindled. Several of the new converts have been confused. Unworthiness has played a great role there. And the follow-up has been generally ineffective, because most of the hosts never went to see their guests face to face, nor really tried hard to interest them. So, exalted leader, I think we can generally stand down from the alert which the prayer breakfast caused us."

"Yes, yes," Balzor agreed. "And our city leader, Alhandra, agrees and sends his congratulations as well. But, my bitter ones, we must always be on the lookout. There are still a couple of churches in our sector that are preaching the Word. Every week a few more people find out the Truth and are saved from the dark eternity that awaits most of their neighbors.

"We've almost done it. Almost. Just a few more years like the last twenty out of the government, the media, the movies, the records, and the unsaved ministers, and then virtually every city in America will be as dark as night, twenty-four hours a day! These people are so confused! It is truly fantastic. To think how simple it would be for them to beat us, if only they could grasp it! And to think of the lies we have to weave in their lives to keep them from it. You are to be congratulated for the work you have done, particularly with this last generation. We really have almost done it. Our task is to keep destroying these local families, while others work on the nation's leaders, in the government and in business. With this two-pronged attack, we cannot lose!"

The demons left that night feeling better than they had in weeks and prepared to take up their positions for Sunday morning, when there were always special duties to perform to distract families from attending church.

SUNDAY, MAY 14 ■ "And does anybody have any prayer requests for this week?" asked Glenn Jamison, the youth minister at Morningside Church. Several of the more than eighty students—they had averaged only about twenty each week a year ago—raised their hands.

The group had finished the morning's lesson on Lazarus and the rich man, from Luke 16. Glenn had pointed out that this was one of several times in the Bible when Jesus himself referred to hell and to the choice people had to make. It had been a difficult lesson, but the kids, as usual, responded with serious attention when he treated them with respect and demanded the same from them. Most of the kids really liked Glenn's combination of playfulness and seriousness, and this had been one of the serious times.

"Yes?" he said, as Bobbie raised her hand.

"I know someone at my school who is pregnant, and I want us all to pray for her and for her baby."

Thomas Briggs, sitting next to Bobbie, was surprised by her request, and he wondered who it might be.

After several additional prayer requests, the group broke up. Some of the students went to the sanctuary to attend the main service. Others left in groups for an early lunch together. Bobbie lingered behind and button-holed Glenn as he neared the door.

"Glenn, the girl I asked the prayer request for . . . Do you think you could meet with her and me and one other friend to discuss her alternatives?"

"Of course, Bobbie." Glenn put down the books he was carrying. "When would you like to get together?"

"How about one day this week, uh, say maybe Wednesday? Would you mind if we came to your office? She's afraid that someone will overhear the conversation in a more crowded place."

"Sure, Bobbie, Wednesday will be fine."

"Thanks, Glenn. She's very confused about what to do, and I'm afraid the rest of us haven't had any experience with this. We'll see you about 4:00 in your office, and I'll call if there is any change." Bobbie hurried off to join her parents for the 11:15 service. Quite often she joined her friends for lunch at this time, after the youth group meeting, but this week she felt the need to worship and to pray with her family. And the sermons of their pastor, Reverend Michael Andrews, usually inspired her. She at least had always understood his sermons, which had not been true of his predecessor.

The congregation of their church had doubled since Reverend Andrews arrived three years earlier. "It's because he speaks the Word, and people have missed it around here, like water," her father had explained. "Once they finally drink some, they want more and more." Now that she was seventeen and had listened to Michael for three years, she certainly understood and agreed with her father. And then Glenn had arrived a year ago and done the same thing for most of the high school students. As she knelt in prayer and their service began, she hoped that the Lord might have the same effect on Amy, on Susan, and on their problems.

It was Balzor's habit on Sunday mornings to inspect personally several of the churches in his sector, alternating between them, at least the ones he could go near.

As he floated down through the cathedral-like ceiling of St. James Church for their midmorning service, he knew that he did not have to fear the wrath of an angel in this particular place. There were so few prayers coming from this church that an angel would never be able to appear. He watched with glee as his demons carried out their work, managing the voices in the pews with complete impunity.

"Imagine!" he thought, "Who would have thought, just one, or at most two, generations ago, that I and my demons would be running around inside this church on Sunday morning? Why, back then it would have been unthinkable. This place used to be alive with worship and prayer. I can remember when there were ten or twenty angels swarming all around this building, and not just on Sundays. No demon in his right mind would have come near this place. But here I am today, inside and enjoying every minute of it!"

Looking down on the congregation, he could see one or two flickers of light inside a few saved souls. But most of them happily looked like they were either asleep or dazed. The sermon appeared to be about halfway over.

"And while Jesus was certainly one of the greatest teachers who ever lived, hasn't it got to be arrogance on the part of the established church over these many centuries to claim that He could be the *only* way to salvation? Jesus said not to boast, and I tell you that it is arrogance and boastfulness which have led the church to proclaim that Jesus provides the only 'Way, Truth, and Life.' It is clear now from scholarly research that that particular passage was added to the Bible several hundred years later, by early church authors who were trying to set up the Christian church as the political counterweight to the Roman Empire.

"How could God provide only *one* vehicle for salvation? Thus, Jesus may be *a* way, but surely there are others. Far be it from us true Christians to boast and to hold our heads above our Buddhist, Hindu, and even our Jewish brothers! Pray daily, as I do, that the One God of All Religions will move mightily among us and save us from such bigoted hypocrisy."

"Bravo, bravo!" clapped Balzor silently from the ceiling. "I couldn't have said it better myself! If that's not confusion, I don't know what is."

He was so pleased that he sent his demons away. "Forget about the voices here. This pastor is doing a great job without us. You can leave here and go find some people who might be going to one of the few real churches left in our sector, and discourage them. These people here are in fine hands."

Balzor wanted to stay to hear more, but he had to pull himself away to go check on some other churches. One place he would steer away from, of course, was Morningside Church. Even from his low altitude, hopping from church to church, he could see the intense white light of the angels who were gathered around Morningside, claiming it as Holy Ground. *Those people pray all the time, and we'll never get through all the angels covering that place. I hate it, but at least we're down to just two or three churches like that in the whole sector. When you think that only twenty years ago there were forty or fifty, we've made great progress!*

7

WEDNESDAY, MAY 17 ■ Amy had been able to set up an appointment with Mrs. Simpson for Wednesday during seventh period, when Bobbie and Susan could also attend. "It's a little unusual to counsel you with two friends present, but it's not unheard of," Mrs. Simpson had said in a friendly voice. "So I'll be glad to see you then."

Now the three of them stood outside her door, and Amy knocked. Mrs. Simpson had been the school nurse for as long as the three of them were in high school, yet she was young. She was respected among the students for her competence, and they appreciated her good natured attempts to be "with it," keeping up as best she could with their latest fads and sayings.

She greeted them with a warm smile, and soon they had pulled up four chairs together in her small office.

"Now what I can do for the three of you?" she asked.

Amy took a deep breath. "Well, Mrs. Simpson, uh, the fact is that I'm pregnant, and I want to find out what you think my options might be. And I asked Bobbie and Susan to come along to hear what you have to say and to help me decide."

Mrs. Simpson's expression turned serious. "You don't have to, Amy, but if you can give me a few more details, I think I can better advise you. And don't worry," she said, trying to ease the tension a bit, "you're not the first girl I've seen with this problem, even this spring."

The three girls looked at each other with surprise, and then Amy described in general about her relationship with Billy. She even recounted their conversation with him in the previous week at the park.

After listening to Amy, Mrs. Simpson said "Well, I think you've already pretty well outlined your options yourself. Of course the choice is ultimately yours alone, but in your case I would definitely recommend an abortion."

All three girls looked intently at Mrs. Simpson. "Why?" Susan finally asked.

"Because Amy is so young, and the father definitely does not want to marry her, nor does he care about the baby. There is no point in putting Amy through the problems and the risks of childbirth when an abortion in the next few weeks can get rid of the problem in a nearly foolproof manner."

Bobbie started to say something, but thought better of it, for the moment. Amy asked, "What do I have to do to have an abortion? Do my parents have to know?"

"How old are you, Amy?" asked Mrs. Simpson.

"Seventeen."

"Then in this state you do not need parental approval for an abortion. Nor do you need anyone else's approval during the first trimester. I assume, looking at you, that you still qualify there." Amy nodded.

"I usually recommend to our girls," making it sound like she did this on a regular basis, "that you go to the clinic on a Friday morning. I can write you an excuse for your classes that day, and you will have the whole weekend to recuperate."

"You mean I can go right from here?" asked Amy. "Without my parents even knowing?"

"Yes," said the nurse. "The medical clinic will send a van right here for you and bring you back here afterwards. You can even have a friend go with you. We've never had two friends attend," she added, smiling at Susan and Bobbie, "but I'm sure they will make an exception in your case. Would you like me to make an appointment for this Friday, or the next?"

"I, uh, I . . . I definitely want to think about it a little longer," said Amy, "but I know I have to decide something quickly, and so I'll definitely get back to you. And thank you so much for all your help."

Out in the hall, Bobbie said "Well, there certainly is no misunderstanding where she is coming from. I had no idea that she was so much in favor of abortions."

"To be fair," said Susan, "it *is* her job—and abortions are perfectly legal, and it may just be the best thing for Amy." Bobbie frowned but didn't say anything more about Mrs. Simpson.

"Well, you're both coming with me after school to meet with Glenn Jamison, right?" Bobbie added. Susan and Amy nodded their heads in agreement.

"And just so you won't think my mind is made up already," Amy added, "I'm really looking forward to meeting this guy, after all you have said about him." But, in fact, Amy had to admit that Mrs. Simpson had made a lot of sense.

Bruce McKinney had called that morning and asked for an appointment with Richard for the afternoon. Richard's secretary had accommodated him at 3:00. They were sitting alone together in Richard's office.

"Now that we have the Tomlinson contract all wrapped up and ready to close, Richard, David and I really need some help. We've got a special favor to ask of you, which is why I've come here, since we've been friends and neighbors for so many years," Bruce began.

"I'm all ears," said Richard. "How can I help you?"

"As you suggested several weeks ago, we went to our bank and asked about a loan, based on the strength of the Tomlinson contract. You wrote an excellent contract, and there is no question in any of our minds that the deal will close, just as soon as the elder Tomlinson's estate is settled. Right?" Richard nodded.

"Well, you know bankers. They are very conservative. They looked at the estate contingency and the stock price contingency and then said they could not help us without personal guarantees.

"Now, Richard, as you know, David and I have to expand or go broke. Our competition has expanded into several new offices in the suburbs, and they are eating our lunch with their new locations and their new agents. Richard, it's just not fair. We're the best securities analysts in town. We have an excellent track record and great guys working with us; but we've got to expand, or we'll be finished and gone in just a few years.

"With office rent so low because of the overbuilding, now is the best time ever to make great office space deals. We've found several spaces we can take over for a song, but we have to sign five-year leases, furnish them, and hire new brokers. The bottom line is that the expansion process alone will cost about $350,000. When you add in the working capital that we already need, the total requirement is just over $500,000. Unfortunately, David and I have mortgaged everything we have to keep the company going, and even though we know we will eventually get a million dollars from Tomlinson, we're not going to survive without some immediate capital, right now."

"So what, specifically, do you have in mind for me to do?" asked Richard.

"David and I are each going to two of our friends—you are one of four—and offering you a proposition we hope you can't refuse. The other three, in fact, are already directors of our company, which we hope, along with you, will show the banks a strong vote of confidence. If you will agree to co-guarantee a loan for us now, we'll pay you a $50,000 financing fee as soon as the Tomlinson deal closes. You, better than the other three, understand how strong the Tomlinson deal is. You should see that it's virtually a risk-free way to make $50,000 in just a few months. And you'll help keep our business afloat at a crucial time."

Richard had to admit that the proposition sounded attractive. He and Janet could certainly use $50,000. They could pay off some of their debt, do some things they had been postponing around the house, and maybe even take a vacation together, to help get their marriage back on track. And he agreed with Bruce that the Tomlinson capital infusion was pretty secure, though, like most business ventures, certainly not guaranteed.

"Well, I'm genuinely flattered that you've asked me," said Richard after a few moments. "I must admit that it does sound appealing. Will the guarantees have to be joint and several?"

Bruce nodded. "The banks require it that way."

"Well, even so, it sounds like it may be something I want to consider. Let me think it through for a day or two, and I'll give you a call. Say, did Hugh McEver's house ever sell?"

"Not that I know of," answered Bruce. "I hear that Betty is getting ready to drop the price by $30,000 or so, which will really make it a bargain. I certainly hope she's successful. I know she needs the money for those kids."

Bruce left a few minutes later, and Richard thought again about all the things he could do with an extra $50,000.

After school, the three girls assembled in the student parking lot, and Bobbie drove them over to Morningside Church, where Glenn Jamison was waiting for them in his office. "Hello, Bobbie. Hello, girls," he smiled and extended his hand to each in turn. "Please come in and sit down. Would any of you like a Coke or some coffee?"

As they sat down, Bobbie said, "I'd like a Coke. How about you?" looking at her friends. With nods from them and a final nod from Glenn, she walked quickly down the hall to the machine and came back with four soft drinks.

After some additional introductions and discussion about the coming end of their junior year, Glenn said to Amy, "Bobbie has, of course, told me why you've come here today, and I certainly want to help.

"Why don't you tell me a little about the situation in your own words?" Glenn asked, leaning forward and listening attentively.

Amy repeated much the same story she had told to Mrs. Simpson earlier that day. She even concluded by telling Glenn that Mrs. Simpson strongly urged her to have an abortion, as early as this Friday, or the next.

"Well, Amy, as you might expect from knowing Bobbie and meeting me here," Glenn began after Amy finished, "my strong advice to you is that abortion is absolutely the wrong thing. God has created a new life inside you. He knows your baby just like He knows you. They will tell you, and I'm sure that Mrs. Simpson already has, that it's 'simple and quick.' Even if there are no complications, Amy, which there very well could be, 'simple and quick' means the death—we actually call it the murder—of the unborn baby.

"We can't always understand God's purpose in our lives. I certainly can't explain to you why you and Billy are the parents of this child. Maybe it's for your sake, to teach you something. Maybe it's for the baby's sake. He or she might grow up to do something very unusual, or just to be a good parent. Or maybe it is for the couple who will surely adopt the baby, if you offer it for adoption, and will love it and care for it. None of us can know. But we believe that God makes all life for a purpose. It is holy and should not be terminated, particularly for convenience.

"I'm deeply sorry that this has happened, for your sake. I know it won't be easy for you, and if you decide to go ahead and have the baby, I'll go with you to talk to your parents, if you would like me to. A lot more people from this church, and these friends who surround you, will do everything we can to support you and to make the situation as positive as possible."

Amy was silent for a long time, looking alternately between Glenn's face and her hands, folded in her lap. After a moment, tears filled her eyes, and she finally spoke. "I hear you, and I really appreciate what you're saying. But, like, I just don't know if I believe it, not yet. All these years I've heard that a fetus is only a thing, not really a baby. And that women have to choose what is best for them in this situation. I'm all mixed up, but I just can't stand the thought of having a baby right now. I've only been seventeen for two months . . ." And then she really started to cry.

Glenn offered her a tissue and moved his chair closer to hers. "Go ahead," he said. "Sometimes it's the best thing just to let it out."

"I'm sorry . . . I've tried so hard to manage this. To seem responsible when I was actually so irresponsible to get myself into this mess. I've tried hard the last few weeks, but it's so difficult. If it wasn't for Susan and Bobbie, I don't know what I would have done." There followed more silence, and finally she asked, "Does it really ever say somewhere in the Bible that a fetus is a baby?"

"Not in precisely those words," Glenn replied. "But throughout the Bible it refers to life as being sacred, and surely that baby is alive within you. Soon you'll be able to feel him or her kick. And the Bible does say, 'Before I knit you together in the womb, I knew you.' That has always meant to me that each one of us has been individually created by God Himself, who has known our spirit since before our parents conceived us; and also that he considers the womb to be a holy place, not to be tampered with."

"Well . . ." Amy took a deep breath and was able to dry her last tears, "I really, really do appreciate what you've said. It's so very hard, and I still don't know what to do. I can see your point that it would be wrong to terminate the baby, if it is a baby. But, like I said, I just can't imagine having a baby now. It just seems so scary, and even with your help, my parents would never understand. They would be so disappointed."

"They'll probably be disappointed in the beginning, yes, Amy. But I can almost promise you that they'll get over it quickly. I'm sure your parents love you so much that even this situation will only strengthen your relationship, after the first few days. And before long they'll be looking forward, as you will, to the birth of your baby."

Amy finished her Coke and slowly stood up to go. "Before you leave, let's pray together," Glenn said. "Here, let's hold hands."

Glenn and Bobbie extended their hands, and Amy and Susan, somewhat self-consciously, took them, forming a circle. Glenn bowed his head, and the others followed. "Dear heavenly Father, I ask a special measure of blessing and protection upon Amy this day. And upon the baby growing in her womb. Please give her the wisdom and the courage she needs to make the right decision for the two lives she now carries in one body. And I thank You for her friends, Susan and Bobbie, who are helping her through this difficult time. Please, Father, bless and protect these girls and their families today. In Jesus' name. Amen."

Amy's eyes were moist again as she shook Glenn's hand and the three of them departed. Walking to the car, Amy said, "Wow! He *is* something. You're right. He is very friendly, but it seems like he can look right through you. Whatever happens out of this, I may want to come back and go to church with you someday."

"That would be great," replied Bobbie. "In fact, we'll pick up either or both of you on any Sunday you want to come. Your houses are right on the way from our house to the church."

That night, tossing in her bed, Amy had to admit that Glenn's argument, too, like Mrs. Simpson's, made a lot of sense. She felt like a knot was tied around her heart, and the confusion in her mind was pulling it tighter and tighter. She fought to stay in control, but she often found herself just wanting to cry and to run away.

FRIDAY, MAY 19 ■ On Friday, Richard called Bruce, without first consulting with Janet, or with anyone else, and told him that he would go ahead and guarantee their loan, as part of a foursome. Bruce replied that one of the men had refused, but the other two were in and that these two had strong financial statements. Richard thought about it for another moment, and decided that the risk was virtually the same, but he might as well ask. "Well, and I don't want you to think that I'm being greedy, but if the three of us help you carry the ball, wouldn't it be fair to increase our fee to $66,000 each?"

There was silence on the line for a few moments. Then Bruce, who knew he was over a barrel, said, "Sure, Richard. That's fair. We had expected to pay $200,000 to get this loan, so we might as well make it worthwhile for each of you. It's a deal."

"Good. Then, to show you that I've earned the extra amount, I'll prepare the papers, *gratis*, and have them over to your office in a couple of days. OK?"

"Sounds great to me, Richard. And David and I really appreciate it. Just don't take too long on the papers because we've got to get that loan as quickly as possible."

"No problem," said Richard, hanging up the phone.

SATURDAY, MAY 20 ■ That warm Saturday afternoon, Susan had challenged Janet to a tennis game, and the men decided to have a game as well. So all four of the Sullivans walked down to the courts at the park in the middle of Devon Drive.

Between sets, when Janet and Susan were sitting and watching Richard and Tommy play, Susan said, "Now, Mom, don't freak! I'm not asking for me . . . but we've been studying in biology, and I wondered what you think about abortions."

Janet looked closely at Susan, trying to read her expression, to see if it really *was* for her, but she could only see an honest question—one that Janet had not exactly expected, however.

"Well, I think that women have the right to choose what's best for their bodies. Sometimes it's just not right or convenient to bring a baby into the world, so an abortion is the best thing. I guess it's regrettable, but sometimes necessary."

Susan, who had of course been present and heard what Glenn and Bobbie had said and had been thinking a lot about it herself, asked, "Why is it regrettable, if it's OK?"

"I . . . uh . . . maybe that was a poor choice of words. But I guess our reproductive systems were set up to have children, so I just mean it's regrettable when one has to be stopped."

"Do you think it's wrong? Does God make us and somehow know us before we are born? Is the fetus a live baby?"

"No . . . no Susan. I don't know about God making us. Sometimes I look around this world and wonder how there could be a God. I certainly don't think that He fashions each one of us. The fetus is just tissue until it can breathe and live on its own. It's not wrong to have an abortion . . . It's just sort of regrettable."

"Well, if God doesn't make us, and there may not be a God, then what is the purpose of life? Why are we here anyway?" Susan pressed, emboldened by the faith she had seen recently in Bobbie.

"Wow! You've been studying more than biology!" Janet smiled, and Susan looked down at her racquet. "I don't know, Susan. I think we're just here. To live and to love each other as best we can. To have kids and to raise them and to do the best we are able. To improve the world and make it a better place for all of us to live. I certainly don't believe that God, if He even exists, gets involved in individual lives with some individual purpose. He certainly never has done that in mine."

Susan was struck by the difference between her mother's belief and that of Bobbie and Glenn. For the first time in her life she questioned whether her mother really had it together in her belief system. *How could it be that there is no purpose to life, other than to exist and to procreate? I want there to be purpose!* she thought. *I want to think that Someone is in charge. I'm almost seventeen, and I don't want to think that I'm growing up for nothing! Mom must have missed something. I better ask some other people. Maybe Dad.*

She said to her mother, "Well, I hear you, but it's hard to imagine that there is no God, and no real purpose to life."

"I didn't say that there's no purpose to life. It's just that we have to make it ourselves . . . I hope that someday you'll meet a good man and you'll fall in love and have kids and raise them well. That's the purpose to life . . . All right!" Janet smiled again. "Enough philosophy. Let's get back to tennis. You're still young. Maybe you'll find more purpose than I have. But don't count on it."

By Saturday evening, Amy was still in mental agony, with the pressure growing on her to make her decision. Billy picked her up at home, and he took her to a quiet continental restaurant—decidedly a cut above their previous dates—for dinner.

After ordering and catching up on small talk, Amy recounted for Billy the arguments she had heard for and against abortion and adoption.

Billy did not jump in immediately, but over the course of their meal together, he repeated his strong position for her to have the abortion. He went back through all of the arguments that both he and Mrs. Simpson had used previously. And Amy had to agree, particularly with no other voice in her head, that he and the school nurse certainly made perfect sense. It really was the wrong time and the wrong situation for her to have a baby, particularly one that neither she nor Billy wanted.

Over dessert, he pushed her for a decision. "Amy, you know an abortion is the right thing. You have no business having a baby now. Neither you nor I want our parents to know. I know you think an abortion is best. Please agree now, and make an appointment with the school nurse on Monday so we can put this behind us."

Her emotional turmoil had become almost intolerable. Already the changes in her body were giving her pause, and they even scared her a bit. Without Susan or Bobbie there, she only heard Billy, and he made so much sense. "OK . . . yes. OK . . ." she nodded her head and tears filled her eyes. "Yes, I'll get the abortion. I'll see Mrs. Simpson on Monday, and I'll do it on Friday. God help me if this is wrong, but I'll do it."

And right then, even with Billy there in a restaurant full of people, she had never felt so alone in her life. She hugged herself, suddenly overcome by a cold chill that enveloped her.

MONDAY, MAY 22 ■ Monday morning, before she even saw Susan or Bobbie, Amy went to the nurse's office and told her decision to Mrs. Simpson. The nurse walked over and put her arm around Amy's shoulder. "That's fine, Amy, I'm sure you've done the right thing. Come back after lunch, and I'll have the forms all prepared. But I'll go ahead and call the clinic and schedule you for Friday morning. The cost, by the way, is $350, and the clinic typically is paid immediately after the procedure. Will that be a problem?" Amy shook her head. "And will you want Bobbie and Susan to go with you? It's fine, but I'll have to write excuses for them as well."

"Yes, I do," said Amy. "I imagine that Susan will join me, but I'm not sure Bobbie will go to the clinic. Neither of them knows about my decision yet, but I'll let you know how many of us will go."

At lunch that day, at a table by themselves, Amy was about to tell Susan and Bobbie her decision. The three of them had not really talked all weekend. The other two girls had been on dates with Drew and Thomas, who were fast becoming steadies with them. Then on Sunday, Amy had driven with her parents to visit her grandmother on her birthday, and Bobbie had gone with her youth group to a late afternoon movie. So this lunch was the first time they had seen each other in a couple of days.

"I've made my decision," Amy announced, once they sat down. "It hasn't been easy, and I completely understand both sides, but I've decided that this is not the time for me to have a baby, and so I'm going to have the abortion, and I've already scheduled it for this Friday with Mrs. Simpson."

It was as if a great burden was being lifted from her, almost as if she had not really made the decision until she actually told her best friends. Now it was out, and her course was set. Susan's reaction was mainly one of relief. She, like Amy, had heard and understood both sides of the argument. She was just glad that it was Amy making the decision, and not herself. Either way, she was now relieved, just to know.

"Do you want us to come with you to the clinic?" asked Susan, indicating her support for her friend.

"Yes, very much. Mrs. Simpson says it's OK. She can arrange it." Silently, Amy looked at Bobbie. Bobbie was looking down at her lunch, but not feeling very hungry. Both of the other girls could see the anguish and the pain on her face.

"Amy, I . . . I . . . you know I think you have made the wrong decision. Now I just don't know what to do, if you are set on an abortion. I love you and want to support you. But I don't know if I can go to an abortion clinic and help you have one. It's an impossible decision I have to make. I know I have to pray about it, and I'll try to tell you something later this week. I wish I could ask my parents about it," raising her hand as Amy started to speak, "but I understand that I can't. So, like you, I'll have to make this decision on my own. This really has been a great couple of weeks, hasn't it?" She tried to smile, as tears filled her eyes.

The professional baseball team in their city had a rare afternoon game that Monday at 4:00, and Richard bought tickets for Tommy and himself. Richard had cleared his calendar, and even picked Tommy up on time as school let out.

Following Janet's advice, he did not push Tommy on any particular subjects. He decided simply to spend time with his son. She had even cautioned him that morning to be prepared for a few jabs from Tommy. After all, he was an adolescent, and all adolescents had to rebel. In Tommy's case, there was apparently some pain inside that needed venting. So Richard had decided to be ready to roll with the punches and not to strike back, no matter what Tommy said.

Somewhat to the surprise of both of them, they actually had a wonderful afternoon together, sitting in the spring sunshine, eating peanuts, and watching their team play last year's division leader.

"That's one thing your grandfather used to always tell me about baseball, Tommy," Richard said early in the game. "Every spring it starts over again. There's a new beginning and everybody thinks their team will win the pennant. Last year is forgotten and hope springs eternal!" As he was saying it, Richard was hoping that the same could be true about their relationship.

In the sixth inning, Tommy just missed a high pop foul ball, which bounced three rows behind them. They shared analyses of the players and of the strategies being employed by the managers. Richard told Tommy about an old girlfriend of his in high school, whom a girl two rows in front of them reminded him of. Near the end of the game, Tommy finally loosened up and was able to laugh about his own game, a month earlier, when he had hoped to play in the infield, but hadn't. "I guess I'm just an outfielder," he tentatively joked about himself to his father, "so I'll have to develop big muscles and start hitting lots of homers across the fence."

Richard smiled and agreed. "You know, it's funny how in Little League the infielders get all the notoriety, but in the majors, it's the outfielders who typically win the games for their team. You're exactly right." By the end of the day, the father and son had experienced more eye contact and discussed more things than in the past three months. The only negative thing about the day was that their team lost a close one, four to three in the ninth.

Driving home from the game, Tommy suddenly asked his father, "Dad, what do you think about homosexuals?"

That was certainly a question for which Richard had not prepared, but he reminded himself to roll with the punches. "Why do you ask, son?"

"Like, you know, we studied homosexuality in our health class several weeks ago, and then two of them came in and talked to us about their lifestyles, and, I don't know, I just thought I'd ask you."

"Well, I don't know. I guess I really never thought about them much. They're obviously people, just like us, some good, some bad. I've never really been able to figure out whether it's something caused by heredity, or by environment, or by friends, or what. I guess it just is an alternative lifestyle. I wouldn't want anyone in our family to be a homosexual, because I think that, no matter what the Gay Rights people say, it's a tough life. And of course this AIDS thing is rampant in the homosexual community, killing many of them. I don't think they should be persecuted, but I also don't think special laws should be written for them. Like many things in life, it's a complex question, and I'm not sure that I have a clear answer one way or the other. I guess it depends on the individual situation and on the individual person."

Richard's answer might have been perfect for an intellectual debate among adults, but unfortunately it was not really what Tommy needed or wanted to hear right then. He yearned for his father to say something definite, so he could hold on to some fixed point in his rapidly spinning social world. Unknowingly, Richard had given the worst answer he could for his fourteen-year-old son. He had thrown the issue back on Tommy to decide, and Tommy on his own was no match for the forces aligned against him.

TUESDAY, MAY 23 ■ "Glenn, I just don't know what to do," Bobbie repeated into the telephone on Tuesday afternoon, after school. She had explained Amy's decision to have the abortion. Now she was trying to decide whether to support her friend or to refuse to go to the abortion clinic on Friday. "I've promised Amy that I won't talk to my parents—you're the only one I can turn to. What do you think?"

"This is about as tough as they come, Bobbie," Glenn hesitated, hoping for inspiration. "Obviously we have to pray. Do you mind if I alert our prayer warrior team, only mentioning her first name, of course?"

"Please, yes. Please do. She's scheduled for first thing on Friday morning."

"Bobbie, I guess if it were me, I'd want to be with my friend. But I don't think I could help her do something which I believed to be so wrong. For her sake you couldn't openly pray or disrupt what was happening at the clinic—you'd just have to be part of it. What a tough choice. But I just can't see you going to an abortion clinic, even with Amy." Glenn hoped that he was right.

"Well, I'll pray again tonight and make my decision in the morning. Thanks a lot for your help. And do call the Prayer Warrior team." Bobbie hung up and thought how simple her life of only a month ago now seemed.

WEDNESDAY, MAY 24 ■ Richard and his paralegal had prepared the unconditional joint and several guarantees which the bank needed for the McKinney and Smith loan. Bruce and David had secured the signatures of the other two guarantors that Wednesday morning, and now the three of them were meeting at the bank for the loan closing.

As a final precaution before leaving for the bank, Richard had called Patrick Tomlinson's attorney, Marty Tsongas, without disclosing the real reason for his call. "Everything is on track with the estate settlement," Marty had assured him.

Within forty minutes all of the documents had been signed and approved by the bank officer and his attorney. The banker, William Butler, gave Bruce a check for $500,000, and they shook hands. "I hope these funds will help continue the success we all have seen from you guys," he concluded in his most friendly banker's voice.

"Can we borrow your conference room for a few minutes?" Richard asked William. Once he was alone with Bruce and David, he pulled out another folder and placed the papers in front of them. "These are the individual notes to secure the fees owed to each of your three guarantors, payable at the time of the Tomlinson capital investment. They are just like the drafts I faxed to you, so please read them over and then sign them."

Back in his office thirty minutes later, Richard put his own note into the safe and congratulated himself on earning $66,000 so easily.

"Amy, I just can't do it," Bobbie said at lunch that day, the pain obvious to her two friends. "I know you think it's just because that's what I've been taught. But this situation has made it all very real to me. I really do believe that there is a baby inside you and that it is wrong to kill him or her. I pray that you will reconsider. In fact, I plan to be praying for you and for your baby that morning. I want to support you. I love you, but I can't help you do this." She paused and looked out at the gathering stormclouds through the tall cafeteria windows. "I've been a mess ever since Monday, not to mention the last two weeks. But I just can't go with you to an abortion clinic. I'm sorry, but I can't. I hope you can understand." Tears filled her eyes, and she wiped them quickly, hoping that no one else in the cafeteria would notice.

"Bobbie, I know what an impossible decision it was for me, so I can't be upset with you. For me, it's not a 'baby'—it's a fetus, something that is not yet really alive and something that no one wants. So I'm going to get rid of it. And then hope that I won't make the same mistake again. God knows I'll be more careful next time!" Amy's last statement reminded Susan that Amy had taken a huge step, separating her from her two friends. "Susan and I will go to the clinic on Friday morning. I know you want to help. I'll see you right after it's over. And don't worry—I feel like everything is going to work out OK."

For you, Bobbie thought, but then she caught herself being spiteful to her friend, and her emotions took another dip on the rollercoaster. She looked up at the ceiling, trying to clear her head and stop her tears.

"I'm meeting Billy after school, and he's going to give me the money to pay for it," added Amy. "I still hope my parents will go away this weekend, but so far they're planning to stay home. I may need you guys to take me out and to run interference for me. We'll figure it all out on Friday afternoon, after it's over."

Nepravel was upset and worried. Starting on Tuesday night, and building all during the day on Wednesday, hundreds of answered prayers had been hitting their voices in Amy, diminishing their intensity and threatening to trigger intervention in their plans by one or more of those blasted angels. Even late that night, as Amy slept, the incoming lights arched across the sky, telling all of the city's demons that someone in Nepravel's sector was the subject of intense prayer.

As he rushed about, bringing in Doubt, False Teaching, and Selfishness, to replenish the voices in Amy for the last two days before her abortion, he cursed the Prayer Warriors at Morningside Church. "There may not be many people at that church, but when they want to, they can really cause problems. We've got to figure out a way to strangle them!" Nepravel hissed, angry that he was missing his regular night at the nearby Platinum Club, where he urged visiting businessmen to forget about their wives and to have a wonderful time in their great city. "Balzor will certainly ask tonight about our plans and about all these prayers, which are ruining the darkness. I'll have to ask for help, to silence some of these prayer people, before an angel gets involved."

8

FRIDAY, MAY 26 ■ Friday morning it was still raining, though the reports said it would clear by the afternoon. "Don't forget, everybody, that I'll be working late tonight," Janet reminded her family at breakfast. "We're having the local test run for this controversial new show '911 Live', and I'm going along, chasing ambulances if you will, until about eleven, I imagine."

"Will it be on TV?" Susan asked, looking for some socks in the laundry room.

"Not tonight. But if all goes well—if that's the right word—it will be on this fall, broadcast live from ten different cities, including ours."

"Neat," said Tommy, turning from the open refrigerator. "And it's going to show, like, what's really happening at that moment, like, right when it's happening? Right?"

"Yes, that's the idea. But first we have to see if it works tonight." She glanced at Richard, who was reading the morning paper at the end of the breakfast room table. The two of them had experienced their first argument in many weeks the night before, when Richard learned that the station's experiment would keep Janet out until almost midnight.

She had explained all about Tom Spence and the others who were concerned about the show. And about Bill Shaw arranging for this "test run." Richard heard, but the voices, which had been diminished by the prayer breakfast, by the Merediths' daily prayers for the Sullivans, and by Richard's own recent thoughts, had spun up again under Nepravel's masterful control. Without any other force to counter them inside Richard, they slowly came back to control his words, urged on as well by his total confusion and guilt about Kristen.

"Janet, I hate it when you work late," he had launched into her the night before. "And on Friday night! I thought we had agreed to spend more time with each other and with the kids. I hope you've noticed how I've tried to do my share. Now here you go again, out all night. You really are married to that job . . ." The last words had really stung her, but her defense was weak, because she was about to spend an evening away. *Why does Richard make such a big issue of this?* she wondered. After so many weeks of relative calm and budding happiness, it sounded to Janet as if she were hearing voices, almost canned voices, from their past.

"I'm sorry," she had said, and meant it. "I didn't plan the timing, but I do think it's an important issue."

"It's always important," Richard snapped, with annoyance in his voice. And that had been the unhappy end to their conversation, which felt unfortunately like many they had suffered before, though not for several weeks. Janet got the message that she was the cause, but she didn't know what she could do, other than to quit her job. Was Richard going to react like this whenever an assignment took her away, even for a few extra hours?

So in the morning they were back to an icy standoff. Janet didn't want a flare-up in front of the children, so she was thankful for Richard's pointed silence. But she knew she would have to talk to him about it, maybe tomorrow, after the test run was over.

"Is either of you doing anything special today?" Janet asked her two teenagers.

Tommy thought for a moment and then shook his head. Susan smiled and lied, "No, nothing in particular." But she thought to herself, *Just skipping class to go with Amy to get an abortion that her parents don't know about . . . nothing significant at all . . .*

Susan and Amy were surprised to find Bobbie waiting for them in Mrs. Simpson's outer office. "Are you going with us?" Amy asked.

"No, I still can't do that," Bobbie replied in a low voice, hoping that Mrs. Simpson wouldn't hear her. "I want you to know again that I wish you wouldn't do this, Amy." Amy grimaced. "I know, you think I'm a broken record. But it's not right to kill your baby." Amy took a step back and folded her hands in front of her. Bobbie paused, but Amy just stared at her while Susan watched them both. "If I can't stop you, then I also want you to know that I love you—both of you—very much." Tears once again flooded her eyes, and Susan felt her own tears coming. "I can't come, but I'm going to cut my classes and find some quiet place to pray. For you, for the baby, for Susan, for me, for Billy . . . for all of us involved in this. I just want it to be over, and you to be OK, and all of us back the way we were, if we can be. . . ." Then Bobbie hugged Amy tightly and left.

As Amy and Susan turned back from watching her leave, Mrs. Simpson entered from her office. "There you are. Good morning. I hear everything is set up for you and will be just fine. I've written the excused absences for both of you, and I'll take them to the office in a minute. The van should be coming around to this side door," she pointed out into the hall, "any time now. Do you have the fee? Do you have any questions?"

"Will we come back here immediately afterwards? Will I feel like going back to class?" asked Amy.

"They usually keep you for an hour or so of observation. You both may want to take your books with you. When you get back here, we'll see how you are and just play it by ear. OK?"

"One more thing," Amy added. "Could you please also write an excuse for Bobbie? She wants to come with us, but she just can't. She's going to cut her classes to pray." Mrs. Simpson looked shocked. "And we don't want her to get in trouble."

Then Mrs. Simpson smiled. "Well, I guess it won't hurt. Sure, Amy, I can do that . . . Oh, there's the van. Good luck, and I'll see you both in a few hours."

■   ■   ■

Nepravel was livid. The barrage of prayers for Amy had only let up slightly during the night, and with the dawn, they had intensified again. Then that Meredith girl's last-minute plea to Amy had been short but powerful. It was lucky he had followed Amy to school and could be there to combat the Truth with the voice of Decisions Made. But the prayers were taking their toll—the voices in Amy were winding down. She was starting to think about that baby again, riding along in the van with Susan and two girls from Riverside High. This might be touch and go, despite the determined front she had put up only yesterday. Nepravel hated their prayers!

And now, worst of all, from his vantage point on top of the van, Nepravel could clearly see what appeared to be the glistening light of at least one angel in the vicinity of the abortion clinic. Oh great! All these prayers for Amy, plus the usual prayers from the believers demonstrating in front of the clinic, had finally produced the divine intervention he so feared, because his horde was not ready for it. Yes, there he was. A huge warrior angel, right over the abortion clinic, his talons poised and his beaks snapping.

Unlike the prayer breakfast, when the demons had prepared and outnumbered the two angels by a huge margin, Nepravel had no help at the abortion clinic that morning, other than the two demons who normally guarded it, and the one who always rode the van. To his dismay, the angel, shouting, "Holy is the Lord God Almighty," caught one of the two clinic's demons who tried to plunge for a bite at his neck. The angel closed his talons around the squirming demon and squeezed tightly. The demon screamed and suddenly exploded into a black fireball, which the angel then hurled at the second demon, who was quickly backing off.

As the van neared the abortion clinic and the angel saw the two demons riding on top, he began to fly in their direction. Nepravel, being a liar but not a fool, knew that alone they were no match for one of God's fiercest warriors, and he beat a fast retreat, followed closely by his companion. The angel returned to his position over the clinic, and Nepravel stood off at a distance and cursed. "Who will now tend to the voices in Amy?" he spat.

"Janet, the guys from Network are out checking the cameras and the sound equipment on the emergency vehicles," Bill said over the intercom. "If there are no problems, they should be back here in time for lunch. Can you join us?"

"Uh, let me see. Sure, Bill, that will be great," Janet replied. "It would be nice to hear Network's view on '911 Live' first hand."

"And, uh, Janet. Let's just keep the lunch group small. We'll save Tom and Connie for this evening. OK?"

Outside the abortion clinic, the four girls in the van were appalled to see that there were ten or twelve protestors on the sidewalk, kept in a roped-off area by two policemen. They had signs that read "Abortion Kills Babies" and "Abortion is Murder."

As the van slowed to pull into the clinic driveway, one of the protestors broke away from the group and made it to the side of the van, shouting, "Please don't kill your babies. Adoption means life for them." The girls blanched. Amy suddenly felt cold and wet. This was the real world. She wasn't a protected little girl any more. She was living the reality of decisions made. At barely seventeen, she was facing life and death. Her stomach started to churn. She and Susan both put their hands to their faces, to hide them.

"Oh, don't worry, they can't see you through the tinted glass," said the driver. "And don't mind them. There's always a few of those crazy Christian fundamentalists here, illegally harassing our clinic. Nobody even notices them anymore." But Amy did.

After the van had left school, Bobbie found an unused office in the PE department, which she presumed would be empty until lunch, at least. She put down her books, turned a chair around, knelt at it, and started to pray for Amy.

At the same time, Glenn Jamison knocked on Michael Andrews' office door. As they had agreed the day before, these two men of God, one the pastor and one the youth leader at Morningside Church, knelt together and prayed for Amy.

All across the city, members of the Morningside Prayer Warrior team, alerted to the approximate time of the scheduled abortion, stopped whatever they were doing and prayed to God for Amy.

He heard. And, as He promised, He answered. Another angel flew down to the clinic. With the one stationed outside, the second entered the clinic to clean out any demons hiding inside. Nepravel cursed even louder as he saw the two lesser demons fleeing through the clinic sidewalls. Afraid that it might be too late, he nevertheless sent his companion to find Balzor and to ask for reinforcements against these two angels. They would not stop shouting praises to God, as their twin eagles' heads searched the area around the clinic for more demons to crush.

Inside, Amy, Susan, and the two other girls were greeted by an efficient-looking nurse in a crisp white uniform. "Welcome to our pregnancy clinic," she smiled warmly. "Everything is ready for you. Here are the forms for the two of you who are actually having procedures this morning. Please read them and fill them out. Then you will sign them when we have our brief interview. We start with your blood work. Patty—we use only first names here—you will be first. Amy, we have several procedure rooms, so the wait won't be long at all. Would you and your friend please have seats here, and you can fill out your forms while I interview Patty."

Amy and Susan were left alone in the tastefully furnished waiting room. Amy quickly read through the forms, checked the appropriate boxes, and put down the clipboard. Like Susan, she tried to pick up a magazine, but she just couldn't focus on it.

All those people outside—she could still hear them shouting every now and then—just to try to stop girls like her. They seemed so serious. And Bobbie, crying over this baby—fetus—inside her. And Glenn Jamison, praying that day for her. Bobbie was even praying now. Maybe Glenn was too. Were all of them right? Could all of these people be so concerned if they weren't right?

Her hands suddenly became damp, and she felt lightheaded.

The voices planted by the demons had almost been silenced by all of the prayers. The angels had taken the area, and there were no demons to whisper in her ear or to spin the voices again. She started to think about the toddlers at the playground. Did she have the courage to have a baby? Could she do it? Imagine bringing a new life into the world! Her mom might understand after a few days, but what about her dad? What about Billy? What about her life? What a disruption. But surely the baby would be cute, and she could make some young married couple so happy. Maybe she could even visit the child some day. . . .

At that moment the spiritual battle had been won by the prayers and by the angels. The demons had retreated. The voices were silenced. Amy was open to hearing and acting on the truth. But angels only rarely talk to humans. And Amy would not have recognized God's voice that morning because His Spirit did not live inside her. What Amy needed was another human being to talk to her. To listen to her new thoughts. To tell her the truth, again, now that the way was prepared for her to hear it. To tell her not only that abortion is murder, but also that God has the power to heal all of her concerns and all of her fears. But, tragically, there was no one. Bobbie had made the difficult decision to stay away. And Susan looked up from her magazine and asked, "Can you believe these new swimsuit colors?"

Just then the nurse came in again, smiled, and said, "All right, Amy, we're all set. It won't take long at all, and you'll be back at school. First please come with me, and we'll go over the forms. Then we'll do the procedure and you'll be on your way." She held out her hand to Amy and smiled. Susan, trying to be supportive, stood up, walked over to Amy, and smiled courageously. Amy started to speak, but then didn't. Almost in a trance, balanced between her new thoughts and her previous commitments, Amy responded to the outstretched hand and the smiles, stood up, and followed the nurse into the procedure room.

After all the emotional turmoil of the previous weeks, the sleepless nights, the interviews, and the impossible decisions, the abortion itself was, for Amy, uneventful. There was some natural uneasiness in preparing for the procedure, and some discomfort once it began. She expected the few jabs of pain during the fifteen minutes that the cutter and suction pump ran, and she was not really surprised. In what seemed to Amy like a very brief time, the doctor and nurse announced that they were finished, and

Amy was rolled into an observation room and made to sit up in a chair. Susan joined her after about fifteen minutes.

Of course the abortion was anything but uneventful for the baby boy whom Amy was carrying in her womb. The two angels on the roof of the clinic screamed in agony as the innocent child was torn apart below them. They flapped their massive wings and raised their mournful cries to heaven; but they had not been empowered to intervene on the human side, so they could do nothing more than writhe in pain at such inhumanity.

Soon the spirits of Amy's boy and of the baby girl being carried by the student from Riverside rose up through the clinic. Nepravel, whose fear for Amy's resolve had turned to utter joy upon seeing the agony of the angels, knew not to venture near them. Innocent children, both born and unborn, have a special place in God's kingdom when they die—they do not suffer the Judgment Seat, but instead are carried to heaven by angels. With these two angels already present, he knew the process would be quick. So he darted around them, just beyond the reach of their beaks and talons, gloating that once again the dark side had won the victory.

"They huff and they puff," Nepravel laughed to himself, as the angels began to move off with their charges, "but in the end we always win! We are just too many for them, and we have too many human dupes and allies. How long before we control it all?" he yelled at them. He was ecstatic, and he made a mental note to embellish his own role in these events at their meeting that night.

While her daughter helped Amy abort her baby, Janet was sitting at her desk and going through a trial of her own—Richard's negative reaction to her need to work late on the special project gnawed at her during the entire morning. She, too, had been trying to mend their marriage the past several weeks, and it galled her that he would become so hostile over this one evening's work, even if it was a Friday. How many times in the past few months had he come home late, with little or no notice? Weren't her job and her responsibilities and her feelings just as important as his? Why did she have to put up with a double standard, when she had a respected position and was earning a good salary? The voices, restarted several days ago by Nepravel, were spinning well on their own now.

Although another voice tried to remind her of her earlier decision to discuss it later, the louder voices demanded that the wrong be righted while it was still fresh in their minds. So she dialed his number. When he answered, she let him know how unfair he had been and how she did not appreciate being treated as if he were the only one who was concerned for their marriage. "I don't appreciate the way you always arrange it that whatever problems we have are only because I have to work, when you are away as much or more than I am," she concluded.

Richard had moved beyond his emotional reaction of the previous evening, and he had even admitted while driving in that morning that her assignment tonight was pretty important. He felt silly that he had reacted so strongly. But now she was attacking on a larger front, and he could not pass up the opportunity to let her know just how he felt in general about her job, since she brought it up.

"OK, I agree that you should work tonight—but I still think, if you feel you have to work somewhere, that you should get a less demanding job with easier hours. You don't really have to work, and I wish you had more time to spend at home. We would all be happier if you did that."

Richard had trouble with his choice of words because what he selfishly really wanted was the Janet of fifteen years ago, who stayed at home, planned their meals, and focused her attention on him and their young family. As much as anything, though Richard could hardly voice it to her, he was jealous of the attention which the station demanded from Janet. Only *he* was supposed to be sitting late at night at the dining room table, working on a pile of papers from the office, not *both* of them. He felt like they were supposed to be husband and wife, but instead they were executive and executive.

"So you want someone who will just stay at home, cook your meals, look after you, and have no aspirations of her own," Janet said, with an edge to her voice.

"*Yes!*" Richard almost screamed, "*Yes. That's it, Just like Kristen, every Tuesday and Thursday!*" but he didn't. He smiled at his own childishness. Instead, he put his hand to his forehead, closed his eyes, and tried to say in a calm voice, "Just more balance, Janet. I feel like we both work too hard, and that can't be good for us or for the kids."

"Well, I think you have a one-sided view of who is supposed to do what. I will gladly compromise and work on trying to save what we have, but it can't be just my responsibility alone."

"OK . . . OK . . . I told you I was sorry for being upset about tonight. Go ahead and do the test run. I know it's important. Tell me about it when you get home. And let's discuss this larger issue when we're together. All right?"

"Agreed, but I don't want it swept under the carpet. I want to talk about it, Richard. Goodbye."

Yes, ma'am! he thought, as he dropped the receiver into its cradle.

If Nepravel had not been at the abortion clinic, he would have been delighted by this almost pointless argument, because for the first time one of them had mentioned the need to "save" their marriage, as if it were lost. Words are so wonderfully powerful, Nepravel well knew. If his plan continued to work, the next time it would be Richard's turn to attack a contrite Janet. Then her turn to attack him, a few days later. If this powerful cycle kept up, Nepravel knew from experience that he could destroy their marriage in just a few months.

"It was no big deal—just a little discomfort," Amy told Bobbie, as she sat in a chair in Nurse Simpson's office. "A few cramps afterwards, but that's about it."

"See, I told you that everything would turn out fine," said Mrs. Simpson, checking Amy's blood pressure. "It always has. Now let me take your temperature, Amy."

As the thermometer went into Amy's mouth, Susan picked up the story. "There were all these protestors out on the sidewalk when we drove up, and we were scared that someone would see us."

"I know," said Bobbie sadly, "my parents have held vigils there in the past."

"They *have?*" Susan questioned, and Mrs. Simpson turned her head to look at Bobbie.

"Then I guess it really is a good thing you didn't tell them," said Susan.

"Yes, I guess so." Bobbie looked down at the floor and felt terribly guilty. Maybe they would have known what to do . . .

"Well, anyway, Amy was great. Never batted an eyelash." Susan smiled at their friend, genuinely relieved and proud. "Afterwards, they watched her for a while. Amy paid, and here we are. All done."

"One less baby to worry about, you might say," Bobbie said, and immediately regretted it, from the frowns on the other three faces. "All right. All right. It's done," she said, raising her hands toward the glares. "I didn't think it was right, but it's done. I'll stop talking about it, and let's just all try to go back to the way we were. OK?" And she managed a smile and squeezed Amy's hand.

"That's all I want, the sooner, the better," Amy smiled back tentatively, as Mrs. Simpson removed the thermometer.

"It's just a shade above normal, but nothing to worry about. Amy, why don't you just rest here for as long as you like so we can be sure that there will be no more bleeding. You girls are welcome to stay with her, or you can go back to class."

"We'll stay," Bobbie said, and sat down with Susan on the couch. She sensed that perhaps more than Amy's body had to heal, and she wanted to be with her two friends.

"Can you come over tonight?" Brent asked Tommy at lunch.

"No, not tonight. I wish I could, but Mom is working late, and Dad made a big deal of asking Susan and me to go out to that place where you cook your own steaks. So I guess I gotta do that. And Saturday morning we're all driving up to the Bryants' new mountain house. I'm gonna have a great time, with only Susan and Amy there!" he added sarcastically.

But in fact he was glad to have a weekend off from their activities. Since his brief discussion with his dad after the ball game, he had felt that perhaps things were moving too fast, that he needed some time to think. So this coming weekend promised to be at least normal, even if it would be boring.

As the regular work day drew to a close, Janet went into the studio dressing room and changed into the jeans and work shirt she had brought from home. Then she met in the conference room with Bill, Tom, and

Connie, who were similarly dressed for their evening of chasing possible emergencies. Soon they were joined by Bob Grissom and Mark Pugh from Network, the producer and director, respectively, of "911 Live."

Bill introduced the network men to Connie and Tom, who had not been at the luncheon with Janet, where Bill had, with carefully chosen words, explained to Bob and Mark some of the concerns that had been expressed about the show. Their reaction had been similar to Bill's, but they agreed with his request to help him solve his internal station problem by inviting two of the dissenters on the test run. Janet did her best to maintain a neutral position through all of the discussion at lunch on the suitability of the show, trying to voice both sides correctly.

Once the introductions in the conference room were completed, Bill Shaw began, "We should have a really good opportunity to test both the concept and the equipment this evening. Mark will be staying here in the studio control booth, directing the show and controlling the helicopter, the reporter/camera teams in the three roving patrols, and the remote control cameras on the emergency vehicles. The five of us will be in our station's van, following closely behind a police car on the north side of the city. All of the vehicles will be hooked together by a two-channel radio link. Hopefully, after all of this preparation, we'll have some 'action' to record."

"We're really looking forward to this trial run, as well," added Bob Grissom. "It should be very similar to the national show which starts this fall. And we are delighted to have you folks along to add your local spin to whatever happens this evening. I probably don't need to say this, but I do want to remind you that we are all just observers. Whatever may happen, we want to remain safe and not get involved. We're there to observe and to report, but not to interact in any way. OK?"

There were nods all around the table. "One question," Tom said. "How did you secure the involvement of our police, emergency rescue, and fire departments for tonight?"

"It was easy, and totally aboveboard, of course," said Mark. "We called your mayor a month ago and asked his permission, pointing out that the footage for the national promotion for the show to be run during the summer will feature clips from tonight's test. Hopefully there will be several opportunities to show your emergency response people in a very favorable light. We also, with his permission, made a sizable contribution to the appropriate retirement funds for the professionals involved."

"Sounds fine. I was just curious."

"Well, if that's it," said Bill, "let's get in the van and head towards the north area precinct to pick up the police car they've assigned us to follow. Mark, I know you have a lot of last-minute things to do here at the station to get ready. Good luck to all of us."

Kristen was anticipating what would apparently be a very boring weekend. She had drawn duty in one of their new subdivisions for most of Saturday, and her regular aerobics workout would fill the late afternoon. But the rest of the weekend looked empty, and she was frankly jealous that Richard and Janet would be spending the weekend with their friends, the Bryants, at a mountain house.

Here it was almost summer, and Richard had still made no concrete move to leave Janet. If he was half as unhappy as he said, then why did he stay with her? Maybe he wasn't really as unhappy as he told her. Maybe he was simply amused to have two women sleeping with him. That thought added anger to her already ripe jealousy. What had begun for her as infatuation and the security of an older man had blossomed over the past months into real affection. She wanted to live with him. She missed him. Even though it was late in the day, she decided to call him.

Richard was putting a few contract files in his briefcase to review at home after dinner with the kids, when his private line rang. He was surprised to hear Kristen, who, after a few initial pleasantries, reminded him again that he had vowed to leave Janet and that she was tired of being just a part-time lover.

Richard, who now regretted his earlier, too easy portrayal of his life with Janet as being so bleak, was afraid to tell Kristen that there had actually been some improvement (at least until this morning, he thought). So he fell back upon the same excuse he had used for months. "Kristen, I know. But the kids, especially Tommy, are going through a difficult time. I think it would devastate them if I suddenly left. You know, maybe if you need more of a relationship—and I would certainly understand it—then maybe you should find someone else who can provide it for you." Richard held his breath, because this was the first time he had ever used her now familiar complaint to try to put some distance between them.

She was silent for a long moment. "No, Richard, that's not what I want. I want you. I don't know if it has dawned on you, but I actually love you. However," and she paused again and spoke slowly, "if I can't have you, then maybe Janet needs to know what a great lover you really are, first hand from me."

Now it was time for Richard to be silent. *Touché*, he thought, as he imagined a phone call from Kristen to Janet.

"No, no," he said. "I'm just thinking of you. I know it's very difficult for us. If it weren't for the kids," he lied, "I would have left Janet long ago. I just don't know what to do. And now I'm late to get home to take the kids to dinner, and I don't know what to tell you."

"Well, Richard, I just want you to know that I'm not happy with this situation. Either way there are consequences. Leave Janet, or stay with Janet. You have to choose. But I can't go on much longer with this in-between situation. I'm not happy. Something has got to change."

Richard's hands and forehead were damp. He was pacing back and forth behind his desk, in front of his huge window. "OK, Kristen, I hear you. Maybe with summer vacation coming we can spend more time together, like when Janet and the kids go to visit her mother. I don't know right now. But I hear you and will try to figure something out."

"All right, Richard, but it seems pretty simple to me. One day soon you're going to have to choose between us. See you Tuesday," and she hung up.

Richard looked out at the city below him. Ultimatums from both women in one day. Indeed there would be consequences! Why couldn't they just rock along? Why did he have to choose? For a moment he imagined himself to be a tightrope walker, perched at that lofty altitude, with a balance bar held between his hands. On one end of the balance bar was Janet—on the other end was Kristen. And there was no net below him . . .

The TV5 news van not only had spacious seating, but also enough television and communication equipment to make it a small studio. For tonight's experiment it had been fitted with a special television link, which could monitor the scene being selected by Mark in the director's booth back at the station, simulating what would be shown in September on the actual live broadcast around the nation.

Bill Shaw drove the van, with Bob Grissom from Network seated up front. Connie, who had the most technical expertise, operated the console in the back, and Janet and Tom occupied swivel seats in the middle. Bob wore a miniature headset, which kept him in contact with Mark back at the station. At 7:30 Mark brought up the "911 Live" logo and cut to John Blevins, the local newscaster who was substituting for the as-yet-unnamed national personality who would host the network show. Behind John were several monitors, and he began a recap of the various live stories in progress around the city, which they had been following for the previous hour.

As the van followed the police car on its regular rounds, Janet and their team watched on the monitor as Mark cut skillfully back and forth between a potentially violent domestic argument on the west side of the city, an ambulance in route to a reported heart attack at a downtown restaurant, and a possible convenience store robbery on the south side. Pointing to the monitor, Bob said to Bill, "I can see now that we're going to have to invest in those wide-angle lenses. Mark is going to have to be able to pull back further to take in an entire area when the emergency vehicles get up close to a building."

Shifting his attention to Mark and pressing the transmit button, which keyed his headset, he said "Mark, these domestic situations are going to be boring if the patrolmen simply pull up to a house and go inside. We'll either have to have several going at one time, so that you can cut back and forth. Or perhaps we can figure out a way for the officers to wear small mini-cameras, or button microphones, so we can pick up the action inside."

"Yeah, I'm taking notes, and I concur on the equipment."

During the first ninety minutes of the test run, Janet had to admit that the pace and the subject matter were similar to many other shows already on television. The fact that it was live did add a dimension of excitement, since no one, including the anchorperson, knew exactly what would happen next. Mark Pugh and John Blevins each did a skillful job of keeping the tempo upbeat during several slow moments. By this time in the evening, several of the original situations were still "in play," and John ran through recaps of each situation after their commercial breaks, as if they were following several football games at once.

Suddenly, over the police net came the code for a possible armed robbery in progress at a fast food restaurant only two exits north of their position on the interstate. An employee had tripped a silent alarm, and the police vehicle in front of them in the left lane turned on its blue lights and sped up to respond.

As the news van accelerated to keep up and turned on its yellow flashing roof lights, the car just ahead of the cruiser in the far left lane swerved quickly to the right, into the middle of the three lanes, to let the two-car convoy pass. Unfortunately, this move and the sudden multicolored flashing lights startled the driver of the car in the middle lane, who slammed on his brakes. The driver of a large tractor trailer, following too closely behind, tried a combination of brakes and a swerve, but swiped a small car in the far right lane and caused the large rig to jackknife.

As the TV5 van gathered speed, directly behind it there was a huge pile-up on the interstate, with several cars swerving and braking successfully, but others not so lucky. Bill caught the first unusual motions in the rearview mirror and swore. As the others spun around to look, he slowed down and moved over to the emergency lane. The police car did the same, and the two officers were already radioing for fire trucks and ambulances over the net.

Because there was now no traffic behind them, the police car turned around on the deserted pavement, and, with its blue light flashing, raced back to the wreckage, where already there was smoke from one fire. Janet and the others sat for a second, stunned by what they saw. Then Bob yelled to Bill, "Come on man, let's go. This is perfect! I can't believe it. Mark, are you getting this!?!"

"Yes . . . the camera on the police cruiser is working perfectly. It's fantastic. Can you give me any details? We'll cut right to this when the commercial ends."

While Bob told Mark their position and the little he knew, Bill turned the van around and drove toward the parked cruiser and the crushed autos. Traffic in the southbound three lanes had also stopped, and people were rushing everywhere, some obviously hurt, some trying to help.

"I wish we had a mobile camera and a reporter with us," Bob said under his breath. Then to Mark, "How soon can you get the chopper here? The road will be jammed."

As Bill brought the van to a stop right in front of the car that had originally applied its brakes, they could see, even in the fading light, that another car, the small one which had been in the right lane, was partially crushed between the first car and the massive cab of the tractor trailer. A young man, bleeding terribly from his head, dragged himself through the smashed window of the driver's door and fell on the concrete, then immediately pulled himself up and staggered around to the other side of the car, looking inside.

"Are you getting this?" Bob almost screamed into his mike. He was answered by the scene in front of them flashing onto their television monitor, from just a slightly different angle, caused by the offset of the camera at the police car's position. And they heard the voice-over by John Blevins, describing the live shot of the obvious carnage on the northern interstate connector. "It's fantastic! Just what we hoped for!" Bob said to all of them. Janet was nearly in shock. This is what they had hoped for? Obvious injury, terrible destruction, and probable death? She opened her mouth to tell him to go to hell, but before she could speak, Tom reached across to open the sliding door. "We've got to go help. I think there's someone still inside that crushed car, and there's gasoline everywhere."

As Tom got up from his seat, Bob turned around and pushed him back. "No you don't. We can't get involved. We're only observers. If we start participating, it won't be real, won't be what's really happening."

While Bob was talking, Janet looked at the man covered with blood and saw him holding a small hand, which was reaching out from the passenger side of what used to be his family's car. With the little strength he had left, the man was kicking the smashed, jammed passenger door, all the time screaming for someone to help him.

"There *is* someone trapped in that car!" Janet yelled. "There's at least one child in there. We've got to help that man!"

"No! You can't! Whatever happens, we can't get involved!" Bob ordered, holding Tom back with his right hand and grabbing Janet's arm.

Tom swore at Bob and shoved him up against the dashboard. Then, almost pushing Janet out ahead of him, he leaped from the van, followed immediately by Connie.

"Don't go over there!" the three of them heard, as they ran toward the car. "Bill, they're ruining this whole thing." Bill Shaw had unlatched his own door, but now he rocked back into his seat. "Mark, can you zoom in on the bleeding man next to the small car? Tell Blevins to say that some motorists are helping an injured man with his family trapped in a car, in a pool of gasoline. Hurry, it may blow up any second."

When they arrived at the car, Janet was horrified to see the small boy—he could only have been five or six—leaning up against the inside of the smashed door, unbelief in his eyes, blood on his face, and his lower body hidden under the crushed dashboard. It had been pushed in and down on him by the force of the collision with the truck cab, as the car had careened all the way around and then been sandwiched between the two vehicles.

He was crying and reaching out to his father, who was trying to pull him free, but without success. "Please help me," his father gasped to Janet and Tom. She could see that he was in terrible pain, with blood almost covering his upper body from the gash in his head. And all of them could smell the gasoline.

Janet, Tom, Connie, and the boy's father all pulled on the crushed door, but it would not budge. The whole car had been smashed to two thirds its normal size. Just then the driver of the truck, who must have been in shock, stumbled and fell from the cab next to them, and started toward the back of his rig.

"What are we going to do?" Janet yelled to Tom, who began circling the car, looking for some alternative.

"Daddy . . . Daddy . . ." the boy moaned and looked up at his father, who was now weeping and looking for more help.

One of the two police officers ran by, and Janet almost tackled him. "There's a little boy trapped in this car! It may catch on fire any second!"

"I've called for all the help in the area. The fire trucks have tools that can cut him free. Right now we've got at least ten people back there in terrible shape. Come on, I'll give you the fire extinguisher out of our patrol car, while I get the first aid kit."

Janet ran with him to the patrol car, and she suddenly noticed the remote camera on the roof, swiveling and focusing on her. She glanced over at the van and saw Bob and Bill sitting in their front-row seats, feeding the station via Bob's mike. *They've probably interrupted our regular show and have actually gone live with this one,* she thought.

Running back to the car with the small extinguisher cradled in her arms like a baby, she saw that the father had slipped to his knees by the car door and was now simply holding his boy's hand and sobbing. As she stopped and took it all in, she found herself praying to a God whom only days before she had told Susan probably didn't exist. "Please, God, spare this little boy. Please don't let there be a fire . . . Please protect his father. And please help all these other people." As she opened her eyes, she was looking right at the remote camera, which was focused on her. "Please, God, not on television . . ." she added.

The distant sirens meant that help might come at last, but neither the boy nor the father might live long enough. The father had collapsed next to the car, and Tom had ripped off his shirt and was using it to press against the deep head wound. "Please, God, please," she prayed, clutching the fire extinguisher more tightly. She could see the red lights of fire engines coming the wrong way down the empty interstate, when from the south she suddenly heard the steady beat of a helicopter.

The chopper came low overhead, and she could read the TV5 logo on its side, even against the glare of its spotlight. It circled once and then began to land, only about fifty yards north of them. Janet would never know whether the explosion was connected to the helicopter's arrival and the resulting wind and blowing debris, but suddenly the back of the car was engulfed in flames. There were screams all around, and the boy began to cry. His father tried to get up, but fell down, and someone started dragging him away to safety.

Janet awoke from her trance, put the fire extinguisher on the pavement, pulled the pin, and walked quickly over to the boy. As the flames advanced from the back of the car, she used the extinguisher to beat them back. But the fire was very hot, and she sensed that her extinguisher would ultimately be no match for it. She looked down at the boy, who stared up at her in wide-eyed horror, screaming. Tears filled her eyes, as she realized she was going to lose him to the flames. Just then Tom arrived, took the extinguisher, pushed her back, and used the last third of it on the advancing fire.

The flames were reaching the front seats, and many of those standing nearby began to turn away from the awful scene. Janet held her hands to her head and screamed a long *No!*, tears streaming down her face.

Then two fire fighters from the first truck, led by Connie, ran up with large portable extinguishers and leveled them at the flames, beating them down. Thirty seconds later, two more men arrived with a high pressure hose from the truck itself and put the fire out.

More emergency vehicles were arriving, and one of the men on the hose yelled that they would start cutting the boy out immediately. Janet ran over to the father, who was still alive, as the men with the cutting tool were pointed toward the car by the police officer, who was still using his portable radio. Out of the corner of her eye she saw a reporter with a camera crew run by, on the way from the helicopter to the wrecked cars and the injured victims.

Connie and Tom joined Janet by the father. The three of them from the station hugged and cried. Janet shook all over and suddenly felt very weak and nauseated. She staggered to the grass strip by the edge of the road, dropped to her knees, and threw up, still crying. As she calmed down a little and looked around, she found Connie in the same position, and Tom lying on his back next to them, his arms over his face. Tom said hoarsely, "I hope they caught us throwing up, live and in color."

The ride back to the studio, an hour later, began in icy silence. Janet was still shaking from the adrenaline coursing through her system. Bob and Bill would not look directly at the three of them in the back of the van.

Finally Bob broke the silence. "Look, I'm sorry for trying to hold you back. That was stupid. You did a courageous thing in helping to rescue that boy. I've never been in exactly that situation before. You were obviously right and I was wrong."

"Apology accepted," Tom said quietly.

"And," Bill added, "we got some *great* shots of what you were doing. They'll look terrific in our public service segments, and the promotions for '911 Live' will now have a really local flair!"

"You mean you're still going to broadcast '911 Live' after seeing what happened tonight?" Connie asked in disbelief. "What if those firefighters hadn't arrived and that little boy had burned up, right on the camera?!?"

"Well, he didn't, and if the fire had gotten any closer, we would have cut away," said Bob, obviously pleased with all that had happened.

"Any closer? *Any closer?*" Janet trembled as she spoke, her voice rising. "How close do you want? Besides his crushed lower body, he has second-degree burns on his head, back, and hands. And his father may die before the night is over. How can you *imagine* putting that in families' living rooms at 7:30 on Friday nights?"

"Janet, you're just upset from being so close to it," Bill consoled her. "No one knew you were going to wind up on the fire brigade. When you see it on the monitor, like we did, you'll understand how great it is. Our audience will love it."

"Yeah, I noticed how you watched it all from the safety of the van," was Janet's last comment to Bill, which foreclosed further discussion.

When they arrived at the television station it was after eleven, but the twenty or so staff on hand greeted them as they walked through the back door with cheers and champagne. Mark Pugh was grinning from ear to ear as he and Bob hugged. "Wasn't that fantastic? Better than I could have ever hoped for," beamed Mark. "We have a few bugs to work out, but for the most part, all of the systems worked perfectly."

Several of her coworkers congratulated Janet on her heroism, but she was not in the mood to be a hero. She wondered about the little boy and his father. She wanted to call Richard and then go to the hospital to check on them.

But before she could collect her things, the back studio in which they were standing was darkened, and the monitors brought up the crash scene again for all of them to relive the night's events. Janet looked up into her own grief-stricken face, looking around desperately for help, as the flames came toward the boy. Only now Tom's Promotion Assistant had already superimposed their TV5 logo and the "911 Live" promotion, and a voice was recommending the show to their entire viewing audience! She suddenly realized that she was going to be used to promote the show she found so offensive.

Janet again felt nauseated and broke away from the other station personnel. As she made her way to the restroom, her coworkers patted her on the back and congratulated her. She spent ten minutes in the restroom, throwing up and crying. Finally she managed enough control to wipe her eyes and to look at herself in the mirror. What a fright! She smiled for the first time in hours. "I guess I really wouldn't have done too well as a fire fighter," she laughed to herself. "But I've got to get to the hospital. I'll call Richard from my car."

Leaving the restroom, she walked down the hall and past the employee break room. She glanced in through the window in the door and saw Tom, Connie, and two other men and a woman sitting around the table inside. She opened the door and walked in, realizing too late that they had their heads bowed in prayer. Embarrassed, pulled toward them, uncomfortable with praying out loud to a nebulous God, she nevertheless listened for a moment. They prayed for the people in the wreck and for the leadership of the network and of the station. She realized that they were actually praying to God to bind Satan and his work at their station! As if Satan were real, and right there at the station! With that unusual new thought etched in her mind, she slipped out to find her street clothes and to head for the hospital.

Kromor, the dark lord of the station, and his horde of demons were hosting Lord Vidor of Network, along with all the demons who had come in from New York for the test run. Lord Vidor, only a lowly lesser demon thirty years ago, was now one of Satan's most powerful captains, because of the unprecedented human destruction he had caused in such a short time. Together, all of these hateful furies were celebrating simultaneously with the "911 Live" crew in the back studio, and they never noticed the concentrated prayers coming from the break room.

9

THURSDAY, JULY 20 ■ The families on Devon Drive had moved smoothly into summer vacation routine. Susan picked up the job she had started the previous summer at the frozen yogurt shop, working part time four out of seven days each week. The family had celebrated her seventeenth birthday a little early, on the weekend when they joined the Bryants at their mountain home.

That weekend had been intense in one sense, but the Sullivans had each found some much needed rest. Janet had slept in the car driving up, since she did not arrive home from the hospital until after one. It had taken much of that day to explain all that had happened, first to Richard, then to the children, then to the Bryants. It seemed so incongruous to be sitting in a rocking chair on the Bryants' long porch, looking across miles of mountain valleys, and describing the frightening events of only a few hours before. The father had survived the night, as had the boy. Janet had met the young wife outside the intensive care unit, and she called several times that weekend to confirm their progress.

Susan and Amy had their own major event to review together, but of course they were not talking about it. Amy was glad that Mrs. Sullivan's experience kept everyone's attention. She discovered a remarkable result from the abortion—she actually felt much better. Although she deferred Tommy's challenge to play tennis, claiming cramps, the truth was that the instant removal of the symptoms of pregnancy, primarily her nausea and fatigue, gave her a real lift. In the short run it seemed to confirm that she had done the right thing.

And Tommy had enjoyed a slow weekend, despite his complaints about being locked up with two girls. His father and Tom Bryant made sure that he at least benefitted from plenty of exercise, including tennis and jogging.

But that had all been six weeks ago, and Tommy now spent much of each day mowing the lawns in the neighborhood with Brent, and several nights a week hanging out with the same group of older boys who had befriended the two of them in May. Sometimes they watched videos, other times they just "hung out." Each set of parents typically thought that their boy was at the home of the other, or at the park, and so far the ruse had worked.

Amy had arranged to babysit for a steady group of young children for the summer, giving their mothers a morning or an afternoon off. She went on one date with Billy as school had ended, but any chance of a relationship between them had died. Perhaps each reminded the other of what had almost happened, and the memory was just too intense to survive a routine of occasional dates. At any rate, as Billy had said goodnight that one evening, they had both sensed that it was their last date.

Susan and Drew, on the other hand, were becoming more and more attached. Drew had a summer job at the local soft drink bottling plant. Sometimes he worked the fill line, and sometimes he assisted on the delivery trucks. The work was exhausting, with long hours, often lasting into the evening, but the pay, especially the overtime, was great. Susan really liked Drew and actually felt in those early weeks of the summer that she might for the first time in her life be falling in love. As far as she could tell, Drew felt the same.

Bobbie and Thomas also saw a lot of each other, and their relationship also deepened as the summer allowed them to spend more time together. Bobbie was working at a camp for disadvantaged inner-city young people, which was both exhausting and exhilarating. Thomas worked as a cashier at the neighborhood hardware store. They enjoyed many evenings together, sometimes on double dates with friends. Each of them used humor—and on one particularly tough night, prayer—to keep their very natural desires for each other in check.

On that Thursday afternoon in mid-July, Janet joined Connie Wright and Tom Spence at the same restaurant where she and Tom had shared lunch three months before. After their intense experience on the night of the test run, they had not really spoken much about "911 Live." The three of them and the prayer partners of that evening had spearheaded a fund drive to help the injured father and son, William and Eddie Barnes, along with all of the other victims of the crash. The network had even contributed. The boy was still in the pediatric hospital, but the father was scheduled to begin work again next week. There was hope that neither of them would suffer permanent physical damage, if the skin grafts took, and the boy learned to walk again despite his damaged nerves.

"So, what's happening with '911 Live,' Janet?" Tom asked as they finished ordering.

"As incredible as it seems to the three of us, I believe Network is going ahead with the show, and still at 7:30 on Fridays. I received a promotion package just yesterday, and as you can imagine, the video shorts contain several shots of us in action."

"Can you see where this is leading, Janet?" Connie now asked. "Do you remember studying about the end of the age in Rome? How the emperors invented more and more live spectacles, each one more bizarre than the last, as their empire fell apart because there were no moral values left in people? Well, '911 Live' is easily comparable to a live Roman spectacle, and when the 911 Channel starts next year, people will be able to watch death, destruction, and debauchery twenty-four hours a day, right from their living rooms."

"I wouldn't have believed it—or I guess I wouldn't have thought about it—except for your bringing it to me, and for our experience that night. It would have sailed right past me, along with all the other new shows. But what can anyone do about it? I mean, this is the national network we're talking about."

"You know Janet, Connie and I have been talking since that night, and praying. It occurs to us that Bill Shaw never really intended to keep an open mind, as he told us. He never actually considered stopping this show. He just hoped that *we* would change and go along with the decision he had already made. If we had liked what we saw that night, then Bill could keep his show, his good relationship with Network, and some of his more experienced employees. We haven't told him this yet—we wanted to talk to you first and see if you will join us—but his plan is not going to work. He's going to lose at least five of us, if he goes ahead with the show. Janet, what about you?"

Just then their orders arrived, so Janet took that extra moment to look around, as if she could find help in the restaurant, and to collect her thoughts.

"I, uh, remember you talking about that when we started, but I didn't know if you still intended to go through with it. When would you resign?"

"Since the show starts in September, we will resign about two weeks before the first episode. If we did it now, it would be lost in the summer doldrums, when no one is focusing on the fall season. If we wait too long, there will be no time for a reaction. We know that it's a long shot, but we're praying that in the midst of all the build-up to the new shows, maybe our action will be taken as 'news' and will actually be picked up and have some effect," explained Tom. "At first we were incensed that we were personally identifiable in the promotion videos. But then we thought how powerful it would be if all three of the station personnel in the promotions resigned simultaneously because of this show! What do you think?"

"Yes, umm, that might have some effect. I, uh, I haven't really thought about it, of course," Janet added as she stirred her chef's salad with her fork. "Do you . . . have you looked into any other positions?"

"No, not yet. And frankly, after we do this, there probably won't be too many jobs open in broadcasting for us, except maybe some Christian programming," said Connie.

Janet had a constructive idea. "Wouldn't it be better if we all stayed put and tried to fight this sort of thing from the inside? Instead of cutting and running? Couldn't we have more impact that way?"

Tom and Connie exchanged glances, and Tom spoke. "We said exactly the same thing, Janet, two years ago, when 'Sex Lives of the Rich and Famous' first came on, with all that bizarre and kinky stuff. We tried. We talked to Bill then. You may remember the short 'minority report' that he let us type and circulate around the station. Basically, Janet, we have come to the conclusion that Bill will do nothing to upset Network or the bottom line, no matter *what* is broadcast into our homes, unless he's threatened with a loss of income or a stink of huge proportions. Frankly, we doubt that our resignations will produce either of those, but it has finally come down to a personal thing. Do we want to be part of an organization which has no sense of its public responsibility and will broadcast *anything* in the name of 'freedom of the press'? In our cases, the answer is simply no."

"When do you plan to tell him?"

"We want to give him one last chance to stop the show or at least to move it to late night. We'll tell him in about a month. If he refuses, then we won't say anything more until we resign, two weeks before the show starts," Connie explained.

"Well, I appreciate your stand, and I appreciate the fact that you have asked me to join you. But I don't know. It's a big step. Other than this problem, I like it here. I may not be so ready to give up on the possibility of changing it from the inside. I'll have to talk it over with my husband and get back to you."

"Janet," Connie looked up from her almost untouched chicken salad, "I urge you to try praying about it too."

While Janet was considering how a moral stand might affect her career, her husband was enjoying another Thursday "lunch" with Kristen, whom he had not seen in two weeks because of his own out-of-town meetings and her real estate continuing education classes.

After putting the pressure on Richard six weeks earlier, Kristen had backed off, waiting to see if he would do anything about leaving Janet. He hadn't, and Kristen finally realized that Richard probably never would, so long as he could "have his cake and eat it too," as she heard herself say. After that thought, a voice seemed to speak to her and to tell her that perhaps it was going to be up to *her* to help him make the move. For his sake, as well as for hers. No specific plan had formed yet, but she was in a better mood, just thinking that perhaps *she* could take the initiative and move their situation along, as both of them really wanted.

He lay back on her king-sized bed, relaxed after their "workout," as he always called it, in honor of the health club where he was supposed to be. She said, "Richard, I've got an out-of-town family, the Hawkins, who may be interested in the McEver house. How about if I bring them over to meet with you and Janet, to encourage them about the neighborhood?"

"You and some clients come over to our house together, to meet Janet?" he asked incredulously.

"Yes, why not?"

"No way. It's too dangerous. You or I might slip up. But listen, I've got some good news."

"You're leaving Janet tomorrow," she suggested, looking down at him, her eyes smiling.

"No. Not that. But in early August, Janet and the kids will drive up to Vermont to visit Janet's parents, like they do every summer, for almost two weeks. They still live on a farm, and the kids love it. As usual, I'll fly up for the last few days and then drive back with them, but that will leave me here, alone, for about ten days." He sat up, grinning, "We'll have to be careful, but I bet we'll be able to spend most nights together, either at your place or at mine!"

She covered herself with the sheet and exaggerated her mild Southern accent. "Why, Mr. Sullivan, I do believe that you have dishonorable intentions in mind where I am concerned," she pouted, smiling.

"You bet I do," he laughed, as he toppled over onto her.

FRIDAY, JULY 21 ■ That Friday evening, Susan and Drew were double dating with Amy and Jay Stembler, the college freshman who went out with Susan the night Amy and Billy left the fraternity party. Jay had unexpectedly called Amy earlier in the week, and they had gone out for a casual dinner together. Tonight the four of them were headed to an early movie and a quick supper afterwards.

At their first dinner, Amy asked Jay why he had called her. Jay responded that Billy had said so many nice things about her, and he had simply wanted to get to know her better. She was curious and pressed on to ask Jay whether he knew about the "little problem" she and Billy had experienced earlier. Jay was bad at lying, and so he told her that he knew. She pressed on, and Jay finally had to admit that most of the boys in their fraternity knew and had actually followed the developments with Billy, including the "good news" of the abortion. Billy, had, in fact, bought a keg of beer for the fraternity house to celebrate on that particular Friday night.

Amy sat back in the restaurant and reflected on her new status with the largest fraternity in the city. She tried to smile, but there were suddenly tears in her eyes. As she reached for her purse to retrieve a tissue, she asked Jay, "And is that really why you asked me out, because you think I'm 'loose'?"

In his heart Jay could not deny that the thought had crossed his mind, but he genuinely believed that he wanted to get to know her, not just expect sex. "No, Amy, it's not. I enjoyed being with you for that little while, and I figured you might be going through a not-so-great time—I've got an older sister, and I know it must not be easy for you—and Billy hasn't asked you out, so I thought I would. That's all. I'd just like to have a date or two and see how we do. Okay?"

Amy appreciated his kindness and his apparent honesty, so she dried her eyes and smiled, thinking to herself that she could probably trust Jay, but *maybe* he was lying. For the first time in her life she experienced a glimpse of the power which exists in granting or withholding sexual favors. She was no longer a "girl." The guys apparently all knew that she was "experienced," and so she had a decision to make with each one—the decision would involve an interplay of words, actions, emotions, and assumptions that had not been in her repertoire only ninety days before. This unexpected feeling was a strange combination of being sick to her stomach and of holding a new power. She would definitely have to think about it. And she was saddened that Susan and Bobbie would probably not be of much help.

Now for their second date on this Friday evening, Jay was driving, and Susan and Drew were in the back seat. The movie was a funny comedy, and they had tried a new fondue restaurant in the same shopping center. They really had a delightful evening together, talking about everything from their baseball team's possible pennant race to the colleges to which the three seniors should apply. Jay was able to act the "older man," sharing his advice from his college search of two years before.

On the way back to Devon Drive, Jay turned into an unfinished new cul-de-sac where there were as yet no houses nor street lights, and parked the car at the far end. He slid over into Amy's bucket seat, with no complaint from her, and in a few minutes they were hugging and kissing. Susan and Drew, who had known each other for much longer, were frankly surprised by the unexpected friendliness of the couple in the front seat, but lost no time in joining them.

Susan, who had grown to like Drew very much, for the first time allowed him the same freedom to explore her body which Amy was obviously granting to Jay. She had decided a week ago, after stopping his advances for a month, that if a safe situation arose in which she were sure they could not possibly "do it," she would at least let him do "a little." She could not think of any reason why not. What was it her mother had said? That there was no real meaning to life? Well, here was a nice boy who cared for her, and she might just love him. Maybe they could find meaning by loving each other. And love obviously included physical intimacy, as every television show and movie she had ever seen had taught her.

But now that he was doing so, she had not counted on the rising tide of emotion, not only in him, but in herself as well. It's hard to go near a flame and not be burned. Voices in all four of them were urging them to go further, but that was just not possible. Finally, as it came close to 11:30, Susan pushed Drew up gently, took a deep breath, refastened herself, and said that they had to get home.

When she was safely in her own bed, with these new, strong feelings playing through her and voices telling her that she was a woman and should experience everything a woman can experience, she picked up the phone beside her bed and dialed Amy. They talked for over an hour. And Nepravel was the delighted third participant on the party line.

SUNDAY, JULY 23 ■ Late that Sunday morning, after they had finished reading the paper and sipping their coffee, Richard and Janet sat down for their usual brunch. Today Janet had prepared ham and cheese omelettes. Janet used this moment of relative quiet to tell Richard about the stand that Tom, Connie, and three others at the station were prepared to make. And about their request that she join them, with the probable consequence that she would lose her job.

"I know you've wanted me to have no job, or a different job, Richard. I haven't made up my mind yet, and I would like to have your input."

Richard thought, *Be careful here.* Like many who complain, half of Richard's derision of her job had really been an attempt to gain sympathy for himself. Yes, he wished she would stay home more and take care of him more. But when confronted with the actual chance that Janet would lose her job, which he knew meant a lot to her (not to mention the income), he was not so sure.

And then the thought struck him of *how* she would leave the station. There might be press conferences and interviews. With her prominence in the promotion video she had told him about, other media would probably pick up on the story and run it. What would that say about him and his law firm? Although they did not represent TV5, they had many media clients, both in broadcasting and in publishing. How would it look in the newspaper if Janet, identified as the "wife of prominent attorney Richard Sullivan," were seen to be siding with a bunch of Christian fundamentalists against the station's perfect right to broadcast the news?

"I think I'd go slow on this one, Janet," he finally said. "I know I've badgered you about being home more, but I *do* think that you—we, really—have been trying harder lately. And I really would hate for you to give up the job you love so much, so long as you—we—can keep this balance. And over such an obscure reason."

"Thanks Richard. That's about the first nice thing you've said about my job in a couple of years. I do appreciate it. The problem is that I basically agree with Tom and Connie. That show should *not* be broadcast into our homes, at least not at 7:30. It *is* too much. I don't think they or we can stop it by resigning. But I would like to try to stop it from the inside. Still, I *do* admire their courage, and I'll think about it a little longer."

"Well, think about it all you want. But don't do anything without us talking again. And don't let Bill Shaw know you're even considering siding with those people," Richard warned her. Then he smiled and asked her when she and the kids were planning to leave for Vermont.

MONDAY, JULY 24 ■ At mid-morning on Monday, Richard received a call from Bruce McKinney. "Has there been any more word from Tomlinson's attorney about the timing of our closing?" he asked.

"No, there hasn't, Bruce," Richard replied, "but in all honesty, I've been so busy that I haven't really pushed him lately. I'll call him today."

"I don't suppose you noticed the article in yesterday's paper about the huge Japanese investment in Apex Textile, did you?"

"No, why? What does it have to do with Tomlinson?"

"Well, apparently the market senses that Apex may now become a real competitor, with modernized robotic production. It may give Fairchild a run for its money, since Fairchild also needs to modernize most of its plants."

"Which means?"

"Which means that the Fairchild stock dropped some on Friday with the rumors, and this morning it has continued to fall. Last Wednesday it was at 32, but right now the tape reads 28. We just need to get Tomlinson's horse in the barn before something unexpected happens."

"OK. I see what you mean. I'll give him a call and try to speed things along, if that's possible. How is everything else going?" Richard asked.

"Just fine, thanks. Our expansion is underway. We'll have a lease for you to review later this week, I think. We've interviewed several new brokers. I hope we'll have our first new office open in the north area by the end of October, if all goes well."

"Great. I'll get back to you on Tomlinson."

One of the things Amy and Susan had discussed on the phone after their last double date was the subject of birth control pills. "I've got to figure out how to get a prescription," Amy explained, "so the same thing doesn't happen again."

Almost casually, Susan said, "If you get some, I'll get some, too."

"What?!?" said Amy. "Have you and Drew . . . ?"

"No, not yet. But I can see how it might happen. And I sure don't want to go through what happened to you," Susan told her. Hearing herself speak those words, she felt as if she were already no longer a virgin.

Nepravel, listening in, nodded, laughed, and said to himself, "A good firstborn. Everything nicely organized. Even her deflowering. How difficult it used to be!" And he laughed again.

"Well, if you're serious, let's call each other's doctors, so they can't recognize our voices, and ask about the procedures. Tell me your doctor's name, and I'll call him on Monday," Amy directed.

So on Monday afternoon Amy drove Susan to her job at the frozen yogurt shop, and they compared notes on what they had found out. Both doctors' offices had reported the same thing: in their state, any girl sixteen or older could obtain a prescription for birth control pills, and that information, at her request, became privileged doctor/patient communication and could not be revealed to her parents, except under court order. Both offices said that a regular patient could just schedule a confidential appointment and come in for a quick examination and obtain a prescription.

It sounded easy, but they admitted that it would take some courage to call the same doctors and nurses who had treated them for sprained ankles and sore throats as little girls, and ask for birth control pills. But they encouraged each other, and Amy finally said, "I'll come over to your house in the morning, when everyone is gone to work, and call for an appointment, if you'll do the same, right afterwards."

It all sounded so grown up and mysterious to Susan. She thought for a moment, smiled, and said, "OK."

By Friday afternoon they both had their first compacts of birth control pills hidden in their rooms. Amy started taking hers as soon as her cycle was right. Susan just looked at the tan package every day and wondered what would happen next. She noted with some relief that they were good if used anytime before the end of three more years.

FRIDAY, JULY 28 ■ The following Friday night Susan had to work until the 10:00 closing at the yogurt shop. Janet took her to the shop after coming home from her own job, because Drew had offered to bring her home, as a late date. On the way over to the yogurt shop, Janet mentioned that Tommy would be at Brent's home that evening, although he was not spending the night.They also talked briefly about their upcoming trip to Vermont in a couple of weeks.

About eight that evening, as Susan was fixing yogurt cones for a young family with two children, she looked up and thought she saw Tommy and Brent in the back seat of an old car, with four other boys, cruising through the shopping center. If her eyes were to be believed, two of the boys she recognized from her own class, who were known for being loners—and a little "strange."

Although one of her friends had told her near the end of the school year that she had seen Tommy with this same crowd, Susan had frankly discounted it as mistaken identity. But there they were tonight, when Tommy was supposed to be at Brent's home, cruising the north side of the city. She made a mental note to ask Tommy about all of this on Saturday.

Drew picked Susan up after work, and they soon pulled into the same dark cul-de-sac near Susan's home and parked behind Jay's car, which was already there, with its windows fogged up. Drew flashed his lights before turning them off.

Another hour of heavy petting ensued. Drew for the first time professed his growing love for Susan, which delighted her. She responded that she felt the same. And although she was not yet ready to do "it," she told him that she loved him and that virtually anything else was fair game. The two of them, although they were both virgins, had experienced enough sex education, fueled by their teenage passion, to contrive several creative ways to spend an hour together. Soon Drew's windows were fogged as well.

SATURDAY, JULY 29 ■ Late Saturday morning, as they were eating bowls of cereal together, Susan asked Tommy if he would like to play tennis before she had to depart for the afternoon shift at the yogurt shop.

Their two paths had diverged somewhat in the preceding months. At their particular ages, their social opportunities were quite different. So Tommy was surprised by her suggestion, but secretly pleased by this apparent attention from his big sister. "Sure," he said. "I just bought some new balls yesterday."

The two of them walked down to the city park an hour later. Susan decided that she didn't want to come on too strongly about the night before, just as they were beginning to play. So as they walked along, she asked some chatty questions about what courses he would be taking next year, what girls he liked, and so on. The majority of his answers were some variation on a muffled grunt.

They played one very even set of tennis, and she realized that soon his increasing strength would overcome her advantage in age and placement. Susan just barely won the set, and as they rested for a moment on a bench under two large oak trees, Susan asked, as casually as she could, "Didn't I see you last night at the shopping center in a car with Brent and some older boys? Wasn't that Derrick and Paul in the car?"

Tommy was so startled by her question that he did not have time to think through that their entire tennis outing had been planned around it. He considered lying to her for a moment, but he looked at her face and did not see either hostility or a setup. So he glanced down at his racquet strings and answered, "Yes. Why?"

"Well, you know that I know those guys—well, I don't *really* know them, but they're in my class," Susan explained slowly. "And I just can't really imagine what you have in common with them. Either you or Brent."

"What exactly do you mean?" Tommy asked, with some obvious hostility in his voice.

"I don't know, exactly. I mean, they're not like, bad, that I know of. It's just that they're sort of, well, I guess . . . loners. Like, I don't think either one of them has ever had a date with a girl, at least not from our school. You know, they're just sort of geeky, I guess."

"And you think that's how I am?"

"No. That's just it. I *don't* think of you like that, which is why I wasn't even sure it was you in the car."

"Well, I happen to like them a lot. And sometimes Brent and I just hang out with them, not that it's any of your business."

"But Tommy, Mom and Dad thought you were at Brent's house last night, and there you were out driving around God knows where. What if something had happened to you?"

Tommy finally connected his sighting last evening with this morning's tennis game. "I can't believe it. You asked me to play tennis for the first time in months, and it was all just to bash me about my friends! You've got some nerve. What are you, some kind of a perfect angel, loved by everyone, checking on us lowly sinners?"

That remark hit closer than he knew, as a visual image of what she and Drew had done together the night before leapt quickly at her. "No, Tommy, That's not it at all. I can *assure* you that I'm no angel. Maybe I did ask to play tennis so that we could talk about it. But you and I have said hardly two words in the last three months, and I *am* your sister. And, as hard as it may be for you to believe, I do care about you, particularly if you start to hang out with guys who can't do you any good."

"Do me any good? What do you mean by that remark?"

"Well, I mean, Tommy, you're sort of a handsome guy, and you ought to have lots of girlfriends. I don't know what the crowd that they are in does, but I don't think they go out very much—I mean with girls—and, well—Look, Tommy, I guess that being a fourteen- or fifteen-year-old boy must be worse than being a girl. I've talked to some of the guys in our class; and I know it was tough, when we were dating older guys who could drive. It *is* hard, but you're almost through it. Everybody eventually comes out the other end of those years, and then I guess you have new problems. Believe me. But what I mean is I would hate to see you get in with boys who . . . well, I can't put my finger on it. I'm sorry, Tommy. But there's just something about those guys that has always given me the creeps."

"Well, thanks a lot, big sister. I really appreciate the lecture. You should definitely major in psychology in college! I've got two parents, which is plenty. I don't need a third. So you can just take all of your advice and stuff it!"

With that, he took their tennis balls and lofted them one at a time as far as he could into the adjoining woods. Without another word, he picked up his gear and jogged off towards home, leaving Susan alone, frustrated and upset on the bench. After five minutes of feeling like an idiot and reflecting on the unexpected anger which her conversation had aroused in Tommy, she stood up slowly, gathered her things, and walked home, thinking.

She wanted to talk to Tommy again. To try to work past his anger. To apologize, if she had to, for "setting up" their tennis game. She again wanted to explain that she had done so out of concern, even love, if he would listen. She was mad at herself—and mad at him.

When she came in the back door, her mother was working on a shopping list. "Where's Tommy?" Susan asked.

"He blew through here a little while ago, dropped his things, and said he was going over to Brent's on his bike. How was your game, and why didn't you come home together?"

"Oh, it was fine. I don't know. Tommy just wanted to jog some. Is Dad here?"

"No, dear. He had to go to the office again, on this beautiful Saturday morning, to work on some documents. I hate it, but he says he has to do it. I guess that there just aren't enough hours in the regular work week, or something."

"Well, I guess I'll go take a shower and get ready for work, then," said Susan.

Sunday, July 30 ■ Between her work schedule, everyone's dates, and weekend activities, Susan never saw Tommy alone again during the entire weekend. It was Sunday afternoon before she could say a few words to her father, but by then she had decided that it was best just to stop meddling and to drop the whole thing. *But I just don't understand what Tommy has in common with those guys,* Susan thought to herself, alone on Sunday evening.

■   ■   ■

Late that same Sunday, Bobbie called Susan. The two of them had not seen each other for several weeks. Susan blamed it on their odd work schedules, but part of the reason was that she and Amy had grown unconsciously apart from Bobbie through their double date activities and purchasing their birth control pills. They had talked about the fact that Bobbie would probably neither approve nor understand either decision.

"Susan, do you have to work next Saturday night?" asked Bobbie.

"Let me see. No, next Saturday I work from morning until early afternoon, which is pretty easy, except at lunch. Why?"

"You may think this sounds crazy, so don't say no when you first hear it. I thought it would be great for you, Amy, and me to have an old-fashioned three-girl slumber party here at my house on Saturday night, like we used to do years ago. You and Amy can both spend the night, we can stay up late and talk, and then you can both come to our youth program and church service with me, like we talked about before. What do you think?"

Bobbie had been right to be cautious. The mention of the word *church* immediately triggered a voice inside Susan, which said, "No fun," and she almost declined. But then she thought about Bobbie and how they had not seen much of each other and how it might actually be fun—as well as a relief from Drew's pressure—to spend a Saturday night with her two best friends, the way they used to.

"Have you asked Amy yet?" Susan inquired.

"No, not yet. I get the impression from our few conversations that she somehow doesn't feel 'worthy' enough to go to church, because of what happened. So I was hoping that you would say yes, and then the two of us could call her."

"OK, Bobbie. That really does sound like fun. Let's put on our old pajamas and sleep in sleeping bags on the floor, like we used to."

"Great," Bobbie exclaimed, obviously happy. "Now let me see if I can make this conference call gizmo work, and we'll both be on the line to Amy."

Amy's reaction was even more negative than Susan's at first. She didn't like the idea of giving up a Saturday night with Jay. But, like Susan, she missed being with Bobbie, and under pressure from both of them, she finally also agreed.

MONDAY, JULY 31 ■ "The tax and estate attorneys tell Marty Tsongas that they should be all wrapped up by the end of the summer, so hopefully we will be able to close in early September. Unfortunately, neither Marty nor I can directly speed up the process, except with phone calls and prodding, which we have both done. How is the Fairchild stock doing?" asked Richard that Monday morning.

Bruce McKinney answered, "It's been in a slow slide these last few weeks, as the Japanese have announced more plans for upgrading Apex. This morning it opened at 24.5. Hopefully the Fairchild board is working on some sort of an investment strategy, to counter these Apex stories. I just hope they hurry up and announce something positive so the stock will stabilize.

"You and me both, Bruce. I promise you I'll keep the pressure on, even if I become a little obnoxious."

"Thanks, Richard. That's what legal friends are for!"

10

SATURDAY, AUGUST 5 ■ That Saturday evening would be the last one when all of the Sullivans were in town for several weeks, since the next Saturday morning Janet and the kids would drive off for Vermont. It had been a beautiful, warm, early August day, and the four of them had gone to swim and to sunbathe at the neighborhood pool, next to the city park. Richard had invited Janet to go to dinner, since they would not be together the next weekend. Susan had the slumber party at Bobbie's house. Tommy was again supposed to be at a movie at the mall, and then Brent was to spend the night at their home.

Nepravel was ecstatic about Tommy and Brent spending another evening with Roger and his crowd. With orientation starting for the new freshman class at the university, Nepravel had a special night planned for these two teenagers, which he hoped would produce even more confusion and guilt in their young minds.

But he had been horrified to learn that both Susan and Amy were going to Bobbie's house—and to her church! How had he missed that arrangement? What had happened to the voices in the two of them? Probably all those answered prayers had dulled them, and he had failed to notice. If anything happened, Balzor would be livid.

Because Bobbie lived in Zloy's neighborhood, Nepravel had alerted Zloy to be on the look out, but he knew it was asking a lot. Although an angel typically did not station himself permanently at the home of a believer, the answered prayers nevertheless kept bringing angels there on a regular basis. A demon *could* get in and do some damage in a believer's home, but the risk of being caught by a roving angel, summoned by prayer, was just too great, except in unusual circumstances. With so many other, easier families targeted for destruction up and down every street, most of the demons steered clear of the believers' homes, for simple self-preservation. And of course none of them would go near Morningside Church, particularly on a Sunday morning, when Amy and Susan would be there. The praise and worship would have angels swarming around, empowered by prayer and just hoping that some demon would stray too close.

So the unfortunate situation for Nepravel was that unless Zloy could slip into the Merediths' home that night to check and to reset the demonic voices, Amy and Susan would be completely out of their control for about eighteen hours. There was no telling what they might hear or learn, particularly in those environments! Nepravel was worried, and dreaded their nightly report session.

When Amy and Susan arrived at Bobbie's home, her mother, Anne, greeted them at the door. They could look through the house and see Mr. Meredith already grilling hamburgers for them in the backyard.

Bobbie had two younger brothers, younger than Tommy. One was at camp, and the other she had convinced her mother to "farm out" for their slumber party. So the Merediths and the three girls enjoyed a pleasant dinner on their back patio together. Bob and Anne Meredith had watched these three girls grow up together since grade school, and they had always enjoyed hosting events for them. They had noticed that in the past two months Bobbie had not seen as much of her two best friends as usual, but they had explained it away by summer job schedules. And they were delighted tonight to have these three good friends enjoying themselves in their home. Bob even thought to himself, as he watched Anne laugh with them about some new fashion foible, what wonderful women the three girls were becoming and how lucky three men would someday be to have them as wives.

After supper, while it was still light, the girls purposefully changed into their pajamas and spread their sleeping bags out on Bobbie's bedroom floor. Anne, getting into the spirit of the slumber party, brought them a tray of milk and cookies. They leaned back on beanbag chairs and began chatting and calling a few of their friends on the telephone.

Meanwhile, Tommy and Brent, always ones who went along with the crowd, were about to go along in a newer, faster, and more ominous lane. Roger had an older friend, Phil, who was already in college, and who had invited Roger and Zane to come with him to an adult book store in a particular area of the downtown where several such stores, and the Platinum Club, were located. The Platinum Club was a "world class" strip club, where a hundred young women at a time, some of them school teachers and secretaries by day, came out for floor shows, completely naked, except for garter belts and high heels. As they danced on tables, men stuffed money into their garter belts. The club was known not only in their city, but throughout the entire region, and businessmen and conventioneers who visited the city often made it a point to visit the Platinum Club while in town. Because of its status, the club was very strict about checking IDs.

But that was not true of the adult book store where Roger's friend Phil had a fraternity brother behind the counter that Saturday evening. After they left the Holcombes' house, supposedly on the way to the mall, Roger told Brent and Tommy that he would try to get them into the adult book store as well, but he could not promise their success. The younger boys had never been in such a place, and they were certainly eager to go.

Richard took Janet to a very fine French restaurant, and they sipped white wine in the quiet bar while waiting for their table to clear. They discussed the upcoming trip to Vermont, and Richard reminded her of the few items that had often been forgotten on previous trips.

■   ■   ■

The three girls had been talking for over an hour when Bobbie asked Amy how she was feeling following her "procedure."

"Fine, just fine. No sweat. Sometimes, every now and then, I do feel like it would have been great to actually have a baby, in the sense of being a mother. But I know it would never have worked for me in any other way. And now," Amy smiled, looking at Susan, "we've made sure that it won't happen again."

"What do you mean?" asked Bobbie, genuinely surprised.

"She means," said Susan, taking a deep breath and looking down at her knees, tucked up in front of her, "that we both now have birth control pills." As she finished, she looked up at Bobbie.

It was again Bobbie's turn to be shocked by the news from her two friends—shocked, saddened, and suddenly feeling left out. "You both . . . both of you . . . now have birth control pills?" asked Bobbie.

Amy and Susan nodded. "I actually haven't started taking mine yet," smiled Susan, a little sheepishly. "But I've got them hidden in my drawer, in case I need them. So that nothing like what happened to Amy will happen to me."

"What do you mean, 'in case you need them'?" asked Bobbie.

"You know very well." Susan smiled even more, diverting her eyes from Bobbie and rearranging her legs. "In case Drew and I decide to go all the way . . . you know . . . make love. We've done about everything else, and I don't see anything wrong with it, by the way, if you love the other person. Drew is such a great guy. I figure one day, maybe soon, we'll do it, and I want to be prepared. But you *must* feel the same way, Bobbie. You and Thomas Briggs. Haven't you been dating pretty heavily this summer?"

"Who are these two guys?" asked Roger's older friend, Phil, as he looked in the back seat of Roger's car, parked around the corner from the Platinum Club.

"It's Zane's brother and a friend. They're cool. Do you think you can get them into the bookstore too?" asked Roger.

"I don't know," said Phil. "Hank will be taking a small chance with the two of you, but these other two are really young. I'll go ask him. Maybe it'll be OK for just a few minutes."

There was a five minute wait, and then Phil returned with the news. "I convinced him to let us all go in for five minutes, while we pick out some videos for tonight. But you two," looking in the backseat, "be ready to jump into one of the curtained booths in the back if *anybody* starts to come through the front door. OK?" The four boys were out of the car in an instant.

Inside the store, Tommy and Brent nodded in Hank's direction, then kept their heads down as much as possible, trying to look "old." But their eyes wandered over video covers, book covers, paraphernalia, and magazines that, frankly, they had not known until then even existed. While they walked from aisle to aisle looking at the merchandise, Hank asked Roger and Phil, "So, are you guys going over to Freddie's place for the party tonight?"

"We'd planned to just rent some videos. But what's happening at Freddie's?"

"A great party, I think. Freddie's got an old house off campus, and it should really be fun. Two or three videos will be going at one time, lots of guys, and some new boys from the incoming freshman class. I'm going over when I get off. Take them," he nodded toward Tommy and Brent at the back of the store and smiled, "and they'll be *real* popular."

Zane, Brent's older brother, had been listening, standing next to his friend Roger. He had taken the plunge into the "alternative lifestyle," and Brent seemed to like it too. But the party being described sounded a little rougher than the small get-togethers they had initiated during the summer, and he was not sure that it was such a good idea for Brent and Tommy to participate.

"Sure, man, that sounds like a great idea," Phil was saying. "We'll get the videos some other night. Let's head on over to the party." He waved his hand and started out the door.

Zane began to say something to Roger, but then decided to go along, because he wanted to see what a college party was like too. So long as they had their own car and could leave the party whenever they wanted, a voice told him that it would be all right. The demons who permanently occupied the adult book store and who had planted that rationalization in Zane's mind, smiled and couldn't wait to hear the reports on Freddie's party at their midnight meeting over the city.

"Yes, sure, Thomas and I have been dating every weekend, plus some on week nights, unless we're both just too tired. And I do certainly know what you're talking about. We like each other a lot. And I guess it hasn't been easy keeping our hands off each other, but so far, for the most part, we've managed."

Just then Zloy darted in through the outside wall of Bobbie's bedroom, spinning around and looking quickly for any sign of an angel. Nervous, only there because of Nepravel's pleading, he slithered up behind Amy to listen for the voices of Unworthiness, Doubt, and Pride, which every demon knew were the keys to keeping out the Word.

Amy and Susan looked at each other. Amy smiled. "So you *have* done something with Thomas!"

It was Bobbie's turn to look down at the floor and blush a little. "Well, yes, a few times we started to touch each other too much, but then we both knew it was wrong and stopped. It wasn't easy, but we've talked about it, and each of us wants to be a virgin when we get married." Bobbie silently prayed for strength and wisdom for how to explain her deepest feelings to her friends.

Amy and Susan looked at each other again, this time incredulously. "Virgins when you get married!" asked Susan, leaning forward and smiling. "Why on earth would you want to wait that long? Nobody does that anymore!"

If it had not been for the mirror on Bobbie's bedroom wall, reflecting the first glimmer of light as the angel came through the wall behind Zloy, he would have been exploded back to hell in a cloud of black smoke. As it was, he just ducked in time, and the angel's talon grazed the top of his smoldering head. His shriek was drowned out by the angel's cry of "Holy is the Lord God of Hosts," and Zloy could only escape by darting under the floor and out through the crawl space at that end of the house. He had accomplished nothing in his brief stay, except to confirm that he should never go back. Amy and Susan were Nepravel's responsibilities. Let him come risk his own neck! Zloy had seen and heard enough.

Bobbie began, speaking slowly, "I realize it's hard to explain, and you may never understand. But for us, having sex before marriage is just like a lot of other things we might do—drinking, smoking, stealing, cheating on an exam. Both Thomas and I feel the power of God's Holy Spirit living inside us, and so we don't want to do *any* of those things, because He doesn't want us to. God truly knows what is best for us—He has always known—and He has said that all of these things are wrong. That we will live a fuller and happier life if we don't do these things. And if we do it God's way, marriage will be better.

"So for Thomas and me it's not a question of giving up sex before marriage. It's rather a question of trying to do the will of our heavenly Father, whose Holy Spirit lives within us. And since that will does not include premarital sex, we try to cut short the things that could get us going beyond the stopping point. It *is* tough, especially since we really like each other. On a couple of occasions we've actually prayed together for God to give us the power to do what we know is right. And you know what's funny? After praying like that with Thomas, I've felt that I loved him and respected him more than I ever would have if we had had sex together."

Bobbie had said so much, and it did make sense. But it was so foreign to anything that Amy or Susan had ever heard. For a few moments neither of them could think of anything to say.

"You mean," Amy finally asked, "that you're sitting there in a parked car with Thomas, and you're hugging and kissing, and as things start to get really hot, you begin *praying*?"

"Yes, a couple of times we've done that." Tears started to come into Bobbie's eyes, as she tried to explain her faith to the two girls who were most important to her. "Again, I know it's hard for you to understand. But you see, I—we—pray all the time for and about all sorts of things. Our families do. The power of God is so great. He can do anything, if you believe in Jesus as your Lord and have the Holy Spirit living inside you. And we know that we can never overcome the temptation to do anything— sex, drinking, whatever—without His help. Relying on our own strength just doesn't work."

Susan had to admit that what Bobbie said sounded logical, if the business about the Holy Spirit were really true. But it was so alien, so foreign to anything she had ever seen on television, or in a movie, or read in a book; it was almost as if Bobbie were telling her things about another planet. Then she thought about all the fun she and Drew were having, and a dim but audible voice asked her why on earth she would want to give that up.

The answer was contained in what Bobbie then said:

"The problem is, I can understand that if you don't have the Holy Spirit living inside you, then the real joy of passing up premarital sex, or any other temptation, probably doesn't make sense to you. Because you're focusing on the instant pleasure. But Thomas and I are focusing on the joy of our Lord, and the fact that he paid the ultimate price for us, so our bodies are not just our own. They belong to Him too. And we're always brought back to 'What would He want for us?'"

Tommy felt uneasy as soon as they walked into the old home that was apparently Freddie's college living quarters. Just looking around, he could tell that this group was made up of committed homosexuals. As confused as he had been about his own sexual orientation over the past several months, it had been one thing to act out fantasies in the relative safety of a friendly basement. But this party was another matter. These college boys—and young men—were obviously smoking pot, drinking, and he wasn't sure what else. When their group walked in, two men were dancing cheek to cheek in the living room, and all heads turned to look over at the four younger boys who came in with Phil.

"So, you and the kids will leave next Saturday, and I'll join you the following Thursday, ten days later," said Richard, as they split a chocolate ice cream pie dessert. "I know you'll have a great time, as usual. Please, of course, be particularly careful when you drive up there."

"Yes, it should be nice this year, especially with the new riding horse Dad has apparently bought. But what about you?" Janet smiled. "Do you eat regularly when we're away? What will you do?"

"Oh . . ." Richard returned her smile and then dabbed at the ice cream with his spoon. "I'll be OK. I'll find something to do to keep me busy. But of course I'll work mainly."

The girls talked on for several more hours at Bobbie's slumber party, but each of them realized that the gulf which separated them on the subjects of premarital sex and birth control pills was so great that there was no real point in bringing it up again, at least not that night. Amy and Susan would try to digest all that Bobbie had told them, but it was not easy. And Bobbie would try to understand how her friends could give in to something she believed would eventually harm them so much; she, too, had a hard time understanding.

Finally, around 2:00 in the morning, they decided that they should get some sleep, if they were going to make it to Bobbie's youth group at 10:00.

Tommy, Brent, Zane, and Roger stayed together, following Phil around Freddie's old Victorian home. They had only been there a few minutes when Freddie himself materialized from the kitchen, wearing leather pants and no shirt. "Welcome, welcome" he smiled. Reaching down into a cooler by his feet, he pulled out a beer for each of the four boys, and said, "Make yourselves right at home."

As soon as Zane popped his beer, he wished he hadn't, because he really thought they should leave. Turning to Phil, who had led them over in his car, Zane said, "Just one quick beer, Phil, and then I really think we need to get these guys home."

"Oh, we only just got here," said Phil. "You can, of course, leave whenever you want, but for now let's go look at the big video screen in the den."

Tommy followed along, being drawn deeper into the house, sipping on his beer. Soon he was seated in front of a large-screen video, watching yet another version of the acts he had seen before during their basement gatherings. As the video kept rolling, and the beer can became emptier, the seat felt more comfortable, and the boys felt more relaxed.

Zane's first instinct had been right—the four of them should never have gone to that party. But the voices drowned out those instincts and encouraged each of them to take just one more little step, to drink just one more sip, to wait just a few more minutes to see what would happen next. Tommy and Brent, besides being uncertain about themselves sexually, were naturally pliable and tended to go along with the crowd. Sadly, tragically, this was the wrong place and the wrong night for two confused fourteen-year-olds who naturally "went with the flow" and liked to please other people. When they finally left almost two hours later, Tommy and Brent were even more confused than ever.

That night over the city, messengers from the adult book store and Freddie's party described their continuing successes. Nepravel emphasized the steady degradation of the two teenage boys and only briefly mentioned that neither Amy nor Susan was a candidate for premarital sex that night, since they were not out on dates.

Zloy had warned Nepravel not to gloss over where the girls were, because he was not about to take even more blame where the Merediths were concerned. When Nepravel passed, Zloy spoke, out of self-preservation, and alerted the broiling mass that the two girls would be out of their control for several hours. And of course he boldly recounted his own heroism in singlehandedly fighting off a warrior angel that very evening in Bobbie's bedroom.

On hearing this, Balzor came screaming down to Nepravel, making an example of him in front of all the others, demanding to know how he had let these two girls, already almost completely under their control, come under the Merediths' influence for so long a period. Nepravel, his back against his cohorts, Balzor glaring down at him, blamed it all on Zloy, protesting that if Zloy could just keep the Merediths quiet and inactive, many of them would have fewer problems.

Zloy was incensed. The two of them started trading taunts and charges. Finally Balzor intervened, screaming, "Enough! Whatever the cause, you've *both* got a problem. Now figure out how to neutralize any damage the Merediths or that Michael Andrews and his cursed church might do, and be quick! Remember, a run-in with an angel is not the only way to be blown back to hell!" He turned and resumed his high place of authority. The meeting continued, and Nepravel and Zloy eyed each other warily.

SUNDAY, AUGUST 6 ■ Glenn Jamison, the leader of the Morningside Church youth ministry, believed that to change teenagers' lives—or any people's lives—required three things: instruction in the power of God, instruction in the wisdom of God, and Christian role models with whom the kids could identify. Glenn and Michael Andrews, his boss and mentor, believed that most churches put people to sleep droning on about the wisdom of God. As important as His wisdom is, Glenn knew that if an individual could only once feel the real *power* of God, he would then pick up God's wisdom out of a simple thirst to know more.

So Glenn and his assistants emphasized teaching about God's power in their Sunday youth group; and they tried to live lives as Christian role models. Just as significantly, they knew how important are peer groups, and so they built their ministry around a core of young people, which changed slightly as the kids moved through school, but which was basically responsible for teaching the gospel to the other students. The result was a youth program that had grown exponentially—the kids knew they were receiving genuine friendship and important instruction, so they came.

"Hi, Amy. Hello, Susan," Glenn greeted them with a warm smile at the door to the large, sloping classroom when the two girls arrived with Bobbie. "Glad you're here. We've got a superb speaker this morning. His name is Price Weeks, and he has a strong message to tell. Come in."

The three girls found their way down to the seats Thomas Briggs was saving for them. Bobbie sat next to Thomas and squeezed his hand.

There was a Bible reading followed by announcements about upcoming events, the number of which frankly startled Susan. Bobbie had said that they saved prayer time until the end, and Glenn rose to introduce their speaker. Price Weeks, it turned out, had graduated from the university seven years earlier in architecture. He worked now with one of the city's best midsize architectural firms. Glenn did not say too much more, and Price, a handsome young man with blond hair, rose in front of the group of more than a hundred teenagers.

After some first remarks and a joke about Glenn, whom he had apparently known for quite a while, Price told them that he could talk about a number of things, but he wanted them to learn that morning about how the power of God had changed him completely. Because, he said, he had been a practicing homosexual.

Amy and Susan looked at each other, as if to say "Oh great, what has this got to do with me?" They underestimated the power of Price's words.

"But I'm not here to talk about homosexuality, as such. That just happens to be what Satan used—and it was very powerful—to trap me, to bind me, to keep me away from the love of God, to fool me, and ultimately, except for God's grace, to completely destroy me. You see, Satan doesn't just walk up to us on a sunny day and say, 'Hi, I'm Satan, and I want to destroy you and your family, and be sure that you spend eternity in hell, not in heaven.' If he did that, then even I would have been smart enough to run in the opposite direction as fast as I could.

"No, Satan has known forever that the straightforward approach doesn't work. He has a better way. He's been deceiving us since the first man and woman. And remember, he *hates* you. He *despises* you. He wants you in hell with him, not in heaven with God and Jesus, where he used to be, but can't go. He can't stand it that you might wind up there forever. But he can't confront you straight on because he knows that you will flee. *So he lies.* He lies about *everything*. And he knows *exactly* what to lie about with each one of us to pull us into a life separated from God by sin. If he can do that to you, then he will win. You will lose. He's got you. You go to hell—forever. And you're miserable here on earth, deep down inside, as well. All he's got to do is keep you so confused and so overtly content and feeling so unworthy and doubting God that you won't take the *very simple* step of turning to God.

"Listen, what is he doing now to lie to *you*? How many of you are already drinking, and partying every weekend, when you ought to be advancing yourselves by studying? Don't you think he loves it when you destroy your brain at sixteen and cut yourself off from all that you could be? He's winning!

"How about your parents? How many of you hate your parents?" There were some nervous laughs and looks around the room. "He loves it when he can get you to believe your parents don't understand you, and he gets your parents to believe you're bad. Then you'll never talk to each other, much less pray together. And you'll never learn anything from the people who could teach you the most, if God were just in there too. Who loses? You and your parents! Who wins? He does, laughing all the way to hell, with all of you! God set up families, and Satan is destroying them. He's lying and winning. Does any of this sound familiar? When was the last time you and your parents got down on your knees together and prayed to your common Father? Trust me: it will work miracles, right here, right now, in your lives. But he can't stand that, so he lies to you, and his voices tell you not to be so stupid. Stupid? *You're only stupid if you listen to him!*

"And, hey, what about sex?" More nervous laughs, but a lot of seriousness, too. "How many of you girls are being pressured to have sex now? How many of you boys are doing that to your girlfriends?" Amy looked down at the floor, and Susan felt herself turning pink. "That's all him. Satan. He's lying to you. Listen, you can't embarrass me on this, after what he convinced me to do. He had voices going in me that said I was the best thing around. I know about the excitement and the professions of love and the thrill. Believe me. It sounds *great*, going in, doesn't it? Fantastic. Fun. If it feels good, do it. He loves me, so it's OK. Right, girls?

"I know, I know. I've heard it all, too. But, *please* hear me. It's not the sex that it's *really* about. Or the liquor. Or the homosexuality. It's all about *you*. He will use *anything* to trap you, and the better it sounds, the better job he's doing on you.

"You know what? You can't win . . . That's right. By yourself, you haven't got a chance. Satan has been at this forever. He will chew you up and spit you out. 'Maybe just a little,' you say. He loves it. 'I can handle this; no sweat,' you say. He cheers. 'I'll stop when I get older and have to be responsible,' you say. He laughs, knowing that you may never be either.

"Kids, hear this, if you don't hear anything else I say this morning. He used all of those tricks on me, and I got to the other side, where you *always* wind up, where it isn't fantastic or even fun. I was at the very bottom. I was in the gutter. I was with the wrong crowd. I knew from the beginning that what I was doing was wrong—or at least a small voice tried to tell me, and I drowned it out with all the 'fun' I was having. I felt terrible about myself, which is what Satan wants. If I ever thought about God, a voice screamed at me that I was unworthy and that God wanted no part of me. Listen. Listen: I was going to hell, both here on earth and eternally." Not a head moved. No one stirred, as the teenagers focused on Price's message. It had really happened to him; this was obviously not an act.

"But that is where Jesus found me. In the gutter. In despair. Contemplating suicide. I found out later that a lot of people had been praying for me. For years. By His grace, He found me. And what I want you to hear is that He changed me. Instantly. Permanently." Price took out his handkerchief and wiped his eyes.

"I finally surrendered all of that old life to Him and asked Him to forgive me for the sin I had committed and for the other men I had led astray. I was at the bottom, and I asked him to come into my life and to lift me up.

"Kids, you don't have to be at the very bottom to ask him into your lives. Please don't go that far. But let me assure you, whether you are aware of it or not, Satan is gunning for you right now. He's after you. And by yourself, you will never defeat him. *You need God and His Holy Spirit in your life.* Let me tell you: walking away from the homosexual lifestyle is not easy. But I did it, in one day, through His power. By the grace of God, I've never looked back. I pray every day that His Holy Spirit will refill me and give me the power to carry on. I have a freedom and a joy in my life now that I can't really express. By surrendering to Him I found perfect freedom. God has me, and I'm His. And I'd like to introduce you to the second greatest joy in my life, my wife, Patti."

Applause filled the room as a short, brunette young woman stood up from where she had been sitting quietly next to Glenn, turned around, smiled, and acknowledged the recognition from the young people.

Glenn walked up front, and there followed a question and answer period, in which Price emphasized again the universality of Satan's attacks. Then there were prayer requests and a ten-minute prayer period, led by the students themselves.

Susan was struck by how personal and specific were the prayers offered by these kids her own age. She had never prayed like this, and certainly never out loud. They were lifting up friends and family to God and praying both thanksgivings and requests in their own lives. One girl stood and prayed for a friend of hers who was considering an abortion. Amy felt warm, and she wondered if these same people had prayed for her. Then the girl prayed for the unborn baby as if it were already a person, asking God that He not allow the baby to be killed in his mother's womb. It was almost too much for Amy, who for the first time opened that corner of her consciousness, shut tight since the morning of her pregnancy test, allowing in the thought that she had in fact taken an innocent child's life. She slumped down in the chair, and both Susan and Bobbie were silently concerned for her.

When the prayers were over, the kids divided up. Some were going to an early lunch. Some stayed behind to talk to Price and his wife. The three friends sat still, letting Amy set the pace for getting up. As she rose, she looked white as a sheet. "I'm sorry, Amy, if that hit too close," Bobbie said. "I really didn't mean for you to be hurt. We never know what people will pray for. Let's go on to the service, where you can sit as much as you want, if you're not feeling well."

Amy mustered a fragile smile and followed Thomas, Bobbie, and Susan to the door. Glenn had managed to work his way there as well, and he handed Bibles to Amy and to Susan. "Here, we'd like you to have these, from our youth group. Someday I hope you'll have read the whole book. But for starters, try reading the Gospel of John."

Both girls returned Glenn's smile and accepted the gifts. "Thanks a lot," each one said, as they followed Bobbie toward the sanctuary.

The four teenagers sat with the Merediths, and the opening hymn began right at 11:15. It was an old and often-heard hymn, which even Susan and Amy recognized, and soon they were caught up in the general praise, singing along with Bobbie and Thomas. Amy found her spirit lifting as she focused for a moment on God, and not on her own problems.

The service lasted about ninety minutes, and Michael Andrews' sermon was on Christian love—tough love, when you care enough about someone to tell him that he is wrong. "We get love and sentimentality mixed up today," he said. "If I truly love someone, then I want God's perfect will in his or her life. And that means that I cannot want him or her to do something which is outside the will of God." Susan listened and thought about Drew and wondered for a moment whether they were really in love.

At the end of the sermon, Michael, as he almost always did, asked everyone to bow in prayer, and then he gave an invitation to those who heard God talking to them that morning, to silently repent and to ask Jesus to come in, to take over, and to be the Lord of their lives. Amy heard the words and knew that God was calling her away from all that Price had talked about. To a life of quiet joy with Him, not worrying about what other people thought or did. She heard, but Doubt was still reacting, diminished as it was. "Could this be real? Bobbie and Thomas and Price are real, but are they being fooled too?" the voice asked her. She heard, but she could not surrender. Not that day. But she heard.

After communion, they ended the service with "Amazing Grace." Amy had been surprised by the many raised hands during all of the singing that morning, but particularly with this closing hymn. As she discreetly looked around, she noticed tears on many of the faces near her, both men and women. She felt the power. She did not have it yet. But she could see what it was doing, from Bobbie to Thomas to Price to all of these adults, standing, singing to God, and weeping. She would not have believed it only twenty-four hours before. Now she had seen it. The question was, did she want it?

As the three girls walked to the car with the Merediths, Anne asked Susan and Amy if they would like to come again sometime.

"I'll be away the next few weekends," responded Susan. "But maybe in the fall, after school starts," she smiled.

"I'd like to come again," said Amy. "I really enjoyed both the youth group and the service. Thank you so much for inviting me. I think I'll come again next Sunday. I'll talk to you this week, Bobbie. Maybe I'll pick you up."

THURSDAY, AUGUST 10 ■ "Janet, we heard that you'll be on vacation for two weeks," Tom Spence said, standing in the door to her office on Thursday morning, "and since we'll have to say something to Bill while you're gone, I thought that I should see where you stand. Are you going to join us?"

Janet motioned for him to come in and to close the door. "Have a seat, Tom. I did talk to my husband, who is an attorney, and I did think about it a lot. I've been meaning to get with you and Connie, but our schedules have just been so crazy. I'm glad you stopped by."

Tom nodded and took a chair across from her. "Tom, I know we won't agree on this, so I might as well tell it like it is. I do think that '911 Live' is wrong to be on the air, particularly when it's scheduled, for all of the same reasons that you, Connie, and the others feel so deeply. But I haven't given up on being able to change things from within, and I'm not ready to sacrifice my job—maybe even my career—over this issue. I'd rather try to influence policies from the inside."

"And just how, exactly, do you plan to do that?" Tom asked quietly.

The truth was that Janet had been practicing what she had already said for a couple of days, thinking that it would be enough. She had not expected his question, and she involuntarily glanced down at her desk. There was an uncomfortable silence. "Well, by letting Bill know that shows like this are not appropriate. And I thought I would maybe write a memo to the chief of programming at the network," she ad-libbed. "I've known her for several years, and I think I can approach her through the children angle, although she's single. Anyway, I'll think about it. And I wish all of you would stay and help fight it with me."

"As you know, Janet, we've already fought those battles, with no success. First they ignore you. Then they humor you and make you think that they're listening. Then they co-opt you into the process, all the time hoping to wear you down. You've seen the process perfectly with '911 Live.' We have no choice left but to give in, or to resign.

"We so wish you would join us, Janet, because it will be real news if *all* of us go. But if some go and some stay, they'll use the old tactic of divide and conquer. We'll be labeled as crazies and forgotten. You'll be the sane voice of moderation. Who knows, Janet, maybe you'll be interviewed after we go or make it to a few local talk shows." As Tom rose to leave, he added, "You better be thinking about what you're going to say, about the show and about us. They won't make it easy for you. You'll find, unfortunately, that once you compromise, it's hard to go back."

"I don't think I'm compromising. I'm just protesting in another way," Janet said forcefully.

Tom smiled. "I hope you're right. God bless you Janet . . . and your family." And he silently closed the door behind him.

FRIDAY, AUGUST 11 ■ Friday evening Richard and Janet packed the items she had assembled plus the big suitcases into the minivan Janet used as her car. Susan had been working extra shifts at the yogurt shop to make up for her coming absence, and she was on again that night. Drew was bringing her home after work, as a last date for two weeks. Tommy was helping load the van. He had been at home and more subdued since the previous Saturday night. Neither parent knew why, exactly, but they were delighted to have him around.

Drew and Susan stopped in the same cul-de-sac on the way home that night and were surprised that Jay's car was not already there. During the week, Susan had asked Drew on the phone one night about Michael Andrews' words on real love and on the will of God. Drew had responded logically that God is a God of love and He wants us to love each other. Drew assured Susan that he loved her very much and that God had given men and women natural urges and ways to express their love for each other. When Susan asked about marriage in relation to those ways, Drew responded that those ideas had been right in Bible times, before modern science, hygiene, birth control, and so on were invented. God did not mean for us to be stagnant, but to advance with the knowledge He has given us. "We know so much more now, Susan. I'm sure if the Bible were written today, it would take all of these changes into account. But old or not, the Bible still says love is the greatest gift, and I certainly love you and want to share that love with you."

Nepravel, who had been working all week to counter what Susan and Amy had heard the previous weekend, had planted that voice in Drew himself, even though Drew lived outside his neighborhood. Balzor had given his personal permission. And through it Drew's simple teenage lust for Susan took on an almost religious quality. The Father of Lies had not missed a trick.

So parked that night in the dark, knowing that they would not see each other for two weeks, their passion elevated to godly love, Drew and Susan almost did "it." But the memory of Amy's ordeal was too fresh in Susan, and so she stopped him. To calm his protests, and to stretch out the excitement, Susan whispered in his ear that she would start taking her birth control pills while on vacation. "And that should give us both something to look forward to when I get back!" She smiled in the dark.

"You got that right," Drew agreed, smiling as he hugged her close, trying to calm his racing heart.

Richard heard Susan come in and lock the front door. Then he turned out the light in their bedroom. Janet, exhausted from a week of work and looking forward to an early start in the morning, nevertheless did her best to feel romantic, since she would not see Richard for over ten days. Richard had been in an unusually good mood all evening, helping with the packing without any complaints.

All summer, since her ultimatum on the day of the "911 Live" test run, he had been pleasantly docile, and even loving toward her. They did seem to have found a new balance in their relationship, and Richard was not as angry. He was trying, through his own will, to grow a relationship with her. Of course he had not been able to end his affair with Kristen, whom he planned to see the next day, once Janet was gone. Richard knew that his future, like his past, had to be with Janet. It was just the continuing present in which Kristen was so important. He simply did not know what to do, and so he did nothing.

That evening the two of them made love in a quiet and peaceful way. It meant a great deal to Janet, who was beginning to conclude that Richard really did love her and was trying. And Richard felt the same way about her. It could have been the signal of a real starting over, if Richard did not have to keep constantly reminding himself not to slip up and utter "Kristen" at the wrong time.

11

WEDNESDAY, AUGUST 16 ■ "Now, what can I do for you?" Bill Shaw asked, as he, Tom Spence, Connie Wright, and four other men and women, also station employees, all settled into the comfortable chairs around their conference room table. Eight color monitors embedded in one of the walls kept their own signal and those of their main competitors in view constantly but silently during their discussion.

"Bill, the six of us have talked among ourselves, watched the promotion videos, and, frankly, prayed about '911 Live.' Of course you know that Connie and I rode along on the test run, with you and Janet. After all this thought, observation, and contemplation, we feel more strongly than ever that this show is totally inappropriate for viewing in our audience's homes, particularly at a time when it might lead to staged acts of violence for the sake of television when so many children will probably be watching. We are here to formally ask you to cancel the show in our city, or at least to tape it for rebroadcast at 11:30, after the news."

"Is that all?"

"Yes."

"And if I won't do either one?"

"Then the six of us, and perhaps others, will resign from our positions."

"I see. Could you please tell me what gives the six of you the right to decide what's best for our audience to see at 7:30 on Friday evenings?"

"That's obviously not a job which belongs to any of us, formally. But common sense and simple decency tell us that you don't bring unedited violence and mayhem into people's living rooms—nor do you set up a weekly stage for deranged people to parade their worst fantasies in front of a national audience."

"That may be what *you* keepers of our moral code think, but the rest of the country can't wait. I thought we might be discussing this subject, so I brought the reports from the preview tests run on sample audiences, using the same videos, I might add, in which you participated. Here," he said, sliding the reports down the table towards Tom. "The viewers *loved* it. Network says this will be one of the hottest—if not *the* hottest—shows of the fall season. It starts in a month, in early September. And you want me to kill it? To call Network and say that we're too squeamish here in this city to view the truth? That we want to censor ourselves? Come on, guys. Are you crazy?"

"Bill, Network should never have come up with this," Connie picked up for Tom. "Of course people will say they like it. So long as it's other people's problems and crashes and deaths we're broadcasting live. But what about the victims? Some things are not decided by majority vote, but by what is simply *right*."

"And who decides what's right, if not the majority?"

"Well, a good place to start is Scripture. Have you ever heard of the Golden Rule? It's pretty useful. Would you want to watch your own child burn to death on television, Bill?"

"Of course not . . . but I guess if it did happen, God forbid, and it was picked up by the show, I'd understand."

"Come on, Bill," Tom said. "*You* might understand, but would you like it? And what about other people?"

"Look, we're not getting anywhere," Bill cut him off. "I'm not going to buck Network, and I'm not going to tape the show and rebroadcast it. It's called '911 Live,' and live it's going to be. So if that's too much for you, you'll just have to resign. By the way, where does Janet stand in all of this?"

"You should ask her yourself, but I don't think she is prepared to resign, although she hates the show," Tom said.

"Well, good. I hate some of our other shows, but I'm not resigning either. Now, anything else? Let me know what you finally decide. Meeting adjourned." And without any attempt at further reconciliation, Bill rose and left by the side door.

"Bruce, this is Richard. I've got good news. Marty called this morning and said the tax people told him they'll have the estate wrapped up by the end of August. So he suggested that we go ahead and schedule our closing for early in September, either just before or after Labor Day, in three to four weeks."

"Sounds great, Richard. And none too soon. We can obviously put the full million to work, and the Fairchild stock seems, for the moment at least, to be holding steady at around 25."

"Well, start updating your closing exhibits, like the accounts payable and receivable, and we'll start working with Marty's law firm to generate the closing documents."

"Go easy on us, Richard," McKinney half-joked, thinking about the probable legal fees.

"Always, Bruce. You know that."

That evening Richard had dinner at Kristen's apartment. He had already spent two nights there since Janet and the kids had left. He had mentioned to Nancy Bryant on Saturday, as they watched Janet pull down the driveway, that he had some touchy contracts in the works and might have to go out of town at any moment, so she should not worry if he were away. He promised to call whenever he wouldn't be there so she could check the house.

"That's fine, Richard," Nancy had said. "Whatever Tom and I can do while Janet's away, just let us know. But we won't be much help next weekend because we're planning a trip to the mountain house. Would you like to come?"

Richard had graciously declined, saying that this was his one annual opportunity to really catch up on his work and his reading.

Now he and Kristen were enjoying a late dinner on her twelfth-floor balcony. There was a spectacular view of the city below them in the dark. This was like a dream to Richard, sipping white wine with this beautiful woman, looking out at all the lights, wondering what he had done to rate so much happiness. The voices were really spinning and had been since Saturday. He recognized that when he was with Janet, he thought his life should remain with her. But when he was with Kristen, he received such an ego stroking that he could—maybe—imagine leaving Janet for this younger woman. But then he thought of the kids and Janet's love for him, and it all got so balled up that the loudest voice told him just not to think about it, especially not during these ten days, when he and Kristen were virtually honeymooners in their own city.

She handed him some more pasta across the small table, not minding that the motion opened her house coat. The light breeze caught her hair. Richard was in heaven, he told himself.

"So, are you happy?" she asked.

"Are you kidding? I've never been happier."

"Me, too. You're a great man Richard. I love you very much." Smiling, she leaned across again, with the same effect, and asked, "Now when do I get to spend the night at your place?"

"Well, I almost hate to risk it, because of the neighbors, but I guess it would be kind of fun. Do you really want to?"

"Absolutely. I want to see what this Janet person gets to see. I want to feel like your wife, if only for one night. I love you so much. I'm terribly jealous of her, but I believe you when you say you *are* going to leave her. And I just want to be able to see all your things, as if we lived together already."

"OK. A weekday would be very tricky. But our closest neighbors, the Bryants, are going to their mountain house this weekend, so we ought to be able to spend Friday night, and maybe Saturday night, at the house. But we'll have to keep the drapes facing the street closed. I don't think that anyone is close enough to see on the other sides."

"Great. So we'll have dinner out on Friday night and then 'sneak' me into your house after it's dark?"

"Sounds good to me. I can't wait to see you in our big jacuzzi tub." He held up his glass for a toast.

"And you with me," she smiled, as their glasses met.

"Janet, I hate to call you while you're on vacation," she heard Bill Shaw's voice in the handset, "but I think that six or seven of our staff may resign over this ridiculous '911 Live' thing, and I just want to hear from you exactly where you stand."

Janet looked out of the big picture window in her parents' farmhouse living room, across the gently rolling Vermont countryside, in the direction of Lake Champlain. Bill's voice and the awful events of that one night seemed out of place, imposed on so much natural beauty. Janet paused, shifting in her mind back to television programming and out of the peace and quiet of the last several days.

"Are you there? Good. I mean, Janet, if you were thinking about resigning, I might have to reconsider this. But these people are just overreacting to almost nothing."

Janet thought, *OK, Bill, if you mean that, then you owe me one.* She finally said, "Bill, I think that '911 Live' stinks. It ought to be thrown in the trash. But I'm a team player, and I'm not going to resign over this. I do think we at the local level should have more input at Network on potentially controversial shows. And I hope '911 Live' doesn't make it. I know that's a terrible thing for the head of your programming department to say, but you asked me, so I'm telling you."

Bill laughed. "Hey, that's fair. We all have our opinions. And I like your idea on the local input. If I propose to Network that they set up an affiliate commission to do just that, would you like to help me get it started and be our first representative?"

Another pause. "Yes, sure. Anything to weed out these problems before they blow up in our collective faces."

"And, Janet, if by some chance I need you to talk to the press or to anyone else about the show and about why you're *not* resigning, can I count on you? Be completely honest, of course, but let them know why you're staying. Will that be OK?"

"I guess so, as long as I can be truthful."

"Sure, sure—no problem at all. Thanks, Janet. Enjoy your well earned vacation. And I won't forget your support when it's time for your annual review and salary discussion. See you in ten days."

You better remember, Janet thought, as she hung up the phone and went to rejoin Susan, Tommy, and her mother, who were waiting in the car for their annual day trip to Montreal.

"Everybody ready?" Janet asked, as she opened the driver's door to their minivan.

"Yes, sure," said her mother, who had a shopping list of possible Christmas presents to look for. "I've got my sweater in case it gets cool and my heart pills, in case I need them."

At the mention of pills, Susan sat up. "Oh, shoot, I forgot my camera . . . I'll be right back," and she was out the door before anyone could argue.

She took the inside stairs to the second floor two at a time, flung open her bedroom door, and reached under the books and magazines inside her travel bag. There she found her new pack of birth control pills; she had been taking one pill every morning since Sunday. She carefully removed a pill, replaced the compact in her bag, and went into the bathroom. Smiling, she lifted a glass of water to the mirror and said to herself, as she swallowed the pill, "Here's looking at you, Drew." Then she grabbed her camera and vaulted down the stairs and back into the car.

■ ■ ■

FRIDAY, AUGUST 18 ■ "You know, as much as I love you, I think there's an element of second childhood in our relationship," Richard laughed as he turned his car down Devon Drive on Friday night. "OK, this is it, get down." He reached over and brought her head into his lap so that she would not be seen in his car by any of the neighbors.

"An interesting place to hide," she smiled, as he turned into his own driveway and operated the garage door opener. There were a few lights on in the Bryants' home, but they were the lights which they left on whenever they were away. Because their driveways and garages faced each other, the Bryants' home was the only one with a clear view of rooms in the Sullivans' house, primarily the kitchen and breakfast room. The view to and from the other neighbors' homes was obscured by distance or by foliage. But Richard had closed the front drapes before leaving for work that morning, just to be sure.

With the garage door safely down, he smiled again and said, "Later . . . this is what you came to see!" Kristen sat up and pulled her overnight bag out of the back seat. She followed Richard in through the small entrance-way at the back of the kitchen.

"So, this is what a Richard and Janet Sullivan house looks like," Kristen said as she stood in the center of the kitchen and slowly turned around. "Nice kitchen. Very homey. Pictures of the kids on the walls. Let's see more!"

Richard led her on a tour of the entire home, through every room. Kristen was impressed by its simple charm and by the understated but high quality in which it was decorated. "I may wish that Janet would go away," she told him, as they neared the end of the tour in the second floor master bedroom, "but I have to give her high marks for homemaking, particularly since she works."

"I didn't bring you here to talk about Janet," Richard said, holding her to him. "Didn't we decide that the plumbing in the jacuzzi tub needs checking?" Then they kissed in the middle of the floor, and she began undressing him.

Nepravel was delighted by Richard's childishness in bringing Kristen to his house. He had frankly not foreseen this fortuitous turn of events, but it played right into the general plan which they had been working on all these years with him. When the demon pulled himself away ninety minutes later, the well-scrubbed couple were sitting in their robes at the breakfast room table, having the desserts they had brought from the restaurant.

SATURDAY, AUGUST 19 ■ Richard and Kristen were just beginning to stir in the late morning when the doorbell rang. "Ohhhh," Richard groaned, "Who can that be?" He walked quickly to the front window of the bedroom and looked down. It was Amy and Bobbie, standing on the front stoop, looking straight up at him!

"Kids. Susan's friends. Let me go see what they want. I thought Amy was out of town with her parents. I hope that everything's OK. *Please* stay up here, out of sight and hearing," Richard whispered, as he put on his robe and started down the stairs.

"I'll slide down the bannister buck naked in five minutes, so start timing," she laughed after him.

Richard ran his hand through his hair on the way past the mirror in the hall, looked out through the glass by the door, smiled, and opened the front door.

"Hi, Mr. Sullivan," Amy smiled back. "How are you?"

"Just fine, ladies. I'm afraid I got in late from the office and was sleeping in, but I had just stirred when you rang the doorbell. What's up? You know Susan's gone."

"Yes, that's why we're here. We'll be spending the night at Bobbie's tonight," Amy said, "and I thought we might miss you with all your work this week. Last night at my house we each wrote a letter to Susan. Would you mind taking them with you when you leave for Vermont this week? And here's your morning paper too."

"Uh, sure, sure." He took the letters and the paper from their outstretched hands. "You were at *your* house last night, Amy? I thought you went to the mountain house."

"My folks did," Amy explained, "and Bobbie's folks are away, too. We didn't want to go, so they let us stay together—last night at our home, tonight at Bobbie's."

"Were you home all night? Did you see anything unusual?" Richard's mind raced back to all of the time he and Kristen had spent together in the kitchen and breakfast room, in plain view of Amy's home, if she or Bobbie had looked.

"No, why, Mr. Sullivan? What do you mean?" Amy asked.

Richard looked closely and could detect no duplicity in either of their expressions. "Well, nothing really. I just meant that you were alone. You should have called me."

The two girls smiled. "Oh, thanks a lot. We were OK. We rented a movie and then talked on the phone in my room most of the night. Everything was fine. And tonight we'll be at Bobbie's." They turned and walked down the front steps. "Have a nice weekend, Mr. Sullivan, and tell Susan and Tommy hello for us when you see them. Goodbye." They waved to him.

"Goodbye, girls. I'll give these letters to Susan. See you next Sunday, when we get home."

Richard felt like he had just dodged a bullet. He closed the door, put the letters on the hall table, poured two coffees in the kitchen, walked up to his room, and handed Kristen a mug. "*That* was close," he said, taking off his robe and joining her on the bed with the paper. "They were next door all night. We're lucky they never saw us. That would have been real easy to explain!" He managed a small laugh, the tension starting to ebb.

"Why, sure," she smiled mischievously, exaggerating her southern accent again, as she took the paper out of his hand, "your cowgirl niece from Texas showed up unexpectedly, and all she wanted to do was ride the horsey . . ."

Nepravel, circling through, smiled as well. "Amy and Bobbie didn't see you, Richard, because it was not time . . . Not quite time . . . but soon!"

That Saturday night, at Amy's insistence, she and Jay double dated with Bobbie and Thomas. "I want to see what you two do!" Amy had told Bobbie, smiling, but also quite seriously curious.

Ever since the previous weekend, from the slumber party to the youth group to the service, Amy had been thinking about what she had seen and heard. She was attracted by these Christian people and their behavior, and she was curious about their beliefs, which seemed to be so strong and confident. So she went to church again with the Merediths on the Sunday after Susan left for Vermont and arranged this weekend to be as much a repeat of the previous two as she could.

Jay was a little on edge, knowing that this particular double date would keep them off the cul-de-sac again. Amy had not let him park there since the slumber party two weeks before. And he knew that these kids were somehow indirectly responsible for Amy's new "go slow" attitude. He obviously didn't appreciate it, and he was so desperate for time with Amy that he had even agreed to go to church with her on Sunday! *I must be crazy,* he thought.

But whatever the teenagers felt, Nepravel was furious. He had heard through Balzor that Susan was in good shape, out of town and taking her pills. But Amy was another matter. He and Zloy had been pulling out all the stops in their repertoire of voices, but she was just hearing the Word too much. And reading it in that blasted Bible Glenn had given her! She was actually reading the Gospel of John in the morning and at night. The demons were appalled, because they knew the typical result.

When they tried Unworthy on her, it almost backfired. She started to think about the abortion and the prayers of the young people, and she considered the possibility that she had actually killed a living baby, part of God's creation. As sometimes happened with Unworthy, when people really hit bottom, they stop defending themselves, and began looking for help. Amy was almost there, so Pride would not be much help in her case, either. Zloy and Nepravel therefore decided to back off and to stick with Doubt and Confusion.

They played up the questions in her mind about how real this could all be, with people actually experiencing this power. How could that be? Luckily, a Christian day school counselor was indicted that week for child abuse, and a prominent married pastor admitted openly to an affair with his secretary of fourteen years. They played these images in front of Amy as often as possible, trying to persuade her that these Christians, like Bobbie and the rest, were basically hypocrites. But unfortunately for the demons, Amy had Bobbie right there, and Amy knew that Bobbie was no hypocrite. So it was a nip and tuck battle for Amy's soul, which could go either way, and Balzor watched the events from his perch over their sector.

The double date was superbly low key, and Amy had to admit she actually had a lot of fun, knowing that the sexual "maneuver" was not even going to come up that night. Then the youth group and the service at Morningside were as powerful as the previous two weeks, and even Jay seemed moved by the strong testimony of a converted drug dealer/hit man. Amy was still feeling her way, checking out everyone involved, listening a little to Doubt, not quite ready to make a commitment, but she obviously liked what she saw in the kids and in the adults associated with Morningside. And she wanted to see more.

THURSDAY, AUGUST 24 ■ Early Thursday morning Richard caught a flight with connections to put him into Burlington at 1:00 that afternoon. Janet, Susan, and Tommy were waiting for him, tanned and looking very happy. There were hugs all around, and since he had only his overnight bag, they went directly to the van.

During the ride to Janet's parents' home, Susan and Tommy told Richard all about the latest news with the Vermont friends they kept up with every summer. There were two families, the Battens and the Wildes, with farms and lots of kids on either side of Janet's parents', and these children enjoyed the Sullivans' visit every summer as well. Tommy and Susan also told their father about the new horse they both rode almost every day. The weather had been great, and Richard noted that Janet looked really good, having benefited from plenty of rest and outdoor activities.

"Everything is fine back home," he announced, "and Susan, here are letters for you from Amy and Bobbie. They brought them over on Saturday." Susan opened them and began reading.

After a huge meal that night, the four adults sat together on the porch and discussed topics ranging from family members to national politics. Richard enjoyed Janet's parents and their simple but dedicated lifestyle as working dairy farmers. It was a world totally foreign to his own experience, except on these visits. But he understood hard work and could see the results every year. He also understood getting up at 4:00 every morning, with hardly a break, and he respected his parents-in-law for their single-minded dedication to all that had to be done on their farm.

While the adults talked on the porch, Tommy watched television alone and reflected on a singular experience of that afternoon. After bringing his dad to his grandparents' home, he took off on his bike for the Battens' farm. Ever since they had been coming to Vermont, Tommy had played with Caroline Batten, who was his age, along with her older and younger brothers. Caroline had always been a tomboy, wearing her blonde hair in pigtails and hitting a baseball as far as any of the boys. But something had happened to her in the past year. Tommy barely recognized her when they arrived. She was rounder and curvy and even seemed to walk differently. It occurred to Tommy on their second day there that Caroline was simply beautiful. When she smiled at him, he felt a strange stiffness in his chest.

Then today, when he arrived at the Battens' farm, he found only Caroline and her mother at home. "Come on, Tommy, let's go feed the chickens," Caroline suggested, as she bounded out the kitchen door. Tommy enjoyed all the farm chores, since he only had to do them for two weeks, and he liked to help. So they started off down the short gravel road which led to the chickens' half of an old barn.

Once out of sight behind the barn, as they came close together to open the gate, Caroline said, "I hate it that you already have to go home on Saturday." And then she leaned over and kissed him. Tommy had to steady himself on the gate, he was so surprised. This wonderful, beautiful girl, whom he had known every summer of his life, must like him! She kissed him!

He had no idea what to do. So in self-defense, he smiled and said, "I hate it, too. And you sure are beautiful, Caroline." And he kissed her back, tentatively putting a hand on her shoulder. For the next five minutes, they kissed and hugged, standing behind the barn. Then they heard her father's tractor coming and had to return to the chores. But Tommy was not sure that his bike wheels ever touched the ground on the way back to his grandparents' house that afternoon. And now, as he sat in front of the television, he was thinking about Caroline, and what this all meant.

Susan, who had left the porch, sat in a big armchair in her room and reread her two letters. Both Bobbie and Amy recounted their activities during the first week of Susan's vacation. But then, almost as if they had planned it, both letters urged her to go slow with the birth control pills. Amy's letter was the more remarkable. She wrote that she had been back to Bobbie's church, and that she was rethinking many things, including her "physical relationship" with Jay. Amy admonished her not to begin taking the pill and not to become physically involved with Drew.

The second time through these letters made Susan even more angry than the first time. "Wonderful advice from girls who hardly even know Drew, and certainly don't know him the way I do!" a voice told her, as she thought of Drew and imagined how far away he was. "Bobbie has her God to keep her happy—at least she sure likes to tell us so—and Amy hops into bed with a college guy she hardly knows—probably two—has an abortion, and then tries to tell me to go slow!"

Almost before she could think it, a voice reminded her that she and Drew had known each other for a year and had been dating for several months. They had expressed their love for each other. Drew was a great guy, and she was *not* going to get pregnant. So why not express her love in the way God—or Nature, or someone—had provided? And, the voice told her, she certainly didn't need Amy and Bobbie to be her new moral policewomen!

■   ■   ■

Later, Richard lay in bed next to Janet as she slept, listening to her breathing and to the total silence of the Vermont night. As often happened to him in settings like this, he wondered what it would be like to give up his law practice in the big city and to move to a smaller city or town. Not Vermont, probably, but one of the towns within a couple of hours of their city. What sort of a life would they have? Could he earn a living? Would there still be a "rat race"? Or would he come home at five in the afternoon and play tennis with Susan or baseball with Tommy? How would the kids grow up differently? Would it be better . . . or boring?

As he reflected on the possibilities, a voice reminded him that Susan and Tommy would be gone to college in a few years. So a home in a small town would be just as empty as a home in the city. Whatever the kids were going to be was pretty much set. There was no reason to think about moving when they had so many friends and opportunities where they were. As he rose up on one elbow and looked across the dark but peaceful countryside outside the second floor window, he felt a distant sadness, as if the choices he made twenty years ago were now unfolding before his eyes, and he was powerless to stop them. But maybe if they moved, there could be a different ending . . .

SATURDAY, AUGUST 26 ■ On Saturday morning they packed the minivan for the trip home, and everyone said a tearful goodbye. "Please fly down for Christmas," Janet told her mother.

"Sure wish you could stay another day and go to church with us tomorrow," Janet's father told Richard, as he did every year.

"It's just too far to drive in one day." Richard smiled and thanked him, as he also did every year. Susan and her parents were surprised to see Caroline Batten there so early in the morning to say goodbye to Tommy. This was a new and unexpected development, but the three of them had the good taste not to press Tommy about her on their trip home.

SUNDAY, AUGUST 27 ■ Late Sunday afternoon the Sullivans arrived home. Amy and her parents heard them drive in next door and came out to help them unpack. Tommy was soon off for Brent's house, and the two girls went up to Susan's room to look at her photographs from the vacation. Nancy talked with Janet while she unloaded the laundry.

Tom went into his garage and returned. "Richard, I found these tools and your jumper cables and bolt cutter up at our mountain house. Remember when I borrowed all of these during our construction?"

"Yea, sure. Here, just put them in the trunk of my car for now," Richard said, tossing Tom his keys, as he gathered a load from the minivan. "I'll sort through all of them later, and at least I'll have the cables if I need them."

Upstairs, Amy and Susan sat on her bed while Susan called Drew to let him know that they had arrived home safely. "Yes, sure, I don't see why not. Give me a little while to get cleaned up. Come over about 6:30. I love you." And Susan hung up the phone.

"Drew asked me out to dinner," Susan smiled at Amy. "How are you and Jay?"

"He's fine. We went to a movie last night. But I've put my foot down about going slow for now, and he doesn't like it."

"Why did you do that? I read your letter, but I don't really understand."

"Well, I've gone to Bobbie's church four Sundays in a row now, counting this morning. Every time I've attended both the youth group and the service, like you did. I don't know, it's like something Glenn said last week. Like I never realized I was thirsty, but suddenly I'm drinking water, and I like it. I don't think I've really changed, maybe, but they're challenging me to think about a lot of stuff, and until I get it figured out, I told Jay I don't want to complicate things even more with sex."

"Well I'm glad for you. And you've obviously had more experiences than I have. But Drew and I love each other, and I'm seventeen, and I'm ready to share that love in any way he wants," Susan said, feeling more certain of herself as she heard her own words. She began to unbutton her shirt, to take a shower.

"Mom," she called downstairs, "Drew and I are going out tonight, so don't count me in for dinner."

"Susan," Amy said, getting up to leave, "I know how stupid this sounds, coming from me, after what I've done, and how you've helped me in the past few months. But having sex is powerful. Just like our parents and teachers have told us, it changes things. Besides babies and diseases, which I know you don't expect," Amy raised her hand as Susan turned to say something, "there's just the change in the relationship itself. I can't really explain it, but it happens. Once you've done it, you can't go back. I do know that. I just wish . . ."

"Look, thanks a lot," Susan interrupted. "You're right. We've been through quite a bit. And in some ways I guess I'm jealous of your experiences. People are different, and Drew is not Billy or Jay. We love each other. I think our relationship will only get better. Now, I have to get ready. See you tomorrow."

Three hours later, parked in the cul-de-sac, after a casual supper at Austin's, where they had caught up on the last two weeks' news, Drew and Susan were now experiencing the pent-up emotion caused by their absence.

Susan pulled back from a long kiss and smiled up at Drew. "I've been taking the birth control pills, just like I promised. I love you so much."

"I love you too," Drew whispered back in her ear, hugging her.

"But I can't imagine making love in a car, Drew. What are we going to do?"

Drew thought for a moment. "I think I can rent a motel room over on the interstate, where no one will know us or ask questions. I can use a fictitious name, pay cash, and then come to get you. No one will ever know."

"A motel room? Do you think you can?" She smiled, imagining how nice that would be. "But we couldn't spend the whole night."

"I know. I'll pay up front in cash, and then we'll just leave in time to get home. It'll work. When . . . ?" He smiled down at her.

"Well, since school starts on Thursday, and I have to work tomorrow night, what about Tuesday?"

"Sounds great to me." Drew returned her smile. "I'll drive over and get the room and then pick you up about 6:30. If I have a problem, I'll call."

Susan snuggled in close to him. "I can't wait. I love you so much. Drew, do you think we can apply to the same colleges this fall? Wouldn't it be great if we could spend four years together at school?"

That thought sounded like a prison term to Drew. But focusing more on Tuesday than on next fall, he hugged her tightly and said, "Yes, that would be fantastic."

"Oh, and be sure to bring a condom," she added. "I've been taking these pills, but it's only been two weeks, and I want to be *real* sure I don't get pregnant!"

12

MONDAY, AUGUST 28 ■ "Bill," Tom Spence said as he stood in front of the station manager's desk, "I understand that '911 Live' is starting in three weeks, on September 15, two weeks before the rest of the new season."

"That's right. They think it's such a strong show that Network is going to use it as the lead-in to introduce the other new shows. And they want to have as many weeks as possible with sunlight, before daylight savings time ends, after which everything will have to be on floodlights."

"Have you considered our request to cancel the show or to move it to later at night?"

"Yes, of course. I've considered it. But I'm not going to do either one."

"Well, I'm sorry for all of us, then, but more importantly I'm sorry for our country. I expect you'll have several resignations on your desk today, effective next Tuesday, the day after Labor Day."

"I'm sorry, too, Tom. You, Connie, and the rest are good people. I respect your opinions, but I obviously don't agree with them."

"Since I'm resigning Bill, I want you to know that this show is the work of the devil. It's that simple. He's using you and Network to even further demean individuals, families, and all the values on which this nation was built. It's so obvious, if you just look back over the last twenty years."

Smiling, Bill responded, "And since you're resigning, Tom, I can finally tell you you're crazy. There's no such thing as the devil, and if there were, he'd have a lot more important things to do than to worry about this one small television station. Please do say at your press conference, if you have one, that the devil is behind this show. I can't wait to hear the reaction!"

As Tom closed the door to Bill Shaw's office, Kromor and his two lieutenants, floating over Bill's desk, gave each other high fives. "The work of the devil! Can you imagine!" Kromor laughed. "I'm sure glad Bill set him straight." And they all laughed again.

"Richard, the news this morning is that a German firm has bought Princeton Textiles, the number three producer, and is planning to do heavy investments in robotics," Bruce said over the phone late that morning, with obvious concern in his voice. "This could mean another beating for Fairchild's stock price. What exactly happens if the price *does* fall below twenty, with the closing so close?"

"It means they can call the closing off, and the deal dies, if the price falls below twenty for a week prior to the scheduled closing. I'm sure they're watching the price, too, Bruce. It gives them the opportunity to cancel the deal or at least to renegotiate it with us. I just can't believe this is happening," Richard said, anger in his voice.

"Hey, I hate it, too, Richard. It's not my fault, you know. I have as much or more to lose as you do. What should we do?"

"You and Patrick Tomlinson struck the original deal, Bruce. This is not a legal question—it's business. Why don't you call Patrick, and you and David get on a plane and go see him? Then I'll do whatever I can to help on the legal end."

"OK. You're right. I'll call him and see what his schedule looks like. Thanks, Richard. I guess you should keep working on the documents, and we'll try to settle the business side. I'll keep you informed about what's happening," and he hung up.

Richard felt his $66,000 fee slipping away, and he hated it. He slammed his fist on the desk, got up, and paced around the office, swearing.

Just before noon Tom Spence stopped by Janet's office. "I realize you've just returned from vacation, but Connie and I want you to know that we're turning in our resignations this afternoon, effective next Tuesday. We hate to leave, but we don't believe we have any other choice."

Janet had hoped that some other solution would be found, and she regretted watching this good group of old friends breaking up. "Do you have any other jobs lined up?" she asked, genuinely concerned.

"Sam Tarrant has found a small station out on the west coast that needs a senior technician. The rest of us will start looking in earnest after our press conference."

"When will that be?"

"Tuesday at noon at the Palace Hotel. That will be about ten days before '911 Live' is scheduled to start—right after Labor Day, so we hope there will be some impact."

"Well, Tom, I have to thank you indirectly for one of the most exciting and disturbing evenings of my life." Her smile turned serious. "But I guess if you are going to blast Network and the station, then we're on opposite sides now."

"Are we Janet?"

"Neither one of us likes that show, but I've chosen to remain inside the system, and you've decided that you have to leave. So I imagine we may butt heads on this one. It's a shame, but it may happen."

"Be careful, Janet. You can start out from what seems like a reasonable position, and pretty soon they'll own your soul, if you're not careful."

"Thanks, Tom. I'm a big girl, and I'll watch out. Don't worry about me. I can handle it. Here, let me give you a hug, for old times' sake. You be careful, too. You've got a family and no job, come Tuesday."

Janet stood up and walked around her desk. They hugged in the middle of her office. "I really respect all seven of you, Tom. Good luck."

He had not been gone more than five minutes when the intercom buzzed from Bill Shaw's office, and he asked Janet to come up.

"It's great to have you back, Janet," Bill said, as she took the seat he offered in his office. "I hope you had a wonderful vacation." She nodded in the affirmative.

"Good, then. Tom Spence came by this morning," Bill continued, "to tell me that seven of them are going to resign, effective next Tuesday."

"Yes, he just left my office with the same news."

"Did he give you any details about their plans?"

"Only that they're planning a press conference for noon that day at the Palace Hotel."

"Great. Thorn Glass from Network and I have been talking, and we've worked out the beginning of a plan. It may involve you, so I'd like your input,"

"Shoot," said Janet, not realizing the irony in her response.

TUESDAY, AUGUST 29 ■ At Tuesday's "lunch," Kristen, who had not seen Richard for almost a week, was again persistent about their future. She had thought more, during his absence in Vermont, about taking matters into her own hands. But she wanted to hear from him first. As she left their bed to fetch some bread and fruit, she turned, and, pulling her hair back with both hands while silhouetted in the bedroom doorway, said, "Richard, the summer is almost over. Your kids will be starting back to school in a matter of days. When are you ever going to tell Janet about us, so that we can get on with *our* life together?"

"Kristen, it's so difficult. I just don't know what to do."

"Well," she asked, as she stretched her body with her hands now over her head, "is it Janet, or is it the kids, who keep you there?"

"Oh, it's the kids," he lied once again, not wanting to tell her the truth, that he and Janet were slowly but steadily improving their relationship.

"So if Janet were gone, but you could still have a good relationship with the children, then that would be OK?" she called from the kitchen.

"Yes, I guess so. But I don't see how that's possible," he said. *And I don't really want it,* he added silently to himself.

"Well, my Texas grandfather had a saying," she said, returning and sitting down across from him on the bed, the bowl of fruit in her lap. "'Be careful what you ask for, 'cause you might get it.'" She smiled and offered him a bunch of grapes. He took them and smiled back, not really understanding, but always delighted to talk with her about almost anything, when he had so many freckles in so many great places to look at.

That afternoon, Bruce McKinney called Richard again. "Patrick Tomlinson has a tough schedule for the next two weeks, but luckily he's coming here at the end of next week, on Friday, to spend the weekend. He was amenable to us getting together on Friday night for supper; and he will even have his attorney with him, on some other business. So David and I would like for you to join us, and the five of us will have a nice dinner. Then maybe we'll relax, do something like the Platinum Club, let our hair down a bit, to strengthen the relationship. Can you make it that night?"

"Let's see. Yes, looks fine. We're having a quiet, stay-at-home Labor Day, after the recent trip to Vermont. Next Friday looks fine. And I haven't been to the Platinum Club in a year. Are you sure it's Tomlinson's cup of tea?"

"Absolutely. He even asked me about it. Said he'd heard of it, but had never been there. And, by the way, Richard, he was very laid back on the telephone. Maybe he's watching the stock and preparing to nail us. But he sounded happy to meet and to have dinner with us, so maybe it will all work out."

"I hope so. The documents are almost ready. We've penciled in the closing date for Friday, September 15."

"We'll all keep our fingers crossed. Goodbye Richard."

Tuesday night Susan was ready for her date with Drew thirty minutes early. She had been imagining this night for a month, and during her bath a voice had reminded her of how lucky she was to be loved by one of the best "catches" in her class. She knew that many other girls were envious of her good fortune. The plan was that he would drive over and rent a room, then pick her up. She told her mother they were going out for supper and would then go to a movie or play miniature golf or "something." As she was brushing her hair in her bathroom, checking her looks for the twentieth time, she smiled to herself at how easy it had become to lie to her parents, in just the few short months since that night with Amy. *Well, not lie, actually*, Nepravel reminded her in her own voice. *It's just better that they not know everything.* And she smiled again.

Drew was right on time, and said hello to Janet and Richard as he waited for Susan to come down. "With school starting Thursday, I guess you, Susan and the rest of your class will be applying for college soon," Richard said. "Where are you planning to apply?"

Before Drew could reply, Susan came down the stairs. Both men thought she looked stunning, even in that evening's casual dress. Richard was pleased that she was growing up to be such a happy, attractive young woman. And Drew was already imagining their evening's activities. Nepravel, who came down with Susan and was now perched above the kitchen cabinets, laughed at the dichotomy in the two men's minds over one woman. "If only *they* could read each other's thoughts!" he smiled to himself.

As Richard watched his daughter and Drew walk out to Drew's car, holding hands, he turned to Janet and said, "Drew seems like such a good guy. I hope Susan stays happy with him. And maybe someday, when the time is right, she'll meet somebody like him and get married. I guess it won't be too long now, Janet. When did we get so old?" he smiled at her.

"Oh, I hope we still have quite a few years before that, Richard. But Drew *is* a nice boy. I think he does well in school. And the main thing is that I trust him with Susan," Janet said, putting their own supper in the oven.

"Did you get the room?" Susan asked, as soon as they were in the car.

"Sure, no problem," he smiled. He pulled the key to room 272 at the Pilgrim Lodge out of his pocket and handed it to her. "The room is on the second floor, and around back. We can park right by the stairs, and no one will see us."

She handled the key like it was something magical. Their very own motel room! She slid over close to Drew and whispered in his ear, "I love you." Nepravel, who wouldn't miss an evening like this for anything except a death, turned up the voices of Lust and Passion in both of them, in case either of them started to have second thoughts. But he knew that at their age, and with so much planning already invested, there was little chance of that.

They rode to the motel without saying much, each lost in imagining what the next few hours would be like. Susan imagined a large, sunny room with a balcony and white curtains blowing in the breeze. Drew imagined Susan.

When they arrived, they parked next to the stairs, as Drew had predicted. At that hour the parking lot was still almost empty. Standing outside the motel room door, Susan giggled when Drew at first couldn't open it. When the door finally opened, the first impression was the stale smell of twenty years' of cigarette smoke. As they walked in, Susan noticed the cheap, dark wood paneling and the two double beds with faded brown bedspreads. Drew closed and locked the door, turned and smiled. Suddenly Susan wanted to run. She felt as if cold water had been thrown on her. This was not what she had been imagining for the past month or in her bath that afternoon. Or in her dreams since she was a little girl. This was not a handsome husband in a magnificent bridal suite at an expensive hotel in Europe. This was a cheap motel room with a high school student who said that he loved her. But did he? And what if he did? Was this how she wanted to make love the first time? What about getting married first?

Nepravel was right there and heard the questions in Susan's mind. Immediately he sought to reassure her and to relax her with the voice of Passion. *Of course he loves me*, she heard herself saying. *And he is so good to me . . . if I don't go through with this after all these plans, I'll never see him again! Mom even said that this is what life is all about.* Drew took her in his arms and kissed her. The voice continued inside her, *Probably we will get married . . . and even if we don't, we love each other . . . not like Amy and Billy . . . and what he is doing feels so good . . . he must love me.*

So the small voice of Truth in her conscience was overwhelmed by the other voices, telling her to give in to her passion. And Susan simply had no other defense to fight with. She was no match for the forces working toward this moment in her life for so many years: the movies and television she watched, the magazines and the ads she read, the CDs she played, even the advice from her mother. All had told her to go ahead, to give in to "true love" and to passion, two of the most revered qualities in America, judging from the time spent selling them. With no counterbalances in her life, how could she really be expected to do anything else?

So for the first time she lay down on a bed with a boy, and even though they were both novices, their lust went on automatic pilot. They had both seen enough movies and television so that there was no mystery about what they were supposed to do. A few minutes later, as Drew fumbled again, this time with the condom, they both laughed and said at the same time, "Just like in sex education class!" That really broke the ice, and, in a strange way, legitimized in Susan's mind what they were doing. They had practiced! The final lie, after so many others, reassured her, in a clear voice, "This is OK. Go ahead. Don't worry about later. He loves you."

Later that night over the city, the dark forces who hate humans were pleased to hear of Susan and Drew's decision to have intercourse. They knew that this one act could now set up other important hurdles to prevent them from hearing about Jesus: guilt, disease, unworthiness, bad company, gossip, and on and on. Until widespread drug use came along to destroy parts of the population, sex had always been their greatest weapon to tempt humans away from a happy life. And it would always be very powerful.

But as pleased as Balzor and his lieutenants were about Drew and Susan, they were just as concerned about Amy, who continued to go to church with Bobbie, read her Bible, and had even started praying, motivated by a desire to help Susan.

"What is your plan to prevent her from becoming a Christian?" Balzor asked Nepravel and Zloy.

"She's still only looking," Nepravel volunteered to his master. "She has not yet decided to submit her life to that cursed Son of God, nor has she prayed the Holy Spirit into her life."

"But if she hangs around with that Meredith girl and continues going to Morningside Church, it could happen any day now. And then we will lose her, and you two will be to blame!"

"We plan," Zloy interjected, "now that Susan has joined her in experiencing sex at seventeen, to use the Sullivan girl to pull Amy back, away from Bobbie and all of her influences."

"Well, you better be quick about it." Balzor dismissed them with a blast of scalding flame and went on to the next demon's nightly report.

THURSDAY, AUGUST 31 ■ Amy, Bobbie, Susan, and Drew started their senior year at Northpark High that Thursday. Susan had decided that she would not volunteer to her two friends what she and Drew had done, given their previous advice, but would instead just let the information drop when the time was right. Since Tuesday night, Susan had felt a strange mixture of gain and loss. She now knew something adults know, but some part of her regretted knowing it, no matter how much she tried to silence those thoughts. Sex was now a part of her relationship with Drew, and, like Amy, Susan was realizing that this meant a complexity and a force she had not anticipated.

Just as significant as the physical loss of her virginity was the sudden difference in their relationship. Drew had already asked her if she wanted to go to the motel again on Saturday night. Was this going to be their standard date now? And she could not shake the feeling that she had done something wrong, no matter how many voices reassured her that she was just fine. As she walked in from the parking lot at school that morning, Drew met her, gave her a quick kiss, and put his arm around her. *It really will be OK,* she thought.

MONDAY, SEPTEMBER 4 ■ The Sullivans enjoyed a low-key Labor Day, joining their neighbors on Monday afternoon at the park to play tennis and softball and to enjoy their traditional neighborhood cookout. Bobbie, Thomas, and Drew joined the neighborhood party. Jay's interest in Amy had waned in the past weeks, so she was alone that weekend, but she didn't mind. There were some interesting guys from other schools at Morningside's youth group, where she was now a regular, and she decided that her social life had not ended with Jay's departure.

Between the trip to Vermont and excuses of one form or another, Tommy had managed not to spend an evening with the older boys since that night at Freddie's house. His experience with Caroline Batten in Vermont had caught his attention, and each had written a letter to the other. In school some of the boys in the crowd with whom he had been spending time almost surrounded him in the hall and asked him when he was going out with them again. He had put them off, too. But here at the Labor Day cookout, Brent told him, as they rode their bikes around the park, that on Friday night the "old gang" with whom they had started, were going to the adult book store again, renting videos, and camping out in his basement, while his parents would be gone.

"I don't know, Brent. That night at Freddie's was pretty heavy. I may want to move on. That group is a little too far out for me. I mean having fun together is OK, but there's this girl, Caroline. I don't know."

"Come on and join us, Tommy. You know it's fun. And it doesn't hurt anybody. We're going to get both girl and boy videos this time."

Tommy, still confused about virtually everything associated with his emotions and wanting to please his friend, agreed in the end to join them, at least this one more time.

TUESDAY, SEPTEMBER 5 ■ On Tuesday morning at 9:00, Tom Spence stopped by Bill Shaw's office to say goodbye. He had cleaned out his desk over the long Labor Day weekend, and this morning he was ending his career with the station where he had worked for longer than he cared to admit.

"I'm sorry, Mr. Spence," Bill's secretary greeted him, "but Mr. Shaw is not in this morning, and we don't expect him until after lunch."

Tom headed downstairs to Janet's office to say goodbye, but she was not in either. Her secretary was more helpful. "She's at a network press conference with Mr. Shaw."

"Press conference?" Tom asked. "Our group has scheduled one at noon. That's the only one I know about. Is there another? Where is it?"

"It's at 10:00, I think, at the Palace Hotel. Bob Grissom, the producer of '911 Live,' flew in early this morning for it." Tom suddenly felt sick to his stomach.

He quickly found all the others who were resigning that morning, or left notes on their desks, then drove downtown to the Palace. On the way he called Connie, who was still at home, and told her what was happening. Because she lived downtown, they arrived at the Palace Hotel at about the same time and met outside the large meeting room, where a sign on a tripod read:

10:00 Network "911 Live" Press Conference
12:00 "911 Live" Press Conference

Inside, the room was packed, and Tom was interested to see that both the other local television stations were covering the event, along with TV5. *Bill must have called them personally,* he thought.

At a little after the appointed hour, Bob Grissom, Bill Shaw, and Janet Sullivan walked up on the small dais, and Bob Grissom addressed his fellow members of the media.

"This fall our network will be kicking off a new show which will utilize the absolute latest in communications technology to bring you the best and most interesting cases of our nation's finest 911 emergency personnel in action, live. We're calling the show '911 Live.' We think it will break new ground in broadcast journalism and set a pace for others to try to emulate, if they can. I have the privilege of being the show's producer. We are very excited about the show's potential to inform our audience of what is happening in our nation's larger cities, *as it happens.* We are proud of this show and the technological challenges we have overcome in order to make it possible. There is a page in the press kit you received this morning that details all of these breakthroughs, as well as the system we will use to link the cities together.

"But there is apparently a small, vocal group who do not agree with us and who want to stop this show for their own purposes. As you may know, we tested all of the command and control concepts for '911 Live' right here in your city two months ago. Two of those who volunteered for that duty, who are avowed Christian fundamentalists, have now decided that the show needs censorship, and they have encouraged others at our local affiliate here, TV5, to quit their jobs over this show. We detest censorship in any form, as I'm sure you do, and we hate to see good people talked into giving up their jobs over a personal opinion.

"But looking beyond these immediate motivations, we can in fact understand how this show may be so new and so dynamic that it might give some people, even good and unprejudiced people, some pause, because of its potential for immediacy.

"And so we have called this press conference to announce three extraordinary steps which we at Network are instituting immediately, in order to show our commitment to broadcast responsibility:

1. We are beginning the show earlier than the rest of the new season so that our audience will have the opportunity to judge its impact as soon as possible, with as little third-party opinion as possible.
2. After the show has been on for eight weeks, in mid-November, we will make ballots available through our major soft drink sponsor on a nationwide basis, and we will allow our audience to vote on whether to keep the show on the air or not. We know of no other previous network commitment to such democracy for a new show. We believe that this pledge speaks for itself in the area of reason and fairness.
3. Finally, in order to ensure the ongoing appropriateness of all of our network's programming, we have created, at the suggestion of your own Bill Shaw, seated behind me, the new Affiliate Advisory Commission, which will review all new shows and concepts to insure that they meet the highest local standards of quality and appropriateness. And I am very pleased to announce that Janet Sullivan, who also participated during our earlier test run at TV5, has agreed to serve as our first chairwoman. Mrs. Sullivan, I might add, also has some problems with '911 Live' in its original format. But she is here today because, unlike the fundamentalists, she is not quitting and is instead working to improve broadcasting from the inside. We salute her and welcome her to this new, important position."

Janet nodded.

"Now, that is the end of my prepared remarks. If you have any questions for me or my colleagues, please go ahead and ask. Oh, and don't forget to watch the first '911 Live' next Friday, September 15, at 7:30. Thank you."

Tom, Connie, and three of the others from their group who arrived at the hotel in time sat in the back of the room, stunned. Tom, who had been around television the longest, had to give it to the network—they had turned every possible negative into a positive statement for the show. He knew their own press conference in ninety minutes would now be an uphill battle, at best. Bob Grissom had signaled his allies in the media that the folks who had called the later conference were the worst types imaginable:

Christian fundamentalists! Even a competing television news department would shelve its normal policy of not discussing another network's shows and carry the story about the TV5 show, if it was a chance to bash the fundamentalists, who were perceived as their common enemy. Yes, Tom had to admit, the early press conference was brilliant and would result in more publicity for '911 Live,' probably on a national basis, than Network could ever have purchased.

A reporter was asking Janet a question about her differences with the show and with the fundamentalists who were quitting.

"Well, I must say that they are good people, many of whom I have known for a long time. I just think they have been almost brainwashed over this one issue." Tom cringed at her choice of words, knowing he would hear them repeated later. "As for the show itself, I worry about what might be broadcast into living rooms at that hour. But Network has already agreed to review the whole concept in November, after our commission is operating and the vote from our viewers is in. I think their approach is very forward thinking and fair. I believe that if changes are warranted, Network will make them."

"Good luck," Tom said, almost loud enough to be heard. He suddenly had a splitting headache and could not believe how Bob and Bill had used Janet so obviously and so quickly. Didn't she see it? Did she really believe what she was saying? What about that little boy, Eddie Barnes, in the burning car? What would *he* say about "911 Live"?

The conference was breaking up. Tom and the other "fundamentalists" sat in the back of the room, not saying a word, as Bill, Janet, and Bob left by the center aisle. Bill stopped to shake Tom's hand, Janet standing behind him. Tom did not stand up, so Bill patted him on the shoulder and wished him good luck.

Tom turned in his chair, looking up at Bill and Janet. "Since we are so fundamental, we have decided to pray between now and our own press conference. And we will pray for you, Bill, and for the station. Thanks for the vote of confidence, Janet. Next time I go to see Eddie Barnes after one of his skin grafts, I'll give him your best."

"That's all right, Tom. I'll do it myself, the next time I go to see him. I'm sorry for you, Tom; I think you really are brainwashed. We'll change the show, but from the inside." And she left with the two men.

Tom and his group filed out and talked in the hall. Connie left to get her car, and the rest of them found an empty, smaller conference room, where they circled some chairs and prayed for the next hour, interceding for the station, its personnel, the network, and the nation.

"Richard, the Fairchild stock price opened at 21 this morning, but already it's at 19.5," Bruce announced. "That's the first time it's been below 20 in several years. I swear, these slow estate tax attorneys! We should have closed our deal months ago."

"I agree," Richard said, "but here we are. Unless Tomlinson or his attorney calls one of us, let's just soldier on as if nothing had happened, and listen to what they have to say on Friday night."

"That's about all we can do. See you then, Richard."

At noon most of the newspaper and television reporters who had covered the earlier meeting reassembled in the same room for the second press conference. Connie had not yet returned, so Tom Spence and the other five members of their group took their seats around the podium, and then Tom rose and started with his prepared remarks.

He made the same case as he and the others had made to the TV5 management over the past several months. He emphasized that they were not advocating censorship, but responsibility. "The government has granted the Network and TV5 the right to broadcast into our homes, and every right also carries responsibilities," he said. "We feel that '911 Live' violates those responsibilities on several counts." And he listed them for the reporters.

As a result of the previous conference, Tom added to his text that each of them had made an individual decision, not aided or coerced by the other. He quickly reviewed their previous frustrations with changing Network policies and called for a public response to both TV5 and to Network to cancel or to reposition the show.

Once he finished his remarks, the reporters started asking questions.

"Is it true that you are all Christian fundamentalists?"

"It happens that we are all Christian believers—I'm not sure how to define a fundamentalist," Tom answered. "But this issue is far broader than any one faith. It has to do with families and simple decency and government licenses. Those are the issues we should be focused on."

"Aren't you calling for internal censorship, which has been a plank of the Christian right wing for years?"

"Again, I'm glad that I'm a Christian, but that's not the issue today. If internal censorship means the decision makers at Network decide not to show a particular show because it is inappropriate or in poor taste, then I guess the answer is yes."

The questions continued on this line for several more minutes, and the conference was becoming a religious debate, when the back door of the room opened and Connie walked in, holding Eddie Barnes' hand. Eddie's father pushed his wheelchair. They came right to the dais, and Eddie, who still had bandages on his neck and the back of his head, smiled and waved to the reporters. Several waved back.

Tom spoke. "We could debate this show all day on theoretical grounds, with little result. Instead, let me introduce you to a very brave and very lucky young man and to his father. We met them in that awful interstate wreck you may have seen 'featured' in the '911 Live' promotions. Ladies and gentlemen, the truth is that but for the grace of God and for two firefighters arriving just when they did, we all would have watched Eddie burned alive, right before our eyes, during that evening's dessert."

There was a gasp from the reporters. Tom continued, "While we of course cannot provide you with the video, since it is not ours, we have obtained these color pictures, taken of the crash and of Eddie, by a motorist who happened to have a camera in his car. We have twenty copies of the set of ten prints. And we ask you to imagine these views live and in color in your home, with your children watching."

The pictures were passed out, and the reporters started directing questions to Eddie, his father, and Connie. The last-minute decision to invite Eddie had the anticipated effect, even on a hardened press corps looking for reasons to shoot holes in their story. After thirty more minutes, Tom was sure that the reporters' stories would at least be balanced and questioning, not just repeating Network's viewpoint. His only regret was to be creating so much publicity for the show, but they had prayed and decided that they had no other choice.

WEDNESDAY, SEPTEMBER 6 ■ "Don't forget that this Friday night I'm going out to dinner with Bruce, David, and their investor," Richard reminded Janet over their breakfast the next morning.

"Hmmm? . . . Oh, yes, thanks . . . Richard, I remember." Janet looked up from the morning newspaper. She had been reading the lead article in the local news section about their dual press conferences. The article had a color picture of Eddie Barnes in his father's car, and the headline read, "'911 Live': Are We Ready For It?"

She held the paper up for Richard to see. "Whatever else happens, you have to admit this has turned into a marketing bonanza for us. Why, I bet most televisions in the city will be tuned in to that first show. Bill can ask almost anything he wants for a sixty-second spot. And maybe we really will get the show cleaned up after a few months—or else killed. It looks like a win-win to me. I wish Tom and the others hadn't quit. So senseless."

Richard listened and gave a yes in agreement. He was interested, but for the moment he was more interested in protecting his $66,000 fee from McKinney and Smith, not to mention his $500,000 loan guarantee.

13

FRIDAY, SEPTEMBER 8 ■ Richard met Bruce McKinney and David Smith in the foyer at Bruce's downtown club at 6:15. They discussed together the fact that the Fairchild stock price had stayed below 20 all week, hovering between 17 and 19 until that afternoon, when there had been an up-tick to 19.5 at the end of the day.

"Marty Tsongas and I have worked through all of the documents," Richard said, "and they're ready to go. Frankly, we could close any time now, contingent on what happens this evening."

They did not have long to wait. Patrick Tomlinson and Marty Tsongas came through the front door right at 6:30. There were greetings and handshakes all around before they adjourned to the small private dining room Bruce had reserved for their dinner meeting.

During the excellent meal, the talk was about the McKinney and Smith expansion plans on the one hand and about the freefall of the Fairchild Textile stock on the other. Patrick Tomlinson, in his early thirties, was trying to fill his father's shoes, with the help of old and trusted advisors like Marty Tsongas. Bruce McKinney had begun the relationship with Patrick's father over ten years ago, when he cold-called him on one day and was given the opportunity to invest 10 percent of Mr. Tomlinson's portfolio for twelve months. Bruce did so well with that assignment that their relationship expanded every year, and Patrick grew up in the business hearing his father's praises for the good work of McKinney and Smith.

So it had been a natural for Bruce to approach Mr. Tomlinson to become an investor in their company, and his son had carried on the negotiations after the unexpected death of his father.

As they sipped their coffee at the end of the meal, Bruce McKinney finally brought them to the crucial purpose of the meeting.

"It goes without saying, Patrick, that with the Fairchild stock price now below 20, you have the opportunity to cancel your investment in our company. Obviously we hope that you won't, because we have made plans and are looking forward to having your input on our board. We assume you've followed the Fairchild stock price as closely as we have, and so we're interested in what you intend to do."

Patrick Tomlinson looked up from his coffee and glanced at Marty Tsongas, then proceeded. "Bruce, I know that none of us expected the Fairchild stock price to fall so precipitously, and it would not have except for the recent foreign acquisitions of its competitors. Unfortunately, as you know better than almost anyone, a major portion of our portfolio is still held in Fairchild stock, so there simply is not as much liquidity as we had all expected when these negotiations began.

"Marty and I and others whom I trust have talked about this situation at length, and we would like to propose to you that you consider doing the same transaction, where we purchase the same amount of McKinney and Smith stock, but that the purchase price will have to be reduced from $1,000,000 to $900,000. If you can live with that change, then we are prepared to go ahead with the closing."

Richard held his breath. Although it would be difficult for Bruce and David, the infusion of $900,000 into their company was certainly much better than no infusion of capital at all.

Bruce and David looked at each other. David asked, "Is the change in the price the only modification we have to make?"

"Yes," said Patrick, "there just isn't enough cash in the till. But otherwise we still think very highly of your firm and want to join you in ownership."

"Well, if David says yes, then I certainly do," said Bruce. David smiled and nodded his head. Richard exhaled a great sigh of relief—he could almost see the $66,000 moving back to his side of the table. There were smiles all around.

Bruce reached across and shook Patrick's hand. "Then that's settled, and Richard and Marty can finish up the paperwork. I'd say that this calls for some celebration and relaxation. What do you say we adjourn to the Platinum Club?"

As Richard was finishing his main course downtown, Tommy was headed out the back door to get on his bike to ride over to Brent's house, his overnight bag strapped to the rack. "Zane's going to take us out for hamburgers, Mom, and then we'll probably rent a movie or two and watch them at Brent's house. His mom and dad will be back around eleven."

"Fine, dear," Janet replied. "If you need anything, just call me here. I guess your father will be in about the same time from his business meeting. And Susan and Drew are at the football game tonight. By the way, why aren't you going to the game?"

"Didn't want to," was his only reply. Tommy sped over to Brent's house, where the Holcombes were backing out of the driveway. He pulled up on his bike and waved to them. Zane was already on the phone to his friends, letting them know that his parents had just left. Ten minutes later, Paul and Derrick arrived with Roger. The six boys piled into Zane's car. Their plan was to eat a simple dinner at the Rathskeller and then head downtown to the adult book store, where the high school seniors would rent videos for their evening together.

Parking was always a problem in the area of the city around the Platinum Club, almost every night of the week. In addition to the huge club itself, there were several bars, restaurants, and adult book stores in the surrounding blocks. Richard, Bruce, and their guests found a space about two blocks from the club, and they began walking along the sidewalk toward the gaudily lighted former warehouse which now paraded naked women for men to watch seven nights a week.

"You won't believe the girls in this place, Patrick," Bruce said. "They are so wholesome looking—and so naked! We should be able to get a table and have one or two dance just for us. Which do you guys like, blondes or brunettes?"

"How about a matched pair?" Patrick volunteered. Everyone laughed. "This place is almost on the national register," Patrick added. "Every conventioneer—well, every male conventioneer—who has ever come to your city, it seems like, has been here. I can't wait. But, hey, Marty, let's not mention this part of our visit to Kate. I don't think she'd understand why I want to see hundreds of naked young women . . ."

"My lips are sealed," Marty smiled, and everyone laughed again.

Just then, as they came to the corner of the building across the street from the Platinum Club, they ran into a group of teenage boys who had been walking up the cross street and whose leader had been turned around, talking to his friends, not watching where he was going. Their paths had been shielded from each other by the building itself, and the two groups literally ran into each other at the corner.

The teenager in the lead was carrying a bag, and in the collision with Bruce McKinney, he dropped it. Three video tapes bounced out onto the sidewalk. "Hey, watch it," the teenager said, swearing loudly. Richard, who had been in the middle of their group and had his shoe stepped on, looked up and saw his son Tommy, with Brent and Zane and three boys whom he did not recognize.

Richard looked at Tommy, who had not spoken, but instead stared back at him. Then he looked at the videos on the sidewalk, at the earrings in Derrick's ear, at the hippie clothes on Paul, again at the titles of the videos, and at the wild look in Roger's eyes. In that one instant he completely understood the last six months of Tommy's life. It was as if a knife pierced his heart, and he lost his breath at the same time.

Tommy, looking in his father's eyes, saw the revelation, the understanding, and the disappointment. It was as if a knife pierced his heart as well, and he lost his breath at the same time. He wanted to cry out to his father that he hadn't wanted to come and that it was all a mistake. *Please, Daddy, take me home, and let's be happy again like we used to be when you and Mom didn't fight. . . .* were the first thoughts in Tommy's mind.

The men sensed the recognition, just as Richard was finally able to speak. "Tommy . . . Brent . . . Zane . . . what are you doing here? Who are these guys? And what are these videos? Look at these." Roger was quickly putting the videos back into the bag, but the subject matter of at least two of them had been obvious to all five men.

"Hi, Mr. Sullivan," Brent spoke up. "Uh, we were just down renting some videos." He stood still and smiled.

Inside Tommy, the bleeding in his heart turned quickly to venom. A voice told him that here was a real chance to hurt his father, the same way he had so often been hurt. He regained his composure and almost leered at his father, "And what are *you* doing here? Aren't you supposed to be at a 'business meeting'? That's what Mom told me. Does she know you're here?"

This was not the sort of conversation Richard's compatriots had come to the Platinum Club to hear, and they moved a few paces away, toward the club, both fascinated and horrified by Richard's plight. Tommy's friends were uneasy as well, and they moved in the direction of Zane's parked car. Tommy and Richard were left on the sidewalk, facing each other.

"Tommy, I'm here on business, but I probably need to take you home," Richard said quietly.

Tommy laughed and said, "Yeah, right. Exactly what business do they do in the Platinum Club, Dad?"

"Tommy, why are you so angry?" was all Richard could think to say.

"You figure it out. Have a great time, Dad." Tommy turned to join his friends. "First one home tell Mom not to wait up!" And he ran off.

Richard, drained and in shock, rejoined his group. "Weren't those the Holcombe boys?" Bruce asked, trying to make conversation.

"Yes. I vaguely remember Janet saying that Tommy was going to be over at their house tonight. I wonder how long he's been doing this?"

"How old is he?" Marty asked.

"Fourteen."

"Mmmm," was all that Marty could say.

Richard, realizing that his family encounter was throwing a damper on an important night, smiled, put his hand on Patrick's shoulder, and said, "Well, boys will be boys. Heaven only knows what I did at that age. Come on—let's go have some fun." And they went inside the Platinum Club. But all night, as the girls danced lewdly on his table, Richard thought about Tommy, the three older boys, and the pictures on the covers of those videos.

SATURDAY, SEPTEMBER 9 ■ On Saturday morning, Richard rose early, despite the previous night's late hour, and went to the office, as was his custom. Only this Saturday morning he had a hard time focusing on cleaning up the files from that week. Instead, a thousand thoughts of Tommy, from when he was a little boy until last night, pulsed in his head. He felt terrible about all the hours and days that were gone forever—the hours and days he could have spent with Tommy, but didn't, because other demands seemed more important at the time. What exactly had Tommy been doing? Was he really a homosex . . . Richard couldn't bring himself to think the word. What about that Caroline Batten in Vermont? What was going on? And how could he not know? How could he be so blind to his own son?

Richard managed to do about a half hour's worth of work in the two hours he sat at his desk. Finally he gave up and drove home, hoping to find Tommy and take him to lunch so they could talk.

But Tommy had already left for Brent's house, Janet told Richard. She acted as if nothing had happened, so Richard presumed he and Tommy had a common secret, at least for now. *Well, in a strange way, maybe that's a start to a relationship,* he thought.

Tommy did not come home until almost dark, and he was careful to stay near Janet until his parents left for his grade's parent support group meeting, scheduled long ago for that same night. So Richard was unable to talk to Tommy one-on-one that day.

Meanwhile, Amy and Bobbie went on a double date. Thomas brought a friend from his high school, Ben Forbes, who shared his faith, as a blind date for Amy. Much to the anger of Zloy and Nepravel, Amy liked Ben and was soon trying to talk him into coming to their youth group the next morning.

But the good news for the demons was that Drew convinced Susan to lie again to her parents and to spend the evening together in another motel room. By the end of that evening, Susan was still dreaming about how they would go to college together, but Drew was simply focusing on the next Saturday night at another motel.

SUNDAY, SEPTEMBER 10 ■ On Sunday morning, Richard remained in their breakfast room until Tommy finally came down, late in the morning. "After you get something to eat, Tommy, let's you and me take a walk to the park." Tommy said nothing, which meant a grudging OK.

It was a beautiful morning, still summer, really, with just a first hint of fall in the lower angle of the sun. As they walked along Devon Drive thirty minutes later, Richard, who had rehearsed this moment in his head fifty times in the past twenty-four hours, said, "Tommy I'm not here to throw stones or to be judgmental. I just want to understand. Do you mind telling me who those boys were you were with on Friday night, and what you were doing?"

Tommy had also rehearsed. One voice told him to hurt his father by telling him the truth. Another voice told him to hurt his father by telling him nothing. *I win, either way,* it occurred to him. No voice could be heard telling him to seek help or love from his father. He decided to give his father pieces of the truth, but he saw no reason to tell his father everything. It was his own business, after all.

So Tommy coyly answered that they were just friends from high school. There followed a thirty-minute cross-examination, as they walked around the park, during which Richard finally pieced together that Tommy had been "doing videos" with his friends for some months, when he and Janet had thought they were elsewhere. "Doing videos" apparently involved some sort of mutual stimulation, and Tommy had enjoyed both "girl" and "boy" videos. In fact, Tommy told his father, he liked both girls and boys, which, as Tommy hoped it would, turned his father's stomach.

The more Tommy tried to be assertive and in control, the more Richard realized the depth of his son's anger and confusion. A couple of times

Richard lost his train of thought, wondering what had happened in just a few short years to the little boy with whom he had played T-ball in the back yard.

Richard had sworn to himself that no matter what Tommy said, he would not lose his temper. For once he kept his control. There was no resolution from their walk and talk. But Richard listened. By the end he didn't know whether Tommy needed professional help or was just part of the "alternative lifestyle" which was bombarding everyone with its legitimacy these days. It never occurred to Richard, of course, that Tommy might need spiritual help from someone strong, like both a natural father and a heavenly Father, to believe in explicitly and to trust. Richard was frankly as confused as Tommy, which didn't help the boy. Did Tommy need psychological help, no help, more fathering, less fathering, what? By the end of their walk, much of their tension was gone, but Richard was now an active part of Tommy's problem, as much as a simple adversary. Both of them sensed Richard's impotence, but neither of them knew what to do.

MONDAY, SEPTEMBER 11 ■ Bruce McKinney called Richard early Monday morning. "Did we do well on Friday night or did we do well?" he asked, the joy obvious in his voice.

"We did well," Richard agreed. "In fact, I just got off the phone with Marty. I'll draft a waiver for them on the stock price, and a modification to the purchase price. Then we need your final payables and inventory to fax to them so we can pro-rate everything to Friday. We seem to be in pretty good shape. I gave him our bank escrow account number so they can wire in the funds."

"That's great, Richard. Thanks for all your help. By the way, how's Tommy?"

"He's fine. Just a little mixed up, I think. But we're working on it." Richard tried to move on. "Does the deal look OK to you?"

"I don't like losing $100,000, but it will be good in the long run to have Patrick as an owner."

"And in the short run, the $900,000 won't hurt," Richard concluded as they said goodbye.

Janet was running late that afternoon. The controversy and the publicity surrounding Friday's upcoming kick-off of "911 Live" were growing so quickly that she was having trouble keeping up. There had been several interviews for Network—even other network—news shows. And with newspaper tie-ins to the local station's involvement in the test run that summer. The local advertising time was all sold, and at a very high rate for an unproven show. Nearly everyone at the station was involved, especially since they had lost seven members from their staff. So Janet was late leaving the station.

As she drove into the garage, she looked at her watch and decided to call for a pizza delivery for the kids. She and Richard could have a salad. After putting her things down, she phoned their favorite pizza restaurant and placed an order. Looking in her wallet, she realized she didn't have enough cash, so she climbed the stairs to ask for a loan from Susan or Tommy.

Janet knocked on Susan's door but heard the water running in her shower. She opened the door. The door to Susan's bathroom was shut, but her purse was on the bed. Hoping to find fifteen dollars, Janet opened it and instead found Susan's birth control packet. She pulled it out, thinking that somehow her own had been misplaced, but the label, from their pharmacy and from their own doctor, clearly read "Susan Sullivan."

Janet sat down on Susan's bed, the container in her hand. She opened it—almost the entire month had been used. She closed it and closed her eyes. "Drew," she whispered.

The water went off in the shower, and a few minutes later the door opened. Susan came into her bedroom, a towel wrapped around her. She was surprised to see her mother on her bed, staring at her. Janet opened her hand, revealing the birth control pills.

"I didn't hear you come in and open my purse," Susan said.

"I was looking for pizza money. Is there something you want to tell me, Susan?"

Susan smiled at the thought and walked to her bureau for a brush. "No, I hadn't exactly planned on telling you about those. But now that you've been through my things and found them, I guess they're no longer a secret. Drew and I are sleeping together. But I'm not pregnant and I won't get a disease, so you don't have to worry."

"Oh, that's great," Janet smiled. "Our seventeen-year-old daughter is sleeping with her boyfriend, but we don't have to worry."

"Mom . . ." Susan turned, anger now in her voice. "It's not like that at all. Drew and I love each other very much."

"How long have you two been having sex, and where?"

"I don't think it's any of your business, but we've been making love for a long time," she lied, "and we usually go to a motel."

The mental image of Susan and Drew at a cheap motel together invaded Janet's mind and almost caused her to jump, physically. She closed her eyes for a moment and then said, "Don't you think your health and happiness are the business of your parents? We love you and don't want anything to happen to you. What if you do become pregnant, or contract AIDS?"

"I won't. Believe me, we know what to do to take the right precautions."

"*If* they all work. But what about your mental health? You're just seventeen. You and Drew are playing with fire."

"Mom, I'm the age of most women when they married a century ago. I know what I'm doing. And besides, I'm just following your advice."

"What?"

"You told me that day when we played tennis that the only meaning to life would be to fall in love with a good man and raise a family. Drew is a good man."

"Not as good as he was a little while ago. Anyway, I meant when you are in your twenties, after college, when you've had a chance to experience other things and get married. Not now, when yesterday you were a little girl."

That remark angered Susan, and she was about to speak when the doorbell rang. "The pizza man must be here," Janet said, rising from the bed. "Here are your pills. I guess one day I'll understand all of this, but for right now I'm very disappointed in you."

"Mom?" Susan asked as Janet reached the door, "Are you going to tell Dad?"

"I don't know. Probably. I'm sure he'll be really pleased."

"Mom, it's not that big a deal."

"Not until you get pregnant, or ill, or die, or have an abortion, or have a baby, or Drew leaves you. You're absolutely right, young woman." And Janet left Susan holding her pills.

Janet decided she would sleep on what she had learned before deciding whether and how to tell Richard. But after Susan and Tommy had gone to bed, she and Richard were sitting alone in the den, both working on stacks of papers brought home from their offices, when Richard said, "Janet, I think Tommy may have been having some fairly significant homosexual experiences with Brent and other boys, and I'm not sure what to do about it."

For the second time in one evening, Janet was speechless. "How . . . how do you know, Richard?"

"Friday night the investor we had dinner with wanted to see the Platinum Club." Janet squinted her eyes a bit, and Richard hurried on. "And since my car was back at the office, and I didn't want to be inhospitable," he shrugged, "I went along with them for a short while." And then Richard recounted the story of their collision with the boys and of his talk with Tommy the previous afternoon. "So I don't know whether it's something he just did as a 'stage' or whether he's permanently homosexual, or bi-sexual, or what. I do know he's angry and confused. Unfortunately, those are the best two adjectives to describe me at this point too. I mean, is this something to be worried about, or just to accept, like the color of his hair? One thing that *is* obvious is that he's been lying to us for some time about what he and his friends were doing and where they've been. So I guess we can't trust him any more."

"Well," Janet started slowly, "before you get too down on Tommy alone, I found out tonight that Susan has been taking birth control pills and that she and Drew have been sleeping together."

Now it was Richard's turn to be speechless again. The same knife that had pierced his heart on Friday night stabbed him again. And again.

Someone kicked him in the stomach, robbing him of his breath. But his mental images worked well, and quickly.

Seeing that he could not speak, Janet continued, "She claims they've been at it for some time, but I don't believe her. The date on the prescription—from our own doctor, by the way—is just last month. I would imagine that they started either just before or after our trip to Vermont."

"Where?" he managed to ask.

"She says in motels."

The mental image of his daughter Susan naked in a motel bed with Drew exploded in his mind. Richard vowed, "I'll kick his butt from one end of the street to the other."

"Well, you better kick Susan's too. She's the one who bought the pills, and it takes two to tango."

Richard slouched back in his chair. Nepravel, who had been watching the discussion from the mantel over the fireplace, smiled. "Isn't it something, Richard, when they grow up to be exactly like you?" he laughed. "You should be proud. Following in their father's footsteps. Don't kick them, Richard—compliment them! And maybe their children—your grandchildren—will do the same, or worse!" and he laughed so hard that he slipped off the mantle and would have fallen to the floor, if gravity had affected him.

After a minute of thinking, Richard said quietly, staring at the floor, "So we have a fourteen-year-old son who may or may not be a homosexual, who lies to us, and who goes places at night we don't know about with people whom we don't know. And we have a seventeen-year-old daughter who is sleeping with her boyfriend, who lies to us, and who goes to motels on a regular basis, also taking birth control pills. Do you think we need help?"

Nepravel stood on the mantel and pointed at Richard, fire leaping from his mouth and eyes, "And what about you and Kristen! Tell her the whole story, Richard! Don't stop with the kids!"

"You may be right, dear," Janet said, the sadness in her voice matching his. She started to tell him that they should have spent more time with their children, but she decided to save that point for another day. The news by itself was depressing enough.

"How do we fight all this, as parents?" Richard said, not realizing that he was looking right at Nepravel. "When did all of this happen? What did we do wrong? Is this how it is with everyone these days? Are there no values left?"

Nepravel almost fell off the mantel again, he was so delighted with Richard and Janet's agony as parents. "You reap what you sow, folks. At least your kids have two parents. Think of all the children trying to make it without the help of good folks like you!" and he smiled in contentment.

"I guess an immediate issue is what we let them do now, this coming weekend," Janet said. "I mean, do they continue to lie about where they are going? Or do we forbid them to see Brent and Drew? Or do we buy them boxes of condoms and wish them 'Safe Sex' as they go out the door? What do we do?"

"I think we need professional help, Janet. This is beyond my experience. Tomorrow can you call their school, maybe the nurse, and see if they can recommend any family therapists?"

"Yes. And I've heard a few names from other mothers. I'll make some calls. I guess we should go as soon as possible. Maybe we can get them to hold off on their sexual urges for one weekend, while we try to sort this out."

TUESDAY, SEPTEMBER 12 ■ Richard was still reeling from their Monday night discussion when he arrived at work on Tuesday. At least he had "lunch" with Kristen to look forward to.

About 11:00 his intercom hummed. Mary said, "It's a Mr. Dowling from California." Richard couldn't quite place the name, but he told her to put him through.

"Hi, Richard. This is Peter Dowling in San Francisco. We met several months ago at a symphony there. I was with Kristen Holloway. Do you remember me?"

"Of course," Richard replied as friendly as he could, remembering the awkwardness of that evening. "How are you, and what can I do for you?"

"I'm fine, thank you. And Kristen certainly said a lot of nice things about you. She must know you pretty well." Richard was silent. "Well, anyway, she suggested that night that I call you if I needed some help in the financial sector of your city, and so I'm following up, if you don't mind."

"How can I help?" Richard asked, mildly curious.

"Well, as you may recall, I'm an investigative reporter for the morning newspaper out here. For over a year I've been working on and off on a possible story about Far West Securities. The rumors have been that they've pledged or sold stocks and bonds held in trust for others to raise money for themselves when times were difficult. Obviously this is quite illegal. The rumors have been around for several years. Apparently they've always been able to replace one sold stock with another, when they had to, so they have never been caught short.

"When I was there earlier this year I was checking out a new part of the story, but I could never confirm it. That story was that Far West had worked out a secret deal with a securities firm in your city, which was doing the same thing, 'swapping' the stocks or bonds each firm needed to pass its quarterly audit by the National Securities Examination Association. In other words, if Far West needed a particular group of stocks or bonds to show the auditors that their physical holdings matched their book records, the firm in your city would express them out for a few days. Then Far West returned the assistance with their holdings when the other firm was audited. The audits are scheduled in advance, so they had time to prepare. And if an occasional spot check by a young auditor produced a discrepancy in the stock register numbers, it was blamed on a typing error, and they promised to correct it. So long as the total volume of assets always matched the books, that was the main thing."

"Sounds ingenious, and, as you say, quite illegal," Richard said. "But what does it have to do with me?"

"Nothing. But yesterday a very unhappy and very recent former employee of Far West called me and gave me a name in your city. He said that this is the name I was looking for when I was there earlier. Have you ever heard of someone named Bruce McKinney?"

Richard's blood froze. "Yes."

"Well, allegedly his firm has been doing these illegal swaps of escrow stocks with Far West for all these years, and I wondered if you might know someone with that firm whom I might call to try to develop a relationship with, so I can slowly try to uncover whether this is all true or not. I'm not asking you to do anything yourself. I thought you might just know a broker or someone with whom I could start."

Richard's legal training finally kicked in. "Peter, I wish you had asked me the name first, instead of telling me the story first. The fact is that I'm the main attorney for McKinney and Smith. Now I know something that may or may not be true, and I wish I didn't know it. I'm going to have to think through my ethical position, but it's obvious that I can't help you in any way."

"What a coincidence," Peter agreed, "in a city as big as yours. Well, I'm sorry, too. I understand, and I guess I did do it backwards. If you have to tell them, how about deleting my name for now, so I can keep working from this end?"

"I'm not sure I can, Peter. This is suddenly quite a mess. But I'll do all I can to protect your identity within the bounds of my responsibilities to them."

"Well, thank you, Richard. I'm sorry for the call, for any number of reasons. I guess I'll have to fly back there again myself and dig around on my own. Goodbye."

Richard swiveled in his chair and looked out across the city in the direction of Bruce's office. He could not believe the conversation and even imagined for a moment that it was some sort of bar association test of his own ethics. But in the pit of his stomach he could imagine that if times were tough enough, Bruce McKinney was at least capable of doing what Peter had described. But had he?

Turning back around, Richard called Kristen's beeper number. He only had to wait forty-five seconds before his own phone rang. "Listen, dear, something *very* important has just come up, and I've got to go out. Just now. I hate it more than you do, but I can't have lunch today. I'll try to make it up to you on Thursday."

"Is it really that important?" she pouted.

"Yes, I'm afraid so. It's business, and I've got to take care of it."

"OK. But I want three hours on Thursday."

"You're on. See you then. I love you. Bye."

Richard pushed the button on his phone for a new line and dialed Bruce's number. The receptionist put him right through.

"I was just heading out the door to grab a bite to eat with one of our trainees, Richard, but I always take your calls. What's up? Is everything all right?"

"I hope so, Bruce, but I need to talk to you, face to face. Can I come over now?" The concern in his voice was apparent.

"Sure, Richard. I'll take my young broker to lunch tomorrow. I'll order us some sandwiches, and we can meet right here over lunch. Is that OK?"

"Yes. Fine. I'll see you shortly."

When Richard arrived in Bruce's paneled office, two club sandwiches and chips were waiting on china plates at the small conference table beside the large window.

"Have a seat and some iced tea and tell me what's up." Bruce smiled and motioned Richard towards the table.

After they both sat down, Richard took a sip of tea and asked, "Bruce, have you ever heard of Far West Securities?"

Bruce paused for an instant, took a sip of his tea, and said, "Yes, they're a large brokerage firm in California, based in San Francisco, I think. Why?" His eyes narrowed a bit.

"Have you ever traded stocks or bonds from your escrow safe with them?"

"Who have you been talking to, Richard?" his eyes narrowed even more.

"I'm in an impossible ethical, and perhaps legal, position at this point, Bruce. I'll probably tell you the name, but for the moment I just want to get to the bottom of the facts. I've known you for years. We're neighbors. I've guaranteed your loan. Now what I want to know—plain, simple, and true—is whether you've been selling or pledging other people's stocks and working with Far West to cover it up?"

"The short answer is yes, Richard, but I want you to hear the rest."

Richard leaned back in his chair, exhaled, and swore. "Bruce, how could you? . . . Wonderful. Tell me the details."

"David and I started pledging a few stocks owned by trusts that never sold anything, over ten years ago. We hated to do it, but we had poured every cent we had into the business, and the banks wouldn't lend us any more money without collateral. It started out very simply. We had a big fee coming in on a Monday, and we had to meet our payroll on the Friday before, so we just took out a short loan to cover the weekend, and it worked perfectly, using the escrow stocks from our safe as collateral.

"We didn't do it again for several months, but then we needed more money for a longer period, or we faced closing our doors, losing our homes, everything. So we took out a thirty-day note, and we made enough money to pay it all back and to retrieve the stocks in plenty of time for the audit.

"We did this on and off, but only when we had to, Richard, for a couple of years. Then at one of our national conventions, I met the owner of Far West Securities—I'll give you his name when we get to that point—and we wound up going out for dinner and drinks one night, just the two of us. We were talking about our business and our problems and having a few rounds, and before long we both had hinted in a roundabout way that we had beefed up our collateral on occasion with stocks readily at hand.

"I don't remember, exactly, but we somehow actually started discussing what we had done, and he lamented how unhelpful it was that we had these quarterly audits when we had to produce the stock certificates. That's when we more or less simultaneously hit upon the idea of helping each other out, to get through the audits when the stocks had been pledged."

Richard reached for his tea again. "How recently have you done this?"

Bruce looked out the window. "I hate to tell you, Richard, but right now we've got a loan for $150,000 at the bank, secured by stocks we don't own."

Richard's chest felt hollow. "So on Friday, among other problems, I'm supposed to give our firm's legal opinion to Patrick Tomlinson about your good standing and the accuracy of all the representations in our financial documents, while you have 'borrowed' your clients' stocks and colluded with another securities firm to defraud a bank and those same clients?"

"You asked and said you wanted the truth. You're our attorney, so I told you."

"Thanks. I appreciate your faith in me . . . Now what in blazes do I do?"

"Look, Richard, David and I don't like this any more than you do. We've hated to do it over the years. And one of the reasons we want the Tomlinson investment is so that we can wipe out that loan and never have to do it again. We obviously haven't told anyone, but we built that loan payoff into the equity infusion from the beginning. Don't worry. The loan is mentioned, just not the specific collateral. So my suggestion to you is that you do nothing, and let the closing occur. David and I will never borrow any funds in this way again—or help Far West again."

"That sounds so simple."

"It is simple. If you blow the whistle and stop the closing, our company will be finished, David and I will lose everything we have, your firm will be out a big legal fee, you will be out your personal financing fee, and you will still be guaranteeing a $500,000 loan at the bank." Bruce paused to let those results sink in.

"Or we can have the closing, the cash will come in, we'll pay off both loans, you will have your fees, our company will be in good shape, no one will have been hurt, and that will be the end of it."

Richard sat quietly and thought. Neither of them had yet touched his sandwich. "But I'll have to lie. I have to certify your standing and your records. And I now know that there is the potential for criminal and civil action against you. What if this reporter keeps digging and uncovers more?"

"I'll call Far West and have whoever is unhappy made happy, so he or she will shut up. Then the trail will die, and after a few weeks, there won't be a trail. No harm, no foul. No one will be out any money, and if something is made of it several years from now, we'll explain it as an overzealous clerk and accept a quiet reprimand. When the public is not hurt, the regulators don't like to make a big fuss—it's bad for the whole industry. Whatever else might happen, anything is better than the disaster that will occur if the closing doesn't take place. Trust me on this, Richard. You are our attorney and are not supposed to reveal privileged information, anyway. No one can ever be mad at you. Just let it all happen like it's set to happen, as if you'd never heard any of this. Then we all come out OK, you included."

"Well, but I've got to give an opinion for the closing . . . Maybe I can play around with the words a bit so that it's not quite as strong as usual, but still legal sounding enough not to raise any suspicions. I don't think they're really looking too hard for problems anyway. They trust us."

"That's right. And they'll be fine, too, or I wouldn't ask you to do this. Everyone, and I mean everyone, comes out OK if the closing goes forward."

"And if you and David also stop this practice, once and for all."

"You have my word, Richard."

"Well, I've got to think it through again, but I guess I can do it, since no one will be hurt."

"That's good. I understand that the papers are to be signed on Thursday morning, and the money wired in first thing on Friday, right?"

"Yes, that's how we've set it up."

"Well then, if that's settled, let's have some lunch."

On the way back to his office, a small voice tried to tell him that mixing his legal work and his investments had created this problem and that he should do the correct thing. But a louder voice reassured him that it would all blow over, everyone would be paid, and no one would be hurt. He just had to change a few words . . .

Back at his office, Richard summoned his paralegal and told her that he wanted to make one last review of the McKinney/Tomlinson documents before expressing them to Marty Tsongas that afternoon. He then went through the opinion letter to be issued by his firm, removed a few absolutes, and added an innocuous-sounding catch-all phrase, stating that their opinion about McKinney and Smith was subject to the "customary requirements for client confidentiality."

Once the document was modified, they expressed the entire package to Marty for his review on the following day. Marty and Patrick would then fly in to sign all the papers during a brief ceremony on Thursday morning.

That night at home, sitting again together with Richard in the den, Janet explained to him about the several psychological and psychiatric programs she had investigated on the telephone that day.

"Most of them want to see all four of us on the first few visits, then break up and do therapy for anywhere from six months to many years. But, you know, Richard, these sounded like programs for really messed up kids—I mean like drug addicts, robbers, and that sort. Do you think Tommy and Susan need that sort of treatment?"

"I don't know, Janet. I'm not feeling very good about my parental judgment right now."

"Do you think we could just talk to them and ask them to stop what they're doing?"

"I would hope so, but I don't hold out much hope that it would last very long. I mean, how do you ever really change someone?"

"Well, I'll call back the two places that sounded the most low key and talk to them again. Then we can decide. But what about this weekend?"

"We'll have to talk to them tomorrow night, I guess."

WEDNESDAY, SEPTEMBER 13 ■ Amy, Bobbie, and Susan sat alone again at lunch on Wednesday. Alone except for Pitow, the demon in charge of the forces of darkness in the school, who hovered above the fourth chair at the table. "I think it's time for another slumber party," Amy announced, "and this time we can do it at my house. I've checked with my parents, and Saturday night will be fine with them. Then we can all go to Morningside Church again. Susan, I think you'd really like it."

The other two girls looked at Susan, who had been acting a little aloof for the past two weeks. "I don't know. Isn't a slumber party a little childish for seniors? I think I'd much rather spend the evening with Drew, maybe even in a motel room, than at a slumber party in a basement."

Bobbie and Amy looked at each other—the put-down had been obvious. "So you and Drew are shacking up in motels now?" Amy asked.

"I wouldn't call it 'shacking up.' We love each other very much, and he is wonderful. My mother even knows, and she hasn't stopped us."

"Your mom knows?" Bobbie asked.

"Yes, she found my pills."

"What about your dad?"

"Not unless Mom told him. I don't know."

"And she didn't say anything at all?"

"Well, she wasn't overjoyed, but she hasn't said we have to stop. How could she, really? She told me this summer that finding and loving a good man is the most important thing in life, so I think she understands us." Pitow nodded in silent and amused agreement.

"My parents still don't know what I went through," said Amy. "I hope someday I can tell them, when I'm older."

"Finding a good man is important," Bobbie added, "but it's not *the* most important. Loving God is the most important. If you do that, the other stuff just comes, according to His will." Pitow was enraged, and rose three feet above the table. He hated it when the few Christians in the school actually spoke up, even in private. But just try it in public! Then they'd see his power!

"Well, maybe," Susan smiled. "But right now I sure am enjoying Drew. You ought to try a motel sometime, Amy. It sure beats parking in a car. You might get back into boys if you had the right place to go." Pitow watched Amy's eyes for a spark of lust, but was terribly disappointed.

"I'm into boys," Amy said, not smiling. "I'm just not into that part of boys right now."

"Well, they say it's just like riding a bicycle, only a lot more fun. Maybe we could double date sometime and get adjoining rooms!"

"Come on, Susan," Bobbie said, "you sound like some kind of hooker. You really need to come to our youth group. Everything I've read, including God's Word, says that you're playing with fire and will regret it, sooner or later. The only questions are how bad the hurt will be, and who will suffer the most."

"Don't you think I know more from experience than you do from books? It's real life. What about you, Amy? Are you a jumper and shouter yet?"

"You aren't going to understand this, Susan," Amy said, "but the Bible I've been reading seems like real life to me. At least I feel like it's telling the real truth to me. And I feel loved and wanted by the people at Bobbie's church. So right now that's a very happy reality for me, and I don't need a motel room with a boy to make me feel good."

"Well, *excuse* me. Let me know," Susan said, getting up to meet Drew, who had just walked into the cafeteria door, "when you're ready to relax again."

As Susan walked away, Bobbie asked Amy, "It's not easy, is it?"

"No, it's not. But I know inside that it's right. In fact, I might ask you and Glenn to pray with me after youth group on Sunday. I may be ready to turn over my life to Jesus. If Susan is the alternative, then I'm running as fast as I can to God!" Pitow was flabbergasted. This is not what Nepravel and Zloy had expected from her. Balzor would be furious!

Bobbie was quietly thrilled by Amy's finding the Lord's power acting in her life, and on the way back to class she said silent prayers for both of her friends.

That afternoon the national crews for "911 Live" arrived at TV5, which would act as the control center each week for the satellite relay back to Network in New York. Janet had arranged for their accommodations and for their appointments at the police, fire, and ambulance stations where the equipment was to be installed. Because of all the controversy surrounding the show, the arrival of the crew was "news," and the local newspapers sent reporters to cover the equipment installation.

Janet rode with the team to the police station. The equipment was familiar from their trial run, except that Mark and Bob had accelerated the purchase of tiny cameras which could actually be worn on the helmet or on the hat of emergency personnel, linked back to their vehicle for up to five hundred feet and amplified back to the station. So now it would actually be possible to go along with 911 personnel into a building, which did not comfort Janet, but at this point she was not prepared to say anything.

By the end of Wednesday it looked as if they would be finished in plenty of time to roll on schedule, an hour before the 7:30 broadcast started, in just two more days.

Janet and Richard talked on the phone later that afternoon, and it seemed that perhaps the program run by the Sequoia Center might be low key but powerful enough to have some effect on their family. So Janet had tentatively signed them all up for an initial interview on the following Tuesday afternoon.

After dinner that night, the parents met and decided that they would ask—it would not be "appropriate" to demand—that their children refrain from their sexual activity that weekend, given their family interview scheduled for Tuesday. And they decided that they would each ask the child of the opposite sex.

So Richard headed upstairs to talk with Susan for the first time about her involvement with Drew, and Janet asked Tommy to turn off the television at the end of his show. She had a fairly easy time with her son, who had not particularly wanted to get back together with his group so soon anyway. At her request, he promised that he would not lie about his activities that weekend and that he would not "do videos" or any other similar behavior until their interview. Tommy was frankly relieved to have his parents ask him to slow down, as tenuous as their request was. And he wanted to figure himself out as much as they did. Although he was not prepared to give up his fun totally, he actually looked forward to their meeting on Tuesday.

Susan was not so happy or so agreeable. Richard tried to control his anger, his disappointment, and his discomfort when talking to her, but all three were clearly just below the surface.

"Susan, this is not easy for me, but I just don't think that you should be . . . sleeping . . . with Drew at age seventeen, with all the risks involved. But I'm in over my head, and your mother and I would like for all four of us to go see a counselor together. We've scheduled a meeting for Tuesday afternoon."

"What on earth are we going to talk about?" Susan asked.

"I honestly don't know. But because we think what you're doing is wrong, and because of this meeting, we'd like you to promise that you and Drew will not . . . sleep together . . . this weekend, until we've all had a chance to hear what the counselor has to say."

"I don't know, Dad," Susan replied, to Richard's astonishment. "I don't think Drew and I are doing anything wrong. I mean, if we use birth control and a condom . . ." Richard felt himself blushing, but noticed that Susan wasn't. ". . . then what's wrong? We're not hurting anyone, and we love each other. Those are the criteria you and Mom have always given me to decide right from wrong. So tell me what's wrong."

Richard had expected her to do as he asked, just as she always had, and not to debate him. She waited for his answer, and to his amazement, he could not think of one. He knew it was wrong for her to be sleeping with Drew, but he could not articulate why. He had to admit that he didn't really know why, especially given the fact that he and Kristen would be enjoying "lunch" together the next day. He quickly suppressed that thought! Why was it wrong? He certainly couldn't say, "Because it says so in the Bible," but that's what he found himself thinking. How unexpectedly bizarre!

"We just think it's wrong for you to be running the risks of disease and pregnancy, Susan. Either one would be terrible."

"But I said we know how to prevent those. And I love him. He's a great guy, and I hope we can go to the same college and maybe get married some day. We're not hurting anyone, and we'll always be careful, I promise."

Richard knew he had lost. It astonished him that he couldn't give his seventeen-year-old daughter any good reasons why she shouldn't be sleeping with her boyfriend in motels! *Maybe there aren't any,* he thought. Maybe she should just do what she wanted, and Tommy should do what he wanted. Maybe that was the way today, a voice told him. But he hung in for one more try, not wanting to face Janet otherwise.

"Look, your old man is at his wit's end. Perhaps I can't tell you now what's wrong. That's why I want to see a counselor. I'll even concede that *maybe* you're right. But can't you please just humor me for one weekend, for old times' sake, and do something else until we see this expert?"

Susan relented, when asked nicely. "Oh, all right, Daddy. I'll do as you've asked this one weekend, but that's all I'll promise. And we'll see what this expert has to say. Now I've got to finish this homework."

Richard rose and kissed her on the forehead, then left, feeling he'd won the battle but lost the war.

At midnight the broiling mass of hateful demons met over the city to review their work during the last twenty-four hours. Tymor asked to address the horde, and Balzor nodded.

"Good news. We've 'helped' a professor at the seminary in the university 'discover' that the story about Jesus, the possessed man, and the herd of swine on the hill was actually a parody of an earlier Greek allegory, and he's going to publish that finding next month in a scholarly journal on religion, discrediting Mark and Luke as the authors!"

Balzor and the others laughed. Plando, one of the streetleaders, spoke up from the ranks. "I was there. It was awful. He ordered us out of that man, and we had to obey. I've never been so humiliated, so we killed those pigs. But, hey! I'm glad to hear now that it never happened!" And they all laughed again.

"We're working with the seminary scholars on more such 'discoveries,' and the press will give us full play with every one," Tymor concluded, to everyone's delight.

But soon Pitow reported on the conversation between the three girls in the high school cafeteria that day. Balzor was furious to learn that Susan, while in excellent shape herself to be permanently theirs, was nevertheless driving Amy toward the Light. He turned on Nepravel and Zloy, who cowered at the edge of the mass.

"What are you going to do?" he asked. "She may be lost to us forever on Sunday!"

Without answering the question, Nepravel countered, as bravely as he could with Balzor hovering directly over him, "It's those prayers. The Meredith girl has the whole youth group and the church Prayer Warriors praying for Amy every day. Look down there."

The demons looked down toward Devon Drive, and even at that late hour they could see the streaks of light, incoming to the Bryants' home, from all over the city.

"All those prayers are silencing the voices as soon as we start them. Unless we stay right there, she won't hear them. And with all those prayers, there's likely to be an angel nearby, so we'll need an army. Is one girl worth all that?"

Balzor backed off a bit and considered for a moment. "No, not with all that we have planned for her neighbors, the Sullivans, in the next few days. We need our best resources there. Let's hope that something keeps her from committing to that Son of God on Sunday so we can work on her again next week." And, much to Nepravel's and Zloy's relief, Balzor turned and resumed his place above the assembled gang of liars and haters, to hear more reports.

14

THURSDAY, SEPTEMBER 14 ■ Patrick Tomlinson and Marty Tsongas flew in on the first flight of the day and were in Richard's office a little before 9:00. Richard and his paralegal had arrived an hour before, and all the closing documents for Patrick's investment were arranged in order on the conference room table.

While the principals sipped coffee in Richard's office, he and Marty went over a few small changes and typos Marty had discovered. Richard's team took care of those in short order, and a little before 10:00 they all entered the conference room to sign the documents. Richard was relieved that Marty did not question any of the subtle additions or deletions he had made after the talk with Bruce McKinney.

Patrick and Bruce executed the papers that were handed to them by Richard and Marty. At one point Patrick looked up from a fifteen-page exhibit and said to Bruce, "It's a good thing we simply trust you, because beyond the basic deal points, this is all Greek to me."

"I feel the same way," Bruce responded with a smile. "And don't worry, you can trust us."

Once everything was signed, Bruce and Patrick shook hands. "Marty will now call our bank and instruct them to wire the funds first thing tomorrow morning," Patrick told Bruce.

"And then I'll deliver the original papers to all concerned," said Richard.

"I'm sorry it's too early for champagne," David said, shaking Patrick's hand, "and I understand you have a plane to catch back home."

"We'll take a rain check at the Platinum Club," Patrick smiled, "after our first board meeting."

For once Richard was going to "lunch" with Kristen truly relaxed, now that the McKinney deal was done. He had not seen her for a week, and the tension of that deal, the problems with his children, and the decision over what to do about Bruce's revelation had all weighed heavily on him. The problems with the kids were still there, but he promised himself that he would not think about these things or about breaking off with Kristen for the next few hours. He would just enjoy the moment. There was a resulting spring to his step, as he said hello to Bart, the doorman at the Park Place apartments.

She did not disappoint him. He had called before leaving the office and told her that they had just closed the McKinney deal, so she had retrieved a bottle of champagne from her refrigerator, and it was cooling in an ice bucket on the coffee table. Knowing that they had time today, she stayed in her business suit, with her hair pinned up—Richard liked to watch her take it down. They never made it to her bedroom, but instead had "lunch" on the sofa.

Later, she was sitting on the sofa, and he on the floor, while she rubbed his neck and shoulders, and they finished the champagne.

"Kristen, I'm afraid that my kids are a mess. We found out some things this weekend that we should have known, or guessed, but didn't. It turns out that Tommy has been having homosexual experiences on and off for months, and Susan has been sleeping with her boyfriend. Obviously, these were big shocks to Janet and me. We've decided that the whole family needs to see a counselor."

"What your family needs is for the mother and father to stop being at each other's throats, and put the kids in a healthy environment," Kristen said, kneading his right shoulder. "I've read lots of articles where the problem kids of unhappy parents instantly improve, once the parents actually split. Kids pick up on the tension between parents, and they can't help but be affected. Don't you think so?"

Richard, making conversation, answered, "Yes, I guess so."

With that opening, Kristen moved to his left shoulder and continued, "You and Janet have got to split up, for the sake of your kids. You'll never be happy together, and the kids will just get worse and worse in that environment. Think how happy they would be if you were happy, Richard. And we know how to make you happy, don't we?" She smiled above him, rubbing his head.

"Seriously, Richard, all *five* of us will be much better off after you and Janet split up and you come to live with me. It might be tough for a few days, or a week, but very shortly they'll get used to it, and then it will all be much happier."

Richard, lost in thought about his children and relaxed from the champagne and the massage, simply said, "You may be right."

"You know I'm right," Kristen said. Then to herself, she thought, *And I know how to make it happen.*

FRIDAY, SEPTEMBER 15 ■ After breakfast on Friday morning, Richard said to Tommy and Susan, "Be sure to be here tonight for the beginning of '911 Live.' Your mother has worked hard and suffered a bit to get it going, and it ought to be really interesting. Will you be here or at the station, dear?"

"I decided that as a member of this new network commission, I want to get the full effect of what it's like to be in the audience for this show, so I can judge it better. I plan to be here, watching it with you."

"See you then, Mom . . . Dad," Tommy said, as he and Susan left for school.

Richard was working at his desk that morning, trying not to think about Susan and Tommy. Their actions were now like a low-level fever for Richard—he could still do his work, but the discomfort was real and never quite went away. It gnawed at him, making him feel his seventeen years as a father had been a failure.

A little after 10:00, his paralegal came to the door. "First National just called," she said. "The Tomlinson wire transfer came through, and the funds are good."

"Great!" Richard exclaimed. "Then you can go ahead and transfer the money to McKinney and Smith, and express original documents to everyone concerned. Thanks. You've done an excellent job on this difficult project."

As she left, he pushed back from his desk and swiveled around to look out at the city. He felt very good. The legal fee for this transaction would be sizable and would really help the firm's bottom line this quarter. And his $66,000 fee was finally assured. He would surprise Janet with the news at supper. Maybe they could take a short vacation and get their marriage back on track.

But first he knew he had to leave Kristen and straighten out the kids. Maybe he could buy Kristen a nice present with some of this money, to ease her pain when he told her that they had to split up. The problems with the kids had finally decided it for Richard. He had to devote his full time to them, and that meant focusing on Janet. He would just have to keep working on their relationship, as he had to admit that Janet was. And that meant dumping Kristen. He finally realized that he could not be a real husband and father while seeing a mistress several days each week.

But when to do it? Maybe the counselor would say something he could use as the reason to bring it up. Or maybe he would just invent something and blame it on the counselor! Either way, he decided, he would have to tell her by the middle of next week that they were through. Surely she would understand, with the kids in trouble. And he tried to imagine what nice thing he could buy for her.

Kristen had lunch in her apartment on that Friday, which was unusual. She was alone. She fixed herself a tall glass of white wine with her salad, which was also unusual. When that glass was gone, she poured another. She had not slept much the night before, and she was building her resolve to do what she knew was the right thing. Or at least that was what the voices in her mind had been telling her.

A little after 1:30, she put down her wine glass and called the television station. "Janet Sullivan, please," she said, and waited.

"This is Janet Sullivan."

"Hi, Janet. We've met, but you don't know me. Who I am is not really important right now. The important thing is that your husband loves me. We've been seeing each other for over six months now. We make love on Tuesdays and Thursdays when you think he's at the health club. He wants to leave you so we can live together. And I'm calling because I'm sure that all of us, including Tommy and Susan, who I understand are having problems now, would be better off if you two would split up."

Janet was silent for a long moment. "Is this a joke? Who are you? Connie, if you're trying to get back at me, or something, I don't appreciate it."

"My name is not Connie, and I'm not joking. Richard and I have been having an affair for months now. We love each other. I don't want to hurt you any more than absolutely necessary, so I won't repeat what he has said about you. He doesn't think you understand him. He wants to be with me, and I want him."

"Who are you?" Janet said, in a low voice filling quickly with anger.

"I'm not going to tell you. Ask Richard, if you like. But I'm telling you the truth. Remember his trip to Atlanta in the spring? Well, I went along, and we had a great time together. And let me describe your bedroom, where we made love when you and the kids were in Vermont."

Kristen went on to describe the Sullivans' bedroom and bath in minute detail, down to Janet's dresser drawer contents. After the first few items, when it was obvious that this woman knew her bedroom better than she did, Janet started to lose control. The humiliation was so great that she felt as if she were being stepped on and compressed into the chair. This woman had been making love to her husband in her bed, only three weeks ago! The fire and the hollowness alternating in her chest made her break out in a sweat, but also made it difficult to speak.

"What do you want from me?" she finally asked, when Kristen finished the description of their kitchen.

"I just want you and Richard to split up, so we can get on with our life together, and you and the children can get on with yours. Believe me, it will be better for everyone."

Janet had started to cry, but the mention of her children brought back the anger. "Please don't tell me what's best for our children, whoever you are!" she spat out. "We—I—am capable of determining that without your help."

"Yeah, it sounds like you've been doing a great job, from what Richard told me when he was here yesterday."

"Yesterday?"

"Yes, like I told you, we make love together at lunch almost every Tuesday and Thursday. Yesterday was particularly nice. We had champagne and celebrated the McKinney closing. Did you think to do that for him at home last night?"

Janet was so hurt, so humiliated, and so angry that she simply hung up the phone and pulled her hand from it as if it were a hot ember. Then she sat and stared at her desk for half an hour.

While his two women were finally talking, Richard received a call himself when he returned from lunch. It was Bruce McKinney, and he sounded breathless, as if he were calling after running a great distance.

"Richard. Listen. I just talked to the owner of Far West Securities. It seems the little scumbag who had been unhappy about being fired took the money we offered him to be quiet, said he would cooperate, and then talked to some hotshot reporter anyway. The morning edition of the San Francisco paper apparently has a lead article on the front of the business section about Far West, and, get this Richard, it mentions us several times as participants in the fraud.

"Our phones have been ringing since 11:00, but both David and I have been out. I called Far West first, and that's the news. You're our attorney, Richard. What do we do?"

Richard swore. "You said this wouldn't happen, Bruce. This is all a mess now."

"Hey. The guy said he would keep quiet, but he lied. Everyone lies today, Richard. Do we issue a statement or deny any knowledge or what? The news folks are all over us."

"Bruce, I'm not real experienced in this area. I need to bring in Court Shullo, who has handled this type of situation before. Don't do anything for the moment. I'll go find Court, brief him, and call you back."

"Make it fast, please."

Richard did not get up right away. He had to think how he was going to dance around what he knew beforehand with Court. He suddenly hoped that Bruce had the good sense not to mention their conversation over lunch on Tuesday to Court. He was picking up the phone to call Bruce back to remind him of that, when his intercom hummed. "It's Marty Tsongas on the phone, Mr. Sullivan."

"Did you tell him I'm here?"

"Yes, sir."

Reluctantly, Richard took the call. "What's this we're hearing out of San Francisco about McKinney and Smith being involved in some scam to cover up securities fraud?"

Richard paused. He had to be careful what he said, he knew. "I'm not quite sure myself, Marty. I just got a call from Bruce, which I have to return. I'll call you back after I talk to him."

"Richard, this smells. In fact, it stinks. Did you know anything about this before our closing?" Silence. "Because if you did, I'll have you up before your state ethics committee—and maybe the district attorney—so fast your head will swim. I hope you have a large errors and omissions policy, although I guess those don't usually cover outright fraud."

"Now Marty, calm down. I said I'd call you back, and I will."

Richard hung up, his shirt becoming wet with perspiration, even in the air conditioning. He had to stop this madness. He had to sit and think. But first he had to call Bruce back and then go find Court Shullo.

"Bruce, why don't you and David at least get out of there and come over here. We can strategize with Court and a small team of attorneys. And Bruce, remember that our lunch discussion never happened. I've got to play dumb, and you've got to back me up, or else I'm finished, too, and can't help either of us."

"I understand, and we're coming there now. See you in fifteen minutes."

Richard walked down the hall and found Court in his office. He briefed him on the information he had received that hour, as if he believed that Bruce could never be involved in any type of scam or fraud. "There must be some mistake," Richard concluded, "but I figured that we ought to bring you in now, just in case.

"Bruce and David are on the way over. Can you assemble two or three guys who are good at damage control and litigation, and with your criminal defense experience, we ought to be able to help them."

"Sure, Richard. I'll go brief Tim and Sandra, and we'll be ready when they get here."

An hour later the attorneys were assembled with Bruce and David in the main conference room. Under client-attorney protection, the two owners were telling their attorneys the truth. Richard took notes and acted as shocked and surprised as the others. But they were professionals and had been through tough situations with clients before. Court was just starting down his first list of recommendations when there was a knock, and Mary, Richard's secretary, opened the door.

"Excuse me, Mr. Sullivan. It's your wife."

Angered by the interruption, he snapped at Mary, "Tell her I'll call her back in an hour or so."

"No, sir. She's here. She says she has to see you."

Richard was astonished. In twenty years of marriage, he could never remember Janet doing something like this, unannounced.

"Uh . . . OK . . . I'll be right there. Please excuse me for just a minute. This must be something pretty important."

"Sure, Richard. We'll take notes and catch you up when you get back," Court offered.

"Where is she?" Richard asked Mary in the hall.

"Sitting in your office. And, Mr. Sullivan, I'm afraid she doesn't look too well," Mary said, trying to be helpful.

As Richard entered his office, he could see Janet's head over the high-backed chair across from his desk. She did not turn as he walked around in front of her. Richard was startled. Mary was right. Janet looked terrible, as if she had been crying and running her fingers through her hair.

"Janet, what's wrong? Are the kids OK?"

She stared straight ahead and, obviously in pain, said, in a low, hoarse whisper, "I guess they're fine. As fine as they can be with a father who sleeps twice a week with his mistress."

Another knife in Richard's heart, for the third time that week. Again his knees were weak, and he felt as if he couldn't breathe. "What?" was all he could say, as he sat down on the front edge of his desk.

She finally moved her eyes to meet his. "I received a call right after lunch from a woman who says that we've met, but she wouldn't tell me who she was. Her voice was vaguely familiar, and I've been sitting in my office for almost an hour, trying to figure out who she is. I think I finally did. It was that young, attractive real estate woman we met at the symphony several months ago, wasn't it, Richard?

"I don't know."

"Yes, you do, you slime ball," Janet's voice began to gain control again. "She, or someone, called up and told me that you had been . . . I can't even say it . . . with her at lunch on Tuesdays and Thursdays, instead of going to your health club." Richard turned pale. "She said you love each other and that it would be better for all of us, especially the children," Janet started to fight back tears, "if you and I split up and let the two of you get on with your life together. Richard—" And now tears streamed down her cheeks, and she did not even bother to wipe them with the wet tissue she clutched in her hand. "Richard, this woman has been in our bedroom. She knows where I keep my things in my own drawers. She said the two of you made love on our bed while I was in Vermont with our children. She said she went with you to Atlanta." The tears fell from her face and puddled on her dress, as she held her head up, not moving, trying to rescue a trace of dignity from her utter humiliation. "Richard, how could you?"

He hung his head, slowly got up, walked around the desk, and collapsed in his chair like a sack. She continued to look at him, not moving, only crying.

"I . . . I . . . " he whispered. "I tried to break up with her many times. I knew it was wrong. But I didn't stop it. I would get mad at you for working so hard at the station, and she made me feel good. I was an idiot. The crazy thing is that all of this trouble with the kids finally made me realize how stupid I've been, and I decided to break up with her next week, after we meet with the counselor."

"I'll try to remember to have champagne for you that night to celebrate, like the two of you apparently did at lunch yesterday. Do you realize, Richard, that it's not just the sex and the humiliation of having another woman with my husband in my own bed? It's your mind and your soul she's taken from us as well. If something was good enough to celebrate, why didn't you celebrate with your family? What else of you have we missed because you've shared it with her and not with us? What's her name, Richard?"

"Kristen. Kristen Holloway."

"That's right. And she is the one in real estate, right? The dark brown hair?"

Richard nodded, still looking down.

Just then his intercom interrupted them. It was Mary. "I'm terribly sorry, Mr. Sullivan, but it's Mr. Tsongas. He *insisted* that I interrupt you. He wouldn't hang up. He said to tell you that if you don't take his call now, the next calls he makes will be to the state ethics committee of the bar association and to the district attorney."

Richard spoke toward the intercom in a calm voice. "Please tell Mr. Tsongas that my wife is here with a problem, that we have a team working on *his* problem, and that I *will* call him back this afternoon, but I can't talk to him now."

"Yes, sir."

"Trouble, Richard?" There was a note of pleasure in her voice.

"Yes, but we'll handle it."

"You always do. Well, Richard, I'm sure that sometime I will want to hear all of the gruesome details about you two, like during our divorce proceedings." Janet straightened her dress and wiped her face, further destroying her make-up. "But for now let's just say that I will be glad to grant you and Kristen your fondest wish. You can be *free*. *Free!* If that's who and what you want, then good riddance. I'll add an adulterous husband to the homosexual son and the slutty daughter I've already been handed this week. Isn't life great? I was so happy, just a few short weeks ago, in Vermont. I remember actually thinking that. Even with you, thinking that we were actually starting to make it work again. You seemed to be trying. I know I was." Her voice gained strength and rose almost to a yell. "And all the time you were with that bimbo! So, goodbye, Richard. If I didn't have to go back to the station and be sure that '911 Live' starts OK, I'd go home and pack your bag one last time. Please don't ever sleep in my house again."

She turned to walk to the door. He could think of nothing to say. "And I'll probably tell our lying children that they came by that trait naturally. No point in holding them to any promises this weekend is there, Richard? Have a great time with Kristen. I hope she knows how to mend your shirts." And she left, slamming the door behind her.

Richard sat in shock for ten minutes. Finally, Mary knocked at his door and came in. She became very worried when he just stared up at her, a vacant glaze in his eyes. "Mr. Sullivan, Mr. Shullo says they're waiting for you in the conference room."

"Yes . . . Fine . . . Please tell them I'll be right there," he whispered, "but I have to go to the restroom first."

His heart was like a cold stone. But his stomach was churning. He could hardly make it, his knees were so weak, but he reached the restroom just in time to become violently ill. He found himself kneeling in front of the toilet, crying like a baby, and throwing up his guts. After ten minutes, the agony subsided a bit, and he washed his face and hands and rinsed out his mouth. He looked at himself in the mirror. He stared. He looked ten years older than at lunch that day.

He cleaned himself up as best he could, stopped by his office for his pad, and entered the conference room. The others had obviously grown impatient waiting for him, but they were shocked nevertheless by his altered appearance. "Are you all right?" Bruce asked, as Richard retook his chair.

He waved his hand and smiled. "Sure. Everything's fine. What did I miss?"

Court went back over the strategy written on the large newsprint pad. Richard listened and took notes, but he had a hard time concentrating.

Finally, when he realized that they were all looking at him, he nodded approval and said, "That sounds fine to me for the weekend. Let's implement it and meet again at, say, 10:00 on Monday morning. OK?" Everyone nodded. "Bruce, I'll stop by your house tonight or in the morning. Court, can I see you for a minute?"

When there were only the two of them in the room, Richard gave Court a piece of paper with Marty Tsongas' name and telephone number on it. "Court, please call Marty. He's the attorney for the Tomlinsons, who just invested almost one million dollars in Bruce's company this morning. He's not happy, as you can imagine. Please tell him that I'm in another meeting, and divulge to him as much or as little as your experience says is OK. Then tell him that I'll get back to him on Monday morning. OK?"

"Sure, Richard. By the way, these guys have really gotten themselves into a mess," said the younger attorney.

"That's why they pay us so much to get them out. Work on it over the weekend, and I'll see you early Monday morning."

It had taken a supreme effort to appear normal and calm during the past hour. Once he had told Mary not to let anyone disturb him and sunk back in his own chair in his empty office, Richard's total hollowness returned. He swiveled and looked out at the late afternoon scene of the city. Everyone seemed to be hurrying somewhere on that Friday afternoon, but he had nowhere to go. He no longer had a home or a family. He had trouble breathing, and his shirt was still damp from his earlier perspiration. For a long time, he just stared.

Nepravel had of course been there all afternoon, joining the two demons who were regularly posted at the law firm. Now the three of them were joined by Balzor himself, who floated into Richard's office through the plate-glass window. "How is it going?" he asked Nepravel.

"Just as you planned, sire—even better, perhaps. Janet has told him never to live in her house again, and she may release the children to do whatever they want this weekend. He's just sitting here, staring out."

"We've got to make him mad—and soon. It's getting late. Nepravel, turn up the voice of Hate."

Richard had been daydreaming, really, his mind wandering among different parts of his problems. He imagined that he might just pull through the difficult business with Tsongas and Tomlinson. It would be close and would depend on how hard they pushed, how much money Tomlinson ultimately lost, and how loyal Bruce was. He might save his legal skin—or he might lose it.

But as important as those problems had been before Janet arrived, they no longer occupied center stage in his mind. His family. He had lost his family. He would never spend the night with all four of them together again. He was still a biological father, but could he ever be a real father to Susan and Tommy again? Lost. All lost. Forever.

And why? *Kristen Holloway,* he heard a voice within him say. *That witch destroyed our family for her own selfish ends. How could I have been so blind to how selfish she is? She called Janet and told her everything, deliberately trying to hurt her. Poor Janet. No wonder she was upset! That stupid, selfish shrew!*

It never occurred to Richard that *he* was responsible for the destruction of his family, at least not in a loud enough voice for him to hear over the other voices. Balzor, Nepravel, and the others pushed the voices further, enraging him even more.

The rest of the law offices were empty. It was after 6:00. Mary almost knocked, but decided that she had interrupted him enough for one day. So she left him a short note, wishing him a happy weekend, and left. Richard stood up and began pacing, becoming madder and madder at Kristen for sticking her nose into his family. What right did she have, after all, to do this to him? And to his kids?

Janet drove back to the station, reminding herself repeatedly that she was a professional. Particularly if she was going to have to make her own living now, she had better do a good job. So she stopped at a restaurant and used the restroom to recreate her face. When she pulled into the station, she vowed that she would not let Richard affect her work, either that night or ever again.

Everything went smoothly. At 6:00 the cameras and microphones on all of the vehicles and emergency personnel were turned on and tested. The link with Network in New York worked well, and the local director, Kevin Jones, was in his chair. Just before 6:30, the vehicles with the special equipment rolled, looking for stories. Janet knew that the same scene was occurring simultaneously in nine other cities across the country.

Once everything was underway, Janet said goodnight to Bill Shaw and the large group gathered at the station to watch the first broadcast. She had explained to Bill her intentions to watch it at home, and he gave her a thumbs-up sign as she waved goodbye through the glass window of the control room.

Kristen felt great after her phone call to Janet. A heavy burden had been lifted from her. As she put away her lunch plates and freshened up for her 3:00 showing that afternoon, it occurred to her that if all went according to her plan, Richard would probably be spending that night, and all his nights from now on, with her.

Later, she hurried home from her appointment, arriving about 5:30. There was no message from Richard on her answering machine, but plenty of messages from her clients. So she started returning their calls.

Richard continued to pace in his office, while Balzor and the demons turned up the pressure. *My children deserve a better life than they're now going to have, and she robbed them of it. What if Janet remarries and the kids wind up liking him more? Blast it all! Kristen has really done it. She deserves a swift kick or a slap in the face!*

She probably thinks I'm going to come over there, fall down on my knees, and thank her. Well, hardly! In fact, I think I'll go over and slap her. Would that be simple enough? Just walk in, slap her, and tell her she's a slut. She needs to feel how I feel. She needs to feel ruined.

Richard picked up his phone and dialed her number. "Hello," she said. He hung up, having verified that she was in her apartment. He grabbed his coat and keys, not bothering with his briefcase. *I'll probably spend the night here,* he thought, and was even more depressed and upset.

Kristen, who didn't like it when a phone caller hung up immediately, glanced up to see that her night chain was locked across the door. Then she called back another of her potential purchasers, wondering what had happened to Richard. It was almost 7:00.

As Richard drove to her apartment, followed closely by Balzor and Nepravel, he became angrier and angrier. His career hung by a string. He was incredibly in debt. His children were running wild. When would he next see his kids, and what would he say, after criticizing their behavior the way he had? That woman!

She'll be in there with the night chain on. How will I get in? Maybe she'll open it. The bolt cutter! Tom Bryant put it in the trunk weeks ago, and I've never moved it. It'll cut through a night chain in an instant. Good luck, he thought.

Richard parked in a visitor space at Park Place and took the bolt cutter out of the trunk. As he walked through the front door with his key, he smiled at Bart and said, holding up the tool, "She locked a trunk and can't open it." The doorman smiled and nodded knowingly.

Janet pulled in at about 7:15. Susan and Tommy already had the television on, tuned to TV5, but they were elsewhere in the house, waiting for the appointed starting time.

She put her things down and freshened up again in front of the mirror. She would not have time to tell the kids about Richard before the show, but maybe they could talk afterwards, or in the morning. It would not be easy, but it had not been an easy week, and it had to be done, since Richard would be moving out immediately.

Kristen was sitting on her sofa in the middle of a conversation with Mr. Robert Bradley, to whom she had shown a house on Tuesday, when she heard the key turn in her front latch. "Hold on just a minute, Mr. Bradley," Kristen said. "I'll be right back." She lay the handset down on its side on the table next to the sofa and walked toward the door.

"Richard, is that you?"

"Take off the chain, Kristen."

Something odd about his voice gave her pause, and she looked out before removing the chain. She could not believe the transformation. The anger in his face, especially his eyes, was overpowering. She stepped back, shocked.

"Take off the chain, Kristen. Right now!"

"Richard, what's happened?" she whispered, her hand at her face.

"What's happened!?" He brought the large bolt cutter up and sliced through the night chain in one stroke.

He flung her door back, walked in, and slammed it. "What's happened!?" he yelled at her. All the time Kristen was backing up, shock on her face.

"You know exactly what's happened, you slut! You called Janet and destroyed our marriage and the woman I love, in one five-minute call— that's what happened!" he yelled in her face. Then he slapped her with his free hand. She screamed. He grabbed her wrist and flung her on the sofa.

Mr. Bradley, who had been listening on the open telephone line, heard the slamming, yelling, the slap, and finally the scream. He became very concerned for the safety of the attractive real estate agent who had been so patient with his wife on Tuesday, and reached over for his hand-held cellular telephone, which had been recharging on his desk. With it he dialed 911.

The operator answered immediately, and Mr. Bradley quickly explained what was happening.

"Do you have the address?" the operator asked.

"No, but I have the telephone number."

"That's OK. Our computer can cross-check for the address instantly." He gave Kristen's home telephone number to the operator.

"I'll dispatch a police unit immediately. Did you say you can hear what's happening?"

"Yes, she apparently put the phone down on the table right next to where he's now standing, and he's yelling so loudly I can hear most of his words."

"Would you mind putting your two handsets together, earpiece to microphone so that we can try to listen in and tape it?"

Mr. Bradley complied, and using the amplification equipment at the 911 emergency center, the operator was able to hear Richard's voice in Kristen's apartment, as he berated her and told her what a slut she was.

Janet, Tommy, and Susan had gathered in their den to watch the beginning of "911 Live." After a brief explanation about the show's groundbreaking concept and a quick look at the new equipment needed to link the cities together, promising more information later, the anchor-man cut to a fire which was burning out of control in an apartment complex in suburban Chicago.

"Hey, this is wild," Tommy said. "You mean this is really happening right now, while we watch?"

"Yes," replied Janet, "as we watch. For good or for ill."

Wrapping her arms around herself and tucking her feet beneath her on the sofa, Susan said, "It sort of gives me the creeps, not knowing what may happen to someone next. Mom, where's Dad? I thought he wanted to see this."

Janet, remembering the most painful afternoon of her life, said, "I'll tell you when this is over. Let's just watch the show for now."

"I don't love you," Richard spat at Kristen. He was still looming over her, the huge bolt cutter in his left hand, as she cowered on the sofa beneath him, sobbing and scared for her life.

"I was going to leave you next week . . . even buy you something nice to make it all right." He laughed derisively.

"But you told me you loved me," Kristen managed to cry.

"Hey, you know what a client told me today? 'Everyone lies.' I guess I lied, Kristen. We used each other pretty well. Only you blew my life apart, and now you're going to have to pay," he said, vaguely imagining that he would slap her a few more times.

"I love you, Richard," she whispered.

"Tell that to my kids, the ones I'll never live with again!" he yelled.

On the internal link between TV5 and New York, Kevin Jones alerted Mark, "Hey, we've got a possible burglary, or violent domestic, with live audio here."

"What? Live audio?" Mark asked from the "911 Live" central control room.

"There's an open telephone line into this apartment. The police are on the way with video, but we can hear this guy yelling and threatening a woman, over her phone, which is right next to where he's standing."

"Fantastic. We'll cut right to you. Get ready."

Kevin threw the switch for the internal intercom back to the studio where the TV5 personnel had assembled to watch the show on their large screen. "They're coming to us next. It could be a hot one. Stand by."

The crowd quieted in anticipation.

As the Sullivans watched from their den, the anchor in New York interrupted the apartment fire story and described the unusual circumstance to which they were now switching.

Suddenly there was a street scene from their city, as the minicam in the police car showed the unit speeding through traffic. As the Park Place apartments came into clear view ahead, the audio was suddenly patched in live.

"Get up, you slut, so I can slap you again," the voice yelled.

"That's awful," Susan said.

"Cool," said Tommy. "I hope the cops get there in time so we can see some of this."

■   ■   ■

"No, Richard, don't," the sobbing woman's voice replied, as the video showed the police car stopping in front of the apartment house.

Richard grabbed Kristen's wrist to pull her up, and in the turning motion, he noticed the phone handset on the sidetable. "What's that?" He released her wrist to reach across for the phone, and in that instant of rising up, she pushed him and ran back to her bedroom, slamming and locking the door.

Forgetting the phone, Richard went after her. "Kristen!" he yelled. "I've got a score to settle with you."

Janet froze, sitting in her den, watching through the microcam on the policeman's helmet, as the two officers entered the elevator. Richard. Kristen. "Ohhhh . . ." she moaned, bringing her hands to her lips. Susan and Tommy turned to look at their mother and had never before seen so much pain on any person's face.

"Come out of there, or I'll knock the door down," the man's voice yelled, somewhat dimmer because it was further away. But the two children nevertheless recognized it.

Susan turned to her mother in horror. "Is that Dad on the television?" she gasped.

Janet, tears streaming down her face, stared at the screen, and could only nod.

"What's he doing?" Tommy asked, equally scared.

Continuing to cry, Janet started to emit a low, chilling wail from inside her soul. Hearing their mother, the children were even more afraid.

"Open this door!" Richard yelled, his anger rising to a new peak because she had run away. He pounded on the door and then began hitting the doorknob with the bolt cutter, trying to break it off.

Kristen, trapped in the bedroom and scared for her life, looked around and saw her purse where she had tossed it on the bed. She ran to it, opened the catch, and pulled out her Sig Sauer automatic pistol. Releasing the safety, her hands slippery from wiping away her tears, she turned, leveled the gun, and yelled toward the door, "Don't come in here, Richard. I've got my gun."

Just as she spoke those words, he struck the doorknob with a heavy blow. The knob broke off, and the door swung open. He pushed it further with his hand, and came through it, intending to yell at her again.

Kristen saw the door fly open and Richard's form come through, leading with the bolt cutter. She fired.

The police officers were coming through Kristen's front door as the gun went off. The noise on the nation's television screens was deafening. Janet screamed. Susan shrieked and began crying. Tommy got up and stood behind his mother, wanting somehow to comfort her. The video image blurred as the police officer dove to the floor.

As the policeman on the floor looked up and the camera recorded what he saw, Richard staggered back into the living room, holding his chest, blood clearly oozing from between his fingers. He looked with wild, uncomprehending eyes toward the police officer, and so his family was looking directly into his face as he slumped to his knees, then fell over on the carpet.

Someone in the crowd in the TV5 studio yelled, "Hey, isn't that Janet Sullivan's husband, Richard?"

"No way," Bill Shaw said. But he looked again and swore loudly. "It *is* Richard! Where's Janet?"

Janet was sobbing hysterically in her seat. Susan was crying and shrieking, biting her fingers. Tommy kept repeating, "Dad! . . . Dad! . . . Dad! . . ." as he paced behind the sofa, crying.

Next to Janet, the telephone began to ring.

Back in Kristen's apartment, Richard tried to speak, to explain that it was all a mistake, that he had only wanted to scare her, as the policeman rolled him over onto his back, and knelt over him. But no sound came from his mouth. As he stared up into the policeman's face and therefore into the microcamera, everything suddenly went very dark for Richard.

But only for an instant. The next moment, Richard's soul rose from his body, free to spend eternity without the confines of a human form. His spirit was shocked, looking down on his former body and on the scene around it. Then he was overcome with a paralyzing fear, as he realized that the black forms of Balzor and Nepravel had surrounded him, and he smelled for the first time the sulfurous stench of their hate for him.

By long tradition, they could not yet speak to him, not until after the Judgment Seat, but he looked at them in his nakedness, knowing exactly who they were and who they represented, and he shook uncontrollably. *This can't be real. There aren't supposed to be demons and a devil. I know that for sure. Everyone knows that*, he said to himself, in a 'voice' he used for the first time. But his eyes and nose told him that they were very real, and both now started to laugh silently, apparently having somehow heard his thoughts.

In another moment a light started to appear, and Richard noticed that the demons shrank back as the light grew brighter. Richard glanced down and saw Kristen standing over his body along with the police, as an officer took the gun from her hand. Then somehow he knew about "911 Live" and that his family had been watching. "Oh, no," his new voice recorded in horror, as he turned toward the growing brilliance of the light.

Richard had never seen such light. The huge angel was descending toward them, his two eagles' heads constantly moving. Richard was in utter awe as the angel came close, and then they started to move away together. He turned and saw that the larger demon was staying behind, but the other one took up position next to him, on the opposite side from the angel.

They traveled together for Richard knew not how long. He fixed on the angel, trying to avoid the staring smile and the awful stench of the demon. Soon they neared a source of light even stronger than the angel's, if that were possible. The demon and the angel pulled away from him, and his spirit continued on toward the light, which ultimately revealed itself as a large, brilliant throne room.

He was propelled into the room, and as he entered, he saw more angels, like the one who had brought him, only these were flying with one set of their wings and covering their faces and feet with the others, screaming, "Holy, Holy, Holy is the Lord God of Hosts." And voices from everywhere were lifting a steady harmony of praise and worship, proclaiming His glory and His righteousness.

Richard, naked, realized that he had arrived alone at the throne of God.

The Light appeared as a large human form, seated on a huge throne. Next to Him, at His right hand, was a white Lamb, alive, but with his throat cut, as if the Lamb had been sacrificed. Richard could barely stand the brilliance. He still could not believe that this was happening. A real God, just like in the Bible! How could it be? Why had no one told him?

In the next moment Richard suddenly began reliving his entire life on earth, from his childhood through school, law school, marriage, children, Kristen, everything. He had no idea how long it took, but the effect was debilitating. In the presence of the perfect God, his own imperfections, lies, sins, and rationalizations cried out their difference from what God had expected of him. Halfway through his life, he hung his head and tried to hide from God, but there was no place to go. He was alone with his Creator, who was judging him, as He had always promised that He would. When his family was reviewed, Richard started to wail, the enormity of his betrayal bared for him to see and to feel.

When his life review was completed, the Light spoke thunderously. "He has sinned and cannot partake of heaven, where there is no sin." Then the Light addressed the Lamb, and asked, "Is his name written in the Book of Life?"

The Lamb, also surrounded by brilliant Light, replied, "No, Father. His sins are not atoned for by the Blood of the Lamb. He did not believe."

"Then he is to be cast into Darkness," were the last words that Richard's soul ever heard God speak, for all of eternity.

He cried out. "There must be a mistake. This can't be! I know I hurt my family, but I didn't kill anyone. I'm no worse than most of the men I know." His spirit started moving away from the throne, but not by his will. "Please. No one told me it would be like this. Please give me another chance. If I had known it would be like this, I would have done differently. What do you want me to do? I'll do it. Anything! Please . . ."

As he left the throne room, he realized that Nepravel was waiting for him. He screamed in terror, but Nepravel laughed a blood-chilling laugh, and Richard heard him for the first time. Now that Richard belonged to him, Nepravel could speak.

Still laughing, Nepravel answered the question Richard had posed to God. "Oh, but someone *did* tell you about all of this. We've just been confusing you. And you bought all of it! You could have escaped your future and gone to heaven, where we can't go. But now you're *ours*, forever!" And his laugh pierced Richard. "Come with me, now, Richard. This is what I live for!" And Richard's soul was led away to an eternity without God.

If demons could hold a party, then that night's meeting over the city qualified. Balzor was exuberant. They had destroyed a prominent figure in the community, driving another nail of disbelief into the people's general sense of decency in their society.

And they were well on the way to destroying Richard's family members, and all of their friends and associates, through what had happened to Richard. Who knew what might soon happen to Susan, Tommy, Amy, Brent, Janet, and all the other humans who had been associated with Richard?

This was truly a great victory for the forces of Darkness. One of several that day. As their meeting broke up, Balzor slowly circled his sector of the city, content that the Light was now almost completely extinguished.

Book Two

FOREWORD

The preceding pages recount what might have happened to Richard Sullivan and his family. Happily, there was actually another outcome. The following pages describe what really happened to them all.

1

TEN YEARS EARLIER ■ Susan and Tommy were asleep in the back seat of the station wagon, dozing after their lunch on the road, as Richard counted down the last few miles to Tarpon Springs, just north of Tampa. Susan was clutching her favorite doll, and Tommy was curled up on his pillow, sucking the two middle fingers of his left hand.

"It shouldn't be too much farther now," Janet said, holding on her lap both a map and the directions to the Petersons' home, which Scott had mailed to Richard the previous week.

Richard and Janet had not seen Scott or Cindy Peterson since their wedding, right after their college graduation. Scott was Richard's roommate during their senior year, and Janet introduced him to Cindy, who was one of her sorority sisters. Scott was known on campus as a "wild man," but he visibly calmed under Cindy's influence, as their romance budded and grew. As so often happened in those days, the two of them were married that June, and both Richard and Janet were in the wedding.

When Richard and Janet were married the following summer, after Richard's first year of law school, Scott was serving in Vietnam, and Cindy was tending to their baby daughter, Lacy, who was born almost nine months to the day after their wedding. So the Petersons were not able to participate in the Sullivans' wedding. In fact, the two couples had not seen each other for the entire intervening period. They kept up by telephone calls, letters, and Christmas cards. But when Richard and Janet had decided to take Susan and Tommy to Disney World that year, they had called the Petersons, and now they were only a few miles from their home.

"Hey, sleepy heads, time to wake up," Janet smiled, as she turned around and shook her children.

"Are we at Disney World yet?" Tommy asked, rubbing his eyes.

"No, dear. That will be tomorrow. Now we're almost to our friends' home, and you'll be able to play with Lacy and Jeff."

Janet had convinced Richard that this was the year to visit Disney World, since Susan was only in the first grade, and they could take her out of school for a few days without a problem. And they would miss some of the rush that would hit Orlando during the regular days of spring vacation. Richard had made partner in the law firm two years before, and he was finally feeling he could relax every now and then, even though the work load was still tremendous.

He and Janet had their eye on a home on Devon Drive, which was supposed to be up for sale that summer. Compared to their small ranch home in the suburbs, the Devon Drive home offered a much larger yard and a wonderful city park nearby. So Richard was working hard to ensure that his income would qualify for the necessary loan. But Janet finally prevailed on the need for a family vacation, and he was frankly glad to be out of the office for a week with his young family.

They had left Friday morning, spent the night on the road, and now it was Saturday afternoon as they pulled into the Petersons' driveway in Tarpon Springs. The Petersons bounded out of their front door as soon as the Sullivans' car was in the driveway, and the four adults embraced and kissed in the front yard. The Petersons' children were each approximately two years older than Susan and Tommy, but they were soon all playing together in the backyard.

"You look great, Janet." Scott held her at arm's length and then gave her another hug. "I can't believe we're finally all back together again after so many years."

"And married life seems to agree with you, too, Richard," Cindy smiled, patting the slight bulge of his stomach.

"No complaints, no complaints at all," Richard laughed. "Janet's the best homemaker in the business!"

Richard and Scott unloaded their overnight bags while Janet and Cindy arranged the kids' sleeping quarters. Soon the four adults were relaxing on the Petersons' patio, drinks in hand, watching the children running and jumping together, joined now by several of the neighborhood kids.

Scott, who had opened an insurance agency with some friends from his army days, had completely adapted to the casual Florida lifestyle. That evening they grilled swordfish steaks for themselves and hamburgers for the kids, while catching up on almost ten years of news.

"I can't believe how tall Susan is," Cindy marveled. "It's hard to tell from her pictures. She's almost as tall as Lacy."

"Jeff has amazingly nice manners." Janet returned the compliment. "I hope in two years that Tommy is behaving as nicely as Jeff is tonight."

After dinner, while Janet and Cindy worked on bedding down the excited children, Richard and Scott nursed another round and continued to catch up with each other.

"Remembering you hanging off the balcony at our dorm," Richard smiled at Scott, "it's hard to picture you married and settled down. You were always the wilder of us, Scott, and I imagined you would be a pilot or something equally challenging."

"Eyes, Richard. I couldn't ever pass the eye test. So I wound up on the ground instead, in-country Vietnam, and that's where my life really changed."

"I bet," Richard said. He had not served in the armed forces because of a high draft lottery number.

"No, Richard, I mean *really* changed. Cindy and I have a strong faith now, which began for me with an experience I had in those days."

"What happened?" Richard asked.

"Well, as you may recall, I received a grazing wound in the right thigh." Scott patted his leg as he spoke. "There's still a chunk missing. It really wasn't that bad, but it got me medivac'd out to a field hospital.

"After my operation, there were six of us in this particular ward. I was the only one from our unit, but the three guys across from me were the only survivors from a patrol the VC had ambushed. In the bed on one end was a white guy who had his right thigh and right hand completely bandaged. On the left end was a black guy whose legs had been shot up much worse than mine. The doctors said he would never walk again. But in the middle bed was another white guy, their buddy, who had his midsection badly torn up and was in a coma. On my second day there, one of the nurses told me that the middle guy—his name was Reese— wasn't expected to live another twenty-four hours.

"Now you knew me in school, Richard. Like you, I don't think I ever darkened the door of a church while we were in college, and I certainly could not boast about my faith then. But it turned out that these three guys were all from the same town—they had played football on the same high school varsity team, and had been active in the Campus Crusade for Christ. And they had all enlisted together.

"Richard, I lay there day after day, night after night, and I watched the white guy and the black guy pray for Reese incessantly. The white guy would kneel on one side and whisper his prayers in Reese's ear. The black guy, who couldn't get out of bed, would reach over and hold on to Reese's arm, and together he and the first guy would pray. The other three of us in the ward started out as skeptical as we could be, and at first we even asked them to keep their prayers quiet, so we could read or sleep. But those two guys never flinched. They told us about the power of prayer and about how the Holy Spirit had already worked miracles in their lives, both back home and in-country.

"Frankly, their prayers were infectious. Within a few days we were all praying for Reese. They talked me into hobbling over with my cane and laying my hands on Reese's head and praying with them.

"Richard, I could not have explained it to you, then. But eight days later, after almost around-the-clock praying, Reese was not only still alive, but he woke up from his coma and smiled. I mean, here this guy was—his whole midsection was spaghetti—and he wakes up and *smiles* at his buddies!"

Richard noticed that Scott's eyes were becoming moist as he retold the story from nine years earlier. "Reese was in terrible pain, but as soon as he could, he began praying with his friends. Richard, a week later, the black guy got up out of his bed, and with the help of my cane, he walked! The doctors and nurses were flabbergasted. They started calling us the 'Prayer Power Ward.' Other men in the hospital began coming to my three new friends and asking them to pray and to lay hands on them. People started being healed, Richard. And just as importantly, they started believing.

"When I saw Mac—that was the black guy—walk, I told all three of them that I'd seen enough. I wanted whatever it was they had, which was not only healing them but giving them such inner strength. They explained to me how simple it was, and that night, with them, I prayed for Jesus to forgive my sins, and I asked Him to come into my life, take it over, and use me as He wanted."

Richard could not believe what he was hearing from his old fraternity brother. *I guess you had to be there to appreciate it*, Richard thought silently to himself, *but Scott has really gone off the deep end.*

"At any rate," Scott continued, "in that hospital the four of us began a friendship that is still flourishing to this day. In fact, they were from near Tampa, and it was with those three guys that I started the insurance business here several years ago. If you and Janet come to church with us in the morning, you can meet each one of them. And unless you look closely, you'll never be able to tell that they spent many months in Army and VA hospitals.

"So when I say that my life changed in Vietnam, that's what I mean. I thank God every day for the little bit of pain I went through in order to receive such a blessing."

"Well, Scott, we'd certainly like to go to church with you in the morning," Richard said, "but we promised the kids we'd get to Disney World as early as possible after spending the night with you. So I think we'd better shove off for Orlando when you guys head to church. But I really appreciate your story, and maybe next time we can make it."

"Sure, Richard, sure. That'll be great," Scott said, knowing that it would probably never happen. "Well, let's go in and see how the kids are doing. It must be time for a goodnight kiss or two."

The next morning the Sullivans packed their station wagon and left for Orlando as the Petersons left for their church. On the way down the interstate, Richard repeated Scott's story to Janet. When he finished, he said, smiling, "Isn't that wild? Imagine. It sounds like something out of a holy roller TV show."

"Yes, it does," agreed Janet. "Cindy mentioned their faith and their church several times in our conversation, but I didn't really pick up on it. Isn't it amazing how people can change?"

"It sure is." Richard shrugged off Scott's experience as some kind of hallucination. But a seed was planted in Richard that might bear fruit many years later.

2

FOUR YEARS EARLIER ■ Janet was feeling a little tense. One of her best friends from growing up in Vermont, Sally Coker, should be driving up any minute to spend the night with them, and Janet had only just arrived home from her new job at the TV5 television station. Although she had been preparing for Sally's arrival for days, her new responsibilities had caused her to work later than expected, and now there were many last-minute preparations to be made. So she said goodbye to the housekeeper who looked after their children in the afternoons and then set about preparing dinner, hoping that the children's homework demands would not be too great that evening.

Sally Coker had been through a tough time with her marriage. Always interested in the outdoors, she and some friends had taken a camping trip to an unpopulated barrier island off the South Carolina coast one fall, several years after college. There she met an ardent outdoorsman, Henry Coker, from Charleston. They hit it off immediately and were married only six months later, in a spectacular outdoor ceremony at one of Charleston's beautiful and historic gardens.

For the next several years, Henry divided his time between his paving company, camping with Sally, and hunting with childhood friends. Sally joined Henry in camping, especially in the early years of their marriage, and then concentrated on raising the three children who came along quickly.

The Sullivans and the Cokers had seen each other during several summers in Vermont, when Janet and Sally returned to their parents' homes for vacations.

But as Janet put the finishing touches on her special chicken dish that Richard liked so much, she thought through what a difficult ordeal Sally had experienced during the past five years. Like a bolt of lightning, Sally was awakened early one morning by a telephone call from Henry, who was in the custody of federal marshals, arrested for attempting to smuggle bales of marijuana into the country on a friend's fishing boat.

Sally thought that Henry was duck hunting that night, but in fact, he and his three friends had rendezvoused off shore with a mother ship and had then transported a full load of marijuana up one of the hundreds of nondescript rivers and creeks that make up that part of the South Carolina coast, to what they thought would be an abandoned shrimping dock. Unfortunately, there had apparently been a tip-off of the federal agents, and Henry and his friends were all arrested, along with a boatload of evidence.

There had then followed a year of legal maneuvering and extremely expensive legal fees, which drained the income from Henry's fledgling company. The Cokers were forced to sell their home and to move into a much smaller rental home in the suburbs.

Almost eighteen months after his arrest, Henry was finally sentenced to five years in prison. He was sent to a minimum security facility in the West, and due to his record of good behavior, he was being paroled this week. Sally had left the kids with friends near Charleston and was driving to meet Henry at the prison. She would be spending the night with Richard and Janet, then driving on in the morning. Although they had spoken on the telephone many times, neither Janet nor Richard had seen Sally since Henry was sentenced to prison, and they wanted to make her feel very welcome.

Richard arrived home a little after six and immediately noticed the wonderful smell of Janet's chicken dish in the oven. *That's how it used to be almost every weekday*, Richard was reminded, *before she took this new job at the television station six months ago. I wonder if she'll really stay there? I know it's selfish of me, and her income is nice, but I certainly did like having her at home.*

Richard and Janet kissed in the kitchen, and he went upstairs to change clothes. Just then Sally drove up, and Janet waved through her large kitchen bay window. She then went out to the garage to welcome her lifelong friend.

After Richard greeted Sally in the entrance hall and her bags were stored in the guest room, he mixed them all drinks, and they sat in the den while Susan, at age thirteen, sipped a Coke with them. Tommy, after a quick hello, elected to watch television in the basement.

"I feel like I'm coming out the end, finally, of a very long tunnel," Sally reflected, thanking Richard for her cranberry juice and soda. "There's not much in general life training from parents or teachers to prepare you for your husband being arrested and taken to prison for almost four years."

With characteristic early teen bluntness, Susan asked. "What exactly did your husband do?" Richard shifted in his chair. Janet looked down, but Sally smiled at Susan.

"I don't mind talking about it in the least. In an incredibly complex way, it's probably about the best thing which has happened to us in our marriage, other than the birth of our three children, of course." And Sally recounted for Susan and her parents all the factual details of their experience.

As Sally was nearing the end of her story, Janet excused herself and put the finishing touches on their dinner in the kitchen. A few minutes later, Tommy joined them. They all enjoyed a chicken dish that Janet's mother had taught her to make. Sally remembered it from when they were childhood friends in Vermont.

Two hours later, when the kids were in bed and Richard had quietly pulled some papers out of his briefcase, signaling that the two women were free to talk without involving him, although he politely listened with one ear, Janet asked Sally, "I can't help but remember your earlier statement that this mess with Henry has been one of the best things that ever happened to your marriage. How on earth could that be possible, Sally?"

"It's hard to explain to someone who hasn't experienced it. But I'll try. Less than a week after he was arrested and released on bail, Henry and I left the children with friends and spent a night alone together in one of the downtown Charleston hotels, just to get away. I was so hurt, angry, and humiliated. Nothing in my background had prepared me for a seemingly loving and respected husband being arrested as a common criminal, with his picture paraded almost daily across the local newspapers. As you can imagine, the telephone calls began immediately after his arrest. First local calls from our friends, then from farther away as our families and long-time friends in other places heard the news.

"Until that night with him in the hotel, I had held in all of my anger and my humiliation, but in that hotel room, I let it out. For a few minutes Henry became angry and defensive, but then he slumped into one of the hotel chairs, put his head in his hands, and started crying, like a baby. I'd never seen Henry cry before. He was sobbing. I was still angry and frustrated, but my heart went out to him. I sat down and put my hands on his knees while he cried.

"After about five minutes, I guess, he regained enough control to tell me that the whole night's trip was supposed to have been a 'sure thing,' a lark. His friend, Bob, who owned the fishing boat, had proposed it to the three other men six weeks earlier at a dove shoot. He told me that because of the recession, his business had been losing money, and his share of the seven-hour boat ride was supposed to be over $150,000.

"He then told me that he loved me deeply, that he had been a fool, and he asked me for my forgiveness. I was so angry I couldn't forgive him, and I told him so. I reminded him that this was all going to hurt our children, who were already being taunted at school by their friends, calling their daddy a criminal. And we could already foresee that we would have to sell the home—and maybe the business.

"Although I appreciated his honesty and knew he was a decent man, I simply couldn't understand his stupidity at risking *everything* for *any* amount of money. We stayed like that for several weeks, almost a month, living together—but I hated it. Then I was introduced to an incredible woman from Savannah who headed up a special support network for wives in my situation. We had a long telephone conversation one day. I imagined she would recommend some therapist or psychologist for me to go see, but instead she asked me whether we had been to talk to our minister about all of this.

"I was shocked. We had been attending a small church for six months with a young minister about our age. It had never occurred to me, I am ashamed to say, to talk to him about this problem. But thanks to her suggestion, we did. I don't know whether she called to prepare him or if he just knew what to say by himself. But the result was that, at our meeting, the Holy Spirit worked a miracle inside me.

"This young minister, Carl Scott, explained to me about forgiveness. For a long time he didn't say anything about our specific situation, but rather reminded us of God's plan for forgiveness for all sins, even those much worse than Henry had committed, through the death and resurrection of His Son. He reminded us that if we are believers in Jesus, then we will receive God's grace, which we don't deserve, rather than God's judgment, which we do deserve. He went on to cite Bible passages in which Jesus specifically told the people of His day to forgive one another, so that His Father could forgive them.

"And the most striking thing Carl told me was that by hating, or not forgiving, someone—anyone—I would not hurt that other individual. Rather, the hate and the unforgiveness would simply consume *me*. I reflected on how awful I felt, and I had to agree with him that the anger was eating me up inside."

Richard put down his papers and was now listening to Sally's story, which obviously moved her greatly. Janet was also fascinated, hardly taking a sip from her drink while Sally spoke.

"Once I agreed with Carl that I wanted to be freed from the devastating power—the bondage, really—of this anger, all three of us knelt in prayer, right there in his office, and he prayed with me to give my anger to the Lord and to forgive Henry for the pain and the problems he had caused.

"And you know what, Janet? As we knelt in prayer and Henry and I quietly wept, I could feel this huge weight being lifted from me. I mean physically. I was suddenly able to hold my shoulders up again. My mind cleared. I saw Henry in a whole new light, with both his strengths and his weaknesses. I suddenly loved him even more and wanted to hold him and to support him in that difficult time.

"Carl suggested—and we kept it up until Henry left for prison—that we pray together, on our knees, holding hands, every day. Janet, I don't know how couples who pray together ever split up. When both partners in a marriage ask their common heavenly Father for forgiveness and guidance and strength to cope with the ills of the day, it binds the two people together in a way I really find difficult to describe. But it happens. It works. By the time Henry had to leave, our faith had broadened and deepened, and we shared that joy during the last few months I had with him at home.

"Listen, it hasn't been easy, at all. The kids and I are renting a two-bedroom house that would fit into a corner of the home we used to own. I had to go back to work. Thank God Henry's brother took over running the business. Henry has a place to come back to for a job, although we had to sell the ownership to his brother to pay the legal fees.

"But you know what, Janet? The other three guys on the boat that morning were also married. Two of them are now divorced. Their wives left them. The third wife is, I think, having an affair. I don't know what's going to happen when her husband comes home. But despite all the pain and all the problems, our marriage is actually much stronger than before this all happened. Our children have backbones. The oldest one has a paper route, and his income helps put food on our table. They have learned so much about life and love and good and evil and forgiveness.

"And every morning, Janet, I've awakened up and said out loud, remembering several of my friends whose husbands and brothers died in the war, 'Thank God he's not dead. Henry is alive and *will* come home. Whatever our problems are, they could be a lot worse. Just look around.' And that, along with the Holy Spirit's in-filling, is how I've made it through each day.

"I'm sorry, Janet and Richard. I've talked too much. But His power has turned what could and should have been a disaster into a great blessing. I have no idea what the future will bring, but I know that Henry is getting out and coming home day after tomorrow. The kids know that too. We're all healthy, thank God. Henry has a job. We don't have much else, but we have each other. And we'll make it, with God's help."

Janet could not help but feel the moisture in her eyes as her old friend finished her moving story. She felt as if she had just read a short story or seen a movie. It was interesting and entertaining, but not immediately relevant to her. She couldn't help thinking it would make a good script for a television docudrama. Janet could never imagine anything like that actually happening to her or to Richard, but she appreciated what Sally and Henry had gone through. Richard and Janet looked at each other across the den, and each one had words of comfort for Sally.

Once again, nothing changed in either Richard or Janet as a direct result of Sally's experience. Yet another seed was planted, and the ground became a bit more fertile, under the simple power of Sally's testimony.

3

ONE YEAR EARLIER ■ When Court and Sandy Shullo moved to town, and Court joined Richard's law firm in criminal litigation, they also joined the Church of Faith, a relatively new and growing church near their home. The Church of Faith had a dynamic young pastor, Stephen Edwards. Court and Sandy had both grown up in homes where the Christian faith was an active part of their families' lives; they were pleased to find a strong and growing church of their denomination, just like Morningside was on the other side of town.

Richard and Janet had been looking for a reason to take the young associate and his wife out to dinner, but their four schedules always seemed to be in conflict. Then Court and Sandy invited the Sullivans to a Friday evening dinner preceded by "Praise the Lord," a joint musical production by their church's young adult forum and their youth group. At first Richard and Janet hesitated, thinking the show would be pretty silly. But Court finally prevailed, and the younger couple drove the Sullivans to the private school where their church had leased production facilities for four performances in one weekend.

Richard was frankly astonished by the quality of the production, both in its original songs, its casting, and its staging. Several of the city's better actors and actresses were interested enough in the event to volunteer their time to the show.

The story line was about a modern family in disarray, with the husband and working wife spending too much time away from the family. Lives were changed, and a tragic near-death was averted because the teenagers in the family learned about the power of the Holy Spirit, and brought faith to their family.

Several of the songs were quite moving, and in the final scene the packed auditorium joined the cast in singing and clapping to the title song, a rousing spiritual.

Immediately after the performance, Stephen Edwards appeared on the darkened stage in a single spotlight, describing how any family or any individual in trouble could call upon the power portrayed in their show by sincerely submitting to the lordship of Jesus Christ. Clearly many of the people in the audience were moved, either by the show, or by Reverend Edwards' short talk, or by both, because Richard noticed that several people near them were using handkerchiefs as the houselights came up.

Richard was also moved by the performance. He identified with the husband who was feeling jealous of his working wife's time. The husband in the play finally turned to the Lord and began praying with his wife. It reminded Richard of the story Sally Coker had told them three years earlier. Janet shared many of Richard's feelings. But for both of them it remained an intellectual question, almost a curiosity. After all, how could people really find everyday power in their lives from the supernatural?

Seated in a Texas-style restaurant after the show, Richard and Janet were surprised to learn that Court and Sandy prayed about all major issues which faced their family and their business lives.

Richard was astonished to find that Court actually prayed every morning in his office and asked for God's involvement in each of his cases.

"You see," Court smiled at Janet and Richard as he cut his steak, "Sandy and I believe that if God is going to be in your life, then He must be in your *whole* life. Otherwise, it's like I'm telling Him that *I* can still be in charge of *certain* parts of my life, which I don't believe I can be."

"And of course," added Sandy, "we gave the raising of our children to Him years ago. In fact, we tell our children that they are *His* children, and we have simply been given the blessing by Him of raising them as best we can, with His help. They are still young now, but we trust Him to guide them and to protect them."

"But Sandy," Janet asked, "do you *really* believe that God is involved in your life every day? I mean in your life, individually? Doesn't He have a lot more important things to do than to be concerned about a single family?"

"Oh I *very much* believe He is involved in our individual lives. I know. I feel His presence and see His work changing me, changing Court, growing our children. I see answers to specific prayers. It's very real and very much what He says in His Word that He will do," Sandy smiled.

After their evening with the Shullos, as Richard and Janet were undressing in their bedroom, Nepravel, who had been spending more time with the Sullivans since Richard and Janet were growing into positions of authority in their firms, turned up the voice of Pride, when he realized to whom and to what Richard and Janet had been exposed that evening.

"Court and Sandy are certainly interesting people, you have to admit," Richard said to Janet as he unlaced his shoes. "I mean, you look at our friends the Petersons, say, or even the Cokers. Both have told us stories over the years about their strong faith. In both of those cases, there was something powerful like Vietnam or Henry's arrest, which you can say explains why those two couples suddenly acquired their new faith. But Court and Sandy are so *normal*! I mean, he's a lawyer, just like me. And here they are praying about everything, and he's in there in his office praying every morning! He seems like such a regular person. And they *do* appear to be awfully happy, and awfully ... well ... I don't know, I guess the word is together. But can you imagine us ..." And here the voice of Pride really kicked in. "Getting on our knees together here at night and praying to God about Tommy's baseball games?" He laughed.

"It's very strange," Janet agreed, as she hung up her dress in their walk-in closet. "All the people we know who really talk about being Christians—I don't mean the people who just go to church—always tell us about the 'power' in their lives, about how they have been changed.

That certainly was never talked about—at least that I remember—in the Catholic schools I went to. All we ever focused on was doing good and confessing our sins and praying that somehow we would wind up in heaven when we died. But these people—and you're right, the Shullos do seem awfully normal otherwise—really seem to feel some inner power, and to have some type of inner peace. I just find it hard to believe it's possible," she concluded, with Nepravel right there helping her to that conclusion.

Ten minutes later they climbed into bed and read for a while. Janet turned out the light on her side of the bed and rolled over with her back to Richard. He finished two more pages in his book, turned out his light and moved up close behind her, putting his arm around her and brushing his lips on her ear.

Her body tensed up and she pulled her elbows into her side. "Not tonight, Richard." Janet exhaled in a voice dripping with fatigue. "It's been a very long week and a very long night. Let's just get some sleep, and maybe tomorrow night we can."

Richard rolled onto his stomach and said, "OK, OK. Good night." But, frustrated, he thought to himself as he tried to go to sleep, *You didn't* used *to be so tired all the time, when you weren't working. That's all I ever hear from you now. Maybe I need to find somebody who's not so tired!*

Nepravel finally left, pleased that Richard and Janet were learning so well the lines he and the other demons were feeding them. "If we can keep this up and nothing interferes," Nepravel congratulated himself as he moved through the bay window toward the Bryants' home, "it shouldn't be too long before one or both of them starts having an affair. Humans, left on their own, are so wonderfully predictable."

4

SATURDAY, JANUARY 14 ■ The fifteen individuals assembled that Saturday morning around the tables in the large Sunday school room at Morningside Church sipped their coffee and talked among themselves. They had all been invited by Michael Andrews, Jim Burnett, and Stephen Edwards, the three ministers whose churches had decided to join together in their effort. At a little past 9:30, Michael Andrews, the pastor of Morningside Church, welcomed them.

"And we are of course pleased and blessed to welcome from Pittsburgh both the Reverend Bryan Hughes and the layman who was in charge of their church's businessmen's prayer breakfast, Roy Wise. Jim and Steve, I'm really glad you could bring with you the men and women from your churches with a heart for evangelism, who want to work for the Lord with our upcoming prayer breakfast. Before we hear from Bryan and Roy, I know we all want to spend some time in prayer."

There followed almost twenty minutes of silent and voiced prayer, as each individual in the room in turn lifted the meeting and its purpose to the Lord for His blessing and His involvement. Michael Andrews, as the host, finished their prayer time and concluded, "Now Lord, send your Holy Spirit to be here among us as the most important member of our team, that we can say and do only what is pleasing to You, to extend Your kingdom here on earth. In Jesus' holy name we pray. Amen."

Bryan Hughes and Roy Wise then described in great detail all the preparation that had gone into their earlier businessmen's prayer breakfast in Pittsburgh. Near the end of his remarks, Reverend Hughes warned them, "You have to realize that what you are planning will make Satan and his forces of deception and darkness very angry. It's one thing for us to preach the Word in our churches—he expects that. He almost laughs that the majority of 'Christians' really just gain enough knowledge of the gospel to be immunized against experiencing the real power of Christ in their lives. But now you're talking about going out into Satan's territory and taking the Word to business leaders, who might then affect many businesses, families, and individual lives. Satan hates that. And you can expect he will do everything he can to attack you and to discredit you and your efforts."

Roy Wise added, "Given what we've told you about our experiences, we recommend that you organize around three distinct functions: all of the events which are necessary prior to the prayer breakfast, the prayer breakfast itself, and the follow-up activities after the prayer breakfast. Since you have three strong churches involved, you could either give each church the responsibility for one function, or you could have each church involved in each function, under a designated leader. However you decide that issue, we urge you, as we have already warned, to begin praying for the prayer breakfast now. As Bryan just said, you can count on Satan and his demons to attack you. And using your own strength alone, you'll be easy prey for them. So the most important thing you can do, however you decide to organize on a human scale, is to pray for the Holy Spirit's involvement, starting right now. It's never too early to begin praying for an event like your prayer breakfast."

Michael Andrews again thanked the two visitors from Pittsburgh for taking time away from their families to help these three churches with the city's first businessmen's prayer breakfast in many years. There followed a question and answer period. After a break, the group reconvened to discuss how to organize their local effort.

Eddie Tatum, a volunteer from Morningside Church, suggested, "I like Roy's idea that we organize by activities. For the greatest learning possible, I believe each of the three churches should be involved in each of the three functions. And I have to admit that until this morning I never realized how much preparation will be necessary if we're serious about winning souls away from Satan in this city. We have a lot to do, so we'd better get organized this morning and get started."

Betsy Chalmers, a member of Stephen Edwards' Church of Faith, suggested that they begin the prayer cover, as Roy had recommended, immediately. "I'm the chairwoman this year of our Prayer Warriors, like the ones here at Morningside. We have almost two hundred people who each take an hour of every day of the week—twenty-four hours a day—to pray for the people and the concerns of our church. The *Prayer Warrior Bulletin* will go out on Tuesday, and we'll begin including the prayer breakfast right away. We'll continue into the follow-up period five months from now."

"And we have a prayer chain at our church," added Jim Burnett, "which we can also enlist immediately."

"Are you having the prayer breakfast in a hotel ballroom?" asked Bryan Hughes.

"Yes, at the Palace Hotel," answered Michael Andrews.

"Then—and I'm not exaggerating—you may want to rent a room in the hotel several days before the prayer breakfast and enlist a volunteer team to pray there and to claim the hotel as holy ground before and during the prayer breakfast."

"That sounds like a good idea. We ought to do it," Eddie Tatum agreed.

The group stayed together for another hour, planning for the prayer breakfast, following most of the suggestions made by the visitors from Pittsburgh.

Thanks to the fervent prayers of the Morningside Prayer Warriors and of other church members, there were always at least twelve angels protecting the church and any event held there, so that no demon would go near the place. Because of that spiritual protection, the early work of the three church groups responsible for the prayer breakfast was able to begin, and was in fact well underway, before any demons learned of it and reported the possibility of such a prayer breakfast to Balzor.

5

TUESDAY, APRIL 18 ■ It was only midafternoon, but already it was gloriously dark to Balzor. One of Satan's most experienced demons, Balzor was not visible to human eyes. But he was no less real. And just like a devastating, invisible wind, he was no less deadly. From his vantage point high above the northwest section of the city—his personal responsibility for forty years now—the sun's position was really irrelevant. His whole area had grown progressively darker during his years there, and he was immensely proud of his accomplishments. As he shifted his dark form and exhaled a breath of broiling sulfur, he watched his minions going about their tasks below, content that the long war was now almost won.

Everything was proceeding according to Balzor's grand strategy: Richard's affair with Kristen, Tommy's growing estrangement from his parents, Amy's fateful date with Billy, and Janet's initial concern with Tom Spence about the upcoming "911 Live." Almost everything, that is. One thing Balzor hadn't counted on was that those in charge of the prayer breakfast would drench all of their plans and activities with prayer. Because they did, the prayer breakfast was different, as was much of what happened afterwards.

WEDNESDAY, MAY 3 ■ Two weeks later, just after Richard came home from work on the Wednesday evening before the prayer breakfast and said hello to Susan, Amy, and Bobbie, who were upstairs talking and doing their homework, Bobbie left to go home in her family's station wagon, and Susan told Amy goodbye in their turnaround. The telephone rang and Tommy answered it. "It's for you, Dad."

"Hello."

"Hi, Richard. This is Bob Meredith. How are you doing?"

"Fine, Bob. Hey, Bobbie just left a few minutes ago, and she should be home very soon."

"Thanks, Richard. Dinner's almost ready, so I'm glad she's on the way. But that's not really the reason I'm calling. Listen, I'd like to pick you up in the morning and drive you to our prayer breakfast. I know it might seem a little bit strange, but it's a tradition we're starting, and I'd like you to be my guest for the ride in."

"Well, that's fine, Bob. But isn't it a lot of trouble? How will my car get to the office?"

"Don't worry. . . . Just bring your keys with you, and we'll have your car parked in your regular garage space when you get to the office."

Richard was stunned and a little concerned about all the trouble involved, but Bob persisted, and so he agreed.

"Great. I'll pick you up tomorrow morning right about 7:00. We're really looking forward to the prayer breakfast. See you then, Richard."

As Richard hung up the phone, he thought, *Someone sure is going to a lot of trouble. I didn't realize a prayer breakfast required so much organization!*

Nepravel, who came through Richard's breakfast room near the end of the conversation, was infuriated. He and the other demons had been battling the prayer breakfast for almost two months now, since they had first learned of it. But, with few exceptions, the organization was very strong; and the prayer support was so intense that they were only able to learn bits and pieces of the details from conversations such as the one he had just overheard. He knew that Balzor, already in a terrible state because of the prayer breakfast, would not like this latest news.

The midnight gathering over the city in those last few hours before the prayer breakfast was chaotic. The demons had never seen Balzor so furious. For two months his anger and frustration had grown, since he had first learned that the prayer breakfast had been in the planning stages for six weeks, without any of his demons picking up a hint from any source.

"You should have suspected something from all the prayers coming from those three churches—and from that infernal church in Pittsburgh!" Balzor had screamed at his lieutenants. ". . . Even if they do pray all the time about everything!"

And the angels. They had started appearing a month before, boldly positioning themselves at the Palace Hotel, around the homes of the prayer breakfast leaders, in the offices and conference rooms where the organizational meetings were held, even taking up roving patrols through the homes of the men who had been invited! The result had been disastrous for Balzor's demons, who were constantly on the defensive, even in their own neighborhoods. They had to be looking over their shoulders to guard against attacks from God's holy angels, who were actually able to reintrench in parts of the city, as if it were forty years ago!

And with each passing day, as it became apparent that the demons would not be able to attack the prayer breakfast directly, the suggestions of Balzor's lieutenants became much less numerous, and each demon stayed as far away from Balzor as possible. But distance was not possible at the midnight meetings.

Looking down from their high vantage point, Balzor and his demons were sickened that night to see so many angels concentrated in their sector of the city. At least forty angels surrounded the Palace Hotel, claiming it as holy ground and daring a demon to be foolhardy enough to venture nearby. In addition, they could see the sharp bolts of angels' light around churches and homes and roving through the neighborhoods, making it very difficult for streetleaders like Zloy and Nepravel to tend to the voices of deception in these last critical hours.

Balzor, enraged by the show of God's power in his sector, was examining his own future and looking for someone to blame. "All streetleaders will check and build up the voices in every invitee tonight. We can see the answered prayers arriving in these homes even now, and we must spin the voices up before these men arrive at that prayer breakfast!"

All the demons nodded silently, except one. "But there are so many angels around now," complained Streetleader Plagor, who was responsible for a neighborhood just to the south of Nepravel's Devon Drive. "I was almost caught twice this evening."

Balzor, whose fury had been pent up for days, locked his demonic gaze on Plagor, rose up, and sailed toward him. Plagor, regretting that he had spoken out, cowered down as Balzor closed in on him, and the other demons around him moved back.

"Those angels missed, but I won't!" screamed Balzor, and the blast of fiery heat he unleashed from his mouth burned Plagor to a crisp. He disappeared in an instant, blown back to hell.

Turning in a circle over the ashes that had been Plagor, Balzor snarled at the rest of his demonic forces, "Now, is anyone else going to complain about my orders to maintain your voices?" There was total silence. "Toron, you're now the streetleader in that neighborhood. Do you have any complaints?" Toron bowed his head in silent submission.

Balzor resumed his normal station. "Without control of the Palace Hotel, we may lose many souls tomorrow. A lot will depend on how much Pride and Confusion can keep spinning in these men before they arrive. But after the prayer breakfast, we'll have to redouble our efforts with those who are not saved at the breakfast. And with any of those who we do lose tomorrow to heaven, we'll have to be sure to isolate them with Apathy and Unworthiness, so they won't affect anyone else. Are there any other reports?"

There was only silence from the demons, except for the normal hissing that accompanied them wherever they went.

"Then be off now to your neighborhoods. Be careful, but turn up those voices!"

All during the night a rotating group of volunteer Prayer Warriors from the three churches maintained a prayer vigil in the room they had rented at the Palace Hotel, praying by name for the salvation of each one of the men who had been invited to the breakfast. Praying for the speaker, Benjamin Fuller. And praying for divine protection during this important battle in their city in the spiritual war.

Nepravel and Zloy were hugging the roof of a bar in the commercial center that separated their two neighborhoods, watching all the incoming prayer cover and knowing that any voices still left turning inside the invitees in their neighborhoods would be weak, at best.

"I haven't seen so many answered prayers in years and years," Zloy cursed. "I'm sure glad it's not like this all the time!"

"You and me both!" agreed Nepravel. "Look, let's work together and protect each other. I'll go with you to your neighborhood and stand watch against angels while you spin up your voices—then you do the same for me."

"Sounds good. It'll take all night that way, but perhaps we'll survive!" grumbled Zloy, as they headed out.

6

THURSDAY, MAY 4 ■ Alarm clocks went off early that morning all over the city, and in Pittsburgh, as believers from the churches arose to pray for the list of men who would be attending the prayer breakfast. Bob Meredith was proud of his daughter, Bobbie, who had asked to be awakened early so she could pray for Susan's father and the other men as well. While Bob dressed, Bobbie knelt by her bed and began praying, adding her voice to the hundreds of other voices seeking God's intervention in their city that morning.

At that precise moment, Nepravel and Zloy finally reached the Sullivans' house, after a tense night of dodging angels in their neighborhoods. While Zloy stood guard on the roof, Nepravel arrived at Richard's side, just minutes before his alarm was set to go off. Nepravel was upset but not surprised to find that the large number of incoming answered prayers had almost completely silenced the important voices of Pride and Disbelief inside Richard.

As Nepravel began to spin them up again, Zloy was focusing on a huge angel who appeared to be coming their way, just above the treetops, from the east. His attention on that one angel was almost his undoing, because this angel was only half of a pair, and the other angel was heading toward Richard's house, sent by all of the prayers, from the west. Only at the last instant did Zloy remember his training and turn to check over his shoulder, just in time to duck the crack of the talons and screams from the eagles' heads of "Holy, Holy, Holy is the Lord God of Hosts!"

"Yiiee!" screamed Zloy as he dodged to his left and spun around, only to face the second angel now closing on him, as the first circled to return.

Nepravel simultaneously heard Zloy's scream and the angel's proclamation. Since all demons are lying cowards, he was not prepared to risk his future by staying with Richard, nor by helping Zloy defend himself. Instead, Nepravel took off through the back of Richard's home and threaded his escape through the woods to the north.

Zloy, desperate to escape the twin attack by the circling angels, dove into a storm sewer outlet on Devon Drive and flew as quickly as he could through the dark tunnels of the city's sewer system.

When Richard's alarm went off that morning, he could not for a moment remember why it was so early. But then he recalled the prayer breakfast with Benjamin Fuller and Bob Meredith's appointment to take him. With the demonic voices only partially working that morning, thanks to all the prayers, he found himself—and it actually surprised him—looking forward to the event.

By the time Bob's car pulled into the driveway, Janet was awake as well. Bob came to the front door and smiled a hello to Janet, whom Richard kissed goodbye, and they walked out to Bob's car.

Richard could not believe it, but there, waiting in the car, were Court Shullo and two men he did not know. As they approached the car, one of the men opened the front passenger door, and Bob Meredith introduced them. "Richard, this is Ricky Knowlton. Ricky is a young accountant who goes to our church and works not far from your office. If you'll give him your car keys, he'll have your car waiting for you in your normal garage space."

"Hi, Ricky," Richard smiled. "Well, here are the keys and my briefcase, and there's the car. I certainly do appreciate your doing this."

"Think nothing of it, Richard. What you're going to hear this morning is so important that I'm delighted to help."

As Ricky headed toward Richard's car, he and Bob climbed into the front seats of Bob's car.

"Hi, Court," Richard said as he buckled himself in. "I had no idea you would be here this morning."

"It's a real privilege to be here, Richard. Do you remember Jim Anderson from the Greene Firm?"

Richard had not immediately recognized Jim, but now he remembered the attorney against whom they had litigated a major insurance case a few years earlier.

"Hi, Jim," Richard said, extending his hand. "I didn't recognize you at this early hour."

"I can imagine," smiled Jim from the back seat with Court. "But I'm sure glad to be here with you."

As they began the fifteen-minute drive to the Palace Hotel, Bob explained to Richard, "Court and Jim just wanted to come along this morning to let you know how important the message you're going to hear this morning can be in your life."

"Richard," Court began, "you know from our evening together a year ago that the first priority for Sandy and me is trying to submit our lives to the Lord. I thought you might like to meet Jim again and hear what he has to say."

Richard, who was beginning to be overwhelmed by all of this attention so early in the morning, nodded to Jim.

Jim, who was a little older than Richard, told the other three men the moving story of his oldest son, who had been estranged from his parents and become a heavy user of alcohol while still in college. Unknown to Jim, his son was on the verge of suicide when a Christian chaplain at the college found him and brought him to his knees in what Jim's son later described as the worst and best all-nighter of his entire life.

Within a week, Jim's son gave his life to the Lord. He was so moved that he came home in the middle of the term to tell his mother and father about how the power of God had changed his life. Jim greeted his son at their front door and could not believe the physical transformation. The three of them spent most of the night staying up, talking and crying, as Jim's son and Jim himself unburdened many years of pent-up misunderstandings and frustrations. His son returned to college the next day, but Jim had called Court, whom he knew to be a Christian, to describe the events of the previous day. And within another two weeks, both Jim and his wife became Christians and joined Court's church.

As they drove up to the Palace Hotel, Jim concluded, "Richard, whatever you may have thought or heard about real Christianity is probably at best only half true. Whatever garbage is in your life, whatever problems you are having with your wife or your children, God wants you to be victorious and happy. You can be, believe me, if you just stop trying to run it all yourself, and, like I did, turn it over to the Father who knows everything you need even before you ask."

They pulled up to the front of the hotel, and all four men got out. But Bob handed his car keys to Court.

"You're not staying?" Richard asked, as Court and Jim re-entered the front seats. "No, Richard, there wasn't room at the prayer breakfast for us this morning. We just wanted you to know how much you mean to us . . . and how much you mean to God." Court smiled as he waved goodbye and started the car.

As Bob escorted Richard into the hotel lobby, they noticed many other cars pulling up and dropping off other men, just as Court and Jim had done. Richard, who had organized events for his civic club, was astonished at the preparation and organization which had gone into delivering so many men to this breakfast so early in the morning. He could not help thinking, *Why are all these men doing this? They must really believe that whatever is going to happen here is important.*

After they received their name badges, Bob led Richard to their table, where he introduced him to the other invitees and hosts who had already arrived. Richard recognized Ben Fuller from his photographs, sitting at the center table in front of the podium with several men whom Richard vaguely recognized as clergy from some local churches.

Richard's seat was marked with a place card, and when he arrived and looked down, he found a brightly colored placemat, as well as an envelope. Looking around the table, he noticed that each man had a different, individually colored placemat. Richard picked up the envelope, and, before opening it, looked more closely at the placemat. Drawn in crayon, in the bottom left hand corner a man was looking up and reaching up with his right hand. In the top right hand corner were clouds and a large forearm and hand reaching down toward the man. Written in the middle were the words, "God loves you, Richard." And in the bottom right-hand corner it was signed Cindy, Scott, Lacy, and Jeff Peterson.

While Richard was trying to imagine how this placemat had arrived at his place, he opened the envelope and found a short note written to him by Henry Coker. The note read, "As I know Sally explained to you years ago, God changed our lives completely. You don't have to go to jail, Richard, to find God. He is right there in that hotel ballroom this morning, looking for you. Don't do what I did for so long, Richard, and tell him no. The greatest decision you will ever make is to say yes to God. Sally and I send you all our love. Henry."

Richard was speechless, and noticed that several of the other men seated at his table were having similar experiences. Holding out the envelope, he turned to Bob Meredith with a questioning look, but Bob only smiled, as Jim Burnett rose to walk to the podium.

Unknown to the hundreds of men arriving at the Palace Hotel, they were being guarded by fifty brilliant angels, both inside and outside the facility. Each angel shouted his individual praise to God. The Prayer Warriors, now numbering over twenty, continued to pray upstairs in their hotel room. And Balzor and his lieutenants stood off at a great distance, cursing the Light.

Following the invocation and the welcome by Jim Burnett, breakfast was served. They all sat down, and Richard asked Bob Meredith how this had all been possible.

"Let's just say there are some people who love you very much, Richard, and who want you to find the peace that only God can give. We checked with Janet to find the names of some people who might have planted seeds in your life years ago. She was a little skeptical, but she gave us some names and phone numbers. When we called them and gave them the opportunity, they jumped at it. In fact, they're probably praying for you right now. And look around. All of these men are loved in exactly the same way as you," Bob explained, motioning throughout the entire ballroom.

Richard almost could not eat the sumptuous breakfast put in front on him, he was so overwhelmed by the car ride, the placemat, and the envelope. He managed to make small talk with the mechanical contractor sitting across from him and with the other men at his table, a few of whom he had met previously, but none of whom he knew well.

As the dishes were being cleared, Stephen Edwards rose and walked to the podium.

"This morning we have with us not only our speaker, but also a fine lady, Paula Lindsay, who is going to sing two songs for us before we hear from Ben Fuller."

Accompanied by the pianist who had played during breakfast, Paula Lindsay walked to the podium, dressed in a conservative black dress with a single strand of pearls, picked up the microphone, and began singing "I Bowed on my Knees and Cried Holy." Richard, not thirty feet away, was pierced by the incredible love radiating from this woman. She was indeed singing, but primarily she was worshiping her Lord. The words of her song moved Richard deeply. Then she began her second song, "He is Here." The depth of her belief was so obvious and the words of the song so powerful that he actually felt himself opening, almost like the bud of a flower, to the sunlight she represented. As she closed her eyes and raised her free hand during the last verse of the song, Richard could see tears in her eyes. It occurred to him that this woman had not been performing, but had instead been singing to her Lord. The rest of them had just been privileged to be there while she did so.

When Paula finished, there was hardly a dry eye in the ballroom. She curtsied humbly to their applause, smiled, and bade them farewell.

Stephen Edwards returned to the podium to introduce Ben Fuller. As the applause began and Ben rose to walk up the three steps to the platform, he said a quiet prayer of thanks to God for all the support he had received from the organizers of this prayer breakfast. And he asked the Holy Spirit to use him and to prepare the hearts of the men in the audience that day for his message.

As Ben reached the podium and looked out across the faces in front of him, he was strongly encouraged. The hall that morning was filled with angels, not demons, and the Holy Spirit was moving mightily in the hearts and minds of these men, preparing them to hear the true story of how a great man of law and commerce had learned that the greatest power imaginable came only by humbling one's self, and by giving up those things that will not last in order to obtain those things that will last forever.

As Ben Fuller began speaking that morning, the voices of deception inside Richard were almost completely silent, dimmed by the prayers, by the obvious love and concern of so many people, and by the message of the two songs Paula Lindsay had sung. Richard, for the first time in his entire adult life, was open to hear the Truth.

Benjamin Fuller described for them his life of acquisition, material gain, love of money, and slighting his family. He described how he sought possessions, corporate power, fame, and constant activity to fill a life he knew was empty. "But the problem was," he said, "no matter what I acquired and no matter what I did, the happiness I thought they would bring only lasted for a short time, and the emptiness returned. So I tried harder and worked harder and stayed at the office longer and made more goals and wrote out more Do Lists."

Encouraged by the Holy Spirit, Fuller admitted to the group that morning something he had never admitted in public before, that there had also been other women. When Richard heard this admission and saw the obvious pain on Fuller's face, he felt a wrenching inside, and his breathing became difficult.

"I was lying to my wife. Every day was a lie to my wife. I kept saying to myself, *she doesn't understand me.* But the truth was that I was not even beginning to meet her needs for real love and affection. So I know now there was no way she could begin to meet what I thought were my physical needs." Fuller pulled out a handkerchief and dried his eyes. Richard felt as if a knife were being turned in his heart.

"I would hardly have known it and never have admitted it," Fuller continued, "But I was a wretched human being, ruining myself, my family, and my business. Because I was breaking God's laws and not fulfilling His plan for me. I did not put Him first in my life. I put myself first. I was not the spiritual head of my family. I didn't even know what that meant. I did not love and honor my wife. I complained about her shortcomings. I did not raise up my children to fear the Lord, as the beginning of their wisdom. I left their training to other people, most of whom taught them that there is no God. And all of these awful things were true because, like Adam and millions of men after him, I was rebelling against God, confident that I was in charge of my own future. But in truth, I was living hell on earth, and heading for hell itself. And worse, I was taking my family with me.

"But then by God's grace, I attended a function not unlike this one. I sat there, and heard the words a man was speaking from a podium just like this one, and I knew that those words were not from him, but from God. I knew that they were meant just for me, as I hope some of you may feel that my words are meant just for you, personally."

Richard tried to wipe the moisture from his eyes without drawing attention to himself.

"Men, God has such a better plan for us than we can ever imagine by ourselves. And certainly better than the media or the movies or our government would trick us into believing is our fate." Leaning forward and moving his hand from side to side as he spoke, Fuller proclaimed, "He has the power to wipe *all* of your garbage away. To change you completely and permanently. To change you eternally. To assure you that you *will* spend eternity with Him in heaven, but also to give you a new life while you are still on earth. Can you imagine that?

"All you have to do is give up. Give up your fruitless efforts to be in control. Give up your rebellion. Become a child again and let your heavenly Father do what He has always wanted to do, through His son Jesus Christ: be the Lord of your life. There is so much good which will unfold for you, as you will hear about in the follow-up sessions in the weeks after this breakfast, so much richness, so much joy. So much love. So much happiness that you cannot imagine . . . so much peace.

"How do you change? How do you become a completely new person? Become the husband your wife needs and wants to give herself to? Become the father who can train and lead his children? Become the businessman who will ask God for His agenda before setting his goals? How do you do that?

"The answer is very simple but very important. Like me, you have probably imagined that all the complex problems in your life require complex solutions. But the one simple solution has been there for two thousand years, and the only reason I can imagine that we don't all grasp for it is that we must be deceived into ignoring it. Don't confuse lack of complexity with lack of power. The answer is right here for anyone who wants the power to change his life this morning." Fuller went on to describe the incredible changes God worked in his life once he asked for forgiveness and let Jesus become the Lord of his life. He spoke for almost thirty minutes and concluded by reminding them that based only on God's justice, he certainly deserved to spend eternity in hell.

"But besides being a God of justice, He is also a God of grace and mercy, and He has provided a way for each one of us to escape the justice we deserve. He let His only son—imagine that—die in our place. And His love is so great that He would have done that for me if I were the only human being alive. How incredible. That someone could love me enough to die in my place—the death I deserve.

"I told you earlier that the answer is right here. And it is. Here is what you have to do. Ask God, with complete sincerity, to forgive you for all of the sins which you have committed. If you really want to lead a new life with His help, then submit yourself for the rest of your life here on earth to His Son, not only as your savior, but also as your Lord. If you want the power of the Holy Spirit in your life, then pray along with me now, as I prayed twenty years ago, and leave this place a completely new person."

Fuller bowed his head in prayer, and the other men in the hall did likewise. Richard was stunned, almost immobile. Listening to Fuller had been like trying to drink from a fire hydrant. Every word had meaning, and every word had meant something to Richard. His heart was laid bare and the awful truth of what he had been doing with Kristen was seared on his conscious mind. He knew he was no spiritual leader for his family. He knew his selfishness was awful. And yet, he had just heard that God had provided a way out from all of this . . . this . . . sin.

Fuller was praying, but Richard was still caught up in the enormity of his sins and didn't feel worthy to pray with all the other men. When Fuller finished praying, Michael Andrews rose to thank him. Richard looked up and saw tears streaming down the face of the mechanical contractor across from him. The banker sitting to his right also had moist eyes, and smiled at him. Obviously every man in the ballroom that morning had been moved deeply by what he had heard. Something tangible had happened. Something real. Richard had heard Fuller's prayer, but he did not honestly know whether he had prayed the prayer himself. The weight of his sins and of his lying to Janet in particular were so very heavy on his soul.

After checking the box on the card in front of him that he would be interested in the follow-up, he could barely stand, because his knees were so weak. No one appeared to be in a rush to leave, and he noticed two or three men in the room who seemed to be sitting and praying by themselves. Finally Bob Meredith touched his elbow, smiled, and said, "Richard, I hope Ben Fuller's message meant something to you."

Richard, almost in a daze, picked up his placemat from the Petersons and his note from Henry Coker and nodded. In not much more than a whisper, he replied, "Yes . . . yes, a great deal. Thank you so much for inviting me."

Bob led Richard through the hotel lobby, shaking hands and talking briefly with several other friends who had attended the prayer breakfast. Once outside, they found Bob's car where Court had left it in the parking lot of the large mall next to the hotel. As they drove to Richard's office, Richard still found it hard to talk, but he managed to ask Bob how he had originally come to his own faith.

Bob explained how during the winter of his junior year in college a series of events with his girlfriend, his grades, and his parents had terribly depressed him. He had seriously contemplated suicide. He had located a hand gun in a pawn shop in their college town. The night before he planned to buy it, a friend from high school, who was attending college in another small campus town two hundred miles away, happened to call him. "I say 'happened' because that's how it seemed at the time. But I know now that nothing like that just 'happens.' The friend heard my pain on the telephone, got in his car, and drove the two hundred miles to my apartment. He then spent the rest of that night sitting on the floor with me in my kitchen, mainly just listening to me.

"He let me talk it all out. And I guess the more I talked about it with him, the more ridiculous it sounded to kill myself. We finally went to sleep about the time the sun came up, and when we woke up in the afternoon, I knew the crisis had passed. I knew it had passed primarily because this friend loved me enough to stop what he was doing and to be with me when I needed him. It was only that afternoon when I really learned, I think because I asked, about his faith. Although we were obviously younger and he did not have all the experiences of Ben Fuller behind him, he nevertheless shared with me many of the same ideas you heard this morning. I guess they were like seeds planted in me because that summer, when we were home for vacation, I prayed with him to ask Jesus into my life. And I have simply never been the same since."

Richard listened to yet another man tell him about love and about the power of God to change a life. At that moment, Doubt was gone. It was simply impossible that so many men whom he knew and respected could have virtually the same experience without this power being real.

Bob pulled up to the curb near the front entrance to the forty-story office building where Richard's law firm was located. In all of his life, Richard could never remember two and a half hours like those he had just experienced. As his mind began to clear, he knew, however, that, although he had been exposed to the Truth and to the power of the Holy Spirit, they were not yet part of his life.

"Robert, thank you for a most moving and important morning. I'll think about all these things, and I'd like to participate in whatever might be planned next," Richard told him, as they shook hands in the car.

"I'll give you a call in a couple of days to let you know what's happening," Bob smiled in reply. Richard left the car and walked in through the revolving door to the elevator lobby in his building.

Although he did not know it, he was accosted in the elevator lobby by Nepravel, who had been waiting for him in the safest place he could find away from the Palace Hotel. Nepravel was ecstatic to see that the Light was not yet flickering inside Richard, and so he still had a chance to turn him away from the Truth.

There was therefore an unseen extra party in the elevator riding up to the thirty-seventh floor with the other occupants, as Nepravel began once again to spin up the deceptive voices of Confusion and Disbelief inside Richard.

The elevator doors opened on his floor, and Richard walked slowly through the glass entranceway of his law firm, still lost in thought about what he had seen and heard that morning. But already a new voice began to ask him, "Could that have all actually been real? Did all of those men really accept Jesus into their lives this morning? How could that be possible?"

He smiled at Mary, his secretary, and entered his office. There on his desk was his briefcase. Seeing his briefcase and looking down at the placemat and the envelope in his hand reminded Richard that this morning ten or more men—he really could not imagine how many—most of whom did not know him at all, had put themselves through all sorts of logistical problems just so that *he* could hear the Truth from Benjamin Fuller. That simple revelation of their unselfish love for him brought back the flood of feelings from the prayer breakfast. Nepravel was astonished when the voices of Confusion and Disbelief stopped spinning inside Richard, even as he was manipulating them.

Richard turned around immediately, throwing his coat on a chair and, without glancing at the messages on his desk, he walked past Mary and down the hall to Court Shullo's office. Court was seated behind his desk reviewing a deposition. Richard asked if he could come in, and Court rose and greeted him with a smile. "Sure, Richard. By all means, come in. How was the prayer breakfast?"

"Court," Richard said with great seriousness on his face, "It was like nothing I have ever experienced before. Benjamin Fuller spoke as if he had written every word just for me." Richard turned and closed the door to Court's office. Court walked around his desk, and Richard met him in the middle of the office.

"Court . . ." Richard looked out the window for a moment, then turned back and looked Court in the eye. "Court, you cannot imagine the things I have done . . . I can't believe God will ever forgive me, but I want to ask Him to . . . I don't know exactly what it is you and Ben Fuller and Bob Meredith have found, but I know that I want it. What do I do? How do I do it? Please help me!"

Nepravel, who had followed Richard into Court's office was horrified. Desperately he tried to restart the voices of Doubt, Confusion, Disbelief, anything. But he was shocked to find that there was simply nothing left to work with inside Richard. The prayers and the events of the past several hours had wiped all of Richard's voices clean. It would take days to start them over again, and Nepravel knew that he didn't have enough time.

Only twice since time began on earth had Nepravel been personally present when a soul was saved by Jesus Christ, and he involuntarily pulled back in both fear and anger. He landed on Court's bookcase, spitting and shrieking vile insults at Court and Richard, knowing that he was helpless now to do anything else and afraid of what was going to happen next.

Court asked, "Richard, are you ready to stop trying to run your own life—to submit to God and let Him provide for you and your family?"

Richard spoke slowly. "I know I've made a mess of the things in my life that matter. Janet. Tommy. Yes, yes, I'm ready. So very ready."

"And, Richard, are you really sorry for these things you have done that you shouldn't have done . . . what the Bible calls sins?"

"Court, I'm so very sorry. I've lied to . . ."

"Richard," Court smiled, raising his hand, "that's between you and God. It's none of my business. Here, kneel with me and let's change your life forever."

Nepravel shrieked from the bookcase and snarled, alternately cringing back against the books and lashing out with his sharp teeth and sulfurous breath at Court, hatred filling him so completely that his eyes turned blood red.

The two men knelt in the middle of the modern office, and Court led Richard in an ancient prayer. Richard listened to Court and then repeated the words from the depth of his heart.

"Dear heavenly Father, I have sinned. I am a sinner. I am separated from Your perfection by my sin. I deserve the wrath of Your judgment. I deserve to die in my sin and to spend eternity separated from You. Please, dear Lord, forgive me for what I have done wrong, and give me the power of the Holy Spirit to conquer my temptations in the future.

"Through Your grace, I want to have a relationship with You through Your Son, Jesus Christ, whom You sent to earth to die for my sins so that I might receive Your forgiveness, instead of Your judgment."

As Court led and Richard prayed these words, Nepravel shrank back in terror, because he heard the distant rush. This was not just one of God's holy angels. He actually saw coming the mighty cleansing flame of the Holy Spirit Himself. This was God Almighty, coming down from heaven, to visit this one repentant sinner, that he might be born again. Nepravel screamed in hate and defeat and fear, backing through the wall, closing his eyes to the searing flame. The invisible flame filled Court's entire office and turned it white with spiritual heat. Nepravel crouched and snarled behind a row of file cabinets in the office hallway.

"This day, right now, I want to submit my life to the Lordship of Jesus Christ. I want to be born again by the power of the Holy Spirit. I want Jesus to run my life. I want to start my life over as Your child. I pray for the power and the grace to know and to serve You more each day. Please, Lord, take me now as Your own, and make of me a new man, to do Your will while on earth, and to be an heir of eternal life with You, not because of what I have done, but by Your love and grace for me. All these things I pray in the name of Him who died so that I might live, Jesus Christ."

The searing flame of the Holy Spirit pierced Richard and turned him an incandescent white for a split second, then passed on through him, leaving behind a small flame of Light which could be seen by any spiritual being. Nepravel looked up from behind the file cabinets and cursed God.

Richard opened his eyes and felt a huge weight lifted from him. He had not seen the Light nor heard the rush, but he knew that something had happened to him. He had given up. He had submitted to God. And suddenly he felt lighter and cleaner than he had felt in years. He looked at Court, and they smiled together.

"Court . . . I . . . I feel new. It's really there. I *want* to be God's! I want to do His will. What do I do now, Court?"

The two men stood up. "First, I want to welcome you to God's kingdom," Court smiled, and he embraced Richard with a hug, which Richard returned. "No day should ever be the same for you now, Richard. You will still, of course, have problems—God doesn't promise us a rose garden—but now you are God's child, and if you call upon His power and His wisdom, they are yours to use in everything you do."

"Court, I feel like a child. What a morning! But I still feel so unworthy. There's so much I have to change. I don't know if I can. What do I do now? I want to shout and go tell Janet what's happened! She'll never believe me."

"Richard, go tell her. And she probably won't believe you. . . . Remember how you were only yesterday. Until the Holy Spirit indwells you, you see things through an old set of eyes. But tell her . . . Share your joy.

"Here, sit down, and let me answer your question. God wants to have a relationship with you through His Son. In business, Richard, I know you tell us here in the firm to develop relationships with influential people and with clients. How do we do that?"

"Well," Richard answered, "we spend time with them, get to know everything we can about them, talk to them, listen to them, try to figure out what's important to them . . . All of that builds the relationship."

"Exactly, Richard, and that's precisely what God wants you to do with Him. Let me tell you how to start. You learn about Him by reading the Word He inspired men to write about Him—the Bible. It's all there. Everything you need for a full life. The more I read it, the more I know it was written for these times. Start your relationship with Him by reading the Gospel of John, then maybe First John, James, Peter, and the many letters of Paul. These were men who knew Jesus personally, and you can find out about Him by reading their words. Do you have a Bible?"

"Yes, sure, at home. I think I can find it. How much should I read?"

"As much as you want. Remember, you're building a relationship, so learn as much as you can. The other way we communicate with God is through prayer. We talk to Him, and He talks to us. I recommend finding a quiet time every day, Richard, usually early in the morning or at night. And there's something about us Type A men getting down on our knees—or on our faces—and praying to our heavenly Father. When she's comfortable, include Janet sometimes, and pray together. Ask Him for forgiveness and for guidance in your life. Then listen. If you're rusty at praying, it might take a few times. But be honest, and tell Him everything that's on your heart. He *will* answer you."

"Build a relationship . . . That seems so simple," Richard said. "Read, talk, and listen. Why didn't anyone ever tell me this before?"

"Well, you have to be ready to hear, and you have to go some place where you might hear it. When was the last time you went to church, Richard?"

Richard grimaced. "A long time ago."

"Well, that's the final thing I was going to tell you. We learn a lot about our heavenly Father through the teachings and the relationships we have here on earth, particularly with other believers. So besides reading the Bible every day and praying every day, you should find a Bible-believing church where you feel at home and become part of the body. From this day forth you are saved, but like all of us, you have so much to learn. We call it our spiritual walk, and we'll be learning from Him and from each other until He takes us home. The body of believers supports each other, teaches each other, and worships together.

"We would love to have you at Church of Faith, or you might try Morningside, which is a little closer to your home, where the Merediths attend. The denomination doesn't matter, as long as the church is founded on the Word. And believe me, Richard, you'll know. You might try several different churches, but then make a decision and put down roots in one community of believers."

Court had finished, and Richard was still overwhelmed that this man had taken so much time with him, from early that morning, to help bring him into the kingdom of God. "Court . . . I . . . I can't thank you and Bob and all the people who worked so hard on the prayer breakfast. . . . It has obviously changed my life. How can I ever repay you?"

Court laughed. "Richard, the greatest joy of my life is telling others about our faith and then seeing results like this morning. Your name is now written in the Book of Life. Do you realize that angels are rejoicing in heaven right now? Yes, I mean it. What joy! You can repay us by calling on us whenever we can help you and by doing what we are all supposed to do: tell others about this new faith that burns inside you."

Court held out his hand. This time Richard embraced him. Nepravel, who had been circling them since the Holy Spirit departed and listening to the Truth being told, spat at them and swore because the deception had ended in Richard. Now they would have to concentrate on confusing him and isolating him before he could tell others.

"Oh, and Richard—" Court said, as Richard opened the door, "—one more thing. Satan hates to lose a soul to God. He will now do everything he can to confuse you and to turn you away from the faith. In the coming weeks you may experience more problems, not less. But unlike before, you now have the power of the Holy Spirit inside you to battle him. Don't try to stand up to Satan on your own—you'll always lose. Pray for the Holy Spirit's help whenever you feel tempted."

"Court, do you really believe that the devil is real?" Richard asked.

"I know it, and so should you. Who do you think has kept you from the Truth you finally heard today? Who do you think is trying to ruin your marriage, your family, and your business? Who do you think gets all those voices going inside you, rationalizing every imaginable sin?"

"How did you know?"

"Richard, he tries to do it to all of us. He's still going to come after you, even though he's lost you today, because he wants to discredit you and to make you ineffective with others. But now you belong to God, and you can fight back with God's miraculous power. Richard, God can do anything, even help us fight Satan.

"In case it hasn't hit you yet, there's a spiritual war going on. Satan wants Janet, Susan, and Tommy. You're now the spiritual head of your family. Rejoice in what has happened today, but get ready to do battle. Like all of us, you'll need all the help you can get, meaning the Holy Spirit and other believers. I'm sorry, Richard—I didn't mean to get so serious, just when you're first feeling the joy and the power of God. But Satan is very definitely here among us, and he would like nothing better than to destroy our loved ones."

Richard, realizing he had a lot to learn, nodded to Court and walked back to his office, where his coat was still thrown over the chair. He smiled at Mary on the way by her desk. "Have you had a good morning, Mr. Sullivan?" she asked.

"The very best one ever," he replied. "I just let God find me!"

He left her with a puzzled look, walked into his office, hung up his coat and sat in his chair. He was about to call Janet and invite her to lunch. Then he remembered that it was Thursday, and he was supposed to see Kristen in ninety minutes.

Kristen had shown a home to clients early that morning and was reviewing her listings at her desk in the office when her phone rang. She put down her coffee and answered.

"Kris. Hi. This is Peter Dowling in San Francisco. How are you?"

"Peter. Long time no see. I'm fine. How are you?" she replied, happy to hear from the man with whom she had had a "fling" at the end of college. He had been a journalism graduate student, a few years older than she was, and now he was working for a big newspaper in California. They had not seen each other in several years.

"Listen, I'm coming out your way this weekend. I wondered if you would like to go out, maybe on Saturday night?"

Kristen hesitated for a second and then said, "Sure. I'd love to see you. I think the symphony is giving the last concert of the season. It should be good. Would you like me to try to get tickets?"

"Sounds great. I arrive tomorrow morning and will be staying at the Carlton Hotel. I'll call you when I get there. It'll be wonderful to see you again."

Kristen could hear the genuine anticipation in his voice, and she remembered the happiness they had shared during their two months together. "Me, too. I'm glad you called. See you on Saturday."

She had barely put down the receiver and picked up her coffee when the phone rang again.

"Kristen. Hi. Listen, something has come up, and I just can't make it to lunch today. I'm sorry, but it's important."

Remembering the teddy she had laid out on her bed that morning and the thoughts she had been having about their "lunch" for days, she was terribly disappointed. "But, Richard, you couldn't come on Tuesday, either, and I was planning something special for us today. Why do you always have to cancel *us*? Why don't you postpone the *other* meeting?" she pushed.

Richard knew it would be impossible to explain on the phone all that had happened to him that morning, and he also knew he had to make a break. He just couldn't see her that day. "I'm sorry. I really am. But this other matter has sort of overwhelmed me. I just can't come."

"I hate it. But if you have to. You *will* be here on Tuesday, right?"

"Uh . . . yes. Sure," Richard replied, not really knowing the answer, but wanting to end the conversation.

"All right. Call me later. I want to see you."

"I will. I'll try to explain better then, when we have time. Goodbye."

Kristen again returned the handset to the telephone. She had so wanted to see Richard. The teddy was out. Could she wait until Tuesday? As she sipped her coffee, she remembered that Peter Dowling had said he would be arriving the next day. She thought to herself, "I wonder what *he's* doing tomorrow? Why do we have to wait until Saturday night to get together? Maybe he just thought it wouldn't be proper to ask me out on such short notice. But what if I ask *him* out!" And she looked in her Rolodex for the telephone number she had kept for him.

Janet was surprised to receive a call from Richard so early in the day. "Is everything all right?" she asked.

"Dear, it's fantastic. I've got to tell you about what happened to me. Are you free for lunch?" he asked quickly.

She couldn't remember the last time her husband had invited her to lunch, and she could hear the excitement in his voice. "Are you talking about the prayer breakfast?" she asked.

"Yes, and more. Can you get free? Say 12:30 at the Cafe Grille? That's about halfway between us."

"Sure, Richard. I'll change something around and be there. My curiosity is up now. Goodbye, dear."

Sitting at his desk, looking out at the city, Richard felt brand new. He felt younger and lighter and happier. He wanted to call people and shout the good news to them. He took out his phone book, looked up a number, and dialed Bob Meredith.

When Bob answered, Richard described what had happened with Court Shullo just thirty minutes earlier.

"Richard, that's wonderful!" Bob said with obvious joy. "Praise God. Let's pray." Richard had never prayed on the telephone before, but he was open to trying anything Bob suggested. So the two men bowed their heads, and Bob thanked God for Richard's deliverance. He then prayed for protection for Richard and his family. He concluded by praying for similar experiences and protection for all the men who had attended the breakfast.

When they finished, Bob said, "Why don't you and Janet have dinner at our home this Saturday? I know that Anne would like to see Janet again. And I think Bobbie has been talking to Susan about trying our church, so why don't you come on Sunday morning as well, all four of you?"

"Bob, you've done so much for me in the last few hours, why don't you let us take you two to dinner?" Richard replied.

"Next time. This time you come to our place, and we'll cook out. Casual. OK?"

"I'll check with Janet at lunch, but it sounds great. I was also going to ask you about your church. Thanks for inviting us. What time does the service begin?"

THAT AFTERNOON ■ Richard arrived early at the Café Grille and found a booth. He could not shake the feeling of being a kid again. He knew that what he had been through and what he had to change were as serious as anything he had ever experienced, but the joy still lingered. And when Janet walked in, for the first time in a long time he smiled at the sight of her.

"Hi, Richard. You look like the little boy who just found the buried treasure," Janet said, returning his smile and sliding into the booth across from him.

"Maybe I did . . . I had to see you today, and tell you what's happened to me," Richard began, reaching across the table and cupping her hands in his. "I can't really explain it, but I found God this morning, Janet. Or He found me. No, really," he continued as she made a questioning face. He went on to tell her about the men who had cared enough about his salvation to ride to the hotel with him, to take his car for him, and to carry his briefcase to his office, without even attending the breakfast themselves.

"And Bob Meredith told me he called you for leads on people from our past who might have a strong belief. These were waiting for me at my place." He handed her the note from Henry Coker and the placemat from the Petersons. "And, Janet, *every* man—I mean hundreds of us—had notes and placemats at our places. Can you imagine what that took to organize? I realized riding over here that all of that unselfish work and love was just a small way for those believers to prepare us for the incredible love of God."

The waitress came and they ordered soup and sandwiches. "Yes," Janet responded when the waitress left, "Bob called me for some names and asked me not to tell you. But I didn't realize they were doing the same thing for every man at the breakfast."

Richard went on to tell Janet all the details of the prayer breakfast, especially Ben Fuller's message. He had just finished when their lunch arrived, and as he took the first spoonful of his clam chowder, he said, "But the most important event happened a little later, at the office."

Richard slowed down and told Janet about praying with Court Shullo. As he spoke, she was at first skeptical, then realized that something powerful had in fact happened to her husband, though she could not really understand it. But he seemed different. She noticed it in his face. And he almost looked as if he was sitting up straighter. It was crazy, she knew, but he looked younger and happier than he had looked just that morning. How could that be? What had happened to him?

"After we prayed, Court told me that I need to pray and to read the Bible daily and to find a church where we feel comfortable—I know that's a leap, Janet, to say 'we,' but I hope you will try it. The whole point is to begin a relationship with the One who made us, who loves us, and who wants to empower us to defeat the devil, who is out to destroy us."

Janet sat for a moment, not speaking. "Wow!" she finally said, smiling and shaking her head once. "You've had quite a morning! In six hours you've acquired a belief in both God and the devil."

"Yes," he replied, looking in her eyes, "because I've seen what God's power has done to and for others. I've also felt His power, for the first time, in me, and I've realized that almost everything I've been doing lately would be an abomination to God if I met Him today. I can only deduce that someone—Court called him Satan—is out to ruin us, to keep us from God."

"Well you certainly seem different, I must admit. What does all this mean, Richard?"

"In some ways, I'm not sure yet." Now it was his turn to be silent for a moment, searching for the right words, then continuing. "Janet, I don't know how it seems to you, but I'm the first to admit, after this morning, that my life—and to a large extent our life—is a mess right now. I . . . I . . . have done some things . . . of which I'm not very proud. I asked God to forgive me this morning. I believe He did, but I still feel like I'm not worthy." Janet frowned. "Believe me, I have a lot to be forgiven for and to change.

"But the main thing is I want to follow Court's advice and begin a relationship with God. Imagine! The same God who hung the stars in the sky wants to have a relationship with me!" Richard smiled. "It's incredible. So I'm going to do the things Court suggested and hope that I hear Him. Oh, and I want to go to church on Sunday. Bob Meredith has invited us over to their home on Saturday night and then to their church on Sunday. Is that OK?"

"Yes . . . but we have those symphony tickets from your office. I think this Saturday's concert is the last one of the season."

"Well, I'd like to go, but Bob sounded like they would really like to see us, and he has done so much for me today—plus Bobbie and Susan are such good friends. I'll ask Mary to find someone else to use the tickets, if that's all right with you, and we'll go to the Merediths."

"Fine. Anne is a nice person, although I don't know her all that well. Bobbie is certainly a fine girl. By the way, when and what are you going to tell our kids about this morning?"

"I'll try to say something to them this weekend. And that's the other thing, Janet. The mess I referred to earlier involves them and me. I don't think I've been a very good father lately; Ben Fuller and Court referred to fathers as the spiritual heads of their households. I know that description doesn't fit me. It struck me, sitting in my office this morning, that if I yearn for a relationship with my heavenly Father, imagine how Susan and Tommy want to have a relationship with me! And how relatively simple it is, compared to knowing God. It will just take time—and the same active steps I want to take to open up to God." Richard was smiling again.

"Maybe God can teach me something, and I can teach them! Wouldn't that be great?"

For the first time Janet could imagine that a real transformation had actually taken place that morning, a real physical event. A miracle. She could not believe what she had just heard Richard say. She thought to herself, *If he really changes like this and his actions follow his words, then there really may be a God! How incredible that this has happened . . .*

As the waitress cleared their plates and brought them coffee, Richard asked, "Well, we've talked a lot about my morning. Is anything going on at the station?"

Another miracle. Richard had asked about her work in a positive way. *What* did *happen to him this morning?* she thought. After a moment of reflection, she said, "Oh, the usual. But the '911 Live' controversy is heating up. These strong Christians—" and she had to pause for another moment to realize that maybe Richard now had a budding faith like Tom Spence "led by a good guy named Tom Spence, want the show stopped or shown later, as I've told you. The latest development is that Bill Shaw is arranging for some of us to ride in or behind city police cars and ambulances in two weeks, when Network does a test run of the concept here on a Friday night, so we can see what the show will really be like."

"I hope by that 'we' that you don't mean 'you'," Richard ventured, as he filled in the credit card charge ticket.

"Well, yes. Tom, Bill Shaw, Connie Wright, and me, along with the network people. Why?"

"It certainly doesn't sound very safe. Especially on a Friday night. I see the police reports, Janet, on occasion. I don't think riding with or behind emergency vehicles at night in this city makes any sense. And—please don't take this as sexist—I'm saying this to you as my wife and the mother of our children. I particularly don't think it's any place for an untrained woman. You just have no idea what you could suddenly find yourself involved in."

"Well, I hadn't really thought about it that way. I just assumed everything would be OK."

"But these people are going to be out looking for trouble, in a way. Couldn't you and Connie, at least, evaluate this program just as well by watching and participating in the control room at the station?"

Janet was silent. She could not remember Richard caring about her job—or even recently about her—in this way. Out of habit, she searched his eyes for duplicity or a put-down, but saw only sincerity. Finally she spoke. "Maybe so, Richard. I'll think about it . . . But right now I think we've both got to get back to work. You know, I don't know how long it will last, but you really are kind of different, and I must say I like it," she smiled.

"Isn't it funny?" He returned her smile, "I do, too!"

■   ■   ■

That night at home, after reading through some papers from the office, Richard went to their bookcase in the den, while the kids dressed for bed, and found a Bible he had been given years before. He looked inside the front cover and found the inscription, "Merry Christmas and may God bless your family. The Petersons." Richard smiled. He returned to his chair and opened it to the Gospel of John, as Court had suggested, and began reading.

It had not been a good day for Nepravel—he had already lost seven men in his small neighborhood alone, and a couple more were wavering. Worse, he knew from experience that once a husband and father had the Light in him, it usually followed that the whole family eventually shook off their deceptions and learned about God's promise of salvation. And, worse yet, most of these men were in positions to influence other men and women in their businesses and in their community. Yes, it had been a very bad day for all of the demons in their sector. Balzor was understandably livid as they gathered for their first meeting after the prayer breakfast. Nepravel knew it was not the time to be a hero by speaking out and trying to blame all their problems on the incredible prayer cover that had brought all the angels.

As he neared their nightly cabal, Nepravel took one last look back at his neighborhood and was sickened to see the white light of prayer coming *from* the Sullivans' home! Richard was apparently praying, and Nepravel was suddenly racked with terror. If Balzor saw that particular light, given his angry state and all the time and plans they had invested in Richard, Nepravel feared this might be his last night on earth for a millennium or more. Those infernal people praying so much! And giving themselves to God! And those angels! Had Balzor seen those angels? They were everywhere! He started to formulate his defense, if he might have even a moment to speak before being blasted . . .

As their meeting began, all of the streetleaders vied with each other to stay as far away from Balzor as possible. Balzor began by asking for reports, and the roll call was frightful. Halfway through, it was obvious that their losses were worse than when Ben Fuller had spoken in Pittsburgh.

It came to be Nepravel's turn. He reported as simply as he could that there were now seven more men in his neighborhood with the Light burning inside them. He saw no reason to mention that he had been present himself when the Holy Spirit indwelt Richard.

He thought his problem might have passed, but Balzor asked, "And what about Richard Sullivan?"

Nepravel paused for an instant, then said, "He accepted Christ today, too, but I think we can isolate and confuse him so he will have no effect on others. He still has not spoken at length with the Holloway woman, and there is potential there to discredit and to defeat him . . ."

He was going to continue, when Balzor cut him off, "Enough! We'll come back to you and Richard Sullivan for a reckoning later. Next!"

Nepravel stopped, dreading Balzor's threat. The reports went on and continued to be dreadful. But as they were nearing the end of the reports, the demons began to hear a haunting sound, like thousands of men crying out, screaming, all blended together. It started like a whisper, but grew in intensity until it became a low roar. It was coming from the center of the city.

Balzor stopped in midsentence when he first heard the sound. He turned in the direction of the source. Nepravel turned, too, and the blackness from which the sound came was radiating, giving off darkness in the same way a human lightbulb gives off light. Nepravel had never seen and had only heard about a lord of the darkness such as this. The Darkness and the agonizing screams were coming towards them. Nepravel glanced back at Balzor, and the fear on his countenance was plain for all to see. Alhandra! This must be the Lord of the City, coming himself to their sector meeting! Such was unheard of. All the demons began to cower in fear, following Balzor's lead.

From a position above them, a voice spoke above the screams of the tortured, which never diminished. "Stop your stupid counting Balzor! It is 215 new Christians—lost to us and going to spend eternity where we belong! How could you!?! In one morning, 215 new Christians! Probably more tomorrow! If we're not careful, they'll start a real revival and set our work back by decades in this city, just when we've almost won! How could you let this happen?"

Nepravel wanted to run, but he knew he couldn't. Alhandra's own lieutenants had surrounded them with a ring of utter darkness and despair.

"But it was the angels," Balzor replied, in a voice that was barely audible over the rising fury of the agonized wails and screams, which now seemed to surround them as well. "They planned everything under prayer cover and prayed constantly for their prayer breakfast. I know it was bad. I was just about to punish my lazy streetleaders for letting it happen. Then I have a plan to recover and to minimize the damage."

"We won't be needing your plan," the Darkness spoke, and Balzor backed up in fright. "I have a small village far to the east of Moscow that needs streetleaders, and with your years of experience, you should be perfect, Balzor!"

"But mighty Lord of the City, this prayer breakfast was not my fault! My streetleaders let us down. They didn't tell . . ."

That was the last they saw of Balzor, as the Darkness reached down out of himself and drew Balzor up and away, leaving nothing where he had been only an instant before. Nepravel was consumed by fear as he felt the presence of Alhandra's lieutenants behind him.

The Darkness bellowed, "Now listen, all of you. I am prepared to blow all of you straight to hell, this instant. No more time on earth. But I need you because you know your neighborhoods, and I am willing to give you one more chance. But one more event like today, and you *all go!*

"From now on Tymor is your new sectorleader. He will be in charge of restarting the voices in as many of those who were saved today as possible, to make them feel unworthy, uncertain, and isolated. Also, you must spend more time on the people around them, being sure that their voices of Pride and Disbelief are always working so that this problem will not spread! Until this crisis has passed, I am sending in extra forces—we will flood your sector with the powers of Darkness and Deception. Some of my own lieutenants will work with you. Each of you will receive at least one experienced demon to assist you in fighting the angels sent by the prayer cover.

"But the responsibility is yours. We are too close to a total victory in this nation—the government, the media, the courts, the industry leaders— almost *all* are ours. And we *will not* allow a revival to start here and to tear down all the walls of deception we have so completely put in place. Can you imagine the disastrous effect if the people in one major city like this one realized what we have been doing and turned back to God? Or if a leader in the media understood how helpful they have been to us in destroying this generation? We *cannot* let that happen! And it could start here, with these men, if you don't stop them! So get to work! Listen to Tymor. I have given him permission, when absolutely necessary, to intervene, not just with the voices, but *directly* in human affairs, on a limited basis. We will provide the cover for the response if there is one. This situation has got to be stopped!"

The dark cloud of hate and anger started to move again, back towards the center of the city. Nepravel was relieved that Alhandra's intervention had apparently saved him, at least for the moment. He was astounded by the authorization of direct intervention. Satan himself must be worried about the outcome in their city, and there must be other battles that a revival here could greatly influence for such a move. The level of spiritual warfare in their city had just been raised by a very significant factor—and the outcome, Nepravel knew, was not always predictable.

Tymor assumed his new position of authority at the center of their meeting, as the wails accompanying Alhandra subsided in the distance. He was obviously pleased with his new position, and all the demons knew that a new sectorleader plus direct attention from Alhandra meant they had better only have good reports in the future, even at the risk of lying.

Tymor told them to expect new demons in their neighborhoods by the next day, and he exhorted them to redouble their efforts, as Alhandra had commanded, with both the saved and the unsaved. Finally he finished and, much later than usual, Nepravel flew back towards his neighborhood, prepared to inventory all of his voices, even while his unsuspecting humans slept.

■   ■   ■

FRIDAY, MAY 5 ■ The next day was Friday, and that evening Amy, Susan, and Bobbie went to dinner and a movie with Billy, Drew, and Thomas.

Richard again sat in their den and read more from the Gospel of John, while Janet finished a novel, and they tried to ignore the beat of the rock music coming from overhead in Tommy's room. Richard used a pen and underlined passages that seemed relevant to him and to his family.

"Janet, I know this sounds incredible, but I'm just overwhelmed by how much God has been trying to talk to me—to all of us. Do you know the word John used to describe Jesus before he became an actual man? He called Him 'The Word!' How's that for emphasizing a desire to communicate with us? Think of all the other descriptions or phrases he could have used. But he chose 'The Word.'

"And the references printed next to the verses in this Bible the Petersons gave us point back to the first of Genesis in the Old Testament. Can you remember how the author described what God did to start the world?"

Janet tried to remember from her school days as a young girl. "Doesn't it say, 'And God said . . .'?" she answered.

"Exactly! Not that He turned around three times. Or waved a magic wand. Or any of a thousand other things. But He *spoke* the world into existence! And He said, 'Let Us make man in *Our* image, according to *Our* likeness.' Jesus was there with God! So here is God who spoke us into being and who sent His Son, whom John calls the Word, to become a man, so that we might learn and see exactly what God's character is! And I've been sitting here for years not listening to God, who wants to talk to me! I must have been a fool."

Janet could only continue to marvel at the transformation in Richard. What he had just said didn't seem all that crucial to her, but it had obviously struck her husband as being very important. Maybe once she finished her novel, she would try reading the Bible again. It had been many years. . . .

Nepravel had been sitting by Richard, trying to start the voices of Unworthiness and Doubt, but the Bible readings and the continuing prayers by the three host church Prayer Warrior teams were making it very difficult. He had just decided to concentrate for the moment on containment, by spinning up the voices in Janet and their children, when another demon suddenly appeared through the den wall. He was larger than Nepravel and carried himself like a fancy courtier from Alhandra, who had been forced to sweep the streets.

"I'm Zoldar, and I've been sent here to help you in this neighborhood," he quickly blurted out, the sulfur almost enveloping him because he spoke so fast. "But right now two angels are about to come by this house, looking for our kind, so I suggest we get out of here and go compare notes in a safer place."

Nepravel broke away from Janet and followed his new "assistant" through the north wall, heading apparently for the night club in the nearby commercial center, as the two angels, summoned by all of the prayers, swept up the street, looking for careless demons to destroy. Because of this interruption and the constant angelic patrols throughout the neighborhood, Nepravel and Zoldar could not return to spin up the voices in Janet, Susan, or Tommy until Sunday evening. They would regret waiting so long.

Since Peter Dowling was visiting in town without a car, Kristen offered, when she called him back, to pick him on Friday up at his hotel. "Let's just have a casual night . . . like old times," she suggested. "In fact, I'll show you some of my favorite spots in 'Little Georgetown,' and then we can go dancing, like we used to. OK?"

Peter readily agreed, delighted at the prospect of seeing Kristen twice. "She must not have a steady friend," he thought to himself, as he hung up for the second time. "That's hard to imagine for a woman as beautiful as Kristen. But maybe I'll get lucky!"

He was waiting outside the Carlton at 7:30 when she drove her European sports sedan under the porte-cochere. He waved, and smiled. He got in beside her, took her hand from the gearshift, kissed it, and asked, "So, how is the 'Queen of Real Estate' in this fair city?"

"Princess, only the 'Princess,'" she laughed. "I haven't been here long enough to be the 'Queen' yet."

"My mistake. And you're much too good looking to be a queen, anyway. Your prince, if I may continue the metaphor, is at your service and ready for an evening at your command!"

Kristen had always enjoyed Peter's sense of humor, and it struck her that she hadn't really laughed with Richard in a long time. It was going to be nice to be out with someone younger, and someone who had liked her very much, before their careers had led them to different cities.

"We've got dinner reservations at Presto's, which I think you'll love. A lot of the city's newspaper people go there, I'm told. Then I thought we'd go dance to some old tunes at Edsel's."

"Sounds great to me. Lead on, fair princess."

She did. They had, in fact, a wonderful, relaxed evening together, as if the five years since their brief affair had not intervened. She found him to be as witty as ever, but now he also seemed to know everything and everybody in the San Francisco area—he had an informed opinion on virtually every topic. And she enjoyed the dancing, which she could never do with Richard. As she pulled up to his hotel again at 1:00 in the morning, he leaned across and kissed her for the third time that night.

"Are you sure you can't come up for a nightcap?" he asked, before opening the door.

She smiled and answered, "Not tonight." But her tone and her expression implied that tomorrow night might be different.

8

SATURDAY, MAY 6 ■ That Saturday was a normal weekend day for the Sullivans. Richard spent the morning at the office, catching up on his contract files. Janet had to do "big shopping," and she coerced Tommy into joining her that morning for the trip to the grocery warehouse. Susan studied in the resulting quiet for a big math test. Tommy was to spend the night again at Brent's, and Amy had invited Susan to spend the night at her home.

Richard had a difficult time concentrating at the office because he kept thinking about Kristen and their next meeting, scheduled as always for Tuesday. He knew he had to break up with her. He had used the index at the back of his Bible to look up what God's Word said about adultery and marriage. As new in the faith as he was, he nevertheless knew that God had a higher standard than adultery. God promised joy or judgment for those who obeyed or rebelled. Richard wanted the joy he had seen in others and had read about in the Bible, and he knew he had to leave Kristen. But how?

He decided to finish his work in time for lunch at home, and he arrived just as Janet and Tommy returned from their shopping. Forty-five minutes later, the four Sullivans sat down to a Saturday lunch of ham sandwiches, and Richard used their meal together to tell Susan and Tommy about his experience on Thursday morning. At first they both thought he was kidding, but as he went on in more detail, obviously still excited two days later, and they noticed their mother's seriousness, they listened with complete attention.

After ten minutes, Richard had hardly eaten a bite, but the others had almost finished their lunches. He neared the end of his story and told them about Court's advice on how to begin a personal relationship with God. Then he slowed down from his earlier enthusiasm, looked down at his sandwich, and continued, "Kids, I . . . this isn't going to be particularly easy for me to say . . . but . . . I . . . I wish I could take the last five years back." Looking up at Tommy, he said, "I wish I had the opportunities I've missed forever to throw the ball, to listen to music, to go to the movies, to watch your games."

Turning to Susan, "And the opportunities to help with homework, to watch your matches, to talk about your dates, to just be together." He started to find it difficult to speak, and the two children, who had never seen their father so vulnerable, softened in their feelings for him. Tommy, in particular, could not believe what he was hearing. At first he had waited for the punch line, but as his father continued, it was obvious that he was sincere.

"In the last two days I've learned about love and about relationships, partly from men who mostly don't know me, but still love me, and partly from our God, who knows me completely, and *still* wants to have a relationship with me! I've been convicted—yes, that's the right word . . . that I have done a *lousy* job of having a relationship with the two of you. And, yes, with your mother as well. I haven't taken the time to be your father, and I'm sorry. You've needed me, and I've let you down. I'm here to ask your forgiveness. I mean it. And simply to tell you that, with God's help and yours, I plan to try to be more of a father, starting now." He ended, looked down again, and sighed, as if he had released a weight from his soul.

No one spoke. Janet didn't know whether to smile or to cry. She was still waiting for some downside to appear. Tommy, despite the defenses he had built up to protect him from disappointment where his father was concerned, acknowledged that his father really appeared to mean what he said. *What will be different, if anything?* he questioned to himself.

Susan, who made the fewest demands on Richard and was the least alienated, suddenly felt as if a new potential source of knowledge and of adult friendship was reaching out to her. It occurred to her that it would be good to have a father who was actually sometimes active in her life, instead of just "there."

Richard raised his head and looked from one to the other, the openness showing on his face. "Wow!" Tommy finally spoke, and Richard smiled. "That sounds OK to me," Tommy said tentatively. "Are we going to start going to church?"

Now all of them smiled, breaking the tension. "Maybe so," Richard responded. "Probably so, in fact. None of you may appreciate this right now, but I frankly want to know more about God—I'm terribly ignorant—and I think the right church will be a good place to start.

"Susan, I don't know if your mom told you, but Bobbie's parents have invited us over for dinner tonight, and then they've asked the four of us to go to church with them in the morning. I hope we can all join them tomorrow, at least to try it," he concluded, looking back and forth between his son and daughter.

Tommy shrugged compliantly. "I guess so. What time should I come home from Brent's?"

"A little before ten."

"I'm spending the night next door at Amy's," Susan said. "But I can probably make it, if you think we should. I know Bobbie has been asking Amy and me to go for months. They have some new sort of youth group, Tommy, that's really supposed to be OK. I've heard other kids talking about it." Richard was pleased to hear Susan's stamp of approval on the idea, to further encourage Tommy.

"Well, beyond church, I just want the two of you to know I'm really going to try to make time for you. And to listen to you. But you've got to help me. Please let me know when you feel like I'm letting you down, so I can do something different. I'm new at this, and it will take your help to make it work. Maybe I can learn some things from you, and you can learn some things from me. OK?" he looked at both of them.

"OK," said Susan.

"OK," said Tommy.

"Thank you," said Richard.

Janet was too overwhelmed to say anything.

Kristen tested her bath water and found it to be just as she liked it. She slipped into the oversized bathtub, a glass of freshly squeezed orange juice next to her and her favorite piano concerto beginning on the CD player. She had just finished her Saturday afternoon aerobics class at the same health club where Richard was supposed to work out, and she was enjoying her usual post-exercise ritual.

Only today there was a new twist. Peter. Since Richard had canceled their "lunch" on Thursday for no good reason, and Peter had unexpectedly arrived, she was compelled to compare the two men and to come to a decision about tonight.

Peter's relative youth and wit had been very refreshing last night. But she admired what Richard had accomplished and his caring for her . . . when he wanted to. That was the problem. In the past few weeks, since their wonderful trip to Atlanta, he had slowly seemed to grow more aloof. But then he would suddenly change and become the adoring older man she had fallen for so quickly. She had even used the word "love" with him. He seemed so unhappy with Janet. Kristen wanted to love him and take care of him, if he would just let her.

But what about tonight, with Peter? she asked herself, as she put down her glass and shaved her left leg over the remaining bubbles in her bath. She could picture how he had looked five years ago, as a graduate student. Unlike Richard's slow and caring way, she remembered Peter as wild and free, but loving all the same. Would he still be the same? She smiled as her curiosity rose, enhanced by the old visual images in her mind, and by the voice of Passion, which the demons had spinning at a fever pitch in her, as well as by Richard's recent inattention. *Well,* she concluded, moving the razor to her right leg, *I guess if the situation presents itself, I should definitely research what differences five years can make! Purely for scientific curiosity, of course,* she smiled to herself.

Kristen's parents still lived in a small town in rural Texas. They had worked and saved all they had to send Kristen to the university. When she was little, they took her to Sunday school and to the occasional revival that came through town in the springtime. Her mother still prayed, every day, for Kristen's salvation. Her parents would have been saddened, but probably not shocked, to learn that in her deliberations about whether to sleep with Richard or Peter, the thought never even crossed Kristen's mind that sleeping with either man was wrong. So complete was her "education," that her only concern was about the timing.

■　　■　　■

"See you in the morning," Janet thought Tommy said, as he headed out the back door for his bike, to spend the night at Brent's. She did hear when he said, "I'll be home about 9:30."

As Janet told him goodbye, Susan came downstairs with a small overnight bag, to walk over to Amy's house. "Is Dad around?" she asked.

"He's in the bathroom shaving," Janet replied, getting some ice water from the refrigerator. "We're leaving in about thirty minutes for the Merediths."

"Mom," Susan asked, "do you think what Dad was talking about this afternoon is real? I mean, can someone really change like that?"

Janet smiled. "I've been asking myself those same questions since lunch on Thursday, when he first told me. I have no idea. I've obviously never experienced what your father seems to have experienced. It's only been two days, so we'll just have to see. But I can tell you that they've been two pretty nice days, and he really does seem to be different."

Susan was intrigued. "That's wild. It'll be interesting to see what happens next!"

"Yes, I guess so. Have a good time tonight at the Bryants', and we'll see you in the morning."

Bob Meredith greeted Richard and Janet at the front door. They walked through to the kitchen, where Anne was cutting the last ingredients for their salad. They exchanged greetings, and Bob invited the Sullivans outside to their back patio, where they found comfortable outdoor chairs and a table set with four places.

The Merediths were a few years older than the Sullivans, but their two boys seemed to keep them young. Janet and Anne had known each other from school functions. Tall and obviously intelligent, Anne had a streak of gray in her hair, which simply made her look distinguished, in an unassuming way. Janet had always found her to be very "down to earth," not trying to impress anyone with wealth or status. She usually had a smile and a helpful suggestion when a school project hit a problem.

"Where are the kids tonight?" Janet asked.

"We've already fed the two boys a couple of hamburgers, and they're watching TV upstairs. Bobbie is going out with Thomas. I think they're going to the ballgame."

Anne appeared in the door with a tray and a pitcher of iced tea. Bobbie answered the door when Thomas arrived, and the two of them said hello to the adults, then left for the game. The two couples sat down in the cool spring evening and talked about their daughters, the boys whom their daughters had been dating recently, school, work, the baseball standings, and other matters. Bob went inside, after starting the gas grill, and returned with a platter.

"I hope you don't mind swordfish steaks. Anne and I really like them, especially on the grill."

"That's great," Richard volunteered. He smiled and thought to himself about another patio cook-out ten years earlier with Scott Peterson, who had also grilled swordfish. Richard made a mental note. "I need to call Scott. He won't believe what's happened."

The dinner was delicious, and after all the dishes were cleared away and the two young boys put to bed, the Merediths and Sullivans returned to their comfortable chairs to finish their coffee.

Bob took a sip to test the temperature, cradled his cup in his lap, and said, "We're sure glad to have you over tonight. We've been meaning to get together for a long time, and it's just great that the prayer breakfast gave us the opportunity. Richard, if you don't mind—and you don't mind either, Janet—would you tell Anne about what happened to you after the breakfast?"

Richard looked at Janet, who smiled and nodded. So Richard again told about his experience in Court's office, feeling the presence of God come into his life. He couldn't help but smile as he told the Merediths all that had happened since, including the family discussion at lunch that day. "I just find that I want to know more about God. His power is now so real to me—I've seen it in so many other good people. I'm like a grown child who suddenly wants to find out more about his heavenly Father, whom he hasn't known for forty years!"

Janet had listened again and noted the obvious joy in the eyes of both Bob and Anne as he spoke—Anne even nodded knowingly when Richard explained a new feeling. Janet was delighted for Richard, but she felt a little left out, and she wanted to know more.

"Bob—or Anne—" Janet said, resting her coffee cup on the arm of her chair, "Susan, Tommy, and I have all been asking what exactly happened to Richard the other morning and what happens next?"

The Merediths looked at each other—Anne nodded to Bob. He leaned forward a bit and tried to speak casually, even though the subject was the most important one on earth.

"Janet, the Bible says that Jesus is the Son of God and that He died to take on the sins of the whole world, so that those who believe in Him will not spend eternity in hell, but instead have everlasting life in heaven with God. It also says, which is implied by what I just paraphrased, that Jesus came to divide. Some will believe and be saved. Others will not, but will instead receive what we all deserve—God's judgment.

"Thursday morning, Richard chose God. He asked God to forgive him for all the sins he has committed. And he acknowledged that he wanted to be born again by an indwelling of the Holy Spirit, accepting Jesus as both his savior and the Lord of his life. When a religious leader asked Jesus point blank what someone must do to be saved, Jesus answered that he must be born again. In other words, he must put off his old self and be born anew through the power of the Holy Spirit. Forty days after Jesus returned to heaven, the Holy Spirit came to earth, which we call Pentecost, and indwelt first the twelve apostles. Those largely uneducated men were endowed with so much power that they collectively turned the world upside down. Individually they were able to accept death by martyrdom, rather than renounce whom and what they had experienced first hand.

"That same Holy Spirit has been indwelling believers ever since, empowering them to overcome temptations and habits and lifestyles and ways of living that have kept them in bondage to the prince of the world, the devil, who hates every one of us, and who only wants ruin and alienation from God for us.

"Well, after the prayer breakfast, Richard chose to cast off the devil and his deceptions and to instead enter into a relationship with God. The Holy Spirit now lives in your husband, Janet, and through God's grace alone, he will never be the same. You, and everyone else, can call upon that same power, if you do what Richard did—what Anne and I did. Which is basically to give up trying to run your own life, ask Jesus for His mercy, and let God take over. It's a wonderful, joyful feeling, being in a relationship that you simply know is right, because the Father who made you is in control."

There was silence as Janet considered what Bob had said. Finally she spoke. "To quote Tommy," Janet smiled, "Wow! That's pretty radical."

"Yes and no," Bob replied. "One of the problems some people have, frankly, is that on one level, the level most people first really experience it, like Richard has, it's not 'radical' or complex at all. It's very simple. There's God and Satan—good and evil—submission and rebellion. All you have to do is choose. In today's complex world, people apparently want complex answers. This one is so simple, but so powerful. People tend to pass it by, missing the miracle of what can happen in their lives, right here, right now."

"Well, while I think about that, what's going to happen next to Richard?" Janet asked.

"Let me take that one," Anne answered, shifting in her chair, and pausing for a moment.

"Richard's spiritual position is now with God, but his human situation is still as it was." Turning to Richard for a moment and smiling, Anne continued, "Like any new believer, Richard has to deal with the life he made for himself without God, now that God has found him. While he has God's peace and joy burning in him, like a small candle, the next few months, or even years, could actually be more difficult, in a human sense, than they would have been otherwise.

"You see, God doesn't promise us an end to all problems. He promises us eternity with Him, and His help in dealing with those problems. So Richard is now beginning what some call his 'Christian walk.' It means that with his salvation now assured, he will try every day to learn more about God and to pattern his life more on God's will."

"Beginning a relationship with the Lord," Richard interjected.

"Exactly," Anne responded. "Imagine, Janet, that Richard is like a tall glass of muddy, dirty water. And each day he can, through God's grace, add one or more drops of clean, clear water in the glass so that a little bit of the muddy water is pushed out. The Bible reading and the prayers and the going to church and the learning from other believers and the making right choices are all those clean, clear drops of spiritual water. And we pray that as time goes by Richard will have less and less of the old self—the muddy water—in him, and more and more of God's will—the healthy clean water. That may sound overly simplistic, but believe me, it really is like what happens to us."

"I can see why that makes sense," Janet said. "But all of you, Richard included, must realize that I *haven't* experienced exactly what you have experienced. I'm seeing it as an outsider. I must admit what I've seen in the last two and a half days in Richard tends to support what you're saying. There does seem to be a real change in him. And I recognize the strength in the two of you—and the same strength in Bobbie, your daughter. Maybe someday I'll feel the same. But, for now, I feel sort of like a spectator. Tell me, what do you think has changed in your marriage because of your faith?"

"First, let me assure you, Janet," Anne said, smiling at her, "that the only thing we believers want is for others to experience the same power of God in their lives. We are delighted for you to be a 'spectator.' In fact, it's a great blessing for your family that Richard now has the Holy Spirit living inside him. You can view that power first hand, every day. But, similarly, don't push your expectations too high. Like you, Richard is also new at this. And he is still a glass filled to the top with a lot of muddy water. Satan is still going to be gunning for him, because he is a new believer, a father, and a business leader. In fact, you both can expect Satan's attacks to step up against all of you. Richard needs your prayers and your support, just as you need his. So help him all that you can.

"Now to answer your question about our marriage. I was not a believer when we were married. I accepted the Lord about five years later. I can only speculate from what I was feeling beforehand and from what has happened to so many of our friends, that we would not be married today unless we shared our faith.

"We were drifting apart. It was nothing terribly dramatic. Neither of us was having an affair or anything, but—and this is what so many of my friends have told me—we were just becoming bored with each other. I have to laugh, thinking about it, as a committed Christian. But that was certainly the case then."

Anne turned to Bob, reached out for his hand, and smiled. "When we think about all that we now share because our relationship is based on our common faith and not just on human attraction, which ultimately *always* will fade, we have to laugh. Laugh, in a sense, and mostly thank God. Can you imagine breaking up a marriage because of *boredom?* Yet that seems to be what gets most of our nonbelieving friends. How can people not believe in the devil, if they reach the conclusion that they must break up their marriage because they are bored?!?"

Richard shifted in his seat, thinking about Kristen and his own conviction over the past several months that his marriage was, in fact, boring. He still did not know how he was going to end his relationship with Kristen, but he knew that he had to do so.

Their conversation continued for more than an hour, sometimes touching on Richard's new belief, sometimes simply recounting their mutual experiences, as the two couples came to know each other better. Before any of them could have imagined, it was after eleven, and the Sullivans rose and thanked the Merediths for a most enjoyable evening.

"Thank you again for inviting me to the prayer breakfast," Richard said, shaking Bob's hand, "and for all that you and so many people did to help me feel God's presence in such a special way."

"I guess we'll see you in the morning," Janet said. "Am I right that Sunday school starts at 10:00, with the service at 11:15?"

"That's it," responded Bob. "You know where Morningside is? We'll meet you outside the main entrance a little before 10:00. OK?"

"We're looking forward to it," said Richard, as he and Janet said a final goodbye and walked to their car.

That same evening, while Richard and Janet missed the symphony and instead went to the Merediths' home, their son Tommy and Brent drove with Zane, Brent's older brother, to pick up Roger and the videos and to have a quick dinner at the food court in the mall. As soon as the boys returned to the Holcombes' empty home after dinner, they headed straight for the basement and the VCR. Just then the doorbell rang, and Roger returned upstairs to welcome two more of his friends, whom he and Zane had invited to the showing. Tommy only vaguely knew these older boys, Derrick and Paul. He had always seen them together, kind of like himself and Brent. Derrick had two small earrings in one ear, and Paul wore clothes that looked like the hippie pictures from his father's college. "I can't wait to see these flicks," announced Derrick, as they positioned themselves in front of the basement television.

After dinner at the Bryants' home, Amy told her parents that she and Susan were going to get some frozen yogurt. Once they were beyond Devon Drive, Amy turned in the opposite direction and headed east across town. "Hey, where are we going?" asked Susan.

"We'll get some yogurt in a little while," answered Amy. "But first I want to buy one of those pregnancy tests, and I don't want to go to a drugstore where we might be recognized. I thought it might be good to have you with me tomorrow morning in case it turns out to be positive."

The girls drove on in silence for several minutes, each considering the gravity of Amy's possible situation. Then Susan broke the silence and described their family meeting at lunch and the apparent transformation of her father.

Amy was startled. Her father, like Susan's, hardly ever talked about God or religion, except in a slightly derogatory manner. "Do you think he means it?" asked Amy.

"I really do, at least for now," answered Susan. "The question is, of course, will it last? But as an immediate result, we're all going to church with Bobbie and her family in the morning. Will you come with us?"

"Go to church?" Amy asked. "What time?"

"We have to leave in time to be there a little before 10:00," Susan answered.

"Well, if the pregnancy test should prove positive, I guess I'll need all the help I can get!" Amy said fatalistically. "I'm not saying yes or no now. We'll see in the morning." And she drove on toward the drugstore.

When Kristen and Peter entered the symphony hall, they took no notice of the young assistant from Richard's law firm and his girlfriend who were sitting in the seats a couple of rows behind them. They enjoyed the symphony immensely and, at Peter's suggestion, they returned to the bar in his hotel for a late-night drink.

Kristen was stunning in a low-cut turquoise dress, with her auburn hair up tight on top of her head. Peter, like most of the men near them, could not take his eyes off her. And she knew it.

They sat together in a booth in the quiet bar at the Carlton Hotel, sipping brandy and laughing over their old times at the university together. Peter occasionally ran his finger up and down Kristen's right forearm as they spoke, and she seemed quite happy with his touch.

After their second brandy, Peter said, "I have one of those personal minibars in my room, and we could continue this conversation in much more comfortable surroundings up there." He looked at her with a mixture of seriousness in his eyes and a smile on his face.

Kristen turned her head, looked in his eyes, read his face, and replied, "That does sound much more interesting than this bar. Let's go," she smiled.

Fifteen minutes later, the minibar door in his room never opened, her turquoise dress thrown haphazardly on a chair, and her hair no longer piled on her head, Kristen and Peter relived the past and explored the present on the king-size bed in his hotel room.

"You're more lovely than I even remember," Peter whispered in her ear as they hugged for the first time again without their clothes, and were egged on by the two demons who had followed them up from the bar. "How can a woman as beautiful as you not be living with someone in this town?"

The thought stunned Kristen, and she tensed for a moment. "Maybe there is someone, Peter," she smiled at him in the dim light from the bathroom. "Maybe I do. But tonight is just for us, so let's not think about anyone else."

And, happy to be with Peter, she never thought about Richard again that night, as Peter quickly reminded her of why she had so much enjoyed their earlier affair.

Late that night, as Tommy climbed into the top bunk in Brent's bedroom, there was a battle of images fighting for prominence in his head. The tapes of the last several hours and his new involvement with the older boys made up one set of powerful visual impressions. His father's confession of faith and admission of failure, sitting at lunch that same afternoon, made up the other set.

The two were at war in Tommy's mind—and although he would not have used these names, they represented a clear division, or choice, between good and evil.

As he lay in the bunk, trying to go to sleep, he thought for the first time in a long while, *I wonder what my father would think, if he knew what I was doing.* And he meant it not to hurt his father, but rather for the first time feeling some sincere tugs of shame and of guilt.

If his father could admit that he himself had done so many wrong things and was truly seeking God now, then it occurred to Tommy that perhaps his father might actually understand some of the rejection and uncertainty Tommy had been feeling.

His defenses were still up, and he knew he would have to watch his father carefully to see whether his actions followed his words. But in a way that he could not really express, just knowing that his father might actually understand him and be there for him, if he needed him, gave him a sense of peace and of having a foundation in his life which had been absent for a long, long time.

As he finally went to sleep, the images were still battling. But at least it was a battle, and no longer a one-sided rout.

9

SUNDAY, MAY 7 ■ Sunday morning, the two girls awoke at Amy's house, and Amy pulled the pregnancy tests out of her drawer while Susan remained in bed. "Well," Amy said, holding the tests up, "wish me luck." And she headed for the bathroom.

It occurred to Susan that she should try praying, and so she said quickly, "Dear God, please don't let Amy be pregnant."

But it was not to be. Within an hour, as the girls dressed, both tests confirmed that Amy was, in fact, pregnant.

When the first test turned positive, Amy sat on the bed, staring at it. Her first emotion was a genuine thrill, that a new life was actually growing *inside her*. How incredible! But then, like a pump evacuating water, the reality of her situation pushed the momentary joy right out of her and kept it out, almost completely. "I can't have a baby now," she heard a voice screaming inside her. Soon she began to cry. "Susan, what am I going to do? My parents will kill me if they find out. How could this happen to me? ... We only did it one time! I wonder what Billy will say!" she laughed derisively, sensing his answer. Turning to Susan, she said, "You can't tell anybody—and certainly not your parents until I figure out what to do. Do you promise?"

"Yes, of course," Susan said, sitting beside Amy and putting her arm around her shoulder. "You, Bobbie, and I will figure out what to do. If you come to church with us this morning, we can sit with Bobbie, and then the three of us will talk about it."

"Do you think we should tell Bobbie?" Amy asked Susan. "She'll be so disappointed. I know she'll want me to have the baby, and I just don't think I can do that."

"Yes, I know. But she already knows what you've done, so I don't think she can be any more disappointed. And we've been best friends for so many years. I think we should try to work this out together. Starting this morning—or as soon as you are comfortable enough to talk about it."

Amy nodded her acquiescence and wiped her tears with the tissue Susan offered. "OK. I guess I'll go to church with you. I certainly need all the help I can get!"

"Now we better go downstairs for breakfast," Susan concluded, smiling as best she could, "or your parents will think something strange is going on."

Kristen awoke slowly that morning, her first impression being that of a man's arm across her body. For an instant she had to think where she was, but then she smiled, remembering how delightful had been her "scientific observation" of Peter, five years older. If anything, he had improved with age!

As she lay in the bed, not moving, while Peter slept, she could not help but think about Richard. They had their usual appointment set for Tuesday. It occurred to her that she would be sleeping with two different men in the space of a little more than forty-eight hours, and the term "loose woman" jumped into her mind, along with the visual image of her mother praying for her. But before she could begin to process that thought, a voice within her told her that she was, in fact, a "modern woman," "liberated," and able to handle such emotional supercharging with no problem.

She smiled at that thought, rolled over, and ran her hand through the hair on Peter's chest. He opened his eyes slightly, and smiled.

"Good morning," she whispered with a smile.

"Good morning . . . Hmmm . . . ," he smiled. "Listen, my flight is not until 2:00, and this is an expensive room. I think we should make the most of my company's investment . . . " And he pulled her to him.

Tom and Nancy Bryant were surprised at breakfast to learn from Susan that the Sullivans were going to church that morning with the Merediths. And they were even more surprised when Amy said that she'd be joining them.

The four Sullivans plus Amy arrived at Morningside Church just before 10:00. Bob and Anne Meredith, along with Bobbie and Thomas Briggs, were waiting for them inside the front door of the large, traditionally built brick sanctuary. After greetings all around, the two couples left for one of the four adult Sunday school classes, and the five young people headed for the large class in which the students themselves, along with Glenn Jamison, led their youth group.

Glenn was standing at the door to the youth group classroom, and Bobbie introduced him to Susan, Tommy, and Amy. Glenn smiled and shook each hand in turn. "Welcome to Morningside. Any friends of Bobbie and Thomas can't be all bad! We're glad you're here and hope you'll always feel welcome to come."

The large classroom was filling up, so they took their seats immediately. Amy, Tommy, and Susan each recognized many other kids their age, either from school or from playing sports. It turned out that it was Bobbie's Sunday to lead the devotion at the beginning, so she rose, walked to the front, and read several passages from the Bible, then gave some brief remarks on what those excerpts from God's Word meant to her. She announced that there would be prayer time after the main program, and then Glenn came up to the front.

"For those of you who are visiting, we often have a guest speaker with us here at Morningside Youth Group. But this morning you're stuck with me," he smiled.

"I want to talk with you for a while this morning about love. About what it is and what it is not.

"I'm talking about the kind of love Jesus describes in Matthew 22, to 'love your neighbor as yourself,' and in Mark 12:31. And in John 3:16

when it says, 'For God so loved the world that He gave His only begotten son, that whoever believes in Him should not perish but have everlasting life.' The love described in those famous passages is not anything like passion. You would probably have little reason to confuse it with that popular notion of love. But it also has nothing to do with something you could more easily confuse it with today, namely a warm and fuzzy feeling—a feeling of attraction or sentimentality which so many times today is characterized as 'love.'

"You see, I'm talking about tough love. Love that goes beyond a warm and fuzzy feeling. There's nothing affectionate or sentimental about dying for someone else. And when Jesus says to love your neighbor as yourself, think for a minute about how it is that you love yourself. Is it a warm and fuzzy feeling? Or is it more that you want the best for yourself in the long run?

"If that is what our Lord means by love—that He wants only the best for us over the long term—and of course the longest term is eternity—then think what that means for your relationships with other people as you try to love them."

Tommy, Amy, and Susan were struck by Glenn's down-to-earth manner and by his ability to communicate a difficult subject in a way they could understand. All the teenagers in the packed classroom listened attentively as Glenn continued.

"Sometimes if you want the best for someone in the long run, your love for them may appear in the short run to be just the opposite of simple affection or of a warm and fuzzy feeling.

"Tough love, for example, has us tell a friend that the beers he drinks on the weekend are hurting his chances for college and spoiling his body and his brain while they are still growing.

"Tough love says that premarital sex is wrong, that no matter how good it may feel at the moment, it is not God's long-term plan for us or for a specific couple. And it changes their relationship because it is not what God wants.

"And so, guys, that means if you're trying to push your girlfriend to have sex, you can't really love her. You may feel affectionate toward her. You may be excited by her. But you can't really *love* her, because having sex with you at age sixteen, seventeen, or eighteen can't possibly be the best thing for her, no matter how great a stud you think you are. Ask yourself, is that what God wants for this daughter of His? If your answer is no, then real love means you don't try it, no matter how excited you get!"

Many of the teenagers squirmed in their seats. Susan and Bobbie, sitting on each side of Amy, consciously refrained from looking at her. "Tough love says that abortion is murder and is therefore wrong, no matter what the inconvenience or the circumstances. It's hard to imagine that the mother of an unborn child can want the best for him or her by committing murder.

"Tough love is not justifying some short-term expediency, like dropping out of school, or failing to do your best, just because it requires a little pain or seems 'unaffectionate'."

Glenn went on to give the kids more examples of how God's real love for them could or could not be reflected in their real love for others. At the end of his remarks, there were questions, and then a prayer time, when many of the students lifted up their friends and families to the Lord. The three newcomers were moved by the clarity and the sincerity of both the discussions and the prayers. None of them had ever been around kids their own age who obviously believed they were literally God's children.

After youth group, the five of them walked to join the adults for the main service.

The class the Merediths and Sullivans attended was led by a local businessman, Monty Ludwig. He was leading an ongoing class on how believers should cope with a world in which virtually every institution denied that the Word of God was important or relevant. This was the first time Richard had ever heard anyone refer to America as a post-Christian society, and it caused him to reflect on his nation's future, without its institutions grounded in the Christian faith. Although Richard had not, until Thursday, considered himself a believer, it now struck him that he had just assumed that the moral teachings of the Bible would always be there in the background.

But now, in this class, he was confronted by the possibility that there would actually soon be no institution left in America attached to the bedrock of those teachings. And in one of those flashes that sometimes hits people as an obvious truth, the term post-Christian explained for Richard the past thirty years' increase in violent crime, drug abuse, child abuse, and other problems. He thought about Susan and Tommy coming to adulthood in a nation without moral principals, and it truly worried him. How had this happened? He was intrigued by Monty's teaching, and he wanted to come back next week to hear more.

As they entered the sanctuary, he was pleased to see that Paula Lindsay was leading the congregation in singing before the service began. He noted this connection with the prayer breakfast to Janet as they sat down, and she nodded her understanding.

The service itself was powerful in both its liturgy and its simplicity. Janet and their children had never experienced this power before. Richard had experienced it but could not name it. The power that moved them was the Holy Spirit, who was present there in the church with them. Amy and the Sullivans could feel, without anyone telling them, that God was there with them. Their hearts felt His presence, and the voices of deception which had been spinning in them took another blow.

And no demon in his right mind would venture near Morningside Church on any occasion, particularly not on a Sunday, when the believers' extra praises summoned even more warrior angels than usual.

Michael Andrews' sermon that morning was on confessing sin. He described the cleansing effect of truthfully and penitently asking God's forgiveness for sins of both commission and omission. "Isn't it sad," he told his congregation, "that psychologists and the press have turned old-fashioned sin, which has been around since Adam and Eve first rebelled against God, into illnesses, addictions, problems with upbringing, problems with teachers, and on and on. If you're told you're the way you are because of your parents, or your teachers, or your economic status, or because of some illness, the implication is that you're stuck with it.

"There's not much good about sin, but the one good thing about sin is that you *can* be forgiven, and the sin can be put behind you. You can give it to God, lay it at the foot of the cross, and let Jesus carry that burden for you. What a blessing. What love for us, that God has provided this way to allow us to start over, to seek His forgiveness, and then to close that chapter of our lives and move on.

"Most of what the newspapers call our nation's problems are simply sin. Plain and simple. At forty years old when you're having an affair and also cheating your company, it's a bit late to blame your parents or your teachers. It's you. It's simple. It's sin. And if you'll take responsibility for your own actions and ask for His forgiveness, then you can, with the power of the Holy Spirit, change, overcome the sin and be different.

"If any one of you in this congregation, or any of you who is visiting, is carrying around with you a terrible burden, either of current sin or of guilt for sins past, and you want to clean up that mess, then I urge you to take those to the Lord in personal prayer. And although it's certainly not necessary, because it's between you and God, if you nevertheless would like for me or one of our ministers to pray with you, then we'll be happy to do so. We will pray with you here, now, during communion—or you may call the office for an appointment during the week. But the main thing is to clean up your past, ask truthfully for God's forgiveness, and then close that chapter of your life and begin again as a new man or a new woman."

Richard felt, while Michael was speaking, that he was the only person in the sanctuary, because Michael's words made so much sense to him, and they were so relevant to his situation with Kristen. The thought of being cleaned up and able to start over again attracted Richard like a magnet, and he made a note to call Michael Andrews early the next week.

Janet, too, was moved, not only by Michael's sermon, but by the service itself. She couldn't exactly put her finger on it, but in her past experience, the emphasis in church worship had seemed to be either on the ritual or on the ministers conducting the service, and the congregation had always been passive. At Morningside it occurred to her, near the end of the service, that the emphasis appeared to be on worshiping the Lord in everything that happened: the liturgy, the singing, the sermon, the prayers. And the congregation was actively part of it all. She noticed that most people had Bibles and followed the readings.

They sang with a vigor she didn't remember in other churches. Many of the people around her took notes during Michael's sermon, and there were even a few "amens" when he made particularly strong points. In short, everyone in the sanctuary appeared to be genuinely interested in worshiping their heavenly Father. Janet's heart was opened, and she was drawn to the sincerity of the worship and the feeling of goodness like a thirsty person to water.

After the service, the Merediths introduced their guests to Michael Andrews at the back of the church, as they were all leaving. He had a warm smile and encouraged them to come back again. Richard and Janet found themselves saying yes simultaneously, and Richard mentioned that he might call during the week. "That'll be fine, Richard," Michael said. "I look forward to meeting with you."

While the Merediths introduced the Sullivans to several other couples in the bright sunshine after the service, Thomas Briggs asked Tommy Sullivan to help him assist his father, who was on usher duty, in straightening up the sanctuary. Amy mentioned to Bobbie that she and Susan would like to talk to her, and the three girls walked several paces off by themselves. "Bobbie, listen. I really appreciate being included this morning," Amy began, "because everything you've told us about your church seems to be true. I liked Glenn Jamison in particular. But what Susan already knows, and I want to tell you, is that I took two pregnancy tests early this morning, and they both turned out positive. So it looks like I'm pregnant."

Bobbie closed her eyes momentarily and said, "Oh, no." Opening her eyes and taking Amy's hand, she paused for a moment and then said, "I'm so sorry. I guess you haven't had time to think through what to do next, but you know I'll be here to help you."

Amy squeezed her hand and tried to smile. "I know, Bobbie. I'm really going to need you and Susan, and you're right, I haven't thought very much past the initial shock . . . But, let's please get together at lunch tomorrow. And, Bobbie, obviously please don't tell anyone about this. *Not anyone,* until we have a chance to talk about it."

"OK. I understand. But I *will* pray about it. And we'll get together tomorrow."

As they were finishing their conversation, the adults walked up.

"Again, Bob and Anne, we can't thank you enough," Richard said, "for all you've done for us in the past few days, from the prayer breakfast to last evening's dinner to the service this morning. For me, these have been four days like I've never experienced before." He turned to his family. "I hope the rest of the Sullivans agree with me."

"I really liked the service," Janet said, "and would like to come back again." Susan nodded her agreement. Tommy said the youth group was "cool."

That evening, as Tommy finished his homework upstairs, Susan watched television, and Janet read, Richard sat at his desk in the den and worked through the family bills. But his mind returned to Kristen and to his problem coming up on Tuesday afternoon. What was he going to do? And what, if anything, was he going to tell Janet? And, knowing that he had now committed completely to Janet and his family, how was it ever going to work out? Could he really be different? What if he failed and all of what he had been hearing for the past four days had no effect on him or his family? As he sat looking at all the bills he had to pay, which was depressing in itself, the voices in his mind led him from worry directly to despair.

Unknown to Richard, as he sat at his desk, he had two invisible visitors at his side. If he could have seen the dark forms or smelled the abominable stink, he would have recoiled in horror. Nepravel and Zoldar were right next to him, and Nepravel was spinning up the voices of Uncertainty and Worry, which were having an immediate effect on Richard.

"Good work," Zoldar congratulated Nepravel, smiling and moving over to Janet, who sat reading a novel in her armchair. Zoldar expected to strengthen her voices of Disbelief and Doubt as a defense against the Word, but he was shocked to find that there were no voices of deception playing in Janet that evening at all! They were all gone! She was defenseless and completely open to hearing the Truth.

Zoldar knew Nepravel had been maintaining the voices in this family for years, and he moved quickly to Susan, who was sitting on the floor, her back against the front of the sofa, watching television. No voices in her either! How could this be? Was the situation worse than Balzor and Tymor had imagined? Where had these people been, and what had they heard? And who had been praying for them?

"Nepravel," Zoldar exclaimed, "there are none of our voices in either of these women. They could be told the Truth about God right now, and they would in all likelihood believe and be lost to us! This isn't just maintenance. We have to rebuild this entire family!" He was obviously annoyed.

"I can't imagine," answered Nepravel. "I knew we would have to start over again with Richard after the prayer breakfast. But what has happened to the others? How could one man—even a husband and father—already have so much effect on his family? They must have gone to a real church. Or there must be many people praying for them, for our voices to be completely silenced. . . . Well, you try to start them again in Janet, and as soon as I finish with Richard, I'll move over to Susan."

Zoldar angrily agreed and settled in behind Janet to replant the voices inside her, while Nepravel returned to creating more worry and despair in Richard.

Richard started to feel even worse about the coming meeting with Kristen and about what might happen to his family in the future. Sitting at his desk, he put his head in his hands. But the voices of deception were not the only supernatural forces now residing in Richard. He had been touched by the Holy Spirit, and the flicker of Light inside him gave a glow which both Nepravel and Zoldar could see—and hate. As he sat with his head in his hands, Richard remembered what both Court and Bob had told him about spiritual warfare, about how he would be attacked, and about the solution. "If you rely on your own power, you will be easy prey," Court had said. "But now you have the power of the Holy Spirit inside you to help you fight."

Without moving, his head still in his hands, Richard began praying for guidance in dealing with Kristen, and protection for his family from the powers of Darkness. Nepravel, right next to Richard, was surprised to see the Light in Richard grow suddenly stronger, and the voices he was rebuilding simply stopped dead. "He's praying!" screamed Nepravel.

"Blast it all!" screeched Zoldar, as the voices he was trying to plant in Janet stopped as well.

As the demons saw the light from Richard's prayers fill the room and then head outward, Nepravel cursed, "He's even praying for that Holloway woman! And you know that angels usually follow up on prayers like these. Come on, we better get out of here before they turn up."

Zoldar spewed out a string of vile curses in frustration as he and Nepravel left the Sullivans' home, their mission unaccomplished.

Ninety minutes later, Richard and Janet had prepared for bed. Richard, in his pajamas, had been in the kitchen, setting up the automatic coffee maker for the morning. He closed the door to their bedroom just as Janet was emerging in her nightgown and robe from their bathroom. He had been agonizing over something for two days, and he finally summoned his courage, walked over to her in the middle of their room, and embraced her in a hug. As they began to part, he looked into her eyes and asked, "I know it may seem strange at first, but would you pray with me?" For some reason he felt more nervous than when he had asked her to marry him.

She smiled. "Of course I will, Richard. What do we do?"

"I'm not sure, but let's kneel here together by the bed." He took her hand in his, and they knelt together on her side of the bed. "Dear heavenly Father, Janet and I come to You tonight to thank You for the many blessings which You have given us . . . Uh, we thank You that by Your grace You have promised us eternal salvation through belief in Your Son, Jesus Christ. We thank You for our marriage and for so much love over so many years. And, uh dear Father, I admit to You, before Janet, that I have not been the best husband I could have been and that there is much for which I must ask your forgiveness. In these times, which have been so difficult for us, I pray that Your Holy Spirit will envelop us and that we will focus on the positive in each other while trying to correct the negative in ourselves. I . . . I love Janet very much, Father, and I ask that You please show me how to make that love grow.

"We thank You for our two wonderful children. Lord, we lift them up and give them to You. We cannot possibly raise them as they should be raised relying on our own strength. So, Lord, we give them to You, trusting Your mercy and Your protection for them, and asking for Your guidance to raise them only in ways that will be pleasing to You. And we pray especially tonight for Tommy, who seems to be going through a difficult time. Please, Lord, fill him with Your grace and Your peace, and give us the knowledge and the patience to lead him back into the family."

As Richard prayed, holding her hand, Janet was drawn to him. She could not help it. Although in all their years of marriage they had never prayed together, it seemed to Janet to be the most natural thing to do. She was attracted to the simultaneous declaration of his submission and of his authority. He was putting himself in submission to their common Father, yet he was praying for his family from a position of authority, as the father and husband. Janet couldn't explain it, but it just seemed the way things ought to be.

When Richard finished praying, he remained kneeling. Janet realized that she should now pray. "Father . . . I . . . I thank You for the transformation of my husband. Please forgive me, too, for not doing my best to help our marriage and our children. Please help me understand more each day what has happened to Richard. And let me experience it, too. We thank You again for all of Your blessings on our family. Please, Lord, don't ever leave us. In Jesus' name, Amen."

When they finished praying, Richard squeezed Janet's hand, smiled at her, looked her directly in the eyes, and said, "I love you so much. I've made a mess of a lot of things. But I want us to be together, and with God's help, we will." He squeezed her hand again, rose, and went into the bathroom to finish getting ready for bed. Janet took off her bathrobe and slipped into their bed. Instead of picking up her book, she folded her hands and thought about the last several days, particularly the day just ending. She could never remember feeling so loved and so secure as she had when Richard finished praying. Not because Richard told her that he loved her. But because Richard told God that he loved her.

Her husband was laying himself bare in front of the Creator of the universe and praying for their marriage. What would it mean to have God involved in their relationship? She realized she could not imagine the future. But she recognized that if God's involvement meant the strong commitment she had heard from Richard tonight, then she could be at peace, for the first time in a long time, about Richard's commitment to her and to his family. Her body shuddered involuntarily with that thought, and she silently thanked God again for all that had happened in the last four days.

When Richard finished brushing his teeth, he looked at himself in the mirror. He realized that he actually looked happier, or somehow better, than he had for weeks, and that made him smile again. It occurred to him that a great question mark had been lifted from him, which had been burdening him terribly for years.

At the beginning of their marriage, he had just assumed that they would always be together. He was young and in love, so it never occurred to him to ask whether they would split up. But then came the bad years, the constant temptations. So many of his friends had affairs or were divorced. And then Janet's job, and her partial focus outside of the home. And finally, Kristen. During all that period he had more and more sensed that perhaps their marriage was not permanent. And thoughts of leaving and of hurting Janet, and not living with Susan and Tommy, and of guilt, had weighed him down simply and slowly over the previous months, almost causing him to bend physically.

But now, closing the medicine cabinet, he realized that as a result of the last four days, he had taken a step that was completely new to their marriage. He had consciously *chosen* to stay with Janet permanently, no matter what. It was not the simplistic assumption of twenty years ago. It was much stronger. It was a conscious decision and a commitment, made, he knew, with God's help, and needing God's support to maintain it. But what a blessing! What a relief from the pain of the previous months. The guilt over Kristen still was there. He still had to deal with her. But he knew in the bottom of his soul that in choosing God he had also chosen Janet and his family. He knew there were still many problems to work out; and he knew there always would be. But the issue of whether he would leave or not was settled forever. And he felt like a new person.

As he turned off the light in the bathroom and made his way toward their bed, it suddenly occurred to him that if Janet and his whole family became believers, then they would spend eternity together in heaven. He had never thought about that before, and it was an incredible revelation. Whatever problems they might have here on earth, he could be with Janet and Susan and Tommy forever in heaven, praising God! And in the next instant, as clearly as any thought he had ever had, he realized that God was looking to him to help bring his family into the kingdom. Suddenly the phrase *spiritual head of the household* had tangible meaning to Richard, and he actually had to sit on the side of their bed for a minute and consider the implications.

"What are you thinking, dear?" Janet asked. Richard slipped under the covers, turned toward her, and told Janet about the two realizations that had hit him just since they had prayed: that he was completely committed to making their marriage work, through good times and bad, and that the four of them could, through God's grace, spend eternity in heaven together.

Janet smiled and put her hand on his shoulder. "Richard, I don't really know how this has all happened, but I am so thankful. I . . . I . . . feel loved and wanted for the first time in a very long time. And I want you to know I love and want you, as well. I'm going to try to be a better wife and mother. But I think I've also heard the message that I can't do those things very well in my own strength. And so I've decided that I'm going to start praying for God's help with our family, too."

Richard smiled as he reached to turn off the light. "Isn't God just amazing? What have we missed all these years?"

In the immediate darkness he turned back to her and put his arm around her shoulder. She snuggled up close to him and in a moment they kissed. He rubbed her back, then her arm, then he moved to her front. Janet moved into him and felt herself giving herself to him in a way she truly had never before experienced.

Richard, for his part, was touching Janet almost as if it were for the first time. He knew now what it was like to be loved totally by God, and he wanted her to know that he loved her in the same way. He knew it was a miracle that their marriage was still together, and he was so moved to be loved by this beautiful, patient woman.

They made love that night with a power and a simultaneous tenderness that was new to both of them—because they really loved each other and had committed their marriage to God, permanently. Janet wanted to please Richard, to give herself to him, because she felt the security of his permanent love. Richard wanted to please Janet and to give himself to her, because he wanted her always to be with him. When their shared release finally and lovingly came, Richard could see the tears in Janet's eyes, and they lay still together in each other's arms, with her tears on his chest.

Richard knew, in one final personal revelation that Sunday, that no previous sexual experience with Janet or anyone else had ever come close. Like a blinding light in the near darkness, it struck him that he had, for the first time, experienced what God meant for the physical union between a husband and wife to be. Everything before had been counterfeit, not even close. For the first time, they had experienced "one flesh," and there was simply no comparison. He lay with his arm around Janet, as she snuggled even closer to him, and he silently praised God, as a single tear escaped the corner of his eye.

10

MONDAY, MAY 8 ■ Riding into work on Monday morning, Richard had still not decided how to handle his "lunch" with Kristen on the next day, and it finally occurred to him that he was in over his head and needed help. Upon reaching the office, he smiled a warm hello to Mary, glanced through the messages on his desk, and picked up the telephone.

"Bob, this is Richard. I know you've seen a lot of me in the past four days, but I've got a problem that's really gnawing at me, and I wondered if I might buy you lunch today."

Bob Meredith heard the pain in Richard's voice and said, "Sure. In fact, I was going to call you later to tell you about the follow-up meetings for the prayer breakfast. So lunch will be fine. Say noon at the Terraces?"

"That will be perfect, Bob. And I really appreciate your help."

Amy had struggled the night before with lack of sleep, cried a lot, and made her list of people to see about her problem. That day she would have lunch with her two best friends, Susan and Bobbie, and together they would lay out the strategy for deciding what to do about her pregnancy.

Janet asked Tom Spence and Connie Wright to stop by her office for a cup of coffee that morning. When they came in and shut the door, Janet motioned them to the two comfortable chairs in front of her desk. She took the fresh cup of coffee Tom offered, walked around her desk, sat down and leaned forward. "Listen. I thought we ought to get together this morning because Richard and I have been talking at home about Bill Shaw's plan, and it has made me think. I definitely want to participate in this upcoming '911 Live' test. But I'm not so sure that any of us, and particularly Connie and I, ought to be chasing police cars on a Friday night in this city. Can't we evaluate the show just as well by watching it in the control room?"

"I guess I never really thought about it," said Connie, "but you may be right. Actually, we may be able to get a broader picture from the station than we could experience in any one isolated situation."

"Well, if it's all right with you both, I'm going to suggest to Bill that we monitor the test run from here," Janet concluded, looking for their approval.

Connie nodded. Tom said, "I'll do it either way. I'll stay here with you and watch the incoming feeds. Or, if Bill still wants to hit the streets, I'll certainly go with him."

"Fair enough," said Janet. "I'll let Bill know. Thanks for coming by."

■　　■　　■

Richard and Bob met at the Terraces Restaurant and were shown to a quiet booth with a view of the river and of the eastern half of the city. Richard began, "I bet when you invited me to breakfast you didn't know you wouldn't be able to get rid of me."

"I'm pleased to help you in any way I can," Bob smiled, "particularly since we are new brothers in Christ. We're now one body, with all of the parts trying to work together."

"Thank you. You obviously have meant a lot to me and my family in a very short time," Richard said, and he glanced down at the menu.

"Think nothing of it. And before we discuss anything else, I want to let you know that starting next week we'll be having several men meeting at my office on Wednesday mornings, as a follow-up to the prayer breakfast, for the next three weeks. We'll start at 7:30 and be out by 8:45. I think you'll learn a lot, and you'll probably be able to share some of your own experiences with the other guys. What do you think?"

"Count me in. It sounds great, and I look forward to joining you. But if the next week is anything like the last few days, I just hope I won't burn out on you," Richard smiled.

Bob returned his smile. "God renews us every day with His Holy Spirit, if we ask Him."

"I know, Bob. And I prayed that very prayer this morning," Richard replied, as the waiter came to take their orders.

After ordering, Bob looked at Richard and asked, "Now, how can I help you?"

"I'm going to tell you about something I've never told anyone, and I think you'll understand why in a minute. It goes without saying that I hope this conversation will just be between you and me, at least for now." Bob nodded his assurance. Richard then spent almost fifteen minutes quietly telling Bob about his affair with Kristen. How it had started, how he had let it continue. How he had been torn and trapped in rationalizations until Thursday. And how he had now made a complete change and commitment to his marriage to Janet, except that he still had to break off with Kristen.

"Bob, I know this has all been my fault. I blame no one but myself. I've asked God for His forgiveness, and I want to go on with a new life. But I must make the break with this woman, and of course I don't know whether or how I should also confess this sin to Janet. I really need help with both of those, but I feel like I've got to say something to Kristen at lunch tomorrow. Until these two issues are resolved, I can't really be in a position to start over. As strongly as I feel about all this, I'm frankly afraid to see her by myself tomorrow. But I certainly don't feel like I can explain to Kristen on the telephone. Judging from my recent track record, I'm not very good at maintaining my resolve to keep my distance from her, once we're together. So it's really just a mess."

Bob thought for a moment while Richard took the first bite of his sandwich. "Richard, I'm sorry this has happened to you, to Kristen, and to Janet. I know it's an awful situation, and I respect your confession and your resolve to change. By way of some reassurance, let me first assure you that only Christ was perfect, not we Christians. There are some other big-time temptations that the devil knows are my weaknesses, and he hits me with them pretty regularly. Paul gave us the best advice concerning temptations like this: He said not to try to fight them, but instead to flee in the opposite direction. Trying to convince yourself that you can stay close to your favorite sin without actually giving in to it is like a moth convincing itself that it can hover safely around a flame—simple flight, tail down and admitting that you are no match for your strongest temptations is absolutely the best defense.

"On those rare occasions when you do have to get close to your temptations, for some unusual reason like this one, then the next best defense is to rely on the Holy Spirit and never on your own powers of determination or rationalization. One trick I have used in a couple of very close situations is that I find it very hard to commit a sin when I am praying to God. So when all else fails, prayer is the last line of defense. I believe God hears those prayers and that his angels react quickly. One last biblical principle to apply in a situation like this one is not to try doing it alone.

"So let's pray here, now. Then I'll tell you what I think, and we'll try to find a solution together."

As he walked down the hall at the end of classes that Monday, Tommy was continuing the debate he had been having with himself since Sunday morning. His experience Saturday night had been so intense, so over-whelming. All the boys had eventually participated together in a group, just like on the video. It had been wild, and he couldn't take his mind off it.

But he had also seen and heard the transformation in his father. And then on Sunday he had been to both youth group and the service at Morningside Church. None of those latter experiences had yet focused him on any specific course of action, but they did remind him that there is a higher standard of living than "if it feels good, do it." And he was feeling slightly less interested in hurting his father, since his father had already admitted his shortcomings to Tommy, in front of their family. And, finally, unknown to him, the deceiving voices that otherwise would be running at a fever pitch in him were almost silent, stilled by those same experiences and by the continuing prayers of believers, including his father.

As he closed his locker, Roger suddenly appeared next to him. "Hey, big guy. The same bunch is going to get together over at Derrick's house this Saturday night. Do you think you can figure out a way to make it?"

Tommy looked at Roger, and the debate raged on inside him. "I'm not sure," Tommy said. "I'm not sure. It seems to me I'm doing something next weekend. Let me check with Brent and my parents, and I'll let you know."

"Well, OK. But I hope you'll be there because we sure did have a lot of fun," Roger concluded.

"Yeah, sure. A lot of fun," Tommy repeated, but he was not smiling.

The meeting over the city that midnight, conducted by their new sectorleader, Tymor, was a reflection of the mixed results the demons had achieved since the prayer breakfast.

On the plus side for Tymor's forces, bent on the destruction of humans, they were successful in beginning to isolate some of the men who gave their lives to the Lord at the prayer breakfast, particularly those who had not yet found a way to join with others in the Body of Christ. Some, despite the Light now shining within them, tried to fight their earlier temptations by themselves, usually were unsuccessful, and then became confused and discouraged. For others, the easiest deception for the demons was simple: busyness. By immersing them in the cares and worries of their daily lives, and spinning up the deceptive voices to remind them of their own importance and of their critical need to help solve problems, the demons kept many of the men from any follow-up activity, which severely limited any effectiveness they might have in leading others to the Truth.

But other reports that night infuriated Tymor and his lieutenants. The initial secondary impact of the prayer breakfast had primarily been on families, given the fact that the prayer breakfast had only been a few days before. Many believing wives, who had been praying for their husbands for years, were brought to their knees in joyful thanksgiving that their prayers had been answered. Strained relationships, which the demons had been pushing, were suddenly healed. Church attendance went up that Sunday, and worst of all, seven additional men who had attended the prayer breakfast without a commitment, had, that Sunday, asked the Son of God into their lives. And the prayer breakfast follow-up program had not even yet begun!

Nepravel let Zoldar report that night, hoping that his status would deflect some of the heat they would receive. While they, too, had experienced some mixed results, the negative report on Richard was particularly upsetting to Tymor and the others. Because his heart was prepared by other believers many years before, and believers around him prayed and were involved, Richard's faith, like that of several other men at the prayer breakfast, was putting down strong roots and already affecting the members of his family.

"We had great plans for Richard Sullivan, as you know," Tymor bellowed at Nepravel and Zoldar. "He seems to be lost to us now, and that is most disturbing, particularly given his potential for affecting others. But he can still be brought down. Concentrate on containment as you have, but also work on those around him, like the Holloway woman, and business associates. He is still new in his faith, while we have been at our work for thousands of years. Find a way to cause him to fall!"

■   ■   ■

Janet knocked once on Bill Shaw's door after checking with his secretary. She went inside and took the seat to which Bill motioned her while he finished his telephone conversation.

"Now, Janet, what can I do for you?" Bill asked, as he put down the telephone.

Janet explained to him the conclusion she, Connie, and Tom had reached that morning.

When she finished, Bill raised both his hands from the desk and smiled. "OK, OK. That's perfectly fine with me. You and Connie can stay here and watch the input in the control room. But I still want to go out to see what it's like firsthand. And I think Bob Grissom will want to go too."

"Then I'm sure Tom Spence will join you. And we'll pray"—Janet noticed the quick turn of his head towards her when she innocently used that term—"that everything goes well and safely for you."

"Janet, when you say 'pray,' have you joined Tom and Connie in their overreaching religious fervor?" Bill asked, somewhat derisively.

Janet was flustered by his question and didn't know how to respond. "It's . . . it's hard to explain. I said 'pray' just then without really thinking about it. I just meant that I hope that everything goes well . . ."

"OK, fine," Bill smiled. "I just wanted to . . ."

Now it was Janet's turn to hold up both her hands. "But . . . now that I think about it, yes, I probably will pray with them. And with my husband, Richard. He's been renewing his faith, and his searching has already had an effect on me. And so," she continued as she stood up to leave, "I probably *will* be praying for you and Tom and everyone else who is out there that night, if that's all right with you?"

"Yeah, yeah, sure. That's just fine," Bill finished their conversation and picked up the next papers from his "in" box. "That will be just swell," he concluded, as Janet closed the door behind her.

TUESDAY, MAY 9 ■ Richard set his alarm and awoke half an hour early Tuesday morning. At Bob's suggestion, without waking Janet, he slipped quietly into their den and read his Bible for fifteen minutes, then knelt on their carpet and prayed for guidance, protection, and the Holy Spirit's indwelling for what would happen that day. And then he prayed for Kristen.

Torgo, the demon for Kristen's neighborhood, happened to be in her apartment early that morning, spinning up the voices of deception that Nepravel had requested. He saw the incoming light from Richard's answered prayer diminish slightly the Darkness of the planted voices, but he was right there to spin them up again.

After Kristen awoke and had her first cup of coffee, she reflected again on her weekend. She had had a wonderful time with Peter, but she frankly had no idea about his love life back in San Francisco. He told her he was still single, but he didn't volunteer any other information, and she didn't ask. When they parted on Sunday afternoon, he encouraged her in a general way to come visit him in San Francisco, but there was nothing specific.

Now it was Tuesday, and she had not seen Richard in over a week. A voice inside her told her that her weekend with Peter had been a great fling, but Richard was right here in her hometown. She loved him, and once he left Janet, she could make him very happy. She replaced her mental images of Peter with those of Richard, and after her bath that morning, she selected her favorite spring outfit, which was both businesslike and strikingly feminine, to wear for him.

Tommy and Brent were walking together from English class to lunch in the cafeteria late that morning when Brent said, "Aren't these videos they're getting just fantastic? Do you think there's any way we can get over to Derrick's house this Saturday night?"

"I like the videos," Tommy replied, kicking an imaginary soccer ball on the hallway floor with a sweep of his foot, "but I can't say I'm interested in getting any further involved with those guys."

"What do you mean? That's half the fun! You don't suddenly think there's anything wrong with it, do you?"

"No . . . Well, I guess I mean I don't know. I know it's supposed to be great and just another lifestyle. But I guess I'm *not* sure it's right, at least for me. So I just want to cool it for one Saturday. Why don't you spend the night with me, and we'll go to a movie or a ball game or something halfway regular?" Tommy asked.

"I'll think about it. I'll think about it," Brent said as they entered the cafeteria line for their trays and silverware.

"You've got the car keys, Richard," Bob said, handing them to him in the parking garage at Kristen's apartment building. "So Anne and I can't leave until you come back. We'll be here praying for you and Kristen. Take as long as you need, but not too long!"

Before leaving for her first appointment that Tuesday morning, Kristen had placed a new bottle of white wine in the refrigerator in case Richard, whom she would see at lunch, was in the mood. But now, as she touched up her make-up a little before noon, she thought back to Richard's call to her car phone only an hour earlier. He had confirmed their date, but he had told her the first thing they had to do was talk. That had sounded ominous to Kristen. But he didn't want to go into any details on the car phone.

As she continued to question in her mind what Richard had meant, her doorbell rang. *Who could that be?* she thought. *Richard has a key. I hope this isn't a problem.* She walked to her front door and looked through the small viewer in the door. It was Richard. *What on earth could this be? He must have lost his key.* And she opened the door.

"Hi, Kristen," Richard began with a smile. "I decided to ring the doorbell because I want our time together to be different from all our other ones, so I wanted to start differently. May I come in?"

Surprised, she nodded, and without saying a word, she opened her door, and stepped back. He walked in, went over to one of the armchairs by her coffee table, and took a seat. She sat down in the chair opposite him and folded her arms across her chest. Leaning forward and putting his hands together, he began "This is probably going to be one of the most difficult conversations of either of our lives. I ask you to listen to what I'm going to say with as much understanding as you can muster under these circumstances. I don't expect you necessarily to be happy today, but I hope you will at least understand me, so that perhaps you can be happy later. And I want to ask you to forgive me."

As Richard continued, he simply couldn't help thinking how beautiful she looked, even in her uncertainty about his intentions. He asked God for the power to overcome these thoughts and to continue without hindrance. "First and foremost, I am not the same man who shared your bed here with you ten days ago.

"You may or may not be able to understand this, but last Thursday morning, before you and I were supposed to get together at lunch, I went to that prayer breakfast I told you about. There, for reasons that really stretch back many years and that I will be happy to share with you in detail some day, but probably not right now, I committed my life to Jesus Christ, asking Him to come into my life, and He has made me a new person."

Kristen frowned and folded her arms more tightly around herself. A voice inside her said, *Oh, give me a break!*

"And the days since last Thursday have been some of the most genuinely happy days of my life. I have felt the Lord's presence in most things that I'm doing; and I really, truly want to do His will.

"As you can, I think, imagine, I don't believe that having an affair is His will for me, or for anyone else. I have asked Him to forgive me, and I am trying, with His help, to begin healing my relationship with Janet and with the children. I now know our affair has crippled that relationship."

Kristen pulled her arms even a notch tighter, and her frown hardened into a scowl.

"Janet doesn't know about our affair yet. I'm grappling through prayer over whether to tell her or not. You could, of course, pick up the telephone and tell her, which I hope you will not do. I recognize that you could. But the first and main step is for us to break off our affair immediately. I know it's the right thing for both of us. It may not seem that way to you now, Kristen. You still mean a great deal to me, but what we have been doing is just wrong.

"And if I were to tell you that I love you, I would now also have to say that in loving you, I must also want the best for you. You're a great person—bright, talented, and generous. And I'm absolutely certain the best thing for you is not to be having an affair with anyone, but instead to be married to a good husband. And my own marriage means that your good husband will never be me."

Kristen's first words since he started speaking were, "That's not what you said a few weeks ago," as a tear formed in her left eye and threatened to run down her cheek.

"I can certainly imagine how my words and actions could have led you to that conclusion. I would also have to add that your own imagination has underscored whatever I may have said or done. But again, I totally admit that I was wrong and that it was my fault. The overriding point now is that the man who said and did those things is no longer me. I don't want that kind of life. I want to try to make my marriage work, and I honestly feel God is already helping me do that. There just is no room in His will for us to be having an affair. And I mean that as being best for both of us."

She could tell that Richard was being honest about his feelings, and he believed what he was saying. But then a voice kicked in and reminded her of how he had used her as an agreeable plaything and was now discarding her when he became tired of her, hiding behind some make-believe story about finding God!

"Well, hallelujah!" Kristen exclaimed sarcastically. "You find God and then have to dump the woman you've kept on the side. That's great, Richard. How do you think that makes *me* feel?!? I don't appreciate being jilted."

Richard looked down at the floor, feeling terrible.

"And I may just call Janet this afternoon, or this evening, or tomorrow. Who knows when it will be, Richard? But you can bet that I will!"

Richard finally spoke again. "Kristen, again, I appreciate that this is my fault and that you have every reason to be angry. But I ask you to think for a few days about all that I've said. I even ask you to imagine to pray about it. I also ask you not to call Janet until you do those things, because you may feel differently. But whatever happens, I will be praying for you. And to repeat what I've already said, I want nothing but the best for you, as well as for Janet, me, our children, and our futures. And that's the simple reason why I'm doing this." Rising from his chair, he concluded, "So I urge you not to call Janet, but instead to move into dating some good man, who might lead you one day to a marriage as happy as mine once was, and now I pray will be again."

Kristen remained seated. Her countenance was almost dark. "You know the way out, Richard. How about leaving my key behind, so I won't have to make another copy to give to the next guy I go out with, when he wants to come over to my apartment to pray with me? Which church are you going to this afternoon? There are several in the neighborhood, any one of which I'm sure will be pleased to have a righteous soul like you walk in the door!"

As Richard removed her key from his key chain, he was cut deeply by her remarks, but he tried his best to ignore them. He said, "I'm anything but righteous by my own actions. *All* of us sin, and I've tried to tell you that I understand how sin ultimately leads to one sort of pain or another. In this case, I'm trying to do the right thing, and to minimize the long-term pain. Despite how you feel now, this is the right thing because it's in God's will. I genuinely wish you the best and hope that one day you will understand."

"Thanks, Dr. Sullivan. I'll remember that. Now will you please leave?"

That same Tuesday afternoon, the three teenage girls began the investigation Amy had decided upon to help her consider what to do about her pregnancy. Their first meeting was with Billy in the park.

THURSDAY, MAY 11 ■ At noon on Thursday, Kristen made a point of not being in her apartment for lunch. There was still an emotional war waging inside her over everything that had happened to her in the past week. She had not yet called Janet. She could not think about her meeting with Richard without becoming angry, even though a small voice in the background kept quietly repeating that Richard had, in fact, been right. She almost called Peter Dowling, but decided that he would think she was chasing him if she volunteered to come to San Francisco that weekend. So, sitting at her work desk and eating a brown-bag lunch, she decided she needed some time and space to think. She called her travel agent and booked a flight to Dallas and then called her mother and gave her the unexpected good news that her daughter would be spending a long weekend back at home.

FRIDAY, MAY 12 ■ On Friday afternoon, Bill Shaw stopped by Janet's office at the station and confirmed that the "911 Live" test run was set to take place in their city in two weeks.

"I've been able to secure three spots for Tom, Bob Grissom, and me, since you and Connie want to stay here in the control room, to ride along in one of the police cars as it cruises on this side of town. Maybe we can set up some kind of communication net, so those of us from TV5 can be in contact while the network people shoot their footage. And they've said we can use their video to promote the show here at home. So it's looking good for two weeks from today. Are you still on?"

"Sure, Bill," Janet answered. "It sounds great. I really appreciate your setting this up, and I hope it goes well."

"Me too," agreed Bill as he headed off down the hall.

SATURDAY, MAY 13 ■ That Saturday morning Richard, for the first time in a long time, stayed home and worked around the house with Janet. For one moment late in the morning all four Sullivans were together in the kitchen, and Richard said, "I'd like to go back to Morningside Church tomorrow morning, and I hope we can all go together again."

"Amy's gone with her parents to their mountain house this weekend," said Susan, "but I'd like to go. Maybe I'll drive myself and go to their youth group. That Glenn Jamison guy is really good."

"Brent's spending the night with me," said Tommy, "but maybe I'll call him and see if he wants to go to youth group, too. Can we ride with you, Susan?" She nodded.

"Well, that's fine," responded Richard. "And, Tommy, by the way, I'm really glad Brent's coming over here for a change. Maybe we can all go out for a hamburger after your game this afternoon. And if you guys need any batting practice before the game, I'm sure your mother will let me take a break from all this spring cleaning to pitch some balls for you."

"Sure, Dad. Can we go to Johnny B. Goode's for burgers?"

Knowing the boys loved this particular restaurant, with its expensive but delicious hamburgers, Richard smiled and said, "Sure, I guess we can. It's the only place left with loud music that I can stand—because the loud music is from when I was your age. And you're welcome to come, too, Susan."

"Thanks, Dad. But I'm going out with Drew."

"I'll go check with Brent about batting practice, Dad," said Tommy. "We'll see you later."

So that Saturday night Tommy and Brent didn't join the older boys for videos, and the next morning the two of them, plus Susan and Bobbie, were at the Morningside youth group when Glenn Jamison gave his lesson on Lazarus and the rich man, from Luke 16. Tommy was intrigued when Glenn pointed out several of the occasions in the Bible when Jesus referred to hell. Tommy vividly remembered just a few weeks earlier when his father had told him, after Mr. McEver died, that the Bible never mentioned hell.

Since Dad's really getting into the Bible now, thought Tommy, *I'll give him these references.* And he wrote them down.

After youth group, instead of going to the main service, Susan, Bobbie, Tommy, and Brent joined several of the other kids for an early lunch together at a popular cafeteria not far from the church.

11

WEDNESDAY, MAY 17 ■ That Wednesday morning and afternoon, Amy, Susan, and Bobbie had their appointments with the school nurse, Mrs. Simpson, and with Glenn Jamison at Morningside Church. They received Mrs. Simpson's advice for Amy to have an abortion, as quickly as possible. And they heard Glenn's advice for Amy to have the baby, whom God had created, and then to seek an adoption.

That afternoon, Bruce McKinney came by Richard's office and proposed that Richard co-guarantee along with three other individuals a $500,000 loan for his company at the bank, until the Tomlinson deal closed. Richard was intrigued by the prospect of earning an additional $50,000 for just signing his name, and he promised his friend Bruce that he would give him an answer in a day or two.

Late that afternoon, after most of the attorneys and staff had gone home, Richard walked down to Court Shullo's office. "Have you got a minute for a 'what if'?" Richard asked, standing outside Court's door.

"Sure, sure, Richard," Court answered. "I was getting tired of reading motions and countermotions anyway," he smiled.

Taking a seat across from Court, Richard said, "As both a lawyer and a Christian, I'd like your advice on a proposition one of my long-standing clients and friends made to me today." And Richard described for Court the background of the McKinney and Smith deal with Patrick Tomlinson, and the attractive proposition Bruce McKinney had made to him that afternoon about co-guaranteeing their company's loan at the bank.

Court listened attentively and made several notes while Richard spoke. When Richard finished, Court thought for a few moments and then replied, "Let me respond as best I understand the situation, first as a Christian and then as a lawyer." Richard nodded his approval.

"Have you ever read Proverbs?" Court asked Richard.

Richard shook his head and said, "I guess I've read one or two isolated extracts, but never the whole book in the Bible."

"Well, most of Proverbs was written by Solomon, David's son, proclaimed by both God and man to be the wisest ruler Israel ever had," Court said. "There are, by the way, thirty-one chapters, and you could do worse than reading one chapter each day of the month, repeated for about six months. But anyway, the point for now is that some large number of times—I forget exactly how many, but it must be three or four—Solomon writes in the course of these thirty-one chapters that a wise man never guarantees a loan for someone else. I try to take note of everything written in the Bible, but I figure that when something is repeated over and over again, it's for a reason. And I bet if you ask any of our attorneys in civil litigation, you'll find that a great part of their work today is created by the fact that so few people have heeded that advice.

"So that's my spiritual input. As a lawyer, it seems to me that you could be putting yourself in a position where you could have a terrible conflict if, God forbid, something negative started happening to this deal. I mean, could you readily give McKinney sound advice, if you had not only our fee, but an additional, personal $50,000 of financing riding on the outcome?"

Richard listened attentively to all Court had to say, his chin resting on the tips of his upturned fingers. When Court finished, Richard smiled and said, "I really appreciate your advice, Court. You've done exactly what I asked. And tonight I think I'll try for the first time doing something Bob Meredith tells me he wishes he had begun doing years ago: I'm going to ask my wife her opinion."

"Sounds good to me," Court smiled. "And let me know if anything changes, or if I can help you in any other way."

Richard nodded, smiled back and said, "And now we both need to go home to our families. That's an order from your senior partner, Court. But thanks for being here."

Ever since the weekend events after the prayer breakfast, Janet had been moved to respond to the changes that she had so visibly seen in Richard. She started by trying to think of ways to be home more of the time. And ways that each of them could become more involved in the other's interests. Driving home that afternoon from work, she thought she might have hit upon such an opportunity.

After dinner that night, as Richard rinsed the plates and she loaded them in the dishwasher, Richard said, "When we get finished, I'd like to ask your opinion about something."

"That's fine," replied Janet. "Because I wanted to ask you something too."

Settled in the den while the kids worked on their homework upstairs, Richard again described for Janet the history and the proposal from Bruce McKinney. Janet listened and interrupted him several times with short clarifying questions.

"We could really use the $50,000, for several specific projects we've talked about together in the past, as well as maybe for a getaway for the family. But it means that I have to personally sign for a big loan, although there will be other guys joining me and the downside risk should be very minimal. What do you think?" Richard finally asked.

As Court had done, Janet took a few moments to think before answering. "We've lived next to Bruce and Diane for years, and we've always enjoyed doing things with them. They've got four cute little children who keep Diane busy all the time. I've always liked doing things with them, Richard, but I've never thought that Bruce had very much business common sense. I mean . . . I don't know . . . it's something about his eyes or the way he's always buying the newest of everything. I can't exactly explain it, but I wouldn't want you—and therefore our family—to risk any money, if the outcome we need depends largely on Bruce."

Richard smiled, almost chuckled. "Well, that's the same sort of scientific investment advice that Bob Meredith told me Anne gives to him! But he also says that she's right virtually all the time. He even told me that it's a Christian principle that husbands should always listen to their wives on issues such as this, that God has given you a sense that we men don't have! Now, I haven't had time to check that out myself, but it sounds as if you and Anne ought to open an investment advisory firm!"

Janet smiled as well. "Anytime, dear. I've thought you've done some crazy things in the past, but I didn't want to say anything. But if you ask, I'll definitely tell you . . . And now, if that's settled, I've got something to ask you." Richard nodded in agreement. "As we've talked about before, in nine days the network and our station are going to conduct the test of the '911 Live' concept here. I took your advice—as long as we're thanking each other for advice—and told Bill Shaw that we didn't think it was good, particularly for Connie and me, to ride around with the emergency vehicles. So he and Tom Spence are going out in a police car, while Connie and I will watch from the control room. I wondered if you would like to join us that night at the station, and then you and I can go out for dinner afterwards? The next day we're all going with the Bryants to their mountain home, but we shouldn't be out too late."

"I think that sounds like a great idea," Richard smiled. "Let's plan on it."

THURSDAY, MAY 18 ■ The next morning, Richard called Bruce and told him that, despite the attractiveness of the offer, Richard just did not feel it was the right thing for him to do. In his explanation, he primarily cited the potential for a legal conflict of interest, and he thanked Bruce for the opportunity.

"But you may soon not have a client or a business to have a conflict with," Bruce told Richard, obviously disappointed. "If we don't get this loan, I don't know if we're going to make it. And one of the other potential guarantors has already declined. If you back out, Richard, it could kill our company."

Richard did not like the escalation of his own implied responsibility for the culmination of many years' past problems. "Now, Bruce," Richard responded, "I think that's a bit of an exaggeration. You're my client, neighbor, and friend. I've helped you every step of the way with Tomlinson, and will continue to do so. But I've got to help you as your attorney, not as an investor in your firm, which I would essentially become if I guaranteed your loan. I understand you're disappointed, but I didn't create the situation you're in. I'm here to help you work it out, but not in that way."

"OK, OK." Bruce backed off on the telephone. "I understand. I'll try to ask someone else, and if I need papers drawn up, I'll give you a call. Thanks for considering it." And he hung up without saying goodbye.

SATURDAY, MAY 20 ■ That warm Saturday afternoon, Susan had challenged Janet to a tennis game, and the men decided to have a game as well. So all four of the Sullivans walked down to the courts at the park in the middle of Devon Drive.

Between sets, when Janet and Susan were sitting and watching Richard and Tommy play, Susan said, "Now, Mom, don't freak! I'm not asking for me . . . but we've been studying in biology, and I wondered what you think about abortions."

Janet looked closely at Susan, trying to read her expression, to see if it really *was* about her. She could only see an honest question—one that Janet had not exactly expected, however.

"Well, if you had asked me that question a few weeks ago, I would have said that women definitely have the right to choose what's best for their bodies. But now, after going to church and Sunday school for a couple of weeks and considering all that has happened to your father and seeing how he has changed, I have been led to reconsider a belief I've held for a long time, about God. *Something* has changed your father, and he believes that it's God. And I must say that everything I've seen and heard so far supports that.

"So if there is a God," Janet continued, bouncing the racquet on the fingers of her free hand, "then we need to listen to Him. And there is apparently some pretty strong evidence in the Bible that God is opposed to abortion.

"I know you went to lunch with your friends and were not in the main service on Sunday, but Michael Andrews preached a great sermon. I think we told you a little bit about it. The sermon was not really about abortion, but he used it to illustrate some points. They made me stop and think. For example, he said that elevating individual convenience over life is going against God, and will undoubtedly lead us as a society to more and more problems in the future. And he pointed out how college enrollment has dropped off dramatically because of all the babies who would have been born, had abortion not been legalized in the early 1970s.

"Anyway, as I said, if you had asked me earlier, I would have said that abortion is just an individual woman's right to decide a personal matter about her own body. But now, in just the past few weeks, I've had to grapple with some new thoughts." Janet sighed and slowed down. She looked toward Richard, playing tennis with Tommy, then she continued.

"You see, as you've heard me say so many times in the past, all those thoughts and decisions came from a belief that there was no God. Or at least that He doesn't become involved in our personal lives. But seeing with my own eyes what has happened to your father, hearing the same story from people like the Merediths, and listening to teaching from men like Michael Andrews, I'm simply forced to say that perhaps there *is* a God. And perhaps He *does* act daily in our lives. And if that's the case, then I'm going to have to rethink my stand on abortion because, like all individual decisions, it has to fit within God's larger plan. And I guess I can't imagine that getting rid of unborn babies fits into God's plan."

There was a long silence between mother and daughter, as Janet continued to look toward Richard, then turned. "We certainly did get off on a serious subject for a tennis match!"

Susan returned her smile. "Yeah, I guess so." As much as her mother's words, Susan appreciated her mother's honesty in sharing her uncertainty and her thought process. It made Susan feel good that her mother could trust her with these very personal thoughts.

"So you see," Janet concluded, picking up their can of tennis balls, "you cannot get a simple answer from me right now, because I don't have one. But I'm working on it. Or perhaps it's better to say that God is working on me. Anyway, I'm thinking about it. Maybe you should ask your father. By the way, why do you ask?"

"Oh, nothing," said Susan, picking up her own racquet.

That Saturday evening, while Bobbie and Susan went on dates with Thomas and Drew, and Tommy went to their school's junior high spring dance, Amy had dinner with Billy and discussed with him what she had learned about abortion and adoption. By the end of the meal, feeling that she could just not imagine having a baby as a high school senior, she agreed with Billy that she should have the abortion and promised to schedule it for the following Friday.

Then on Sunday morning, she and her parents left and drove ninety miles south of their city to celebrate her grandmother's birthday. As they had backed out of their garage, they waved at the Sullivans, who were apparently on their way again to Morningside Church.

SUNDAY, MAY 21 ■ Amy's grandmother lived in a beautiful old two-story home on the outskirts of a small and once-thriving farm town. Her grandfather had been one of the two bankers in the town, and he had built a nice home on a large corner lot, from which her grandmother had always grown what seemed to Amy to be an amazing variety of fruits and vegetables, which she canned and gave to her three children and six grandchildren.

This was her grandmother's first birthday since her grandfather's death. Amy knew it was an issue for her father, his older brother, and his older sister, that their mother should move from her large home to more modest surroundings. Among her father's generation, that subject would be the main topic for discussion on the large veranda, and in the comfortable kitchen.

Amy had not seen several of her cousins for quite a while. She was looking forward to being with them again in the large home, which was filled with memories for her of Christmases and of summer vacations when she was a little girl. But she was not prepared for her cousin Catherine, the daughter of her father's older brother. Catherine was seven years her senior—and very pregnant with her second child.

Catherine was, of course, the main topic of conversation among the women. Amy's mother and her Aunt Lois doted over their niece whenever they were together. Amy found it difficult to escape the almost continuous conversation on childbirth and on young children. Once Amy was present when her own father was very complimentary of Catherine and told her how fine she looked in her modern, good-looking maternity dress. *I wonder what they would say to me in six months*, Amy wondered, *if we were back here for Thanksgiving—and I were the one in the maternity dress*?!

For Amy, the effect of being with Catherine for that entire day was one of simultaneous attraction and repulsion. Her cousin seemed so happy, even with the increased inconvenience in her seventh month of pregnancy. Amy had never noticed it before, but it really was true that pregnant women had a special "glow." And Catherine seemed so maternal to her, shepherding her two-year-old around his great-grandmother's home.

Amy thought about the life growing inside of herself, and she longed to share her secret with Catherine. She asked her as many questions about being pregnant as she could, without seeming to be too intently interested. Catherine was a walking advertisement for pregnancy and childbirth. Several times during the day, Amy found herself warming to the possibility of actually carrying the baby to full term.

But then she reflected upon Catherine's older age, her college education, her seemingly loving husband who was a well paid engineer, and then voices inside her brought Amy back to what it would be like to be an unwed eighteen-year-old mother, with no high school education and a dismal future.

Amy spent the entire day on an emotional roller coaster. And driving home with her parents, she was glad that she had made her decision to have the abortion, if only to end the uncertainty and the emotional swings within her.

At youth group that Sunday morning, Glenn Jamison reminded the kids about the movie to which they were all invited that afternoon. He also announced that the church had hired a new director for the junior high ministry, a young lady named Carrie Wagner, whom he had known for several years. "Carrie will be joining us late in the summer, after she graduates from college and has a bit of a vacation. We're really looking forward to having her here to concentrate on working with those of you in junior high."

As they were leaving the room after the meeting, Glenn asked Tommy if he would like to join him some morning that week for an early breakfast, before Tommy had to be in school. Tommy, obviously happy to be asked, told Glenn he would certainly like to go.

"Great. I'll give you a call tomorrow afternoon to set it up. OK?" Then, turning to Bobbie and Susan, Glenn motioned them aside in the hallway.

"Has your friend Amy come to a decision yet about her baby?" he asked.

The two girls looked at each other, and then Bobbie responded, "Not that we know of. She and Billy were going out for dinner last night, but then she had to go to her grandmother's this morning, and we haven't talked with her. I've been praying for her and for the baby. Obviously she has to make a decision soon, and we'll let you know."

"Please. My wife and I have been praying, too, that she will choose adoption."

After Susan prepared for bed that evening, she picked up the novel she was reading and climbed into bed as usual. Then, thinking for a moment, she closed the book, placed it on her night table, stepped out of bed and, for the first time, knelt in prayer. The long exposure to Bobbie's faith, the last three weeks in church, the conversation the day before with her mother, and Bobbie's comment that morning that she had been praying for Amy, all led Susan to this new position, on her knees, bowing her head to her heavenly Father.

She had little experience and no training in how to pray, but her heart was sincere and her agony for her friend was very real. She asked God for His help and His blessing, that Amy would choose the right path, for her, whichever that was. And she prayed that neither Amy nor any of her other friends would have to go through such an experience again.

Nepravel, who happened to be next door, running up the voices of Doubt, False Teaching, and Selfishness, to bolster Amy's decision in favor of abortion, was angered to see two streams of light going up from the Sullivans' house and being answered immediately by more brilliant streams from heaven to earth, each attacking and diminishing his hard work on the voices of deception inside the teenager. Because of Susan's prayers, added to the others building up on Amy's behalf, Nepravel had to spend extra time at the Bryants' home, further slowing him down in his regular rounds. And further making him nervous about the possible appearance of one or more angels at Amy's abortion.

MONDAY, MAY 22 ■ As she sat at lunch in their school cafeteria the next day, Susan was amazed by what she thought was the power of prayer. Amy announced to her two friends her final decision to have the abortion, and she told them that it was all set for Friday morning. Bobbie tried to argue, and tears formed in her eyes, as she considered whether she could join Amy at the abortion clinic. Susan, for her part, was amazed that God had already apparently answered her first attempt at a serious prayer, from only the night before, that Amy would choose the right path. *That's amazing,* Susan thought quietly to herself. *Dad and Glenn Jamison are right. The power of prayer seems to be incredible. I'm a little surprised that Amy has chosen abortion, but I'm glad that my prayer has been answered.*

Tommy had now made it through two weekends without joining the older boys in "doing videos." In one part of his mind, he knew that he was better off for not participating. But the pressure was building inside him again, from the visual images of the wildly pornographic videos, to the excitement of being with the other boys, to the voices of rationalization that Nepravel had spinning at a loud pace in him, countering as best Nepravel could the presence of a believing father in the family.

That Monday afternoon, Tommy really enjoyed the professional baseball game his father took him to as a special afternoon together. While the chasm between Tommy and his father had not closed, the distance had certainly narrowed over the last few weeks. His father had, in fact, consciously taken more time with him, in everything from homework to sports to just sitting for a while and talking together in the evenings. And something about his father's new openness and vulnerability, which Tommy could daily see coming from his father's new faith, actually made Richard stronger and more trustworthy in his son's eyes.

So the baseball game that afternoon was very enjoyable for both of them. Riding home in the car, they talked about how close Tommy had come to catching a high pop fly that bounced only three rows behind them.

But the pressure from the other side was also building and building in Tommy, and finally he asked his father, as they entered the interstate, "Dad, what do you think about homosexuals?"

"Why do you ask, son?"

"Like, you know, we studied homosexuality in our health class several weeks ago, and then two of them came in and talked to us about their lifestyles . . . and, I don't know . . . I just thought I'd ask you."

"Well, I don't know. I guess I've never really thought about them much. They're obviously people just like us, some good, some bad. I've never really been able to figure out whether it's something caused by heredity or by environment or by friends, or what. But by coincidence I do happen to know what the Bible says about it, which I now believe is the best place to begin on any difficult subject like this, because I started on Paul's letters the other night, the first one, the one to the Romans.

"I had frankly never realized that the Bible specifically mentions homosexuality, but it does, in both the Old and the New Testaments. I don't remember exactly where, but I think it's near the end of the first chapter of Romans. It says that both men and women committed homosexual acts with each other and received a punishment inside themselves for doing so. I referred to the Bible notes on the subject, and they led me back to Deuteronomy, I think. There it again says that homosexuality is wrong and actually calls it an 'abomination to God.'

"So, it looks like God is very much opposed to it, and, judging from the homosexuals I have known and the ones we see on television, if it really is an 'alternative lifestyle,' it appears to be a very unhappy one. They all seem to be angry or upset about something. And of course the AIDS epidemic has been devastating to the homosexual community, which is awful. So the Bible says it's an abomination. All of the homosexuals I know fit on a narrow scale from unhappy to angry—and AIDS is killing them at alarming rates. All in all, it doesn't sound like a very positive lifestyle!"

"No, it doesn't," Tommy agreed. His father's arguments, which Tommy had never really heard before, made a lot of sense, and certainly gave him some reasons to pause and consider before joining his friends again.

TUESDAY, MAY 23 ■ Tuesday morning Richard received a call from Bruce McKinney. "Richard, is there any way you'll reconsider helping us out with that loan guarantee?" Bruce asked.

"Bruce, I really wish I could, but I just don't think it's possible, for several reasons. Why?" Richard answered.

"It's just not fair. We're so close to closing the Tomlinson investment, but we haven't been able to arrange a short-term loan with our bank, because we're loaned out. Only one of our prospects would guarantee the loan, which wasn't good enough for the bank. It's a real mess because we're about to run out of operating cash, and I just don't know what to do."

"That does sound bad, Bruce." Richard could hear the agony in Bruce's voice. Closer to home, he could imagine that his legal fee for his work on the Tomlinson matter might now be in jeopardy. "I'll call Marty Tsongas again for the latest reading on the estate settlement, and I'll try to hurry him up. Perhaps you should try another bank."

"OK. Let me know what Marty says. As you know, banks are all about the same, and I don't hold out much hope for a loan. But I'll make a few calls," Bruce concluded and said goodbye.

As Richard rode down the elevator to a luncheon appointment that Tuesday, he noted that it had been exactly two weeks since his meeting with Kristen to break up their relationship. He had had no further contact with Kristen, which he knew was the right thing to do. But he was still concerned about her, and he imagined that he would call her again after more time had passed.

But more to the point, during these past two weeks he had also lived in constant but slightly decreasing fear of a telephone call from Kristen to Janet. Every evening when he returned from work, and every time Janet had answered the phone at the house, he worried that Janet would confront him with news that might end their marriage. He knew in his mind and in his heart that he was finished with Kristen. More importantly, he knew he had been born again after the prayer breakfast, and that he was a new man. And he hoped Janet recognized the differences in him. But he also knew it would be impossible for her not to be devastated by news of what he had done, and he frankly didn't know what to do. Every day he suffered through the agony of whether he should take the initiative and tell Janet, or hope that Kristen would calm down, that it would all blow over, and that Janet would simply never know.

Bob and Anne Meredith had shared his anxiety when they left the garage at Kristen's apartment that day. Anne had told him that if she were Janet, she would never want to know. Bob had said Richard might feel better if he told Janet all that had happened and asked for her forgiveness—but he also understood the risk to their marriage. They had finally suggested that Richard talk to Michael Andrews about it, when the two of them met.

Richard had called the office at the Morningside Church on the Monday morning following their first visit. The church secretary, who had been very helpful, explained that for the next two weeks Reverend Andrews had an unusual schedule of conferences. Unless it was an emergency, she asked that their meeting be arranged near the end of the month. Richard had of course agreed, and he looked forward to meeting with Reverend Andrews on the following Wednesday. In the meantime, he continued to keep his marriage in his nightly prayers, asking God for His blessing and His mercy.

"Hello."

"Peter, hi. This is Kristen. How are you?"

"Kristen! I'm just great. How are you?"

"I'm OK . . . OK. Listen, I was thinking that I need a break, and I might use some of my frequent flyer miles and come out to San Francisco for the weekend. Are you going to be there?"

"Sure. Absolutely. When are you planning to arrive?"

"Well, I thought I would catch an early flight on Friday morning, so I can arrive in time to do some shopping. I'm sure I could be there for lunch, if you'll be free."

"That sounds great. Some friends and I were planning to go sailing in the bay on Saturday afternoon. Would you like to join us?"

"Yes. That would be great. I'll bring some sailing clothes. Listen, Peter. Can you recommend a decent hotel that's not too expensive?"

"Well . . . why don't you just stay with me?"

There was a pause on the line, and Peter held his breath. "I . . . uh . . . that sounds great. Are you sure it will be no trouble?"

Peter smiled. "No trouble at all. Call me when you know your flight information, and I'll meet you downtown at the airport express terminal."

THURSDAY, MAY 25 ■ Susan had wavered on whether or not to talk to her father about abortion. After the discussion with her mother on Saturday afternoon, she had meant to ask her father the same question, in order to help Amy. But then on Monday at lunch Amy announced her decision, and for the next few days Susan decided that the issue was closed.

But now that it was Thursday evening and she would secretly be going with Amy to the abortion clinic in only a few hours, she changed her mind again and decided that she would like to know what her father thought. So after dinner she picked up her biology book as a cover and joined her parents in the den, where her father was looking through a legal brief, and her mother was reviewing the last month's local news ratings.

"Dad, I asked Mom this question on Saturday, and she suggested that I ask you. We've been studying childbirth in biology, and I wondered what you personally think about abortion?"

Richard put down his brief and glanced at Janet, who returned his look without changing her expression. For a second he thought to himself, *First Tommy and homosexuals on Monday, now Susan and abortions on Thursday. Suddenly there sure are a lot of questions!* But then the thought occurred to him, *Maybe that's what Ben Fuller and others have meant about being the "spiritual head of the family." I don't know. But here goes.*

To Susan, who had taken a seat in an armchair next to him, he said, "Well, legally, abortion is of course the law of the land, and so I would have to defend any woman's right to have one. And I recognize it's a very difficult subject. But recently, from reading God's Word and praying and listening to men like Michael Andrews, I've come to a new recognition of how important it is, both for us individually and for our nation, to try to follow God's will for us. And, Susan, I cannot imagine that God wants us to kill defenseless, unborn babies in their mothers' wombs."

"But how do you know that they are really babies? Our biology teacher has insisted that we call them 'fetuses.'"

"Well, as your mother may have told you, a couple of weeks ago, Michael Andrews gave a sermon on the future of our country, and he mentioned abortion as one of the 'watershed' issues, like slavery was before our Civil War. The sides now being drawn on this fundamental moral issue, unfortunately, allow for little compromise. And he mentioned that in the Psalms . . . I took some notes and I can look up the exact reference for you . . . it mentions how God 'knits us together in our mother's womb.' That indicates to me that God thinks of us as individuals, created by Him, whether we are born yet or not." Susan listened silently and waited for him to say more.

"And then, I've been reading through some literature Court Shullo gave me from the Foundation for the Family. It was started by a medical doctor, Samuel Morris, ten years ago, as a nonprofit organization to support the role of the family in our nation. The article I read corresponded with my reading in the Gospels over the past few weeks. It pointed out how in the first chapter of the third Gospel, the author/doctor, named Luke, described when Mary visited her cousin, Elizabeth. They were both pregnant, but Elizabeth was further along in her term. He writes that John, who was the unborn baby in Elizabeth's womb, jumped when Mary spoke. Now Luke was a doctor, but he did not write that the 'fetus' in Elizabeth jumped. He was inspired by God to write that the 'baby' jumped.

"I haven't done an exhaustive study of biblical references on this subject, but it would be great if you would do it, and we could talk about it again. I guess the bottom line is that I think they're living babies from the moment of conception, simply because God already knows us. He must agonize over the millions and millions of these babies who are killed every year throughout the world. I wonder how long He can let it go on, frankly, before He does something."

Susan said in a low voice, looking at the floor, "I never thought of it that way."

"Nor did I," Janet added from across the room. Smiling, she said to Richard, "In most ways living with you has become easier since God got hold of you that morning, but in a few ways it has become more difficult. I have to think more."

"Well," Richard smiled and put his hand on Susan's knee, trying to break the sadness of his last statement. "Let me tell you this. I assume that you ask this question not about yourself, but rather for your biology class. But let me tell you that if, God forbid, any of your friends or acquaintances ever become pregnant, we have many, many wonderful couples who are desperate for babies and who have asked our law firm to help them find a healthy little boy or girl. So if anyone ever asks you, please let her know that we can arrange for all of the mother's medical expenses to be paid and for the baby to find a very nice home."

"Really? I had no idea your law firm could do that," Susan said, obviously surprised.

"Yes, of course. In fact we have a young attorney, Kathy Thomas, who does little else but arrange such adoptions. She's a fine young woman, and she does a very good job of matching the right couple with the right mother."

Susan smiled and thanked her father, wishing that she had asked him her questions before the abortion was arranged, when she first learned that Amy was pregnant. And she made a mental note that her father might be a reasonably good source of information in the future as well. But she didn't feel she could call Amy and talk about what she had just learned, since it would reopen the painful decision that her friend had already made.

12

FRIDAY, MAY 26 ■ Friday morning Janet reminded the kids that she and Richard would both be staying late at the station for the "911 Live" test run, then going out to dinner together. Tommy had a baseball game that night. Susan volunteered to take him, knowing that her parents would be out, and she made it into a date with Drew. But that morning as she ate her breakfast with her family, Susan had the more immediate concern of Amy's upcoming abortion on her mind.

Amy, Bobbie, and Susan met outside Mrs. Simpson's office that morning, and Bobbie made her last-minute plea to Amy, which Amy refused to hear. Shortly afterward Amy and Susan were in the van headed for the abortion clinic, while Bobbie found an office in the PE Department in which to pray.

Susan remained silent, wanting to support and respect her friend's decision, even though her father's words had come immediately to her mind again when she had awakened that morning.

Nepravel was livid. The barrage of prayers for Amy had let up only slightly during the night. With the dawn, they had intensified again. Then the Meredith girl's last minute plea to Amy had been short but powerful. It was lucky that he had followed Amy to school and could be there to combat Truth with the voice of Decisions Made. But the prayers were taking their toll—the voices in Amy were winding down. She was starting to think about the baby again, and about her cousin Catherine, as she rode along in the van with Susan and two girls from Riverside High. This might be touch and go, despite the determined front she had put up only the day before. Nepravel hated their prayers!

And now, worst of all, from his vantage point on top of the van, Nepravel could clearly see what appeared to be the glistening light of at least one angel in the vicinity of the abortion clinic. Oh, great! All these prayers for Amy and the usual prayers from the believers demonstrating in front of the clinic had finally produced the divine intervention he so feared, because his horde was not ready for it. Yes, there he was. A huge warrior angel right over the abortion clinic, his talons poised and his beaks snapping.

As the van neared the abortion clinic and the angel saw the two demons riding on top, he began to fly in their direction. Nepravel, being a liar but not a fool, knew that alone they were no match for one of God's fiercest warriors, and he beat a fast retreat, followed closely by his companion. The angel returned to his position over the clinic, and Nepravel stood off at a distance and cursed. "Now who will tend to the voices in Amy?" he spat.

The van made it through the demonstrators outside the abortion clinic, and the four girls went inside. There they were greeted by an efficient-looking nurse in a crisp white uniform. She welcomed all the girls and began the process of filling out the forms, then starting the blood tests for the two girls who would be having the abortions that morning.

All across the city, members of the Morningside Prayer Warrior team, alerted to the approximate time of the scheduled abortion, stopped whatever they were doing and prayed to God for Amy.

He heard. And, as He promised, He answered. Another angel flew down to the clinic. With the one stationed outside, the second angel entered the clinic to clean out any demons hiding inside. Nepravel cursed even louder as he saw the two lesser demons fleeing through the clinic's side walls.

Amy and Susan were nervous, but they took their seats as the nurse began with the girl from Riverside High. Amy quickly read through the forms, checked the appropriate boxes, and put down the clipboard. Like Susan, she tried to pick up a magazine, but she just couldn't focus on it.

All those people outside—she could still hear them shouting every now and then—were just to try to stop girls like her. They seemed so serious. And Bobbie cried over this baby—fetus—inside her. And Glenn Jamison was praying last week for her. Bobbie was even praying now—maybe Glenn was too. Were all of them right? Could all these people be so concerned if they weren't right? Her hands suddenly became damp, and she felt lightheaded. The voices planted by the demons had almost been silenced by all the prayers. The angels had taken the area, and there were no demons to whisper in her ear or to spin the voices again. She started to think about the toddlers at the playground. She thought again about her cousin Catherine and her two children. Did she herself have the courage to have a baby? Could she do it? Imagine bringing a new life into the world! Her mom might understand after a few days, but what about her dad? What about Billy? What about her life? What a disruption. But surely the baby would be cute, and she could make some young married couple very happy. Maybe she could even visit the child some day . . .

At that moment the spiritual battle was won by the prayers and by the angels. The demons had retreated. The voices were silenced. Amy was open to hearing and acting on the Truth. But angels only rarely talk to humans.

Susan, who had been wrestling most of the night and all of the morning with her father's information, was flipping through a magazine, trying not to think about what they were doing. Just then, she and Amy heard the whirring sound of the cutter and suction pump slicing into the other girl's baby, and the magazine Susan was holding opened simultaneously to an advertisement with two young toddlers chasing a puppy across a playground.

Susan could stand it no longer. She looked up at Amy, who was also listening to the machine at work, and said, "Amy, I know this is the worst possible time I could tell you this, and I've tried so very hard to hold it in. But last night my father told me that they have many, many couples who desperately want newborn babies—and they can arrange for everything, all of the medical expenses and everything. I hate to tell you this now, but I think Bobbie is right, that this abortion is wrong. I know it's easy for me to say, but I wish you weren't having it."

Amy sat quietly, listening to the machine in the other room and looking at Susan, the tears running down Susan's cheeks, and the magazine open on her lap to the two toddlers.

"I . . . I know. I've gone back and forth myself." And now Amy closed her eyes as her own tears started to come. "It would be so hard to have a baby. It would mess up my life completely. But then I think about all those little babies and the life that is actually growing inside me, right now, and I hear that machine in there sucking the life out of that girl. And I just go round and round . . . But maybe if you and Bobbie will help me . . . maybe I *can* make it. I don't know. How will I ever tell my parents? Oh, God, please help me."

Susan moved over and sat in the chair next to Amy. She took her hand. Amy continued, "I . . . what a mess. If I don't have this abortion, everybody is going to be mad at me."

"But Bobbie and I won't," Susan smiled through her tears. "And I don't imagine that God will be either."

Feeling a new resolve growing inside her, gathering strength from Susan's strength, Amy managed a small smile too. "If I don't have this abortion now, you do realize that you're going to have a lot to learn about with me," Amy said, squeezing Susan's hand. "Because, 'I don't know nothin' about birthin' no babies.'" She smiled again, breaking the awful tension they had both been under for so long.

Just then the nurse walked in and was surprised to see the two girls holding hands, crying, and smiling. She said, "All right, Amy. We're all set. It won't take long at all, and you'll be back at school."

Amy interrupted her, "That's OK. I can be back at school much sooner, because I've decided not to have the abortion."

"What? But it's all set up. You've reserved our time, and it's unheard of for a girl of your age to stop an abortion at this point. Surely it's the best thing for you in your situation," the nurse said, trying to sound stern.

"I'm sure you're right. It probably is unheard of. But now you're hearing it." She smiled, still holding Susan's hand. "I don't want to have the abortion. If it costs me something, I'll pay it. But please just get us back to school, either by that van or a taxi, or I'll call someone or whatever." And she took the forms from the clipboard, tore them into four pieces, and handed them to the nurse.

"Well, there's a fifty-dollar cancellation fee within twenty-four hours of the scheduled time, so you must pay that."

Amy let go of Susan's hand, wiped the tears from her cheeks with the back of her own hand, took out her purse, and gave the nurse fifty dollars.

Obviously displeased, the nurse took the money and said, "Fine. I'll get you a receipt. The van will leave in about an hour, after the waiting period following the first procedure."

"We don't want to wait that long," Susan said. "I'll call Morningside Church, and I bet Glenn Jamison or someone can come and take us back to school."

Amy nodded. Susan asked the nurse if there was a phone which she could use. Doubly displeased but unable to fight it, the nurse said, "Yes, I guess there is. Come, follow me."

Nepravel, standing off at a distance for his own safety, saw the angels over the abortion clinic scream in agony as the first baby was killed. The angels flapped their massive wings and raised their mournful cries to heaven. Nepravel loved it and assumed that both babies were suffering the same fate.

"They huff and they puff," Nepravel laughed to himself as the spirit of the first baby rose and was taken by one of the angels to her special place in heaven, "but in the end, we always win! We're just too many for them, and we have too many dupes and allies. How long before we control it all!?!" he yelled at the angels.

Just then he noticed the front door of the clinic open, which was most unusual, and Amy and Susan walked out, down the steps and onto the sidewalk, where a brief discussion with the protestors brought hugs and kisses and shouts of praise. A few minutes later a car pulled up and stopped in front of the clinic, and Nepravel recognized Glenn Jamison from Morningside Church, who got out, came around the car, and hugged Amy, then Susan. Then all of them, including the demonstrators, gathered in a circle on the sidewalk and prayed together!

Nepravel was livid. He cursed Richard Sullivan and the Morningside Church. Somehow Sullivan's daughter must have squelched the abortion. He was just starting to think about what he would say at their midnight gathering, when he noticed the remaining angel leaving the clinic, empowered by the prayers of the believers on the street, and heading right for him. Without further thought, he flew as fast as he could in the opposite direction.

Nurse Simpson was sitting at her desk, finishing the week's paperwork, when her door opened and Amy and Susan walked in. Surprised, she looked at her watch and said, "My goodness, how can you be back so soon? That was quick."

"It was quick . . ." Amy smiled, obviously pleased, "because I didn't have the abortion. I decided not to. I'm not sure how I'll do it—and I hope you'll help me—but I'm going to have this baby." And the excitement in her voice was genuine, even to Nurse Simpson.

"You didn't? Why not? And how did you get back here?"

"I called Morningside Church," said Susan, "and someone came and got us and brought us back to school."

"You mean you didn't get the abortion I set up for you, and then you rode in an unauthorized vehicle during school hours?" Mrs. Simpson asked, her anger obviously rising. "Do you realize that you've damaged our relationship with the clinic, which may make it more difficult for other girls in the future to have the procedure? And if anything had happened to you in that car, I would have been held responsible."

Amy looked down at the floor for a moment. She was suddenly struck by the bizarre truth that it was OK for her to have an abortion without her parents knowing it, on school time, but it was not OK for her to ride in a car driven by a minister! She looked up at Susan and then turned to Mrs. Simpson. She said quietly, "And do you realize that a baby is still alive inside me, which would be dead now if we had followed through with the abortion? It seems to me like a small price to pay for a human life."

After Susan and Amy left in the van, Bobbie alternated between praying and reading her Bible in the vacant PE department office. Suddenly the door to the office opened and her two friends walked in, smiling. Bobbie, who had been praying on her knees, looked up and could not believe that Susan and Amy were back from the abortion clinic so soon. As she stood up, but before she could speak, Amy hurried to her and hugged her tightly. While they hugged, Susan came up behind Amy and looked into Bobbie's eyes, smiling. "We looked all over the school, and finally figured out you might be here. Amy didn't have the abortion," Susan said.

Bobbie couldn't believe it. She started to jump for joy while Amy was still hugging her, then remembered Amy's condition and stopped. So she hugged her tightly and said, "Praise God. Oh, Amy, I'm so happy. I mean I'm so sorry for you. But I'm so happy for you too. What are you going to do? How can I help? I should call the church and tell Glenn."

"Well, to start with, Glenn already knows, because we called him and he brought us back to school," Amy said, finally releasing enough pressure to look Bobbie in the eyes. "As for all the rest of it, I don't know. But I've taken you and Susan at your word that you'll help me. I've taken on—I mean we've taken on—a huge responsibility. We've got a lot of things to do, starting I guess with my parents and Billy and this attorney who works with Susan's dad who arranges adoptions, and I really don't know what. I'm so happy and so scared at the same time. I don't know whether to laugh or to cry. Do any of you have any ideas what we should do first?" Amy asked.

"Yes," Bobbie said. "First we ought to pray. To thank God for what He has done today in your life, and in our lives, and to ask Him for His guidance and protection for you and your baby, starting right now."

Amy nodded, and the three girls formed a circle in the middle of the small office, held hands, and prayed. For the first time, both Amy and Susan prayed out loud with Bobbie, giving the next eight months to the Lord and asking for His wisdom and protection.

As the regular work day drew to a close, Richard knew he had to leave on time in order to be at TV5 for the warm-up to the test run for "911 Live." Since they were leaving to spend the weekend in the mountains with the Bryants the next morning, Richard promised himself that he would not take a lot of work home that evening. So for the first time in longer than he could remember, he actually left his briefcase on the floor of his office, next to his desk. He put on his navy blue suit coat, said goodbye to Mary, and left, just a little after five.

As he waited for the elevator with both hands free, he couldn't help thinking of the image of a prisoner, escaping without his ball and chain to weigh him down. *I ought to do this more often,* he thought, with a smile.

Over at TV5, Bill Shaw was introducing Janet, Tom Spence, and Connie Wright to Bob Grissom and to Mark Pugh, the producer and director, respectively, of "911 Live." Once the introductions in the conference room were completed, Bill began, "We should have a really good opportunity to test both the concept and the equipment this evening. Mark, Janet, and Connie will be staying here in the studio control booth, directing the show and controlling the helicopter, the reporter/camera teams in the three roving patrols, and the remote control cameras on the emergency vehicles. Since there will just be the three of us actually going out on the street, we'll be in the back seat of a police car on the north side of the city. All the vehicles will be hooked together by a two-channel radio link. Bob and Mark will have a direct link as the network representatives, and I'll have a TV5 headphone through which Janet and I can talk. Hopefully, after all of this preparation, we'll have some 'action' to record."

"We're really looking forward to this trial run, as well," added Bob Grissom. "It should be very close to the feel of the national show that starts this fall, and we're delighted to have you folks coming along and helping in the control booth, to add your local spin to whatever happens this evening. I probably don't need to say this, but I do want to remind us that we are all just observers. Whatever may happen, I want us to remain safe and not to get involved. We're there to observe and to report, but not to interact in any way. OK?" he concluded, looking particularly at Tom and Bill.

There were nods all around the table. "Well, if that's it," said Bill, "the three of us will head out to the north area precinct to pick up the police car they've assigned for us to ride in. Mark, I know you have a lot of last minute things to do here at the station to get ready, as do Janet and Connie. Good luck to all of us."

As the six of them split up, Janet stopped Bill and said, "I really appreciate the way you've arranged for our involvement in this test run, to get first-hand experience." Bill smiled and nodded. Janet continued, "Richard and I are planning to go out to dinner after the show, so I invited him to come down and watch what's happening, back in the studio with everyone else from the station who is here. I hope that's OK."

"Sure, Janet. That's fine. Richard is always welcome. Let's just keep our fingers crossed that everything goes well." He smiled one more time, then turned and headed out the door to catch up with Tom and Bob.

As Kristen took out her wallet to purchase the scarf she needed against the cold breeze from San Francisco Bay, she glanced for a second at the key to Peter's apartment at the bottom of her purse. That brought a smile.

Peter had met her late that morning and had taken her to his loft apartment in downtown San Francisco. She had smiled at the slightly eccentric, masculine touches in what was definitely a bachelor pad, complete with king-sized bed. They kissed in the bedroom after she had hung up her clothes, but when she moved to kiss him again, he pulled back and said with an exaggerated English accent, "Now, Princess Kristen, you may be here for a fairytale weekend, but the good Prince Peter has to earn money to pay for his apartment and other items he finds convenient, which means he has to work. They are expecting me to show up around 1:00 this afternoon to work on the Saturday morning edition, so we just have time to grab a bite to eat."

She frowned but let him go. He continued, "After lunch, you can go shopping and then come back to the apartment. Here's a spare key. You can then take a bath, make yourself lovely, whatever the right term is. And I'll show up about seven and be more than glad to pick up right where we're now leaving off."

He bowed. She curtsied. And, laughing together, they left for lunch.

For the night's test run of "911 Live," the police car in which the three men were riding with two officers from the north precinct had been fitted with special equipment in the trunk, making a live television link possible. Bob Grissom and the others could watch a small hand-held monitor in the back seat and see whatever scene Mark was following from the director's booth back at the station. By actually being in the police car, they could see, hear, and feel exactly what the emergency personnel were seeing, hearing, and feeling, supposedly one of the show's strong points. They could compare the two—live and televised—to test the validity of their reporting style.

Bob Grissom and Bill Shaw wore miniature headsets linking them back to Mark and Janet in the control room. At 7:30 Mark brought up the "911 Live" logo and cut to John Blevins, the local newscaster who was substituting for the as-yet-unnamed national personality who would host the network show. Behind John were several monitors, and he began a recap of the various live stories in progress around the city, which they had been monitoring for the previous hour.

Richard had arrived at the studio in plenty of time to watch all of the preparations being made and to marvel at the behind- the-scenes chaos which somehow always turned into a respectable television show for public consumption over the airways. Although he did not understand everything Janet was doing, he still found himself being quite proud of the responsibilities which she was obviously handling well, working with the various people necessary to direct and to produce such a complex under-taking. This was certainly her world, and he did not try to intervene in any way. Rather, he stood on the sidelines and watched, having an occasional chat with the few station personnel he knew.

In the back of the police car, Bob was sitting in the middle of the seat, with the small monitor on his knees. Bill Shaw was on his right, with Tom Spence on his left. Bob talked to Mark over the headset about the need for additional equipment when the national show was underway, including wider angle lenses on the minicameras, and button microphones. Bill Shaw told Janet over their radio link that they should always know the names of the emergency personnel on duty on any given Friday evening, so they could add a local visual overlay whenever the national show might cut to their city, identifying the police officers, fire fighters, or emergency medical personnel involved in a particular situation. Janet made a note that it would be good to create a local visual overlay identifying their city, which they could also add whenever the network cut to them.

The three television men had been introduced to their police officer hosts and escorts upon arrival at the north precinct. The officer driving their patrol car that evening was Pete Talmadge, who had been on the force for six years. His partner in the right hand seat, Doug Higgins, was younger. As they drove around, the three television men, particularly Tom Spence, who was not wearing a headset, asked them about their back-grounds and why they risked their lives every day as police officers. "Somebody's got to do it," Talmadge replied. And, smiling, he continued, "And where else could I have so much fun with wonderful people like Officer Higgins here? Why, you should hear his stories about growing up. You guys should do a documentary on this man alone. He was a hero in his neighborhood by the time he was twelve!" The admiration for his partner was obvious in Talmadge's voice, despite the good natured joking. Higgins smiled, but didn't say anything.

As the sun started down, Tom asked the younger officer, "Why do you guys go out at night? Isn't it more dangerous than during the daytime?"

This time Higgins replied. "Yes and no. A lot of times policemen get in trouble when they let their defenses down. That's easier to do in the daytime, like when you stop somebody going ten miles an hour too fast, walk up to the car in the middle of the afternoon, and get blown away. At night, we assume that everybody we deal with is a bad guy, and we take as many precautions as we can. It keeps us focused, you might say."

Tom asked, and they all learned, that Officer Talmadge had a wife and two young children, the older about to start first grade in the fall. Higgins had only been married eighteen months, and he and his wife were expecting their first child in September. Tom made some personal notes on the pad he was carrying, in case there was a reason to expand the human interest side of the program that night.

During the first ninety minutes of the test run, Janet had to admit that the pace and the subject matter were similar to many other shows already on television. The fact that it was live did add a dimension of excitement, since no one, including the anchorperson, knew exactly what would happen next. Mark Pugh and John Blevins skillfully kept the tempo upbeat during several slow moments. By this time in the evening, several of the original situations were still "in play", and John ran through the recaps of each situation after their commercial breaks, as if they were following several football games at once.

Suddenly over the police radio came the code for a possible armed robbery in progress at a fast-food restaurant. The location was only two exits north on the interstate from their present position. The officer driving the patrol car turned on the blue lights and sped up to respond.

As the patrol car accelerated, the car just ahead of it on the interstate swerved quickly to the right, into the middle of the three lanes, to let the patrol car pass. The driver of the car already in the middle lane, seeing the car swerve in front of him and the blue lights from the patrol car pass him, was startled. But there were no van and no yellow flashing lights next to him, and he could see that he had room to maneuver if he had to. So he slowed with his brake as a caution, but he did not slam them on. The driver of the large tractor trailer behind that car was able to slow down without a problem. There was, therefore, no wreck on the interstate that night.

The three television men could feel the adrenaline starting to pump in their veins as the patrol car sped up the interstate, its lights flashing and siren blaring. Exiting the interstate, Talmadge killed the siren and the blue lights. They were now on a four-lane main street, with low-rise suburban commercial development on both sides. The fast-food restaurant was located only two blocks from the interstate, and as they came down a slight grade, they had an excellent view of the store.

Just after a white, four-door sedan pulled out of the restaurant parking lot, still a block away, their dispatcher radioed that the manager of the store had called to report a single armed gunman had just driven off in a white sedan with approximately three hundred dollars out of their cash register.

"Tell them we've got the suspect car in sight and will be in pursuit on Route 36," Talmadge said to Higgins.

Higgins reached for the radio microphone while Talmadge turned on the blue flashing lights and siren and accelerated toward the white sedan.

Immediately upon seeing the patrol car behind him, the driver of the white car accelerated rapidly around three cars in front of him and took off up the street at an increasing speed.

"We're in hot pursuit west on Route 36," Higgins said into the microphone. "Request back-up assistance."

The two professionals in the front seat automatically helped each other with the difficult task of chasing a car at high speed on a crowded city street. The three television men in the back hung on as best they could, and Bob Grissom was delighted to see that the picture coming over the television on his lap exactly corresponded to what they could see out the front window of the patrol car, as the minicam bolted to the light bar on the roof faithfully recorded their chase, even in the increasing darkness.

"How are you guys doing?" Mark asked from the control room. "Fine," answered Bob Grissom. "I'm holding onto Bill and Tom, and they're holding onto the doors. The picture looks great!"

"Tell central we may have to break this off," Talmadge yelled to Higgins. "This is getting too dangerous for the conditions on this street, and we've got these passengers with us."

Higgins picked up the microphone and was about to repeat his senior partner's message when the white sedan suddenly veered to the right, up and into what appeared to be a large, vacant construction site, and stopped in a cloud of dust.

Talmadge turned into the same driveway, and their headlights momentarily reflected off a large sign announcing that a new shopping center was to be built on that site. Talmadge brought the patrol car to a stop about thirty feet from the white sedan, parked parallel to the street in the large dirt lot. He stopped almost perpendicular to the street so that from his driver's side window and from Tom Spence's window behind him, there was an excellent view of the car, from which there had been no movement since it stopped.

The veteran officer quickly turned on the spotlight attached to his patrol car next to his outside mirror and swiveled its light onto the sedan. He rolled down his window and cracked his door, but did not get out. Higgins also cracked his door, and both men drew their service revolvers. Talmadge nodded at Higgins, who picked up a second microphone, attached to a loudspeaker, and said, "You in the car, throw out your weapon, open the door, and get out real slow, with your hands in the air."

The window on the driver's side of the sedan began to roll down, and Talmadge leveled his service revolver on the car through his own open window. A single large-caliber hand gun was thrown out of the driver's window, about ten feet, and then the driver's door was cracked, and a voice yelled, "OK. Don't shoot. I'm coming out."

The driver's door opened, and a single man in his early twenties got out, raised his hands, and stood by the open door.

"Be careful," Talmadge said to Higgins. "I don't like this. It's been too easy. You go around on the right, and I'll circle in from the left."

The two officers opened their doors further and got out. "Stand right there with your hands up!" Talmadge yelled at the man by the car, as the senior officer moved slowly out from behind his own open door, all the time keeping his revolver pointed toward the car.

In the back seat, the three television men could glance back and forth from the reality directly in front of them to the monitor in Bob Grissom's lap. Grissom was doing his best to feed a narrative of what was happening back to Mark Pugh in the control room.

At the station, Richard and twenty or so of the station staff had been watching all the coverage that evening, but the drama of this live chase, accompanied by Bob Grissom's occasional narration, was by far the most interesting. Now they were all looking at the white sedan, bathed in the light from the stationary spotlight. They could see the car and the gunman with his hands raised. Unseen off camera, the two officers approached the car and the gunman from opposite sides, coming up on the rear of the car.

The three television men watched from the patrol car only a few feet away. Suddenly and without warning, both back doors of the white car opened, and there were bright blasts and loud cracks from two automatic machine guns, firing on the police officers at close range. Though their reactions were quick, they were not fast enough for the fire power leveled at them. Each man was hit several times, and the two gunmen kept firing. The driver leapt in the air and clapped his hands for joy. Bill Shaw in the back seat screamed, "Oh, my God!" so loudly that it almost knocked Janet off of her chair in the control room. Everyone in the station had seen the flashes of gunfire, but they didn't know the results. As soon as the firing finally stopped, Bill Shaw whispered into his headset, "Janet! They've shot both officers, probably killed them. We're here all alone. Get help! Get some help, quick!"

Janet reached for the telephone by her elbow and, keeping her eyes on the monitor, which still showed the car and the gunman, she dialed 911.

Everyone watching then saw the standing gunman point directly toward the side of the car where the spotlight was stationed, and the second gunman, crouched down behind the driver's seat, let fly another long burst from his machine gun to put out the spotlight. The burst of machine gun fire sprayed all over the patrol car, smashing the spotlight, but also breaking glass in the windows and ricocheting off the door posts and all the other metal in the car.

Because of the angle at which they were parked, the structure of the car somewhat protected Bill and Bob, but not Tom Spence, who was directly in the line of fire, seated almost directly behind the spotlight. A direct shot grazed his upper left temple, but a ricochet off the open door post entered his upper chest, near his lungs, just missing his heart. The sound of the breaking glass and the ricocheting was deafening to all three men, who simultaneously tried to slide down in their seat. Both Janet and Mark heard screams over their headsets from Bill and Bob. Then suddenly there was silence.

The minicamera on the roof, which had miraculously been spared any damage, quickly adjusted to the new low-light situation without the spotlight, and once again everyone at the station could see the car, though it was not as clear without the help of the extra light. The driver walked over and picked up his revolver from the ground where he had thrown it, then started walking toward the patrol car.

Mark Pugh found that he still had control of the minicam by radio, and as the gunman walked first over to investigate Officer Talmadge on the ground and then toward the patrol car, Mark was able to follow him with the camera.

While that was happening, the three television men in the back seat didn't know whether to look out or to stay down. "I've been shot," Tom hoarsely whispered, trying to reach his right hand toward his chest, but unable to do so because Bob had fallen across him as the bullets ricocheted through the car.

"Tom's been shot. What's happening? Please somebody get some help," Bill pleaded across his headset to Janet. Janet noticed that her hands began to shake as she held the telephone receiver and relayed Bill's news and his plea to the 911 dispatcher. On the other end of the line, the dispatcher assured her that backup help would be there in less than two minutes, and she relayed this word to Bill through her headset.

In the back studio, all the staff and Richard were on their feet, glued to the large monitor and hearing the internal communications being broadcast across the headsets and through large speakers set up for that purpose.

Meanwhile the gunman, having kicked once at Talmadge's motionless body, turned toward the patrol car and immediately dropped into a shooter's stance when he saw the small red light on the minicam. For a moment he stared, and even in the near darkness the excellent minicam lens was able to pick up his facial expressions, as he realized what he was seeing. He relaxed a bit, but kept his revolver pointed toward the car, then walked in that direction.

"We can't see anything, and Tom is bleeding like crazy. What's happening?" Bill whispered.

"He's . . . he's walking toward the patrol car," Janet whispered back.

The gunman was looking at the camera, which was looking at him, and not until he was right up to the car did he notice what looked like bodies in the back seat. "What's this?" he said out loud and opened the door next to where Tom lay. When he did so, the release of the pressure on Tom's lower body caused him to move, creating great pain, and he groaned. Bill and Bob moved slightly as well. The gunman, now bathed eerily in the glow from the overhead light inside the patrol car, yelled this time, pointing his gun right at Bob's head, "Who are you!?!"

Bob Grissom, lying partly on top of Tom and feeling the blood oozing between the fingers of his left hand, staring down the barrel of a .357 magnum revolver, with a wild killer on the other end, could not say anything at first, but finally whispered, "Television."

Mark had been able to swivel the camera and refocus it up close, and from its position just above the gunman's head, with the light coming out of the patrol car, everyone in the studio could again see the recognition on the gunman's face. He actually smiled as he realized what was happening.

"Television! You mean we're on television?" Bill didn't know whether to say yes or no, afraid of the possible reaction from either answer. But the gunman leaned in the car and shoved the barrel of the revolver right up against his head and yelled again, "Are we on television?" Bill closed his eyes and nodded once.

The gunman pulled out of the back seat and yelled toward his friends in the car, "Hey, guys. We've been on television all this time!"

To the horror of everyone in the station, the gunman backed a few paces away from the car, smiled toward the camera and used his free hand to smooth down the hair on his head. "What channel?" he asked in Bob's direction.

Hoarsely the producer replied, "Five."

"Hey, guys, we're on TV5." He smiled at the minicam again and flashed his revolver in front of his face. "Hi, Louise. This was for all the Diablos!"

Then leaning down again into the back seat of the patrol car, where Bill Shaw was also now staring back at him, he laughed and pointed his revolver at the three men in turn. "Hey, pukeheads. You want I should blow your heads off on television?"

Back in the studio, everyone heard the audio coming across the headset, which had fallen around Bob's neck, and Janet felt as if a knife were turning in her stomach.

"Turn off the camera. Please turn off the camera," she pleaded with Mark.

"No, not on your life. This is awful, but we've got to get it," he yelled back at her.

Bill closed his eyes again and shook his head slowly. In the distance, they could hear what sounded like several police sirens.

"Yeah, you're probably right," the gunman said, pulling his revolver back.

"We love to kill policemen, like we did tonight, but we probably shouldn't hurt the television men, particularly since you've been so good to us," he smiled, nodding down toward Tom, whose chest was now completely covered in blood.

Turning and running back toward his car, the gunman kicked Officer Talmadge's body, then yelled back to the patrol car, "Thanks a lot. We'll be sure to watch your show. Come on, guys." And he got back in on the driver's side, started the engine, and sped out of the lot, west on Route 36.

Richard was in bad shape, but he was driving because he was in better shape than Janet, who sat next to him in the car, and Connie, who was in the back seat. They both burst into tears about a minute after the gunmen drove off, the other police cars arrived, and Bill confirmed with what energy he had left that Officer Talmadge was apparently dead, that young Officer Higgins was terribly wounded and probably wouldn't make it, and that their own Tom Spence was also badly wounded and covered in blood, almost unable to breathe. An ambulance screamed up right behind the patrol cars. Richard was now driving the three of them to the large county hospital where Tom and the two police officers were being taken at high speed.

"Oh, Richard, I feel so terrible," Janet said holding his handkerchief to her face. "Tom and those poor police officers! And who knows, if you hadn't said something, maybe it would have been Connie and me too."

"I just can't believe there are people like that in the world," Connie volunteered in a low voice from the back seat. "People who say there is no devil should watch the tape of what we just saw." She shook her head, trying to fight back her own tears as well.

They arrived at the hospital only minutes after the ambulance. They parked and walked unsteadily into the emergency room, where they were confronted by a police officer, who told them they would have to stay in the waiting room until he had more information. He was obviously upset by the night's events as well, and though he was pleasant, he was also firm.

"Do you know whether the hospital has a chapel?" Connie asked. Her question seemed to melt him a bit.

"Yeah, there's one just out the door of the waiting room and down the hall on the left. You're welcome to go there, and I'll come and tell you any news. Please pray for these guys," the officer said.

"We will," Connie said, and she opened the door to the hallway for Richard and Janet.

The small nondenominational chapel had a center aisle with four rows of pews on each side, three seats per pew. The pews faced a large, beautiful stained-glass window, which took up most of the end wall and was back lit from the other side. No one was in the chapel at the time, so the three of them went to the front row. Richard and Janet knelt on the right, and Connie on the left. They began to pray.

Over the next thirty minutes, more of the Christian believers from the television station, hearing about what had happened, came to the hospital and found their way to the chapel, along with their spouses. At one point the police officer opened the door to the chapel and simply announced to those inside that Officer Talmadge was, in fact, pronounced dead on arrival at the hospital. He added that Tom Spence and Officer Higgins were both in operating rooms, hanging on by threads. Soon the chapel was nearly full, and prayers both vocal and silent were lifted up for Tom, for Officer Higgins, for the soul of Officer Talmadge, for their families, for the gunmen, and for all members of the city's emergency teams.

After a while, Janet whispered to Richard that she was going to go look for Tom's wife in the waiting room. Richard nodded, and then slipped out of the chapel with her. Janet, who knew Sandy Spence from several pleasant meetings when she had visited Tom at the station, found her sitting in a back corner of the waiting room, holding hands with a young, pregnant woman. The two of them had their heads bowed in prayer. Janet and Richard walked up quietly and waited for the two women to stop praying. Sandy recognized Janet and stood up, and they hugged. Janet introduced Richard, and Sandy introduced Florence Higgins. Both of the wives had obviously been crying, but Sandy mastered a difficult smile and said to Richard and Janet, "Florence and I had never met before, but we quickly found that we both know the Lord. And so we've been sitting here, talking and praying together for our husbands."

"There are quite a few people praying with you and for you in the chapel down the hall," Janet said. "Is it all right if we sit and talk and pray with you?"

"Sure. Certainly. Please," Florence said, moving her coat to a vacant chair further away so that the four of them could form a small circle.

They talked for the next hour, and both Richard and Janet were frankly amazed by the strength these two women were finding at this almost impossible time in their lives. Both obviously wanted their husbands to live. But both also expressed that their husbands knew the Lord, and that if, God forbid, either one or both of them did pass away that night, they would instantly be in heaven with Christ.

"And you see," Sandy said to Janet, her eyes filled with tears, "I know someday I will definitely see him again, and we'll spend eternity together, which will make whatever happens tonight, as awful as it may be, seem like only a moment."

Janet listened and was frankly overwhelmed by what had happened in the last several hours, not to mention the last several weeks. She was particularly awed by the strength and the testimonies of these two women, in whom it was obvious, even to Janet, that the Holy Spirit lived.

A little after midnight, Bill Shaw, Bob Grissom, and Mark Pugh entered the waiting room. Richard, Janet, and the two wives rose to meet them. Bill and Bob had been taken to the police station to make their preliminary statements. When the interrogating officer realized that most of the action was recorded on video tape, he sent a patrol car to the television station to secure a copy of the tape for safekeeping. At that point, Mark also made a statement. Then they went to the hospital, where Bill and Bob were treated for some minor cuts from flying glass. Now they joined the vigil in the waiting room. Everyone knew, without saying so explicitly, that it was not time to talk about the future of "911 Live." That would come later.

At one in the morning a surgeon joined them and told them that both men were out of surgery, though there was a good chance that both would have to go back within the next few days, if they made it. They were being moved to intensive care for observation and recovery. When asked, he reluctantly estimated that Tom's chances of surviving were about fifty-fifty, while Officer Higgins' prospects were not as good, due to the number of rounds he had taken. If they survived, both men would be in intensive care for many days. He suggested that all of them, including the men's wives, go home and try to get some sleep, because they could not do much at that point.

There were a few questions, and then the surgeon left. Connie suggested to all of them that they begin a rotating prayer vigil, and Richard was surprised when Janet volunteered for them to take the first watch. One of the other Christians from the station said he would go home, shower, and then come back to relieve the Sullivans in an hour.

The police officer who met them when they arrived at the hospital told Richard the department was already taking care of Mrs. Talmadge and that he would be sure that Sandy Spence and Florence Higgins arrived home safely. Everyone said a sad goodbye and then left for home.

Janet and Richard returned to the now empty chapel. They sat in the front pew, and Janet turned to her husband. "Richard, before we begin praying again for these men and their families, I want you to pray with me. I know now that there must be a God, because only God could have changed you in the way He has in the past few weeks, and only God could give those women the strength they have. I don't understand how things like tonight happen. Maybe someday I will. But I know that He lives in you, the Merediths, and those two women. And I want Him to forgive me for doubting His existence for so long, for raising our children without knowing Him, and for trying to do everything and be everything myself. Richard—" And she took her husband's hand. "I want to be His child, too, like you are. I want to be able to pray to Him for these men as one of His own, like Sandy and Florence. I want to know that we will be together forever, no matter what happens here on earth. What do I do?"

Richard described what he had done with Court Shullo three weeks before. She nodded, and they knelt on the floor in front of the pew. As best he could, holding her hand, Richard led Janet in the same prayer which he had prayed with Court. Janet, broken by the love she had seen in Richard and the strength she had seen in Sandy, gave herself to the Lord early that morning.

Invisible to both of them, yet very real, the Holy Spirit visited the chapel at that moment and filled it with a brilliant glory that paled the beautiful stained glass into insignificance. Janet was touched by His power, and an invisible eternal flame began to burn in her, matching the one in Richard.

As she finished praying, she thought she had cried all that she could in one night, yet there were apparently a few tears still left inside her. She squeezed her husband's hand even tighter, as she felt the cleansing of her entire past taking place in an instant, and she was born again.

They remained kneeling, holding hands, for several more minutes, then Janet looked at Richard, and they smiled and hugged. They bowed their heads and began praying for the two men in intensive care—and for the men who had put them there.

13

SATURDAY, MAY 27 ■ Richard and Janet did not return home until a little after 3:00 in the morning. They had called home on several occasions during the long night at the hospital and confirmed that Susan and Tommy were home safely from Tommy's baseball game and from Susan's date. When it appeared they would actually be quite late, Richard called to let them know, and Susan said it would be OK. Tommy came on the line to speak to his father.

"Hey, Dad, you know that double play I almost made, but screwed up at the beginning of the season? Well, it happened again, and this time I made a great throw to first base. We cut off the runner and stopped what looked like a rally for them. We wound up winning five to four. Isn't that great?"

Richard smiled, surrounded by the mayhem and the distress of the emergency room, to know that his children were safe and that his son had made his first double play. Richard choked a little bit and said, "Yes, Tommy, that's just wonderful. I can't wait to hear all the details tomorrow on the way to the Bryants' mountain home."

The original plan had been for the two families to leave no later than 9:00 for the Bryants' home. But Richard and Janet didn't wake up until 8:30. While Janet called the hospital to check on the two men, Richard quickly donned his jogging clothes and walked over to the Bryants' home, where he knocked on their back door.

Inside, Richard explained to Tom and Nancy all that had happened the night before and asked if they had room in their minivan to take Susan and Tommy with them, while he and Janet checked at the hospital again and then drove up separately in a few hours.

"That'll be fine, Richard," Tom said, offering to share his eggs and bacon with Richard. "You and Janet do what you have to do, and we'll take care of Susan and Tommy until you get there. We'll try to leave a little clay on the courts for you guys. It sounds like you need a rest, so come up and relax as soon as you can."

Richard returned home and found the kids dressed and Janet in her bathrobe, throwing together some breakfast. "They're still both alive, and there has been no change in their situation," Janet said. She had apparently given a brief account to Susan and Tommy, who were unusually subdued for a Saturday morning.

"It's fine with Tom and Nancy to take the kids with them," Richard said, looking at Susan and Tommy. "Once your mom and I get cleaned up and packed, we'll swing by the hospital and then come on up to the mountains. Tom gave me a map, and we should be there just a few hours behind you. OK?"

"Sure," said Tommy. "But don't be too late, because I really want to play some tennis with you."

An hour later, Richard and Janet found themselves back at the hospital, but this time in the waiting room outside the intensive care unit. Sandy and Florence were there, as were some people whom Richard and Janet didn't know, who were personal friends of the two families. As they entered the waiting room, Sandy stood up and walked over to them. "He's still alive," she said, "and the doctors say that there's hope." Lowering her voice, she continued, "Officer Higgins is still hanging on, too. But he's apparently in very bad shape. Florence and I pray for both of our husbands every few minutes, and Connie tells me there are still people praying downstairs in the chapel."

After a few minutes of conversation, Janet said, taking Sandy's hand, "We hate to leave, but we've had this weekend set up with our neighbors and with our kids for weeks. Obviously you'll be in our prayers, and we'll come straight here when we get back in town tomorrow night. We'll find out the telephone number here and call every few hours to check, if you don't mind."

"That will be fine, Janet. And please do go away with your family. Take all the time you can with them—there's precious little of it. There's really nothing any of us can do now, except pray. And as long as you're doing that, we'll be in good shape," Sandy smiled.

Kristen awoke early that morning in San Francisco, due to the time difference, and slipped out of Peter's king-sized bed, descending the stairs to his kitchen. After looking around the kitchen for a while, she started a pot of coffee and then, dressed in only a large t-shirt, started making a cheese omelette, bacon, and English muffins.

As the smell from her work drifted upstairs, she heard the floorboards creak when Peter stood up next to the bed and came downstairs, dressed only in his shorts, with a towel around his shoulders taken from the bathroom.

Smiling, she poured him a cup of coffee, handed it to him, and said, "Breakfast is almost ready, but I can't find the grits."

He returned her smile. "We don't got no grits. But if it will keep you around, I'll send out for some now."

She smiled even more and thought to herself how nice it was to be wanted.

"But look," he continued, surveying the stove, "there's nothing healthy in this whole breakfast you've fixed. Are you trying to kill us?"

"Oh, but it will taste *so* good. And I've got to do my part to keep your strength up. If you're going to keep pleasing me, we've got to feed you hearty food!"

Coming around the island in the middle of the kitchen, he pulled her to him.

"Will food like this keep for a while?" he asked, looking down at her and smiling.

Her own feelings starting to match his, she managed to ask as he carried her over to the large sofa in the living room, "Do you have a microwave?"

The drive up to their mountain house took about three hours, and the Bryants made it with Amy and the two Sullivan teenagers with no problem, even though their minivan was a bit crowded. Tom Bryant, who had loved all sports as a child and still enjoyed tennis, golf, and jogging in his midforties, had never had a son. Amy was their only child. Over the years he had enjoyed being included in some of Tommy's sporting events, and had even volunteered to coach Tommy's soccer team when Tommy was in third grade. Nancy Bryant knew Tommy was her husband's surrogate son, so she volunteered to sit in the middle seat of the van to chat with the two teenage girls while "the boys" took the front seats to discuss whatever it was that men and boys discussed. Her insight proved a wise one, because Tommy soon opened up. In no time her husband knew everything about Tommy's baseball team and all of its players. As she listened to the two of them talking, she knew her husband loved playing this role.

Nancy used the time to read a few pages in the novel she was nursing and to catch up on what she could find out about Amy and Amy's two best friends, who would shortly be seniors in high school. Aware of a growing aloofness in Amy over the past few weeks, Nancy hoped that perhaps this weekend she could find out what had been bothering her daughter. But she received no clue during their drive.

Nancy couldn't believe that their only child was seventeen and soon to be a senior. She and Tom had always wanted more children, but it was not to be. After years of trying, they'd considered adoption, but the waiting and/or the cost just appeared to be too great. So they decided to concentrate on raising Amy as best they could. And having only one child freed some financial resources, making, for example, their mountain home more possible.

By the time they arrived and unpacked, everyone was hungry for lunch. Not long after inhaling some sandwiches, Tommy was changing into his tennis gear and challenging Tom Bryant to a match. Tom smiled and said, "Hey, when you get to be my age, you've got to wait a few minutes after lunch. Call down to the tennis center and see if you can reserve a court for three o'clock. Maybe your dad will be here by then, so we can play round robin, if the girls don't join us."

Richard and Janet did, in fact, arrive just before three. While Tommy impatiently watched the "Game of the Week" on television, dressed in his tennis clothes, Tom and Nancy gave Richard and Janet a brief tour of their new home. There were three bedrooms and two porches. Susan and Amy shared the upstairs bedroom, and the couples had bedrooms on either side of the living room, while Tommy had his choice of the sofas.

Pushed by Tommy, the men were soon out the door in their tennis clothes, leaving the house to the two wives and their two daughters.

Nancy Bryant asked Janet to sit with her on the sofa in the living room, looking out across the wide expanse of mountains and the long valley, leading to another range in the distance. Janet then told Nancy in more detail about the "911 Live" test during the previous night and morning.

Janet, who was a bit tired, but more than happy to describe the events, was just getting into the story when Amy and Susan walked in from the porch and sat down in two chairs across from their mothers. They listened to Janet's story as well. Susan was very interested to hear her mother's testimony about praying to receive the Lord into her life that morning. It interested her to know that both of her parents not only now believed in God, but also expressed their faith to others.

When Janet finished and Nancy had asked a few questions, Susan and Amy looked at each other, Susan nodded, and Amy said to her mother, "Mom, I know Mrs. Sullivan has been through a lot. But I've got to tell you something, and it's just as good that Susan and her mother are here."

Nancy Bryant suddenly felt she was about to find out what had been bothering Amy for the last few weeks. She leaned forward on the sofa, looked at Amy, and said, "What is it, dear?"

"Well, Susan and I haven't been able to think of any easy way to say this, so I'll just say it. I'm pregnant. A little over a month . . ."

As Amy continued, her mother brought her hands to her mouth and exclaimed quietly, "Oh, God." Janet rocked back in her seat, crossed her legs, and looked back and forth between Susan and Amy.

". . . and yesterday morning I went to an abortion clinic with Susan to get rid of the baby, but then I couldn't do it. Susan says that her dad knows attorneys who can arrange for adoptions and even arrange to have the new parents pay for all of the medical costs. . ."

Now it was Janet's turn to bring her hands to her cheeks as she realized that her daughter had been to an abortion clinic the previous morning. And she suddenly understood all of Susan's recent questions about abortion. *Good grief,* she thought, *what have our daughters been through by themselves in the past few weeks?*

". . . and so I know I've made a mess of all this, and I'm to blame, but I couldn't kill the baby growing inside me. And after being so incredibly irresponsible to get this way, I've tried my best to be responsible and to do only the right things." Finally the tears started to fill her eyes. "But I hope you and Dad can still love me, even though I've done this terrible and stupid thing. I'm just so very, very, very sorry."

During the few minutes while Amy had been talking, her mother's emotions had changed from shock to disappointment to anger to sympathy to tenderness. As Amy sat crying quietly, Nancy stood up, walked over to her, and stretched out her hands. Amy stood up, a questioning look on her face. Nancy took her and held her, and Amy cried like a little girl on her mother's shoulder.

Janet, seeing that Susan was also in pain, went over to her daughter, and they also hugged, while Amy cried.

"Well, I knew something was bothering you," Nancy said, stroking Amy's hair. "Now I know what it is. I know it took great courage, first to go to the abortion clinic and then to leave it. I agree with you that you've been pretty stupid, but I also think you've been very brave. I certainly don't know all the answers now, but we'll do our best to work through them as a family."

The four women sat down again and spent the next thirty minutes talking through the details and the options as Amy and Susan understood them. Then Nancy said, "Well, obviously we have to get your father involved. And apparently perhaps Mr. Sullivan as well," Nancy said, turning to Janet. "I guess we need to tell them today. Amy, do you have any ideas about how to do that?"

"I hoped you would," Amy said, looking at her mother.

"Well, I guess the direct method like you used with us is the best way. The men should be coming back from the tennis court any minute, and we'll just have to tell them."

"Is there any way we can keep Tommy out of it, at least for now?" Amy asked.

"Yes," said Janet. "Susan, why don't you go change into your tennis gear and challenge Tommy to a singles match? He's been wanting to play for days. So keep him on the court, and tell the men that we asked for them to come back."

Susan looked at Amy and asked, "Do you need me here?"

"I'd certainly like for you to be here, but if Mom will help, that'll be OK. And you're probably the only one who can keep Tommy on the tennis court."

So Susan agreed with their plan and went to change her clothes.

When the two men returned from tennis, their wives had a pitcher of iced tea and glasses waiting for them on the porch. Nancy met Tom at the door and said, "Before you and Richard take your showers, come sit out in the fresh air on the porch."

As the four adults were putting sugar and lemon in their tea, Amy came out and took a seat with them. Janet had to admire her courage and her strength. She silently said a prayer for the Bryant family as the adults sat down. Amy said, "Dad, there's something I have to tell you, and I think this is about the best time and place to do it."

As she repeated virtually the same words she had spoken to the women a little over an hour before, her father frowned at first, then never changed from what appeared to be a completely normal expression while Amy continued. Occasionally he glanced at the other adults. It appeared to him that Richard was hearing this news for the first time as well, but he quickly realized that Nancy and Janet already knew the whole story.

When Amy finished, this time without crying, only her countenance indicating how sorry she was, Tom Bryant leaned forward in his chair, looked sternly at Amy, and said, "Amy, I love you, and I can't imagine what you have been through in the past several weeks. I wish you weren't pregnant, and I wish that whatever I could have done to prevent you from having sex with that college boy, I had done it. And I can't believe you could have almost had an abortion while we thought you were safely at school. But we don't have to go into those things now." Amy held her breath as he continued. So did her mother.

"I wish we could turn the clock back and not have to go through this, but we can't. I certainly can't condemn you for something which, but for the grace of God, could have easily have happened to me at your age. Obviously we'll stick by you, and support you, and help you in every way that we can. It's not going to be very easy, but you've already shown what you're made of by deciding at the last minute not to have the abortion. If your mother and I were a little younger, we would think about raising the child ourselves. But I guess that may not be possible. Anyway, I'll be interested in talking to you, Richard, about this adoption situation—with Amy of course—and we'll find out all the details. Parts of the coming months may be a mess, but parts of them should bring us some joy. So we'll just do our best and get through it."

Amy, who had assumed that her father would be very angry and would lecture her, was prepared to take his reprimand. She could not believe what he had just said. Nancy stood up and went over to Amy and put her arm around her. Looking at her husband, she said, "Thank you, Tom."

Richard said, "I'll check with Kathy Thomas on Monday about the details of the adoption process, including the latest prospects. I may even have a particular couple in mind myself. I believe this will all work out. I assume that Susan has known about this for some time, given her recent questions on abortion. And I assume that Janet just heard about it a little while ago. I just want you to know, Amy, that all of the Sullivans will support you completely in any way we can."

Amy, looking at the floor of the porch, managed to say, "Thank you, Dad. And thank you, Mr. Sullivan. Mr. Sullivan, I know this may sound strange coming from me—and, Dad, you may not understand it, but, Mr. Sullivan, would you pray for us?"

"Of course, Amy. In fact, even though it may seem a little awkward at first, let's join together and hold hands."

All five of them stood on the porch. A bit self-consciously, they joined hands. But quickly the self-consciousness faded as they bowed their heads and Richard began to pray. "Dear heavenly Father, we turn to You at this difficult time for Amy and her family. We first thank You for Amy's courage in saving the life of her baby yesterday. We ask Your blessing and guidance for her and for her parents as they work through what we all know may be difficult times in the coming months. But we know that if we put our trust in You, You can lead us through any problem, any period that seems difficult to us, because nothing is difficult for You.

"Dear Lord, I ask a special blessing on Tom and Nancy this afternoon, that they will continue to open their hearts to Amy's needs as they grow more complex in the coming months. And I ask You to give all of us the wisdom to know Your will concerning the adoption of this child. We know You already have the perfect parents and the perfect home picked out for him or her, and we ask You to guide us to that family. Bless us and keep us, and fill us with your Holy Spirit as we consider what must be done. In Jesus' name."

"And dear heavenly Father," added Janet, "we particularly thank You for Tom and Richard, that they are men of understanding, humility, and strength. Finally, dear Lord, we also ask Your blessings on the family of Officer Talmadge, and on Officer Higgins and Tom Spence, and on their families, that You will heal their wounds and give peace to their families. In Jesus' name."

Richard waited for a moment, as they continued to bow their heads, and Amy finally prayed, "Thank You God for my parents and for the Sullivans and for my friends, Susan and Bobbie. Thank You for leading me in the right way yesterday, with their help. God, I know I've . . . uh . . . made a mess of this, but I ask that this child will be born healthy and that he or she will be a gift to some wonderful couple." Amy started to choke up, and the others found it hard to fight back their tears. "And, Lord, please forgive me and make it possible, when this is all over, for me to lead a normal life and find a husband who loves me and to have children of my own." At this point she began to sob and released her mother's hand so that she could wipe her eyes.

Richard gave a concluding prayer. "And now, Lord, bless us and keep us as we seek Your will in all that we do. In Jesus' name. Amen."

This time it was her father who hugged Amy to him as she cried. The other adults moved off and left the two of them on the porch together.

Late that evening, the two girls sat up in their night clothes and talked in their bedroom for almost an hour about the events of the past few weeks and, particularly, of the past two days. Amy finally turned out the light on the table between their beds. Looking out through the large sliding glass door to the private deck on their side of the house, she could hardly tell where the lights on the mountains stopped and the stars began on that clear and moonless night.

"Come look at this, Susan," Amy said, as she rose from her bed and slid open the door. In the darkness the two girls walked out on the deck, immediately surrounded by more stars than they could ever see in the city.

"To think that God made all of those millions of stars, and He made the little baby inside me! Can you imagine Him? And I wonder what He has in store for the person who is growing inside me. . . ?"

"It's incredible," Susan agreed. They were quiet together for several minutes.

"I've been so lucky to have you and Bobbie." Amy finally broke the silence. "And your father has really helped. He seems so different from how he used to be. What do you think happened to him?"

"He says he asked God to forgive him for all the things he had ever done wrong, and he asked Jesus to come into his life and to take it over. I think it really happened, Amy."

"Me, too . . . Do you think that teenagers can ask for the same thing?"

"I would think so . . . Sure."

"Well, I know I did the wrong thing by having sex with Billy, and I've hurt my parents, no matter what they say. And I can't have this baby and figure out the adoption and then start over again, all on my own. I need God, as well as my parents. I need His help."

"My Dad calls it a relationship with God. I think that's what we need. And I feel it, too, looking at all the mess in the world today," Susan said.

There was another silence. Amy asked, "Do you think you and I could pray for God to forgive me and to help us? Do you know what to say to ask God for what your dad has found?"

"Not exactly, but we need Him so badly, I think He'll hear us." The two girls knelt on the deck in the starlight. Susan began their prayer.

"Dear God, Amy and I come to You tonight and ask for Your help. First, please forgive both of us for things we've done wrong. Please come and be with us. Please even live within us. My father says that Your Son Jesus died so that those who believe in Him can go to heaven and be with you forever. Glenn has also told us about Him, how He loves people, even when they do bad things, if they are really sorry for what they've done. And that He can help us through difficult times. Please, God, Amy and I ask you to forgive us for all the things that we've done wrong . . ."

Amy added, "Please, God . . ."

". . . and we thank You for all You've done for us through Your Son. We don't know exactly what to say, but we want to give ourselves and Amy's baby to You tonight, Lord. We can't make it through the next months unless You help us. Please, God, protect us and be with us. And guide us in all that we do. In Jesus' name. Amen."

The physical darkness did not register it, but the spiritual darkness retreated two more steps that instant, as the blinding white Light of the Holy Spirit descended onto the two teenage girls as they knelt in prayer, touching each of them with His power and branding them as His own forever. Each girl felt a sudden chill as the Spirit moved through her. They looked up simultaneously, feeling the sensation of a cool breeze together.

"There's no wind tonight." Amy smiled at Susan. She took Susan's hand and said, "I want to pray some more for my baby and my parents. Do you mind? You can stay or go back to bed. And thank you again."

"I'll stay," Susan smiled. "And, as crazy as this sounds, let's also pray that someday we each find a husband like Glenn, or maybe even like my dad. Someone with real faith, in a world which is so very difficult."

SUNDAY, MAY 28 ■ Sunday at the Bryants' was a lot more normal than Saturday. The adults and the two girls decided not to let Tommy in on Amy's condition for a bit longer. At Sunday lunch they celebrated Susan's seventeenth birthday a few days early, and Janet found herself praying that God would help her daughter escape the problems that Amy had found during her seventeenth year.

Driving home late that afternoon, Richard and Janet finally had a chance to discuss their "911 Live" experience.

"Can you imagine having what we saw Friday night pumped nonstop and without editing into homes in America?," Janet asked.

Richard took his eyes from the wheel for a second to look at her and say, "No, I can't."

"Well, hopefully after what Bob Grissom went through in the back of that police car and the awful consequences of the whole thing, including the death, so far, of at least one fine police officer, Network will reconsider the whole project."

"I certainly hope so," Richard agreed. "But knowing how big corporations sometimes work, I wouldn't necessarily count on it."

"Then I'll have to talk to Bill Shaw about not showing it here, or changing it somehow. Or putting it on very late at night. I don't know, Richard. I can't believe God wants us to see a steady diet of actual death and violence. Surely a show like that will make us almost uncaring when we're confronted by the same problems in our own lives. It makes death and destruction the norm."

"Well, do what you can at the station. I'm not an expert in this area of the law, Janet, as you know, and I'm not necessarily advocating or committing to anything. But I have to believe that what we saw Friday night can be challenged in court on all sorts of statutes: morality, maybe even pornography. If all else fails, maybe we can talk to the group of which Tom Spence was—I mean is—a member, about filing some sort of legal action. But I hate to do that, because it'll bring all the 'free speech' folks out of the woodwork, raining their wrath down upon us."

Janet, very pleased and still slightly amazed to find Richard supportive of anything she did, particularly associated with her work, smiled at him from the passenger seat and said, "If it comes to that, Richard, I'm sure that you, with God's help, can do it."

That evening, Richard and Janet dropped their children at home on the way in from the mountains and then drove to the hospital. Sandy and Florence were there, sitting in the waiting room outside the ICU. Janet had called on Saturday afternoon and received a "no change" report from Sandy. Now the two smiling wives greeted them.

"The doctors think my husband is going to make it," Florence said, taking Janet's hand.

"And Tom is much better, though he's not out of the woods yet and may have to have another operation tomorrow or Tuesday," Sandy added. "The team is continuing to pray in the chapel, and we know the Lord has answered all of these prayers. I think, in fact, that many families on the police force and many churches are praying as well. So we're very much encouraged."

"Is there a slot for us in the prayer vigil?" Janet asked.

"I'm pretty sure there is," answered Sandy. "Connie is in charge, and I think there's a schedule outside the chapel. I'm sure they would very much appreciate your joining them."

"Thanks, Sandy. We'll check on the way out. We've got to go now because we've been away all weekend, as you know. But we'll be praying for both Tom and Doug, and we're so pleased to hear about their progress."

As Kristen left San Francisco that night on the late flight home, she reflected on her wonderful weekend with Peter. They had been sailing in the Bay, shopping, dining in nice restaurants, and enjoying each other in his loft apartment.

Now a question came to her mind: *What next?* He insisted that he had to stay in San Francisco, and she felt that she must not leave the base of real estate contacts and referrals she had developed over the years. It would be hard to build a lasting relationship from so far away, and if neither of them would move, their long-term prospects were dim. But maybe there was a solution in the future, she told herself, as she tried to fall asleep on the plane.

As she thought more about her relationship with Peter, it occurred to her that she now thought only two or three times every day about Richard and about what had happened to their relationship.

When Amy returned home from the mountains, she called Bobbie and told her all that had happened.

"I'm so glad," Bobbie said, her voice obviously relieved and excited. "I can't wait to hear more about your prayer time last night. And I guess we'll have 'expanded' strategy sessions together now, including your parents and Mr. Sullivan, huh?"

"Yes, I think so. And you were right. I should have involved them weeks ago. It could have saved us all a lot of trouble and a lot of problems. I just had no idea my parents would be so understanding."

"They love you, Amy. By the way, have you told Billy, yet?"

"No, not yet. I think we're supposed to go out this coming weekend, and I'll tell him then."

"Well, let me know if I can help you. And, by the way, youth group was great this morning. I'm sorry you and Susan missed it. Glenn introduced Carrie Wagner, who will be joining our church in the early fall. She seems really nice, and I think you'll enjoy knowing her."

14

M ONDAY, MAY 29 ■ Richard's first stop that morning was by the office of his young associate, Kathy Thomas, whom he found in a telephone conversation. Seeing him, she waved him in, and in less than a minute she finished and greeted him.

"Kathy, I know a teenage girl who may be a candidate to give up her baby for adoption. Do you have anything already written up that I can give to her and her family about how it all typically works?"

"Yes, I do, Richard," Kathy replied, rising and walking over to her credenza. "Here's a short paper that explains it. It's called an 'identified adoption.' Basically, the mother, and in this state, the father, enter into a contact with a couple to place the baby with the couple within one week after the birth. Typically the couple agree to pay all of the medical expenses associated with the pregnancy and with the childbirth. The only real risk for them is that in this evolving area of the law, the courts typically give the mother the absolute right to renege on the contract after the baby is born, if she wants to. And it's usually pretty tough, in that case, for the couple to get their money back. But we've found with proper preparation, that situation almost never happens, and despite what you sometimes read in the paper, everyone associated with the adoption usually winds up happy."

"I've heard that you have a list of potential parent couples. Is that accurate?"

"Absolutely. We can go through quite a list. I usually do a preliminary screening myself and then give the expectant mother summaries on five to seven couples. She and I then work through them, and usually we find one or two for her to consider seriously. If she doesn't like any of them, I bring her five more."

"Well, I may also have a candidate couple in mind. What about confidentiality?"

"In some cases we act as a buffer between the parties. But frankly these days we find that both the girl and the couple often appreciate knowing each other. Once the adoption is completed, the mother has no legal recourse, and that's usually the end of the relationship. But in the beginning, it sometimes seems to make both parties feel better to meet each other."

"Thanks, Kathy. You've been most helpful, as always. Listen, how about giving me a couple of copies of your summary, and sometime this week I may have you meet with the girl, at least, and maybe her parents."

After lunch, Richard called Janet and learned that Tom Spence and Officer Higgins were both making slow, but steady, progress. The hospital had scheduled the second operation for Officer Higgins in the morning, and Janet volunteered to pray for them at 9:00 that evening. Richard told her that he would like to join her, and then she let him know that the funeral for Officer Talmadge was scheduled for the next afternoon at three. Janet told him that she understood Bob Grissom would be flying back into the city and would attend the funeral.

Richard's next call was to Marty Tsongas. "Marty, hi. This is Richard Sullivan. Listen, if you've got an update on our deal, please let me know, but I'm really calling on another matter."

"The timing doesn't seem to have changed on Mr. Tomlinson's estate, Richard. But they do seem to be making progress. We may have a more definitive final date by the end of this week, and if we do, I'll call you. What else can I help you with?"

"Somewhere in the back of my mind I seem to remember that you or Patrick Tomlinson mentioned in passing that he and his wife had been unable to have children and that they were trying to arrange an adoption. Was I imagining that, or am I right?"

Marty laughed. "No, counselor, you aren't imagining things quite yet. You still probably have a few good years left. That is the case. And, in fact, Patrick and Kate are almost desperate to have children, but the doctors have told them that it's unlikely they will ever be able to do so naturally."

"OK. Thanks, Marty. That's great. Listen, I may have a candidate for them in a wonderful teenage girl whom our family happens to know very well. It's a difficult situation, as they all are, but her family will, I think, be supportive of her. She already had the courage to walk out of an abortion clinic just minutes before the baby was to be terminated. So for a lot of reasons, we'd like to help her."

"That does sound promising, Richard."

"I wanted to call you first, Marty, not just to be sure I was accurate, but also to seek your OK to have one of our attorneys talk either to you or to Patrick directly, given the fact that we're working on this other deal. I want to be sure that communication on the adoption is OK with you."

"By all means, Richard. Go ahead and call Patrick directly, and I hope you're successful."

"Well, it wouldn't be fair to move the Tomlinsons to the head of the list, and for some unknown reason they may not even be the right potential parents, but I at least want to put their names in the pot with the attorney here in our office who handles a lot of adoptions. So if you're talking to Patrick in the next day or two, you might tell him that Kathy Thomas from our office will probably be calling him."

"I'm sure he'll appreciate the call. And so do I," Marty said, and he told Richard goodbye.

TUESDAY, MAY 30 ■ That Tuesday morning, Glenn Jamison picked Tommy up a little after 7:00 and took him out for breakfast at the Twenty-four Hour Cafe, not far from Northpark High. Tommy had never been to breakfast one-on-one with a nonfamily adult, and he was very happy to be there with all of the businessmen and businesswomen having their "power breakfasts."

For Glenn's part, a large part of his ministry was relationship building so that the teenagers at Morningside Church had an adult alternative who was feeding them the Word of God, as a balance to all of the other things which they were being fed by the media, their friends, and others.

All during breakfast, Glenn asked Tommy a lot of questions, trying to get to know him better. Finally, when the food on their plates had almost disappeared, Glenn asked, "How about God? Is God a part of your life, Tommy?"

"I don't know, Glenn," answered Tommy. "But He sure has become a part of my dad's life lately. Dad has been reading the Bible and praying and trying to help Susan and me understand about God ever since he went to that prayer breakfast."

"Tommy, that's great. Do you know how lucky you are to have a father like that?"

"Yeah, I guess so. And the amazing thing is that he really has changed. But as for me, I don't know. I mean I'm just fourteen years old, and I guess I've got a lot of time to think about God and stuff like that. I mean, I like your church and the youth group, and I like talking with Dad about God, so I guess, yes, He's in my life; but I don't really think about it too much."

"I understand, Tommy. Again, you're just blessed to have a father and a church where you can at least hear about your heavenly Father. So many kids today don't have a chance to hear that. But let me tell you, from my experience you're right at the age where your life is going to start filling up with something. Hopefully it will be God, and His will for you. But it could just as easily—in fact, more easily—be drugs, sex, pornography, rock music, alcohol, violence—I mean, it's just terrible what's out there. And most kids these days seem to wind up being influenced by some or all of them. It's true for people at any age, but particularly at your age, that each one of us is kind of like a glass, and we can fill ourselves up with one thing or the other. And I just pray, and I urge you, that fourteen is not too early to be thinking about what you're filling yourself with. Is it going to be God, or is it going to be something else, and particularly something else that can hurt you or maybe even destroy you? I know this is kind of serious for a Tuesday morning breakfast, but all I ask is that you think about it."

"Yeah. OK. Sure." Thinking about his experiences with the videos and the older boys, Tommy was surprised to realize that Glenn had described him exactly. His glass was, in fact, filling up with something which was not good. "Yeah, I'll think about it. And thanks a lot for breakfast."

"Hey, I enjoyed it. We'll do it again soon, and I hope I'll see you on Sunday morning."

"Me, too."

■   ■   ■

"Janet, could you join Bob Grissom and me for lunch today?" Bill Shaw asked her Tuesday morning. "He's coming back to go to the funeral for the police officer, and he said he wanted to talk with a few of us about '911 Live.'"

"That's fine, Bill. Can Connie Wright and Phil Tenneyson come too? Phil has shared Tom and Connie's views, and with Tom in the hospital, I think it would be good for Phil to be there."

"Well, I hadn't planned on this being a big meeting. If we invite them, we should probably have sandwiches in the conference room."

"That's fine with me, Bill. Their group really began this discussion, and I certainly don't want them to be cut out of any later talks. You said you would be fair-handed, so I think you need to invite them."

"OK, OK. I'll invite them. Unless I call you back, I'll see you in the conference room at noon. What kind of sandwich would you like?"

Bob Grissom still had two Band-aids on his forehead where the flying glass cut him on Friday night. He and Bill were already seated in the conference room at noon when Janet entered. Bob greeted her pleasantly, and soon Connie Wright and Phil Tenneyson joined them. Five styrofoam-covered sandwich plates were on the table, and soft drinks were lined up on the credenza. After everyone began eating, Bob started speaking. "Obviously it was a great tragedy, what happened here on Friday night. Bill and I were right in the middle of it, and of course it's terrible about Officer Talmadge, whose funeral I'm attending this afternoon. By the way, our network is donating a thousand dollars to the memorial education fund for his children, and a thousand to the police department retirement fund. And I understand that Tom Spence and the other officer are at least holding their own at the hospital. Bill, do you know whether there are any leads on catching those guys?"

"I called the chief investigator on the case this morning. He said that with our video they could positively identify the driver. And they found the stolen white sedan late the next morning, abandoned. But so far there has been no trace of the man himself."

Bob nodded. "Well, hopefully they'll catch him, along with his friends who pulled the triggers. I'll never forget his face as long as I live. Anyway, let's talk about the new show.

"Mark Pugh and I met yesterday with the entire production staff in New York, along with the head of network programming. They all watched the tape of the complete show, and I have to say that they, as well as we, were very impressed.

"Except for what happened to us, which was obviously an anomaly anyway, because we wouldn't be there when the real show is airing, they think that the test run proved the concept is not only valid, but exciting and workable."

Janet looked at Connie and Phil, who had put down their sandwiches and were listening with obvious disbelief.

"We've talked to our technical people, and they can insert a thirty-second delay, which will allow us to black-out either a part of the screen, or the entire screen, if something really awful happens right in front of the camera. But, for example, we never saw those machine gun shots actually hitting the officers, because the minicam was focused on the car when they were firing. We've also decided to implement a policy that if, like what happened to us, the camera or any other part of our production becomes the focus of what is happening, we'll cut away so that we do not affect the action by our presence.

"When you think about it, with no visual on the police officers and none of the close-ups of what was happening to us, it was really a pretty tame show." Bob smiled and looked around the table.

Connie spoke. "Mr. Grissom, we sat and watched at least three hoodlums kill one officer and badly wound another, plus our colleague, Tom Spence, live and in color. How can you possibly say it was 'tame,' and propose that we broadcast it into living rooms all across the nation? Can't you see that a steady diet of murder and violence from this show, plus the copycats and variations that will inevitably spring up, will have an effect on all of us? On our whole society?"

"Look . . . Connie, isn't it? Our job is to show our viewers what's really happening, if they want to see it. It's not my job to think about what might happen in our society at some time in the future."

The debate began and went on for about thirty minutes. Janet said little in the beginning, letting Connie and Phil carry the argument. But Bob and Bill continued to put them down and to act as if a live television show broadcast coast to coast to tens of millions of people was no more important than a single handbill posted on a fence. It was all "free speech" and was separate from any consequences on society, which were other people's responsibility to monitor and to mold. As Janet listened to the debate, she couldn't help thinking of the strong women she had recently met. Besides Connie, there were Anne Meredith, Sandy Spence, Florence Higgins, and even Amy Bryant. She said a silent prayer, asking God to give her just a portion of the courage and resolve she had seen in these women.

Finally, when it was apparent that neither side would change the mind of the other, Janet did something neither Bill Shaw nor Bob Grissom expected: She took a stand. "Bill, I know you pay my salary, with help from Bob. And I want to work here for a long time and do a good job for this station and this network. But what you have been saying today is, in my opinion, a crock of garbage. What we saw Friday night should not be in our viewers' homes, live and without editing. I don't know exactly where it says so, but it *must* be that we have a responsibility about what we show. We can't just shrug it off by saying 'it's what's happening.' I hope your decision is not set in stone and that you will reconsider it or modify the program some more . . . something. And if you don't want to think about 'society,' just focus on Mrs. Talmadge and her children in a little while at the funeral. And think about all the other innocent people who will die if our society becomes totally numb to the reality of violence and death." With that, she stood up, nodded at both of them, and left the room.

WEDNESDAY, MAY 31 ■ "So . . . I'm so glad we're finally able to meet for lunch," Michael Andrews said, extending his hand to Richard and smiling. "Here, please pull up a chair and sit down. I usually just try to have an informal lunch in my office when I'm getting to know people, and I'm sorry my schedule has been so crazy for the past couple of weeks. But I'm delighted that you're here now."

"Thank you very much," Richard replied. "I'm also glad we have the opportunity to get to share some time together."

"Is that order OK?" Michael's secretary asked, preparing to leave the two men alone.

"Yes, it looks just right. Tuna salad on toasted rye bread," Richard said. "Always my favorite." She smiled and left, closing Michael's office door behind her.

There then followed a very pleasant, relaxed lunch, during which Richard told Michael about his personal history and how that history had changed, starting only a few weeks before at the prayer breakfast. "I can't thank you and your church enough for sponsoring the prayer breakfast," Richard said. "It's really hard to describe to you what a difference God has already made, not only in my life, but in the lives of our family members and friends. My wife, Janet, asked Christ to come into her life early Saturday morning, when we were dealing with the tragedy. And I think there are already some subtle differences in our children, just as the Bible promises, and just as you have indicated in the sermons we've heard here. By the way, we're really enjoying Morningside Church. That young man who runs your youth group has been a tremendous blessing to our children, and we'd like to find out more details on how to join the church."

Michael sat back in his chair, smiled, and said, "We give God all the praise for changing lives like yours so totally. I thank Him that we can be just a small part of what He does, and I have to tell you that it has really rekindled my own spirit to see all the effects of the prayer breakfast. Lord willing, we'll do another one, either in the fall or next spring."

"Well, I hope I can help when it happens. If nothing more than driving someone's car to his garage, I'd like to help other men find what I've found."

Michael laughed. "Don't worry. All you have to say is 'I want to help' around here, and you'll have lots of folks beating a path to your door. But one of the things we've consciously sought as the church has grown is to spread out all the responsibilities among various lay leaders and to change the roles every year. The last thing we want is for any small group to be perceived as running this church. Because we firmly believe that only God runs this church."

Richard looked at his watch and realized that Michael probably had another appointment coming soon. "Listen, Michael, there is one pretty serious thing I'd like to talk to you about for just a few minutes, if I might."

Michael leaned forward again, put his hands on the table, and said, "By all means."

Richard took his time and slowly unburdened the story of his relationship with Kristen and of how God had convicted him of his sin and how he had asked for His forgiveness the morning of the prayer breakfast. Michael listened without saying anything. Richard went on to describe how Bob and Anne Meredith had volunteered to pray for him when he met with Kristen to break off their relationship. When Richard finally finished, he continued, "But, Michael, here's what I want to ask you. I know my relationship with Kristen is completely a thing of the past. I know I'm now a new man, and I pray that with the help of the Holy Spirit inside me, I'll be able to fight any temptation in that area again. I truly love Janet, probably more now than I ever have. And I just want God's best for her and our whole family.

"But what do I do about either telling or not telling Janet about my affair with Kristen? On the one hand, as a believer, I feel that I should come clean not only with God but also with her. I guess I still feel guilty about what I did. I feel I should tell her, in order to get rid of my guilt and to start our relationship over again with a clean slate.

"But on the other hand, I know it would hurt her terribly to find out what I was doing. That's no longer me, I know. But it was only weeks ago, and she may feel she can never trust me again. I'm just caught in the middle, and I so much want to do the right thing . . . to do what God wants me to do. And, frankly, I'm still living in fear that Kristen, the other woman, will just up and call Janet one day and tell her all about us. How will I appear to Janet then? Can you possibly help me?"

Michael briefly looked down at his hands, folded in front of him on the table, then looked up again at Richard. "You've really got a dilemma, Richard. I know. It seems to both of us that there are merits in both paths, yet there are also risks in both paths. I agree with you that it's a very difficult situation.

"The first thing to do in a situation like this is to pray about it, seeking God's wisdom and His guidance. The second thing is to really put your affair with Kristen and the guilt you have from it behind you. If you have truly confessed this sin to God and asked for His forgiveness, then you are forgiven. And, as I think I said in one of the first sermons you may have heard, you need to close that chapter on yourself and to go on. That's the one good thing about sin. We can be washed spotlessly clean by God's Holy Spirit when we really repent and turn away from it. So either pray again, if you feel you must, to ask God's forgiveness for this sin. If you have done so, then that's enough. Stop. Don't do it again. It's gone, and as the hymn says, 'Jesus took my burdens, and he rolled them in the sea.'" Michael smiled.

Turning serious again, he continued, "It's my strong advice that you should *not* tell Janet these things, unless she has a really strong, mature faith. We do think we can handle a lot, but the actual reality is then more difficult than we first appreciate. She may not be able to accept it, and your marriage could be damaged. If it is really behind you, then let it go.

"But if you pray earnestly and still feel led to tell her, and you believe her faith can withstand the terrible shock, then as you seek God's guidance, you might consider something I have recommended to several men—and unfortunately not a few women—in similar situations, people who had mature Christian spouses. You might consider finding a quiet time with your wife and simply reminding her of how you feel about her and of how much your marriage means to you. You might then remind her of what happened to you after the prayer breakfast and how you know you are a completely new person, through God's grace.

"Then simply tell her that there are some things you did before God found you and remade you, but while you were married to her, of which you are not proud. You can be general, but let her know that these were serious things. Tell her that they are completely behind you, that you know you have been forgiven by God, and that they will have no impact on you in the future. But they happened.

"Then give her the choice. Tell her that if she wants to know about them, you will tell her and ask for her forgiveness as well. But if she wants to leave them buried with the old man, which you hope she will, then you will do that too. I of course can't predict how she will answer, and that is the danger, but she should recognize your honesty and your desire both to be open with her and to protect her. Whatever then happens, the choice will have been hers, and she will know that. We both hope she will let those events die with the old man, but even more important will be your willingness to be vulnerable."

Richard listened intently to Michael and thought that his suggestions sounded good. He honestly did not know which course to take. But he also knew he had to pray before making a final decision.

"Thank you so much for your words of advice, for the lunch, for this church, and for the prayer breakfast," Richard said, as Michael's secretary knocked on the door. "Our whole family now looks forward to attending church and youth group on Sunday, and that in itself is a miracle," Richard smiled in conclusion.

The two men shook hands and Richard left, wondering how he had ever lived before knowing God.

The reports that night at the cabal over the city were mixed, but in Nepravel's and Zoldar's cases, they were almost all negative. It had been a bad week for the demonic forces where the Sullivans and their friends were concerned, and Nepravel and Zoldar knew it was all Richard's fault. Amy's canceled abortion and Janet's confession of faith, both in less than twenty-four hours, had almost been the fiery end of Nepravel on Saturday night. Then there were Amy and Susan. And now Janet was beginning to intervene on "911 Live," and Richard was seeking a permanent healing for their marital problems. It was a mess, and Nepravel expected to be blasted again by Tymor at this night's meeting.

But to his surprise, when it came Nepravel's turn, Tymor was unusually calm. "You need not report tonight, Nepravel and Zoldar. Lord Alhandra is quite aware of what has been going on with Richard Sullivan, his family, and his friends. With my help, he has devised a plan that you will carry out to destroy Richard Sullivan's faith. We cannot tolerate his meddling anymore. He is becoming very troublesome, and he is upsetting other plans made long ago. Tell me, Nepravel, what would you say is Richard Sullivan's greatest weakness?" All of the other demons were as silent as their persistent hissing would allow.

Nepravel, hoping that he was not being set up for a fatal trick, thought for a moment, and then said, "I . . . it seems to me, master, that in the past his greatest weakness has been the Holloway woman."

"Very good, Nepravel," Tymor agreed. "And what would you say is now his greatest desire?"

Nepravel again thought for a moment. "To tell other people about his faith?"

"Exactly! Very good, Nepravel. You may survive this one yet. We have devised a plan, which you will carry out, to utterly confuse and disillusion him. It may take several weeks, but we're confident that you will carry it out correctly, Nepravel. Unless you are tired of your time here on earth."

Nepravel received the clear message and listened intently as Tymor explained what he was to do.

FRIDAY, JUNE 2 ■ Amy had been able to dodge Billy's phone calls on the Friday of her abortion appointment, and then she had been out of town with her parents over the weekend. On Tuesday evening when Billy finally caught her, she simply told him that she had "missed her appointment" at the clinic, but she confirmed that she looked forward to their dinner date on the coming Friday evening, as he had suggested sometime earlier.

Amy convinced her father not to say anything to Billy when he picked her up that evening, because she felt she should be the first to tell him of her decision. Tom Bryant reluctantly agreed and remained politely civil to Billy for the few minutes when they were together before Amy came down. Billy assumed that it was his imagination, but it did seem to him that Mr. Bryant was looking at him quite a lot.

Now Amy and Billy were sitting in Austin's Restaurant. They gave their waitress their orders; when she left, Billy finally said to Amy, "Well, if you missed your appointment last week, did you make it today?"

Without answering at first, Amy reached into her purse, which was beside her in the booth, and pulled out the $350 in the envelope Billy had given her the week before. She slid it across the table to him. He immediately knew what it was and said, "What is this? What are you doing?"

"To put it as simply as I can, I didn't have the abortion, and I'm not going to have it. Instead, I'm going to have the baby."

"What?!?"

Amy continued calmly, "Yes, Billy. I told you back a long time ago that this was going to be my decision, though I certainly sought your input. I know you wanted me to have the abortion, but I decided it was wrong to do it. So I'm going to go through with bearing our child, God willing; and I even paid the fifty-dollar abortion cancellation fee myself, because I knew it was not what you wanted.

"By the way, my family knows what we've done and knows of my decision. . . ."

"You mean your father knew when I was there this evening that I'm the father of this child?"

"Yes, Billy. He had some things he wanted to say to you, but I asked him not to. And I know he'll be all right, as the weeks go on. In fact, since we've been working through what all this means, I really feel closer to him and to my mother than I have in a long time.

"I'm not going to ask you to do anything else or to be involved in any other way. I know you're leaving next week, at the end of the term, and going out West to take that job on the ranch. As far as I'm concerned, you'll have nothing else to worry about, nor any further part in this."

She could see his facial tension relax a bit. She continued, "But there is one more thing you have to do." The tension returned.

"For an adoption to be legal in this state, apparently the father as well as the mother has to agree. Do you remember Susan Sullivan, who double dated with us that night? Well, her father is an attorney, and there's a nice-sounding lady attorney in his office. I've talked to her on the telephone, and she's going to try to help me. But you have to sign a form. In fact, she said it would be best if we signed it together, in front of witnesses. So here is her telephone number." Amy slid a piece of paper across the table to Billy. "You need to call her on Monday and set up a time to pick me up; then we'll go down to their office and sign these papers. Since we all get out of school for summer vacation next week, we ought to be able to do it before you leave town. OK?"

"So all you want me to do is sign a paper saying that it's all right for someone to adopt this child? That's it?"

"That's it. Between the adopting couple and my family, I think the medical costs will be covered. You can go on out West. In fact, you can go on with your life as if none of this ever happened. I just hope you'll think about me and your child the next time you're tempted to do what we did. And I'm going to make it through the next months by believing that God has some purpose for this child inside of me, whom you and I have conceived, which will make all the pain and all the trouble and all of the cost worth it."

Billy, chastised by Amy's statements and frankly amazed by her strength, was nevertheless pleased that his role in all of this could end with his signature next week. "Yeah, sure, I'll call this Miss Thomas next week, and we'll set it up. Listen, Amy, thanks. And I'm just as sorry that all this has happened as you are."

"Sure, Billy. I'm sure you are."

Tommy and Brent opened the back doors of Mr. Festa's car, and thanked Taylor's father for the ride to Brent's house that Friday evening. Their baseball coach had hosted an early evening cookout for the boys on their baseball team, now that their season was over, and Tommy was returning to Brent's home to spend the night as their school year wound down to its last couple of days.

Walking up the front steps of the Holcombes' home, Tommy suddenly stopped and asked, "Hey, isn't that Derrick's car?" He pointed to the single car parked in the turnaround at the side of the house.

"Yeah, I guess it is. I told you our folks went to the lake with some friends tonight. I guess Zane must have invited Derrick over."

"But I told you I don't want to get involved in all of that anymore. At least not now."

"What's the matter, Tommy? Don't you like the videos?" Brent asked, a little sarcastically.

"Yes, you know I like them. But I don't want to be involved with those guys any more. I don't think it's right."

"Well you sure thought it was OK just a few weeks ago! What's the matter? It's fun. Nobody gets hurt. Hey, we could be doing a lot worse things!"

"I know, Brent. I know. But I just don't feel good inside about it. Maybe I can't really explain it to you. But when I was doing it with them every weekend, it got to the point where that was all I was thinking about, almost all the time. It sort of took me over, and I really didn't want to think about anything else, or do anything else, and that scared me. I still want to see those videos as much as ever. How couldn't I? But I have to believe that God—yes—God, has more for me—and for you—to do with our lives than to get so involved with these guys and those videos all the time."

"Well, I like watching them and enjoy what we do. I don't think it's any big deal," Brent replied.

"Brent, you're my best friend. You can obviously do whatever you want. More than anything, I'm mixed up about all this. Maybe I can't explain it correctly to you, but I just have this feeling I shouldn't be doing this. That God has other and better things that he wants me to do. I'm sorry, but that's how I feel."

"So, then, are you coming inside?"

"Not if I'm going to be sitting alone watching television or something while you're in the basement with those guys. I'd be happy to do something with you as long as you don't try to push me to go into the basement."

"Well, I'm going to watch the videos. They've got some new ones which sound fantastic."

"Well, I . . . I guess I'll just go home. See you tomorrow." And Tommy picked up his overnight bag, turned, and walked toward his home in the dark.

Tom Spence was moved from the ICU to a private room in the hospital on Friday. Officer Higgins was still in the ICU, but his prognosis improved after the second operation, and the prayer vigil was called off at noon, after fifteen of the participants assembled in the small chapel to thank God for His mercy and His blessings.

Late that Saturday morning, Richard and Janet drove down to the hospital to visit with Tom. Sandy had told them on the phone that he was still very weak but that he would enjoy their visit very much, if it were not too long.

Tom's right eye, half of his nose, and his mouth were the only parts of his head that were not bandaged. Still, he managed to smile when the Sullivans walked through the door.

"It was nice of you to help protect the city's police car with your body," Richard quipped, as Janet first hugged Sandy and then took Tom's right hand in hers.

"I guess it was the least I could do for all that I was being paid," Tom replied in a soft voice, returning their smiles.

"We hear good news about Officer Higgins."

"Yes, Sandy and I have asked that he be moved to this room just as soon as he can leave the ICU."

"Tom, we're so glad to see you sitting up and smiling! I know you're in no shape to hear much of this," Janet said, "and you may not believe it, but Connie, Phil, and I met with Bill Shaw and Bob Grissom on Tuesday, and Network has already decided to go ahead with '911 Live.'"

"I haven't seen the tape and don't really remember what happened after I was shot. How bad was it?"

"Pretty bad. We'll bring you a copy of the tape when the doctor says you can stand it. Network's one concession to the close-up violence you suffered is a thirty-second delay, to delete or to mask really nasty parts. And a commitment to cut away if they feel they are being set up on purpose, as a stage for violence."

"But who makes those decisions, Janet?" Tom asked. "So long as the same people produce the show, it will probably take something far beyond plain gruesome to provoke a black-out or a cutaway."

"I know, Tom . . . At least you would have been proud of me. I told them exactly what I thought about the show. I may be fired before I even have a chance to join the group opposing it!"

"I hope not, Janet. I hope we can stop or modify it without anything like that ever happening to any of us."

"I'm going to do a little quiet investigation myself," Richard added. "I was there in the studio, Tom, and I saw it all. Once you have your strength back and I've got some facts, we'll sit together with your group and see what perhaps we can do to put some pressure on Network. But for now, you need your rest, so Janet and I had better go."

"Thank you, Richard. We would really appreciate any help you can give us. Sandy, could you lead us in prayer before Richard and Janet leave?"

15

MONDAY, JULY 17 ■ The families on Devon Drive had made a smooth transition into a summer vacation routine. Susan picked up the job which she had started the previous summer at the frozen yogurt shop, working part time four out of seven days each week. Bobbie worked hard at an inner city camp, and Amy's schedule of nearby babysitting jobs was perfect for her special situation.

Tommy and Brent mowed lawns together to earn money, but their relationship suffered somewhat from their differences on the videos. They enjoyed all sorts of other activities together, from tennis to swimming; but on the nights Brent elected to "do videos" with the older boys, Tommy would not participate. Tommy continued to believe that he was doing the right thing, but he also didn't want to upset his friendship with Brent; and he wanted to see the pornography. He was fourteen. But he had decided, thanks to the input from Glenn and his father, that "doing videos" was wrong; and he was trying his best to live up to his decision, despite all the pressures on him to go along.

The Sullivans continued to attend Morningside Church, and Amy joined them every Sunday morning. Each week a few more drops of clean, spiritual water replaced the muddy water in the figurative glasses of their hearts and minds, spiritual water dropped there by the youth group meetings, the adult Sunday school classes, and Michael Andrews' sermons. At the end of June, Richard and Janet began attending six weeks of Wednesday evening classes to become members of the church.

Tom Spence finally went home after two more weeks in the hospital, and Doug Higgins followed a week later, though still in a wheelchair. The doctors hoped that, with physical therapy, he would walk again. But both men and their families were simply glad for them to be alive and improving. Blessings were counted daily in the two homes.

Billy and Amy met with Kathy Thomas, briefly joined by Richard, back in early June. All of the adoption approval papers were signed, and Kathy began putting together a list of possible adoptive parents for Amy to consider. At Richard's suggestion, Kathy called the Tomlinsons, and they enthusiastically responded to her request for information on themselves. Kathy agreed with Richard that they appeared to be a fine and potentially well matched couple for Amy's child; she placed them on the list of seven couples for Amy and her parents to consider, and they then made it through to the short list of three couples to interview. Patrick and Kate would fly into town later that week for their meeting with all three Bryants.

Monday morning Richard received a call from Bruce McKinney and David Smith, calling together on a speaker phone from their office.

"Richard," Bruce began, "our company's cash position is critical. Without the Tomlinson investment or a short-term loan like we proposed to you, we've basically run out of cash, trying to finance our expansion from within. Please don't repeat this, obviously, but we may not be able to make our payroll in two weeks. Patrick Tomlinson seems like our best hope because he's already conceptually onboard, and he knows us well. Do you think if we offered him a better deal—say to buy more of the company for less money—he could move faster?"

"I don't know, Bruce. He wants to invest now, but he also wants to wait to be sure that his father's estate has no surprises. Perhaps if the offer were strong enough, he would go ahead and borrow the money to invest with you, pending the estate settlement. By coincidence I happen to know that he and his wife will be in town on Thursday about another matter. Why don't you just give him a call and ask for a meeting? If he says OK, I'll call Marty and clear it with him; or he can come too."

"All right, Richard, we'll do that," David replied. "And listen, just to add to the problem, Fairchild stock is down four points today on news of a huge Japanese investment in their major competitor. We really need to move Tomlinson along, for all these reasons."

"OK. Call me after you talk to Patrick. I think he and his wife are flying in early Thursday," Richard concluded.

Richard had asked two of their firm's summer interns, Bill Evans and Linda McPhail, to research recent decisions on local obscenity cases. That morning they reported their findings, sitting together in the firm's legal library.

"Since the definition of obscenity is not black or white," Linda began, "the case law is not totally clear either."

"But it does appear—and here are the relevant decisions—" Bill continued, "that the courts do allow local communities to set and to enforce standards for obscene behavior."

"So we have to find out what standards our community has set—I presume that means our city and county governments—and then be able to show that '911 Live' could be expected to violate those standards on a regular basis?" Richard asked.

"I think so," Linda nodded. "We've already requested copies of the relevant ordinances from our metropolitan governments, and we should be able to review them this week. This whole area is, again, very gray. A final ruling could hang on whether the show is portrayed as 'entertainment' or as 'news.' But from what we've read so far, we really should be able to mount a strong case, at least to put in front of a judge for a temporary injunction."

"And what if we can find fifty other attorneys across the nation who will file similar suits on the same day in their communities?" Richard asked. "Keep on digging, and let me know what you find out about the local ordinances."

■   ■   ■

At their family dinner that night, Tom Bryant asked Amy, "Are you sure you want your mother and me to be at these three interviews you've got coming up this week? We know the decision is ultimately yours, and we don't want you to feel that we're interfering."

"Oh no, Dad," Amy replied. She had really appreciated the quiet but solid support from her parents over the past month, while she, Bobbie, and Susan read and discussed as much as they could find out about pregnancy, and Amy began regular checkups with an obstetrician, Tommy Glenn. "I don't feel you're interfering. This decision is so important. I want you both to help me."

"Fine! Then we'll be delighted to meet with you and these couples," Nancy said. "And we'll try to help you ask the right questions so that you can make the best decision."

"Thanks. I really need your help. Now I've got two questions."

"What are they, dear?" Nancy asked.

"I know we decided to wait to tell other people until I really start to show and until I'm safely through the first three months. But could I call my cousin Catherine and tell her? She must be due any day now, and I really want to share this time with her. I even thought that maybe I could visit her, right after her baby is born to understand what she's going through."

"That's a good idea, Amy," Tom answered. "Give her a call tonight. And, if she and her husband are amenable, it's certainly OK with us for you to visit her. She could probably use your help, in fact, with their two-year-old. What was your other question?"

"Would you two come with me one Sunday to Morningside Church? Their youth group leader, Glenn Jamison, has helped me so much, and their services are so good. I think you'll really like Michael Andrews. I'm feeling so much closer to God, thanks to Bobbie and Susan and Mr. and Mrs. Sullivan. Couldn't you just try it once or twice?"

Tom, who had not been to church in years, given that Sunday mornings usually meant golf or tennis, was nevertheless moved by his daughter's request. He had noticed changes in Amy that went beyond her pregnancy, and she had told both of them about what had apparently been a complete transformation in Richard. Unknown to him, their family had been the object of daily prayers from both the Sullivans and the Merediths, and the voices that earlier might have deterred him were playing at a much lower volume than before.

To Nancy's surprise, Tom smiled and said, "Sure, Amy. I think we'd be glad to join you. What about this Sunday?".

Amy returned his smile. "Great! Thanks, Dad. I do think it will mean a lot to you. It certainly has to me. And as soon as supper's over, I'm going to call Catherine!"

TUESDAY, JULY 18 ■ The next evening Richard and Janet drove over to Tom and Sandy Spence's home for dessert and coffee with the group of believers from the television station. Their purpose in gathering was twofold: to thank God for the healing of Tom and Officer Higgins, who was already walking with a cane, and to discuss possible action on "911 Live."

After thirty minutes of pleasant conversation around a buffet filled with delicious desserts, one brought by each of the seven families represented, the group moved to Tom's living room, where they joined hands in a large circle and prayed together, thanking God for His blessings, and asking Him for His continued guidance. They ended by singing several praise songs, with Phil Tenneyson's wife playing the piano on which Sandy Spence occasionally practiced.

After the songs, they went for more coffee, and then the group sat in chairs and on the floor, as Tom began the second part of their meeting.

"Sandy and I thank all of you again for your prayers and your support through all of this. I feel almost 100 percent again, and I'm looking forward to starting back at the station on Monday. I've obviously been a bit out of the loop, here at home, although all of you have kept me up to date. Janet, do you have anything new to add about the show?"

"Not much. Bill tells me that it's scheduled to start early in September. Except for the thirty-second delay and the cut-out policy on 'set-ups,' there have been no changes from what we saw here. I'm still sure that really awful stuff will be broadcast, almost live, into our homes, early every Friday night. Bill keeps saying the show is designed to show people what's 'really happening' and to honor our nation's emergency personnel. But I hear from friends in New York that the talk in the network halls is still about 'immediate realism' and 'ratings'; I think that translates into 'let's hope there's at least a few good shoot-outs, fires, and wrecks every week.'"

"Well, I guess we're going to have to meet with Bill when I get back and tell him that we still oppose the show—even more so after the test run; and tell him that we ultimately will quit if the show is aired here in this format. If you still all agree?"

There were nods and affirmations around the living room.

Richard, who had been silent to that point, asked, "Tom, I assume that if the network can do a thirty-second delay, they could just as well do a longer delay, right?"

Connie Wright, who had more technical experience than Tom, answered for him. "That should be no problem. Why?"

"Well, I'm obviously an outsider, and I don't want to interfere in what you're doing unless you think it's appropriate. But I worry that your threat of quitting, as serious as it is to each one of you and your families, will not be taken seriously or as much of a real threat by the station, and certainly not by the network. I deeply admire and understand your firm principle, but I don't know how effective it will be. What if we could bring pressure to bear to really change the show? Would you be interested in pursuing that, even if we ultimately fail?"

"Of course, Richard," Tom answered for all of them. "Our goal has always been to change the show or to stop it, not to lose our jobs. We just feel like we have no other way to threaten them."

"Well, maybe there is another way," Richard said, and he spent ten minutes describing a strategy that had formed slowly in his mind over the previous few weeks as he prayed with Janet every night about this situation. "I don't have any idea whether it will work," he concluded, "but I'm willing to give it a try if you are."

There was immediate consensus for him to proceed as he had described.

"Janet," Richard said, turning to his wife, "you may quickly have a real conflict with the station. After I do a little more investigation, you unfortunately may have to resign, or at least offer to, before we really do anything concrete. I don't think Bill would appreciate the husband of his programming director filing lawsuits against his network. Hopefully it won't come to that, but I think you have to be fully prepared to do it. Can you handle that if you have to?"

Janet hesitated for a moment, then spoke slowly. "I would hate to lose my job, because I love what I do. But I've seen enough to know that this show just can't go on. So, yes, if I have to, I'll quit." Tom and Connie, who had initiated the early meetings with Janet on this subject, were amazed but not surprised by her transformation, and by the strength with which she now spoke.

Back at home later that night, Richard asked Janet to join him in their den after Susan and Tommy had gone to bed.

"I don't know where this '911 Live' situation is headed, but as I mentioned earlier, it could become kind of difficult, maybe for both of us, to take a stand against the network and the station. I think everyone tonight, including me, was impressed with your pain and sincerity in offering to resign if you have to. But since this could become one of the toughest things we've ever done together, I want our relationship to be completely right, and strong, before we try to tackle it so that we're not open to attack, either by men or by spiritual forces. And for me to feel that way, there's something I have to say to you."

Janet became quite worried. "Please tell me, dear. What is it?"

"I think you know the differences in me—in both of us—since the prayer breakfast two months ago. I believe I'm a new man, and I pray for God's strength to continue building a relationship with Him. But there were some things, some serious things, which I did before God changed me, but still while we were married, that I am frankly very ashamed of. I've given them to Him at the foot of the cross, and I've asked for His forgiveness. I feel that He has forgiven me. I believe—and with His help I'll be successful—that these things will never have an effect on me again. I'm ashamed to think of them now. I've put them behind me and moved on. But here's the thing . . ." Richard shifted forward in his chair and looked directly at his wife.

"If you want me to tell you about them, I will, because I want you to know me completely, and I don't want to keep any secrets from you. Then I will ask for your forgiveness. But if you will let them die with the old man whom I buried that day, then I think that would be best. It's up . . ."

While Richard spoke, Janet could see and hear his pain. She had no real idea what he was talking about, but she knew it had to be something pretty serious, and the thought crossed her mind that it probably involved another woman—or women. Or could he have done something improper or illegal at work? Or what could it be?

As he continued to speak, she placed her fingers on his lips, stopping him in midsentence. "Whatever these things are, are they really behind you? Are they gone forever?"

"With God's help, absolutely yes."

She paused, looking at him. "Then I think that's good enough for me. I do know you're a different person from two months ago, certainly a completely different person from the man I married. It sounds like whoever did these things is no longer you. So I'll love the Richard who has been changed, like me, by God. Let's just hang together for the next few decades," she smiled, "because I don't think it's going to get any easier, and I know I'm going to need you."

"And I'm going to need you, too, Janet. I know that now. I love you so very much. What a miracle that God put us together almost twenty years ago and that we're still together. And only in the past few months have I thought to thank Him for you."

Standing up, Janet smiled again, once more amazed by the power of the Holy Spirit to change people, starting with Richard. He had just said, in essence, that he trusted the strength and the permanence of their relationship enough to bare his worst faults to her. Yet he had done it in a way which let her know what he thought was best. Janet felt both loved and protected. "Come on to bed, dear," she said, pulling him up close to her, smiling, and unbuttoning his shirt. "Isn't it wonderful that God has designed it so that *we* can do anything, and it's not a sin! Got any ideas?"

WEDNESDAY, JULY 19 ■ Wednesday morning Richard called information in Minnesota and obtained the Foundation for the Family telephone number. He knew that it would probably take time to get through to Dr. Samuel Morris himself, so he wound up leaving a lengthy message with Dr. Morris' executive assistant, hoping that the founder of this well-known force for family values might return his call within a few days.

He was therefore pleasantly surprised when Dr. Morris called him back after lunch. Richard took a few minutes to explain the general purpose of his call, which interested Dr. Morris, as Richard had prayed that it would. Checking their schedules, they agreed that Richard could fly in for a meeting on the following Monday.

■   ■   ■

That evening Susan was hurrying to put the dinner dishes in the dishwasher before her date with Drew, and Janet was putting the leftovers in containers, when the phone rang. Janet answered. After a pause, she said towards the den, "Richard, it's for you. It's someone named Kristen Holloway."

Sitting in his usual armchair, just taking out a file from his briefcase, Richard's heart skipped a beat, and he instantly felt lightheaded. Moving over to the telephone on the side table, he answered, as Janet hung up in the kitchen. "Hello."

"Hi, Richard. This is Kristen. Remember me?" she said, with just a hint of sarcasm in her voice.

"Yes, of course. How are you?"

"Not as good as when we were together, but I'm making it. Notice that I'm not calling Janet, but you. I hope you've also noticed that I haven't called Janet—though I've picked up the phone to do so quite a few times."

"Yes, I have," Richard said, closing his eyes, as his stomach twisted into a knot. He wondered where this conversation was leading, with Janet standing in the next room.

"Well, you can relax. I'm calling for a perfectly legitimate reason. I have a buyer—a couple with three teenagers—who are interested in purchasing Betty McEver's house just down from you. They started asking me about the neighborhood and the schools and the kids, and I told them I knew you and that your family could probably give them all the information they need. So my question is, could we set an appointment, maybe even for tomorrow evening, for us to meet with you and Janet and to let them ask you some questions?"

Richard could feel the knot unwind one notch, though he was still wary and unsure of himself. "Just a minute," he responded. "Let me ask Janet."

Covering the mouthpiece, he said to Janet, who had walked into the den, "Kristen Holloway is a real estate agent who handled a big sale for a client of ours several months ago. She thinks she may have a family who is interested in Betty McEver's house, but they want to find out more about the neighborhood. She wants to know if we can meet with them, perhaps tomorrow evening."

Janet reflected on her schedule and on the state of her house, which was not too bad. "Sure. Anything to help Betty, after all that she's been through. Say about 7:30?"

"Kristen? Yes, that'll be fine. Is 7:30 tomorrow evening OK? . . . Good. We'll see you then. Yes, I look forward to seeing you too. Goodbye."

Richard put the phone down and realized that his palms were quite damp. "Thanks, Janet. From what I remember, Kristen is a nice person; and it will be good to meet some potential new neighbors." But inside, he already dreaded the thought of Kristen in their home.

Janet smiled. "I'm just glad she remembered where you live."

■   ■   ■

THURSDAY, JULY 20 ∎ Bruce McKinney worked out with Patrick Tomlinson that he and David Smith could meet with Patrick early Thursday afternoon, after Patrick and his wife Kate met with Amy Bryant, her parents, and Kathy Thomas in the morning. Even though that first meeting was scheduled next door at the Bryants' home, Richard decided he would not attend, even briefly, so that Amy could always feel that she made her decision on her own, with only the help of her parents. Instead, he and Janet spent some extra prayer time that morning, asking God to give the Bryants a clear message on whom He had chosen to raise the baby Amy would have in six more months.

This interview was the second of the three that Kathy Thomas had arranged for Amy. Each was with a couple from out of town, though the Tomlinsons were traveling the farthest.

The Tomlinsons arrived at the Bryants' home right on time, in an airport rental car. As the Bryants greeted them at the door, Kathy Thomas did her best to put everyone at ease. "I know this is in some ways an almost impossible situation," she said, as they walked into the living room, where Nancy had coffee waiting. "Please just be yourselves, feel at home. Everyone should feel free to ask any questions he or she thinks are important. The Tomlinsons know they would be responsible to pay for all the costs of Amy's medical care while she is pregnant, including the birth of the baby; and Amy knows that she would be responsible to give the baby to the Tomlinsons within one week after the birth. Beyond that, let's talk and get to know each other."

Amy and her parents had read the information on the Tomlinsons, so they knew that the couple were in their early thirties, that they had both grown up in Cincinnati, and that Patrick was in line to inherit a large amount of money from his father's estate, with which he planned to continue his father's practice of investing in various companies.

Likewise, the Tomlinsons had seen pictures of both Amy and Billy, and they had read brief histories on both of the natural parents-to-be.

Patrick began, "Kate and I want to thank you for inviting us into your home. We've been trying for many years to have a child of our own, and the doctors finally told us over a year ago that it would simply never be possible for us. We now very much want to have several children by adoption, so hopefully, if this child comes to live with us, he or she will someday have several brothers or sisters."

"Patrick," Tom Bryant said, "we've of course read about your financial capabilities, so that's not an issue. But tell Amy something about how you were raised—both of you—and about how you would plan to raise this child, if you become the adoptive parents."

Kate and Patrick smiled. "Well, I'll go first," he said. "Obviously I did not go hungry when I was little. But my father and mother, who are now both dead, raised both of us—I'm three years older than my sister—to respect the value of all we had. I worked in the neighborhood to save money to buy a car when I was a teenager, finally earning enough after my senior year of high school, when I spent the summer on a survey crew for a local engineering firm, cutting trees and clearing paths. Talk about fun! Anyway, as you may have read, I won an ROTC scholarship when I was in college, because I had always loved sailing, and I wanted to go into the Navy. So I spent four years after school as a communications officer, defending the East Coast. Kate and I 're-met' when I was home on leave during my last year—we had vaguely known each other in high school, though she was four years younger—and we were married right after I got out. That was almost eight years ago, and here we are. I began helping my father with several businesses when I returned home to Cincinnati, and hopefully I will do as much for my family and for our community as he did." Patrick ended, and turned to Kate.

"My story is much simpler," she began, directing her smile to Amy. "My parents were both teachers; in fact, they still are. My father teaches political science at the university, and my mother is now the lower school principal at a local day school. I was raised with two sisters, one older, one younger, in a pretty simple environment. My Dad is sort of an anomaly for a university professor; he's conservative and raised us that way. We went to church most Sundays, and in high school we had fairly strict rules. When I went off to college I have to admit I had a pretty good time; I finally got serious in my last two years, expecting to be a teacher myself. But then I ran into Patrick at a party over Christmas vacation of my senior year, and we were married the next summer. I've been active in all sorts of civic groups, and in our church; but of course what I really want is the chance to raise some wonderful children."

"So you go to church?" Amy asked.

"Yes. I guess I'm very lucky. I can't remember a time when I didn't know the Lord. From when I was a little girl, my parents raised me to trust in Him, and that's what I've done." Placing her hand on her husband's knee next to her, she continued, "Patrick doesn't yet share as strong a faith as I feel, but he comes with me to church most Sundays, and I'm praying for him! How about you, Amy?"

"Well, we haven't been big churchgoers," Amy said, looking back and forth between her parents, "but lately I've felt God's presence so much in what has happened to me, even this pregnancy. Several of us go to a neat youth group here. And Mom and Dad don't even know this, but a month ago I gave all of this to God—the baby, my health, the mess I've made, the adoption, all of it—and asked Jesus to come into my life and to guide me. I mean, how can a seventeen-year-old girl handle all of this, without God and her parents?"

Kate looked at Patrick and then said, "That's a really strong testimony, Amy; you've got a lot of strength. I know God will bless your prayers. And you should know I did the same thing, a year ago, when we found we could not have children. I prayed then and have continued to pray every day, giving our problem to Him and asking Him to lead us to the right mother and child."

A special moment passed between Amy and Kate as they looked at each other, but everyone in the room felt it. After a few seconds, Nancy broke the silence by asking if anyone wanted more coffee.

An hour later, after the families really came to know each other, Patrick reminded Kate that they had to eat lunch and he had to be dropped at Richard's office, while she spent a few hours shopping.

As the Tomlinsons rose to leave, everyone shook hands and said goodbye. "I'll be back in touch with you in a few days," Kathy Thomas concluded, walking them to the door with the Bryants, "after our next interview."

Patrick and Kate smiled and waved a final goodbye.

Richard had worked hard at concentrating on his contract documents that morning, trying to keep his mind off Kristen's visit to their home that evening. He knew his relationship with Janet was stronger and more secure than it had ever been, but he did not want any slip-up to hurt her, especially now that he loved her like never before. He prayed twice, sitting at his desk, that God would protect them all at their meeting that night. And then he called Bob Meredith and asked that he and Anne also pray.

Kathy Thomas dropped by his office a little after noon to report that the meeting between the Bryants and the Tomlinsons had gone quite well. "One more interview tomorrow afternoon, and we should either have a first choice from Amy or a new list of candidates from me. I'm really enjoying working with their family, Richard, and I can certainly see why you want to help them," she concluded, as she rushed to a luncheon meeting with another client.

"Thanks for your hard work, Kathy," Richard replied.

"Oh, and Patrick Tomlinson said he would meet you here at two."

"Thank you for setting us up with the Bryants, Richard," Patrick said, as he shook Richard's hand in their conference room.

"Well, I hope everything went well. Soon the decision will be up to Amy, with her parents' help," Richard responded, showing him to a chair.

"She's one mature lady, that Amy," Patrick continued. "And she really seems to have a relationship with God. It's amazing. She might even move me to pray that we can raise her baby."

"I hope you're serious, Patrick, because that's exactly how I feel."

"I am. You should have heard Amy and Kate. I've never said this before about any meeting, anywhere; but I think God . . . or some spirit . . . or something . . . was there. It was like at one point there was a seventh person in the room."

"I know, I know. I've felt His presence lately in several meetings when we've prayed. Isn't it incredible?" Richard asked.

Bruce McKinney cleared his throat, obviously a bit displeased by the lack of attention.

"I'm sorry, Bruce," Patrick said, smiling and extending his hand across the table to him and to David Smith. "You've got four children yourself, so you can understand how emotional and wound up we get. So close, we hope, to adopting our first."

"I understand completely," Bruce continued with a smile, "because our four have gotten in the nasty habit of wanting to eat several times a day; and to do that I have to make some money, which is tough right now."

"Please, tell me," Patrick said, his attention turned fully now to the business before them. "And, by the way, Marty couldn't come today, but we have his blessing to discuss anything and everything; I've simply promised him that I'll consult with him on any tentative decisions we might reach before they become binding on our side. Is that OK?"

"Fair enough," David said, as they all nodded their approval.

"So, Bruce and David, tell me why you've dragged me away from protecting your city's best stores from my wife," Patrick said, leaning back in the comfortable chair and looking from man to man.

"Patrick, we're in a significant cash bind. It's as simple as that. Believing that your cash investment is coming, we've made plans for our needed expansion; we haven't leased any additional space yet, of course, but just the planning part has cost us extra money. And the monthly interest on our debt, instead of equity, is horrendous. Our closing has dragged on and on, and the continuing cash cost has just hit us at a terrible time. Frankly, we tried to obtain a short-term loan at the bank, based on our contract, but without additional personal guarantees, which we could not obtain . . ." Bruce glanced momentarily at Richard, who returned his look without changing his expression. "We were unsuccessful."

"How bad is it?" Patrick asked.

David answered, "Right now, we don't know how we're going to meet our payroll next Friday."

"What do you propose to do?" Patrick asked seriously.

This time Bruce spoke. "No one else could help us as fast as you potentially can; you're already way up the learning curve on our company, and we believe you want to be part of what we're building here. David and I have talked, and we'd be willing to sell you, now, the controlling interest in our company, say 55 percent, for the same $1 million we've agreed on for the smaller share. We'll take back a management contract, and if you don't like what we're doing, you can fire us after a year. We think that's a hell of an offer."

Based on the numbers he had seen, Patrick also knew that it was an attractive offer. He thought for almost a minute in silence. Then he leaned forward and addressed the three men across the table from him.

"Bruce, David, Richard, I'm painfully aware of your problem; I've run companies myself and know how precious cash is to them. And I also know that, based on what you've shared with me about your company and its future, you have in fact made me a very strong offer.

"Now let me tell you my problem, which you may or may not understand. Before my father passed away, he made me promise that I would listen to the advice of Marty Tsongas for at least five years, and," Patrick smiled, "to the advice of my wife for as long as we live. He told me that everyone thought he was such a brilliant investor, but that he had only invested in companies that both he and my mother felt were run by the right people."

Bruce and David leaned back in their chairs.

Patrick continued, "In this case, I have promised both Marty and Kate that we won't go into debt before my father's estate is settled. Both of them asked me, independently, to do so, and I gave my word. As much as I want to help you and as much as I admire your company, I can't start my own business career by breaking my word to the two people who are closest to me and to my father. So if you need a lot of cash before the attorneys and accountants get completely finished with his estate, I'm afraid I just can't help you."

"But now the conditions have changed," Bruce started to argue. "We've just made you an offer that none of those three people could have foreseen. Surely you can modify your commitment now that this new offer is on the table."

"But Bruce, the promise was to avoid debt, no matter how attractive the situation might be."

"Aw, come on, Patrick. Investors go into debt every day. This is a fantastic opportunity for you!"

"Bruce, I've told you my reason and declined your offer, though I obviously appreciate it." Starting to show just a hint of anger, Patrick continued, "If you can't understand the commitment I've made, then perhaps I should rethink who I want to invest with when the money *does* become available."

"OK, OK!" David spoke up, trying to save their position in Patrick's eyes. "We certainly understand. We make and execute trades every day based only on our word, and we completely understand the importance of a promise. It's just that these are tough times for us, when we can see the goal line is so close."

"Yes, I understand," Patrick agreed, calming down himself. "I wish I could help you. I don't want anything to happen to you. But you'll have to find the short-term money somewhere else."

Ten more minutes of pleasant conversation followed, with David focusing Patrick back on the bright prospects for their firm, once his equity was invested, while Bruce said little more. He sat staring at Patrick and occasionally looked at Richard.

Finally Patrick looked at his watch and realized that he had to meet his wife downstairs for the drive to the airport. He rose and extended his hand across the table. "Thanks so much to all three of you. I hope everything stays on track for our closing."

While Richard escorted him to the elevator, Patrick continued, "And Richard, we hope to hear good news from you or Kathy on the adoption in the next few days."

"We'll see, Patrick. We'll see. As you know, it's up to Amy."

When Richard returned from seeing Patrick to the elevator, he closed the door to the conference room and said to his clients, "I'm sorry Patrick can't help now. Will you guys be able to make it a couple of more months without his equity or the loan you had hoped for?"

"What do you think, Richard?" Bruce almost leapt up, snapping angrily. "What exactly do you think I've been trying to get through to your thick lawyer brain for six weeks? We have *no* cash, and we can't get any! That means *over*—bankruptcy—close the doors! You got the picture now, Christian counsellor?"

"Come on, Bruce," David complained, rising to Richard's defense. "Richard and Patrick both have their reasons for not being able to help us. We just haven't found the right investor yet. But that's no reason to attack Richard, who has helped us so much over the years."

"Thanks, David," Richard said. "If you guys would rather have another law firm help you, I'd be glad to turn over the files. Just say to whom and when."

"No . . . I'm sorry, Richard. I didn't mean that. You've been great, and we've been neighbors for years," Bruce said, sitting back in his chair and appearing genuinely to regret his remarks. "It's just so frustrating. And unfortunately, it's not as simple as just finding the right investor."

Bruce and David exchanged glances. David nodded. Bruce asked, "Richard, what would be the consequences to us of hypothetically telling you something that may not be exactly right about our firm?"

"What do you mean?" Richard asked. The two partners looked at each other again. Bruce continued.

"Patrick really was our last chance. We have no idea where to get next Friday's payroll; but even worse, we need some significant cash to clear up some other discrepancies before next Wednesday. And we need to know what happens if we tell you some things that may not be exactly 'cricket' about that particular need."

"Well, it depends on how 'un-cricket' they are. While I'm your attorney, you can tell me and members of our firm your darkest secrets, and we cannot be forced to reveal them, even if they're somehow criminal in nature. But they could affect my ability to give a clean opinion on you in civil matters, like the Tomlinson deal, for example. So that could affect our ability to close the deal if they insist on a clean opinion from us."

"OK. Thanks, Richard," Bruce said, looking at David and standing up. "We'll think about it. And while you're praying so much, pray that we find some quick investment money. And, again, I'm sorry I blew up a little while ago," he concluded, extending his hand.

A few minutes later they were gone, leaving Richard wondering what, in fact, was not exactly 'cricket' about McKinney and Smith.

■   ■   ■

Despite his prayers and his intellectual assurance, Richard still could not help his growing nervousness as their dinner ended that evening and they made last-minute preparations to receive Kristen and her clients at 7:30.

Right at the appointed time the doorbell rang, and Richard could feel a knot in his stomach. The adrenaline was pumping through him as Janet walked to open the front door.

"Hi, Janet. I'm Kristen Holloway." His smiling former mistress introduced herself to his wife, as Richard came into the entrance foyer. "Hello, Richard. I'd like you both to meet Dennis and Patricia Hawkins and their three boys—Eric, Matt, and William."

There were greetings all around, including Susan and Tommy. Eric would be a senior in high school in the fall, and the two other boys were a year older and younger than Tommy.

As they all walked into the den, Richard suggested, "Since it's still light outside, why don't you kids walk down to the park? You can show the Hawkins' boys the tennis courts and the pool."

Susan, whose instant reaction was that Eric appeared to be interesting, immediately concurred, and all five of them were soon out the door.

The adults sat in the den, and Janet offered coffee all around. Richard took his usual armchair, and the three guests sat on the long sofa, leaving Janet and Kristen, Richard noticed, right next to each other, when Janet returned to her chair.

Kristen took the lead. "Dennis and Patti are moving in from Seattle; he'll be working at First National Bank. It's a tough move with boys their age, and so they want to find a neighborhood where there will be a lot for them to do and many potential friends to meet quickly. I immediately thought of the McEver house, and I obviously think this is one of the best neighborhoods in the city. We really appreciate your taking the time to meet with us." She smiled, turning to Janet. "I know the Hawkinses have some questions they want to ask you."

Returning the smiles and addressing Kristen first and then the Hawkinses, Janet said, "It's our pleasure to have you. We really like Northpark High School and the neighborhood. We hope you can join us here. Please, ask us any questions you like."

Forty-five pleasant and productive minutes of discussion followed, led by the two wives, about all aspects of the school, the neighborhood, and the city. The Hawkinses learned a lot, and the Sullivans soon felt that these would be welcome new neighbors. After an initial nervous period, Richard's tension subsided; and it soon seemed almost normal for Kristen and Janet to be chatting together. Richard noticed that he didn't talk much, and he wondered if it was because he feared he might accidentally say the wrong thing.

The kids came home; Susan and Eric joined the adults in the den while the three younger boys went upstairs to Tommy's room.

"If we move forward on this house and then have some more questions, will you be here all summer?" Dennis asked.

"Except for two weeks in early August when Janet and the kids go to Vermont and I join them for the last few days," Richard replied.

"I know we've got to go," Patti said, "but we've asked everything else. Do you attend a church nearby?"

"Yes," Richard and Janet answered together, then smiled. Richard nodded, and Janet told the Hawkinses about Morningside Church and about how much all of its ministries had meant to them. "We hope to be official members before we leave for Vermont."

"And they've got a really good youth group, Eric," Susan volunteered. "I think you'd really like it. You can meet lots of kids there, from different schools. Will you be here this Sunday?"

"Yes, we're here for two weeks before we go back to pack up. What time do you meet?"

While the two older teenagers continued talking about plans for Sunday, Richard added his invitation to the parents to join them at church as well. Dennis replied, "We'll probably take you up on it. Can we give you a call tomorrow?"

Patti called upstairs for her boys, and the two families began saying goodnight, the process spilling out onto the Sullivans' front yard in the warm July evening.

"Thank you for your help, Richard and Janet," Kristen concluded, shaking hands with each. "I hope we'll have some new neighbors for you."

"We hope so too," Janet replied, smiling. "And please let us know whenever we can help you."

Looking at Richard, Kristen returned the smile and said, "Oh, I certainly will."

SATURDAY, JULY 22 ■ Tommy was delighted to be invited to join all three of the Hawkins boys on Saturday night to show them the nearest mall to their potential new home and to see a science fiction war movie. With their approval, he invited Brent, and Tommy was pleased that his best friend joined them.

When Eric called to invite Tommy, he talked first to Susan, and he had asked her to join him to see a different movie. "I'd really like to," she replied, "but I'm already busy this Saturday." Realizing that her next words might put her in hot water with Drew, she nevertheless added, "Please ask me again. I work a couple of different nights every week at a frozen yogurt shop, but otherwise I try to be free." He had agreed to call her again, much to her delight.

Finally Susan and I have a date to ourselves, Drew thought, as he pulled up in front of the Sullivans home that Saturday night. In the weeks since Susan and Bobbie had quietly told him about Amy's situation, the two girls had made a point of including Amy in much of what they did, given that Amy's social life, at least among Billy's college friends, had dried up instantly. That had been fine with Drew to a point; he certainly liked Amy and wanted to be helpful. But four- and five-person dates did get old after a while! When he called Susan on Monday to make plans for this night, including a romantic movie, he put his foot down and insisted that Bobbie and Thomas look out for Amy. Susan agreed.

To avoid the lines they went to the early show and then to a casual dinner at Austin's. As she seemed to do every weekend now, Susan again invited Drew to come to the youth group she thought so much of. "I work so hard during the week," he told her in his standard reply. "Sunday is one day I can sleep late, so I just don't think your youth group is for me."

"Well, I think you'd really like it, and it won't hurt you." She smiled. He knew from the number of times she had asked him that she was quite serious.

After dinner, as they started towards Susan's home in his car, Drew was still thinking about the three incredible love scenes in the movie two hours before. He couldn't help being aroused; and frankly Susan was moved, too, though the nudity on the screen was more of a shock to her than a turn-on.

Four blocks from her home, Drew turned into a new cul-de-sac which was not quite finished and which had no streetlights. Parking the car, he slid over to Susan's side of the front seat, put his arm around her, and kissed her, which he had done many times before.

She smiled at him, and they talked about the events of the last week; Susan even told him generally about the visit by the Hawkinses. He leaned down and kissed her again, then whispered, "Susan, I love you so much." She could hear and feel his quickened breathing, and she tried to do what she had been doing for six weeks now in this situation, which was to remember Glenn Jamison's words about real love meaning that you want the best for someone. *And this can't be the best for me, so does Drew really love me?* she thought.

"Please, Susan. I love you and need you," Drew almost moaned.

Susan could feel her own emotions kicking in, and she knew she had to say something, or she might not be able to stop him or herself. "Drew, no. I'm not ready for that."

He kept his arm around her and whispered, "Oh come on, Susan. We're seniors in high school and we love each other. Why not? You mean more to me than anyone ever has. I'm not talking about making love; I just want to feel close to you . . ."

"Drew, I believe you when you tell me you love me. I think you mean it. But I don't know that either of us knows exactly what love is. Maybe it means different things to each of us. Whatever it means, I feel just as attracted to you as you do to me. You're wonderful to me. But I think it's wrong for us to have sex, and I can't get past that. So I hope you can understand it. It's very difficult for me, too; but I think we have to do what's right."

"Susan, you're so beautiful. You drive me crazy. Please, let's just make each other feel good and share our love. . . ."

Finally he had gone too far, and she smiled. "Oh come on, Drew. I know this sounds old-fashioned, but if you really love me, please don't push me any further." More sternly she added, "I want to *just* as much as you do, but I think it's *wrong*. So please just stop. OK?"

"OK, OK," he said, moving back, obviously frustrated, "but if you ever change your mind, let me know!"

"You'll be the first I'll call," she smiled in the glow from the radio, "but don't count on it any time soon."

Drew was very frustrated, but he was also very impressed with her strength. She definitely had something he had not seen in other girls!

SUNDAY, JULY 23 ■ Sunday morning, as Richard Sullivan and Dennis Hawkins had agreed on Friday, the Hawkinses met the Sullivans at the entrance to Morningside Church. As they were shaking hands, Amy walked up with her parents, who were on their first visit to the church as well. There were greetings all around, and then the six teenagers were off to youth group. The four adult visitors accompanied Richard and Janet to Sunday school and then to the service.

Just before the opening hymn, Janet whispered to Richard, who was sitting on the aisle, "Isn't that Kristen Holloway up front on the other aisle?" She nodded toward the front of the sanctuary. To Richard's surprise, Janet was right.

"You should go invite her to sit with us, especially with the Hawkinses here," Janet continued.

"But the service is about to start."

"You can walk over during the hymn. Richard, it's rude not to ask her."

Reluctantly Richard agreed, and soon he was sitting in church with Janet on one side of him and Kristen on the other. As Michael Andrews began the congregational prayers, it occurred to Richard that there must be some reason for Kristen to be there. He simply was not sure whether the reason was from God or from Satan. Rather than try to reason or to fight on his own, he knew he had to have God's help, either to reveal His plan or to protect Richard's family from Satan's plan.

So during the entire service Richard never ceased praying, silently to himself, for God's revelation and/or protection. He hoped that by bathing his family in prayer, he could either understand God's will or avoid Satan's attack.

Paula Lindsay was particularly moving in her offertory song that morning, and the entire congregation rose to its feet and sang "I Surrender All" with her. Then Michael preached on the necessity for Christians to forgive all those who may have sinned against them, in the same way that God forgives sinners when they repent and turn to Him. "Unless we truly forgive others," he said, "we carry around bitterness inside. This bitterness does not hurt the one who has wronged us at all; but it tears us apart. And, worst of all, it poisons our relationships with everyone else, particularly God." The congregation was clearly moved by the force of his words.

"That was quite a service," Patti Hawkins told Janet as they walked towards their cars. "I can see why you were drawn to this church. I hope we can come back after we pack up in Seattle and get settled in here."

"Then are you buying Betty's house?" Janet asked.

"We've made an offer, and Kristen tells us we have a good chance."

"I hope to know something tomorrow morning," Kristen responded, smiling at the other women.

Everyone said goodbye, and Richard drove his family home. Susan announced in the car that Eric had invited her to see a movie on Monday night, which obviously pleased her. And twice more that Sunday after-noon, Richard prayed for guidance and protection concerning Kristen and their family.

Late that Sunday night, after Diane and the four children were in bed, Bruce McKinney was still sitting in the same armchair in which only a few months before he had looked enviously through a new European car catalog. Their den was almost completely dark, both physically and spiritually. Nepravel and Zoldar, who had been working steadily on Bruce, both for his own destruction and as part of their plan for Richard, could not have been more pleased. Tonight they had Doubt and Failure with them, and the four demons had fertile ground in which to plant their destructive voices. And with the tapering off of the prayer cover after the prayer breakfast, they had more and more time in which to work, with less and less fear of interfering angels.

"I'm going to lose everything," Bruce heard his own inner voice telling him. "The business, home, cars, boat, *everything*. And when they send me to jail, I'll probably lose Diane. And won't the kids be proud to watch their daddy go off to prison?

"We came *so* close. A few months. The cash investment. If the accoun-tants and attorneys had only done their jobs. Or if we could only have gotten the short-term loan. Thanks, Richard Sullivan—another attorney! Blast him to hell! No one had to know! We could have paid it all back and no one would ever have known. With Tomlinson's investment—thanks, Tomlinson!—we would never have had to use those 'borrowed' stocks again. No more need to use Far West Securities to fool the regulators. So *close!*

"Now I'm finished. Not just the things. Diane will be so disappointed. My parents and brothers. Our kids. What will they go through? What will jail be like? How long will the process take? How will we pay for it all? Wouldn't I be better off dead?"

Bruce thought about the chrome .38 special revolver he kept by his bed and the loaded cylinder in his top bureau drawer. And he thought about his $2 million insurance policy.

"I don't think there's an exclusion for suicide after the first two years. I better check the policy tomorrow." And he realized with a little surprise that he was calmly considering the details of his own death.

The demons loved it, knowing how great it would be to escort him to hell, and urged him on with more voices of Despair. It was after two in the morning when he lay down next to Diane, and it was after three when he finally dozed off for a few hours of fitful sleep.

16

MONDAY, JULY 24 ■ Richard had to wake up early Monday morning to catch a flight to Minneapolis to visit Dr. Samuel Morris at the Foundation for the Family. The offices were located in a large campus-like setting in a suburb of the city not too far from the airport. The taxi let Richard off at a four-story central building, modern in its exterior architecture, and he took the elevator to the top floor.

"Hello, Mr. Sullivan, I'm Dee Thompson, Dr. Morris' assistant," a gracious woman greeted him as he exited the elevator. "Please come with me to his office. Can I get you some coffee?"

Dr. Morris' office was actually a combination office, conference room, and library, sprawling through space large enough for four or five normal offices. There were windows on three sides, separated in most cases by book shelves, and, in some cases, by photographs, banners, or other memorabilia of ten years of service in promoting the value of the family to society.

Dr. Morris and another man rose from the conference table next to one window wall, and the founder of the foundation greeted Richard warmly with outstretched hand.

"Thank you for coming so far, Mr. Sullivan. We're delighted to meet you. Let me introduce you to Tom Morgan, who is our ace in-house legal counsel. Given that you're an attorney and that what you mentioned on the phone could apparently have some legal overtones, I asked Tom to join us."

"Please call me Richard, and I'm very glad to be here with both of you," he greeted his hosts. "What a wonderful view you have from this office."

"Yes, we are blessed in many, many ways. Please sit down. Dee will also be joining us. We've been together since just after the Flood, and I unfortunately travel so much that I like for her to be in on these meetings, so she can provide continuity, plus her own good ideas. But do you need some coffee?"

"No, thank you. I'm fine."

The four of them sat at one end of the conference table. Dr. Morris insisted that Richard take an inside seat so he could enjoy the view. Dr. Morris opened their meeting with prayer, asking for God's guidance in all of their deliberations that morning. "Now, how can we help?" he asked.

Richard took several minutes to describe for them the history of "911 Live" and how his city had been chosen not only for input to the national show but also for a test run of the concept.

Tom Morgan interrupted him. "We've heard something about this show already, but we frankly didn't believe it. You mean the network actually proposes to broadcast live shots of whatever crimes and disasters are happening, without editing? At 7:30 on Friday nights?"

"That was the original plan. After what happened during the test—which I'll tell you about in a minute—they've decided to insert a thirty-second delay, with the ability to black out all or a part of the screen. And they've 'promised' to cut away from a story if they suspect it's an event staged for the camera."

"That won't be easy to tell in the heat of the moment," Dr. Morris said in disgust. "Since it will be live, what will they do? Say, 'We're sorry. We didn't mean to show you that violence; we now feel it was staged.' No way that will happen."

Richard went on to tell them about the test run, and he produced a VHS cassette from his briefcase. Dee inserted it into the VCR set up for their meeting. Richard fast scanned through many of the segments, pausing enough to give them a sense of the show. Then they watched the sequence with the police officers and the white sedan in its entirety, through to the end, when Mark Pugh panned the minicamera mounted on the police car around the area after the white car had sped off, finding the bodies of the two officers on the ground, clearly drenched in their own blood.

"And this is what they propose to put on national TV in less than two months?" Dr. Morris asked, as the tape ended.

"That's right, with only the caveats I just mentioned," Richard replied.

"I say this every few years, but I'm always proven wrong later: Surely this can't be broadcast on our nation's licensed television stations!?!"

"They certainly plan to. They claim that the purpose of the show is to honor our emergency response personnel, which is an admirable goal. But the finished product appears to honor violence and death."

Tom Morgan spoke. "You mentioned on the phone to Dr. Morris that you had some ideas concerning this show. Is now the time to hear them?"

"Absolutely," Richard answered. And they spent the next two hours, including lunch, discussing "911 Live" and Richard's thoughts on the show. By the end of their time together, they had formulated a plan, using some of Richard's ideas and some from his three hosts, which would involve a trip to New York for the two attorneys.

"Hello."

"Mrs. Tomlinson?"

"Yes."

"Hi. This is Amy Bryant. How are you?"

"I'm fine Amy. How are you this morning?"

"Oh, I'm fine, thank you. Listen, I'm calling from Kathy Thomas' office. She's going to call your husband in a few minutes, but I asked and she said it was OK for me to call you. I wanted you to know that I've been thinking and praying about this decision for several days . . . and I've finally decided that I want you and your husband to raise my baby."

Kate Tomlinson's heart leapt with joy. "Oh Amy, really? Oh, praise God! I've been praying too; and I felt so good about our meeting, like He wanted us to meet. That's so wonderful, dear. I promise you—and Him—that we'll love that baby and do everything we can for him or her. Thank you so much. I can't tell you how happy you've made us."

"I feel really good about it too. Knowing that you believe in God means a lot to me. There has to be a reason why I'm going through this, and I think I can get through it better if I know the baby is going to be in your home."

"Thank you, Amy. You can be sure that we know your baby is a gift straight from God, and we'll treat him or her that way."

"I'm going to visit my cousin in a few days. After that, do you think it would be OK for me to visit you, if I pay for my ticket? Just for a day or two? I want to see where he'll be, just so I can visualize the home he'll be in and the yard he'll play in. Do you think that would be OK?"

"As far as I'm concerned, it's perfect. Let's let Patrick and Kathy talk, and then I'll call you back later at home. We might even be able to find an airline ticket for you! Should I tell Patrick to call Kathy at the office?"

"Yes, she's here and waiting to talk to him."

"I'll call and give him the good news. Then he'll call you. And Amy, thank you again. And God bless you."

Monday evening Kristen sat working at her breakfast room table, the summer sunset still gathering strength outside her balcony window. She had finished delivering the accepted contract on the McEver home back to the Hawkinses, so that sale appeared to be going well. And now she was going through her prospects file for a home she expected to list for sale in the same neighborhood. But she was not alone. Torgo, the demon for her neighborhood, was playing his part in Alhandra's plan for Richard.

I really enjoyed Morningside Church yesterday morning, she found herself thinking. *I can see why I've heard so much about it. But those folks really believe. Like the people at those revivals when I was a girl. And like my parents, praying for me every day! It must be nice to have that kind of simple, unsophisticated faith. I doubt I could ever really be like that. Life's too complicated to believe that sort of simple stuff. Still, though, there is an attraction.*

And Richard. He looked good yesterday. But what does he see in that Janet? I mean she's OK, but nothing great. They're so 'homey' together—I never thought of him that way. Smiling, with a mental image of Richard pouncing on her in the bed in Atlanta, she heard a voice say, *I guess I can see why not!* She thought for a moment about Peter in San Francisco; they had enjoyed another three day "fling" together when he was in town following up on the securities story. But he lived so far away.

Maybe I ought to go to Morningside Church more often. Worst case, I'll meet some other halfway decent people, maybe even an eligible bachelor! Maybe even get some business—it's not exactly the poorest church in the city. Best case, Richard will get used to seeing me, and somehow we'll wind up back together, permanently . . . Yes, I think some more Sundays at Morningside won't hurt!

When Richard had called Mary, his secretary, from the airport in Minneapolis the day before, she told him about Amy's choice of the Tomlinsons to adopt her baby.

"That's wonderful, Mary. Please thank Kathy Thomas, and when I get home I'll drop by the Bryants'."

"And one more thing," she added. "Bruce McKinney has called twice today. He says he and Mr. Smith need to talk to you just as soon as possible."

Richard then tried to catch Bruce at his office, but they did not speak until the evening. Bruce sounded terrible on the telephone. They set a meeting for 9:00 the next morning in Richard's office.

TUESDAY, JULY 25 ■ When Bruce and David entered his office, Richard knew something was very wrong. David was slow, almost lethargic, and collapsed in the chair in front of Richard's desk. Bruce was wound up, like a prize fighter with no one to fight, looking as if he had not slept for several days. Despite Richard's invitation to sit, Bruce elected to stand behind a chair, as Richard took his seat, and Bruce began to speak.

"Richard, this is it. We're finished. I don't know how we'll pay you, but we've got to shut down our company." Bruce spoke quickly, as if he had rehearsed these lines and was almost out of breath.

Richard frowned from behind his desk. "Wait a minute, guys. It can't be that bad. You've got a legitimate cash crisis. Maybe we have to file a reorganization for short-term relief from your creditors. If Patrick will work with us, and you can get over the negative PR, a bankruptcy judge will surely grant our request on the strength of your contract. The cavalry is on the way in; we just don't know exactly when. But that's no reason to shut down completely—Unless you think you can't survive the bad press, which admittedly could be significant."

Bruce began pacing behind the two chairs; David looked down at his hands. Richard could not remember seeing anyone look more defeated.

"*That* PR we could probably survive," Bruce said, turning and standing behind David's chair, looking at Richard. "But not when they find out that we've been borrowing money for years, using clients' stock as collateral."

"What?" Richard exclaimed, sitting up straight in his chair.

"It's what we asked you about on Thursday," Bruce continued. "The 'un-cricket' part. For several years we've been using escrowed stocks and bonds, which we're supposed to keep untouched for our clients in our safe, to pledge as collateral for loans at the bank. Right now we owe $150,000, due this week, and we can't cover it. We might be able to pay the interest and roll the note over for sixty days, but there's another little problem."

"Wait a minute," Richard interrupted. "Surely what you're talking about is not just a business problem. I'm not a securities expert, but what you've done must be illegal."

"*Bingo,* Richard! I knew all those degrees on your wall must be good for something. Your old clients McKinney and Smith are *crooks!* Or so everyone will say."

David Smith slumped even further in his chair and looked almost dead. Richard knew he had to stop and think, but Bruce did not give him the chance.

"And the only reason we're telling you this and having to destroy twenty years of hard work, other than the fact that Tomlinson is a Boy Scout and you're a Christian, is that tomorrow the National Securities Examination Association is going to pull an unscheduled audit on us—it's the first time we've ever been selected for what they call a 'high level check of the staff auditors'—and we only found out about it last week.

"Unfortunately, the firm with which we usually swap securities to handle these audits is having its regular quarterly audit this week as well. So it can't loan us the stocks we need to cover. And tomorrow or Thursday the auditors will go to Mother McKinney's cupboard, and a whole bunch of the bones will be missing. And they won't like that at all. Not at all . . ."

As Bruce finished, he looked over and past Richard, to the view outside, as if he were in a daze.

"You mean there's another firm involved with you? A conspiracy to defraud?" Richard asked.

Bruce was silent for a moment, just staring. "What. Oh, yeah. Another firm. Far West Securities. A conspiracy. That's good. Hear that, David? We've been in a conspiracy all this time!"

"That's just legal jargon, as you know," Richard said, standing up himself. "Bruce, David, I'm sorry for both of you, and your firm. But this is not just a business matter any more. I've got to get help from guys who handle this sort of problem on a more regular basis. I'm going to call in Court Shullo and Tim Granger. OK?"

"Whatever. By the way, Far West is going to be in for a little surprise by Friday. We haven't told them about our unscheduled audit problem yet. We figured that we could offer to 'cooperate' or whatever you call it. Maybe the law will be a little easier on us. What do you think?" Bruce asked, still staring out the window.

"I don't know. I don't know," Richard said, walking back into his office after asking Mary to summon his two associates.

He walked over beside his desk but remained standing, so that he could look Bruce in the eye.

"Let me ask you something. Were you going to go ahead and take Patrick Tomlinson's cash, or let me guarantee your loan, knowing that you've been doing this illegal 'swapping' for years?"

Defiantly, Bruce turned toward Richard. "Of course. If either one of you had done the right thing—the sensible thing—we wouldn't be in this mess. We would have paid off *all* of our debt, not just the part collateralized by these securities, and that would have been the end of it. We would never have had to do it again, and no one ever would have known. But you and Tomlinson were too squeamish—too good and principled—to make a sensible investment. So now David and I are finished, not to mention our families and employees!"

"Wait a minute, Bruce," Richard countered. "Anyone at Far West could have turned you in, even years from now, just as you're about to do to them, and then Patrick's money or my guarantee would be down the tubes. Did you ever . . ."

Richard was interrupted by a knock, as Court and Tim came into the office. They sensed the tension and closed the door behind them. Richard stopped talking, turned around to look out the window, and then addressed his associates, turning back as he began.

"Court, Tim, meet Bruce McKinney and David Smith. They've been clients here since we started the firm. Bruce is also my neighbor. Unfortunately they've run into a couple of big problems beyond my recent experience to handle, and we need your help. Let's all move over to my conference table."

The five men sat at the small table in Richard's office. David looked as if he should almost be carried across the room. Richard described to Court and Tim what he had just learned from his clients. If they were shocked, they didn't show it, but instead began taking copious notes on their legal pads.

An hour later, after many questions and exchanges of details, with David only occasionally speaking and even Bruce starting to run out of energy, Court suggested that they take a break for an hour, to give the three attorneys a chance to discuss their options.

"Why don't you both come back at noon, and we'll have some sandwiches brought in?" Richard said. "And then we can discuss what to do. We may have some steps for you to take right after lunch, since the regulators are due to arrive in the morning."

Nancy Bryant had set aside that day to drive Amy to her cousin Catherine's home. Her niece was due to deliver her baby any day, and all the Bryants believed that it would be a good change for Amy to live for a couple of weeks with Catherine and her husband.

"She can be a great help to Catherine when the baby comes," Tom said when he and Nancy discussed it again the previous night. "And living the reality of two little children may cement Amy's resolve to let the Tomlinsons take her baby, when the time comes, in case she has any doubts."

Nancy was very proud of all that Amy and her friends had accomplished in the past month and told her so as they drove down the interstate. Amy was signed up to take birthing classes in six weeks, and Susan was going to be her primary coach, with Bobbie and Tom as substitutes. Nancy felt good about the Tomlinsons as well, and she believed they would give Amy's baby—she couldn't bring herself to say 'my grandchild'—a good and loving home.

"And thanks for encouraging us to go to Morningside Church on Sunday, Amy," Nancy said. "I remembered feelings I haven't felt since I was a teenager myself. That sermon was really powerful, and the singing was wonderful. I plan to go back, even while you are at Catherine's."

Amy smiled and thought again about the amazing differences since Susan helped her decide not to have the abortion.

When Bruce McKinney and David Smith returned to Richard's office a little after noon, they found sandwiches and sodas on the credenza, and the three attorneys at work around the table. The energy levels of the two men seemed to have evened out during their absence. Bruce was more subdued, and David looked as if he would survive the afternoon.

As they picked up their sandwiches and took their seats, Court began, "We've made a preliminary checklist of things we have to do and bases we have to cover between now and tomorrow afternoon, if possible. There's a lot to do, and it won't be pretty. We're into damage control here, trying to win for you the best possible position before the federal attorneys. With your approval, Tim and I will go see a friend we know in the securities office at the Federal Courthouse, and we'll work to plea bargain the lightest punishment we can in exchange for your voluntarily coming forward and cooperating with them.

"If you agree to that approach, then you need to tell us in great detail *all* that you've been doing, so we can communicate the situation clearly and they don't later try to nail you with something new. If that all appears to be going OK for you, then we'll call you here, and you can set in motion the other items on the list for today; and one or both of us will greet the auditors with you at your office in the morning."

"Please be sure to emphasize to the federal attorneys how voluntary it all is," Bruce said bitterly.

After spending another hour with the four men, Richard temporarily excused himself to work on other matters while Court and Tim made their final preparations to head to the federal attorney's office. He stopped by Kathy Thomas' office and found her finishing a draft agreement for the Bryant-Tomlinson adoption.

"You've helped to make several people very happy, Kathy, and I really appreciate your work."

"Well, we're not finished yet, but I do feel really good about this one. After I finish this draft, I'm going to fax it to Mr. Bryant for his review and then to Mr. Tsongas to go over with Mr. Tomlinson. I don't foresee any problems," Kathy replied.

"After what I've been through this morning, Kathy, I may quit corporate work and come help you make people happy!" Richard smiled, as he left her to work.

Walking down the hall toward the law library, Richard realized how close he had come to guaranteeing a $500,000 loan for McKinney and Smith. "If it hadn't been for the advice of Court and Janet, I would have done it," he thought to himself. "And now I'd probably be in almost the same boat they're in. And if it wasn't me, then it was almost the Tomlinsons. What if that deal had closed? Good Lord, I wonder what I would have done if all of this had *then* come out!?! "

When those thoughts sank in, Richard found a quiet corner in the law library and said a lengthy prayer of thanks for protection and for believers like Court, Janet, and Kate. And he asked for God's help for Bruce, David, and their families.

Janet was surprised to see Richard pull into their garage a little after six that evening. She had only just arrived from the station herself, and she had not had time to add the vegetables to the roast beef Susan had started an hour earlier.

"I like your new summer hours," Janet greeted him as he came through the door. "Are we going to play tennis before dinner?"

"I wish," Richard said, giving her a kiss on the cheek. "In a minute we need to go next door to the McKinneys. I promised Bruce we would go over while he breaks some news to Diane that isn't particularly good."

"Does it involve you?"

"Only as his attorney, thanks to some earlier advice from you and Court. But it's pretty serious, and I told him we'd be there by 6:15."

"Susan," Janet said, walking to the door of the den, "can you please cut these vegetables and add them to the roast while your father and I go over to the McKinneys?"

"Sure. Hi, Dad. Listen, I had a great time with Eric Hawkins last night. He's cool. He should do real well at Northpark."

"I'm glad to hear it. And I'm glad you've found someone to keep Drew honest. Nothing like a little competition . . . we should be back by about seven. Where's Tommy?"

"He's still at the pool with Brent and the younger Hawkins boys. Patti called me at work and dropped them off about three," Janet answered.

As Richard and Janet walked down their own driveway on the way to the McKinneys' home, Janet asked Richard what had happened.

"I'd rather you hear it directly from Bruce, but it's not good. I'm afraid there are criminal violations involved."

"Oh, no. You mean prison?"

"Perhaps."

"Then we'd better pray for them." As they stood outside the McKinneys' front door, before knocking, they quietly said a prayer for the McKinney family and for the Smith family as well.

Diane came to the front door. "Hi. Come on in," she smiled as she opened the door. "Bruce called a little while ago and said he was held up at the club but that you had some things to tell me. Is everything OK?"

"He said that *I* had some things to tell you?" Richard asked. "I thought he was going to meet us here."

"I'm just telling you what he said. He asked us to go ahead and for you to start without him, and he said he'd be here in a little while. Is everything OK?"

Richard felt trapped as they took seats in the living room. Three of the McKinneys' children, all of whom were younger than Tommy, ran through, playing cowboys. Diane instructed the oldest to keep the rest occupied in the den or outside. Then she turned to Richard, obviously expecting him to tell her something important.

Richard looked at Janet, then began. "Diane, I'm sorry. I guess I misunderstood Bruce. I thought he was going to be here to tell you what has happened today, but I'll try to go ahead if that's what he wants. How much do you know about Bruce's business?"

"Almost nothing, Richard. He tends to keep his office work separate from our family, so I'm afraid I don't know very much at all. I wish I did. I've asked, but Bruce has always said I wouldn't understand."

Richard admitted to himself he had held the same attitude until finding out what a great resource his wife could be. So he started gently, explaining the role Bruce's firm was supposed to play in keeping other people's securities safe in escrow. He then went on to describe the financial pressures on Bruce's company, both historic and immediate, and the solution Bruce and David had enlisted to get them through the tight cash periods.

"Unfortunately, what they have been doing is both wrong and illegal. In the next few days many investors will probably lose about $150,000 worth of stocks, which Bruce pledged to the bank to cover their company's loan. And the regulators will probably shut down their firm, if we have not already done that voluntarily in the morning."

"So you're saying Bruce is going to lose his company completely and may also be arrested?"

"At this point, Diane, both of those seem probable, although we'll do everything we can to help him—and David—to minimize the negative consequences."

"Like prison?"

Richard nodded. Janet moved over to sit next to Diane on the sofa and to hold her hand. "And he had you come tell me all this?"

"Apparently. I'm sorry."

Diane turned to Janet and put her free hand on her own forehead, "It's so strange. It's almost like I knew something like this might happen. He never tells me anything, and money just appears. One minute he has none; the next minute everything is OK. What are we going to do?"

Janet, who was as appalled as Diane, was thinking about the McKinneys' four young children, and said, "We have some friends in Charleston who went through something similar a few years ago. I know it won't be easy for you. I'll give you her number, and we should call her together. Do you go to church? Can a pastor help?"

Diane shook her head. Her middle boy came in and complained that the others had ganged up on him. "Mommy's busy right now, dear . . ." Janet could see that Diane was fighting back the tears ". . . please run outside for a little while and play in the yard. OK?"

Just then Bruce's car turned into their driveway, and in a few minutes he came in through the garage. It was immediately obvious to the three of them that he had been drinking heavily.

"So, did you get it all out on the table, able attorney?" Bruce slurred. Diane was clearly embarrassed, and she rose to stand beside him. "Isn't it great, dear? We're going to lose everything . . . and all because of attorneys— they delayed the investment, they killed the loan, they wrote the laws. The rest of us get screwed!"

"Bruce, please. Richard is our friend and neighbor. He's just been trying to help," Diane pleaded.

"Oh, I know how he's been helping! He's been a *big* help."

"Now that you're here, Bruce, I guess you want to talk to Diane alone. I've given her most of the details. Janet and I have to get home to have supper with the kids. Will you be all right, Diane?"

She nodded as the Sullivans stood to leave. "Thank you Richard—and Janet. I'm sorry. He should be OK in the morning. I'll call you if there's a problem. And I guess tomorrow we have to start working through the rest of this."

"Court Shullo is planning to meet you at your office at 8:30 in the morning, Bruce," Richard said.

"Yeah, yeah. I'll be there. Have a great night, Richard."

17

WEDNESDAY, AUGUST 9 ■ The last month of summer had begun, and the Sullivans were packing for their two-week vacation with Janet's parents in Vermont. She and the teenagers would delay their normal departure by one day so they could be accepted as official members at Morningside Church on Sunday morning in a special service.

Amy had spent two weeks with her cousin Catherine, who gave birth to a healthy baby girl on Amy's third night with them. Amy had helped their family tremendously, looking after the two-year-old boy and observing childbirth and its aftermath first hand. After a week in their home, she definitely knew that adoption was right for her; she wanted to have her baby, but she knew that she was not yet ready for the responsibilities of raising a family by herself.

Two days after returning from her cousin's home, Amy flew to Cincinnati to visit with the Tomlinsons. On the telephone she reported to her mother that everything was fine, and she was due home on Saturday afternoon.

Richard's original timetable to work on the "911 Live" situation had been delayed by the McKinney and Smith problems, but he was again following up on the summer interns' research.

Susan was now dividing her free time between Drew and Eric. The Hawkinses were not going to close on their purchase and move into their new home for two more weeks, but the family had packed up in Seattle and were living in an apartment not far from the Sullivans. And the two younger boys almost lived with Tommy; they had all become close friends, including Brent; and Tommy had not even been invited to "do videos" for over a month. Richard and Janet remarked that he seemed like a new person, changed remarkably from just four months earlier.

Kristen continued to attend Morningside Church, as did the Bryants and the Hawkinses. She usually sat by herself, and though she was always friendly, she did not try to push herself on any of the other couples. Richard noticed that he began looking for her when he walked into the sanctuary before each Sunday's service, and he occasionally heard a small voice whispering, "Watch out."

McKinney and Smith had closed its doors the day after the two owners made their admission to Richard. There had been a series of articles in the daily newspaper, relating each day's new revelations of fraud and wrongdoing. Richard noticed that there were soon companion pieces written by a reporter in San Francisco, Peter Dowling, who was apparently following the same debacle with Far West Securities. Richard asked Mary to cut and save all the relevant articles.

The McKinney and Smith families pulled together as best they could under the circumstances. They had changed to unlisted telephone numbers after Diane received a threatening call from an investor who lost his savings because of Bruce's crime. The men's days were filled with motions and filings and pleas and depositions. The two wives dodged reporters outside their homes for the first week until the novelty wore off. And the children received taunts at school. After two weeks, even though Richard's firm was doing its best to keep the costs down, it was apparent that they would have to sell their homes to pay their mounting bills. Diane put in an application to teach that fall, since her certificate was still good for one more year.

It was Wednesday evening, and Richard took Janet out for their traditional pre-vacation dinner together, since they would not see each other for almost two weeks, after Sunday morning, until he flew up to Vermont to join them.

After ordering, Janet said, "I took Diane McKinney to lunch today, to get her out of the house. Susan stayed with her kids. She says their marriage is just kind of on automatic pilot. Bruce comes home after all the legal proceedings, obviously depressed, has a few drinks, and doesn't say much. She says he looks terrible and he won't communicate. She has no other means of support, other than a possible teaching job this fall, and she doesn't know what to do. He only addresses issues on a crisis basis, like the need to sell their home, which they apparently listed for sale yesterday."

"What a mess," Richard said, reaching out for her hand. "And, literally, but for the grace of God and your good sense, there go I . . . we. Has Diane talked to Sally Coker in Charleston?"

"Yes, that first weekend. But the McKinney marriage appears to be different, not as strong. Sally and I have talked, and I think we should invite the Cokers to fly in right after we get back from Vermont. They can stay with us, and maybe over a weekend they can help the McKinneys— and the Smiths. And maybe we can all go to church together. Richard, it's so obvious that Bruce and Diane need God in their lives and in their marriage, especially now. But I don't know how to tell her."

"Try saying just that. I've talked to Bruce a couple of times in the office about what God has done for us, but he bristles. I think we're almost too close to them. I like your idea of inviting the Cokers. Maybe they'll listen to people from hundreds of miles away who have been through something similar . . . But, look, as concerned as we both are about them, I didn't bring you here just to talk about the McKinneys."

Janet smiled. "And why did you bring me here?"

"I feel like we've had a crazy three weeks—a crazy summer, really, starting back with the '911 Live' night and Amy's news—and I just wanted to take a quiet moment before you and the kids leave to tell you how much I love you and how much you mean to me. I've never been as happy as I have been the past months—since I asked Christ into my life—and I know that our marriage is a big part of that happiness. And I just wanted to tell you."

"Thank you, dear," Janet replied, squeezing his hand across the table. "I can't tell you how much you mean to me either. And how much you've changed. And I've changed, thank God. And what about Tommy? He seems so much happier. Glenn Jamison has filled in the few cracks in his self-esteem that you've missed. Even Susan has a stronger inner peace. As you said once, how did we manage to live before God found us?"

"How sweet! You both make me sick!" Nepravel screamed, only six inches from Janet's face. "Isn't He wonderful! Isn't life grand with God! Well," he sneered, turning to Zoldar, who was hovering next to Richard, "let's see how he does one-on-one with the Holloway woman in her apartment. And if she doesn't bring him down, we'll just have to ask Mr. McKinney to get rid of him! You witch! See how your life looks with a husband in disgrace—or dead! Come on, Zoldar. Are the voices planted again in Richard?"

"Yes, and if these believers continue to cut back on their prayers for each other, as has happened over the summer, our voices should build up well over the next few weeks."

"Good. It's almost time to break this 'superstar' and get him out of the way of our plans," Nepravel concluded, as they moved off to load down Bruce and Diane McKinney with more worries and despair.

"There's one other thing, Janet," Richard said. "While you're in Vermont, I'm going to try to schedule a meeting with the network honchos, plus Tom Morgan from The Foundation for the Family, assuming that all of our research is finished and written up. So before you go, you probably should say something to Bill Shaw."

"You mean offer to resign?"

Richard nodded. "You should tell him that I intend to meet with Network, and that my goal is to stop or to change '911 Live.' Under those circumstances, you should give him the option of accepting your resignation."

Janet took a deep breath and exhaled. "I know I sounded brave at Tom Spence's house a few weeks ago. And I'll do it. But I hate to lose my job. I like what I do."

"I know. And you're very good at it. In all the confusion that night at the station, I don't think I told you how proud I was, watching you handle all of those assignments and people. And if you want me to stop this, I will. I can't imagine this show on TV as it's now formatted, but I'll stop working on it if you say so."

"No, Richard, we both know the Lord wants us to fight this. And I also know, deep inside, that He is in charge of everything, from our family to where I work. So, as He tells us, I will trust in Him. And I'll talk to Bill in the morning."

THURSDAY, AUGUST 10 ■ "Hello, Richard. This is Kristen."

Richard swiveled around in his chair and glanced out at the morning sun reflecting off of the other tall buildings in their central downtown district. The wrong mental image of Kristen leapt into his mind, which had not happened for three months. He was surprised, but he let it linger, knowing that it was a mistake, but doing it anyway. Sort of like innocently savoring the memory of an old movie he would never see again, he heard a voice say.

"Hello, Kristen. What can I do for you?"

"I see in the MLS computer that a house that must be right next to you on Devon Drive has gone on the market. It lists the owners as the McKinneys. Isn't he the one involved in that securities mess with the other firm in San Francisco? I may have a family who's interested if the home is in good shape. Can you tell me something about it?"

"Sure, I'd be glad to." And he did.

"I'm glad you've been coming to Morningside Church," he continued, when their discussion about the McKinney house was concluded. A small voice kept telling him to hang up, that he was playing with fire, but a louder voice said he was a strong Christian now, and he should be able to talk to Kristen, particularly about their church, with no problem.

"I'm enjoying it too. There are many nice people there every Sunday, and the service is very moving. The Hawkinses have also enjoyed it. By the way, thank you again for your help on that sale."

"It was our pleasure. If you'll be there, Janet and I, along with about sixty others, will become members of the church at the late service this Sunday."

"I plan to be there. That's great, Richard. Congratulations."

"Thanks. We've really enjoyed the new member classes. They've confirmed again much of what I had heard in the follow-up to the prayer breakfast."

"Isn't it about time for Janet and the kids to leave for vacation? Vermont, isn't it?" Kristen asked.

"Yes, in fact right after the service. They'll be gone for two weeks . . ." Richard felt a tingling in the back of his neck as he continued ". . . and I'll be 'batching' it for ten days."

She laughed. "Well, maybe I'll have you over for dinner, just for old times sake."

She finally crossed a line where he would not follow, not yet. "I don't think that would be such a good idea, Kristen. But thanks . . . Let me know if I can help you with the McKinney house. Unfortunately, they need to sell it."

"OK. Thanks. I'll call you."

"Bill, can I see you for a minute?" Janet asked from his office door.

"Sure. What's up? Are we going to switch the times of the local and national news again?"

She smiled. "No. Not that. We'll leave them alone for at least six months. But I do have something I want to tell you." He motioned to a chair in front of his desk and put down his pen.

"I imagine that Tom and Connie have been in to talk with you about the possibility that they and others might resign their jobs if '911 Live' goes on as planned," she began. He nodded.

"Well, Richard was also really disturbed by what he saw that night here, and he'll probably be calling Network to ask for a meeting in New York to discuss possible legal action . . ." Bill Shaw sat up and stared at Janet ". . . against the show. No one is paying him to do this. He simply believes it's right. And so do I, by the way."

Bill swore. "When will you people ever quit?"

"I'm not sure we've even started yet, actually," Janet replied. "But, anyway, he and I think I should offer to resign, effective immediately, so that you don't have to worry about a potential conflict of interest on my part."

Bill swore again. "Why won't you leave this thing alone? What did we all do with ourselves before Network invented '911 Live'? I mean, are you bored here?"

Janet sat back in her chair and answered in a quiet voice, "No, I like it here. I just think the show is wrong—dead wrong."

"I know. I know. I've heard it all before. Look, aren't you about to go on vacation?"

"Yes, for two weeks, starting Monday."

"Fine. Fine. Take three weeks if you have to. Don't resign. Just go on vacation. Tell Richard to do whatever he's going to do while you're away. And if I have to fire you, I'll call you," he ended with a smile.

"Thanks, Bill. I really want to stay. And so do the others. I hope we can work out something so that's possible."

"So do I. Believe me, so do I. Now go do some honest work for the last day and a half you're here!" And he made a motion towards the door.

She returned his smile. "It would have been terrible if that guy had shot you in the car. You're getting soft in your old age."

After she left, Bill picked up the telephone and called Bob Grissom in New York.

Bob was therefore not surprised on Friday when he read a phone message slip asking him to call Richard Sullivan. *I guess I better find out what's on his mind,* he thought, as he picked up the phone.

Richard reminded Bob of his relationship to the station through Janet and asked if Bob's wounds had all healed. Bob responded in the affirmative and asked about Tom Spence and Officer Higgins.

Once the pleasantries were out of the way, Bob said, "I heard from Bill Shaw that I should expect a call from you about '911 Live.' Something about legal action?"

"Not necessarily," Richard said, hating to start out on the defensive. "I'd just like to meet with you and one of your in-house attorneys to discuss some ideas we have to improve the show, so legal action won't be necessary."

"Look, I don't like being threatened, and particularly by an attorney whose wife works for one of our affiliates."

Richard knew that Bob had to be aware of Janet's offer to resign if Bill had called him. So he ignored that jab.

"You may consider it a threat. We consider it a way to ensure that the show does what you *say* you want—to honor our nation's emergency personnel—with as few problems as possible. I've been to see the Foundation for the Family, and I'd like you to meet with me and their attorney, Tom Morgan."

"Oh, great. You've involved them too. That was a mistake. We don't exactly see eye to eye on a lot of things."

"It's funny. They said exactly the same thing about you at first. But now they want to meet with us. How about sometime next week?"

There was a pause. Richard knew that Bob was not pleased, but that he also could not afford to ignore the offer of a meeting. "I'm on the coast until Wednesday late, and Thursday I'll be catching up. How about Friday morning, a week from today?"

"That's fine with me. I'll check with Tom, and if there's a problem, I'll call. Otherwise, we'll see you Friday morning. Say, eleven?"

"Yeah, fine. I'll grab our attorney and see you then. Goodbye."

SUNDAY, AUGUST 13 ■ Richard and Janet greeted friends, old and new, at the reception in the parish hall following the special service that Sunday for the new members. The Merediths, Bryants, Hawkinses, and several other couples congratulated them in the line for the covered-dish lunch. Even the Shullos made a special trip to share in the joy of the day. Court embraced Richard with a special hug, and both men remembered their hug in Court's office the morning when Richard submitted his life to Christ.

"I can't tell you what that day has meant to our entire family," Richard told both Court and Bob. "And Janet and I have been trying to walk our Christian walk every day, reading and learning more about Him." Richard was telling the truth from the bottom of his heart; but if one listened closely, perhaps due to the accomplishments celebrated on that Sunday, there was also just a hint of pride in what he was saying.

"Congratulations to you both," Kristen said, shaking their hands. "I hope I can take the next new member class and join you in a few months."

"You'll enjoy the class, Kristen," Janet responded. "There's so much to learn about our faith."

"And luckily there are also many good teachers." Kristen smiled at Richard.

"There's a ham in the refrigerator and four boxes of pretzels in the pantry," Janet reminded Richard, as they put the last few things in the minivan that afternoon.

"And we'll look after him as best we can," Nancy Bryant smiled, standing with Tom and Amy in the turnaround. Amy was beginning to show her condition, but she also looked very healthy.

"Did you have a good time with the Tomlinsons?" Richard asked.

"Yes, very much. They're really nice people, with a nice house. And she, at least, really loves God. By the way, Mr. Sullivan, Mr. Tomlinson asked me to tell you that he owes you now on two counts. He said you would know what he meant."

"Well, I didn't do much in either case. But it was nice of him to say so. How are you feeling?"

"Fine." She smiled, "But I guess I'm starting to feel a little bit like I'm pregnant."

"You'll be fine. You look great. We're all praying for you and that baby," Richard smiled back.

Soon everything was loaded, and there were hugs all around between the two families. Richard kissed Janet goodbye. "I love you and I'll see you in ten days. Goodbye kids."

Richard and the Bryants waved as Janet pulled out of the driveway. "Can I interest you in a home-cooked meal tonight, Richard?" Nancy asked.

"Definitely sometime this week, thanks. But tonight I'm going to try to work through the pile on my desk at the office, which I've been ignoring for a couple of weeks," Richard replied.

"Maybe we should invite the McKinneys and all of us get together," Tom suggested. "How about Wednesday night?"

"Sounds great. Nancy, just let me know."

TUESDAY, AUGUST 15 ■ Richard worked late both Sunday and Monday evenings. By Tuesday when he drove up his driveway, he knew he missed his family and the activity his teenage children brought to their life. The house was just so quiet and empty. Of other humans. But Nepravel and Zoldar were spending every free moment they had with Richard, stirring up voices in him, voices that could deceive him even with the Light burning inside him.

He wished now that he had accepted Bob Meredith's invitation to a new couples' Bible study that night, which Bob and Anne were hosting as part of the Morningside outreach. Richard had said he would feel uncomfortable at the first meeting as the only single in a couples group, but he promised that they would attend once Janet returned.

He called Vermont, but his father-in-law said the family had driven into town for some ice cream.

As had already happened several times in the quiet since Sunday, he thought of Kristen. He knew that her apartment was only twenty minutes away. He could go see her. Not to *do* anything with her, just to talk. After all, a voice said, they had been very close, and it might be nice to hear about what she had been doing. Of course they couldn't go out together, so he would have to see her in her apartment . . .

The mental image of Kristen together with him painted itself clearly on his mind, and he realized what was happening. He slid out of his armchair and knelt there in his den, praying for God's protection against temptation. And protection for his family.

"Blast. He's praying again!" Nepravel spat. "The voices have almost stopped turning."

"Well, we'll wait until he finishes, and then we'll start them again," Zoldar responded from his lookout position. "We have too much invested in him to quit now. Even if we have to let everyone else in the neighborhood get saved this week, we've got to stick with Richard's destruction!"

As soon as he finished praying, Nepravel went right back to work, and within an hour Richard was feeling restless again. By now it was late, and he called Vermont and had a long conversation with Janet, catching up on their trip and on their first full day's activities.

WEDNESDAY, AUGUST 16 ■ On Wednesday morning Richard and his two interns had a conference call with Tom Morgan at the foundation, in final preparation for their meeting with Network in New York on Friday. The attorneys agreed to meet at the airport and to drive into the city together, to discuss any last-minute considerations.

A little before noon, Richard's phone rang. "Hi. It's Kristen. How are you enjoying being single?"

"Hi, Kristen. I'm actually kind of lonely. It's not very glamorous at all. I miss my family."

"Welcome to the club," she said with enough levity to avoid being offensive. "Isn't single life great? Listen, why don't we get together and have dinner? Nothing romantic, I just mean to talk. For old times' sake. And besides, your church has made me think about some things, and I'd like to talk with you about them."

He didn't say no. "Tonight I'm going next door to the Bryants for an early dinner with the McKinneys. By the way, how is their house looking?"

"I'm afraid it's a bit overpriced, but I have two families who may be interested, if Mr. McKinney will get realistic on his price."

"Anyway, I have to get up early Friday to fly to New York, so I don't want to do anything Thursday night. But maybe Friday or Saturday. Do you think we could behave ourselves if I said yes?" He asked the question in jest, but one small voice was trying to break through all the others and ask it in earnest.

"If we have to," she said with just enough seduction in her voice to make it interesting.

"Kristen, if we get together, which I'm still not committing to, we would definitely have to behave ourselves. I love Janet very much and don't want to do anything to hurt her."

"Neither do I. We'll just have dinner and talk. Which night?"

"I've still got to think about it. It may be really dumb for us to get together, even though I'm sure nothing will happen. I tell you what. I don't know exactly how long I may be in New York. I'll call you from there, or from the airport, when I know what's happening."

"OK, Richard. Let's do get together. I really want to see you."

Nancy Bryant made a delicious curry, and Amy volunteered to stay with the McKinney children so that the five adults could get together for dinner. Everyone steered clear of discussing Bruce's problem, though he brought it up several times himself.

"You should see the home buyers circling like sharks who smell blood! They know we've got to sell because of this mess, and they're circling in for the kill. They want us to give the house away! We've lived here fifteen years! No way."

Diane warned Tom and Richard when she first found them alone in the den that Bruce had already had two drinks before leaving home. And Diane also shared with them her worry because Bruce no longer went anywhere or did anything. He was too embarrassed to go to their club, where many of his former investors spent their time. Other than their boat, which was also for sale, and an occasional jog, he had never been interested in outdoor activities. Stocks and bonds had been his life. And the McKinneys were not members of a church. So Diane despaired that Bruce was becoming a recluse, on top of their other problems. "Please, if you can think of anything to do or can include him in anything, please help him," she quietly pleaded.

The opportunity came that night, although in an unusual way. As they were finishing their coffee and were talking about the upcoming elections, it was still early. Bruce changed the subject of their conversation to the "good old days" in their neighborhood, when the husbands were younger and did more things together.

"Remember after that 5K race on Labor Day—when was that? Five years ago?—when we all went down to the Platinum Club together? Was that a ball? How many of us were there? Twelve, maybe . . . Say I haven't been back there since. I hear they've changed it all around. What say we go down there tonight, guys? We haven't had a boys' night out in years. What do you say?"

"I don't know, Bruce," Tom began. But behind Bruce, Diane was nodding her encouraging approval, which everyone saw except her husband.

Nancy, who under normal circumstances would not be pleased about Tom going to such a place, understood Diane's wish for her husband to have some diversion, and said, "Sure, why not, Tom? It would be fun for you three to spend some time together. And at least we'll know where you are." She smiled.

"Go ahead, honey. Have some fun," Diane said to Bruce.

"What about you, Richard? Do we need to call Janet?" Bruce asked. "Remember, it's just like the shopping these girls do: It's all right to look all you want, but you can't touch the merchandise or take it home!" he laughed.

Without planning on it or really thinking about it, Richard found himself joining hundreds of other men—mostly conventioneers, he imagined—at the Platinum Club. The three men stood at the bar, waiting for a table, while a hundred or more completely nude young women danced on the stage, on two runways, and on individual tables.

Bruce was ecstatic, pointing out the particular attributes of this woman or that. Within a few minutes they were shown to a table, and soon Bruce had arranged for a beautiful, natural blonde young lady to dance directly above them on their table.

Richard was confused. He knew he should not be there. This was not what God had in mind, either for these women or for these men. Two or three times a voice tried to ask him how he would feel if his daughter Susan were dancing here for extra money in a couple of years; but that voice was blown away by the visual images. He wanted to leave, but Diane had virtually begged them to take Bruce. He felt trapped and smiled a "What-are-we-doing-here?" smile at Tom, who shrugged and yelled over the roar of the dance beat, "Just relax and enjoy it. I guess it won't hurt us!"

So Richard sat and watched. And watched. At least three of the young women near them reminded him of Kristen. And the deceptive voices, which had been building slowly inside him, started spinning faster and stronger. The Platinum Club was one of Nepravel's favorite places. As they sat next to Richard, Nepravel told Zoldar that it was their local "banana peel," because so many men unsuspectingly slipped up there and wound up doing things they had never intended to do. Zoldar chuckled as Nepravel fed pure Passion into the deceptive mixture of Rationalization and Invincibility, already playing full tilt in Richard.

By the time Richard made it home, after too many drinks, too much noise, and too many visual images, he was primed, if not cocked, for the bigger event which Nepravel had in mind.

FRIDAY, AUGUST 18 ■ Friday morning Richard and Tom Morgan met in the Executive Club at LaGuardia Airport and took a cab into the city. "We've done our research, and I've got our list of names if we get that far," Tom told Richard, as they threaded along that hour's best route to Manhattan.

"I've never prayed in a taxi before," Richard said, "but why don't we start?" And he and Tom each lifted up a prayer for their meeting with the network that morning, asking for the Holy Spirit to prepare the hearts and the minds of those with whom they would be meeting and to guide and protect them throughout the process.

"Good morning, gentlemen." Bob Grissom offered his hand as Richard and Tom were shown into his large corner office on the fifty-fifth floor of Network's headquarters building. "Please, have a seat at the table by the window. The others should be here in just a minute. Can we get you some coffee?"

The three of them confined themselves to pleasantries and to updates on those who had been wounded during the test run until Mark Pugh and a woman with a legal pad joined them in Bob's office. He made the introductions. "This is Mark Pugh, the executive director of '911 Live,' and Sheila Alston, one of our most able attorneys. Mark, Sheila, please meet Richard Sullivan and Tom Morgan."

There followed another five minutes of general discussion about the network and its prospects for the fall season, which led Bob to the case at hand.

"And of course we're planning for '911 Live' to be our flagship for Friday night. The new technology we're debuting will be so powerful that we're going to open '911 Live' two weeks before the rest of the fall line-up, to create an audience early, to anchor that night. And that's really just a month from now."

"All the equipment is ready to ship to the ten cities we've chosen," Mark added, "and we should begin on-site testing in each city within two weeks, to check for any problems or coverage dead spots."

"That is, of course, if you'll allow us to put the show on." Bob smiled, launching the first volley of the meeting.

Richard returned his smile and nodded. "If it were up to us, the show would be canceled. We think it's one of the worst things imaginable for television, certainly as it's now formatted. So we've at least established that you think it's the best and we think it's the worst. Luckily for you, the decision is not up to us, and we know it. So we can't allow it, or cancel it. But hopefully you will listen to our opinions and maybe even agree with us that what we're here to propose actually has some advantages for Network."

"You've got the floor, counsellor. Please continue," Bob said, as Mark and Sheila sat stonefaced, their arms folded.

"We've taken at face value what Bill Shaw has been saying, supported by the promotional material Janet has received from the Network PR staff, that the point of '911 Live' is to honor emergency response personnel in America, by showing them in as realistic a setting as possible. We assume that it is not the purpose of the show to honor violence or to create opportunities for death or destruction. Are we right?"

The three network people looked at each other. Mark shrugged non-committally. Sheila said, "I really have no idea. That's not my area."

Bob finally spoke. "I would say you're very close."

"Good," Richard continued, "because I took those words from your own promotional letter of June 18. So we all agree on the goal or the purpose of the show. Now we're deeply concerned about the probability of unexpected and uncontrolled violence, crime, and even murder, right on our families' television screens."

Mark started to speak, "But it's . . ."

". . . what's really happening." Richard finished his sentence. "We know. But unless the goal is to show violence for violence's sake, which you say it is not, then you can still show 'what's really happening'; only you can be a little selective about it."

"What do you mean?" Bob asked.

"We have a couple of suggestions to make, both of which we believe can actually make the show better, if violence is not the primary goal. First, we ask you to extend the broadcast delay from thirty seconds to ten minutes. That will accomplish several things. It will of course let actual violence be edited, masked, deleted, or simply not shown. It will also allow you more time to see how a particular segment develops before airing it, not just from the point of view of cutting out any staged acts, which should be much more obvious after ten minutes, but also to tighten up the presentations and to show the most interesting stories possible.

"We checked with the regulators, and we tentatively believe that you can still use the name 'Live,' even with the delay, if you run a short notification at the beginning of the show. We believe the result will be a show that even better portrays our emergency personnel at work, without the worst problems that we now foresee."

The network personnel had shared some glances while Richard spoke, but had said nothing. "Is there more?" Bob asked.

"Yes. No offense, Mark, but we don't think the broadcast/no broadcast decision on a particular segment should be left up to any one person. Rather, we propose a three-person editorial panel, which will work with the director, live, during each show, to decide whether some feed is just too violent or too objectionable to be shown, or whether it could be shown with masking.

"The members of this panel will all be paid for each show. They will receive training from each of the three groups whom they represent so that their diversity has a chance to gel into unity. Three pools of panel members will be appointed by Network, by the Emergency Personnel Association of America, and by the Foundation for the Family. During the four-month trial period we propose, all three members must agree on any segment, or it can't be shown. It's our hope that after a few weeks they will come to share a sense of what works for everyone so that the mechanics will smooth out."

"So you want the Foundation for the Family to censor our show?" Sheila asked in a calm but displeased tone.

"No," Tom Morgan interjected. "We want the foundation plus the other two representatives to help you decide what to show. And this is obviously all voluntary. We propose a four-month trial; but you could stop any time, because there won't be a contract or an agreement."

"Does the foundation want credit on the show for this input?" Sheila asked.

"No, just the opposite. That's the last part of what we have to propose," Richard continued. "Right now the Foundation for the Family and most of the networks do not agree on what is appropriate for television. I have convinced Dr. Morris, the founder of the foundation, that this arrangement could create an opportunity for the foundation and your network to share ideas and value concepts in a real working environment. Who knows where that might lead? You might actually find that you can help each other in many ways, once you start working together.

"He has agreed and is ready to meet you in this halfway position for the trial period. But he recommends that neither you nor the foundation publicize your working together during this sensitive period. If you both benefit and like what's happening, you can continue it and go public after four months. If it doesn't work, then neither of you has lost much, except a little time and money."

"So who would the foundation's editorial panel members be? Would they all be ministers? Do they live anywhere near New York?" Bob asked.

Tom opened his briefcase and withdrew two typed pages of names and addresses and passed them across the table to Bob. "Here is a list of people we recommend. As you will see, most are business people. Some have backgrounds in broadcasting. Only two are ordained ministers. All of them live in the New York metropolitan area. And none of them works for the foundation."

Looking down the list, Bob was impressed. He recognized several of the names. "You've done your homework," he said, passing the list to Mark and Sheila.

"We know that for you to agree with us, we can't just threaten, we have to bring value to the table," Richard said. "All of those people can help enhance your show, and/or Network, as well as help accomplish our goal of limiting the crime and violence on television in our homes. There's a remote possibility that this situation could turn from confrontation to win/win, to use the current buzzwords," Richard finished with a smile.

"And just so we know, Mr. Sullivan," Sheila asked, "what is the threat part of your message today?"

"Fifty nearly identical but locally tailored obscenity lawsuits in fifty cities. And a suit seeking a federal injunction with the FCC. All of these are in the late drafting stages and can be filed in a few days. And a license battle next year when you seek renewal," Richard replied.

"I see. So you *are* serious."

Both Richard and Tom nodded.

"If we agreed to this, how soon could these people be ready to join us for training?" Mark asked.

"We still haven't contacted all of them. And you will probably want to narrow down to a working pool of seven to ten so that a manageable group will be available every Friday. But the ones to whom we have already spoken are ready to begin. Many are recently retired and are frankly looking for something to do. And the Emergency Personnel Association has a large chapter here. The senior staff is ready to join us."

"Well, whatever else," Bob said, "let me thank you for putting together a proposal that is at least balanced. The three of us don't make decisions like this by ourselves, but our voices obviously carry a lot of weight. Do you have a written summary of your proposal?"

Tom handed Bob a letter from Dr. Morris, with an attachment containing the points they had discussed.

"Thank you. This may seem a little odd, but why don't you let us talk here. You can go next door and make calls or watch any of eighty channels, and we'll see if we have any additional questions before you leave."

Richard and Tom agreed and each man found a phone in the vacant conference room across the hall. Twenty minutes later Bob came across and asked them to return to his office, which they did.

Sitting down again, Bob said, "As strange as this may sound, we basically like your ideas. In fact, we think maybe the broadcast delay should be twelve to fifteen minutes, but we'll think more about it. We've got to check with a larger group here, but I think we may all be able to work together, pretty much as you have proposed."

"That's great," Richard beamed, looking around the room and saving an extra smile for Tom. Even Mark was smiling, as best he could. Richard continued, "We want to keep it as low key and as 'unlegal' as possible. Bob, the foundation has talented broadcast people, as you know. Dr. Morris can assign two or three of them to a team, and they will fly here for a week or ten days to help get the initial process rolling with you, once you say 'go.' How does that sound?"

"Fine. We'll touch bases here on our end, and I should be able to call you no later than Monday afternoon. Thanks a lot."

Rising and shaking hands, Richard said, "Thank you . . . and now Tom and I can catch earlier flights, before the weekend rush."

Back in the Executive Club at the airport, where the staff was reworking their tickets, Richard asked Tom the question that had been on their minds since the meeting: "Can you believe that they accepted our offer? Just like that? God is so incredible! I figured we would be battling until late in the afternoon and maybe filing lawsuits on Monday. It just shows you that nothing is impossible if God is involved."

"I know, Richard. It was great. And you were wonderful with your presentation. You never became argumentative, but you spoke with conviction. A great job!" Tom complimented his new friend.

"Thanks, Tom. You did very well too. And thanks to whoever put together that list of names."

"Dr. Morris did it himself. He handpicked each person."

"Well, I hope they officially accept. And then I hope it works—for many reasons. Not the least of which is my wife's job!"

Tom's flight was called, and the two attorneys shook hands and promised to talk on Monday. Then Richard went to a phone and called

Vermont. Janet was in her parents' home, having a late lunch. "You won't believe it, dear, but I think they're going to accept our proposal."

"Oh, Richard, that's great! I bet you did a super job. You're so close there in New York—why don't you run up?" she laughed.

"Too much to do, but I'll be there next week. They're calling my plane. I'll call you again tonight or tomorrow. But let's quickly pray." And for the second time in his life, Richard prayed on the telephone, thanking God for His blessings.

Kristen wasn't sure herself exactly what she wanted to happen, but she knew she wanted to see Richard. She still missed the time they had spent together, and she at least wanted to spend a few hours talking with him.

When she called his office that Friday afternoon, the receptionist said that Richard was still out of town, but offered her the option of leaving a message for him on their new voice mail system. She accepted. After the taped introduction, she said, "Richard, this is me. If you get back in time today, let's get together tonight. I want to talk about us."

Flying back by himself on the plane, Richard was very happy. Although he knew that there was not yet a final agreement to work together, he believed that Bob Grissom understood the advantages of doing so and would follow through positively.

Richard again said a prayer of thanks to God for His action. In Richard's mind, the results from their meeting had truly been a miracle, better than he ever could have imagined. He knew that God had prepared the way and been present with them.

But Richard also had to admit that his years of training and preparation had served him well for doing the Lord's work. He recognized that he had put together a pretty strong combination of carrot and stick to get Network's attention. And his negotiating skills had come in handy. As a new Christian, Richard was thrilled that he had apparently won the first battle God had given him. He hoped there would be more! He was ready to help God whenever God needed his help! And, not realizing it, with his excitement and understandable thoughts about his own important role, Richard was cocking the hammer of his sexual ego, which had been so well primed at the Platinum Club only two nights before.

Nepravel arrived at the office before Richard did, late that afternoon. He had one piece of quick business to do. Although it only took an instant, his action was the first time in many years that he had been authorized to physically change something outside of a human body. He stopped by the firm's voice mail computer and changed one word on Kristen's message to Richard.

Even though he was driving from the airport against the traffic, Richard did not make it back to his office until almost 5:30. He decided on the way in, despite his excitement, that it would be best if he didn't go over to

Kristen's apartment. It just wouldn't be right. From his carphone he called Bob Meredith's home, but his call was answered by a tape machine. He left a message, asking whether Bob and Anne would like to join him on short notice for dinner. Then he called Tom Spence and gave him a report on their meeting in New York. Tom was obviously pleased, and Richard promised to give him a full report as soon as he heard again from Bob Grissom. He arrived at his office before he had time to call Kristen.

Mary had waited for him and handed him a stack of messages. She reminded him that there were also some messages on their new voice mail system. He briefly told her about their meeting and then sent her home to her family.

Standing beside his desk, flipping through his messages, he touched the buttons on his phone to activate the voice mail playback. After five messages on legal cases, he heard, "Richard, this is me. If you get back in time today, let's get together tonight. I want to talk about God."

He played Kristen's message back again. He felt a rush. Kristen was reaching out, and he was the right person to lead her to the Lord. Given their earlier relationship and the important work which God already had him doing, there was no question that he was meant to help her find salvation.

He called her apartment but again hit a tape machine. "Hi, Kristen. I got your message, and I'll be over. Probably about 7:30. See you then."

One more call. He hoped that the Merediths would be home. But no luck. Yet another taped answer. So he left a second message on their machine: "Since I called you earlier, Kristen has called and said she wants to talk about God. Isn't that great? So I'm going over there tonight and won't be able to get together with you. I need some suggestions, by the way, on books or literature to give to people who are interested in the Lord, like Kristen. Call me at home if you get in this afternoon, or I'll see you at church on Sunday. Have a great weekend."

It never failed to amaze Richard how the world had functioned only a few years before without tape machines, voice mail, and fax machines. Well, he had left enough messages for one day; it had been a very good day, and the rest could wait. He went home to shower and to change before driving over to Kristen's apartment.

Kristen arrived home from an appointment and was very pleased to find Richard's message on her machine. She immediately started her bath water, and she put two bottles of wine in the refrigerator. Before leaving the kitchen she put two steaks in the microwave to defrost and two potatoes in the oven.

Unseen by her, a stormcloud of darkness was descending on her apartment. Besides Torgo, Zoldar had already arrived. Nepravel was with Richard, making certain that Richard heard how important he was and regularly flashing visual images from the Platinum Club and from his past experiences with Kristen, just to set the stage in his mind. And while

Richard shaved and splashed on his best aftershave, he told himself, "I have a chance to save Kristen tonight!"

Right at 7:30, Bart, the doorman, rang up on the intercom that Mr. Sullivan was on the way up. Kristen made a last pass at her hair in the mirror and smiled. She switched off the ringer on her telephone so that the machine in her bedroom would answer without disturbing them. She was very happy. The doorbell rang, and she opened the door. Zoldar and Torgo were ready on her side of the door, Nepravel on the other.

Richard was struck immediately by how good Kristen looked, in her low-cut dark green dress which accentuated her auburn hair and her . . . freckles. Oh, all those freckles! How Richard suddenly remembered all those wonderful freckles, in an explosive visual image from six months earlier. He smiled and stared. She did the same. "Come in," she finally laughed, breaking the electricity of the moment. He felt his mind starting to grow fuzzy, even before he spoke a single word. "What's happening?" a tiny voice was able to ask, before it was completely drowned out by a flood of rationalizations.

"Hi," he managed to say, as he walked in. "How are you?"

"I'm fine. It was a rough day, but I might have sold one home this afternoon. How about you? Did your meeting go well? Would you like some wine?"

"Uh, yeah, sure, that would be fine. And today went great." As Kristen walked to the kitchen, he followed behind her, smelling her perfume. "The meeting we had in New York went incredibly well." And Richard began describing to Kristen the history of "911 Live" as they moved back into her living room and sat on the sofa with their wine glasses. He then moved on to share the intimate details of the meeting, which he had not yet done with Janet, telling Kristen how God had definitely intervened for them that day. As he retold the story, his natural joy spilled over into his ego: They had done great work for the Lord that day!

Kristen listened attentively for almost twenty minutes, sipping her wine, her feet tucked up under her, sitting only a few inches from Richard. She smiled at the appropriate times and let him know how impressed she was as his story unfolded.

While Richard was talking, he sipped his wine, but he drank deeply from Kristen's whole presence, her knees almost touching him, her smile so close, her breasts . . . He had all night, a voice told him. Janet was far away. He shook the voices off.

"But that's enough about me and my day," he smiled. "I got your message that you want us to talk about God."

"You did? I'm happy to talk about God, but that's not the message I left on your voice mail. I said that I wanted to talk about us."

"Oh," Richard said, not imagining that they were both right. He was at a loss for words since that was the reason he had come.

"Your new voice mail must not be real clear," Kristen offered, leaning forward and taking his glass, then walking to the kitchen to refill it. "I've thawed two steaks," she said as she poured the wine. "We can start them anytime."

As she sat down again on the sofa, even closer, crossing her legs, she noticed that Richard had a faraway look, like his eyes were glazed over. "Are you OK?" she smiled.

"Me? Oh, yeah, fine." But he had been listening to a voice which reminded him that they were not exactly virgins together. If he slept with her tonight, it wouldn't be that big a deal, because they had already done it so many times before. It was just sort of a repeat. And Janet had said she didn't want to know. And she was so far away . . . And Kristen looked so good . . .

They talked for another twenty minutes, sitting next to each other. Richard watched the rise and fall of her chest with each breath she took. She laughed once and brushed her hair back with her hand. Richard didn't say much, but he eventually heard a low roar in his ears, and he felt even more lightheaded.

Kristen had been talking about them, and she came to her conclusion. "What should I do, Richard? Should I pine away until I'm old and gray," she smiled, "hoping that someday you'll be mine? Should I move out of town? Should I join a convent? What do you recommend for someone who still loves you so much?"

The voices and the images were screaming inside Richard. If he had been rational, he would have said that he loved his wife very much, that he did not want to commit adultery, that he would never imagine to hurt her or to sin against God . . . but it was almost impossible for him to be rational. This was not a thought-out affair, like earlier. This was just plain passion, simple lust. He was alone with a beautiful woman whom he had already slept with, she still wanted him, his wife was far away, and this day he had already proved himself to be invincible. It was a loaded gun, primed and cocked. And now the demons were adding the images and the voices to trigger the explosion.

"Go ahead. No one will ever know. Look at her. Remember how good she is? Go ahead. It's no big deal. You've already done it with her . . ."

To answer her question, Richard put his glass down on the coffee table, in slow motion, as if he were watching himself do it, then leaned across and took her in his arms, and without saying a word, he kissed her. She kissed him back, opening her mouth and putting her arms around his neck. She murmured and leaned back, bringing him with her. Richard could feel the electric reaction in both of them as he lay on top of her. He moved to kiss her neck.

"Ms. Holloway," the doorman called over the intercom, "is it OK if some folks named Meredith come up?"

Richard flinched, as if he were physically pulled back by the scruff of his neck. His heart raced. It was as if scales were suddenly taken from his eyes and he could see. Although the three demons in the room, bent on his destruction, were, of course, not visible to him, he instantly and for the first time in his life felt their presence, as if they were lying on his back, which Nepravel was. He jumped again and felt an icy chill.

"What is that?" Kristen asked out loud, but the doorman could not hear her.

"Ms. Holloway, is it all right if the Merediths come up?"

Richard moved off Kristen and sat with his head in his hands, shaking. "Yes, Kristen. Please tell him it's OK."

"Who are they?"

"Friends of mine," he said in a barely audible whisper, as the reality of what had just happened and what had almost happened started to sink into Richard's heart and into his mind.

"*Friends of yours?* You invited friends of yours to come with you tonight?"

"No. I didn't. But thank God, and I mean that more than you'll ever know, they're here. Please tell him to let them in."

Obviously angry, Kristen got up and walked over to the intercom. "It's all right, Bart. Send them up," she said.

Richard stood up, feeling weak, drained. He tried to look at Kristen, but then diverted his eyes. He took out his handkerchief and wiped her lipstick and make-up from his face. Feeling like a fool, he stuffed it back in his pocket.

Kristen retreated to her bedroom, and the doorbell rang. Richard walked over and opened it. Bob and Anne were standing outside, Bibles in hand. Before they could say anything, Richard stepped out and hugged Anne, his eyes closed, tears forming. Then he hugged Bob. He felt so weak that he was afraid he might fall. They sensed his frailty and helped him walk back into Kristen's apartment, closing the door behind them.

Bob more or less deposited Richard in the large chair by the coffee table, and Richard sat shaking his head, his heart pounding, tears rolling down his cheeks, unable to say anything yet, except "Thank you," which he whispered to his friends several times.

The bedroom door opened and Kristen came out, her make-up fresh. She stood at the entrance to the living room, expecting Richard to introduce them.

"Hi, Kristen. I'm Bob Meredith. This is my wife, Anne. We've heard a lot about you and seen you, I think, at church. We heard that you're interested in learning more about God, so we thought we'd come see if we could help."

"Yes, well, I'm glad to meet you. But I think there was a misunderstanding tonight. I guess I'm interested in learning more about God, someday, but I never meant tonight. Somehow the message got mixed up. Would you like some wine?"

"I'm sorry if we came at the wrong time. Richard, are you OK?" Bob asked, as Richard wiped his eyes.

"Yes, I'm fine," Richard said, starting to regain his strength and looking up at them. "And, believe me, you came at *exactly* the right time." He managed a smile. "Kristen, I don't know what was going on, but we almost made a *big* mistake."

Kristen shrugged her shoulders and looked uninterested. There was a long silence while everyone thought about what Richard had said. Then Anne smiled and turned to Kristen. "Do you have any tea? Or a soft drink?"

"Sure," Kristen said, "I'll put some water on." And she walked into the kitchen, followed by Anne.

"Bob, you can't imagine how happy I am to see you both," Richard smiled again. "I was within a few minutes of doing something I would have regretted for longer than I care to think about. What a fool I've been tonight. I can't imagine what happened to me."

"Richard, what happened to you is that you came here. The result was pretty predictable after that. None of us can withstand Satan on our own—try to do it yourself, and you'll fail every time. This Book tells us to flee, which wasn't exactly your move tonight," he smiled. "And if you can't flee, then pray for God's help, because the forces of darkness are too much for us humans. We need God's help, or we'll fail."

"That's crystal clear now, Bob. But sixty minutes ago I thought I was in complete control, able to do anything on my own, a real soldier for God. And look how close I came to being finished!"

"You're right. How long have you been a believer now? A little over three months? And from what I've seen and heard you *have* been a soldier for God. You've changed and already affected others. You're a husband, a father, and a business leader. Don't you think Satan would love to bring you down? To dishonor you, and therefore God, whom you profess, in your own eyes and in the eyes of your family and friends? You're a perfect target. You've felt God enough to be effective, but you haven't learned enough to know when you're getting outside His protection. It can happen because you stop reading the Word, or forget to pray; or maybe pride makes you forget the true source of your strength—anyway, once you move outside His will, anything can happen. The wisest Christian knows when to turn tail and to run as fast as he can from temptation, because he can't beat it on his own."

"I may be a slow learner, but tonight I got the message, believe me! Bob, when you came, I actually think I felt the presence of evil spirits. Is that possible, or am I crazy?"

"It's probable. Maybe we should get the ladies back in here and pray."

While Richard and Bob were talking, Anne was speaking with Kristen in the kitchen, as she ran water in the teapot. "Please don't be upset, either with Richard or with us. We've known about your relationship since right after Richard surrendered his life to Christ. Our intent is not to judge either of you, but to help both of you."

Kristen frowned but said nothing.

"It's a long story, but before I met Bob, or knew the Lord, I had an affair with a married man. At first I didn't know he was married, but even after I found out, I let him talk me into continuing for over a month before I broke it off. Three months later he left his wife and child for another, even younger woman, and I've lived with my part in that tragedy for many years. So I know some of what you're feeling, in every sense.

"And I have one simple message for you, Kristen," Anne smiled. "God loves you more than any man can or ever will. First find a relationship with Him, and then the right man to be your husband will probably come along, if it's His will. But whatever else happens on earth, you'll know the greatest love in the universe."

Kristen finally spoke. "OK. Thanks, Anne. As you can imagine, I'm a little mixed up right now and don't know how to handle your being here. I didn't really mean for anything to happen tonight with Richard, but I did ask him to come here, and I . . . I . . . just don't know what to do. I'm embarrassed. I'm hurt . . . There's a man in California I've been seeing. Maybe he's the one. I just don't know . . ."

"You've had enough for one night, dear," Anne smiled, as the water began to boil, "but please remember what I said about God's love. Find Him first, which we'll be glad to help you do, if you want our help, and the rest should come along, in His time."

Anne and Kristen rejoined the men, and Bob told them that they needed to pray together. Somewhat self-consciously, Kristen joined them on her knees in the living room, and Bob began by thanking God for His mercy and His presence in their lives that night. Anne thanked Him and asked for His angels' protection for Richard and Kristen. Nepravel and the other two demons had been circling around them all this time. They were screaming insults and snapping their sharp teeth at the Merediths, angry over their intrusion. At Anne's mention of angels, the demons looked at each other and decided to leave. Instantly Kristen felt the first positive moment of healing in her relationship with Richard, as they continued to pray together.

Richard prayed a long prayer of thanks for their protection that night and for God answering his prayers, even though he had violated God's will. He fervently asked for forgiveness and for guidance in the future for him and for Kristen. And finally he prayed for Janet and his family, that he would again be the husband and father they needed.

Hearing Richard pray to God for her and for his family added to the healing process that had just begun inside Kristen. She understood for the first time the depth of his love for his wife, and she recognized as well his genuine concern for her. When Richard finished, Kristen found the strength to pray out loud for the first time since she was a little girl, asking God for His forgiveness and for His help in fighting temptation in the future. She felt awkward at first, but soon her heart was pouring out her grief, as she went on to ask for God's guidance in her life. The other three souls kneeling there with her shared the sincerity of her pain. As she finished unburdening her soul, her voice cracked, and tears flowed down her cheeks.

Bob closed their prayers, and they stood up. Anne hugged Kristen. Then they went into the kitchen and fixed four new cups of tea. The four of them talked together for almost an hour, mostly about what had just happened, but sometimes simply talking about whatever came up, from their new mission church to the first inklings of a pennant race that year.

Finally Richard announced that he was very tired after fighting two battles in one day and that they should call it a night.

"Kristen, I'm so glad I'm leaving with the Merediths." He smiled, his hand holding hers, "We dodged a bullet, tonight, barely. But we dodged it, only by the grace of God. As I hope you know, I wish you the best and can't wait to see you in church. But let's don't ever get together like this again! Like I said that day when we broke up, God has better plans for both of us. Let's see what those are. But they don't include us being together. It's that simple. I really love Janet, and I want to be with her. And I thank God again that nothing more happened tonight."

Kristen tried her best to smile back. "OK, Richard. I promise. No more invitations. And I *do* want to know more about God."

Anne said, "Call me, please, Kristen. I would love to have lunch with you and tell you about what God has done for us. And there's a businesswomen's breakfast group at our church which meets every week; I think you'll really like them."

"Thank you, Anne. And thank you, too, Bob. You're an unusual pair of party crashers!"

As the three of them exited the elevator into the garage at Kristen's apartment, Richard said, "I can't thank you enough for coming. What led you to drive over here?"

Bob answered, "You should thank Anne. When we arrived home and heard your two messages, I didn't think that much about them, but Anne wouldn't let go. She called your home and Kristen's, and only heard answering machines. She told me you shouldn't be left by yourself and that even if she had to come here on her own, she was going to check on you. So of course I had to drive her!"

"I just felt that something wasn't right. Richard, don't ever put yourself in a position like that again. I know men, and I know how God made you, though I've never known why. That's one of the first things I'm going to ask Him when I get to heaven!"

Richard smiled and hugged her again. "Well, I'm sure glad that God made *you*! What a day! Thank you and God bless you."

"One last piece of advice," Anne offered.

"You can give me all the advice you want," Richard said.

"Go be with your wife."

As he drove home, Richard thought about all that had happened from the time he had caught his plane that morning. He prayed aloud in the car, asking for God's forgiveness, protection, and blessing on him and on his family.

The house was dark when he arrived home, and empty. He turned on the lights and made a phone call. Then he went up to the attic and got out his suitcase and his suitbag. Thirty minutes later he made another call.

"Janet? Hi. I know it's a little late, but I've got some news."

"Hi. Is everything all right?"

"Oh, yes. Everything is just fine. Just fine. But I'm coming up there tomorrow morning. There's an early flight with connections; it'll get me there at 12:30. Can you meet the plane?"

"Are you sure you're all right? Are you staying for the whole week?"

Smiling, thinking about Janet and his children, he assured her, "Yes, I'm fine. Everything is fine, thank God. And, yes, I'm coming for the whole week. I can't wait to hold you."

Nepravel didn't want to attend their meeting that night, but he knew that absence was grounds for immediate and permanent banishment to hell. Not that it made much difference; he imagined he was headed there, anyway.

He and the other two demons had been completely surprised by the Merediths' arrival at Kristen's apartment. They had orchestrated Richard and Kristen to do exactly what Alhandra had planned, but then those cursed people with their Bibles had shown up!

"You'd better report," Nepravel said to Zoldar as they flew up to the meeting, trailing black sulfur behind them. "You're at least one of Alhandra's lieutenants."

"But it's your neighborhood and it was your assignment," Zoldar countered.

"He gave it to both of us."

"But you're responsible."

The two demons fought like that until the meeting started, and when their turn came, Zoldar actually shoved Nepravel forward. Nepravel slowly explained all that they did, exactly according to the plan, and how well it worked, as Lord Alhandra had foreseen, when, totally unexpectedly, the Merediths appeared and ruined everything.

Tymor followed the report, expecting to hear about Richard's fall. He could not believe it when he heard Nepravel's conclusion.

"So I'm supposed to tell Lord Alhandra that you've failed, that his plan did not work?!?" Tymor screamed.

"I . . . we . . . his plan *did* work. Tell him that," Nepravel was emboldened to say, in what he assumed were his last seconds on earth. "But God must have answered his prayers for protection. I don't know. But how else could the Merediths have been led there?"

Tymor calmed down just a bit, since Nepravel had given him the possibility of an out with Alhandra. But he was still very angry. "I will report your failure to Lord Alhandra. He may have other plans for you.

In the meantime, keep working on McKinney, and try not to screw *that* up!"

Nepravel bowed and moved back in among the others, shoving Zoldar as he did so.

18

THURSDAY, SEPTEMBER 14 ■ Richard spent a wonderful week with his family in Vermont—hiking, swimming, eating ice cream, and relaxing. Janet could never remember being hugged the way Richard took her in his arms at the airport and held her for so long. She didn't know whether it was the absence or his New York trip, but something made Richard even more interested and seemingly in love with her than he had been for the past several wonderful months. She could not explain it, but her whole being returned his joy, measure for measure; and their love grew broader and deeper.

On the next Monday afternoon Bob Grissom called his office, and Richard returned the call from the porch of his parents-in-law's home. Bob said that Network would agree to their proposal if they could begin training the editorial panel immediately so that there would be no delay, because their first broadcast date was already fixed.

Richard agreed, said a prayer of thanks, and then called Tom Morgan at the foundation, so that he and Dr. Morris could pull the members of their team together. Tom was overjoyed, and again they prayed for God's blessings.

Finally Richard called Tom Spence, whose courage had begun this particular journey and thanked him for his strength, including his time in the hospital. Tom reminded Richard of the source of all their strength, and the two of them also prayed.

Their family week in Vermont went well, and Tommy ended it for them on a pleasant note when they saw him and Caroline Batten kissing goodbye behind the tool shed on the morning of their departure.

After their return, Amy, Susan, and Bobbie began six weeks of birthing classes, one night each week. Janet told Richard after the third session that, based on Susan's remarks, birthing class might be the best form of teenage abstinence training ever devised!

The Hawkinses moved in down the street, and Susan found herself spending more time with Eric, who also became a regular at Morningside youth group. Carrie Wagner, right out of college, joined the youth ministry team to work with the junior high students, and Tommy fell in love with her on the first Sunday. Despite her focus with the younger teens, she quickly became close friends with Amy, Susan, and Bobbie, and even attended their final two birthing classes with them.

The school year started again, and all the families with children on Devon Drive shifted back into the familiar routine. Despite her condition, which was now very apparent, Amy was allowed to stay with her class for her senior year. She talked with the Tomlinsons about once every week, giving them progress reports on the baby. They told her that the nursery in their home was nearing completion.

Kristen was still searching for God, attending Morningside Church twice in that month and joining Anne at the businesswomen's breakfast one morning. She also visited Peter Dowling in San Francisco for a long weekend, staying with him and trying to determine whether she should make the commitment to move there.

It was now the Thursday before the first national broadcast of "911 Live," and Janet and the crew at the station were in full preparation for the event, which had become a legitimate news feature, because of the new technology and the local involvement.

With only a few bumps along the way, the integration and training of members for the editorial panel went smoothly, and Bob Grissom reported to Richard early in the week that they were actually enjoying their relationship with the members from the Foundation for the Family. But he quickly added that the real test of what they were doing would come on Friday night, when they went live.

"Richard, I don't know how much longer I can take the uncertainty and the not knowing," Bruce McKinney said, sitting with David in Richard's office that Thursday, his head in his hands. "They won't tell us exactly what they're going to prosecute us on, and the investors' attorneys won't talk to us either, waiting to see whether insurance will cover their claims. We're just stuck, tortured in limbo, not knowing what to do or when the real resolution will even begin."

"I know, I know," Richard agreed. "It seems like at least half of the punishment is the waiting. Court says we should hear something from the federal attorneys next week, now that the summer is over."

David Smith, who was working two jobs as a waiter and a cab driver to help feed his family, said, "I hope so. The waiting is killing us."

Richard looked from David, who at least was working, to Bruce, who was letting Diane work while he stayed home in the afternoons with their children—and who looked terrible. Bruce said, "Anything but this waiting—even hell might be better, huh Richard?"

Richard knew that Bruce was taunting him for his faith. Bruce had met with the Cokers when they visited in late August, but he let it be known that he wanted no part of hearing about God. Diane was much more receptive. On two occasions, including the Sunday with the Cokers, she attended Morningside Church with her children.

In response to Bruce, Richard smiled and looked right at him, "No, Bruce, I don't think so. Waiting eventually gets over. Hell never does."

"Well, you can't tell that by us. I feel like we're there already."

Richard made a mental note to ask Janet again what they might do to help Diane and her children. And also a note to talk to Court about hurrying up the legal process before Bruce or David snapped under the strain.

■   ■   ■

FRIDAY, SEPTEMBER 15 ■ That Friday night Janet and Richard came home early, and Richard cooked hamburgers outside on the grill. They invited the Bryants, Hawkinses and McKinneys over for dinner and to watch the first edition of "911 Live." Bruce didn't come, but the others did; with the kids running around outside, the neighbors settled in front of the television a little before 7:30.

Janet unexpectedly stood up and asked them to pray with her, and she thanked God for His daily involvement in their lives, and for making such a difference, by using her husband and many others, in everything around them, especially in this show. She finished by praying for protection for everyone involved in the production that night and particularly for the emergency personnel.

She sat down, with a nod and a smile from Richard, as the show began. For ninety minutes they were shown police chases, fires in progress, the rescue of a woman from a car in a flash flood, an ambulance ride for a heart attack victim, and more. From their own city there was an ongoing story on the police stopping a case of potential domestic violence, and one could feel the uncertainty of the police officers as they left that particular home.

If there were, in fact, set-ups of staged crimes for the cameras or outbursts of raw violence, they never made it to the screen. "The panel must be working," Richard thought, as the show entered its last thirty minutes.

At the conclusion, Janet asked her neighbors for their opinions on the show. Everyone agreed that while it was not a first choice for family viewing, the show was at least tastefully done, with no overt violence; and the added dimension of actually being live did add a lot to the production. They basically enjoyed it because no one knew what was going to happen next.

An hour later, when everyone left, Janet called Bill at the station. He reported that an instant national poll had produced basically the same results and Network staff was very happy.

Janet hugged Richard, smiled, and said, "Thank you, dear, for all your help."

Smiling back, and hugging her, he replied, "Thank God, not me. He gave me the words. All I did was speak them."

19

THURSDAY, DECEMBER 21 ■ Christmas fell on a Monday that year, and it was the last Thursday before the holiday. Bruce McKinney hardly came out of his home any more, except to attend legal meetings, which had not gone well for them. The federal regulators had decided to make an example out of their case, to deter others, and they were not interested in a light plea bargain. And civil cases were still lining up over the lost funds.

In October Bruce finally gave in to pressure and lowered the asking price on their home, and a contract was executed a week later. Now, much to his disgust, they would be moving to a small rental home on the Wednesday after Christmas.

Amy was very pregnant, her baby due in less than a month. The Tomlinsons came to visit her at Thanksgiving and assured Amy that everything was ready for the baby back at their home. Despite her discomfort, Amy was healthy and in good spirits. She attended church every week with her two best friends and prayed daily for her baby.

Kristen and Peter exchanged visits in the fall, staying in each other's apartments. Kristen decided to accept Peter's invitation to visit him for the long Christmas weekend. Their relationship, she realized, would not go any further with so many miles between them; and on the flight out she resolved to decide over the weekend whether to move permanently to San Francisco or to end their romantic involvement. She arrived in San Francisco that afternoon, and they were finishing a candlelit dinner in his apartment, looking out at the Bay.

"Peter, I really enjoy being with you in every way. Do you think that if I moved here, we would have a chance at a real relationship?"

"You mean like marriage?"

"Eventually, yes. Not right away. But if I uprooted my life and moved here, I would want to know that we had a better than even chance of winding up together permanently."

"Well, I like you too. And I guess we're getting to the age when we have to think about the future. But before we go on, there's something I was going to tell you tonight anyway, and I guess now is as good a time as any, though the news isn't good."

"What is it, Peter?" Kristen asked with a sinking feeling, leaning forward in her chair at the table.

"I think from now on we're going to have to use a condom, Kristen," he said, looking down at his glass to avoid her eyes.

"Why? I've been taking the pill for years, as you know."

"Well. Look, this isn't easy, and I only just found out yesterday . . . When I first moved here right after graduate school, it was a pretty wild scene. It still is, but back then it was *really* wild. I got in with a group through a friend at the paper, and—well, we had some pretty loose parties. Sometimes they went on for days in houses up in the mountains. There were about twelve of us regulars, men and women, and any number of others who would drop in and out."

"What are you talking about, Peter? That was years ago, right?"

"I'm talking about group sex. Orgies, I guess. Everyone doing everything with everybody. And, yes, it was years ago. But here's the thing. Two of the regulars, a man and a woman, have now turned up to be HIV positive."

"Oh no," Kristen gasped. "Did you . . . ?"

"Sure. Many times."

"With *both* of them?"

"Look, at those parties, everyone was zonked, and we all tried all sorts of things. It didn't necessarily mean you were gay; we just did whatever felt good at the time."

Kristen had turned pale, and her throat was suddenly dry. "So you may be HIV positive?"

"I'm not now; I was tested yesterday afternoon. But I thought I ought to tell you so that we can take the necessary precautions."

Kristen sat in silence. What had she been doing? What had she been thinking? Why had no one warned her? She might very well already be carrying inside her the seed of her own death. What a fool she had been. All of those thoughts burst upon her in one long single flash.

"Take the necessary precautions?" she asked bitterly. "Why didn't you tell me?"

"Hey, I only found out myself yesterday. Do you think I'm happy?"

"I mean about the group sex. The AC/DC stuff. Why didn't you tell me?"

"Well, it was a long time ago. And I haven't asked you about your past sex life. What are you, suddenly some kind of a virgin or something?"

No, but I wish to God I was! The thought exploded on her mind. *What have I done to myself for all these years*? she again thought. Suddenly she knew what she had to do. To Peter she said, "We won't have to take any more precautions because we aren't going to sleep together again. In fact, I'm not going to sleep *here* any more."

She stood up, put down her napkin, walked up the stairs to his bedroom, and began packing. "Please call me a taxi, Peter."

Still sitting at the table, stunned by her reaction, and not wanting to lose her, he said, "Oh, come on Kristen. Please don't overreact. It's not that big a deal."

She leaned over the loft rail and said in a loud voice, almost in a scream, "Overreact? No big deal? Peter, death is a *very* big deal! Now call me a taxi!"

That same Thursday night Nepravel and Zoldar were continuing to build an utter despair in Bruce McKinney to push him over the edge. With little to stop them other than the daily prayers from the Sullivans, the voices inside Bruce were spinning at a fever pitch. The louder they played, the more depressed he became.

Sitting in his armchair, alone again late that night, he heard a voice tell him that he was a total failure. "My family has to move out of our home two days after Christmas. How bad is that? What a provider I am! And this time next year I'll be in jail. And bankrupt. How will Diane and the kids make it? And all because of those stupid attorneys and their picking. It's not fair. We *almost* made it. Those attorneys! And the most self-righteous one lives right next door and pretends to be our friend. I know he laughs at us behind our backs. A lot of help he's been!"

His head spinning from depression and alcohol, Bruce finally fell asleep in his armchair, where his seven-year-old son found him the next morning.

FRIDAY, DECEMBER 22 ■ It was early Friday evening, and there was a bustle of Christmas activity on Devon Drive. The Hawkinses were hosting a Christmas party for the younger teenagers, and Tommy and Brent were there, dancing in the basement with a group from their class.

Tom Bryant was returning late from a business trip, so Janet suggested to Nancy that they go to the mall to finish their Christmas shopping. Susan volunteered to stay with Amy, and the two teenagers decided to use the evening to wrap presents together at Amy's house.

That left Richard at home by himself until Janet returned from the mall. So he also decided to wrap some presents, after eating a microwave supper. He was standing at the breakfast room table, wrapping a present for Tommy at about 7:30, when the doorbell rang. He went to the door and looked out through the window by the door. It was Kristen.

Next door Diane was more worried than usual. Because of the school holidays she had been home all day, and she noticed that Bruce started drinking early in the afternoon; now he was sitting again in his armchair, just staring, as if he were listening to voices, which he was. Nepravel and Zoldar were both there, working Bruce down into a wretched pit of despair.

She tried to interest him in helping her or in playing with the kids, but he grunted his displeasure. Almost in tears, she went into their bedroom, closed the door, and for the first time in her adult life dropped to her knees, and prayed.

"Can I come in, please?" Kristen asked, tear streaks visible on her cheeks.

"Of course," Richard said, opening the door wider. She walked in and sat on the sofa in their den, her coat and her purse next to her.

"Would you like some coffee, or a drink of some sort?" he asked.

"A soft drink would be fine, thank you," she smiled, though it was obvious that it was an effort.

Richard returned from the kitchen, handed her the glass, and sat next to her in the armchair. "Now, what has happened to you?"

"I've just landed on the first flight I could get out of San Francisco this morning. With the Christmas rush, the first two were full, but I got the last seat on the third one, and I drove right here from the airport." She took a long sip from her drink and then told him all about Peter, starting months before, and about his revelation of the night before. It took her almost ten minutes to complete the story, and he was appalled by the last news. "So I spent the night in a motel at the San Francisco airport, and here I am."

"Kristen, that's awful. What do you want me to do?"

Diane finished praying and went upstairs to put the young ones to bed. They were already wound up about Christmas, and she knew she would have to read them several stories. As she walked through their den, Bruce stood up and went into their bedroom, without saying anything to her.

Bruce went first to his bedside table and pulled out his chrome .38 special, then to his dresser for the loaded cylinder. The voices told him that he had seen and heard enough. Someone had to pay for what had happened to him and to his family. And his family would be much better off with his insurance money than they were with him.

As Diane finished reading the first story to their little boys, she heard their front door close. She stood up and looked out the second-story window and saw Bruce walking down their driveway, without a coat. In the light from the turnaround, she clearly saw the gleam from the chrome revolver in his hand.

"Oh no!" she gasped, her breath knocked out of her.

"What is it Mommy? Is it Santa Claus?" her youngest asked.

"No, no. I'll be right back." And she ran to the telephone in the upstairs hall and dialed 911.

Kristen said, "Richard, all night and all day on the plane I've been thinking about what Anne Meredith said that night at my apartment. She said that I had to first find the love of God and a relationship with Him before I could find the real love of any man. And I realize today that she gave me the best advice I've had since I left home; but I've ignored it, until now. Richard, I'm done. I can't run my life any more. I've made a terrible mess of it, and I want to give it to God. I need His help so badly." She started to cry softly. "Please, what is it that the Merediths and you and the others have? And how do I get it? How can I start over, with Him?"

"It's Jesus Christ, Kristen. And He's right here. He can heal you and give you a new relationship with God and an inner joy like you've never known. As you saw that night, we can still be tempted to go astray. But you can belong to God forever. And whatever happens, either with this HIV situation or with anything else, you'll know that you'll spend eternity in heaven with Him."

"Oh Richard, how do I do that? I'm so tired of trying to do it all myself . . . "

Just then the front door opened and they heard a man's voice yell, "Richard, where are you?" Without waiting for an answer, the man came toward the light in the den. Richard and Kristen, frozen by the abruptness of the interruption, were suddenly confronted by Bruce McKinney, unshaven, in a rage, and carrying a large revolver, standing in the door from the hall to the den.

"There you are, you self-righteous lawyer jerk. Who's that, and what have you done to make *her* cry? You're gifted in that area, aren't you?"

Richard and Kristen were speechless. "Well, I've had enough. Enough of you and enough of this messed-up world. You wouldn't help me when I needed you." He raised the gun and pointed it at Richard, whose heart began pounding. "And so now we're going to see what's really on the other side of this life, you and me."

Nepravel and Zoldar, who came in with Bruce, knew full well what was on the other side and looked at each other in glee, anticipating that they would at least have Bruce to introduce to hell that night.

"Bruce, what about Diane?" Richard said, trying to think of anything to say. Kristen, realizing after a few seconds what was happening, also remembered that her purse was beside her on the sofa, covered by her coat. How had she tossed it? Was it open? Could she get to her automatic?

"Diane will be much better off with the insurance money than she will with a failure of a husband locked in jail . . ."

Kristen inched her right hand toward the purse under her coat, trying not to move too quickly. She silently prayed for guidance. Yes, the purse was open toward her. She slowly slid her hand into it, feeling for the cold metal of the Sig Sauer P-230.

"We'll see in a second whether all those prayers have done you any good, Richard," Bruce said, leveling the gun at Richard's head. Kristen moved her hand faster; her breathing had stopped.

Just then the door from the garage flew open, and Susan ran in. She started to speak to her father, then saw Kristen on the sofa and Bruce McKinney in the other door, pointing a gun at her father and swinging it towards her.

"No, Bruce, don't shoot! It's Susan!" Richard yelled. Bruce swung the gun back toward Richard, then again toward Susan. Kristen finally put her hand on her own automatic and slowly started pulling it out of the purse, bringing her left hand across her body to be ready to cock it.

"Daddy, what's . . . ? Mr. McKinney, why? . . . Oh, Daddy, Amy's water just broke, and she's gone into labor. She's crying and in terrible pain. Please come and help! She's got to go to the hospital!"

Richard turned back to Bruce. The gun was still leveled at his head. Richard asked silently for God's help and then spoke, suddenly feeling the power to confront death: "Bruce, your family needs *you*, not money. They need a husband and father for forty more years, whatever happens in the next five. They and we love you and want only the best for you. More importantly, God loves you and wants the best for you, if you'll let Him work in your life. But right now Amy needs our help. She's alone next door, scared to death, and about to have a baby, to bring a new life into this world. Do you remember when Diane had your boys? We've got to help her. What will it be, Bruce? You've got to choose. Will it be death? Or life?"

Bruce held the gun on Richard, while Kristen and Susan watched. No one breathed. They could all hear sirens in the background, coming closer. Nepravel and Zoldar urged Bruce on to pull the trigger. Richard, Kristen, and Susan could see Bruce thinking, and then his countenance visibly changed. The visual image of Amy needing them, just as Diane had needed him years ago, and the prayers, stopped the deceptive voices. He lowered the gun, put it on the bookcase, and said calmly, "What do you want me to do, Richard?"

Kristen breathed again and shoved her own gun back into her purse. Susan ran to her father, who stood up and hugged her, then motioned to Bruce. "We've got to drive Amy to the hospital. Bruce, write a note for Tom and Nancy, or stay in their home, whichever you want. And, whether you like it or not," Richard smiled at him for the first time, "pray!"

Bruce nodded and said quietly "OK. I'll do it. Let me call Diane first, and tell her that everything's OK, and about Amy."

"Susan, Kristen, come on," Richard said, hurrying out the door to the garage, just as a police car and an ambulance pulled into their driveway. Two policemen jumped out, weapons drawn, and ran toward them.

"Stop! Who are you? . . . We had a report of a man with a gun coming in the direction of these houses. Are you OK?"

"Yes, officer, we're fine. I'm Richard Sullivan; here's my ID. I think there was a mistake on that report. But we do have a teenage girl in unexpected sudden labor, and we could really use that ambulance to get her to the hospital."

As they put away their weapons, the two officers looked at each other and at the paramedic, who had run up while Richard was talking. "Sure. That's fine. Where is she?"

Susan lead the paramedics to Amy, who was lying on the living room floor, breathing as she had learned in her birthing class, crying, and praying. "We've got help, Amy. Everything's going to be all right," Susan said, smiling and holding Amy's hand, as the paramedics unfolded the last parts of their stretcher.

Two minutes later Amy was in the ambulance, and the group was standing outside its open back doors, deciding who would drive to the hospital in which cars. The lead paramedic took Amy's blood pressure and fitted her with a portable fetal monitor.

"I can drive Susan in my car," Kristen said to Richard, ". . . if you want."

"Hey!" the paramedic yelled to his partner. "This baby is in distress! Let's roll!"

"Can I go?" Richard asked, as the driver slammed the first door shut. "One adult. That's all. Let's go."

Richard jumped inside, and the driver slammed the second door behind him. Kristen grabbed Susan, and they ran to Kristen's car. The police car and the ambulance took off together, blue and red lights flashing.

Nepravel and Zoldar were defeated. They were used to winning against humans, and they hated the bitter taste of defeat. The prayers. The infernal prayers! The humans had constantly sought God's help, and He had answered them! As the emergency vehicles sped off, the two demons let out wails of anger and of hate, knowing that their fates were sealed.

Amy had heard the paramedic's words about her baby, and between the pain of the contractions, which were already starting to come closer together, she gasped, "What is it, Mr. Sullivan?"

Richard, kneeling by Amy, looked up at the paramedic, who was seated at Amy's head, watching the vital signs on both Amy and her baby. The paramedic answered, "This is on a relay back to the hospital for their analysis, but as best I can tell, the umbilical cord must be wrapped around the baby's neck. Every time she has a contraction and has to push, it wraps the cord tighter, cutting off oxygen to the baby's brain and throwing it into distress." Lowering his voice for only Richard to hear, he said, "I've seen this before, and it's not good. We've got several miles to go, and her contractions are coming closer and closer. The baby may not make it."

That was simply not acceptable to Richard. He took Amy's hand in his and said to her, "Amy, I'm going to pray out loud so you can pray along with me. I know it's going to be hard, but try not to push."

Then Richard began to pray. "Dear God, we call upon Your mighty power tonight. We lift up Amy and her baby to You now, asking You to intervene, to guard and protect this baby, as You did Your own Son almost two thousand years ago tonight. Dear God, please hear our prayer, and save this baby, that he might do Your work in his time . . ."

Roy Johnson had recently retired from a Christian publishing company, and he was one of the three editorial panel members for "911 Live" that night in New York. One of their "spotters," who scanned the raw feeds from the ten cities, announced over the panel's headphones, "We've got a young mother with an unborn baby in distress in an ambulance, with a guy praying for them."

"Let's see it," Roy asked. The monitor came on in front of them, and there were Richard and Amy in the red glow inside the ambulance. Richard was just telling Amy that he was going to pray, and then he began.

"Looks good to me," Roy said to his fellow panel members.

"Isn't it a little mundane?" the woman from Network asked.

"Now, Gloria, it's almost Christmas, and this is probably the last segment we'll get on tonight. I went along with you on that drug bust in

Chicago, despite the violence. I vote we show people doing what we've been doing for thousands of years, praying when we're in distress. And besides, look for yourself. It's 'what's really happening!'" he smiled.

She thought for a moment and then returned his smile. "OK. Sure. It's Christmas. Let's do it. All right with you, Don?"

The third member of their panel nodded his agreement. Roy called over his microphone and spoke to the director, who said to the technician, "OK on the feed from the ambulance. Back it up and start it from the top after this commercial. Give our anchor the details."

At 8:30 that night, the Friday before Christmas, "911 Live" broadcast into millions of homes in America the truth that millions of Americans had forgotten: that the power to do anything and everything rests only in God, not humanity.

On their screens the show's viewers saw Amy and heard the paramedic give his early assessment of the difficult situation. Then they saw Amy's tears and Richard taking her hand, as he started to pray.

And all across America, people stopped what they were doing that night and began to pray with Richard.

Cynthia Weeks was looking out her living room window in Des Moines, as her two younger children put the finishing touches on a snowman with their father; their creation stood in the spotlight created by their outside lights. Behind her, their teenager suddenly said, "Hey, Mom, there's a guy *praying* on '911 Live' for a baby!"

She turned away from the window and immediately saw Richard, Amy, and the paramedic, as Richard began to pray for God's help for Amy's baby. Cynthia listened for a moment, then reached for her telephone and called the three lead numbers on their church's prayer chain. Within three minutes over fifty members of her church were watching the same scene and interceding for God's mercy.

Across America, members of church prayer chains called each other to be sure that all were watching, and thousands of voices were added to the prayers for Amy's baby.

Kristen's elderly parents, watching on an old black and white television set at their farm in Texas, saw that the ambulance was in Kristen's city. They joined hands on their sofa, bowed their heads, and prayed.

Lou Thompson hated being so far from home so close to Christmas, but the same snow storm had disrupted the airline schedule, and he had to spend an extra night in a budget motel frequented by salesmen such as himself.

As he spoke to his wife on the phone, he used the remote control by the bed to flip through the TV channels. He was suddenly struck by the face of a teenage girl, tears running down her cheeks, as a man held her hand and bowed his head praying, a siren going in the background.

"Honey, do you have the television on?" he asked. "Flip to Network . . ." They both watched for a few minutes and listened to Richard's prayer, as they finished their conversation.

When he hung up the phone, Lou continued to watch the television, and his heart melted at the situation, thinking of his own teenage daughter and listening to the man in the ambulance pray so fervently. With tears filling his own eyes, Lou Thompson knelt by the bed in his motel room far from home, and for the first time in many years prayed to the God whom he had known so well in his youth.

Marty Tsongas came home late from the office and was walking through his den on the way to change clothes, when he looked at what his kids had on TV and saw Richard Sullivan praying with a girl in an ambulance. He rushed to the phone and called the Tomlinsons. "It's on Channel 7. Yeah, I promise it's Richard. . . . You see it now? Is that Amy Bryant? Oh, no." And Marty called his wife into their bedroom, where they began praying.

Scott and Cindy Peterson in Tampa, changing channels that evening, suddenly saw Richard. They watched for a few moments and then joined him on their knees.

Kate Tomlinson changed channels when Patrick got Marty's call, and she gasped to see Richard and Amy on the screen in her living room. When she realized what was happening, she ran to Patrick, and they both knelt, bowing their heads and praying for their baby.

When Tom Bryant came within range of the local dialing area, he called home on his car phone to let his family know that he was on the way. He was surprised to hear Bruce McKinney on the other end; thirty seconds later he had changed his destination. And, having seen Richard do it on other occasions, he began to pray for his daughter.

Following behind the ambulance in Kristen's car, Susan asked Kristen to pray with her. Susan bowed her head while Kristen drove. Unknown to Susan, Kristen not only prayed for Amy and her baby, but also for herself, asking God for His forgiveness and committing to Him that from now on she would turn to His Son as the Lord of her life. Unseen by them in the darkness, the blinding Light of the Holy Spirit visited her car on the interstate that night.

All over America, in homes, at airports, in hotels, wherever there were televisions tuned to Network, believers joined in praying to their common Father, united in asking for His protection for this helpless baby.

■   ■   ■

As Janet and Nancy were descending the escalator to the second floor of King Department Store in the mall, Janet turned around and was talking to Nancy, when suddenly she heard her husband Richard, as if he were there, saying, "Dear Father, You know the courage of this girl, how she chose not to have an abortion. Please visit her now and protect her baby . . ." Janet saw the shock on Nancy's face, and she turned to face forward.

They could see a wall of hundreds of color televisions for sale, all tuned to TV5. There in front of them were Richard and Amy, and Richard's voice was reaching out to everyone in the video section of the store, praising God and asking for His help. They ran up to the huge thirty-six-inch screen. Many people noticed the overlay identifying their city on the screen, which had originally been Janet's idea.

As Richard's voice could clearly be heard praying, people stopped talking to salesmen and watched. A crowd started to gather; no one could use the escalator without seeing and hearing Richard's fervent prayers, which never stopped. In one corner of the video section a small group had formed and was praying together.

"Come on, we've got to go to the hospital," Nancy said, pulling on Janet.

"But which one?" Janet asked.

"Memorial," one of the people who had been watching said. The two women ran through the mall for Janet's car.

Millions of believers, and others, united in prayer that night, focused on an unborn baby, fighting for his life in his mother's womb. And as He has promised, God heard the prayers of His people.

God, who created time, was not affected by the network delay. He heard the prayers across time. He responded.

One of God's mighty angels, the same one who had chased Nepravel away from the abortion clinic, flew down and intercepted the ambulance. As Richard prayed and Amy gasped and millions of others asked for God's mercy, Richard laid his hand on Amy's stomach, and the angel reached inside her. With the same powerful talon he used to grasp and to explode demons, this angel tenderly and gently pulled the umbilical cord away from the baby's neck, loosening it and allowing the life-giving blood to reach the baby's brain unhindered.

The paramedic checked his readings during Amy's next two contractions and then said to Richard. "Hey, I hate to interrupt your prayer, but the baby isn't in distress any more. All of the readings are normal. I can't believe it. It's a miracle! I've never seen anything like it."

Unknown to him, all over America millions of people heard his report, and they cheered, hugged, and wept. Many kept on praying, praising God and asking for His continued help for Amy and her baby.

Patrick Tomlinson hugged Kate and then picked up the phone to make airline reservations.

Kristen's father asked her mother, "I wonder if Kristen knows those people?"

The ambulance made it safely to the hospital, and the paramedics wheeled Amy and the unseen angel, still grasping the baby's umbilical chord with his talon, into the operating room. As standard procedure in such cases, the doctors performed a Caesarian section, and Nancy arrived in time to sign the necessary papers.

"911 Live" went off the air at 9:00, but Network was flooded with so many calls that at 9:45 they ran a crawl across the bottom of that evening's Friday Night Movie: "At 9:20 the young woman on '911 Live' gave birth to a healthy, seven-pound baby boy. Mother and son are both doing fine."

The instant overnight polls registered that, due to the word-of-mouth calls, the last thirty-minute segment of "911 Live" drew the largest audience the Network had ever experienced on a Friday night.

Epilogue

So Richard Sullivan did not die that year. In fact he lived to be quite an old man, in love with Janet and loved by both of their children, and by their seven grandchildren. After he submitted to the Son of God as his own Lord, he also accepted his God-given responsibility to be the spiritual head of his family. By doing so, he not only changed the eternal lives of his wife, his children, and his grandchildren, but also, through them, of hundreds of other people.

When Richard's immortal soul did finally pass to the next life, he was taken, like everyone, to the Judgment Seat. There God kept His promise that "all who believe in Him shall not perish, but have everlasting life." The Blood of Jesus atoned for Richard's many sins and imperfections, and he was welcomed into heaven with millions of other believers. Eventually he was joined there by Janet, Susan, Tommy, and five of their grandchildren, where they're spending eternity in complete joy, praising God.

The boy grew up in Cincinnati with fine parents in a good home. He somehow knew—he always believed—that he had been touched by God, even before he was born.

Thirty-five years later, in one of his nation's darkest times, Patrick Tomlinson, Jr., began and led a mighty revival—the most sweeping in the nation since the late nineteenth century. Millions of people were led away from the lies of Satan, who was bent on their destruction and instead turned to the one true God who created them in His own image and who loved them.

And this revival brought the nation to the moment when people finally realized that neither government nor any other program conceived by humans could answer the overwhelming problems of that day. People finally realized again what the founders of the nation had known so well, that each individual and nation must be founded on God and on His will if they are to survive and to prosper.

Patrick Tomlinson, Jr., was alive and able to be the spark to light God's cleansing fire of national revival only because Richard Sullivan had believed. And Richard Sullivan had believed only because many other believers, over many years, most not seeing any results at all, had nevertheless told Richard the same true story about God and about the power of a life submitted to Him.

Despite the forces arrayed against them, their voices could not be silenced.